THE JESS WILLIAMS TRILOGY

THE
JESS WILLIAMS
TRILOGY

THE RECKONING
BROTHER'S KEEPER
SINS OF THE FATHER

ROBERT J. THOMAS

Copyright© 2017 by Robert J. Thomas

A Jess Williams Novel.
Westerns. Revenge. Violence. Action. Adventure.
ISBN-10: 1940108535
ISBN-13: 9781940108537

TABLE OF CONTENTS

!

THE RECKONING

A Jess Williams Western

FIRST IN THE SERIES

This one is for Mom, Blanche T. Thomas,
Whom we lost in October of 2002.
She will be missed by many, but especially by her three sonsAnthony, Daniel
and me.
We love you, Mom!

PROLOGUE

Year 2002

"What's the number?" asked Dave.

"Forty-nine hundredths of a second!" Pat replied loudly since the two of them were wearing shooting earmuffs.

"Not bad, but still not good enough!" said Dave.

The two shots were so close together they sounded like one shot, but there were definitely two shots flying out of the barrel of Dave Walters' custom-built competition pistol. Dave pulled the first shot by thumbing the specially designed hammer back as he drew the pistol and the second shot was fanned by the middle finger of his left hand. The two balloon targets were about five feet apart and about fifteen feet away. He was shooting the customary wax bullets, which were used for competition fast draw.

Dave holstered his pistol and drew and fired two more shots. "How about that time?" he asked.

"Forty-seven hundredths of a second. It's getting hot out here. How much longer?"

"I'm finished!"

Dave had been at it for two hours, trying to get his first shot down under the four-tenths of a second mark. That's where he needed to be in order to seriously compete in the world championship title for fast draw. Dave had been competing in fast draw competitions for several years now and he had won some matches, but he was hell-bent on being the Fast Draw Champion of the World. Pat Johnson was his good friend and also competed in the competitions. They had spent the last two hours at the Shooting Corral, a local gun range with a specialty. It had an area where competitors in fast draw and cowboy action shooting could ply their trade and practice.

"Hey, you did okay," said Pat as the two of them removed their earmuffs. "Maybe after you pick up that new pistol you ordered, you'll break the four-tenths of a second mark."

"I sure hope so. My wife has been giving me a real assful about buying a new gun. She wanted some new bedroom furniture and she's getting impatient."

"Tell her that when you become the new Fast Draw Champion of the World, you'll be able to buy her a whole house full of furniture," said Pat.

"Sure I will. You sure know how to help a guy out."

"So, when are you getting it?"

"I called Bob Graham today and he said it's ready. Want to go with me?"

"You bet! I'd love to meet Graham. I hear he's one of the top custom gun builders in the country. Maybe I can get him to build me one."

"Okay," said Dave, as he threw his stuff into the trunk of his car and closed it. "I'll pick you up on Saturday."

"I'll be waiting. And breakfast is on you this time."

Dave picked Pat up on Saturday at seven in the morning. They stopped to have breakfast and then drove the hundred fifty miles to Bob Graham's house. Graham had been building custom competition guns for years and he was a skilled craftsman. He could build anything you needed or wanted. He was an artist extraordinaire. He greeted them at the front door with his usual wide grin.

"Morning, fellows. How was your drive?"

"Just fine," replied Dave. "This is my good friend Pat Johnson. He's a shooter, too."

"Well, I've got the gun all set and ready for you to check out."

"Great," replied Dave. "You did say this morning that you got the FD7 model holster from Mernickle Custom Holsters, right?"

"It just came in yesterday; it's in the box here," said Graham as he opened the box. "It fits the gun beautifully. I think you're going to like the way it handles. Bob Mernickle sure knows how to work leather into a functional yet beautiful piece of art."

Graham walked into another room and came back out with the newly custom-built pistol in a plastic case. When Dave opened the case, his expression was one of a kid who had just gotten the gift he had always wanted for Christmas. The gun was beautiful. When Dave ordered the gun, he asked Graham, who was also an accomplished artist, to carve him a custom set of handgrips for the new gun. The handgrips were carved from the stag horns of the sambar deer from India.

"You like those handgrips, Dave?" asked Graham.

"They're beautiful. The way the grips flare out at the bottom just makes the gun feel so much more comfortable in my hand."

"They're not just pretty; they're functional. You'll find that they help get the gun out of the holster much easier than the stock grips the gun originally came with."

Dave looked the gun over some more. It was perfectly balanced. Graham explained how he had lathed the barrel small enough to be able to fit an aluminum shroud over the steel barrel. That made the gun lighter, perfectly balanced and easier to draw. It allowed the gun to shoot live .45-caliber ammunition as well as wax bullets, which was something else Dave had expressly wanted.

Graham explained to Dave that he started with a Ruger Blackhawk .41 Magnum caliber single-shot revolver and customized just about everything. There was not much original left of the gun. Besides changing out the barrel and making it a .45-caliber, he cut the trigger guard in half and changed the trigger to one that was about three times as wide as the original. He installed a special fanning-type hammer that could also be thumb-cocked. The hammer rose straight up instead of curving back, which made it much easier to fan. Graham replaced many of the gun's original parts with aluminum to lighten it. Any part that was not changed to aluminum was nickel-plated. It truly was a work of art.

"Bob, I think he's going to drool all over that gun," Pat said jokingly.

Graham patted Dave on the shoulder. "Go ahead and put the holster on and try it out. I think you'll like the way it just glides out of the holster."

Dave picked up the holster and looked it over. It, too, was a work of art. Bob Mernickle was born to work magic on leather, Dave thought to himself. He gently slipped the gun into the holster and it fit perfectly. He worked the action of the gun and it was smooth. He dry-fired the gun several times, both thumbing and fanning it. It worked better than he had ever dreamed it might.

"I love it!" Dave exclaimed, as he placed his hand on Graham's shoulder. "With this gun and this holster, I know I can get a chance at the championship title now."

"Probably. As long as I'm not competing at the same time," said Graham playfully. They all laughed. The men and women who competed in fast draw were fierce competitors, but also a friendly bunch who believed in good sportsmanship. Dave thanked Graham again and packed up his new pistol and holster. Pat spoke with Graham for a few minutes about building a custom gun for him.

They drove back and Dave dropped Pat off in the late afternoon and headed home, his new pistol and holster in the trunk of his car. When he got home, he took the gun out of the case and looked it over once more. He read the serial number on the side of the gun: 40-01079. He looked the holster over once more and took note of the serial number stamped on the back of the holster: SN020679. The name "BOB MERNICKLE CUSTOM HOLSTERS" was stamped on the back as well as the model number, FD7, and the words "MADE IN CANADA." He put the gun in the holster and hung it up in his stand-up gun locker and locked it.

He was watching television when his wife came in the door. He waited for her to say something first since he didn't know how mad she still was over the purchase of a new gun and holster instead of the new furniture she had been asking for. After she put her things away, she walked up behind Dave, who was sitting in an old ragged recliner with several holes in the leather.

"Well," she said sarcastically, "you're going to show me anyway, so why don't you just do it now and get it over with?"

Dave jumped up out of the recliner and headed for the gun locker with a boyish grin on his face. Before he got around the corner, he heard her shout, "And I *am* going to get that new furniture before you get any more guns or holsters, agreed?"

"Agreed!" Dave hollered from the bedroom. He spun the dial on the gun case and opened the door with his combination. He reached in to take the holster off the hook and his hand met nothing but air. He let out a gasp of absolute horror and stepped back until he reached the foot of the bed. He let out a loud moan as he sat down on the edge of the bed. Horror washed over him as the realization of what he was experiencing right now finally took hold of him. The new gun and holster he'd placed in his gun locker not more than an hour ago were gone!

Dave didn't sleep very well that night. He tossed and turned repeatedly and he had several nightmares throughout the night. He woke earlier than usual and he was sweating profusely. He got up and went into the bathroom to wash his face with some cool water. As he did, he thought about the nightmares. Most of them were somewhat vague in his mind now, but he remembered one very vividly. It involved a little girl lying in a pile of hay—with a bullet hole in the middle of her forehead.

CHAPTER ONE

May 1876

Jess Williams wasn't unlike most young men growing up in Kansas in the late 1800s. He worked on the family farm and did odd jobs around town for extra money to help his family. He never had much time for play. He'd just turned fourteen a few months earlier. He was a slender young man, standing five feet eight inches tall.

His father, John, had built their ranch from the ground up. He started with only eight head of cattle and his herd had now grown to over a hundred head. He had crops planted on about thirty acres of fertile rich black soil. John hadn't always been a farmer and a rancher. He worked cattle drives when he was younger and he served as sheriff in a few small towns in Texas where he grew up. Not tough towns though. His duties mostly consisted of breaking up fights in saloons and locking up the drunks who couldn't let go of the bar without falling flat on their asses.

After his last job as sheriff in a little town in Texas called Sparta, he'd decided to pack up and just roam around until he found somewhere he could call home. After almost a year of wandering around, he found some land just five miles outside a small town called Black Creek, in the state of Kansas. Good fertile land and the Black Creek ran right through the middle of the property. He spent some time in the town and rode around the area visiting some of the other ranchers and farmers. Everyone he talked to seemed downright friendly. He liked the area and he decided he was going to spend the rest of his life there. He was sure of it. He spent some nights camped out on the land that he planned to settle on. One night, just before dusk, when he was getting a campfire started to cook some beans and salt pork, he actually picked out the site for the family cemetery. There was a giant oak tree about five hundred feet from where he decided he would build the house. The oak tree would provide some shade for future gravesites. John was a planner in life for sure.

John first met Jess's mom, Becky, in town. He thought she was just about the prettiest woman he had ever laid eyes on. He decided right then and there he was going to marry her. John was just that way. He decided quickly about what he wanted to do and then he would set out to do it. He still had some money he had saved from his work as a sheriff, but it wasn't enough to build the house. He worked several odd jobs around town and for some of the surrounding ranches to earn enough money to buy the lumber and materials he needed to build the house. Of course, he preferred working in town since it gave him more opportunities to see Becky.

Becky was a seamstress and a darn good one. She had a little shop behind Jim Smythe's general store where the townspeople could drop off their clothes for repair or be fitted for new ones. Mr. Smythe didn't charge her any rent. Instead, he took a small cut of what money she made and, of course, he had all his clothes tailored for free. Becky first saw John when he came into the general store for supplies. She knew right off he was different from most men. She was interested, but certainly had no idea that he had already fallen deeply in love with her.

⚐ ⚑

Jess's sister, Samantha, was seven and full of brimstone and hellfire. She was always getting into trouble and usually getting away with everything. Although she sometimes helped Jess with chores, she usually caused him more work and grief. Mostly, she would tag along with him and bug him until he just wanted to thump her on the back of the head. The only thing that stopped him from doing so was the knowledge that he would get a switch taken to his back-side. That was something he worked really hard to steer clear of. It was close to noon on a typical day around the ranch and Becky was in the house making some lunch for Jess to take out to his pa. Jess had finished throwing some hay in the stables to feed the cattle and he was walking up to the house to see if his mother had the food ready when Samantha came out of the stables with her hands full of hay. She was jumping up and down, each time letting a little hay drop here and there. Jess knew she was just egging him on.

"One of these days I'm going to thump you good, Samantha," he warned her, giving her a look of dissatisfaction.

"I don't think so, 'cause you know pa will switch your behind real good," she replied giggling. Jess gave her the evil eye for a moment and turned around and headed for the house. Just as he walked in, his mother was wrapping John's lunch in a cloth.

"I'll bet your pa is mighty hungry by now, Jess," said Becky. "You get this out to him right away, you hear?"

"I'll get it straight out to him, I promise."

"Make sure you do."

"Can I ride the paint today?"

"Didn't your father already tell you that you could?"

"Yeah, but I was just checking."

"Then I'm sure it's okay." Jess took the lunch from his ma and headed for the stables to saddle up the paint.

Jess had the paint saddled up and out of the stable in less than five minutes. Out of the six horses they owned, Jess had always liked the paint the best. He was a gentle horse and Jess gave him a few apples or carrots every day. Jess always loved riding out on the ranch. Sometimes he would imagine he was on his own and roaming around the country going from one town to another. He was always wondering about what he would do when he grew up. Would he stay and work the ranch or go off and do something different? Maybe he'd be a sheriff like his pa had been or maybe he'd own his own business in town. Of course, like most young boys, Jess would imagine himself as a gunfighter, and of course, the fastest gunfighter alive. Whenever Jess got some free time from his chores, he would find himself down by the creek drawing the hand-carved wooden pistol that his pa had made for him. He'd asked his pa a while back to teach him how to shoot a real pistol, but John said he was still too young for that.

It only took fifteen minutes before Jess found his pa. He was looking over a new calf that seemed to be lost and not doing very well.

"About time you got here, Jess," said John. "My stomach's been growling like a bear that just came out from a long winter nap."

"Sorry, Pa," replied Jess nervously. "I got here as soon as I could… honest. I never stopped or anything, I rode straight out here. The biscuits Ma made you are still warm and she put some honey in a jar to go with them."

John looked at Jess and gave him a big smile. "Don't get your britches all up in a bunch," laughed John. "Get down off that horse and let's have a biscuit or two." Jess always liked it when Pa let him have lunch with him out on the range.

"Jess, don't forget to stack up some more hay in the barn and stable tonight before supper," said John, as he finished his lunch.

"Okay, Pa. If I get done early enough, can I go down to the creek and mess around a bit?" asked Jess with a pleading look on his face. John knew exactly what that meant.

"I guess so. As long as you get all of your chores finished."

"Will you come down to the creek and help me practice a little?"

"Maybe after dinner. We'll see what kind of a mood your ma is in. She's still mad about me carving out that wooden pistol."

"How come she's so dead set against it?"

"Well, let's just say she has her reasons."

Jess got back to the ranch as quickly as he could so he could finish his chores and go down to the creek to practice with his wooden pistol. On the way back, he imagined himself a sheriff tracking down a bad guy who had robbed a bank in some town. When he arrived back at the ranch, he brushed down the paint and put him in his stall. Then he finished the chores his pa had told him to do.

Jess went over to the stables and got out his homemade wooden pistol and holster. He'd made the holster himself out of some scrap leather his pa had given him. He fashioned the holster a little different from most holsters. He attached it to the belt at an angle so the barrel of the pistol pointed slightly forward. He fashioned the belt so the gun rode lower on the hip and he tied it down to his thigh with a strip of leather. He ran down to the creek and began to practice.

This time he imagined he was a sheriff in a small town and he had been called out on the street by a gunslinger wanted by the law. Of course, he out-drew the gunslinger. He was there about a half hour when he heard his ma call him for supper. As he walked up toward the stable to put the wooden pistol away, he wondered if his pa would come back down to the creek after supper so he could show him how good he was doing on his own.

Dinner consisted of beef stew and bread. Becky was a pretty good cook. For dessert they had apple pie. Jess ate a good helping of stew and then a big slice of pie. John finished his pie, washing it down with another cup of hot coffee, and pushed himself away from the table.

"Damn fine meal, woman. I don't know anyone who can make apple pie quite like you," said John with a look of pride on his face.

Becky blushed a little. She was very modest. "You're quite the charmer, Mr. Williams. Quite the charmer indeed."

Jess looked at his father. "Pa, do you think you could go down to the creek with me for a little while?" he asked nervously. His ma gave him the look she always gave him when he mentioned going down by the creek. She knew what that meant, and it wasn't fishing. Jess kept looking at his pa, figuring if he looked at his ma it would just get her started.

"You know I really don't like you fooling around with that gun, Jess," she said. Jess kept looking at his pa, waiting for a sign.

"Sweetheart," John said, as he got up from the dinner table, "you are about the best cook around these here parts. I don't know anyone who can bake a pie like you can. Course, women are good at certain things and men are good at other things. Women have to be good cooks else they won't ever get a man. On the other hand, men who don't know how to shoot a gun may never live to get married to a wonderful woman like you in the first place. Matter of fact, if I'd never learned to shoot a pistol, I wouldn't be here today. You know that to be a fact." As he finished his last word he walked around slowly to Becky at the other end of the table and gave her a kiss on the cheek.

"Well, I still don't like it and you know it."

"He's going to learn anyway. So he might as well learn it right."

Jess was already up and out the door heading for the stable to get his wooden pistol. He was excited that his pa was finally going to show him how to handle a gun, even if it was only a wooden one.

John stopped at Samantha's seat and gave her a kiss on top of her head. Just as he reached the door, and without looking back he said, "By the way, you ought not be kicking your brother under the table like that at supper."

It was Samantha's turn to blush now. She dropped her head a little and looked at her empty plate. "Yes, Pa," she replied sheepishly.

Just as John walked out the door he heard Becky quietly say, "Quite the charmer indeed, Mr. Williams…indeed." John met Jess between the house and the stable and they both headed down to the creek. The creek wasn't very big. It was only about six to ten feet across and very shallow except for a few deep pools here and there.

"Pa, when are you gonna let me shoot a real pistol?"

"When I think you're ready, Jess…and not one minute before," he replied firmly.

"But I've been practicing with this here wooden pistol for months now," he reasoned, a pleading look in his eyes.

"I know. But you have to understand. You just turned fourteen a few months back. I'm still your pa and I'll decide when you're ready. Understand?"

"Yes, sir. I understand," he agreed reluctantly, his eyes glancing down at the ground.

"Okay, now, let's see you draw a few times."

Jess got himself ready. He made sure the holster was tight and positioned in the right place. He drew the wooden pistol several times. Each time he reholstered the gun as quickly as he drew it. The first time he drew, John was actually quite surprised with his hand speed, though he shouldn't have been.

"How am I doing, Pa?"

"Not bad, son…not bad at all, but speed isn't the only important thing."

"Well, Pa, if I was in a gunfight, I'd want to be faster than the other guy so I wouldn't get shot."

"Yeah, but if you were one half of a second faster than the other guy, and you missed with your first shot, who would be lying on the street, gut shot, and looking up at the sky wondering what the heck had happened?" he countered with a look of experience on his face.

Jess thought about that for a moment and said, "I think I get what you mean, Pa."

"Okay, Jess, here is your first and most important lesson. Drawing fast is important; there's no doubt about that. But shooting straight and true is just as important. I've seen my share of gunfights. You wouldn't want to know how many times the quicker man lay dead in the street. Sure, if you're that much faster than the guy you're facing, you might get off another shot before he pulls the trigger, but not many men are that fast. You have to make your first shot count every time. Understand?"

"I think so, Pa."

"Also remember this," John continued. "Most men don't have nerves of steel. They're afraid of dying even though they will never admit it. When it comes down to the last second before the draw, most men will be sweating bullets or pissing themselves. A lot of times their first shot goes astray and the next thing that happens is they're lying dead in the street. You have to be cool and deliberate in a gunfight. You have to focus on your target and make sure the first shot counts or it just might be your last."

"How'd you get to know so much about gun fighting, Pa?"

"Watching a lot of people who thought they were real fast get shot real dead," he answered matter-of-factly.

"I guess I'm lucky to have a good teacher like you, Pa."

"Just remember what I said about making that first shot count. I'm going to go up and have a cup of coffee and another slice of that apple pie with your mother. You can stay down here for a few more minutes, but then you get back and hit the sack, okay? You have chores to do in the morning and I need to send you into town tomorrow for some supplies."

"Okay. Thanks, Pa," he said excitedly.

John turned and started to head up to the house. He was still surprised about how fast Jess could draw the wooden pistol, but he admitted to himself silently that he shouldn't be. That kind of speed was born and bred into the boy, but Jess had no idea of the truth of the matter.

Jess thought a lot about what his pa had told him, especially about how some men were quicker on the draw, but still lost a gunfight by missing with their first shot. He practiced for another fifteen minutes and then he headed for the stables to put his gun away. He turned in for the night. As he slowly fell asleep, he imagined he was drawing his pistol slowly and deliberately. He imagined he was a sheriff in a big town and he had to stop a gunfight and…

CHAPTER TWO

Jess woke up at the first sign of daylight peeking into his window. He dressed and headed for the barn and stables to do his chores. He threw hay, did some milking and picked some fresh eggs for breakfast. John was in the stables messing around with the saddles and changing some worn-out cinch straps. He planned to start plowing a few extra acres today. Becky was already cooking a huge breakfast. Jess could smell the bacon all the way out in the barn and his stomach started growling. While he was picking eggs in the chicken coop, Samantha came in and started bothering the hens.

"Samantha, stop fooling around and make yourself useful for a change," Jess complained. "Here, take these eggs in to Ma for breakfast."

Samantha stopped and looked at Jess as if she could burn a hole right through his head with her stare. Then, she smiled and politely said, "Okay."

Jess was a little startled by her reaction, but glad to see her finally willing to do something productive. Jess finished in the coop and then heard his ma call everyone for breakfast. Just as he stepped out of the coop, he heard a crunch under his boot. When he lifted his boot, he discovered a smashed egg. Samantha had put it right in his path knowing he would either step on it or have to carry it into the house. He shook his head.

When Jess got to the table, all the others were already filling their plates. Becky had cooked bacon, eggs, ham, biscuits and honey, and it all looked good.

After finishing his plate and taking another swallow of his coffee, John looked up. "Jess, don't forget, you have to go into town today and pick up some supplies," he said. "Your ma's got the list. And make sure you stop in and see Sheriff Diggs to ask him if he needs any more steaks."

"Sure thing, Pa." Jess went out and got the wagon hooked up to the paint and returned to get the list from his ma.

"Jess, I need those supplies back here in good time so I can get them all put away and have supper ready in time," instructed Becky. "You know how your pa can be if supper is late."

"I won't be late."

Jess climbed up into the wagon, slapped the reins on the rear of the paint and headed for town. It was about a five-mile ride into town and Jess enjoyed every mile of it. The road was a winding one and it followed Black Creek almost all the way. He was about two miles from town when he noticed a cloud of dust in the distance. Jess watched the cloud of dust getting closer and closer. The road was lined with just enough trees that he couldn't make out who or what was coming. Finally, between the trees, he spotted three riders. Several moments passed before he rounded the last curve in the road before meeting up with them.

He saw three men on horseback. He reined in the paint and stopped the wagon. The three men rode up to the front of the paint and stopped. They didn't say anything at first. They just looked Jess over and then looked at one another, with slightly evil grins on their faces. Jess could tell right off he didn't like these men.

The man in the middle was the youngest. He looked to be in his early twenties. He wore a pair of pearl-handled six-guns that were strapped low and tied down tight. The man to Jess's left was older, probably in his thirties and had a busy beard. He wore a single six-shooter in a left-handed holster.

The man to Jess's right was by far the oldest. He was probably in his late forties or early fifties. He was clean looking with a neatly trimmed mustache. He wore a yellow bandanna around his neck, and he had what looked like a new pair of boots on. He was wearing a six-shooter, but Jess noticed he also had a double-barreled shotgun lying across his lap. Jess wondered if he rode like that all the time or if he had taken it out only because he'd seen someone coming. The older man's grin had changed to somewhat of a smile, but Jess's first impression of him was the same as the other two men. He didn't like him.

The older man spoke first and asked, "Where you going, boy?"

"Just going into town to get supplies," replied Jess.

"What kind of supplies, kid?" the youngest one asked.

"I got a list," he said in a sharp tone.

"Kind of mouthy for a boy your age," said the grubby one with the bushy beard.

The older man took over the conversation again. "You from around here, boy?"

"Yeah."

"Where from?"

"Down the road, that way," said Jess, pointing backward, not taking his eyes off the men.

"You got family, boy?"

"Yeah."

"They live down the road that way, too?" the older man asked, as he nodded in the direction Jess had pointed in.

"Yeah."

"You're not very friendly, are you, boy?" asked the older man.

"Not with strangers."

"Hell, we ain't strangers, boy," the youngest one cut in. "We've been talking now for almost a whole minute! Hell, that almost makes us friends!"

"We ain't friends," countered Jess.

"You sure ain't very neighborly, boy," said the older man. "We're just trying to be friendly and all."

"You don't seem very friendly to me," replied Jess. "Besides, I got to get to town, else I'll be late getting back and my pa will be sore at me."

"Maybe we'll stop and see your pa and tell him what bad manners you got, boy," the youngest one groused.

"My pa ain't got time for strangers. He's too busy," he argued. Jess slapped the reins on the paint and the paint responded by walking right through the three men who had been sitting in their saddles in a straight line across the road. The oldest man moved to the creek side and the other two moved over to the left just enough for him to get through. As he was passing the two men on his left, he glanced over in their direction, not directly at them though, keeping his eyes low as if he was looking at the ground. He could see both of them clearly out of his side vision, especially the one who looked like a gunslinger.

That's when Jess noticed something odd. The youngest man's left boot heel was missing. They were old boots, but Jess wondered why he hadn't gotten the boot fixed in town. After a minute or so, Jess looked back. The three men were still sitting in the road watching him and talking to one another. He made up his mind right then and there. He was going to tell Sheriff Diggs about these men when he got to town. When he looked back a second time, the three men had turned their horses around and continued down the road. Good riddance, he thought to himself.

As Jess rounded the last turn and headed down the main street of town, he finally relaxed. He was worried the three men might come after him. He headed straight for Smythe's general store and tied the wagon up in back. He walked around the front of the store and went in.

"Hey, Jess. How are you and the rest of the family?" asked Jim Smythe with a happy smile.

"They're just dandy, sir. Pa sent me in to pick up some supplies. I got the list here." Jess handed the list to him and Jim went about picking the stuff out for him and stacking it in wooden boxes to carry out.

"Are you going to look over the candy counter today?" asked Jim, looking in the direction of the front counter where he displayed all the hard candy in nice clean jars.

"Yes, sir!" Jess replied eagerly. "I'll pick some out when I get back. Right now I have to go see Sheriff Diggs."

"He might be a little cranky just yet," said Jim. "He had to run three drifters out of town this morning. Also, the hothead Red Carter came into town last night and kept the saloon open all night. He got himself pretty drunk and started a fight in Andy's saloon with one of the hands from the Hansen ranch not more than a half hour ago. He had to lock Red up. Red wasn't too happy about the sheriff cracking his skull with the butt of the shotgun he carries."

Jess stopped and turned around before he got to the front door. "I'll bet it was the same three men I met on the road earlier on the way into town."

"Probably was. They rode out toward your place."

"I was going to tell the sheriff about them anyway. I didn't like them much."

"Not much to like," agreed Jim.

"Why did the sheriff run them out of town?"

"He figured them for trouble, just from the looks of them," he replied. "Sheriff Diggs never let them get off their horses. He met them in the street with that shotgun of his and told them they weren't welcome to stop, and to keep on riding. Besides, he knew that Red was sleeping it off in the jail and when he let him out, he knew that Red would end up right back in the saloon. If the three drifters went to the saloon, the sheriff knew he'd be picking up some bodies. You know how Red is; thinks he's the fastest thing in these here parts."

"Yeah, and one day he'll get himself shot, that's for sure," claimed Jess.

Red Carter was the only son on one of the biggest ranches in the area, the "Carter D," and Red was pretty fast with a pistol. He had gotten into a gunfight a few years earlier against some drifter who challenged him after Red won his money in a hot game of poker. Red planted a bullet in the drifter's chest before the man got off a shot. Then, last year the drifter's brother came to town to settle up the score and Red disposed of him even more easily. That officially made Red a gunslinger. Most of the townsfolk were afraid of him and steered clear of him when he was in town.

Jess walked out the front door and headed for Sheriff Diggs' office. When he opened the door, the sheriff was filling out some papers. His double-barreled shotgun was lying across his desk, always within easy reach. Jess saw Red lying on the bunk in the cell, still sleeping it off.

"Howdy, Sheriff," he said as he entered the jail.

The sheriff looked up and smiled at Jess. He had always liked him. He had always liked his mom, too. Everyone in town knew not to mess with Becky or they would have to answer to the sheriff.

"Well, how's my favorite young fella?" asked Sheriff Diggs.

"Just fine. I heard you were having a bad day."

"I was, till you came through that door. How's your pa? And how is my little Becky?"

"They're both just dandy, Sheriff."

"That's good to hear, Jess."

"Oh, I think I'm just gonna puke or something listening to you two carry on," Red Carter said, while propping himself up on the bunk in the jail cell. "My head hurts like hell, Sheriff."

"You're lucky I didn't take that empty head of yours clean off. I've about had it with you coming into town and always causing trouble," barked Diggs angrily.

"I'm warning you, Sheriff. If you ever hit me with that shotgun again, I swear I'll kill you!" threatened Red.

"Shut your yap before it gets you into more trouble," warned the sheriff. "As a matter of fact, you can stay in there for another day now just for getting smart with me."

Red grumbled something under his breath, but the sheriff wasn't listening to him. He turned his attention back to Jess. "Is your pa cutting up some more steaks soon?" he asked.

"Yes, sir. He told me to ask if you wanted some more."

"Tell your pa to cut me up a few extra this time," said the sheriff smiling.

"Yes, sir. I sure will, Sheriff. I ran into three men on the trail this morning. I think they must have been the same men you chased out of town earlier."

"How'd you hear about them?"

"Jim Smythe over at the general store told me about them."

"Well, you stay away from them. They're nothing but trouble. I'm sure of that," claimed Diggs. "I've been looking through my wanted posters to see if I have anything on them."

"Last I seen of them, they were headed down the road toward my pa's ranch. I hope they don't cause my pa any trouble," he said with a worried look on his face.

"They'll probably just keep riding, heading for the next town. I'll tell you what though. After I finish up a few more things around here, I'll ride out to your pa's ranch and make sure that things are okay."

"Thanks, Sheriff," he replied gratefully.

Jess felt a little better as he left the sheriff's office and walked back to the general store. Mr. Smythe had everything in one pile and Jess made quick work of loading up the wagon. He went back in to get the bill to take to his pa. Jim smiled at him and darted his eyes over to the candy counter as he handed Jess the bill.

"Well, are you going to pick up a few pieces of that candy?" asked Jim.

"Yes, sir," he said smiling, as he looked over the candy counter. Jess picked out three different flavors of sugar sticks. Two sticks for him and one for his sister. He climbed up in the wagon and headed back to the ranch, his thoughts on the three men he'd met on the trail. He had a bad feeling and just couldn't shake it off.

CHAPTER THREE

Jess rode back to the ranch and turned left onto the path going up to the house. The house sat about fifteen hundred feet back off the main trail. As he was riding up the path to the house, he looked over to the right to see if his pa was still plowing. He spotted the horse and plow still sitting in the middle of the field, but not his pa. He pulled the wagon up to the front of the house so he could unload the supplies. It seemed unusually quiet around the house. He was hungry so he tied the paint to the front porch railing and quickly headed up the steps.

He swung the screen door open and just as he was about to say how hungry he was he was frozen in a complete state of horror. He stood there motionless, his eyes fixed to the grisly scene before him. He couldn't speak even though his mouth was stuck open. Tears began to well up in his eyes. His knees almost buckled, but somehow he caught himself. His muscles began to tremble and shake. The carnage before him was almost unbearable to look at, but he couldn't turn his gaze away.

His mother's body was hanging in the doorway going to the sleeping quarters of the house. The ropes that were tied around her wrists were tied to nails at the top corners of the doorway. There was a huge pool of blood on the floor surrounding her feet. Within the pool of blood was her dress, which was torn and ripped. The dress was soaked in blood. Her body had been slashed and stabbed repeatedly, and her throat had been cut. Her face was black and blue and one eye was so full of blood you couldn't tell if the eye was still there. Jess's legs finally buckled and he dropped to his knees.

It took him several attempts, but he finally got the strength to slowly stand up. His legs were still trembling and he almost fell to his knees again. He knew he had to tear himself away from the grisly scene in the doorway. He finally found the will to turn away and go back out the front door. He looked out to where his pa had been plowing. The horse and plow were there, but he still couldn't see his pa anywhere. He started to walk in that direction. As he did, he saw something on the ground behind the plow.

As he reached the horse and plow, he saw that it was his pa's body lying beside the plow. Jess knelt down next to his pa. John had been shot several times, one shot in the chest, one in the stomach, and two in the head. After what seemed like an eternity, Jess gathered enough strength to stand back up. He stumbled backward from his pa toward the house a few dozen steps and then he fell backward into the deep rich black soil. He looked up at the sky and the tears streamed down both sides of his head. He stayed that way for almost five minutes, wondering if anyone was looking down on him right now. He finally got the strength to stand back up and he slowly turned around and walked toward the house. He stopped about two hundred feet from the house, not sure if he could summon the courage to go back in there. Then, all of a sudden, he realized that he had not found his sister Samantha yet.

Jess took a few steps toward the house and then stopped as if he had hit an invisible wall. He swallowed hard and wiped the tears from his eyes. He knew he had to look for Samantha and that meant he had to go back into the house, but he couldn't gather the courage to do it. He decided to go to the back of the house and look in the windows. He walked around the back of the house and got within two feet of the first window. He leaned his back against the outside wall and tried to gain the courage to look inside.

He slowly stepped up to the window of his pa's room and looked inside. There was no sign of Samantha. He made his way over to the other window and looked inside, but Samantha was not there. He turned toward the barn and stable and walked over to the barn.

The door was already open. He walked into the barn and called out his sister's name. He looked around and was getting ready to climb the ladder to the top floor when he saw her arm sticking out of a pile of hay. Tears of fear filled his eyes again as he walked toward her. He knelt down and began to clear the hay from Samantha's body. Her clothes were torn apart. Jess sobbed uncontrollably. She had been beaten to a pulp and shot, a single bullet hole in the middle of her forehead.

He picked her up and carried her body out of the barn. As he stepped outside, he stopped for a moment and looked out toward his pa's body. He went around to the front of the house and up the steps and laid his sister's body gently down on the porch. Then, he sat down on the steps of the porch, laid his face on his arms, and sobbed for what seemed like an eternity. He couldn't believe this was happening. He wondered if this was just a bad dream and he would wake up soon. How could anyone do something like this? This just can't be happening, he thought to himself.

He wasn't sure if he had fallen asleep or was simply still in a daze when he began to hear the beating of hooves on the ground. He lifted his head as Sheriff Diggs quickly reined up his horse in front of the house and dismounted. As soon as Sheriff Diggs hit the ground, he knew things were bad. He had already seen Samantha's body lying motionless on the porch. He ran up the steps of the front porch to get to Samantha's body to see if there was any chance that she was alive. There wasn't.

"My god, Jess, what in the hell happened here?" Jess tried to mouth the words, but he couldn't speak. He just sobbed more loudly.

"Where is your father, Jess?"

Jess lifted his head, tears still streaming from his eyes. He slowly pointed toward the field where he'd found his pa's dead body earlier. The sheriff saw the horse with the plow sitting still out in the middle of the field. He could just barely make out what looked like a body on the ground behind the horse and plow. He began to head down the steps to run out to check where Jess was pointing, but before he got to the bottom step, Jess grabbed the sheriff's arm and stopped him in his tracks.

The sheriff knelt down and put his hand on Jess's shoulder. "I've got to go out there, Jess,"

Jess looked at the sheriff and shook his head as if to say no. He tilted his head slightly back and to the right. "Inside," he sobbed so low that the sheriff didn't catch what he had said for a second or two. "Ma," added Jess weakly.

The sheriff started back up the steps to look inside the house. As he opened the screen door, he gasped and froze. He stopped breathing for several seconds and then he slowly let the air out of his lungs. "Damn it," he whispered under his breath.

He glanced back out at Jess still sitting on the steps, his head back down on his arms. They were crossed on his knees. The sheriff fought back the tears welling up in his eyes. His throat felt like he had tried to swallow an apple whole. Becky had been like a daughter to him. He walked toward her, but stopped abruptly. He noticed boot prints in the blood on the floor. There were four distinct sets of boot prints. Jess was one of the four sets of boot prints, but he noticed something odd about one of the other boot prints. Some of the prints were made from a boot with a missing heel, a left heel. He scanned the rest of the room and spotted the murder weapon. A large kitchen knife covered with blood lay on the floor of the kitchen area, about ten feet from the body. There were no boot prints in that area so the sheriff surmised that it had been thrown over there.

He walked over to the body. Another wave of sadness, along with sheer hatred for the people responsible for this gruesome scene pulsated through his body, stopping him in his tracks again. If he ever found them, he would just shoot them where they stood. No trial. Then he would drag their bodies out in the woods and let the buzzards and coyotes pick their bones clean. They deserved nothing less.

He walked closer to Becky and squeezed past her to get around to the back of her body. When he got behind the body, he looked up at the nails and rope that tied her to the doorway. He decided to cut the body down. He went inside Becky's sleeping room and got a large blanket. He wrapped it around the body as best he could and reached down and pulled out the knife he always kept in his right boot. He carefully cut down Becky's body and placed it on her bed. He grabbed another blanket and made sure that she was completely covered. He grabbed another blanket to cover Samantha's body outside.

He walked back outside where Jess was still sitting on the steps. He gently placed the blanket on Samantha. Jess had stopped crying and had lifted his head up, looking out across the ranch toward the main road. The sheriff touched Jess's shoulder as he went down the steps and headed out to the field where John's body was. As he got close to the body he noticed one set of boot prints going in both directions. They were made from the same boots with the missing left heel. He looked over the body and surmised that whoever had done this had shot John with a rifle from a distance and then walked up and finished him with a few shots from a pistol. John's body was behind the plow and there was no evidence that it had been dragged there. Surely if he had seen anyone coming up the ranch road he would have walked toward the house to see who it was. He probably never saw it coming. The sheriff walked back to the front of the house and looked at the footprints. Near as he could tell, there had been three men. He found the prints from the boot with the missing heel again. He turned to walk over to the steps and when he looked up at Jess, he was startled by what he saw.

Jess stared straight ahead with a look that the sheriff had seen more than once in his lifetime. It was not a look that should be on any man's face, much less a boy's. He walked back up the steps and sat next to Jess again, putting his arm around him. He knew there was nothing he could say or do to comfort Jess in this moment, so he just sat there with his arm around him for a while. While the sheriff sat there, he thought about what he had to do next. He wanted to hit the trail and look for these murderers, but he would have to go into town and get some help. The blood on the floor was mostly dry except for the thick puddle that was around Becky's feet, so they had a good head start. He decided he would load up the bodies in the wagon and take the bodies and Jess to town. He knew he had to break the blank stare that Jess still had on his face. The sheriff could only imagine what thoughts could be going through his head.

"Jess?" asked Sheriff Diggs. Jess said nothing.

"Jess?" asked Diggs, a little louder. Jess still didn't respond. "Jess, I have to take the bodies into town, and you have to go with me."

Jess slowly turned his head to look at the sheriff. His voice was broken and quivering badly as he spoke. "Why would anyone want to kill my ma and pa, and little Samantha? Why? What sort of people would do something like this?" The sheriff knew there was no logical explanation he could give a fourteen-year-old boy that would make any sense, and yet, he had to tell him something.

"There are a lot of good men in the world, Jess," he explained thoughtfully. "Unfortunately, there are some really bad men, too. There are men who kill just for the sake of killing and the pure pleasure it gives their cold, black hearts. It never makes any sense, no matter how old you get or how many times you see it." Jess looked away from the sheriff and looked straight out at nothing again.

"Jess, why don't you sit here while I go get the horse loose from the plow and stable him?" the sheriff suggested. Jess nodded.

The sheriff walked out into the field and unhitched the horse. When he was finished, he met Jess back at the front porch and told him to put the horse in the barn and feed the stock. He figured that would give him enough time to load the bodies into the wagon without Jess being around. He quickly unloaded the supplies from the wagon and loaded up Becky and Samantha. Then he drove the wagon out to John's body. Jess was coming out from the stables when the sheriff got back to the front porch.

"Time to go, Jess." He nodded as he looked in the back of the wagon at the three bodies. He crawled up in the wagon and took his seat next to the sheriff. As he sat down, he looked at the boot prints in the soft dirt in front of the house. He noticed a left boot print with a missing boot heel. He planted that picture deeply into his mind.

It was a long ride back to town. Jess never said a word. He kept going over and over in his mind what had happened. He thought about the boot print with the missing left heel. He pictured the three men again in his mind. He never wanted to forget what they looked like. He would burn their images into his brain and remember everything he could about them.

It was getting close to dusk when they pulled into town. The sheriff stopped the wagon in front of the general store. Jim had come out on the porch to see what the sheriff was doing, driving a wagon back to town with Jess next to him in the front seat. The sheriff explained what had happened and Jim fought back the tears.

"Jim, can you take their bodies over to the undertaker? I need to get Jess here set up for the night. Then I need to round up some men for a posse to head out at first light and hunt down the bastards that did this."

"Of course, Sheriff, whatever you need. Are you going to put him up in the hotel?"

"Yeah, just for a few days until I can sort all this out."

"Sheriff, I have a better idea. Why don't you take the bodies over to the undertaker and let Sara and me take care of Jess? We have an extra room upstairs. He shouldn't be alone at a time like this. We can keep a close eye on him that way."

"That sounds fine to me, Jim. I'm sure he would be better off here than at the hotel. You sure your wife won't mind?"

"Not at all. Becky was like a daughter to us and Jess is like family. We'd be more than happy to look after him," he replied firmly.

Sheriff Diggs looked at Jess. "Would you rather stay with Jim and Sara?" he asked.

Jess shook his head affirming that it was okay with him. He, too, had always considered Jim and Sara as family. He looked in the back of the wagon as he stepped down from it. There was no sobbing, but tears were coming from his eyes.

"I'm tired," said Jess, barely audible.

"You go in and Sara will fix you some supper."

"I'm not hungry," he said flatly. "I just want to go to sleep."

"That's okay, Jess," agreed Jim. "Whatever you need."

"Sara!" Jim called out to his wife.

"I'm right here," Sara said softly, tears streaming from her eyes. "I've been standing here all this time. Jess, you come on in and I'll set up your bed right away, okay?"

Jess nodded and followed Sara up the stairs.

"You go ahead and get comfortable," said Sara. "I'll get you a glass of water just in case you get thirsty later."

"Thank you, ma'am," he said politely. He got undressed and got into bed. The sheets felt clean and cool to him and yet they did not comfort him in the least. Sara brought him a glass of water and set it down on a little table next to the bed. She put her hand on his head just for a moment as if to let him know that she would be right there if he needed anything. Sara closed the door most of the way, leaving it open just enough so she could hear him in the night. Jess lay there thinking about all that had happened. He slowly started to doze off. Just before he fell asleep, he imagined he was hunting down the killers who had murdered his family and that he would kill every last one of them. And, he would make them suffer.

CHAPTER FOUR

Jess tossed and turned that night. His mind replayed the horrors over and over again. He woke several times. Each time he did, Sara was right there to comfort him. He finally woke to the smell of freshly brewed coffee and bacon. For a brief moment, when he first opened his eyes, he hoped it was all a bad dream. Then he realized where he was and it all came back to him again in a thundering rush. He just stared at the ceiling. He wasn't sure how he could or even if he could deal with what had happened. Then his thoughts turned to the men responsible. He knew he had to see justice done. He didn't quite know how yet. He only knew that he had to make things right. There would be plenty of time to figure it all out. For now, he had to survive. He had to figure out what to do today, next week, and next month. He was a planner in life, just like his pa had been.

He got dressed and splashed his face with some cool, clean water Sara had left in a large bowl on the table by his bed. It felt good on his face. As he lifted his head up in the mirror and reached for a small towel, he noticed something different about the way he looked. It was surely his reflection in the mirror, but it didn't quite look like him. He was different in some odd sort of way that he couldn't quite put his finger on. He headed down the stairs to the kitchen where Jim was sitting at the table sipping hot coffee, an empty plate in front of him.

Sara was standing over the hot stove and when she heard Jess come into the room, she turned around to see him. "How about some eggs and bacon, Jess?" Sara asked.

"I don't know. I'm not sure I'm hungry yet."

"Jess, you haven't eaten since early yesterday," pleaded Jim. "You've got to be mighty hungry by now."

"Well, I guess so," he replied, talking so low they could hardly hear the words.

"Then let Sara fix you a plate of vittles. You've got to eat eventually." Sara put a plate of eggs, bacon and biscuits in front of Jess.

"Thanks, ma'am," he said.

"You're welcome, Jess. If you need anything else, you just say so." Jess picked up a biscuit and began to pull it apart. He put a small piece of it in his mouth and began chewing it, a strange blank stare in his eyes. Sara fixed herself a plate and sat down next to Jess, hoping she could coax him into eating some more.

"It sure looks good," said Jess, "but I just can't seem to eat much. If you'll excuse me, I'd like to go out and sit on the back steps." Jess got up from the table and looked at his plate and then looked over at Sara. "Sorry, ma'am," he said.

Sara put her hand on his arm gently. "It's okay, Jess," Sara replied. "I understand. You can eat whenever you're ready."

"Thanks," he said, as he walked down the back hallway and out the back door and sat on the steps of the porch. The view behind the store was less than exceptional. There was junk cluttered all around. The view off in the distance was much more pleasing. He could see rolling hills, most of them covered with trees. As he viewed the scenery, he realized to himself that the men who had killed his family could be hiding in those hills right now. He didn't even realize it yet, but his subconscious was mapping out his destiny and his future. Sara slowly picked at her eggs while looking down the hallway watching Jess on the back porch. Jim and Sara had not been able to have their own children and Sara had always been partial to Jess and had always treated him like her own son.

"It's hard to even imagine what that boy is going through," said Sara, her head hanging down looking at her food, which she hadn't touched yet.

"I know," added Jim. "Sara, did you notice something different about him this morning? I mean, I know his family being murdered and all has him all tore up inside, but something else is different about him. I swear he even looks older to me this morning."

Sara hung her head and closed her eyes. Tears welled up in her eyes as she looked up at Jim. "Last night, we put a fourteen-year-old grieving boy to bed," she said sadly. "But this morning, there is a fourteen-year-old young man with hatred and raw vengeance in his heart sitting on our back steps. I'm afraid for him, Jim, deathly afraid."

"I felt it too, Sara. Something has changed him on the inside. We'll have to help him as much as we can. That's all we can do."

Sara was crying quietly. She could feel in her soul what was manifesting itself in this fourteen-year-old boy and she knew there was nothing that she or anyone else in the world could do to stop it. She mourned for him more than for his family who would all be buried in the ground today. His family lost their lives. Jess, however, had lost his very heart and soul.

The burial went as well as burials go. Jim gathered a few of the townspeople and the preacher, and hauled the bodies of John, Becky and Samantha back out to the ranch to be buried in the little cemetery plot John had spotted that very first night he had stayed on his land. The graves were dug in silence and the bodies placed in their gravesites. The preacher said a prayer over each of them and some of the men from town shoveled dirt until the graves were filled. Someone fixed up three wooden crosses for the graves and Jim pounded them into the ground with a rock. Sara cried the whole time. Jess, however, watched all this in a strange silence. He never spoke a word nor shed another tear. It was as if he'd already let them go and this was all just a formality, something that needed to be done. Jim came up beside him and put his hand on Jess's shoulder.

"We should be getting back to town," Jim told him softly. "There is no more we can do for them. The Lord will take care of their souls."

"I'm not going back. I'm staying right here," replied Jess firmly.

"Jess, you can't stay here and run this ranch all by yourself. There's too much to do for one man, much less a fourteen-year-old boy."

"I'm not a boy anymore. They took care of that," Jess replied, not really signifying who they were, but Jim and Sara both knew whom he was referring to.

"I know, Jess," argued Jim, "but taking care of a ranch is an awful lot of responsibility to take on. Are you sure you're ready for all that?"

"I guess I'll have to be," he replied, a tone of finality to his voice.

Jim shook his head in frustration. "Okay," he said reluctantly. "But you promise me that if you have any trouble or need any help, you'll let us know, all right?"

"I will…I promise."

"The sheriff and his posse will be back in a day or so," Jim said. "We'll let him know that you're out here. Is there anything else we can do for you right now?"

"No, I just need some time to myself."

"Okay then. Just don't forget, if you need anything…" Jim started saying when Sara took Jim's arm and he knew that meant for him to shut up.

"Thanks for everything," said Jess. "I won't forget it. Pa always told me to repay kindness with the same."

"Your pa was a smart man, Jess, and a damn good one," said Jim. "We're all gonna miss him, your ma and Samantha, too. We won't forget them ever."

"I won't forget either," Jess said as he turned his stare from the gravesite to the rolling hills out past the field that his pa was plowing when he was shot down in his tracks. "I won't ever forget."

"Well, we'd best be going, Jess," said Jim.

Jim and Sara got into the back of the preacher's wagon and the few other townspeople followed them back to town. Jess found himself all alone for the first time in his life. It was a strange feeling. He didn't like it, but he knew he had to get used to it. He sat down in front of the three fresh gravesites. He sat there for almost an hour. He kept thinking about how he and Samantha had always fought and how she used to aggravate him to no end. He wished she were there right now to do it again, but that wasn't going to happen, ever again.

He remembered his ma and how she was always there to help him with anything. His thoughts turned to his pa, how he had finally come down to the creek to teach him how to draw the wooden pistol he'd carved for him. He was just going to have to finish learning all by himself. But not with the wooden pistol his pa had carved. No, he would begin practicing with his pa's .45 that was in the box under his pa's bed. Before it was just a challenge to see how fast he could draw; now there was a need. He had to learn to be the best. Without really knowing or planning it, his mind was formulating a mission. He would hunt down the people who had savagely murdered his entire family and kill them, one by one, and he would have no mercy. He would kill them in the most vicious way he could. They would suffer. His pa had always told him there were some pretty bad people in the world, but he never realized just how bad. People that bad had no right to live, as far as he was concerned.

Jess finally got up and said a little prayer over his family. After the prayer, he made his solemn promise to them. He made an oath that he would not rest until he tracked down and killed everyone responsible for their deaths. He walked back up to the house and went inside. Someone had cleaned up the large pool of blood where his ma's body hung. Only a dark stain remained.

The smell of food surprised him. There was a fire in the stove and Jess found some fried chicken in a pot along with some biscuits. Sara. She was a good person and he was thankful to have her as a friend. He wouldn't go hungry tonight, but tomorrow he would have to fend for himself. He would have to do everything by himself now.

He felt the loneliness begin to set in as he sat at the table alone and ate. He decided first thing in the morning he would go out and finish plowing the field his pa had started on. He figured he would have to run the ranch for the next year or so. Then, he would ride out and carry out the deadly oath he had made to his family. He would let the sheriff go after the men, but if he didn't catch them, he would go after them himself. If the sheriff caught them, they would hang, and he would watch. Regardless, they would be reckoned with. Deep within himself, he hoped for the latter.

He finished the meal and then noticed there was a pie sitting by the window. It was an apple pie. Sara. Jess decided to have some later. Right now, he figured he would go out and check the stock and throw some extra hay and then go down to the creek and practice with his pa's pistol.

He headed out to the barn and threw some hay. He turned around to put the pitchfork back into the pile when he noticed a slight glimmer off to his right. The reflection was coming from the wall where his pa always hung his hat. What he saw hanging on the peg was the most spectacular and unusual-looking pistol and holster he had ever seen. He walked over to it and picked it up off the peg. The holster was brown and had a finish to it he had never seen on any leather before. On the back of the holster was a name stamped into the leather. BOB MERNICKLE CUSTOM HOLSTERS. He also saw the words MADE IN CANADA. Another unusual feature of the holster was that it had no place to hold bullets. The pistol had a polished finish on it that was as perfect as any he had ever seen.

Jess strapped the holster on and it fit perfectly, as if it had been made for him. The holster held the pistol a little more out from his leg than a regular holster. The gun rode on Jess's right leg perfectly. The holster didn't cover as much of the gun as most holsters did. There was a nice one-inch-wide leg strap that fit Jess's leg perfectly. Jess unhooked the hammer strap and pulled the gun out. The first thing he noticed was how easily the gun seemed to glide out of the holster. It was as if the holster was greased, but it wasn't. He reached inside the holster and felt the inside. It had a real smooth feel to it and it was harder than normal, which allowed the gun to glide out of the holster more easily. Then he noticed there were no front or rear sights on the gun.

He looked the gun over carefully and saw some printing stamped on it. On one side by the trigger he read the words RUGER BLACKHAWK .41 MAGNUM CALIBER. On the other side of the gun was a number: 40-01079. The handgrips were made out of some type of material he had never seen before. It looked like some type of horn material and the grips flared out at the bottom so as to make the gun extremely easy to grip.

Jess decided to take the gun into the house to study it some more. When he got in the house, he placed the gun and holster on the kitchen table. He sat there for several minutes trying to take all this in and wondering where this unusual gun had come from. He picked it up again. The gun was extremely light compared to the few pistols he had ever been able to hold. His pa's gun was a Colt .45 Peacemaker and he figured it had to weigh twice as much as this gun. He didn't know much about pistols, but he knew after handling this one for a few minutes that it was like no other pistol he had ever seen. This was something unique and special. He knew he would have to keep this gun and holster hidden for now. He walked outside and quickly went back to the barn and climbed up the ladder to the top floor. His pa had kept some wooden boxes there and he gently placed the gun and holster into one of the boxes and placed some more boxes around it to hide it.

He went back to the house and decided to have some of the apple pie Sara had left him. Before he cut it, he decided to make himself some coffee to go with it. The coffee was strong but good, and the pie was even better. As he sat there, he thought some more about the pistol. It couldn't have been his pa's gun or it wouldn't have been hanging on a peg in the barn. It would have been in the box with his pa's other gun.

By now, the sun was getting low in the sky. Jess decided against practicing this late and decided to turn in early for the night. He had a field to plow come morning. He had some more coffee and then he went into his pa's room and got the shotgun from the corner and took it into his bedroom along with a few extra shells. If anyone tried to bother him that night or the killers returned, he would be ready. He would never be surprised by anyone like his family had been. He promised himself that he would always have a gun by his side at all times and always be on the ready. As he fell off to sleep, he imagined he was tracking his family's killers across the country. And he saw the pistol he'd found in the barn strapped to his waist. It looked like it belonged there.

He dreamed that night, but not nightmares. He dreamed good dreams of his family. He woke often though that night as he would for the rest of his life. The slightest sound would awaken him. His senses seemed more aware without him really knowing it. He would always be ready…always.

CHAPTER FIVE

Jess woke up before sunrise. Before he got out of bed, he thought about the pistol in the barn. All the same thoughts about the pistol and holster ran through his head again. He got up and cooked himself some breakfast. While he ate, he thought of all the things he would have to do on his own. He continued to plan out what he would do. He would work the ranch for the next two years. He would be a little over sixteen by that time and he planned to be the quickest draw with a pistol anyone had ever seen. In the meantime, he would plant crops and sell them. He would sell off the livestock and stash away all the money and use it to do what he needed to do, what he knew he had to do.

It was a hot dusty day and he never figured plowing a field would be such hard work. He earned a new respect for his pa. It was just after high noon and he decided to stop and eat. After eating a simple meal of ham and a piece of apple pie, he went back at it again. When he finished for the day, he walked back to the house after throwing some hay and looked at the blisters beginning to form on his hands. He figured that he'd better wear the leather gloves his pa had in the barn or else he wouldn't be able to practice drawing a pistol in the evening, and that was something that he'd promised himself he would do every night.

After dinner, he went into his pa's room and got the wooden box out from under the bed. He took it to the table and opened it up. Inside, he found his pa's Colt .45 Peacemaker and the holster to go with it. He also found four boxes of .45 slugs in the bottom of the box. He strapped the gun and holster on and went down to the creek. Even with the blisters, he practiced for two hours straight. The first hour and a half he drew and dry fired the gun. Then, he loaded the pistol and spent the last half hour using live ammunition. His practice took on a new fervor. It was not just a game anymore. Now it was something he had to do to make sure that he survived. He decided that the next day he would start practicing with both his pa's pistol and the one he'd found in the barn.

When he finished practicing, he took his pa's gun and holster and put it back in the house. Then, he climbed up in the top of the barn and looked at the pistol and holster he'd found. He decided to take it into the house. He finally turned in and as he lay there that night, he figured he would practice with his pa's pistol for the first part of his practice every night and then switch to the new pistol for the rest of his practice.

The next day found him back out plowing the field. It was just before noon when he noticed a dust cloud on the main road. He stopped and reached over to grab his pa's rifle out of the scabbard that he kept strapped to the plow horse. The Winchester .44-40 still looked like new. He also had his pa's double-barreled shotgun tied to the horse. He watched the group of riders turn down the ranch road. He counted four of them. He finally caught a glimpse of who was approaching. It was Sheriff Diggs with three other men. They rode right up to the plow rig and Jess walked around the rig after putting the shotgun down.

"Hi, Jess," said Sheriff Diggs. "I sure didn't expect to find you out here and especially never expected to see you working the field. Hell, I thought someone was trying to squat and I'd have to run him off. I figured you would still be at Jim and Sara's. You expecting trouble?" he asked, nodding at the rifle and shotgun leaning on the plow.

"I wasn't expecting any, but if it came, I'd be ready for it," he replied. "I decided to stay here and work the ranch. Got to be a man and do a man's work now, Sheriff. They didn't leave me much choice about that, the way I figure." The sheriff knew who "they" were. "I reckon you didn't find them unless you had to kill them and bury their carcasses out on the trail."

"No such luck," replied Sheriff Diggs sadly. "I would have loved to bury the bastards if I'd found them. We did find out who they were with the help of some other unfortunate people they robbed not more than ten miles from here. I also got some news from the sheriff in a little town about twenty miles east of here. They stopped there for a drink and someone overheard them bragging about how they killed some people and raped some women. The sheriff didn't have any wanted posters on them, but he did get a look at them and he gave me a pretty good description. We had a local artist in town draw up some wanted posters and I showed them to the couple that was robbed. They were able to identify all three of them. I need you to look at them to see if they are the same three men you met on the trail that day." Jess took the drawings from the sheriff and looked at them, the look on his face hardening as he did. It was the same three men.

"The youngest one," the sheriff continued as Jess looked over the drawings, "is Randy Hastings. He's the one with the missing boot heel. He carries two six-guns with pearl handles. The other one is Blake Taggert. He's the one with the bushy beard, unless he's shaved it off by now, but I doubt it. He carries a left-handed six-shooter. The oldest one is Hank Beard. He always wears a yellow bandana. He carries a six-shooter, but his specialty is a double-barreled shotgun. Hear tell, he's killed several men with it."

Jess looked up at the sheriff with a blank, hard look. "These are the three men I met on the trail, Sheriff. I'm sure of it. The drawings are a good likeness, that's for sure. Can I keep these?"

"Of course," replied Diggs. "Jess, is there anything else I can do for you right now? Can we help with some of the work here? Running a ranch is a lot of responsibility for a young man."

"Thanks, Sheriff," he replied flatly, "but I can take care of the ranch and myself just fine."

"All right, then. You take care, Jess," the sheriff said as he and his three deputies started to turn their horses around. Just then Jess stopped the sheriff and asked him the one question the sheriff hoped he would never ask, and yet somehow he knew that he would.

"Sheriff, you said they bragged about raping some women, meaning more than one. Does that mean they raped my little sister Samantha?"

Sheriff Diggs' eyes fell to the ground. He didn't want to answer the question, but there was no way he could avoid it. He knew that in his heart. Jess deserved to know the truth no matter how terrible. The sheriff was a man who always figured the truth was the best way out of a bad situation. His eyes slowly rose from the ground and he looked Jess straight in the eyes and told him the cold, terrible truth.

"Yes. I had hoped not to have to tell you about it," he replied sympathetically. "But the truth is those bastards did rape Samantha. I'm sorry to have to tell you that."

Jess's eyes glazed over and darkness seemed to emanate from the back of them. The sheriff had seen the look that he had in his eyes all too often lately. He knew the look: rage, revenge, love, hate, all wrapped up in one look. He saw it in these eyes of a boy not yet fifteen. He knew what Jess had on his mind and he knew there was nothing that he, nor anyone else for that matter, could do to change it.

Jess never changed his look and never lost his lock on the sheriff's eyes. "Thanks for your honesty, Sheriff."

"You're welcome. I only wish I could have done more."

"That's okay. You're a good man, Sheriff, and I figure I owe you one," he replied. "I know you've done your best. I'll take care of it from here." The sheriff didn't have to try to figure out what that meant.

Sheriff Diggs and his men turned their horses and headed back down the ranch road out to the main trail leading into Black Creek. As they did, the other three men with the sheriff tipped their hats at Jess as if to say they understood what he was going through. Jess simply nodded back.

As the men rode away, one of them looked over at the sheriff with an apprehensive look on his face. "Did you see what that boy had in his eyes?" the man asked. "I ain't never seen that much rage and coldness in any man's eyes, much less a boy."

"I know," replied the sheriff, "but he ain't no boy anymore. Hell, it's only been a few days since I've seen him and I swear he looks five years older already. And by the look in his eyes, he'll damn well do it, that's for sure. I've seen that look before and it ain't a good look. I wouldn't want to be any of those three bastards."

Jess watched the sheriff and his three deputies ride off down the main road until they were out of sight. He went back to plowing the field as if nothing had happened. He thought about his sister Samantha. He thought of the fear and helplessness she must have gone through as she was being raped and murdered. He could hardly contain the rage within him, but he continued to plow, never stopping. The rage would fuel him. The rage would keep him going. The rage would always be his edge.

He finished plowing for the day. He walked back to the house with the rifle in one hand and the shotgun in the other. When he got to the porch, he noticed a large box sitting on it. He looked inside. He found several loaves of bread, a dozen biscuits, an apple pie and a big pot of stew. Sara. He had been so busy he'd never seen her drop it off.

He finished supper and got his pa's gun and holster along with the new pistol and holster he'd found and went out to the creek for his nightly practice. He spent the next two hours practicing. First, he practiced with his pa's gun. He would draw the gun over and over again. Sometimes he thumbed the hammer and sometimes he fanned the hammer. His pa's gun was much heavier than the other gun and much harder to get out of the holster quickly. He noticed as soon as he strapped the new gun on, everything worked so much smoother and faster. The very design of the new gun and holster made it much easier to draw it quicker. Fanning the gun was easier, too, with the tall hammer that stuck straight up. Jess looked at the pistol where it had .41 MAGNUM CALIBER stamped on it.

He took six .45-caliber shells out of the box of ammo and put them into the pistol. They fit perfectly. He took them back out and even tried to put the lead end of one of the bullets into the front of the barrel of the gun. It looked as if it was the correct caliber. Somehow, and he would never find out why, someone had the wrong caliber stamped on this pistol. He loaded the gun again and placed it back in the holster. He drew and fired at a tree across the creek. He was amazed at how much easier and quicker his draw was with the new pistol. He finished his practice with the new gun, going through almost fifty rounds of ammo, and went back to the house. After making some coffee to go along with a nice piece of Sara's apple pie, he went to bed with his pa's loaded .45 next to him on the bed.

In the morning he decided to go into town for some supplies. He stopped at the general store and thanked Sara for the food and Jim for all his help. He ordered some supplies he thought he needed, and some .45 cartridges for his pa's gun.

"Why do you need bullets, Jess?" asked Jim.

"Just doing some target shooting down by the creek."

"You need a dozen boxes for target shootin'?"

"You do if you plan on target shooting a lot. I hope you'll allow me credit like my pa."

"Why, of course, Jess. By the way, did you know that your pa had some money in the bank? I'm not saying that so you'll pay me in cash, I just thought you should know."

"No, I never knew my pa had any money saved," he replied.

"Well, go see Mr. Jameson at the bank and I'm sure he will let you know all about it."

"Thanks, Mr. Smythe."

The bank was small and there were only three windows, with one man working the only window that was open. Mr. Jameson was sitting behind a desk over to the left of the teller windows. As he spotted Jess, he got up immediately. "Good afternoon, Jess. I'm really sorry about what happened to your family," said Mr. Jameson. "What can I do to help you today?"

"Jim Smythe says my pa had some money in your bank and that it probably belongs to me. Is that right?"

"That's right, Jess. Why don't we go look at the account and see how much is there? He was a good man, your pa," said Jameson kindly.

"That's nice of you to say, Mr. Jameson, sir." Jameson went behind his desk and picked out a ledger book from the shelf. He leafed through some pages and found what he was looking for.

"Oh…yes…hmm…here we go," Jameson said in his low banker voice. "Yes, he has…or I guess you have…two hundred seventy-two dollars and sixteen cents. Do you need some of the money right now?"

"Well, I don't rightly know just yet," he replied, as he thought about it for a moment. "How about if I take out twenty dollars for now? That way I can pay off my pa's bill and pay cash for my supplies. I guess I can use credit when I really have to. Better to pay my way if I can, don't you think?"

"Absolutely. Banks are for borrowing money when you don't have it and credit is for people who can't pay right away. The less you use of either is a good way for a man to live, Jess."

"I agree."

Mr. Jameson filled out a slip of paper for Jess. "Here, take this to the teller and he'll get you your money."

"Thanks, Mr. Jameson. You've been a real big help. This will be my bank from now on."

"Why, thank you, Jess. That's a mighty nice thing to say."

Jess walked out of the bank and headed to the general store. He loaded up his supplies and paid in cash even over Jim's repeated objections. Jim was a little more than curious when Jess also asked for two-dozen boxes of .45-caliber rounds instead of the original dozen he had asked for when he first came in. Jess figured as long as he had the money, he might as well get plenty. He knew he was going to use that much and more.

"Jess, what in the hell are you going to do with all these bullets?" asked Jim awkwardly.

"Like I said, just doing some target shootin' down at the creek. As a matter of fact, do you have some empty bottles I could have to use for targets?"

"Well…yes. You'll find all you want behind the store, but you be careful with your target shootin', you hear?" cautioned a worried Jim. "We don't want anything happening to you."

"Oh, I'll be careful. Honest. My pa was starting to show me how to shoot just before…well, you know."

"I know, but just be careful, okay? You promise me," Jim pleaded.

"I can promise you this: I plan on being real careful for the rest of my life," he replied emphatically, as he walked out and picked up a dozen or so of the bottles on the ground out back and headed back to the ranch.

Jess finished the farm work, had supper and went down to the creek with his pa's gun strapped on. He carried the new gun and holster over his left shoulder. He set up some bottles across the creek. Some he stood on the ground and some were stuck upside down on branches waving in the slight breeze. He began the practice that would become a ritual for the next two years. He would draw the guns several times very slowly, but very deliberately. That way he made sure he was doing everything just right. He would dry fire both guns, going through the entire motion perfectly, cocking the pistol on the draw and then squeezing the trigger as he pointed the gun at the target. Then he would load the gun with .45 cartridges and go through the same motions again, firing live rounds. He would do it slowly at first and then finish with fast draws. He would repeat everything over and over again relentlessly. It didn't take long before he ran out of ammunition. He made another run into town to pick up a few supplies and another two-dozen boxes of .45 cartridges.

While he was at the general store, Sheriff Diggs walked in. "How's my favorite young man, Jess?" Diggs said, smiling.

"Hi, Sheriff. I'm just fine."

Sheriff Diggs counted out the twenty-four boxes of .45 cartridges sitting on the counter and gave Jess a curious look. "Twenty-four boxes of cartridges? Jess, what the hell are you doing with all this ammunition?" the sheriff asked curiously. "I heard you're buying poor Jim clean out,"

"I'm just doing some target practice," he replied evasively. "A man has to know how to use a gun these days."

"How's it going so far?" asked Sheriff Diggs.

"Pretty good so far."

"Well, you be careful with guns, Jess. They ain't toys, you know."

"I know, Sheriff. I'll be careful."

"Especially with that shotgun there," said Sheriff Diggs, as he nodded to the back of the wagon where Jess had put his pa's .44-40 rifle and double-barreled shotgun.

Jess picked up his supplies and the boxes of cartridges and loaded them in the wagon. He climbed up in the seat, slapped the reins on the paint's rear and headed out of town and back to the ranch.

Jim looked at Sheriff Diggs. "You need anything, Sheriff?" asked Jim.

"Not really. I was just checking on Jess," said Sheriff Diggs. "He makes me nervous messing with his pa's guns. I don't like him getting that close to a pistol at his age, especially with what's happened and all. There's something going on in that boy's head and I don't think it's anything good either."

"Hell, Sheriff, his whole family was murdered in cold blood and he saw it with his own eyes," expressed Jim. "That would put a change in anyone's life including you, the hard case that you are."

The sheriff laughed at that and agreed. "Well, let me know what he buys from you in the way of ammunition, okay?" asked Diggs. "I want to keep an eye on him. He's really starting to worry me."

"Sure thing, Sheriff. Sara and I only want the best for him too, but he is a man now and he's going to have to find his own way."

"I know. I just don't want it to be the wrong way," cautioned Sheriff Diggs.

The sheriff walked out and looked down the main street. He could see Jess turning the corner out of town. He had a real bad feeling growing in the back of his head about Jess. Yet somehow, he knew there was nothing he could do about it. He knew the boy was holding a real rage about what had happened to his family and he understood that. He just wondered how all that rage would find its way out of the young man. Then he slowly hung his head and shuddered inside as he came to the realization that he already knew the answer to that question.

CHAPTER SIX

For the next two years, Jess pretty much followed the same routine every day. He worked the ranch, taking care of the stock and working the fields. He sold off small groups of cattle here and there and put the money in the bank. He made many trips to town for supplies and ammunition. Every evening, he went down to the creek and practiced with his pa's .45 and the new pistol. He was getting pretty fast with his pa's gun, but he was like greased lightning when he drew his new gun. His accuracy was getting much better, too. He rarely missed a bottle, whether it was standing still or even waving in the breeze hanging on a branch. He had even taken to throwing bottles up in the air and hitting them on the way down. He made it more difficult by wearing a hat while looking straight ahead and not up and then only drawing the gun when the bottle came into his field of view. This only gave him a fraction of a second to hit the target. At first, he missed most of the bottles. Later on, he rarely missed one.

He learned to point and shoot accurately. He learned to rapid fire and to fan the trigger, especially the second shot, which would become his trademark shot. He would cock the hammer back as he pulled the pistol out for the first shot and then use the middle finger of his left hand to fan the second shot a split second later. Before he drew, his right hand was down by the butt of his pistol and his left hand was just above his right hand, ready to fan the second shot. He would even go upstream and throw several bottles in the creek and run back and wait for them to come into his side vision. When they did, he drew and blasted them out of the water, one by one.

The new gun seemed to jump out of the holster with the least bit of effort. He was well on his way to being the fastest man to draw and shoot a pistol because he had an advantage that no other man had: the gun. Without it, he could learn to draw as fast as any of the best. But with it, he would become unbeatable.

Not only did he practice with pistols; he practiced with the rifle and the shotgun. With the shotgun, he made a special holster that was strapped to his back so that the handle of the shotgun stuck up just over his right shoulder. He practiced loading both shells into the shotgun in one fluid motion. He sewed some pockets into his shirt that held two shotgun shells together so that he could grab and reload the shotgun quickly. He had to carry his pistol cartridges in his front pants pockets since the holster had no holders for bullets. He didn't understand why, but it didn't matter to him. He learned to throw a knife. He made a scabbard for the knife and tucked it behind him under the holster and tied it in place with a small leather thong.

During all this time, the sheriff came out to talk to Jess several times. He knew what Jess was planning and he knew it from the start. About a week before Jess was ready to head out for the trail, he decided to pay a visit to Sheriff Diggs and see if there was any news about the three men who had murdered his family. As he walked into the sheriff's office, the sheriff was checking out the lock on one of his three jail cells.

"Need help with that, Sheriff?" asked Jess.

The sheriff turned around. "Well it's about time you came to visit me," exclaimed Diggs. "Naw, I'll get the blacksmith down here to fix it. Damn thing won't stay locked and I sure can't have that. What can I do for ya?"

"I'm just checking one last time to see if you've heard anything new about the three men who killed my family."

"Actually, you're in luck. I just got some information on them. Remember the one with the missing boot heel?"

"I remember every one of them, Sheriff," he replied candidly.

"Well, Sheriff Manley, up in Tarkenton, about four hundred miles northwest of here, says someone fitting his description got into a shootout with a local hothead there and got himself wounded. He killed the other man, but he needed surgery to remove a bullet from his left thigh so he's been recuperating up in the town's local cathouse for the last couple of weeks. I've got no information on the other two, but at least it's a start."

"Why doesn't the sheriff arrest him and lock him up?"

Sheriff Diggs let out a sigh as he sat down behind his desk. "Jess, you need to understand that most lawmen are not tough men. Some of them can't even handle a gun; and quite frankly, most of the lawmen in small towns just do it for the money so they don't starve. They can't handle or won't handle most hardened criminals."

"Then they need to get new lawmen."

"No one else will take the jobs in those small towns," said Diggs shaking his head. "I ain't saying it's right. I'm only telling you how it really is, okay?" Jess just shook his head, not wanting to understand how things really were.

"Anyway," the sheriff continued, "he's the one called Randy Hastings. The only murder he's known to have committed is your family, although I have to believe he's guilty of more. The wanted poster says there's a five-hundred-dollar bounty on his head, dead or alive. I thought about heading up there and seeing if I can bring him in."

"No, don't bother, Sheriff," Jess replied sharply. "Leave him to me."

Sheriff Diggs had a look of frustration on his face as he took on a fatherly tone. "Jess, don't talk that way. Hell, Jess, I know what you've been planning since that day I met you at the house when you were plowing the fields. I've watched you come into town and buy every round of ammunition Jim Smythe has ordered over the last two years. I know about your practicing with your pa's gun and I know what's in that skull of yours. But it just ain't a good idea to go off and hunt men down and kill 'em. It'll change your life forever. It'll turn you into a cold-blooded killer and you'll never be able to come back from that. Once you start, you can't stop and then you'll end up dead before it's over. Trust me, I've seen it over and over again and I don't want to see it happen to you."

"Sheriff, I understand what you're trying to do, and I appreciate it. I really do," he said thoughtfully. "But you have to understand something. I died inside that day I sat on the porch of my pa's house after finding my entire family murdered. That's the day I changed, not today. I have only one mission left in life and it's to hunt those bastards down and make them pay. I'll kill every one of them along with anyone else who gets in my way. Look in these eyes, Sheriff. What do you see?" He walked closer to the sheriff.

The sheriff looked into Jess's eyes, which were black and cold, devoid of anything but death and vengeance. Diggs lowered his eyes to the paperwork on his desk, a sad look on his face, even though he understood. "Okay, here is everything I have on Randy Hastings. As soon as I get anything on the other two, I'll get it to you. You just promise me you're gonna be careful. These men are cold and callous killers, Jess," replied the sheriff.

"Thanks, Sheriff," he said, as he took the copy of the wanted poster on Randy Hastings. "You can be sure of one thing. Their killing days are coming to an end." Jess said it with such a meaning in his voice that the sheriff truly believed it.

Jess headed over to the bank to see Mr. Jameson. He wanted to go over the account before he left town. He had sold everything that he figured he wouldn't need and now had over nine hundred dollars in the bank. As always, Mr. Jameson was working at the desk. He was always glad to see Jess because he was usually bringing money to deposit. "Howdy, Jess. Making a deposit again?" he asked.

"Not today actually. I need to take some money out."

"Well, how much do you need, Jess?"

"I'd like two hundred dollars."

"All right," said Jameson, as he filled out a slip for him to take to the teller. Jess remained seated. "Anything else I can do for you today, Jess?"

"I was wondering how I can get money when I'm on the trail."

Jameson explained how he could wire for money if he needed any while away. Then Jess went to the general store and visited with Jim and Sara. He explained that he would be leaving town and he paid up his bill and purchased all the boxes of .45 cartridges Jim had in stock, as well as rounds for the rifle and more shotgun shells. He told Jim and Sara that he would stop by the next week and see them one more time before he left. Then he headed out of town and back to the ranch. Jim and Sara stood on the front porch of the store watching Jess ride out.

Sara looked up at Jim with tears in her eyes. "Do you think we should tell him?" asked Sara.

"I don't know, Sara. I've got to think about it. We can decide before he leaves next week."

"He deserves to know, Jim," she pleaded. "We should tell him before he finds out for himself."

"We'll see, Sara. We'll see."

Jess went back to the ranch and spent his last week there. The last week at the ranch was a week full of memories. He spent a lot of time sitting at the gravesite remembering all the good times. Jess knew that someday he would come back, but not for a while. He knew he was in for a long and hard journey. On the last day, he made his last breakfast in the cabin, saddled up and headed for town to say his last goodbyes. Before he climbed into the saddle he strapped his new gun on, put his pa's rifle in the scabbard and put the shotgun into the special back holster he had made from his pa's scraps of leather. He stuck his pa's Colt .45 Peacemaker in the front of his holster belt. He checked his knife; it was sharp and in its place strapped to the back of his gun belt. He was ready. He was ready for anything or anybody. Yet, he had something more. Something most men didn't have. He had rage—and he had reason. Jess looked over the ranch once more before he started down the ranch road toward the main trail leading into Black Creek.

Something happened to him when he rode down the trail. Something he couldn't quite put a finger on. His life instantly changed forever at that moment. He felt like he had crossed an imaginary line of some sort. There was no feeling inside him one way or another. There was nothing he was afraid of and nothing that could stand in his way. God help the men he hunted or anyone who got in his way. They were destined for death, and he was destined to do the killing. It felt right.

CHAPTER SEVEN

On his way into Black Creek, Jess stopped along the way at his old favorite spot by the big boulder at the bend in the creek. Not for himself though, just for his horse to drink. While Gray drank, Jess remembered the confrontation with the three men on that fateful day. He could picture them as if they were there in front of him right now. Gray finished drinking and Jess continued toward town. As soon as he rode around the last bend toward town, he noticed it was busier than usual. People were gathering together and talking to one another. He noticed one man who ran across the street to the saloon. He put himself on high alert. He pulled up in the front of Jim and Sara's general store. He dismounted and was tying up Gray when Jim walked out of the store.

"Jess, I have some bad news for you..." He stopped in mid-sentence. "What the hell?" he said, surprised to see Jess with a gun and holster strapped to his waist, another pistol tucked in the front of the holster, and a shotgun handle sticking up from behind his back. Jim stared at him for a few seconds before he spoke again. "Jess, are you okay?" he asked in a concerned tone.

"Yes, sir. I'm just fine."

Jim was looking Jess over and he finally got a good look at the gun strapped around his waist. It was like no other pistol and holster he'd ever seen before. "Jess, where the hell did you get that holster? And what kind of gun is that?" asked Jim.

"I found it in the bottom of my pa's lock box," he replied, not wanting to explain how he had really found the gun.

"That doesn't look like any pistol I've ever seen before. I've never seen a holster quite like that either," said Jim, still looking at the pistol and holster Jess was wearing.

"Jim, you said you had some bad news? What is it?" he asked, trying to get Jim to tell him what was going on.

Jim hesitated, still not sure what to make of Jess. "Oh, I'm sorry to have to tell you this, but the sheriff was shot dead not more than a half hour ago," replied Jim, still staring at the pistol and holster Jess was wearing. If Jess was surprised, he didn't show it, but Jim could see a coldness washing across Jess's face and a darkness looming in the back of his eyes.

"Who did it?" he demanded in a harsh tone.

"That no-good son of a bitch Red Carter. He came into town and got drunk again at Andy's saloon and he was trying to pick a fight with some drifter. The sheriff went into the saloon and warned Red he was going to put him in jail again. Red told the sheriff he wasn't going to let him crack him on the head again with that shotgun. The sheriff gave him his last warning and Red skinned leather and shot him. Then he went back to drinking at the bar again like nothing happened. That cold-blooded bastard is still over there drinking."

"And the drifter?"

"Folks say he high-tailed it out of there before the shootout. Sara went over to Doc Johnson's place to see if she could help, but the sheriff was dead before they got him there. Shot right through the heart. I swear it seems like it's always the good ones who go down," Jim replied sadly.

"Not today," said Jess coldly as he turned around and headed for the doctor's office to see for himself. As he walked away, and without looking back at Jim he said, "Jim, let me know if Red tries to leave town while I go over to the doctor's office."

"Well, okay. I guess so," Jim replied, a little worried about the different way Jess was acting.

Jess walked down to see Doc Johnson, who was a fair doctor, but not a great one. When Jess arrived, he saw the sheriff lying still on the table. There was blood all over him and his shirt was torn open. The doctor was standing over him with a grim look on his face and Sara was sitting in a chair in the corner of the small room with her head in her hands sobbing.

Doc Johnson looked up at Jess. "He never had a chance," he said gravely.

Jess nodded at him, but said nothing. The doctor pulled a sheet up over the sheriff. Sara had slowed her sobbing only because she noticed that Jess had come in. She looked up at Jess with tears streaming from her red eyes, but before she could say anything, she noticed what Jess was wearing. She was speechless for a moment and she just kept looking back and forth between him and the gun strapped around his waist.

"Jess. What? Why are you wearing that?" she said as she nodded to the gun. "And where did you get such a thing?"

"That's not important," replied Jess. "Are you okay?"

"Yes, I'm not hurt, if that's what you mean."

"All right then. You stay in here with the doc, okay?"

"Okay, but why?" she asked. "The doctor doesn't need my help now."

"Just do as I say, please." he insisted. She nodded and started sobbing again. Doc Johnson said nothing else. He kept staring at Jess, startled at the change in the young man that up until now, he had always thought of as a young kid.

Jess walked out and headed across the street straight for Andy's saloon. He wasn't really thinking about what he was going to do. He just knew he had to deal with Red Carter. This town had been good to him and his family. They were there when he needed them and they were terrified of Red Carter. They would be even more terrified now, since there was no law in town and no one was going to step up to replace the sheriff after what Red had done. He stopped in the middle of the street. He looked up and down the main road. He glanced over to the general store and saw Jim standing just outside the door, watching. He looked over his shoulder and saw Sara watching him out of the doctor's office window. He scanned the street down to the sheriff's office and then back to the saloon. He realized that once he went in there, his life would take another turn and there would be no coming back from it. He was ready.

He walked through the swinging doors and as soon as he stepped inside, he stopped to check his surroundings. There were four men at a poker table, but they weren't really playing cards anymore. They were just going through the motions, terrified that Red Carter would start in on them next. The barkeep was standing behind the bar cleaning up just so he'd have something to do.

Red Carter was standing at the bar with a bottle of whiskey and a shot glass. He looked up at Jess. "Why, little Jess Williams," Red said sarcastically. "What the hell are you doin' in a saloon? And what the hell is all that you've got on you? Are you wearing a six-shooter now?"

Jess didn't reply. He simply glared at Red.

"What the hell you got behind you?" continued Red. "Is that a shotgun? Are you goin' rabbit hunting or something? Speak up, boy. I'm talkin' to you!"

Jess looked him straight in the eyes with no discernable emotion. "You shouldn't have killed the sheriff, Red. He was my friend and a good man and he didn't deserve to be shot down like that."

"The hell he didn't. He was gonna crack me on the head with that damn shotgun again."

"You still shouldn't have killed him."

"What the hell is it to you, boy? You gonna do something about it? Oh, you ain't really going rabbit hunting are you? You mean to tell me that you came in here to square off with me for killing a two-bit sheriff? You gotta be kidding me, boy. You ain't got the gonads to face me or any other man for that matter."

The barkeep, William, who hadn't said anything up to now, finally got up enough courage to speak. "Jess, you do us all a favor and go on home," he said. "We've had enough killing here today. Red, you leave the boy alone."

"You shut the hell up, barkeep, or there'll be some more killing real soon, starting with you!" hollered Red. The barkeep quickly went back to minding his business.

Jess moved over to the left side of the saloon. He knew that Sara was still looking out of the window across the street, and he didn't want to chance a stray bullet hitting her. He moved toward a corner where no one could get behind him while he never took his eyes off Red. Finally Red realized Jess was serious. He moved himself away from the bar a little, straightened up his stance and dropped his hand a little closer to the butt of his pistol.

"Boy, why don't you go home now before you get hurt? I ain't never shot a boy, but if you plan on pulling for that gun you got, I'll kill you for sure. Don't you ever doubt it, not for one second."

"Your killing days are over," replied Jess with coldness in his voice.

The cheeks on Red's face quivered. His ears turned a cherry red and he was about all out of what little patience he had left. "Why, you cocky little bastard! You think you can come in here and threaten me? I ain't scared of no man, much less a wet-behind-the-ears little shithead punk like you. You've got about five seconds to clear out of here before you catch a case of lead poisoning from this lead pusher I got on my right hip!"

"Then I guess you've got about five seconds to live. So I gotta ask, what are you planning on doing with the time you have left?" His eyes locked firmly on Red's.

"I guess I'm gonna kill me a punk-ass kid."

Red moved his hand a little closer to the butt of his pistol. Jess had already placed his hands into position without Red even knowing it. Jess could see in Red's eyes that he was going to draw. Jess never moved. He waited until Red went for the pistol and Jess still never moved. Red finally got his hand on the butt of his pistol and pulled. Red's gun barrel just cleared the top of his holster and then the gun fell backward and Red's hand was no longer holding it. Instead, his hand was clutching his chest where the bullet from Jess's pistol had burned through his heart, exploding it instantly. Red slumped to his knees. He gazed at Jess with a look of utter surprise. An instant later, he was lying facedown in a pool of blood not more than ten feet from the drying pool of blood that had been left from Sheriff Diggs' body. Jess watched Red's death with no emotion. After Red fell to the floor, he put his gun back in his holster in one quick, smooth movement.

"Jesus Christ!" exclaimed the barkeep. "I ain't ever seen anyone draw like that before. If I hadn't seen if for myself, I would have thought you drew on him before he had a chance. Jess, you're lucky you got a witness or else they'd say it wasn't a fair fight."

Jess said nothing. He just looked at the body lying facedown on the floor. He walked over to it and using his left boot he rolled Red over. He unbelted his holster and reached down and picked up Red's gun and stuck it back in the holster. He checked Red's pockets and found about fifty dollars and he placed ten dollars of it on the bar.

"This should help pay for any damages."

"I don't know if you should be taking his stuff, Jess. It doesn't seem right," said William.

"He won't need it anymore. Besides, as far as I see it, I've earned it. Is that his horse out there?" William nodded.

"I'll be taking that, too, then."

"Don't matter to me. I mind my own business, Jess."

"I'll be selling the horse and saddle. If you need any more money to clean up or fix any damages, you see Mr. Jameson at the bank and he'll give you the money, okay?"

"Sure thing, but this is more than enough." Jess walked out of the saloon and Sara was standing in the middle of the street with her hands over her mouth.

"Oh my Lord, Jess. What have you done?" she asked.

"I did what was needed, Sara. I've got some business to take care of. When I'm done, I'll stop by and see you and Jim before I leave, okay?"

Sara nodded and headed down the street toward the general store. Jess walked the horse over to the stables and sold the horse and saddle. He sold the rifle he'd found on Red's horse to the gunsmith and he took the money to Jameson and deposited it. He kept Red's .45. He figured it was always good to have extra weapons handy. Then he walked over to Jim and Sara's store. He found Jim behind the counter and Sara sitting in a chair at the end of the counter by the small wood stove that they used to heat up the front of the store. They both looked up at Jess when he walked in, as if they didn't even know him anymore.

"Jess," said Jim, "I know what you're planning to do. It's no life for a young man. Is there any way we can talk you out of this?"

Jess looked Jim straight in the eyes and gave him a simple one-word answer. "No."

Sara wiped more tears from her eyes and said, "Jess, you just killed a man over at the saloon and you don't seem the slightest bit bothered by it. I swear you are not the same boy."

"I'm not a boy anymore and I'm surely not the same person you knew before. Red Carter needed to be killed and I won't apologize for it to anyone. I only hope that you won't hate me for it."

"We could never hate you, Jess," Sara said. "We will always consider you family. We just don't want to see you turn to this way of life. Using a gun is not a good way to live. It's a good way to die."

"I don't plan on dying, but I'm not afraid of it either."

"Jess, where in the hell did you get that gun?" asked Jim.

Jess let his palm touch the butt of the pistol. "Let's just say it came to me."

"Was it your pa's?" pressed Jim.

"I'm not rightly sure, but it's my gun now. Anyway, I have to leave now. The sheriff told me last week that he had a lead on one of the men who killed my family. He said that he was involved in a shooting up in Tarkenton about two hundred miles northwest of here. I intend to hunt the bastard down and kill him."

"Like Red Carter?" asked Sara, still wiping tears from her eyes.

"Yes, only worse," he replied ominously. "I plan on letting that son of a bitch die a little bit slower."

"Oh, Jess," said Sara almost in a whisper. Jim looked at Sara and knew what she was thinking. She figured it was time to tell Jess something she would never reveal if his family were still alive, but there was no reason to hold back the truth any longer.

"Jess, there is something that we need to tell you," she said, still trying to compose herself. "Your parents swore us to never tell you about this, but now they're gone and we think you should know."

"Know what?"

"Jess, you have other family," interjected Jim.

Jess turned and studied Jim with a look of disbelief. "What the hell are you talking about?" he asked intensely, a bewildered look on his face. "I don't have any other family. My family was murdered."

Jim hung his head and began to speak in a quiet, deliberate tone. "Jess, John Williams was a good man and a better friend, but he wasn't your real pa…"

"That's not true!" retorted Jess, cutting Jim off in mid-sentence.

Jim cleared his throat and gathered his emotions so he could continue. "Jess, your real father was a man by the name of Ed Sloan. He's a gunslinger and a gambler who was taken with your ma the minute he saw her. I tried to tell her he was no good for her, but she wouldn't listen. Don't blame your ma, Jess. She was young and he was as slick as they come. She spent some time with him and she ended up pregnant with you…and your brother, Tim." Jess sat down in the other chair, stunned by this revelation of another part of his family he had never known about.

Jim cleared his throat and continued. "After your ma had the two of you, your real father took off with your twin brother and a gal from Dixie's he'd gotten close to while your ma was with child. Her name was Sally. He was a no-good son of a bitch and he hurt your ma. Last we heard about your brother, he'd taken up gunslinging. I hear tell he's mighty fast with a pistol. Your father, Ed, is even faster. The two of them are no good and you should think twice before you have anything to do with them if you have any sense, Jess. Anyway, we figured you had a right to know."

Jess couldn't believe what he was hearing. The thought of all this just balled his nerves up in a knot that found its way to his throat. Then, he made a decision right then and there. He couldn't let all this distract him now. He would have to deal with it later.

He stood up and looked at Jim and Sara. "Do you know where they are now?"

"Last we heard they were both in Wichita. That was quite a while ago though. They could be almost anywhere by now."

"Thanks for telling me, but I still have to go."

"No you don't," cried Sara, almost desperately. "You can stay here with us."

Jess thought for a moment, but he knew in his mind there was no turning back now. His mind was made up. Sara and Jim saw the look in his eyes and they both realized it, too. They both knew he was going to live or die by the gun. Sara stood up and walked to Jess and gave him a long hug. Jess turned to Jim and extended his hand. Jim shook Jess's hand, hoping it wouldn't be the last time he did so.

"I'm going to miss the both of you. I'll keep in touch and if you need anything, tell Jameson over at the bank. He'll know where I am most of the time," said Jess.

Jess hung his head for a moment. Without another word he walked down the steps and to his horse, climbed up in the saddle and headed out of Black Creek. He never looked back.

Jim and Sara stood on the front porch of the store watching him ride away. They were holding hands and exchanging glances. Sara looked at Jim as Jess finally turned the corner. "Do you think we'll ever see him again?" she asked.

"I hope so, Sara. I surely hope so."

"Me too," she said, starting to cry again.

As Jess turned the corner at the end of the street, his thoughts turned to what Jim and Sara had just told him about his brother and father. He knew he would eventually track them down, but not until he finished his business at hand. He made up his mind right then and there that he would always consider John as his real pa no matter what else was true.

His thoughts turned to Randy Hastings. There was one thing he was sure of. He knew that Randy Hastings was one of the three men who had murdered his family. He also knew he was going to find him, confront him, and then kill him. Of that, he was certain. His journey had begun. It would not be over until all three of the men who had murdered his family were in their graves. Only then would justice be served. He rode out of Black Creek and headed for Tarkenton. Destiny would meet him there…at least part of it.

CHAPTER EIGHT

Jess rode all day, watching the landscape change as he went along. He had never been anywhere away from his home and was seeing everything for the first time. He stopped along a creek for some lunch that consisted of the jerky and biscuits Sara had given him. He continued along until he found a nice place to bed down for the night. He picked a site several hundred feet off the trail in a clump of trees and bushes to give him plenty of cover. He leaned his saddle against the largest of the trees to give his back some cover while he slept. He started a very small fire and warmed up some beans. He had another biscuit with the beans and then he made some coffee. Just after dark, he leaned back against the saddle to sleep. He covered himself with a light blanket, not because he was cold, but mostly to cover his weapons in case someone came in the night. He laid the shotgun across his lap and he slept with his gun strapped on. He did not sleep well that night.

He rose at dawn and made some coffee, salt pork and pan bread. Then he took some time to practice with his pistol, which was something he would do every day. He broke camp and saddled up and headed back to the trail. Gray was a sturdy horse but Jess didn't push him hard.

He rode for three days to reach the outskirts of Tarkenton, where he camped about two miles outside of town. After breaking camp in the morning, he rode up to the end of the main street. He stopped for a few minutes to look the town over. It was small, with only about fifteen buildings. There were several people along the street and a couple of people standing together in front of a building. He dismounted and walked his horse into town. One of the first buildings he came to was the livery. When he and Gray approached it, a young boy came out and greeted him.

"Howdy, mister! Do you need me to take care of your horse?"

"What's your name, son?" asked Jess.

"Billy. And yours?"

"It's nice to meet you, Billy. My name is Jess and I'd like you to take care of my horse, Gray, here. He's had a long, hard ride and he needs a good brushing and some of your best feed. If you promise to take extra care of him, there's a dollar a day in it for you."

"Golly, a whole dollar each day? That's more than I make in any day, mister. You got yourself a deal, only don't say anything to the owner. He's a mean old cuss. And don't tell him about the good feed or he'll want to charge you extra for it," said Billy excitedly.

"You've got a deal, son. Where does a man get a decent room and a good meal around here?"

"You can get both at the same place. The town hotel has rooms and they serve some pretty good food. It's right across from the saloon. Right over there," he said, pointing over to the hotel.

"Thanks, Billy. Is Sheriff Manley around?"

"Yeah, he's probably over at the saloon. He ain't much of a sheriff though. Scared of his own shadow."

Jess remembered the little speech that Sheriff Diggs had given him about some of the small-town lawmen not really willing and able to do their jobs. He tossed Billy a silver dollar and he caught it and quickly dropped it into his front pocket. He smiled and took Gray into the livery.

Jess looked down the street and spotted the saloon. He felt his stomach growl and decided to go to the hotel and get a hot bath and some grub before he spoke to the sheriff. He walked into the hotel and up to the counter.

The desk clerk smiled nervously. "Need a room?" he asked.

"Yeah, and if you throw in a hot bath and a good meal, I'll consider you a friend."

"Well, we can take care of all that right here. Dining room is right in the back. I'll give you room twelve upstairs with a view of the street. I'll take your stuff up to your room if you want," said the clerk. Jess signed the register and paid the clerk for one day, not knowing how long he would be in town.

"I'll take my stuff up myself and I don't want any visitors. I also don't want anyone in my room, not even to clean the sheets. Understand?" he said firmly.

The clerk looked at him kind of funny and smiled. "No problem, it's your room as long as you're paying for it. I'll have someone prepare you a nice hot bath."

"Thanks. I'll be down in a few minutes after I get settled in my room. Make the water extra hot."

"Hot and clean and an extra towel to boot. You look like you've been on the trail for a while."

"Long enough," said Jess, as he took the key and went upstairs. He looked out the window to see what view he had and to see if anyone could come in the window easily.

He never realized just how good a hot bath could feel, especially when you haven't had the chance to get one for a few days. He soaked until the water started to cool. He kept his gun within easy reach by pulling a table up to the tub and putting the gun on it. He got dressed and headed to get something to eat. The dining room was small and there were only a few people inside eating.

A barkeep stood behind the bar and looked up at Jess as he entered the room. "You hungry?" he asked.

"As a bear," replied Jess, rubbing his stomach. "What have you got on the menu today?"

"We only have one special a day. Today is ham and potatoes and it's really good."

"Then I guess I'm eating ham and potatoes."

"Martha will be out in a minute to get your order."

Jess sat down at a table in the corner, away from the door and the few people who were in the dining room.

The barkeep kept looking Jess over, paying close attention to the shotgun Jess had strapped to his back. He came over to his table with a pot of coffee and poured him a cup of it. "You expecting trouble, son?" the barkeep asked.

"Why do you ask?"

"You sure got enough hardware hanging on you. Are you one of those bounty hunters?"

"I could be. Is there someone in town who has a bounty on his head?"

The barkeep smiled. "Hell, there's always someone in this town that needs hunting. If you're looking for trouble, you'll sure find plenty of it here."

"I ain't exactly looking for trouble, but I ain't shying away from it either."

"Well, enjoy your lunch. Martha will be out soon."

Less than a minute later, a young girl with dark red hair came out of the kitchen, stopped at a table and dropped off two plates of food. As she did, she noticed Jess sitting at the table in the corner. She smiled as she headed toward him. The smile turned to a look of concern when she spotted the butt of the shotgun sticking up over his right shoulder. She almost paused, but continued.

"What can I get for you today?" she asked.

"I've given it a lot of thought and decided to take the special," he said smiling.

Martha smiled again. "So, Sam told you about the special already, did he?"

"Yes. I'm afraid he beat you to it. You wouldn't happen to have any apple pie today, would you?"

"You're in luck, fresh baked this morning. You'll like it. It's the best apple pie anywhere around here."

"You make it?"

"Of course. Don't I look like a woman who can make great apple pie?" she asked smartly, her hands on her hips now.

"As a matter of fact, you do look just like a woman who can make great apple pie."

Martha turned and walked back into the kitchen. Jess tried the coffee. It was just how he liked it, hot and strong. Jess turned his glance toward the door as he saw a man enter the doorway. The man acted like he wasn't sure if he was going to come in or not. He carried a single six-shooter slung extra low, but not tied down. Jess sized him up and figured him for a local troublemaker and one who was not as fast with a gun as he thought he was.

The man was Scott Vogan, a local ranch hand who worked for a ranch called the Last C. He came into town a few times a week to get serviced at the local cathouse, as well as drunk, and raise a little hell. Scott had a slight crush on the waitress, Martha, which is what kept him coming back to the hotel.

The barkeep, Sam, noticed Vogan standing in the doorway. "Scott," Sam said with a stern voice, "I thought I told you not to come back in here today."

"Yeah, well you ain't the owner here and what you say don't mean shit," argued Vogan, as he walked over to the bar and leaned on it. "Now give me a shot of that good stuff you keep under the bar."

"All right, but this is the last one today and I mean it. You want any more and you'll have to see the boss. I don't care how tough you think you are."

"Well, that's a start, barkeep," Vogan said with an ugly sneer.

Martha came out carrying Jess's plate of food. As she walked toward his table, she noticed Vogan. She ignored his stare and continued toward Jess.

"It sure looks and smells good," Jess said.

"You'll like it. You want some more coffee?"

"Yes and keep it coming."

"Hey, Martha," Scott hollered across the room. "How about you take the rest of the afternoon off and spend some time with me? I'll make it well worth your while."

Martha shot Vogan a glaring look. "I've got work to do, Scott," she said tensely. "And even if I didn't, I wouldn't spend any of my time with the likes of you. I thought I'd made that quite clear to you on more than one occasion. I'm not one of them whores down at Julie's place that you can buy for a few silver dollars. Now leave me alone, you hear?"

Jess took another sip of coffee and looked up at Martha. "Problem?" he asked.

"Nothing I can't handle. What's your name? I haven't seen you around here before."

"I'm not from around here. My name is Jess, Jess Williams."

"Well, it's nice to meet you Jess Williams. Welcome to Tarkenton," said Martha smiling.

"Thanks, but I don't plan on staying around too long. I'm looking for someone, a man by the name of Randy Hastings. Heard of him?"

"Who hasn't? Just about everyone around here knows Randy. He's a pain in the ass and a cold-blooded killer. He came to town a few weeks ago with two other men. He killed one of the local toughs and then decided to stick around and make the rest of us miserable. He's not someone you want to mess with. He'd just as soon kill you as look at you. What's your business with him?"

"Personal," he replied bluntly.

"Well, you watch yourself around him," she warned as she walked back into the kitchen.

Jess nodded and took a bite of the ham. It was so tender he could cut it with a fork. During the conversation with Martha, Scott was leaning sideways on the bar listening to them. He was jealous and it showed by the scrunched-up scowl on his face. As soon as Martha walked away from Jess, Vogan picked up his drink and started to walk over to Jess's table. Jess was listening to his footsteps and paying attention to everything in the room. He was listening for any sound of a gun being slid out of a holster or a hammer being eared back. He heard neither.

"What's your name, son?" asked Scott in a snide tone. Scott slowly walked around the table to face Jess.

Jess put his fork down and looked up at him with a cold stare that seemed to make the man take a step back. "I'm not your son and my name ain't any of your business," replied Jess, with a harsh voice and a cold look on his face. "Anything else you want to ask that you've got no business asking about in the first place?"

"You're a cocky little son of a bitch, ain't ya?"

"Mister, let me make this real easy for you to understand," Jess said sharply. "My business ain't your business. I just had me a nice hot bath and now I'm trying to enjoy a good hot meal, which is something I haven't for a while. Now, I plan to eat this meal before it gets cold. So if you're looking for trouble let's get it over with right quick. If not, haul your ass back over to the bar and don't make me tell you twice, because if I have to, I'm grabbing some iron and I'd suggest you do the same."

Jess said all of this so matter-of-factly that it took Vogan totally by surprise. He knew when to fold up and move on and this was surely one of those times. "Didn't mean to rile you up, mister," he said as he headed back to the bar and leaned on it, looking at his empty glass.

The barkeep had a smirk on his face. He'd enjoyed watching Vogan get his ass ripped. "Would you like another shot, Scott?" Sam asked sarcastically, knowing that his nerves might need a little settling after all.

"Hell, yeah, might as well. And wipe that damn smirk off your face."

Jess finished his meal and Martha brought him a nice slab of apple pie. She had watched the confrontation between Jess and Scott from the doorway and she had a smile on her face when she glanced over at Vogan.

Vogan was leaning on the bar, just looking down at the shot glass. Jess savored the pie and another hot cup of coffee, paid his bill and headed down the street to the saloon to find Sheriff Manley. After Jess left, Martha came back out from the kitchen. Scott was still nursing his wounded pride along with his whiskey. She walked up behind the bar and started to help Sam wash a few glasses. Scott watched her and wondered what she thought of him after he'd been told off by a young kid who barely looked like he'd reached manhood yet.

"He didn't look all that tough," said Vogan.

Martha eyed him quizzically. "Then why'd you back down?" she asked. "You're always looking for trouble. You had it right in the palm of your hand."

Scott let his gaze fall back to his drink.

"Yeah," added Sam, "for a man always looking to give someone a hard time, you sure got a case of the frights."

"Nobody asked your opinion," muttered Vogan. "I just didn't think it right to shoot a kid. Hell, he can't be more than sixteen or so."

"He may be young, but he ain't no kid," replied Sam with a knowing look.

"Hell, yes, he is," chided Vogan. "You saw him. He's still wet behind the ears, for Christ's sake."

"Sam's right," interjected Martha. "He might be a little wet behind the ears, but there's something different about that young man. You can see it in his eyes and tell by his demeanor."

"Hell, that punk didn't scare me," said Vogan. "I've taken on tougher men than him and I'm still standing."

"You tell yourself whatever you want," she said as she walked back to the kitchen.

Jess walked into the saloon and quickly looked around. The place was dirty and reeked of cheap whiskey and cigar smoke. The barkeep gave Jess a look and then glanced over at the men playing cards. One of the men looked to be in his fifties and had a tin star on his shirt. He nodded at the barkeep as if to say that he had noticed Jess and then went back to playing his hand.

The barkeep looked back to Jess and asked, "Can I help you, mister?"

"I'm looking for Sheriff Manley." Jess looked over to the man with the badge. "I assume that would be you?"

"You assumed right, son. Now just wait until I finish this hand. I've been losing at this game all day and I think this hand will make me whole," bragged Manley as he finished his hand. He lost. "Damn it!" carped Manley, throwing his cards on the table. "How can I be such a lousy player?"

"Maybe you ain't such a lousy player," said one of the other men at the table. "Maybe it's just that we're better at the game than you, Sheriff."

"Kiss my ass," groused Manley. "I'll get my money back tonight from you cheatin' bastards."

"Aw, come on, Sheriff," said one of the other men in the game. "We've been playing fair. You just keep playing lousy like always."

"Well, you can still kiss my ass," the sheriff countered as he pushed back his chair from the table and looked up at Jess.

"What can I do for you, stranger?" the sheriff asked.

"I'm looking for a man who goes by the name of Randy Hastings. What can you tell me about him?"

"That you shouldn't be looking for him," replied Manley directly. "He ain't nothin' but trouble. He's wanted by the law and has a bounty on his head. What's your business with him?"

"If he's who I think he is, he's one of the three men who murdered my family."

Sheriff Manley put his head down for a moment and let out a long sigh, then said, "He was heard bragging one night at the saloon after having a few too many that he had raped and killed some women some years back. No one knew if he was just braggin' or tellin' the truth. He killed one of the local boys here in the saloon recently. Wish he would just take off and leave this place for good."

"Do you know where he is now?"

"Left town a few days ago, but he told a few people that he'd be back. You're kinda young for a bounty hunter, ain't ya?"

"I never said I was."

"Sure do look like one. Why the shotgun? And where did you get a pistol and holster like that?"

"I came here to ask the questions, not answer them," he replied crossly. "What is the bounty on Hastings?"

"Kind of a smart-ass for such a young one," observed Manley.

"Maybe. Now what about the bounty?"

"Five hundred dollars the last time I checked."

"I'll be collecting it when he comes back to town."

"I thought you said you weren't a bounty hunter."

"I never said I wasn't."

"There's that smart-ass thing again."

"Don't push me on it, Sheriff," Jess warned.

"I'm the one wearing the star."

"Yeah, and you had a murderer in your town and you didn't do a damn thing to arrest him," complained Jess angrily.

"Don't you tell me how to do my job," Manley snapped back.

"Then don't make me do yours."

"You gonna go at Hastings?"

"I thought I made that pretty clear."

"You seem kinda sure about how things are gonna turn out. Hastings ain't gonna surrender that easy, especially to a young one like you."

"Who said I was going to ask him to surrender? I'm staying over at the hotel. I expect you'll let me know when he comes back to town."

"And just why in the hell should I do that?" demanded Manley, getting agitated at Jess's harsh demeanor.

"Well, Sheriff, if you won't do your job, at least be man enough to let someone else do it for you. Now I expect you to let me know when he comes to town. If not, you'll answer to me."

"Who the hell do you think you are, talking to me like that!" cried out Manley, embarrassed.

Jess took another step toward Manley and spoke calmly and directly. "I'm the man who plans on killing at least one man before I leave your town. It's up to you whether or not it's more than one. Enjoy the rest of your game, Sheriff."

Jess turned and walked out of the saloon, ignoring the curse words coming from the sheriff's mouth. He had already figured that Sheriff Manley was nothing more than a coward and he wasn't going to waste any time on him. He had also noticed that

Scott Vogan had sauntered into the bar during his discussion with Manley. Vogan had leaned on the bar, saying nothing and listening closely. Jess knew that he would probably have to deal with Vogan before he left town, but that would be Vogan's choice. Manley had watched Jess walk out of the saloon and then slowly slid his chair back up to the card table. The other three men at the table were getting ready to start on Manley about the kid telling him off.

"Don't even start on me," Manley advised.

"Start what?" one of the men said, acting as if he didn't know what the sheriff meant.

"You know damn well what I mean!" argued Manley. "Damn young kid thinks he can come in here and tell me what to do."

"I think that's exactly what he did, Sheriff," one of the men said and all three of them started to chuckle.

"Kiss my ass, the bunch of you," muttered Manley.

They started up the game again and one of the men got a serious tone in his voice. "You know, Sheriff, I saw something in that young man. I don't think I'd cross him if I were you."

"What the hell you talking about?" asked Manley.

"I don't know. It's just a feeling. The way he carries himself and that gun he's wearing. Did you ever see anything like that before?"

"I heard of some gunslingers making up their own holsters, but I never seen one like that," one of the other men said.

"Well, I ain't messing with that kid anyway," said Sheriff Manley. "This damn job don't pay enough. I just run in the drunks and sweep out the jail. If the town wants more than that, they can hire themselves another sheriff."

Jess took a stroll around town and checked out the buildings and back entrances to them. He wanted to know more about his surroundings before Hastings came back to town. He stopped at the livery to check on Gray.

"How's he doing?" Jess asked Billy. The stable boy had been brushing Gray down when Jess walked up.

"He's doing fine, mister," he replied. "He sure likes apples. I hope it's okay that I gave him a few earlier."

"He loves apples," he said. "Just don't give him too many; he's quite the hog. I'll be staying in town a few more days over at the hotel. How would you like to make another ten dollars?"

"Golly, ten dollars! That's a lot of money. What do I have to do for it?" he said excitedly.

"All you have to do is let me know when Hastings gets back to town."

"What if he finds out I told you?" he asked, a worried look on his face. "He'll beat me for sure and I'll lose my job. I need this job, mister. I have to help my ma. She's got a bum leg and she can't do much work. Besides, how am I supposed to let you know without getting caught?"

"I'll tell you how, Billy. I'm staying at the hotel in room twelve. If it's late at night, just knock on my door three times, wait a few seconds, and knock twice more. If it's during the day, just find me and look me in the eyes from a distance. I'll know what that means. And I'll make it twenty dollars instead. How's that?"

"Well, my ma can sure use twenty dollars."

"Thanks, Billy. I owe you," he said as he turned to walk out. Before he got to the front door, he turned and said, "Hey, Billy?"

"Yeah?"

"I never saw a dead man give anyone a beating," he said with a knowing look.

Jess went back to the hotel and picked up his clean set of clothes. He went to his room and packed his clothes in his bag. He always had to be ready to move in an instant. After that, he went back down to the dining room of the hotel and had supper. He turned in early and arranged his room very carefully. He put the chair in front of the door and put his pistol on the table next to his bed. The bed was comfortable, much more so than the cold, hard ground he had been sleeping on the last several days. He drifted off to sleep wondering how he would kill Randy Hastings. He wanted to make him suffer as much as possible. He imagined putting the last bullet between his eyes.

CHAPTER NINE

Jess rose before dawn, dressed and went down to the dining room. A few people were already eating. He sat down in the corner again. Before long, Martha came out of the kitchen and took a few orders and then she noticed him. She brought him a cup and poured him some coffee.

"Are you hungry this morning?" asked Martha.

"How about some scrambled eggs and a pile of bacon?"

"Be right out with it," she said smiling.

"Still got any of that apple pie left for dessert?" he asked before she walked away.

"I saved a piece just for you."

"And maybe you could throw in some flapjacks, too?"

"My, my, aren't we hungry this morning?" she asked playfully.

"I'm still a growing boy," he replied, shrugging his shoulders. Martha laughed as she headed for the kitchen.

Jess finished breakfast and washed it down with several cups of coffee. He noticed Sheriff Manley eating at another table. Jess left Martha a nice tip and once again she smiled. It was the best tip she'd ever gotten waiting tables. She walked over and began cleaning off Sheriff Manley's table. He had been joined by one of his poker pals, a man by the name of Ron Butler.

"Well, Martha, what do you think about our new young guest we have in town?" the sheriff asked.

"I don't rightly know yet, Sheriff, but he seems like a mighty interesting young man. I think he acts a lot older than he really is."

"What do you mean by that?"

"Sheriff, he may be all of sixteen or seventeen, but he acts more like a man of twenty. He backed down Scott Vogan yesterday and the look in his eyes when he was doing it…well…it scared Vogan, and quite frankly, it scared me a little, too."

"Really? What kind of look?"

"The kind of look that could burn a hole straight through you," she replied frankly. "A look of torment and hatred all rolled up into one. If that look didn't kill you, I'm sure he would in a heartbeat. Yet, he seems like such a nice young man. It's a little strange, like he's two people all wrapped up as one."

"Well, you don't have to worry about him much longer," said the sheriff. "He's looking for Randy Hastings."

"He told me that yesterday," she said fatefully. "I sure wouldn't want to be him."

"You mean our young guest over there?"

"No, I'm saying I wouldn't want to be Randy Hastings," replied Martha with caution.

Ron Butler finally chimed in. "Hastings is pretty damn fast with those twin six-shooters," said Butler. "I watched him draw in that gunfight over at the saloon and he was pretty quick. Hastings won't be a pushover when it comes to a gunfight."

"Call it a hunch, but I think Hastings may have met his match," she said as she walked back to the kitchen.

"What do you think, Sheriff?" asked Butler.

"I don't know, but I'll put ten bucks on Hastings if you'll take the bet," said the sheriff. Butler thought about what Martha had said about the young man called Jess Williams and took the bet.

Jess went out on the porch of the hotel and sat in one of the chairs. He watched the town wake up and the local townspeople going about their daily business. Sheriff Manley left the hotel and headed for the saloon. Jess took another stroll around town and stopped in to see Billy at the livery. The old man who owned the livery was there and he was yelling at Billy for taking too much time caring for Jess's horse. Jess showed up just as the old man slapped Billy on the back of the head.

"Damn it, boy, quit fussing over that damn horse and clean up this shit here!" hollered the old man. "I ain't telling you again, you hear?"

"Yes, sir. I'll get it right now."

"Well, see to it that you do," grumbled the old man.

Billy grabbed a shovel and started to scoop up the horse droppings. Jess walked into the livery. The old man noticed him when Jess said good morning to Billy. The boy just nodded at Jess and kept working for fear he'd get another slap on the head.

"What can I do for you?" the old man asked in a grumpy voice.

"Well, first off, you can stop slapping the boy around. That horse he's fussing over is mine. I expect him to be taken care of properly, and I made him promise me to do so." Jess didn't mention the extra money he was paying Billy to take care of Gray, thinking the old man would just take it away from Billy if he found out.

"Hell, that boy ain't got a lick of sense that ain't been beat into him. Besides, what's it to you anyway?" barked the old man.

Jess looked at Billy and smiled. "Well, let's just say that I've taken a liking to the boy and don't want to see him mistreated. You got a problem with that?" he asked, turning to glare at the old man.

The old man looked at Jess and didn't say anything for a moment or two, studying him. "Sure, if that's what makes you happy," replied the old man in a softer tone of voice.

"I'm glad we have an understanding. And Billy, don't forget a few apples for Gray today."

"No problem," said Billy with a big smile on his face.

"So what're you in town for anyway?" asked the old man, spitting some tobacco juice on the ground.

"I'm looking for a man by the name of Randy Hastings. You know him?"

"Hell, yes, I know him. I take care of his horse. He should be back tomorrow. What's your business with him?"

"Personal."

The old man laughed, "Hope it's not too personal."

"Why do you say that?"

"You'll find out when he gets back in town," replied the old man with a strange smile on his face.

"I suppose I will." Jess replied, glaring at the old man, who quickly wiped the strange smile off his face.

⚞⚟

Scott Vogan and Saul Littman had been bellied up to the bar in the Spurs Saloon for at least two hours now. They shared a bottle of whiskey and neither of the two was feeling much pain. Ray, the barkeep, didn't like Vogan, but he didn't say anything to him because he knew that Littman was a hired gun with a nasty disposition and he was pretty good with a pistol.

"So who was this punk who gave you a hatful of shit today?" Saul asked Vogan.

"I never saw him around before. I think I overheard the sheriff say his name was Jess Williams or something like that."

"Why didn't you just pull leather on him and smack a bullet into his smart mouth?"

"I don't rightly know. I guess it was the look in his eyes. It was unnatural like. I thought maybe he was just plumb loco."

"Hells-fire! A look ain't ever killed anyone as far as I know."

"I suppose so, but you had to see it for yourself," explained Vogan in a defensive tone. "I'm telling you, it wasn't normal. I think the kid's got the devil inside him or something."

Saul laughed at the notion. "You leave that little shithead to me. I'll straighten him out right quick." Saul looked up just in time to see Ray with a funny look on his face. "What the hell you smirking about?" asked Saul.

"Nothing," replied Ray, sheepishly.

"Don't give me that shit. I saw that little smirk on your face. You best tell me what you think is so funny else I'll wipe that smirk off your face with the butt of my pistol."

Ray was a barkeep, not a fighter, so he answered timidly. "I was just remembering how Sam over at the hotel bar was telling me about how that Williams kid backed Scott down yesterday. According to Sam, he's got the look of death in his eyes. I saw it yesterday with my own eyes when he was talkin' to the sheriff."

"Hell, ain't no kid that young gonna be that fast with a pistol. And looks don't kill," argued Saul. "He comes in here, I'll show you how to handle a punk-ass kid. Now get us another bottle of that whiskey. And make sure it's a full one this time."

Jess left the livery, walked back to the hotel and paid for another night. Then he headed for the saloon. He walked in and noticed the sheriff playing a game of poker at the same table as before. He also noticed Vogan at the bar along with several other men. There was one at the far end of the bar next to Scott that Jess picked up on right away. He looked like trouble. He was a tall, slender man wearing a hat that looked too big on him and two pistols worn low and tied down. Jess kept an eye on the men as he walked to the bar and ordered a beer. Ray brought Jess a cold beer. Jess took a long drink and noticed an empty table over in the corner. He went over to it and sat down, deftly removing his hammer strap as he did.

Scott and the man with the oversized hat turned around at the bar facing Jess's table. Vogan, feeling braver after several shots of whiskey and having Littman with him, decided to pay Jess back for humiliating him earlier in the hotel bar.

"So, what are you really in town for, mister?" asked Vogan sharply and looking directly at Jess.

"I'm looking for someone."

"Anyone I know?"

"Could be."

"Could be?"

"That's what I said," he replied harshly.

"So, who you looking for?"

"His name is Randy Hastings. You know him?"

"Maybe."

"Maybe?"

"That's what I said," Vogan replied sarcastically.

"Hey, you're the one who asked, and frankly, I don't really care."

"You don't really care about what?"

"Neither."

"What do you mean, neither?"

"I don't care if you know him and I don't care if you tell me," countered Jess.

The smirk on Vogan's face suddenly disappeared and he got a more serious tone in his voice. "Yeah, I heard of him," he admitted. "He's out of town right now, but he'll be back any day now." Jess simply nodded and didn't respond.

Vogan pushed some more. "So why are you looking for him?"

"It's personal."

"You and him friends then?"

"Not exactly."

"Well, Hastings ain't someone to mess with."

"Is that right?"

"Yeah, and he don't take kindly to strangers either."

"We ain't exactly strangers."

"So he knows you then?"

"No, we've only met once before and I don't think he'd remember me," replied Jess cagily.

Saul Littman had been listening to all of this, letting Vogan have his fun. Saul put his drink down, took his hat off and set it on the bar. He reached into his front pocket and took out a half-smoked cigar and lit it. He took a long drag and blew the smoke slowly up toward the ceiling. He took another sip of the whiskey, all the while studying Jess. He looked at the shotgun handle sticking up over Jess's right shoulder and took some time to examine the gun strapped to his waist. Jess ignored his stare, but he was well aware of it.

Saul, without taking his stare off Jess, hollered to the barkeep, "Ray, pour me another."

Ray filled the shot glass and Saul reached back, picked it up, tipped his head back and downed the whiskey. He set the glass down on the bar with a hard thump. He hollered at the barkeep again. "Ray, one more time." Ray filled the glass again as Saul stared straight at Jess.

"So tell me, what do you use that shotgun for?" asked Saul.

Jess still didn't look directly at Saul. He took one quick glance around the saloon and took another sip of his beer and put the glass down gently. Then, he slowly lifted his eyes and locked them onto Saul's. He figured Vogan was going to be involved in this, but he'd already decided that this man was the one to worry about first.

"And you are?" asked Jess calmly.

"Who wants to know?" he replied nastily.

"Well, when a man asks me a question, I figure I deserve to know his name before I feel a need to answer him."

Saul's cocky smile turned to a nasty scowl. "You're quite an arrogant little bastard, ain't you?"

"Yeah, I've heard that," he replied, smiling at Saul now, which only got deeper under his skin.

"What if I don't feel like telling you my name?"

"Well, then I guess I don't feel like answering your question."

Saul smiled cynically. He looked over at Vogan who was watching as if he enjoyed the banter. "Well, if you must know, my name is Saul Littman," he replied as if the name was important to everyone listening. "What's yours?"

"Jess Williams."

"Never heard of you before."

"And that matters?"

"So, now that we know each other, what's the shotgun for?"

"Shootin' rabbits, and sometimes people."

"So, how many people have you killed so far?" asked Saul.

"One."

"Only one?" he asked sarcastically.

"So far."

Saul laughed and so did Vogan.

"And did you kill him with that shotgun or with that fancy-looking lead pusher you got there?" asked Saul.

"Does it really matter?"

"Guess not. You pretty good with that pistol?"

"Good enough."

"You sure?"

"Pretty sure."

"And how good is that?"

"How good do I need to be?"

"I don't know," sneered Saul. "Maybe good enough to take me."

Jess noticed an immediate change in Saul and knew that things were coming to a head quickly.

"Ray," Saul hollered back at the barkeep, "you forgot to wipe up that dirty table he's sitting at. I can see spilt beer on the table. Is that any way to run a place?"

Ray, who had been watching and listening to the banter between Jess and the two at the bar, was caught completely off guard by the question. "Huh…oh yeah…I'll get it," Ray said as he started to walk over to where he had left a towel to wipe the tables down.

"Don't bother," said Saul, as he reached for the towel that was lying only a few feet away from him, "I'm sure he wouldn't mind cleaning up his own table." Saul picked up the towel and threw it at Jess.

What happened in the next few seconds was something that no man in the bar would ever forget. The towel was in the air heading for Jess as he reached back with his right hand and found the handle of his bowie knife. He brought the knife out of its sheath and up, going straight for the towel. In one quick, fluid motion, Jess caught the towel on the point of the knife and slammed the knife down into the table. As he did he stood up facing both men. Saul had begun to move his hand toward his right pistol and Vogan's hand was moving for his gun at the same time. Jess drew his pistol, thumbing the first shot, which hit Saul square in the chest. Before the hammer hit the firing pin, Jess's left hand began its movement toward the gun with the middle finger hanging down. Jess fanned the second shot and the bullet slammed into Vogan's chest just above his heart.

Both shots were kill shots, and yet, they were only a fraction of a second apart. Before the two men hit the floor dead, Jess stepped to his right and placed his back against the wall and took a quick glance around to see if anyone else was going to be involved. He quickly glanced over at the sheriff, who had a stunned look on his face.

Ray, the barkeep, was the first to speak. "Damn, I can't believe what I just saw. I saw it, but I still don't believe it."

Jess replaced the two spent cartridges and holstered his pistol. He sat back down at his table, able to see the entire place including the door, and took another sip of his beer. Sheriff Manley slowly rose from his chair and walked over to the two dead men lying on the floor. Vogan had fallen face-forward while Saul had slunk down, banging the back of his head on the bar before hitting the floor. Manley looked up at Jess and just stared at him for what seemed to be forever. The sheriff took in a deep breath and let it out slowly. Then he spoke. "So, you say you're looking for Randy Hastings, hey?"

"I thought I already made myself clear on that matter, Sheriff."

"Well, you'll surely find him now."

"Why's that?"

"Because Hastings only has a few friends around these parts, and you just killed two of 'em. I imagine he'll be looking for you once he gets back in town. Sure as hell hope I don't miss that fight. You gonna pay to bury these men?"

"Is there any bounty on either of them?"

"Don't believe so."

"Well then, I'll be taking their horses, saddles, guns and any cash they have on them. You can tell the undertaker to bury them and I'll pay for it out of what I get for the sale of their belongings. Tell him nothing fancy, only what's necessary."

"Why the hell should I?"

"Because if you're not gonna enforce the law, then at least you can clean up the mess after someone else takes care of it for you," he said bluntly.

Jess stood up, walked over to the two dead men and stripped them of their valuables. He walked the two men's horses over to the stables and tied them up and left a note for Billy. Sheriff Manley walked back to his table. Ron had a funny grin on his face.

"What's that big grin for?" asked Manley.

"Just wondering if you want to cancel your bet?"

"I ain't canceling anything," he muttered. "That kid got lucky is all."

"What I just saw wasn't luck, Sheriff," submitted Butler. "That boy is faster than a whore running out of a church on Sunday morning."

"Kiss my ass and deal me a winning hand for a change," groused Manley, as he sat back down. He sure hoped he got a good hand because he had a feeling that he was gonna lose some money to Ron Butler soon.

Jess headed back to his room and went straight up and turned in for the night. When he woke, he splashed some water on his face and headed down for breakfast. Martha took his order and the place was eerily quiet. Sheriff Manley was sipping coffee with one of the men Jess had noticed at the poker table the prior night. They both glanced at him repeatedly.

"Well, I heard you had quite a night last night," said Martha as she set Jess's breakfast on the table.

"It would seem so."

"Everyone in town is talking about it. They said you were fast, really fast."

"Is that what they're saying?"

"Yes," she repeated cautiously. "Why don't you leave town while you're ahead? You seem like a fairly nice young man, except for the fact that you just killed two men."

"Why, thank you, Martha. I think you're a fairly nice woman, too. But I can't leave town until Randy Hastings is dead. I'm not looking for a fight with anyone else. I didn't ask for one last night. It wasn't my choice."

"There are two men dead, just the same."

"They made an error in judgment."

"And you won't?"

"No."

"How can you be so sure?"

"A good man knows his abilities."

"Oh, and they didn't?"

"That's kind of obvious now, isn't it?"

"And you do?"

"Yes."

"It must be nice to be so sure of yourself."

"It does help," he replied flatly.

Martha turned and walked back into the kitchen. Jess finished his breakfast and headed out to the porch to sit. He wasn't there more than five minutes when Billy walked across the street and up to him.

"I got your note about the horses. What should I tell the old man?" Billy asked, referring to the owner of the livery.

"Tell him to sell the one horse and saddle or buy it himself. He can take ten percent and he better not even think about cheating me."

"Okay," Billy said as he turned away. He stopped suddenly and turned back to Jess. "What about the other horse?"

"Oh, that one's yours to keep, Billy. You pick out which one you want. Every young man needs a horse and now you've got one."

"Thanks, Mr. Williams!" exclaimed a very excited Billy. "I never had me a horse. I don't know how to thank you. Can I pay you something for him? I don't have much money, but what I got, you can have."

"Tell you what, Billy, you can pay me one silver dollar when I leave town. How's that?"

"That's just fine. Wait till my ma finds out I got me a horse. She won't believe it. Thanks again, Mr. Williams."

"Just don't forget about our little secret," he reminded Billy.

"I won't. You can be sure of that."

Billy headed back to the livery and Jess sat on the porch outside the hotel for a while. Then he went up to his room and took a little nap. As he lay there, he thought about Randy Hastings and what he and the other two men had done to his family. Whenever he had any doubts about what he was doing, he thought of his little sister, Samantha, lying with a bullet hole in her head, and pictured his ma hanging in the doorway above a pool of drying blood. Whenever he thought of those things, he knew what he was doing was not only right; it was justified.

CHAPTER TEN

Jess woke before daylight and headed downstairs to the café. He sat down just as Sheriff Manley walked in. The sheriff noticed Jess and sat at a table at the other side of the room. Martha finally came out of the kitchen and stopped by the sheriff's table and took his order. Another man came in and sat next to Manley. Jess recognized him at once as the man who played poker with Manley in the saloon. Martha walked up to Jess's table and her normal smile was replaced with a frown.

"I guess you didn't take my advice about leaving town while you're still alive," she said dryly.

"Guess not. I just couldn't pass up another helping of those biscuits."

"Biscuits ain't worth dying for, no matter how good they are."

"Some men have died for less."

"You're probably right. None of it makes any sense to me, no matter how much I try to understand it. I suppose it must be something that men just think they have to do."

"Maybe so."

"You want the same as yesterday?"

"You bet. And don't hold back on those biscuits. I could eat a dozen of them," he answered as Martha headed back into the kitchen.

Jess thought for a minute and then got up and walked over to Sheriff Manley's table. "Sheriff, I'd like to come over and talk to you at your office later today."

The sheriff waited a minute to look up at Jess. When he did, he had an odd look of both fear and anger on his face. "Well, I suppose that would be okay," he replied. "Say about noon?"

"Noon it is."

"Can I ask what this is about?"

"I'll let you know when I see you."

Jess went back to his table to eat his breakfast. After that, he took a stroll around town again, stopping in to visit Billy and check on Gray. Then he went to his room to take a short nap. His eyes opened before the first knock. He had unconsciously heard the noise of footsteps while he was dozing. He had the double-barreled shotgun up and ready before the knock on his door was finished.

"Who is it?" he asked.

"It's Billy," said a quiet voice. "Please open the door before anyone sees me." Jess got up and slowly opened the door to let Billy in.

"Hastings came back," said Billy nervously.

"When?"

"About ten minutes ago, but he left already."

"He left? Why and where to?"

"Well, he saw the horse you gave me," he explained. "He noticed it right away and asked about it. The old man told him what had happened and he got really mad when he found out you killed his two friends. He took off for the Last C ranch. He told me to tell the sheriff that he'll be coming back to town later today and if you're still here, he is going to shoot you down like a dog. I'm really scared."

"Don't be," Jess replied calmly. "I plan on seeing the sheriff today at noon. You go find the sheriff and tell him everything you just told me and then go back to work like nothing else happened. As far as anyone else is concerned, we never talked. Okay?"

"Okay. But I'm still scared. Are you sure you can take him? He's pretty fast."

"There's not much I'm certain about in life, Billy, but there is one thing I'm sure of and that is before this day is over, Randy

Hastings will be dead." Billy nodded and headed out to find the sheriff like he was told.

Jess spent a few minutes getting his gear ready, knowing he would probably leave town soon after he killed Hastings. He walked down to the general store and picked up some supplies and packed his saddlebags. He noticed the townspeople staring at him and he knew it was because they detected what was about to happen. He headed over to the sheriff's office to talk to Manley about the other two men he was hunting. Manley was sitting on the front porch in a chair when he arrived.

"Sheriff, do you have any information about Randy Hastings' other two partners that he came to town with originally?"

"Not really. They didn't stay long after they hit town. I heard Hastings say something about meeting them down in Red Rock, Texas, later."

"You got any wanted posters on those two?" asked Jess.

"Don't think so."

"When is the last time you looked at any wanted posters?"

"Hell, I don't know," he answered agitatedly. "It's not like I keep a schedule to look at them," retorted Sheriff Manley.

"Maybe you should."

"Well maybe you oughta…" the sheriff never finished what he was about to say after he saw the expression in Jess's eyes quickly change, a dark look coming forth.

"Here are some sketches of them I got from Sheriff Diggs over in Black Creek," said Jess, as he reached into his front pocket and pulled out the two drawings. "Why don't you take a look at any posters you have and see if any match up?"

"Ain't you got something bigger to worry about?" the sheriff asked sarcastically.

"Like what?"

"Like getting shot dead this afternoon," replied Manley. "You know, Hastings is just plain mean and he don't fight fair. He'll probably have some help with him. He didn't ride out to the Last C ranch just to visit 'cause he was lonely. He'll most likely bring back a couple of toughs with him."

"That'll be his choice," barked Jess. "They might even get me, but not before I get Hastings; you can bet on that."

The sheriff's expression changed to more of a look of respect for Jess. It had been a long time since the sheriff had seen such confidence and tenacity, especially in someone so young. "You sure got the gonads of a grown man, I'll give you that. You'd better hope that those gonads don't get you killed."

"You let me worry about that, Sheriff."

"Well, I'll check my posters for you. You be on the lookout for trouble though 'cause it's coming at you for sure."

"I suppose so, but I'm ready."

"I'll just bet you are," the sheriff replied, nodding his head.

Jess walked away and headed for the saloon. He figured that was probably where Hastings would look for him when he returned to town. He took a seat at the table in the corner. He had a good view of the batwing doors and the street so he could see trouble coming early. Ray brought Jess a beer and set it down on the table. Jess thanked him and took a long, slow drink as Ray wiped up the table.

"What are you going to do when Hastings gets back in town later?" asked Ray.

"Kill him," he replied candidly.

"I guess that's one way of handling it."

"I reckon it is."

"He'll probably have help with him."

"I already figured as much. It'll be their choice to throw in with him, not mine. Whoever does is going to die with him."

"Well, good luck, Jess. I hope you get to ride out of here."

"Me too, since I have two more men to hunt down after Hastings," he said, glancing up at Ray with a determined look.

There were at least a dozen people in the bar. That was more than usual this early in the afternoon, but they knew that the show would soon begin. They'd heard about the gunfight between Jess and the other two men the prior day and knew Jess was good enough to give Hastings a challenge. Jess had been sitting there for about two hours when all of a sudden a few more men rushed into the saloon. When they did, Jess could tell that trouble wasn't far behind. He knew by the way the men were looking at him. He stood up and walked over to the end of the bar by the wall so no one could get behind him. All of a sudden it got real quiet in the saloon. Jess removed his hammer strap from his pistol. He had a clear view of the swinging doors as well as the door to the other end of the bar going to the back of the saloon. He knew he would have to keep an eye on both doors.

Jess heard spurs jingling and footsteps coming up the stairs. A man wearing a six-shooter tied down low walked in and made his way to the opposite end of the bar. Jess noticed that the man had already removed his hammer strap. He was slightly heavyset and acted like he'd been drinking. He ordered a whiskey from the barkeep while keeping a close eye on Jess. Then, the moment Jess was waiting for finally happened. He heard footsteps this time, but no spurs. Jess stared at the man as he came through the door. He wanted to make sure who it was and he wanted it to be Randy Hastings. He wasn't disappointed. He remembered the two pearl-handled Colts that Hastings had been wearing on that fateful day he met him out on the road going into Black Creek, Kansas. He was still wearing the Colts, tied down tight and low on both legs. A flood of emotions hit Jess. He felt excitement, hatred, revenge and satisfaction all rolled up as one.

Hastings glanced over at his friend at the bar and the friend looked over at Jess, letting Hastings know which one of the men in the saloon had been looking for him. Hastings would have been able to easily pick him out anyway. The strange-looking pistol and holster and the shotgun handle sticking up behind Jess's back were dead giveaways, but that's not how he would have known; the look on Jess's face was enough. It was a look that would make most men shudder with fear, but Hastings wasn't like most men; he was a cold-blooded killer.

Hastings took a moment to look him over. Jess glared back at him. Hastings had a cocky smirk on his face. It was eerily quiet in the saloon as Jess and Hastings just continued to stare at one another for what seemed an eternity. Jess was savoring the moment of finally catching up with one of the men who had murdered his family. Hastings was curiously wondering why this young man was hunting him. No one said a word until Hastings decided to break the silence.

"I heard you've been looking for me."

"You heard right."

"I also heard you killed two of my friends."

"That almost makes us even."

"Do I know you?" Hastings asked inquisitively. "What's your name, boy?"

"You don't remember me, do you?" asked Jess.

"Now why would I remember you?"

"We met once before."

"Really? Where was that?"

"Black Creek, Kansas."

"Okay. Black Creek, Kansas. Now who in the hell are you?"

"My name is Jess Williams."

"Well, Jess Williams, what's your beef with me?"

"Almost two years ago, three men murdered my family. They shot my pa down like a bunch of cowards. Then they raped and murdered my ma, but that wasn't enough; they also raped and murdered my little seven-year-old sister. You were one of those three men. I remember you from the road that day. I was riding in the wagon. Does that help your memory? Do you remember me now? Do you remember murdering my family?"

Hastings never flinched. He just stood there, with that same smirk still on his face. The truth was, he did remember that day. He just wasn't about to admit it.

"Mind if I have a drink first?" asked Hastings.

"Go ahead." Jess watched Hastings slowly walk to the bar and order a whiskey. Jess noticed that Hastings had gotten his left boot heel fixed.

"I see you got your left boot fixed," observed Jess.

"How'd you know that?"

"I saw it that day on the trail into town."

"Really?"

"I saw your tracks in the dirt in front of my pa's house, too."

"You don't say."

"I saw your tracks in the blood on the floor where you killed my ma."

"Maybe I ain't the only one who's ever lost a boot heel."

"Maybe not, but you're wearing the same two pearl-handled Colts," replied Jess firmly.

Hastings downed his whiskey and glared at Jess. "You know, you've made some serious accusations," he said in a sinister way. "You got any proof?"

"Don't need any."

"Really?"

"Really."

"Why not?" asked Hastings.

"You're wanted by the law, dead or alive."

"Well, if I was one of those three men, and I'm not saying I was, what the hell do you plan on doing about it anyway?" replied Hastings, showing no remorse at all.

"I plan to do what I promised my family I'd do. I plan to shoot you down like the dog you are; and I plan to make you suffer like my family did."

Hastings was getting a little agitated now. Jess could see his ears actually starting to turn red.

"Better men than you have tried and died. You sure you still want to do this? I believe you are outgunned and outclassed."

Jess looked around the bar and back at Hastings. "Are all of these men in the saloon throwing in with you or just the chubby one down at the end of the bar?" Hastings' friend straightened up at the insult.

"Just me and my friend over there. The rest of these men are only here to watch you die."

"Well then, I'm neither outgunned nor outclassed," Jess replied defiantly. "The only ones who are going to die here today are you and your friend if he reaches for his pistol. Now, I don't know about you, but I'm done talking unless you want to confess before I kill you. Not that it will matter much. I don't plan on taking you in alive. I'm just killing you and collecting the five-hundred-dollar bounty on your sorry ass."

Hastings put his right hand down by the butt of his gun. "You know what, punk? I'm the one that put that bullet in your sister's head. What do you think about that?"

"I think your day of reckoning has finally arrived."

Everything happened at lightning speed. Hastings and his friend both went for their guns at the same time. Jess drew and shot the man at the end of bar first, the bullet ripping through his chest. He didn't turn his body; he just snapped off the shot from the hip, keeping the gun close to his side. The man had just barely gotten his hand on the butt of his pistol. As Jess brought the pistol back toward Hastings, he fanned the next shot with his left hand and the slug hit Hastings in the left arm, but that was no mistake. Hastings hadn't quite gotten his gun out of the holster when Jess's first shot hit him. Hastings dropped his gun and grabbed his left arm where he'd been hit. Jess slowly walked forward and shot him in his right arm. Hastings let out another scream.

"You bastard!" wailed Hastings.

Jess said nothing as he slowly moved toward Hastings, who continued to back up. Jess fired another shot that hit him in the gut. He fell back against the wall and slid down to the floor. He was screaming in pain, trying vainly to cover his stomach wound. Jess smiled at him as he shot him in the left kneecap, shattering it into little pieces. His sixth shot took out the right kneecap, with bits of blood and bone splattering Hastings in the face. Jess walked up to him and looked at him for a moment, as he wormed around on the floor holding his gut with both hands, which wasn't easy since both his arms had been shot. There was blood all over. The only noise in the bar was coming from Hastings, who was moaning and cursing. Everyone else in the bar was silent, watching the event unfold.

Jess reloaded quickly and watched the room carefully. If anyone tried anything, he still had his pa's Peacemaker tucked in his front belt. Then, Jess brought the pistol in line with Hastings' forehead and pulled the hammer back slowly, allowing the killer to hear all four clicks of the hammer separately.

"What do you think my sister felt when you put that bullet in her head? Ever wonder if you will actually hear the gunshot or what it will feel like? Well, you're about to find out because that's exactly what's going to happen next," Jess said with deadly intent.

The bullet sprayed Hastings' brains all over the wall and floor. It was an ugly sight, but not one that hadn't been seen before by most of the men in the bar. Jess replaced the spent cartridge, holstered his gun and walked back to the bar to take another long drink from his beer. No one said a word. He looked over at the barkeep and Ray brought him another beer.

Sheriff Manley walked into the saloon. He was surprised by what he saw, but he sure wouldn't miss Hastings. He'd been nothing but trouble since he'd arrived in town. Manley walked over to the bar and Ray brought him a shot of whiskey. Manley slugged it down and turned around to survey the scene. The man at the end of the bar was lying faceup on the floor in a pool of blood, shot in the middle of the chest. Hastings' head was still leaning up against the wall and there were pieces of his brain matter all over the wall and floor.

Manley turned back around to the bar and ordered another whiskey. "Well, I guess you did what you came here to do," he said.

"I suppose I did," replied Jess.

"Don't suppose you feel bad about it neither, do you?" Manley asked, already knowing the answer.

"Not even a little."

"Well, you earned six hundred dollars in the process," offered Manley.

"I thought the bounty was five hundred," said Jess.

"Well, I looked through those wanted posters like you asked me. I found another poster on Hastings and, wouldn't you know, they raised it. I also found a wanted poster on one of the other two men you're looking for. The man's name is Hank Beard. He's wanted for murder and two bank robberies. The last bank robbery was in a town called Halstad down in Texas. There's a three-hundred-dollar bounty on his head. I also found an old telegraph notice from the sheriff in Halstad. The notice said that Beard had been spotted around a small town called Timber, about one hundred miles southeast of Halstad. I got nothin' on the other guy you showed me. I'm sure he'll surface sooner or later though. Those types usually do. Hell, he may even be with Beard. Suppose you're leaving town and heading down that way?"

"Matter of fact, I've decided to stay here tonight and leave tomorrow. I have one more thing to do."

"Can you do me a favor?" asked Manley.

"What?"

"Try not shootin' anyone else before you go?"

"I'll sure try, Sheriff."

Jess finished his beer and headed to his room to turn in for the night. He felt good about killing Hastings. That man had no business living after what he had done to other people. He hadn't wanted to kill Hastings' chubby friend, but that was his choice. As he dozed off, Jess kept thinking about Texas and a little town called Timber, and what he would find there. Hopefully, he would find the next part of his destiny.

Back in Black Creek, Kansas, the funeral for Red Carter was a quiet and solemn one. No one from town came to the funeral. No one really liked Red except for Dick Carter, his father. Carter owned the largest ranch in the area, the "Carter D." He was a hard man who had no problem with stepping on anybody who tried to get in his way. He'd bought out some of the smaller ranches around his, and the ones he couldn't buy, he simply forced the owners out. Carter didn't have much use for Red either, but Red was his only son and he loved him despite all the problems Red had caused him.

Dick Carter had mixed emotions about Jess Williams. Jess had worked for him on the ranch doing odd jobs and he had always liked the kid, but that was before. He felt bad for what happened to him and his family. And he was sorry about Red killing the sheriff, but that was still no excuse to kill his only son; at least in his mind it wasn't. Dick needed something and he needed it real bad. That something was revenge and that's why he hired the two best gun handlers he could find. Their job was to kill Jess, and it didn't matter to Dick Carter how they did it. They could kill him when they found him or they could drag his ass back to Carter so he could personally hang Jess himself. The two men were Frank Reedy and Todd Spicer and Dick was meeting with them that afternoon.

They were both hard men and fast with a pistol. Each had killed his share of men in his line of work. Frank Reedy was a former lawman who had turned to bounty hunting because it was more profitable, at least most of the time. He wasn't really a bad man, just one who had lost his way in a land where you lived and died by the gun. Todd Spicer was different. He was just plain mean and he had no conscience about anything. He killed for money and he could change sides depending on who paid the most. They had worked as a team for the last three years and they split all their earnings right down the middle. They both knew that Carter was one of the largest ranch owners in the area and could pay big money, which is why they dropped what they were doing and hightailed it to Carter's ranch.

They arrived at the ranch after two days of hard riding. They were met by one of Carter's foremen who took care of their horses and arranged for them to have a nice hot bath and good meal before meeting with Dick. That was just fine with them.

"Must be pretty important for Carter to give us the royal treatment like this," Spicer said, as he soaked in the tub next to Reedy. A young cowboy was bringing in more buckets of hot water and adding them to their tubs. The foreman had also put a good bottle of whiskey and two glasses on the table between the two tubs.

"Yeah, this ain't bad at all, partner," said Reedy. "You know, I've been sitting here thinking and I have a hunch I know what he wants."

"Really, how the hell you know that? You got a crystal ball in that tub of yours?"

"I don't need no crystal ball, you idiot. Don't you ever read the papers or listen to what's going on?"

"I only read the numbers on the money we get paid and I only listen to what I want to hear," he said as he shook some water from his head.

"You're one hell of a partner, Spicer. I don't quite know what I'd do without you."

"Probably starve and have to beg for food."

"Then you don't know that Dick Carter's only boy Red bit the dust recently?" asked Reedy.

"Hell, I didn't even know Carter had a son."

"I'm sure glad I'm the brains of this outfit," said Reedy, as he lay back in the tub after scrubbing his feet with a brush. "Anyway, I guess some young kid put a slug into Carter's boy, Red."

"Why the hell did he do that?"

"I guess it had something to do with the fact that Red killed old Sheriff Diggs, who was the sheriff here in Black Creek. For some reason, that riled the boy and he came to town and braced Red and killed him for it."

"Did he back shoot him?"

"The way I heard it, he faced him fair and square," replied Reedy. "I heard he was damn fast, too."

"You figure Carter wants to hire us to go after the kid who killed Red?"

"You catch on real quick sometimes," said Reedy sarcastically.

"Don't make me pay that young cowpoke to throw a bucket of hot water on your sorry ass," retorted Spicer.

"Too bad about Sheriff Diggs though. I worked with him a few times and he was a pretty good law dog. Tough but fair."

"Don't get all mushy on me. Pour me another shot of that good stuff and let's get on to our little parley with Carter. Maybe we can separate him from some of his money."

They both finished their baths and got dressed. Carter's foreman led them up to the main house. It was a grand-looking place with huge rooms and high ceilings. The foreman led them to a room that had a nice spread of food laid out and told them to make themselves comfortable. He said Carter would be in to see them in a little while. They both dug in and filled up. The food was as good as the whiskey. They were sitting down, sipping on some more good whiskey when the door opened and a large man with graying hair entered. Dick Carter wasn't what you would call fat or heavy. He was big boned and made of muscle. He was over six feet tall and weighed almost three hundred pounds and not one pound of it was fat. He tried to force a smile, but they could see the look of torment on his face.

"Welcome, boys. I hope my foreman has treated you well so far?" he asked.

"Hell, we ain't been treated this good in a long time," said Reedy. "A nice hot bath, the best whiskey I can remember and all this good grub. What else could a man ask for?"

"How about three thousand dollars?" Carter said, almost nonchalantly. Spicer, who had been gnawing on a chicken leg, almost choked.

"Excuse me?" said Spicer with a mouth full of chicken. "Did I hear you right? Did you just say three thousand dollars?"

"That's exactly what I said, three thousand dollars," he replied bluntly. "You would each get paid a five-hundred-dollar advance and then one thousand dollars each when you finish the job." Carter poured himself a glass of whiskey. Spicer glanced quickly at Reedy and swallowed the mouthful of chicken.

"And all we have to do for it is hunt down the kid who killed your son, Red?" asked Reedy.

Carter looked surprised. "So you know about what happened?"

"I can read and I hear things," added Reedy.

"Well, do you boys want the job?"

"Hell, yes!" replied Spicer, who had put the chicken leg down and was already figuring what he could do with his half of three thousand dollars.

"Hold on there, partner," Reedy hesitated. "I'd like to at least find out who it is he wants us to hunt down. Who is this kid who shot your boy?"

"His name is Jess Williams," replied Carter. "His family owns a small ranch the other side of town. He's the one who shot my boy and now he's got to pay."

"Don't you mean used to own a small ranch on the other side of town?" asked Reedy.

Both Carter and Spicer turned to Reedy with a surprised look on their faces.

"So you heard about what happened to his family," Carter said, not really asking since he sensed that Reedy already knew all about it.

"Like I said, I read and I hear things."

"Well, that doesn't matter none to me," countered Carter. "My boy didn't have anything to do with his family being murdered. I even hired Jess to do odd jobs around here to help him out 'cause I felt sorry for him. He had no right to kill my boy and he damned well is going to pay for it." Spicer just sat there listening to the conversation between Reedy and Carter.

"Well, do you want the job or not?" asked Carter plainly, leaning forward in his chair.

"Three thousand dollars is a whole lot of money," said Reedy. "You want him dead or alive?"

"I don't really give a shit," replied Carter. "You can kill him, hang him or bring him back to me and I'll hang him myself. It doesn't really matter to me as long as he ends up dead just like my son. I won't rest until that happens."

"I don't know about my partner, but I'll take the job for that kind of money," said Spicer.

"I'd really like the both of you to take the job. I hear you work pretty well as a team and you don't fail to bring back your man, which is why I sent for you. I'll hire just one of you if I have to, but I'd much rather have you both on the job."

Reedy knew that his partner would take the job alone anyway and as long as it was going to happen, he might as well cut himself in for a part of the action. He felt odd though. Something about this job just stuck in his craw like when a piece of meat got stuck between his teeth and he just couldn't get it out, no matter how hard he worked at it. But three thousand dollars was a lot of money, especially for just one man—or boy. That kind of money was hard to turn down under any circumstances.

"Okay, we're in. Do you have any idea where he is?" asked Reedy.

"I hear he headed out to Tarkenton to look for one of the men who killed his family," replied Carter.

"Yeah, at least that's a start," said Reedy. "Can you give us a description of the boy?"

"You can't miss him. He's wearing a pistol and a holster that sticks out like a sore thumb. I didn't see it, but those that did said it was like no other pistol and holster they'd ever seen before. Other than that, he's about sixteen, dark hair, slender, and wears a sawed-off shotgun strapped to his back so that the butt sticks up over his shoulder."

"That would separate him from the crowd," said Reedy. "We'll head out first thing in the morning. Mind if we bunk down here tonight?"

"I've got a nice room for you boys," said Carter, smiling for the first time in a while. "And I'll make sure you're provisioned up real good when you leave tomorrow. Anything you need to get the job done, you just ask for it."

"I wouldn't mind a few bottles of this fine whiskey to take along with us. A man gets mighty thirsty on the trail," Spicer said with a grin.

"I'll have a case of it on the packhorse along with food, ammunition and water. I'll give you the cash in the morning before you leave."

They shook hands with Carter to seal the deal and Carter left them in the room. They ate and drank some more and then turned in for the night. In the morning, Carter paid them five hundred dollars each in cash and supplied them with a packhorse loaded with everything they could possibly need. They left Carter's ranch and headed in the direction of Tarkenton, but both men had enough experience at chasing men down to know that anything could have made Jess detour. Once they reached the outskirts of town, they found a campsite where they decided to stay overnight. They would go into Tarkenton in the morning. Their hope was that Jess would still be in town when they arrived. They could make their kill, collect their money and move on to the next job.

Both men settled in just before dark and Reedy was pouring them each another cup of coffee when he gave Spicer a concerned look. "You know what, partner? I'm still not sure about this job. It doesn't set well with me," he said as he put the pot back on the fire. He had become increasingly uncomfortable about the job.

"A job is a job, Frank. Hell, I told you if you want to back out, I'll do the job myself. Just give me the five hundred dollars Carter already paid you and head out tomorrow. Then, after I kill that kid, I'll collect the other two thousand dollars. Hell, that's more money than I made all of last year."

"It's just that the kid doesn't seem all that bad. They said it was a fair fight and that Red drew on the kid first," argued Reedy.

"Now who the hell told you that?" he asked skeptically.

"I talked to the owner of the general store back in Black Creek when I went there to get us some more supplies before we met with

Carter. He's known the kid since he was a baby. He told me the whole story about his family and all."

"Well, he ain't no baby now," retorted Spicer. "He's a man killer, and we've been hired to take him down."

"Let's not forget about Red killing the sheriff either," added Reedy. "You know I don't stand for killing a lawman."

"Frank, you gonna shine up that old badge of yours and pin it back on?" he asked sarcastically.

"I ain't saying that. I'm just saying there are a lot of things I don't like about this job. It doesn't feel right. Hell, if my family was murdered like that, I'd track down the men who did it and shoot 'em down like dogs, too."

"Hell, so would I, but that's got nothing to do with the job we've been hired for. The kid killed Red Carter and Red didn't have anything to do with the kid's family being murdered. And now Red's dad wants him dead and he's willing to pay three thousand dollars to get the job done, whether we do it or someone else does. It seems pretty plain and simple to me. What part of that don't you understand?"

"I'll tell you what, Todd. I'll go into Tarkenton with you, but I want to talk with the kid before we finish the job. I'm not going in there and putting him down without hearing his side of all of this. Good enough?"

"Suit yourself, Frank. Just remember, once you're done talking, if you ain't in, turn around and leave your share of the money and I'll finish the job myself."

"Can't ask for more than that, I guess," replied Reedy as he put a few more pieces of wood on the fire and both men turned in.

CHAPTER ELEVEN

In the morning, Jess woke and gathered his things and headed to the dining room. He had breakfast and thanked Martha for her hospitality. He asked Martha about Billy's ma and how she got the bad leg. Jess had spotted her a few times down at the stables talking to Billy. She told him the story of how Billy was playing in the street when a bunch of hooligans raced their horses through town and Billy's ma had to grab him and pull him out of the way of the horses, unfortunately, not before she had her leg broken by one of the horses. They had no money for a doctor and she had to set the bone herself. It never healed right and she limped ever since. Jess walked over to the stables and found Billy, who was brushing down a horse.

"Hey, Billy, got my horse ready?" he asked.

"Morning Mr. Williams," he said excitedly. "I can have him ready to go in just a few minutes." Billy went about getting Gray ready.

"Billy, how's your ma doing lately? I noticed her visiting you a few times. Does she have a job?"

"Well, she cleans houses, but has a hard time getting much work," he replied sadly. "That bum leg sure slows her down a lot. She can't get around very well, but we do the best we can. That's why I work here so much. The twenty dollars you said you were going to pay me will sure help a lot. We still have a deal, don't we?"

"Yes, we do, but I figure I need to change the deal a little."

A worried look came over Billy's face, as if he was about to be let down.

"Actually, I figure with all the risks you took, I should pay you... say...how about one hundred dollars?"

Billy's mouth opened, but nothing came out right away. Finally, he responded, "Why would you give me that much money?"

"I figure maybe your ma could go and see a good doctor and set that leg right."

"Mr. Williams, you've got a friend for life for sure," exclaimed Billy.

"Well, Billy, I need all the friends I can get. Listen, if you need more money for your ma's leg, you just get hold of a man named Jameson at the bank in Black Creek, Kansas. He'll know how to reach me and I'll do what I can to help. Killing bad men seems to pay off right nicely."

"As long as you don't get shot doing it," he agreed with a grin.

"Can't argue with you on that point, Billy. Listen, you take care of yourself and your ma, okay?"

"Sure thing. Where are you headed?"

"Heading for Texas. Seems one of the other men I'm looking for has been seen down there in a little town called Timber."

"Boy, I wouldn't want to be him, that's for sure."

"No, you surely wouldn't." Jess took the reins from Billy and walked his horse down to the sheriff's office. As Billy watched Jess, he thought to himself that he wanted to grow up to be just like him. A bounty hunter who was fast with a gun and could still be a nice fellow.

Sheriff Manley was sitting out in front. He looked sober and seemed to be in a surprisingly good mood.

"Good morning to you, Mr. Williams. I suppose you're heading for Timber?"

"Yeah, got a date with a dead man there."

"Well, I want to thank you for cleaning up the town here a little. I know I ain't the best sheriff in these parts, but what you did will make my job a lot easier for sure."

"I guess there's a silver lining in every cloud. Sheriff, will you do me one more favor?"

"Sure, you name it."

"Take five hundred dollars of my bounty money and wire it to my bank in Black Creek, Kansas," he said, handing Manley a piece of paper. "Take the other hundred and give it to the boy at the stables."

"Billy?" asked Manley, a look of puzzlement slowly forming on his face.

"Yeah, he and his ma need the help, especially with her bad leg and all, and he did take good care of my horse." The sheriff grinned. He had gained a lot of respect for this young man, Jess Williams. Truth be known, Manley always had a soft spot in his heart for Billy and his ma. If he had been doing his job right, maybe that accident with the horses would've never happened. He had always felt a little guilty about it.

"That's a mighty nice thing for you to do, Mr. Williams, mighty nice. If you ever come back to my little town, look me up; I'd like to buy you a drink."

"Thanks, Sheriff. You take care."

"I will and you do the same."

Jess climbed up in the saddle and headed slowly down the main street. Martha was standing in the doorway and she waved goodbye. Jess smiled and tipped his hat at her. As he rode out of town, he thought that maybe he would come back again and take Manley up on his drink offer. That way he would get another chance to see Martha, but not yet, not until he finished his task and killed the other two men he was hunting.

Hank Beard and Blake Taggert had left Tarkenton about two weeks after they arrived there. They headed for Red Rock first. Blake still had some family there. The plan was for all three of them to meet up at the Taggert house in Red Rock after a while. Hank was in Red Rock for less than a week when he heard from his old pal Ben Grady, who was in Timber, Texas. Grady had wired a message to Taggert's family for Hank, figuring they would get it to him sooner or later. Hank wired him back and they continued to send some messages back and forth. Ben Grady had a plan to rob the man he worked for in Timber and wanted Hank in on the deal. Hank thought it was a good way to make some quick money so he had agreed to meet Grady.

"So, are you heading for Timber?" Taggert asked Beard.

"I guess so. We're running low on funds. Hell, we haven't robbed anyone or anything in a while. We'll have to do something soon or we'll all have to get real jobs."

"No chance of that happening," replied Taggert plainly. "I ain't working for money as long as I can take someone else's."

"Hey, barkeep, how about two more whiskeys?" asked Beard, waving at the barkeep. Beard and Taggert had been bellied up to the bar in one of the saloons in Red Rock for over two hours and both of them had had their shares of whiskey.

"Well, one of us has got to do something," added Beard. "That dog Randy hasn't done a thing but chase the skirts back in Tarkenton. I ain't seen any money from him or you."

"Simmer down," replied Taggert. "I told you I had a plan to rob that family out on the other side of town. I hear they keep their money hidden in the house 'cause they're afraid of putting the money in the bank."

"Yeah, well, planning is one thing and doing is another. You best get to it and real soon."

"You can count on it," he replied deviously. "You know what else they got there?"

"What?"

"A nice young pretty daughter," he replied with an evil smile on his face. "She looks to be about fourteen and pretty as a cactus flower."

"You just can't pass up a pretty face, can you? Why can't you pick on some older women instead of the young ones? I didn't like what you did to that little one back in Black Creek."

"Hastings was the one who shot her after I was finished with her," he argued, as if that made what he did okay. "Anyway, I hear this family has several hundred dollars stashed."

"We can sure use it," said Beard. "I'm going to head for Timber in the next few days and if that works out as planned, we'll have enough money to take care of all three of us for quite some time." They finished their whiskeys and ordered two more.

Jess headed southwest and made camp at dusk. He woke at dawn and rode for about two weeks without seeing a soul. That kind of solitude bothered some men, but he rather enjoyed it. It gave him a lot of time to think and to practice with his pistol. One morning, he had ridden only about two hours before he finally crested the top of a hill and looked down on a lovely sight. There was a large meadow with a river running through it. The river meandered through the meadow and just before it headed back into a wooded area, it took a ninety-degree turn.

Right at the point of the turn, Jess spotted a tent with a smoke-stack poking through the top of it. A horse was grazing in the meadow untied and a rocking chair sat outside the tent. It was about noon and Jess figured he had to be close to Timber. He figured that whoever was living in the tent might know something about the man he was hunting. Jess made his way down to the camp. When he was about one hundred yards from the tent, he heard a low, raspy voice holler out, "That's close enough, mister!"

Jess reined up Gray and stopped. He could see a man peeking out of the front of the tent. He was holding a long rifle that looked like an old beat-up buffalo gun.

Jess got down from his horse. "I mean no harm," he explained. "Just need a cup of coffee and maybe some talk, that's all. I'm not looking for any trouble."

"Well, come on then and let me get a good look at ya," said the raspy voice.

Jess slowly walked up to the front of the tent. A rough-looking man with a bushy beard came out and looked him over intently. Jess stood very still, not wanting to set the man off, especially while he had that rifle pointed at him.

"You one of them bounty hunters?" asked the man.

"I don't really think of myself as a bounty hunter."

"Sure do look like one."

"I've been told that before."

"Who you looking for?"

"I'm looking for a man by the name of Hank Beard. You know him?"

"Name don't ring a bell, but I'm not good with names anyway," he said. He put the rifle down as if he was no longer worried about Jess's intentions.

"Speaking of names, mine's River Bend Bill. What's yours?" he asked.

"Jess Williams."

"Nice to meet ya, Jess Williams."

"How long have you been living out here?" he asked, looking at the raggedy old tent.

"Oh, 'bout five years or so. I can't recall for sure. How 'bout that coffee? I got the pot, if you got the coffee." Jess tied Gray off and got out some coffee. After Jess poured them each a cup, he showed him the drawings of Hank Beard, but Bill didn't recognize him.

"So, how'd you get the name of River Bend Bill?" Jess asked.

"Well, I suppose it's 'cause of where I live. Right here, by this bend in the river. Can't live in town; they'd just throw me out."

"Why?"

"Well, it's a long story. You see there's a woman by the name of Patti Nate in town. I guess I kinda like her, but so does the sheriff, Mark Steele. Every time I go into town and try to talk with her, he gets all riled up and runs my ass out of town. I keep going back and he just keeps running me out. I think she's sweet on him, but she was with me first, so I figure I'll keep trying as long as she ain't hitched to him yet."

"Sounds like you got a fight on your hands. I wish you luck."

"Yeah, thanks. I'd a whupped his ass already, exceptin' he wears that badge and that gives him a lot of leeway, you know. Plus, I think she's impressed with that badge. Course I guess most women are, don't ya think?"

"I reckon you're right about that, Bill. Besides your problem with the sheriff, is he a good lawman?"

"It pains me to say it, but yeah, he keeps the peace and takes no shit. Maybe he'll have some information on your fellow."

"What's it like in town?"

"It's usually a pretty quiet town, but right now a few of the ranchers are feuding over water rights. Been a few gunfights between the ranch hands so if you go into town, you'd best be careful. Them boys don't care who they pick a fight with after they've been drinking. Town's about two miles straight thataway, through the woods. When you see Sheriff Steele, tell him River Bend Bill says hi. That'll get his dander up," Bill said with a smirk.

"I'll be sure to do that. Thanks for the company and good luck with Patti Nate."

"Hey, you stop in the saloon and have a drink on me and say hi to Patti. She works there. Tell her River Bend Bill still loves her and he'll be in to see her soon."

"I'll be sure to tell her."

Jess left the bag of coffee there and rode through the woods until he came to a clearing by a road. He could see the town about half a mile away. He walked his horse into town. It did seem like a quiet place with not much going on; but then again, the town wasn't much to begin with. There were only about a dozen buildings. He stopped at the only saloon and tied up Gray and walked inside after looking down both sides of the main street. He walked in and up to the bar and ordered a drink. He noticed that there were men sitting at several tables and four men standing at the bar. Jess could feel tension in the room. He took his usual spot, always at the end of the bar and always in the corner with a wall to his backside. They all eyed him as he walked in, but they were paying more attention to each other at the moment.

Another man walked into the saloon and Jess felt the tension in the room tighten up even more. He could smell trouble. The man joined the other four men standing at the bar. He ordered a drink and turned around to face one of the tables where three men had been sharing a bottle of whiskey.

"Since when did you let girls drink in this saloon, Jed?" the new man asked the barkeep. The other four men turned around. The barkeep was nervous and heading slowly toward the end of the bar where Jess had spotted a short double-barreled shotgun.

"I don't want no trouble in here, Johnson. You heard the sheriff the last time you started a fight in here," the barkeep said as he reached for the butt of the shotgun.

"Well, you wouldn't have any trouble if you didn't let girls drink in here. Ain't that right boys?" asked Johnson sarcastically. All four of the other men nodded. The three men sitting quietly at the table didn't say a word. They worked for the Triple Bar ranch, which owned most of the land that the river flowed through. They just finished their drinks, left some money on the table, stood up slowly and started to leave.

"Where you girls goin' now? Down to the store to get some lace for them britches?" asked Johnson, still trying to goad them. One of the three men stopped and turned slowly. He didn't say anything for a moment as if he was contemplating what his next move would be. The other two men stopped and turned. The air was heavy enough to cut with a knife.

"Johnson," the man said, "you know we can't have any trouble or we'll lose our jobs, and we all got families to feed. Why don't you give it up and leave it alone?"

"Because I don't give a shit about your families or your jobs. If your damn boss wasn't such a hard-ass, maybe we wouldn't have a problem."

"We can't control that. And you know full well that it's his water, even Judge Hawkins said so. Why don't you just let it drop?" replied the man.

"I don't know. Maybe I'm just a hard-ass, like your boss."

Just when Jess figured things were about to blow, a tall lanky man walked into the saloon. He wore a badge on the front of his shirt. It was Sheriff Mark Steele. When he walked into the room, it was obvious that he was immediately in control of the situation.

"What's going on, boys?" the sheriff asked, in a very quiet, yet deliberate tone.

"Johnson's been trying to pick a fight again and those boys were just trying to leave, Sheriff," Jed offered quickly, before anyone else could speak.

"That right, Johnson?" asked Sheriff Steele.

"This is unfinished business and you know it, Sheriff," retorted Johnson. He was getting mad and nervous at the same time. He was obviously afraid of Sheriff Steele, as were the other four men who were with him. Jess could see that.

"When I ask a question, I expect an answer, not an explanation to a question I didn't ask. So, what's the answer?" The sheriff's voice was firm as a steel blade.

"I...I guess that's right, Sheriff...but..." Johnson began to say when the sheriff cut him off mid-sentence.

"Okay now, I want you boys to unbuckle those gun belts so that Jed here can deliver them to me at the jail, which is where you boys are going for the rest of the day," ordered the sheriff.

"But, Sheriff...that ain't right!" retorted Johnson angrily.

"I ain't going to ask you again, boys, and you know I mean it," the sheriff answered, his hand going to the butt of his pistol. The look on his face said he would use it if he had to.

"Damn it!" hollered Johnson, as he unbuckled his gun belt and let it fall to the floor. The other four quietly followed suit.

"Thanks, Sheriff. We didn't want any more trouble. We'll be going now," offered the man from the other group.

"Good day, gentlemen," said Sheriff Steele. "And thanks for not acting like these fools. Tell your boss I appreciate it." Sheriff Steele was leading the five men out of the saloon when Jess spoke up.

"Sheriff, could I get a word with you later?"

"Sure thing, stranger," replied Steele. "I was wondering who you were anyway. Give me about an hour to lock these hooligans up, then come see me at the jail."

"Thanks, Sheriff."

Jess drank his beer and ordered another one. He asked Jed where he could find a room for the night then thanked him and headed down to the jail. Sheriff Steele was sitting at his desk writing when Jess knocked on the half-open door.

"Come on in," he said.

"Hi, Sheriff," said Jess, as he stuck his hand out and shook hands with him. "My name is Jess Williams. I'm looking for a man by the name of Hank Beard." Jess pulled the sketch of Beard from his front pocket and showed it to him. "He's one of the three men who murdered my family and raped my ma and little sister. He's got a bounty on his head and I heard he was last seen in this area. Do you have any information on him?"

"Raped your little sister?" Steele asked with a disgusted look. "How old was she?"

"Seven," he said as his gut knotted up.

"Damn. A man who would do something like that should be shot on sight. No judge, no jury, no trial, just shot," said Steele.

"He will be, Sheriff. As soon as I find him."

"You a bounty hunter?"

"No, not really."

"Could've fooled me. You sure look like one although you seem awfully young to be in the bounty-hunting business. Well, this picture doesn't ring any bells, but let me look through some posters and ask around. How about I meet you at the saloon around suppertime and let you know what I find out. They have good food there and I know the cook real well. Can you leave the sketch?"

"Sure, but I need it back. I'll see you later, Sheriff." Jess started to walk out and stopped and turned around. "Oh, I almost forgot. A friend of yours said to say hello to you."

"A friend? Who might that be?"

"River Bend Bill," Jess replied, smiling.

The sheriff shook his head in disgust. "That old codger can kiss my ass," he said sharply. "You tell him exactly that when you see him again and tell him not to show up in town or I'll lock his ass up and throw away the key!"

"If I get the chance to see him again, I will."

Jess left the sheriff's office and headed for the only hotel in town. He stopped at the livery, but there was no one there, so he brushed Gray down and stabled him. He got a room and took a nice hot bath. He decided he would try the food at the saloon since the sheriff had recommended it. He headed down to the saloon to wait for the sheriff. There were a dozen or so men in the place. Jess picked the table in the corner at the end of the bar and sat down to have a cold beer before eating. There was one man who was standing at the bar and paying a little more attention to Jess than normal and Jess knew it. The man was short, but lean and tough looking. He wore a single six-shooter. Jess counted four notches on the man's gun handle. If they were honest notches, that made him a very dangerous man. It wasn't long before the man put his drink down and turned to face his table.

"So, which ranch you working for, son?" asked the man.

Jess looked up to face him. He figured him for a gunslinger or a hired gun. His demeanor and the way he acted told Jess all he needed to know about him. He had to be careful with this one. It was just something that he could see in the man's eyes.

"I'm not working for any ranch; I'm here looking for someone."

The man kept looking at Jess, studying him. He was intrigued by the pistol and holster Jess wore. "You a bounty hunter?"

"Maybe. What's it to you if I am?"

"That depends on whether or not you're hunting any of my friends," replied the man.

"I'm looking for a man by the name of Hank Beard. Is he one of your friends?"

The man stiffened a little and Jess immediately picked up on it. "As a matter of fact, I do know Hank. We've worked together a few times."

Jess figured that any man who could be friends with a cold-blooded killer like Hank Beard had to be just as bad as Beard. Jess deftly removed his hammer strap and slowly stood up from his table, keeping a careful watch on the man's gun hand. Some of the men left the bar slowly and the rest moved around a little and watched, sensing that a gunfight was about to take place. Jess watched the room out of the corner of his eyes, but never took his eyes off the man.

"You didn't work with him on any jobs in the town of Black Creek, Kansas, did you?" asked Jess with a hint of anger in his voice.

"Depends what the job was."

"Murdering my pa and raping and killing my ma and my little sister," clarified Jess crossly.

The man seemed to think a moment about what he had told him. "He never mentioned any of that to me, so it ain't any of my business. I don't cotton to raping women myself, but I don't judge other men."

"The way I see it, any man who would have anything to do with a man like Hank Beard ain't much better than Beard himself," Jess barked.

"Hey, you kiss my ass, kid. If you've got a lick of sense, you'll get the hell out of town and forget about hunting Beard. He ain't worth dying for."

"I'm not the one who's going to die."

"You sure about that?"

"I believe that's what I said," snapped Jess.

The man took a step away from the bar and removed his hammer strap. When he noticed that Jess's hammer strap was already removed, the man smiled. "Pretty fancy pistol and holster you got there," he observed.

"Guess so."

"You'd better know how to use it."

"I do."

"How old are you?"

"What does that matter?"

"Well, you look awful young to be wearing all those guns you have on."

"I need every one of them."

The man looked at Jess's pistol again. "Where did you buy a pistol like that?"

"I didn't."

"Didn't what?"

"I didn't buy it."

"Then where did you get it?"

"I found it."

"Where?"

"You sure ask a lot of questions."

"Just asking."

"You should be asking yourself one question."

"Yeah, what should I be asking myself?"

"Am I ready to die today?"

"Are you?"

Jess took two steps closer to the man and stared deep into his eyes. "I'm always ready to die," he warned with an ominous look. "And I'm willing to take you with me."

"You talk mighty tough for a kid."

"I ain't a kid anymore." A few men in the bar began to move out of the way, sensing that lead would soon be flying.

The man began to slowly move his hand down closer to the butt of his pistol, all the while staring into Jess's eyes, trying to get a read on him. He couldn't see anything but a darkness that seemed to slowly edge forward. Jess did the same and he saw a sign in the man's eyes just before he went for his pistol.

The man was fast, but a fraction of a second later, he was dead. Jess's shot was right on target, dead center in the middle of his chest. The man had barely cleared leather. He fell back onto a table, bounced off it and landed facedown, dead.

Jess holstered his gun after checking the room and replacing the spent cartridge. The saloon had gone silent for a whole minute. The men in the saloon just stared at him as if they couldn't believe what they had just witnessed. Most of them had seen their share of gunfights and some of the gunslingers they saw were pretty fast. They had seen men shoot off their toes and empty their guns without hitting the men in front of them. Most men just weren't cool-headed and fearless. But this young man was not only cool-headed and fearless; he was faster than anyone they had ever seen before. Most of the men swore they didn't even see Jess draw his pistol. One moment, his gun was in the holster; and then, before they realized anything had happened, it was pointed at the other man, with smoke still coming from the barrel. Jess sat down at his table again.

It wasn't long before Sheriff Steele came into the saloon. He walked up to the body lying on the floor and then looked over at Jess. "This your work, son?" he asked.

"I'm afraid so, Sheriff."

"Boy, you don't waste any time. You've been in town less than two hours and I already have a man to bury. How long you plan on staying?"

"No longer than I have to, Sheriff."

"That's good, because you just killed Ben Grady. He was a hired gun working for the Mason ranch. Paul Mason was paying Ben here good money for his skills with a pistol. You must be damn good with that gun of yours because Ben here was one of the best. I was avoiding going up against him as long as I could."

"He's damn good," said the barkeep, who was still staring at Jess, having a hard time believing what he had just seen. "Grady never even had a chance."

Just then, Jess noticed a woman standing in the doorway behind the bar leading to the kitchen area. She was much older than him, but quite attractive. She was slender and had beautiful blonde hair that hung down to her shoulders. She was wiping her hands with a towel and she acted as if it wasn't the first dead man she had seen, which was true. "Well, Sheriff, seems like you got more paperwork to do," she said.

"Guess so, Patti. And you know how I hate paperwork."

"Well, it wasn't his fault," she said nodding in Jess's direction. "Ben drew first and this young man finished it. I watched it from behind the doorway. I have to say, it was something to see, for sure."

"Why thank you, ma'am," Jess said politely.

"Well, at least someone around here has manners. What's your name, young man?"

"Jess Williams, ma'am. Sorry for the trouble."

"I've seen trouble before and I plan on seeing it again, Jess. My name is Patti. Can I get you some dinner?"

"If you don't mind. I'd love some grub," he replied. "Sheriff here says you're a great cook."

"Well, he's right," boasted Patti proudly. "I'll bring you something right out. Meat and potatoes man, am I right?"

"Yes, ma'am, and some hot biscuits if you got some."

Patti went back into the kitchen to fix Jess a plate of food while the sheriff and Jed carried Ben Grady's body out of the saloon. Jed had the floor cleaned up before Patti brought out the food. Sheriff Steele sat down with Jess and ordered a beer. Patti brought out two big plates of food and plenty of hot biscuits.

"I figured both of you were hungry," she said as she put the plates on the table.

"Thank you. By the way, would your last name be Nate?" asked Jess.

"Why, yes it is. How did you know that?"

"An old friend of yours said to say hi to you if I had a chance to meet you." Sheriff Steele looked up at Jess with a glaring look in his eyes, but Jess was ignoring him.

"Really, and who might that be?" asked Patti, wondering who Jess might know that was a friend of hers.

"River Bend Bill," he replied, now turning to see the look on Steele's face. Jess could see the sheriff was less than happy. Patti's surprised look went from Jess to the sheriff and all she could say as she turned and started back toward the kitchen was "Oh, not this again!"

CHAPTER TWELVE

Sheriff Mark Steele was definitely a hard case, one who didn't fool around with people causing him trouble or breaking the law. He'd rather lock them up as talk to them. If they resisted, he'd just as soon shoot them. He had lived in Timber for ten years now. He moved to Timber from another small town in Texas where his father had been a lawman. His father had always carried a shotgun along with a .45 pistol. Steele didn't carry a shotgun much, only when he was facing a crowd, and he'd only had to do that twice so far. Once when he had a cowhand in jail who had raped one of the girls in town while in a drunken stupor, and another time when he was trying to break up a fight between the ranch hands of two competing landowners. They were always fighting over the water rights concerning the only river that flowed year-round through Timber and the surrounding area. He was good enough with his pistol skills to handle most situations. It was his attitude, however, that always carried him through trouble.

He had a confident air about him that most men could sense right off. He showed no fear in a gunfight even though, as most men did, he surely feared getting shot, even when he took a bullet in the left shoulder five years back when he tried to get a hotheaded gunslinger to give up his gun and go to jail willingly. He simply stuffed a bar towel in his shirt, told a few men in the saloon to carry the body over to the undertaker's office and then walked over to the doctor's office. After the doctor fixed him up, he went right back to work, doing his final check for the night around town. He hurt like hell, but he would never show it. He figured that's what the townspeople expected out of a sheriff and he wasn't going to give anything less.

He did have a soft spot for the ladies though, especially Patti. He'd had an ongoing battle with River Bend Bill over the years concerning Patti. Every time Steele had Patti convinced to marry him, Bill would show up just long enough to spoil it. He couldn't understand why any woman, especially a good-looking woman like Patti Nate, would ever give an old codger like River Bend Bill a second look or even the time of day. He was dirty, dressed like an old farmer and just plain smelled most of the time. Steele was sure that he was finally winning Patti over and he wasn't about to let old Bill mess it up this time. He was on the lookout for him. He even put the word out on the street with the other men in town to let him know if River Bend Bill showed up anywhere in town.

Sheriff Steele had risen extra early that day and went to his office to check some paperwork that he had been avoiding for days. He hated paperwork and wished he could afford a deputy to do it. He had told Jess the night before at the saloon that he hadn't found anything yet on Hank Beard. He didn't know Ben Grady and Hank Beard had been friends. Then again, he hadn't known much about Ben Grady either, except for the fact that he was a hired gun and rarely came into town. He finished his work and headed over to the saloon to get a bite of breakfast. The fact that he'd get a chance to see to Patti again was just the icing on the cake. He walked in and sat down at a table and Jed brought him a hot cup of coffee.

"Hey, Sheriff, how's your day going so far?" asked Jed.

"So far, so good."

"Want some breakfast?"

"You bet. Is Patti working this morning?"

"Of course, I won't find a better cook in this town. I'll let her know you're here. You want your usual?"

"Tell her to throw in a little extra bacon this morning, Jed." Jed went in the back to let Patti know the sheriff was in. She came out a few minutes later with a plate of food for him.

"Good morning, Sheriff," she said with a teasing smile across her lips. "How's your day going so far? Anyone get shot yet? Have you run anyone out of town this morning?" He knew that Patti was referring to River Bend Bill. She seemed to like the fact that two men were pursuing her and the sheriff knew it. What he didn't know is Patti didn't really love River Bend Bill. She was just playing one against the other. Her real love was for Mark Steele and she figured he would find that out in due time. She knew she would end up marrying Steele, and the fact that the sheriff didn't know that yet was something she enjoyed. She knew most men usually had to learn things the hard way.

"No, I haven't shot anyone or run anyone out of town yet, but you can bet I'll run that old varmint out of town if he shows up," he warned. "What in the hell do you see in that old codger anyway?"

"Oh, he's not all that bad and he's always so polite to me. Much like that young man, Jess, who kept calling me ma'am last night."

"You mean the young man who shot a man dead and then ate dinner five minutes later?"

"Well, he was nice. Who is he, by the way?"

"I don't know yet. All I know is what he told me. He said he's looking for a man by the name of Hank Beard. Beard is one of three men who killed his family and raped his ma and little sister. What kind of man could rape and kill a little seven-year-old girl?"

"The kind who ought to be hung, but only after someone takes a knife to a particular area first," she said with certainty in her voice. The sheriff winced, knowing just exactly what she meant. Just then, Jess walked in the saloon and came over and sat down with the sheriff.

"Good morning, Mr. Williams. Can I get you some breakfast this morning?"

"Yes, ma'am, and some hot coffee if it's not too much bother."

"See what I mean," exclaimed Patti, looking at the sheriff. "Polite and nice, just like River Bend Bill."

117

Sheriff Steele spit the bacon out of his mouth. "Nice, my ass!" he exclaimed.

"I'm just saying," she replied, walking into the back.

"Did I miss something?" asked Jess.

"You should have missed seeing River Bend Bill," Sheriff Steele snapped back.

"Sorry, Sheriff. I didn't know it would cause that much trouble."

"Well, it's not your fault," he admitted with a look of irritation on his face.

"Did you find out anything on Hank Beard yet?"

"Sorry, but no. I looked through all my wanted posters this morning and didn't find anything on him. I don't always get every wanted poster though. I guess you want this sketch back," the sheriff said, pulling the picture out of his pocket and setting it down on the table in front of Jess. Jess glared at it for a moment, feeling hatred for the man. Patti walked up to the table and set the plate of food for Jess down. She couldn't help but notice the picture of Hank Beard.

"I've seen that man before. He's been in here a couple of times. Is that the man you're looking for?"

"Yes," he replied quickly. "Please tell me anything you know about him. Do you know where he is now? Do you know if he works for someone in the area, one of the ranchers maybe?"

"Whoa, hold your horses, young man," she replied. "I don't know a thing about him. He's only been in here a couple of times in the middle of the afternoon and he only has one or two beers. He never came in at night or hung around with any of the locals. He did have a beer with Ben Grady one of the times he was in here. They only talked a few minutes and then this guy in the picture left. Ben stayed around a few more minutes and then left. Is this the guy who did those terrible things to your family?"

"Yes, he's one of the two still alive, but after I catch up with him, there will be only one left."

"Well, after hearing what he did to your little sister, I hope you do to him what you did to Ben Grady last night."

"That would be too good for this man," he said with a deadly look on his face. "He won't die so quickly. He's going to feel a lot of pain before he meets his maker."

Jess turned to Steele. "Sheriff, what do you think Beard and Grady were up to?" he asked.

"Who knows for sure? I didn't know the two knew each other. Besides, Ben didn't come into town all that much. They must have been planning something. I'm sure that whatever it was, it wasn't anything good."

"Well, I guess it doesn't really matter. I just need to find him and put him down for good."

"I have no doubt that you will do just that, Jess," replied Sheriff Steele. "I have no doubt at all."

⊸ ⊱

Hank Beard had been on the trail for several days now. He was tired, dirty and hungry, and he didn't like to be any of those things. He wiped the sweat from his forehead with his yellow bandana. He could hardly see the color now. It looked more like a faint brown. He hadn't had a chance to take a bath since he left Timber to check out the stagecoach that ran the money from the Mason ranch to the bank in town. The Mason ranch was one of the largest and richest in the area and Paul Mason was a very wealthy man.

Beard and Grady had figured that they could score big, holding up the stagecoach that carried Mason's money long before it ever got to the bank. Grady had helped load the money in the box for Mason and even rode shotgun for the stagecoach a few times. Beard had spent the last several days checking out the route and waiting for the coach to make a run. When it finally did, he was certain that he had picked a great spot to hold it up.

There was a sharp bend in the trail, which forced the coach to slow down to a crawl. There was a rock cliff just off to the right edge of the road and a clump of trees on the other side no more than fifty feet from the trail. It was a perfect ambush spot. Hank figured they could take out the two lead guards instantly and probably take out the shotgun rider and driver before they could get off a shot.

He was heading back to Timber to meet with Grady and firm up when they would hit the stagecoach. He had no idea that Grady was dead yet, and no idea that someone was hunting him. He stopped along a creek and rinsed out his bandana and washed his face off. It felt good. He climbed back in the saddle and placed his shotgun back across his lap as he always did. He figured that he was about an hour from Timber and decided to keep riding until he got there. His thoughts turned to his pals. He pictured Hastings chasing a skirt back in Tarkenton and Blake Taggert murdering another family and raping and killing another young girl.

Frank Reedy and Todd Spicer rode into Tarkenton in the morning. They stopped at the livery and stabled their horses. Then, they headed down to the sheriff's office. Sheriff Manley was just coming out of his office when they got there.

"Hi, Sheriff," said Reedy, "got a minute?"

"Maybe," replied Sheriff Manley. "Depends on what this is about. I haven't had my breakfast yet."

"It's about a man we're looking for," replied Reedy. "Well, a kid really by the name of Jess Williams."

That got Manley's attention immediately. "Well, come on in then," he said, as he walked back into his office followed by the two men. "What business do you have with Jess Williams?"

"To be honest, Sheriff," answered Reedy, "we've been hired to bring him back to Black Creek, Kansas, to answer for the murder of a man there."

"Really? He didn't seem like a murderer to me. Who'd he kill?"

"A man by the name of Red Carter," interjected Spicer.

"And who hired you?" asked Manley.

"Red's father, Dick Carter," replied Reedy.

"Well, it doesn't matter anyway," said Manley. "He left town a couple of days ago. He was involved in a few gunfights while he was here, but they were both fair fights, although it didn't really seem like it."

"Really? What do you mean by that?" asked Reedy.

"The two men he killed never had a chance, from what I hear. Those who saw the shooting said the kid was so fast the other men never got their lead pushers out of their holsters."

"Well, that don't matter, Sheriff," Spicer snapped back. "He's a murderer and we plan to take him back to Black Creek when we find him."

"Suit yourself, but I wouldn't go up against that young man. He's just too damn fast. You boys will find yourself planted in the ground if you plan to brace that boy," said the sheriff almost proudly. The sheriff's stomach growled and he walked out and left Reedy and Spicer in his office.

Reedy looked at his partner. "That bad feeling I had about this whole thing just got worse," he said apprehensively.

"Hey, like I keep telling you, ride out any time you like. Just don't forget to leave your share of the money," groused Spicer. They walked out of the sheriff's office and hollered out to the sheriff who was almost across the street. "Hey, Sheriff," asked Reedy, "did Williams say where he was headed?"

"No, he didn't say. He just rode out. Sorry I can't be any more help." Manley had lied, not wanting these men to have any more information about Jess's whereabouts.

They headed for the stables to get their horses and try to decide what to do next. The stable boy, Billy, got their horses saddled and brought them out to Reedy and Spicer who had been talking about Jess.

Billy had overheard Jess's name. "You know Jess Williams?" he asked as Reedy and Spicer quickly exchanged glances.

"Yeah, we know him," replied Spicer. "He's a good friend of ours and we're looking for him. We did some work together and we owe him his share of the money."

"You guys bounty hunters, too?" asked Billy keenly.

"Yes. You could say that," replied Reedy. "Do you know where he was headed when he left town?"

"Sure, he said he was heading for Timber, Texas. He heard that one of the other men he's looking for was down there. Did you hear about the gunfight?" Billy replied excitedly.

"No, why don't you tell us about it," replied Reedy.

"Jess squared off with two men at the same time in a gunfight and they never had a chance. Jess was so fast you could hardly see him draw. Ain't no one faster than Jess Williams, that's for sure. When you guys see him, tell him Billy and his ma said hi. He gave me money to get my ma's bum leg fixed up. He sure is a good friend to have."

"Thanks, kid," replied Reedy. "We'll tell him you said hi."

Reedy and Spicer rode out of town heading for Timber. They rode for a while in silence. Reedy was thinking about this young man, Jess Williams. Spicer was thinking about the money he was about to make.

Reedy finally broke the long silence. "You know what, Todd? The more I learn about his kid, the more I like him. I mean, how bad can this kid be when he gives some stable boy enough money to get his ma's leg fixed? That doesn't sound like a cold-blooded killer to me."

"Hey, I've known cold-blooded killers who would buy kids candy," retorted Spicer. "Even the worst of men have a heart some-times. But that don't make them nice men. Besides, it just doesn't matter. We're getting paid to kill him or bring him back. We're not getting paid to judge him."

"Well, I'll go along until we finally meet up with him. When we do, I want to talk to him first," said Reedy. Spicer just shook his head, wondering if his partner was going soft on him.

Jess spent the remainder of the day walking around town. He had some dinner and turned in early. He decided not to go to the saloon for a drink, opting instead to go to his room and get a good night's sleep.

Hank Beard finally arrived in Timber late that same night. He didn't stop in the saloon for a drink either. He was tired and went straight to the hotel and got a room for the night. He had no idea that Ben Grady had been shot dead. He also had no idea that his room was just two doors down from the young man who had killed him. Fate has a funny way of arranging things sometimes.

CHAPTER THIRTEEN

Timber was a quiet town in the morning. Jess got up at daybreak, saddled Gray and took an early ride around the area, checking things out. It was early afternoon when he stopped in at River Bend Bill's and had a cup of coffee with him. He took two pounds of fresh coffee to his new friend and Bill couldn't say enough about how nice it was for him to do that. Bill didn't have much money and sometimes he couldn't even afford to buy coffee.

"Well," said Jess, "I gave the sheriff and Patti your messages."

"I would have loved to be there when you did," laughed Bill. "What did Patti say when you told her?"

"Something like, 'Oh no, not this again!'"

"Hah! I'll bet the sheriff was pissed as hell, wasn't he?"

"I thought he was going to spit blood," Jess said with a smile. "I hope you're not thinking about going into town any time soon. The sheriff has men watching for you and he'll throw you in the hoosegow for sure if you show up. I think I'd wait a while if I were you."

"Maybe. Hell, I got nothin' but time anyway."

Bill lifted his cup to his lips for another sip of fine coffee when he noticed a small cloud of dust over the other side of the river. He stood up and so did Jess. They spotted four riders following a large man wearing a hat that looked too big for him. They were heading into Timber. Bill recognized the lead rider as Paul Mason.

"I wonder what he's heading into town for. He never comes to town unless there's some kind of trouble."

"Actually there was a little trouble the day before yesterday," replied Jess. "I killed a man by the name of Ben Grady."

River Bend Bill gave him a disconcerted look. "You drew down on Ben Grady and lived to tell about it?" he asked excitedly.

"He drew first. I didn't start the fight. I only finished it."

"You beat Ben Grady to the draw?" he asked again.

"How many times do you want me to tell you?"

"Well, it ain't finished," River Bend Bill said as he sat back down. "It ain't finished until Paul Mason says it's finished. He was paying Ben Grady a lot of money to be his lead hired gun. He's gonna be mighty pissed off. He ain't bringing those four riders into town for no Sunday meetin'."

"Maybe I should head back to town and see if the sheriff needs any help," Jess contemplated with a worried look on his face.

"Hell, it ain't your job. Have another cup of this fine coffee."

"It might not be my job, but I caused it. Actually, Grady caused it, but I don't like anyone paying for my doings." Jess gulped down his coffee and got on his horse and headed straight back to town.

Paul Mason was mad as hell. He had been paying Ben Grady ten times what he was paying any of his other hired guns. Of course, Grady was ten times as good as any of them. Mason lived by a few hard-and-fast rules in his life. One of them was you get what you pay for. If you want the best, you have to pay for the best. And Grady was the best. At least, he had been the best he could find, up until now.

Mason had a temper hotter than most branding irons. When one of his hands came back to the ranch after hearing how a young kid shot Ben Grady dead in a fair gunfight, Mason got so mad he punched the ranch hand who told him about it and stormed outside and shot the first thing he saw, which happened to be the man's horse. He shot the horse three times and then threw his gun as far as he could. He spent the remainder of the day cursing and giving everyone a hard time while he gathered up a group of men to ride with him into town. They arrived in Timber in the early afternoon. Mason was leading the group by a few feet, not because he ordered the men to stay behind him, but because they were all afraid of what he might do if they took the lead. They rode up to the sheriff's office, but didn't dismount.

Mason yelled out from his horse. "Sheriff Steele, I know you're in there," he growled. "Come on out. I want to talk to you." The other four men just sat on their horses.

The door of the sheriff's office opened up, but Steele didn't appear right away. He stayed back a little for a moment to see if things would explode right away. When they didn't, he slowly walked out of the doorway. He was holding a double-barreled sawed-off shotgun. He was wearing his pistol and he also had another Colt .45 stuck in his belt. He believed in being prepared.

"What can I do for you, Mr. Mason?" Sheriff Steele calmly asked.

"You can start by telling me who killed Ben Grady. Then, you can point him out to me so I can kill the bastard."

"You know I won't stand for that, Mason," countered Sheriff Steele. "Ben Grady was killed in a fair fight. As a matter of fact, he drew on the kid first."

"You're crazy, Sheriff," Mason bit back. "You know there ain't no one fast enough to take down Grady, especially some wet-behind-the-ears young kid. Hell, you were afraid of going up against Grady yourself! If I have to, I'll have each one of these men challenge this kid one at a time in a fair fight. You can't do anything about that now, can you?"

"Well, no, but if you do that, Ralph the undertaker will be a happy man."

"Really! Why is that?" Mason asked infuriated, still clutching the reins of his horse so tightly the horse was jerking his head up and down.

"Because he'll be making four new wooden boxes to put your men in and maybe even one for you. Hell, Mason, you know as well as I do that Grady could take any two of your men at the same time and not even break a sweat. This kid took Grady down and Grady never got his pistol out of his holster. Add to that, the fact Ben Grady went for his gun first."

"Sheriff, I don't give a damn about any of that," snapped Mason. "Now, I'm not asking you again. Where is this dirtball of a kid?"

"First off, don't threaten me, Mason," retorted Steele angrily. "You should know by now that I don't react too kindly to threats. Besides, he's not here right now. Seems he took an early ride this morning. He'll probably be back sometime later this afternoon."

Mason glared at Sheriff Steele. "Sheriff, we'll be over in the saloon having a drink. We can wait, but when I leave today, that kid will be in a box and I'll even pay for it!" hollered Mason, as if he wanted the whole town to hear.

"I'm afraid you just might pay for it," said Steele, meaning something altogether different, but Mason and his group didn't hear him. They had already turned their horses around and headed across the street to the saloon. They dismounted and walked in and bellied up to the bar.

"Jed, get us a bottle of your best whiskey and four glasses," barked Mason, "and make it fast."

"Yes, sir, Mr. Mason, right away," replied Jed, as he went into the back room and brought out two bottles of his best whiskey. He knew from experience that one bottle was not going to be enough. Ray, one of the four men that Mason brought with him, and the fastest of the four with a pistol, poured a shot for Mason and himself.

"I'd sure like to get the first crack at that kid, Mr. Mason," Ray said enthusiastically.

"That's fine by me, Ray," replied Mason. "I know you and Ben were good friends. That's why I brought you along. The fact you're the next best man I have with a pistol wasn't lost on me when I picked you."

"Hey, what about us?" asked one of the other men.

"You'll all get your chance after Ray here. Whoever plugs him gets a hundred-dollar bonus in his pay envelope next month." They all smiled at that, but Ray was smiling the most. He was going to get the first crack at this kid everyone claimed was fast and he was sure he could take him. He had no way of knowing just how wrong he was. Mason and his men settled in for the wait and Sheriff Steele watched the saloon from his office window. He knew today was going to be a day he would more than earn the small salary the town paid him. Hopefully, at the end of the day, he could spend some of it on a drink, which he was sure he was going to need by then.

※ ※

There were bad men and there were really bad men. These were men who would kill without remorse or rob people of their life's work and sleep like a baby with no regret for its actions. However, Blake Taggert didn't belong to that class of men. He was in a class all by himself. He was just plain evil to the bone. If ever God made mistakes, Blake Taggert was surely one of them. There was absolutely nothing good about Taggert. He had killed his first man when he was just twelve. That man was his father. His father was a mean ornery cuss who beat Blake's mother; and whenever he felt like it, he'd beat on Blake. One night, he took a bottle and broke it over Blake's head. It cut Blake's head so bad that the blood just kept running in his eyes and he could hardly see. Blake was used to the violence, but for some reason something snapped inside him that night. Maybe the knock on his head did something to change him or maybe he was just a bad seed and he had finally had all he could take from his father. Blake went over to the fireplace and took down the Winchester rifle that his father always kept there and shot his father four times. When his mother screamed at him, he shot her three times. He saddled up the best horse, took all the money his parents had stashed in the house and never looked back. Truth be known, no one ever figured out Blake was the one who killed his parents. Everyone thought Blake had been kidnapped and killed or had run off after finding his parents murdered. No one really cared, so the matter was just considered another unsolved murder.

While Beard was on his way to Timber, Blake had done what he said he had planned. He rode out to the homestead outside of Red Rock and murdered the family he told Hank about. He walked into the house about midnight and used the pillow to shoot the couple and then he raped the young daughter. The worst part about it was he dragged the daughter into her parents' bedroom and raped her right there on the bloody bed between her dead parents' bodies. Before he was finished with her, she was covered in her parents' blood and she was almost in a catatonic state from the shock of what was happening to her.

Then, when he was finished with her, he took his pistol, stuck it in between her legs, and fired one shot. The shot was somewhat muffled and the bullet passed out of her stomach, along with some of her insides. He watched the life drain out of the girl and then he smiled at his work. He ransacked the house until he found the money. They had over six hundred dollars stashed in several different places and when Blake was satisfied he'd found all the money, he headed back to Red Rock, making sure no one saw him return. It was several days before the bodies were discovered, but no one had a clue as to who would do such a horrible thing. Blake just smiled to himself when he heard the men talk about it at the saloon. "Blew the girl's innards right out!" he heard one of the old men say.

᚜ ᚛

Jess arrived back in Timber shortly after Mason and his hired guns went to the saloon. He took the back way into town and slid up to the side window of Steele's office. He could see Steele sitting in a chair and looking out the window. "Afternoon, Sheriff. You having a bad day?" asked Jess.

"Christ, Jess!" exclaimed a surprised Sheriff Steele. "Don't ever sneak up on a man like that unless you plan on getting shot!" Steele relaxed a little. "Actually, I'm watching trouble right now over there at the saloon. Why don't you come on in? I can see all five of them and they're all bellied up to the bar and not looking this way."

Jess quickly walked into the sheriff's office. "So, is this a result of what happened between me and Grady the other day?" he asked.

"You have a keen sense of perception for as young a man as you are. Yeah, old Mason and his group are over there waiting for you to come back to town. Then, they plan on making sure you're dead before they leave."

"Not very friendly people, hey, Sheriff?" Jess asked sarcastically.

"Paul Mason is a lot of things: rich, tough, married to a beautiful young woman, but definitely not friendly."

"Did you explain it was a fair fight and that Grady drew first?"

"No, and I didn't tell him about the time my father gave me my first horse either since I didn't think he was interested in either of those stories," the sheriff said mockingly. "Of course I told him. He just didn't give a shit."

"Well, what do you suggest, Sheriff?"

"Well, it seems to me you've got two choices: head out of town and put some distance between you and Mason or go over there and probably get shot. I'll be glad to stall them for as long as I can."

Jess thought about it for a minute. "I haven't finished what I came here to do. So, I guess I'll just have to go over there and have a little talk with Mason."

"Damn it! I just knew you were going to say that. Listen Jess, I've known Mason for a long time. He's not a man to be messing with. He said he plans on seeing you dead for killing Grady and he'll damn sure try. You won't talk him out of it, if that's what you're thinking."

"We won't know until I try, now will we? Besides, if I start running from trouble now, I'll be running forever and that's not going to happen. You can join me if you want; it's your choice. It's not your fight and I won't ask you to involve yourself in the matter. I believe in a man taking care of his own problems." He stated it as plainly as he could.

"Maybe, but I'm still the sheriff in town and I won't stand for any gunplay unless it's fair. That's what I get paid for. So, I guess I'll just tag along for the hell of it. It's either that or do more paperwork."

Jess knew Sheriff Steele would involve himself; it was just in the nature of a man like him to never shy away from a problem. Steele grabbed a few more shotgun shells and put them in his front pocket. He noticed Jess had two pockets sewed into his shirt that held two shells in just the right place.

"Kind of handy," said Steele, as he nodded at Jess's shirt as out the twelve-gauge shotgun shells into his own pocket.

"I like to be prepared, Sheriff."

They both seemed ready and they looked at each other for a moment as if to wonder how their two lives had seemed to cross paths at this moment in time. Then they nodded at each other and walked out onto the front porch of the sheriff's office. They took a look around the street and up at the rooftops to make sure no one was ready to take a shot at them. As they walked across the street, and without taking his eyes off the front doors of the saloon, Steele said, "I sure hope you're as good as Jed said you was." There was no answer from Jess. He had other things to concentrate on.

As they walked up the two steps to the porch in front of the saloon, Steele could see that the four men who had ridden in with Mason had turned around with their backs to the bar. As Jess and Steele walked in, the two of them split up. Jess went to the right and Steele to the left. Steele could hardly hear it when Jess said to him in a whisper, "The two on the left are yours, if you want in." The room was so quiet they could have heard a cockroach fart.

Finally, Mason finished his drink and slowly turned around to face Jess and Sheriff Steele. "Sheriff," said Mason, as he shot a look at Jess. "Is that the young man responsible for killing Ben Grady?"

"As a matter of fact, yes, he is," answered Steele, setting the twelve-gauge on a table, but still within his reach.

Mason looked Jess over for a moment. He was looking at a young man who looked to be not more than seventeen years old; however, Mason could sense there was more to this young man than a cursory glance could tell. "So, you're the kid who outdrew Ben Grady?" he asked.

"Yep, that would be me," said Jess, not taking his eyes off Paul Mason. Jess realized right off Mason was the man who controlled the other four hired guns in the saloon, who were all staring at Jess. He knew they would do nothing without Mason's approval.

"You know what, son? Ben Grady was my best man. You have to realize just how hard it is for me to believe that a young kid like you outdrew him. Hell, boy, you ain't lived as long as Ben Grady was hiring his gun out. The sheriff here claims it was a fair fight," an angry Mason spoke.

Sheriff Steele didn't move or say one word, but a voice from behind the bar spoke up. It was Jed, the barkeep. "Mr. Mason," he said. "I saw the fight and it was a fair one. Ben drew on Jess first. Jess here drew that gun so fast I could hardly see it. Grady never even had a chance. His gun damn near fell back inside the holster. The only reason it didn't was Grady fell back and his pistol fell out of his hand and on the floor. I'm telling you, I saw it and I still don't believe it."

Mason listened to Jed's recount of the gunfight, but it only made him angrier. There was no way he could replace Ben Grady unless he could hire this young man who had killed him. He didn't think that was possible and he wasn't sure in his mind that this kid was all that good. Maybe he'd just gotten off a lucky shot. He didn't know and he didn't really care. All he cared about was that he had lost his best man and because of that he would lose a lot of money over the next year or so it would take to replace him.

"Well, son," groused Mason. "It seems like we have a problem."

Jess cocked his head a little and smiled at Mason, which only made him angrier. "I don't seem to have a problem," replied Jess.

Mason took a step forward. "You don't see that you have a problem?" he asked.

Jess thought about if for another moment. He looked at the other four men standing at the bar and then back at Mason. "No, not really," replied Jess calmly.

Mason started peeling his leather gloves off, one finger at a time, while trying to stare Jess down. Jess didn't flinch or show the slightest sign of being nervous.

"How old are you, son?" asked Mason.

"Sixteen."

"Only sixteen?"

"Yes, sir."

"How long have you been using that pistol?"

"Long enough, I guess."

"You guess?" an annoyed Mason questioned.

"That's what I said."

"Where'd you get a gun like that?"

"Found it."

"Well, son, how the hell did you make it to sixteen with an attitude like that?"

"I didn't know I had an attitude."

Steele was trying to hold in a laugh although he didn't know how he could laugh at a time like this. Here he was listening to this young man facing up to an old, tough, rich ranch baron and the kid was either toying with Mason or just didn't care about answering his questions. Steele had never seen anyone talk to Mason like this before and he kind of liked it.

Mason, however, didn't like it one bit. His ears were beginning to turn red. He was losing what little patience he had left with Jess. "Damn it, kid," yelled Mason. "You're really starting to piss me off. Now, here's the deal. I believe in an eye for an eye. Now, the sheriff here says he won't stand for anything but a fair fight. If it was up to me and the sheriff wasn't here, I'd have just shot you on sight when I found out who you were. As you can plainly see, I brought out four of my best men. Ray here is the best of the four. Grady was a good friend of Ray's, and Ray here wants to make you answer for killing Grady. You understand what I'm saying?"

Jess never took his eyes off Mason. He could see Ray, who was to Mason's right, and he watched him out of the corner of his eye. But his main focus was on Paul Mason. He stared deeply into Mason's eyes. It was the kind of stare that looked through a man, yet still allowed him to see everything else in the room.

Then, after a moment of tense silence following Mason's little speech, Jess spoke in a very low, soft and deliberate tone with no telltale sign of fear. "Mr. Mason, I guess you've had your say and now I'll have mine," he said slowly. "I didn't know Ben Grady and I sure didn't pick a fight with him. He drew on me first and for no reason, so that meant he was nothing short of a murderer. Now, you paid him to be a hired gun, which is no different than a murderer. That, Mr. Mason, makes you a murderer too, which in my book, puts you on the wrong side of right. Now, to make matters even worse, you come to town hell-bent to kill me just for defending myself. Was I supposed to just let him shoot me so you could be in a better mood today? Maybe no one ever taught you right from wrong, but more likely than that, I figure you just don't give a shit. So, now here's my deal, and you listen really close because I don't have a habit of repeating myself. You see, Mr. Mason, it really doesn't matter if you have Ray challenge me first or if you have one of the others do it. It doesn't even matter if you have all four of your men take me on at one time.

"You see, the only thing that really matters here, is I'm going to put the first bullet square in your chest about a split second after anyone moves in this room, including Jed behind the bar there. Do you understand that? No matter what happens today, you die. Maybe me, maybe the sheriff here and maybe everyone in this room will die, but make no mistake about this, you are going to be the first one to die here today. Now, that's the deal. I don't have another thing to say about it, so don't ask me any more questions. I've wasted enough of my time with you already." Jess had now altered Mason's entire game plan and Mason was not happy about it.

Mason was a man who hadn't been talked to in this manner for more years than he could remember. That, along with his temper, was the only explanation for what happened next. The only thing anyone could hear before Mason went for his gun was, "You bastard…"

Mason's hand was moving. Jess stole a glance at Ray and determined that Ray was going for Steele. Jess figured that Steele was in now, like it or not, and Jess would let him handle Ray and the other man. Mason's hand never got a grip on the pearl handle of his Colt .45. Jess's shot caught him square in the chest. The other four men were all going for their guns. Jess's second shot hit the man to Mason's immediate right and his third shot hit the man next to him. He had fanned the second and third shots with his left hand. The sheriff had caught his first man, Ray, before he got his gun leveled at Steele, but he took a shot in the left shoulder before he caught the second man. Within a few seconds, five men lay dead on the floor and the smoke was heavy in the air from the gunpowder. Steele couldn't help but notice Jess had shot Mason and the man next to him before he got his first shot off. Jed just stood behind the bar at one end like a statue.

"Jesus Goddamn Christ," he said, almost in a whisper.

Steele was somewhat in shock himself, partly because he had been shot, but mostly because he couldn't believe the speed of Jess's gun hand. He knew a lot of men who were considered fast at skinning leather; but the truth was, it was mostly that they were cool headed and didn't miss with their first shot. The ones who were considered fast were the ones who stayed cool under pressure and made their first shot count, but this was different. Jess was not only cool under pressure; he was blazingly fast and accurate. Jess had pulled off all three shots in less than a second and he made every one of them count. Jed threw the sheriff a bar towel after he finally broke himself from his trance and Steele tucked it under his shirt where the bullet had passed through his shoulder. He winced a little at the pain it caused.

"Jess, I thought Jed here was exaggerating a little when he told me how fast you were, but now that I've seen it for myself, even I can't believe it," exclaimed Sheriff Steele. "How in the hell did you ever learn to shoot that fast?"

"Practice, Sheriff, lots and lots of practice," he replied as he replaced the spent cartridges and holstered his pistol. Sheriff Steele shot Jess a strange look. Jess noticed the bottles of fine whiskey on the bar. "Sheriff, how about I buy you a drink. It doesn't look like these boys are gonna finish that bottle and it sure looks like a good one at that."

"That's one of my best bottles," offered Jed. "Mr. Mason only drinks the best and he had me order it special. It's really good whiskey."

"Well, I guess I can have a drink or maybe two before I go to the doctor. Hell, this doesn't look too bad," said Steele, as he checked his shoulder where he had taken a bullet.

Sheriff Steele and Jess finished the bottle without another word and Jed just looked at the both of them, thinking that he had just witnessed something not too many people would ever get to see. When the bottle was empty, the sheriff went to see the doctor and Jess sat down at a table and looked at the five dead bodies lying on the floor. He wondered if Sheriff Steele hadn't thrown in with him if he would be lying on the floor dead right now. The sheriff had sent the undertaker and some men over to carry the bodies out and clean up. Jess watched, showing no emotion. He finally spotted Patti looking in from the back door of the saloon. He looked at her and smiled a little. So little, you could hardly tell. After the bodies were all removed and Jed had mopped up most of the blood, Patti came in and sat down next to Jess.

"I've seen a lot of shootin' in my days, but nothing like that," said Patti, a bewildered look on her face. "You're not just any young man, are you, Jess Williams? There is something very special about you. Maybe you were born to it or maybe destiny has just singled you out for something special, but you're not like other men. I'm glad I had the chance to meet someone like you."

"Thanks, Patti," he said. "I wonder about it myself sometimes. I figure that you're a special woman, too, and I'm glad I got to meet you."

Patti stood up and smiled down at him. "How about something to eat?" she asked.

"That sounds like a great idea."

Patti nodded and went back in the kitchen and fixed Jess a plate of the day's special. A few men were starting to filter into the saloon now. They had heard about the gunfight and they were quiet and just sat around and talked among themselves; every once in a while, they would glance over at Jess. He heard them, but he didn't listen. He knew what they were talking about and figured they'd be talking about it for the rest of their lives. They'd be telling the story about how they were there the day that Jess Williams took down three men in one gunfight. Jess continued to eat his food, and when he finished, he went to his room and stayed there for the remainder of the day.

CHAPTER FOURTEEN

Hank Beard left Timber about an hour after Jess rode out to have some coffee with River Bend Bill. Their paths never crossed even though they had just spent the night in the same hotel with only one room separating them. Here was the man Jess was looking for and he had been in a bed less than thirty feet away. Beard hadn't talked with anyone and had no idea Jess was in town or that he was looking for him. He had other things on his mind. He was focused on the planned robbery of Mason's money coach and he wanted to talk to Grady and finish up their plans. He knew Grady wasn't in town because when he was, Grady's horse was always in the same place at the stable and it hadn't been there when Beard had arrived. And because Grady didn't often come to town, he didn't think this unusual. Beard knew that Grady usually stayed out at the Mason ranch and close to his boss since Mason had his share of enemies.

Hank spent most of his day checking out some hiding places within a mile or so out of town, just in case. Little did he know he was at one point within half a mile from River Bend Bill's camp while Jess was visiting. He knew about Bill's place and he avoided it because he didn't want anyone to know what he was up to. Hank figured the less people knew the better. He eventually arrived at the Mason ranch just about sundown. The shootout in the saloon between Steele, Jess and Mason and his four hired guns was already history and people were talking about it.

Word had already reached the Mason ranch and Mason's widow was already finished with her grieving. She shed a few tears, but the truth was she had fallen out of love a long time ago. He cheated on her and treated her like a tool that he kept around when the need struck him. She wouldn't miss him. She would miss the young Paul Mason she had fallen in love with years earlier, but not the man who had become so wealthy that he paid more attention to his money than his wife. Before the end of the day, she had already started to rearrange the ranch to fit her desires and she had even thrown out some of his things. After Hank stabled his horse, hoping he could bed down for the night and visit with Grady, he walked up to the bunkhouse for a cup of coffee and asked if anyone knew where Grady was.

"Didn't you hear? Ben's dead and so is Mr. Mason," said a tall lanky cowhand by the name of Luke. "Hell, we don't even know if we have a job anymore."

Several of the men in the bunkhouse told the story to Hank about this young bounty hunter killing Ben and then facing down Mason and four other hired guns. They talked about how Ben never cleared his gun from its holster and how Sheriff Steele had thrown in with the kid against Mason. Beard listened to the story intently, taking it all in and having a hard time believing it. He was listening especially hard when one of the men told of Jess asking Grady if he knew a man by the name of Hank Beard and that he was looking for him.

"Did the Williams kid say why he was looking for me?" asked Hank.

"Said something about you killing his family and all," replied one of the hands.

"Said you killed and raped his little sister. You didn't do none of that, did ya, Hank?" asked one of the other hands.

"Hell, he's talking out his ass," Hank lied. "I ain't raped any women and I sure ain't raped no little girls. I can get all the women I want, anytime I want." Beard took another swallow of his coffee. The hands were all watching him and wondering what he was going to do about the kid who was gunning for him.

"You boys mind me bunking down here tonight?" asked Hank. "I don't need much, just a spot to lay my bedroll."

"Sure, that's fine, I guess," said one of them. "But if that kid comes gunnin' for ya here, you're on your own. None of us is tangling with the guy that took down Ben Grady."

"Don't worry, boys," said Hank. "I take care of my own business. I ain't scared of no boy even if he did take down Grady. He comes in here looking for me, you just let me handle him."

Hank sounded pretty convincing, but the hands could tell he was worried. He knew how fast Grady was, and anyone who could take him in a fair fight had to be pretty damn good. Hank figured right then and there he would try to find the kid and ambush him. Hell, he'd blow a hole in him with his shotgun before the kid even knew what hit him. He'd do it while the kid was asleep.

He finished his coffee and lay down on his bedroll. He was trying to figure out who he would ask to go in with him on the stage robbery now that Grady was dead. Even with Paul Mason dead, his widow would still run the ranch and be able to run the money into the bank in Timber. He already had it all planned out so maybe he would cut himself in for sixty percent instead of fifty. That would leave him with enough money to last him for years.

His thoughts turned to the kid who was gunning for him. He figured it must be someone related to the family he and his other two partners murdered. That wasn't the first family they had killed and it wasn't the first time Blake Taggert had raped a woman, but it was the first time Taggert had raped a little girl. He and Hank had gotten into a real bad argument about it and Hank told him if he ever did that again it would be the last job they would do together. He didn't care what Taggert did on his own; he just didn't want anything like that tied to him. Hank had no problem with robbing and killing people though. He was the one who took the kitchen knife to Jess's ma. He stabbed her while she was screaming and he kept stabbing her, over and over again. Hank dozed off to a light sleep. He had his twelve-gauge lying next to him under his blanket with his hand on it. He knew someone was hunting him and he wasn't going down easy.

Frank Reedy and Todd Spicer finally approached Timber about noon the next day. They had ridden hard to try to get to Timber before Jess left. They argued all morning about what they would do when they finally caught up to him. The only thing they agreed on was that Spicer would let Reedy talk to him first. After that, if Reedy didn't want any part of it, he would just leave and let Spicer do what he was hired to do. Reedy agreed with that only because of professional courtesy, one bounty hunter to another.

Jess was having some lunch in the saloon and watched as Reedy and Spicer rode into town. He didn't know either of them, but he knew they were up to something. He watched the two men through the saloon window as they rode up to the sheriff's office and dismounted. They stopped on the porch again and spoke to one another for a minute and then went inside. Steele was doing what he loathed more than anything, paperwork. There were five new corpses and that always meant paperwork. He looked up from his desk and knew in an instant he was looking at two bounty hunters. He could always tell. Bounty hunters were always heavily armed and had a look in their eyes that most men didn't. These two were no exception.

"Can I help you gentlemen?" asked Sheriff Steele.

"Well, I'll be damned," said Reedy. "Mark Steele, when did you pin on a badge?"

Steele stood up to get a closer look at Reedy. "I'll be damned if it ain't Frank Reedy," he exclaimed. "How in the hell have you been? It must be ten, no fifteen years since I last saw you. It's been ten years since I pinned on a badge. What happened to yours? Last time I saw you, you were wearing a United States Marshals badge."

"Hell, being a marshal doesn't pay enough. Bounty hunting pays a lot more and the risk is the same or sometimes less. Plus, we're both doing the same job except I get paid better." He paused to chuckle. "You ought to try it. We could use another hand. There are lots of bad guys out there that need catching, Sheriff."

"It's not for me, at least not yet," replied Steele. "Being sheriff ain't all bad. I get an office and I don't have to spend my nights on the trail sleeping on hard ground. I sleep in a nice warm comfy bed every night."

"That ain't all bad either, I guess," admitted Reedy. "Sheriff, this is my partner, Todd Spicer." Steele shook Spicer's hand.

"Sheriff," Reedy continued, "we're looking for a young man, about sixteen or seventeen years old. His name is Jess Williams." Frank noticed a change in Steele immediately. "You know him, Sheriff?"

"Yes, I do," replied Steele cautiously. "What's your business with him?"

"We've been hired to bring him back to Black Creek, Kansas, for the murder of a man there," replied Reedy.

"Who'd he murder?"

"A man by the name of Red Carter."

"And who hired you two to bring him back?"

"His father, Dick Carter," replied Reedy, knowing what Sheriff Steele would think. "Red Carter was his only son."

"Murdered? You sure about that?" asked Sheriff Steele. "Jess doesn't seem like a young man who would murder someone. Kill for sure, but not murder."

"I guess you must know him then. Sounds like you've taken a liking to the kid."

"I guess you might say that. You get to know someone who comes to your town and ends up killing four men in a few days. All fair fights, I might add. That's why I'm having a hard time believing he would murder someone. Hell, he wouldn't have to murder anybody."

"What do you mean by that?" asked Spicer.

"The kid's so damn fast with that gun of his, all he'd have to do is call a man out," replied Steele. "I've got to tell you that kid's got an unnatural ability to draw and shoot a pistol and hit what he's aiming at. Have you got a legal warrant on him?"

"We don't need any warrant, Sheriff," interjected Spicer. "We've been paid to bring him back dead or alive and that's what we aim to do, one way or another. It'll be up to him if it has to go down bad."

Steele shook his head. "This ain't right and you boys know it," complained Steele. "I ain't letting you men just take this kid because some rich rancher hired you to do it. You have no warrant or legal paperwork on him. I'm sorry, but if you attempt to take him, you'll have to deal with me along with the kid. Otherwise, go back to Kansas and get a warrant. Frank, you should know better."

Spicer was losing patience and Reedy knew he had to offer up something else. "Sheriff, we just want to talk with him first," pleaded Reedy. "At least give us that and then we'll see how it goes. How's that sound?"

"Sounds like the first sensible thing you've said up to now. I think he's over at the saloon getting a bite to eat. You boys need to understand something though. This kid ain't one to be messed with. And I'm not kidding about his shooting ability. You boys had better think twice about what you're doing."

Steele walked them both over to the saloon. Jess watched the sheriff come out of his office with the two men in tow. He slipped the hammer strap off his gun, straightened himself in his chair and slid it back enough for his gun to clear the table if he had the need to use it. He trusted the sheriff, but not these other two men. There were half a dozen men in the saloon and they noticed the change in Jess and saw him remove the hammer strap. He watched the sheriff come through the door first and kept his eyes on the two men, one on each side of the sheriff.

"Afternoon, Jess," said Sheriff Steele. "These two men say they have business with you. They say you murdered a man back in Black Creek, Kansas, by the name of Red Carter and they've been paid to take you back there for questioning. They don't have a warrant or any legal papers on you, so you don't have to go back with them or even talk to them if you don't want to. I know one of these men, Jess. He's always been a fair man and he says he just wants to talk to you first. So, what do you think?"

Jess didn't look at the sheriff yet; he kept his gaze on the two men standing behind him. "Sheriff, I don't mind talking with them, but first there are a few things you need to know. Red Carter shot the sheriff of our town and for no good reason. The sheriff was just trying to take him into custody again. Sheriff Diggs was a good man and a good friend to my family. That's probably why they don't have a warrant for my arrest. Red Carter was a murderer and I called him out fair and killed him fair. Now, that being said, what do you two want with me?"

Spicer was getting frustrated with all the talking. "I'm going over to the bar to get a drink, Frank," said Spicer impatiently. "Let me know when you're done talking to the kid. And don't forget; leave your five hundred on the bar if you walk away from this."

Reedy nodded at Spicer and then turned his attention to Jess. "Listen, kid," he said, as he sat down in front of Jess. "We've been chasing your tail for a while now and everywhere you go, people end up dying. And yet, everyone says you're an okay fellow. I haven't run into one person yet who said you started any fight except the ones with Red Carter and another guy you shot by the name of Randy Hastings. So, I gotta ask you, kid, did you shoot Red Carter fair and square, just like you said?"

"Yes, sir," he replied bluntly. "I started the fight with Red Carter and I called him out, but only because he killed the sheriff in cold blood. I also let him draw first. Then, I shot him dead. That's the truth."

Reedy sat back in his chair and thought for a moment. "Okay, I believe you're telling me the truth. Answer me one more question just for my own satisfaction. The man you shot, repeatedly I might add, back in Tarkenton, Kansas, by the name of Randy Hastings. Was he one of the men who murdered your family?"

"Yes, sir, he was, and I ain't sorry I killed him. I'm here looking for one of the other two, a man by the name of Hank Beard. When I find him, I plan to kill him like the dog he is."

Reedy looked into Jess's eyes and he saw the look of a young man who was already a hardened killer and a hunter of men. Reedy knew he could not take this young man back to Black Creek and hand him over to Dick Carter. Of course, Reedy saw something else in Jess's eyes and his own self-preservation was also a large part of his decision. He knew Jess wasn't going to let two men or even an army of men take him anywhere. Reedy wanted to live another day to do another job. He knew if he tried to take Jess back, that wouldn't happen. Reedy stood up and walked over to the bar next to Spicer and dug into his pocket and placed the five hundred dollars that Carter had paid him in advance on the bar.

"This young man ain't a murderer and I won't have anything else to do with taking him back to Carter," Reedy stated firmly. "It ain't right and I've been trying to tell you that all along. Why don't we both go back to Kansas and tell Carter we couldn't find him?"

"You're going soft in your old age, Frank," said Spicer, as he put the money in his front pocket. "A job is a job. We don't ask questions or make judgments about the men we hunt. Hell, you'd better go back to wearing a badge and leave bounty hunting to guys like me who don't give a rat's ass whether or not a man is good, bad, guilty or innocent. We just bring them in and collect our money." Todd finished his drink and turned to face Jess sitting at the table.

Reedy said in a low voice that only Spicer could hear, "Don't do it, Todd. I'm telling you, this kid will drop you dead. You can't outdraw him. It ain't worth it."

"Bullshit, Frank. I'm gonna make a total of three thousand dollars when this job is finished. I ain't walking away from that much money," snapped Spicer.

He stepped away from the bar and looked straight at Jess. Sheriff Steele had sat down at a table next to Jess. If this was going to be a confrontation between two men, he wouldn't interfere. His job now was to keep the odds even and to make sure Reedy didn't change his mind and throw in with Spicer at the last minute. He moaned, but it wasn't from the shoulder wound he had gotten yesterday; it was from the thought of more paperwork he was now sure he would have to do, and soon.

CHAPTER FIFTEEN

"Son, stand up so I can talk to you, face-to-face," demanded Spicer. Jess slowly stood up, glancing at Steele. It was a look that told Steele he need not get involved in this. Then his eyes locked on Spicer's. The look in Jess's eyes unnerved Spicer momentarily, but Spicer was a hardened man who had faced death many times and survived.

"I only got one question, boy," said Spicer. "You going back willingly or do I have to drag you back there behind my horse?"

"No." Jess stated flatly.

"No, what? No, you ain't going back or no, you ain't going back dragged behind my horse? Which is it?"

"Neither."

"Well, then just what do you think you're going to do?"

"Probably shoot you, unless you suddenly come to your senses."

Reedy looked at Steele, who almost let out a little chuckle at that comment.

"You think you can take me, kid?" Spicer spat.

"Yes."

"You're that certain?"

"Nothing is certain in life."

"But you think you're that fast, eh?"

"Yes."

"Frank, you sure you don't want in on this one?" Spicer asked Reedy, glancing back at him, now seeming just a little unsure that he wanted to take Jess on alone after seeing Jess's demeanor.

"Like I told you, Todd, I don't agree with this job. It had a stink right from the beginning. Leave it alone and let's go back to Kansas. I'm telling you, this kid will drop you before you even know it happened. I feel it in my gut," urged Reedy.

Spicer turned his stare back to Jess, who hadn't moved except to move his gun hand into position. "Well, kid, this is your last chance," prodded Spicer. "Either you go back to Kansas with me willingly or I'll have to pack you on a mule bent over. What do you say?"

"That's just not gonna happen," he answered plainly.

Bounty hunters were a tough lot. They would face odds that most men wouldn't. Most bounty hunters were pretty good with a gun and Todd Spicer was better than most. Bounty hunters were the type of men who stayed cool while facing death and Spicer was better than most at that, too. But most men just couldn't walk away from a gunfight once they were in. It was a matter of honor. Most men would rather die and have people talk about how tough they were instead of walking away and having people talk about how they had turned tail and run like yellow dogs. That kind of thing would follow a man around forever. These things, along with the thought of three thousand dollars, made Todd Spicer do what at any other moment in his life he would have known he shouldn't do. He had as good a sense about people as Frank Reedy did and he knew he was about to bite off more than he could chew, but he just couldn't stop himself now.

Spicer went for his gun and it was a strange thing from his perspective. He felt himself reaching for his gun and even felt his thumb touch the hammer. Then, he felt a hard thump on his chest, heard a loud noise and saw a flash in front of him. He never blinked. He couldn't understand how it had happened so fast. He never even saw Jess draw his gun, yet here he was with a hole in his chest and the kid was standing there with his gun pointed at him. It was all over and he hadn't seen any of it. He let go of his gun, which had never even made it out of the holster. He glanced over at Steele who had a look of disbelief on his face and then he dropped to his knees, both of his hands trying to stop the blood that was now gushing from his chest. Todd Spicer finally fell face first onto the floor, dead before he hit it. Sheriff Steele, who had stood up after Spicer had been shot, sat back down again.

"Damn it, Jess, you ain't natural," said Steele, shaking his head.

Reedy walked over to Spicer's body, turned him over, and began to talk to him as if somehow he could hear him from the great beyond. "I told ya not to take him on, but would you listen? Hell, no, you stubborn son of a bitch. And now, there you are lying in your own blood, deader than dead. Damn it!" Reedy kept shaking his head in disgust as he reached into Spicer's front pocket where he had tucked the five hundred dollars Reedy had put down on the bar. He pulled out the money along with Spicer's five hundred and put the thousand dollars in his front pocket. He would take the money back to Carter and tell him what had happened. He wanted no part of the money or Dick Carter. Then he sat down in a chair next to Spicer's body.

"Sorry, Sheriff, seems like you got more paperwork to do," said Jess, as he sat down at the table. "It wasn't my call. I didn't want it."

"I know," replied Steele. "It seems like men just keep coming to you to get themselves killed. Hell, maybe you should become a preacher?"

"Now, why would I want to go and do something like that, Sheriff?"

"So you could read them their last rites before you kill them," replied Steele. Jess almost smiled at that.

"Mr. Reedy, do you want him buried here or are you taking him back to Kansas?" asked Sheriff Steele.

"Hell, might as well bury him here. You do have a cemetery for idiots, don't you?" he asked.

"Sure do," replied Steele. "Most of the men buried there were idiots the day they died. The rest of them were drunk and stupid."

"Well, just add one more to it. I'll pay the undertaker on my way out of town. I'll take it out of his share of the money. I think Dick Carter would say okay, not that I give a shit anyway."

Jess and Steele walked out together. Jess spent the remainder of the day walking around town and asking a few townspeople if they knew anything about Beard, but no one did. He had supper, checked on Gray, and then went up to his room early, forgoing the saloon. He planned to ride out to some of the ranches the next morning to ask about Beard. He fell asleep and dreamed of little Samantha. She was throwing hay around the yard and throwing chicken eggs on the ground, agitating Jess as usual, except this time, she had a bullet hole in her head.

※ ※

Beard spent the day hanging around the Mason ranch. He had decided to go into town at night and try to ambush Jess. He even spoke with Mason's widow to see if she would hire him on. He didn't really want a job. It was just a ploy to show he had a reason for hanging around. He left the Mason ranch before dark and rode within a mile of Timber. He made a fire and heated some coffee and waited until late before he snuck into town. He wanted to make sure that most of the townspeople were in bed and out of the saloon. He planned to sneak into Jess's room and ambush him. He would shoot him while he was sleeping and head out of town in the dark, hoping that by the time people woke and found out what had happened he would have a good head start. He hoped it would be enough time for him to hide in the hills near the small ravine he had spotted the other day.

It was three in the morning when Beard tied his horse up to the pole on the back porch of the hotel. Sheriff Steele had already made his last rounds and was turned in for the night. Jed was still cleaning up the saloon, but there were no paying customers inside. The last of them had left over an hour earlier. The desk clerk in the hotel was up in his room, asleep. Beard tried to be as quiet as he could. He went into the lobby, stepped behind the counter and checked out the names on the register. He found the name he was looking for. Jess Williams was the name next to room number 201.

Beard thought that almost funny since he had stayed in room 203 just the other night.

This hotel was like most small hotels in many small towns: drafty, in dire need of a coat of paint and creaky, especially the floorboards. That fact had not gone unnoticed by Jess. He paid attention to many of the littlest details concerning his surroundings. He noticed that the third step going to the second floor had a squeak to it. He was also aware that the floor just five feet from his door squeaked ever so lightly when you stepped there, and he'd made a mental note of the fact that the top of the door to his room stuck a little. Not enough to stop anyone from opening the door, but just enough that when the door was opened, the top would hold slightly so when anyone continued to push on the door, it would pop open and cause the all-too-flimsy door to shake a little.

Jess never heard that third step, although Beard paused for a full minute when he hit it and it squeaked. And Jess never consciously heard the slight squeak of the floor by his door, although it broke a bead of sweat on Beard's forehead. He waited for another minute or two after that one. He was standing just outside of Jess's room, trying to hold his breath and not move. He was waiting to see if anyone had heard the floor squeak before he made his move into Jess's room. He also took this time to gather up enough courage to make his move.

Sometimes when asleep, a sound out of the ordinary can wake a man up even without his really consciously hearing the sound. That's what the squeak outside Jess's door was like. Jess didn't consciously hear it, but his subconscious did, and his brain began giving out signals to let him know that something was awry. It didn't wake him. It just put him on the edge of awake.

Now, when the door did that little shaky thing when Beard finally got the nerve to push it open, well, that was another thing. Jess was always prepared for an ambush. When he slept, he slept with his shotgun by his bed within easy reach and his pistol right next to his right hip. He always slept on his back and he always moved the bed so that he had a clear view of the door when he opened his eyes. Those things, along with the squeaky floor and the shaky door, were what spelled bad news for Hank Beard, although Hank didn't yet realize it.

Beard pushed the door and noticed that it was stuck a little at the top. He had already made the decision to open the door and even though his brain was telling his body he should stop, his body weight was already in motion. It was something that he just can't stop in time, even though he knew he should. Beard threw open the door and raised his shotgun to put a load of buckshot into Jess, but things didn't quite go the way he'd planned.

Jess was awake and had his pistol trained on the door before it was open enough to see who was coming in. The next thing Jess's eyes saw in the dim light was a shotgun barrel. That was all he needed to know. Jess's first shot was right through that flimsy door just as it was flying open. The shot hit Beard in his left side, knocking him off balance. By then, the door was fully open and Beard was totally exposed. Jess's second shot hit him in his right shoulder, which caused him to drop the shotgun as he fell against the wall a second time, this time falling on his ass. By now, Jess was standing up and hovering over Beard, trying to see in the dim light.

The noise had awoken just about everybody in the hotel, including the desk clerk who was quickly coming down the hall with an oil lamp. He stopped outside of Jess's room and called into the room. "Mr. Williams," he said, "are you okay?"

"Yes, I'm fine," replied Jess. "Bring that lamp a little closer and be careful while stepping over the trash."

The clerk stepped inside Jess's room and held the light up high to see the room better. He gasped when he saw a large man sitting against the wall, bleeding from both sides.

"Can you hold that light a little closer to his face?" asked Jess.

The desk clerk put the lamp as close as his shaking arm would allow him. Jess recognized the man as Hank Beard, the man he had been looking for. Jess never took his eyes off Beard and he never looked at the desk clerk. He simply said to the clerk, "Leave that lamp on the table there, and shut the door on your way out." The desk clerk, not one to argue, especially with the young man who had already killed several men over the last few days, did what he was told and left.

Hank was bleeding pretty badly. His pistol was still in its holster and he thought about trying to go for it, even with a bad shoulder. He looked up at Jess. "Do I know you, son?" asked Beard, lying about it.

"You should."

"Well, I don't," replied Beard, still lying.

"So, you're going to lie about it, too?"

"I ain't lying," spat Beard.

"Why'd you come in my room with a damn shotgun?"

"I got lost."

"Lost?"

"Yeah, I stayed in the room two doors down from here the other day. I thought I was going into my room."

"There's an old woman staying in that room tonight."

"How do you know that?"

"I pay attention."

"Well, what now?"

"You don't remember me?"

"Remember what?"

"Meeting a young boy in a wagon back in Black Creek, Kansas?" Jess reminded him.

"Maybe," Beard responded.

"Maybe right before you went to that young man's home and murdered his family," Jess said angrily.

"I don't know if I remember that," Beard lied. He knew what Jess was talking about. He just didn't want to admit it.

"You're one of the men who murdered my family."

"So, who are you?"

"I'm that young boy in the wagon you met that day by the creek."

"Well, if you're hunting me for the bounty, I'll pay you twice what I'm worth," pleaded Beard, trying to buy his way out of a bad situation.

"You don't seem to be listening to me. That family you murdered…that was my family. The man you shot down was my pa. The woman you butchered in the house was my ma and the little girl you beat, raped and shot was my little seven-year-old sister, Samantha."

Beard knew he was done for. "I never touched your little sister. That was Taggert's doing. I didn't like it none and I told him so." Beard said, still pleading.

"And you think that makes you innocent?" asked an infuriated Jess. "You didn't stop him. You were there. Even if you didn't do any of the killings, you're just as guilty as the other two men."

"Listen, you can't talk Taggert out of anything once he's made up his mind about something," said Beard.

"Well, I guess that's just a bad break for you. Now, you wanted to buy your way out of this, so I'm gonna give you that chance."

"How much?" asked Beard, thinking he might get out of this thing yet.

"Money ain't what I'm here to collect."

"Then what is it if it ain't money?"

"I'm here to collect your soul and your life along with it," he replied menacingly. "And it's not going to feel good either."

"You'd shoot an unarmed man? That just ain't legal, no matter what I've done."

"You weren't unarmed when you came in here with that shotgun. You weren't unarmed when you shot my pa and killed my ma and little sister."

"But you can't just shoot me while I'm sitting here," pleaded Beard. "Hell, you've done shot me twice already. I can't draw. I can hardly move my gun hand. That just ain't fair."

"You want a fair fight after sneaking into my room in the middle of the night and trying to plug me with that shotgun there? You think that was fair?"

"I heard how fast you were. I needed an edge."

"You want fair?" asked Jess. "Hell, I'll give you fair. You don't deserve it, but I'll give it to you. It will make killing you even more satisfying." Jess holstered his pistol.

"What are you going to do?" asked a confused Beard.

"Go ahead, take your pistol out of that holster," said Jess.

Beard was frenzied now. He wasn't sure what Jess was planning, but he also knew his choices were running out. He'd bleed out soon and he knew it. He slowly pulled his pistol out of his holster and laid it on his lap. "Okay, now what?" he asked.

"Pick it up with your gun hand and point it at me," demanded Jess. "Make sure you aim real good because you're only going to get one shot, if you're lucky."

"Is this some kind of a trick?" asked a confused Beard. "You want me to point this pistol at you?"

"Well, at least your hearing's not gone yet," said Jess. "Come on, point the gun, but don't try to pull the trigger yet." Beard slowly raised the pistol and pointed it right at Jess's chest. His hands were a little shaky, but at this short distance he couldn't miss.

"Okay, now you've got fair," said Jess. "Your gun is pointed at my chest. My gun is still in its holster. Now all you have to do is pull the hammer back and pull the trigger before I draw and plug you. That's fair, don't you think? Hell, you can even use both hands to steady yourself if you want to."

Beard knew his options were quickly running out. He was bleeding out fast now since his heart was beating rapidly, and he knew he would begin to lose consciousness soon. Besides, he figured he had at least a pretty good chance now. He had his gun pointed straight at Jess and had both hands holding the gun steady. No matter how fast Jess was, Beard figured he had at least a fifty-fifty chance of living through this. He thought Jess stupid for giving him this much of a chance. Beard looked into Jess's eyes. For a split second, just before his thumb began to pull back on the hammer of his pistol, Beard realized he was doomed. Some subconscious thought told him this was the end. A split second was all it took. Before Beard had the hammer back far enough to cock, Jess slicked his pistol out and shot him right where he had planned to, straight in the groin.

Beard let out a scream and dropped the gun in his lap, which only added to the pain. "Damn it!" he shrieked. "You ain't supposed to shoot a man in his privates! It ain't right!"

"You're no man," he retorted angrily. "You're a cold-blooded killer and you don't deserve right. You deserve what you got and you deserve what you've got coming next."

"Just finish it!" bawled Beard. "I've had enough. I don't give two shits about you and your dead family. I enjoyed killing them! How do you like that?"

"I'll finish you when you tell me where Taggert is."

"Go screw yourself!" hollered Beard. Jess took a step closer to him and put a slug into his left kneecap. He screamed with excruciating pain.

"Tell me where Taggert is or I'll gut shoot you and watch you die slowly," Jess threatened with an ominous look.

"He's in Red Rock, Texas, south of here, you bastard! Now finish it!" begged Beard.

Jess walked up to Beard who was starting to lose consciousness. Jess put his pistol on his forehead and looked into his eyes. There was no look of fear, just a pleading look that said to finish it. Jess pulled the trigger and Beard's brain matter splattered onto the wall behind him. Jess wiped his gun off on Beard's shirt and placed it back in his holster after replacing the spent cartridges. He felt no remorse. He felt good that another part of his mission was finished. He had only one more to go.

CHAPTER SIXTEEN

Jess stared at Beard slumped against the wall, all shot to hell. He knew what he had just done would be thought of as terrible, unless people knew the whole story. He couldn't worry about that now. He still had one more task and that was to find Blake Taggert and kill him. And now he had a lead, a town called Red Rock. Jess would head out first thing in the morning. He heard footsteps coming up the stairs and he knew the first one to come in the room would be the sheriff. Steele had his gun drawn, but down at his side. Steele was certain that if anyone was dead in this room, it wasn't going to be Jess Williams. He glanced at Jess and then took a long look at Beard. He had seen plenty of men shot up before, but this was the worst he had ever witnessed. He looked back at Jess.

"Son, I believe you've got a mean streak in you. I'm going to go out on a limb and assume the head shot was last?" Jess nodded.

"Good, otherwise I'd have to start wondering about your sanity."

"Well, maybe I am a little crazy, but at least I got a reason," he said defensively.

"I can't argue with that. Did you get what you wanted?"

"I sure did."

"Did he tell you anything about the other man you're looking for?"

"Yes, as a matter of fact, he told me he was in Red Rock, Texas. Do you know where that is, Sheriff?"

"It's about a ten-day ride south of here. How'd you drag that out of him?"

"I traded him."

"Traded him? For what?" he asked dubiously.

"A bullet in the head."

"Maybe we should talk about that crazy thing again."

"Maybe."

"Suppose you're heading to Red Rock then, huh?"

"First thing in the morning, Sheriff. Besides, I figure that I'm beginning to wear out my welcome here."

"I have to admit I am tired of burying people lately. I could use a break from all that paperwork, too."

"Well, Sheriff, I am sorry for putting you out, but this was going to happen somewhere and your town just happened to be the place. I suppose you could blame Beard for coming here."

"Hell, I'm not blaming anyone, Jess," he explained. "I don't blame you for doing what you did. I would have done the same thing. Maybe not quite as violently as you, but I would've plugged this one for sure. I'd also hunt down that guy Taggert and put a bullet in his sorry ass, too. Don't feel like you've done anything wrong. Actually, you probably saved a few lives today by killing this one here. I have a hunch he wasn't going to start attending church on a regular basis anytime soon."

"Thanks, Sheriff. I'll tell you this. You've made a friend for life," Jess said sincerely. "If you ever need anything, you can call on me. I'll be here as fast as a horse can carry me."

"I'll remember that," he replied keenly. "I can't think of anyone I'd rather have in a pinch backing me up. I won't hesitate to call on you, and that's a fact."

Jess saddled up and rode out of town at first light. He had never fallen back to sleep after killing Beard. As he rode past the sheriff's office, he noticed Steele at his desk. Steele looked up and Jess nodded at him. Steele thought to himself, as he watched this young man who had become a hardened killer at such a young age, that he was surely glad that he wasn't this Blake Taggert fellow. He also wondered how many more men would fall into their own pools of blood for getting in his way. He knew one thing for sure. Jess wasn't ever going to quit killing men. There were too many gunslingers out there who would like to take out someone with a reputation and Jess was gaining one rapidly. Steele laughed to himself when he thought about men who cut notches in their gun handle for every man they killed. Hell, if Jess did that, it sure would mess up that beautiful pistol he had.

※ ※

There was a lot of discussion about the savage murder of the family outside of Red Rock. It was the daily talk at just about every place the townsfolk gathered. Taggert stood at the bar and listened to all the threats.

"If I caught that bastard, I'd cut his balls off and watch him bleed to death," said one man.

"Hell, not me," said another, "I'd ram my rifle right up his ass and let one go!"

The talk didn't bother Taggert. Hell, nothing bothered Taggert. He'd quit caring about life a long time ago. He wasn't really afraid of dying. He simply wasn't going to do anything that would hasten it. He figured that every time he cheated death it gave him one more chance to kill someone else or have his way with another young girl, and the younger, the better in his mind.

No one suspected Taggert as the one who did the killings. His family had lived around this area all their lives and Blake had been in and out of town every few years. It was also where he went between his crimes, kind of a hideout for him. Actually, this was the first time he had done any killing around Red Rock, except for the time he had killed his own family.

The first time he had returned to town after killing his family, everyone was still telling him how sorry they were for what had happened and that they had never caught the culprits who had done it. Blake always found that somewhat funny, although he wasn't sure why. So, whenever he came home, he was welcomed and no one ever thought anything bad of him. Little did he know things were about to change. His final destiny was heading for him and it had a name: Jess Williams.

Jess enjoyed being out on the trail. He wasn't in any hurry since he had a long way to go before he got to Red Rock. He wasn't worried about Taggert leaving town before he got there. He'd just get a lead on him and follow him for the rest of his life until he found him or died trying.

He knew that he was gaining a reputation with a gun and that soon, someone would challenge him just for the status of beating him to the draw. Maybe one day there would be a bounty on his head and men would hunt him down for the money. Either way, he realized then and there that his life's path had been chosen for him. He would hunt down the worst of men for the bounties on their heads.

Jess worked his way south into Texas going around towns unless he needed supplies. On the fourth day, he camped a few miles outside what looked like a fairly large town. He ate a simple meal and kept a low fire. He rode into Largo, Texas, about an hour after daylight. There were plenty of hotels and eating establishments and what looked like a new livery. He stabled his horse and paid the man working the livery an extra dollar per day to get Gray some extra care and the best grain the man had. The livery worker, a small black man by the name of Earl, had a huge smile on his face when Jess gave him the extra dollar.

"Thank you, sir. I'll make sure I take real good care of your horse. He'll get a good brushing and a bucket of my best grain."

"You're a good man, Earl," he said smiling. "Maybe you could tell me the best place to get a good meal and to bunk down for the night?"

"I sure can," he said. "Bridger's Café is the best place for food, course that's 'cause my wife does most the cookin' there."

"Can she make good biscuits?"

"Oh my Lord, she can make the best biscuits in the whole state of Texas and I ain't just saying that 'cause she's my woman," he said proudly.

"How about the best hotel?"

"They are all about the same," he observed. "Bridger's Hotel is probably the cleanest, but any of them are okay. You staying a while or just passing through?"

"Probably just passing through, but I never know for sure. Can you point me in the direction of the sheriff's office?"

Earl looked down at the ground and cleared his throat. "Well, his office is right over there," said Earl, pointing in the direction of the sheriff's office. "If you're only staying overnight, maybe it's best not to bother him."

"Really?" he asked. "Why is that?"

"Well," he replied nervously, "don't say I said so, but he can get pretty ornery pretty fast. I once saw him shoot a man just for calling him a jackass."

"Really?" replied Jess.

"Sure did. I watched him do it. Right over there at the Mustang Bar."

"I'll keep that in mind. I'm not here looking for any trouble. I just need to ask him a few questions about a man I'm looking for."

"Good luck, and make sure you smile when you talk to him. It just might keep him from getting pissed off."

Jess headed over to the sheriff's office. It wasn't far from the livery and while he was walking down the street, he thought about his decision to be a bounty hunter. He figured he would ask the sheriff for any bounty information on wanted men. A deputy was sitting in a chair just outside the door to the sheriff's office. Jess walked up slowly and stopped short of going up the one step to the sidewalk in front. He sized the deputy up in a second and he could see the attitude on the deputy's face.

"Whatcha need, mister?" the deputy asked in a slow sarcastic drawl.

"I'd like to talk to the sheriff for a minute if that's possible. If he's busy, I can come back later."

"What's your name?" the deputy asked, in the same smart-alecky drawl.

"Jess Williams."

Jess could see an immediate change in the deputy's eyes. The deputy sat straight up and his eyes strangely went first to Jess's gun and then to Jess's eyes. Jess could see fear in the deputy's eyes, but along with that, a look of respect. It was obvious to Jess his reputation had already spread deeper into Texas.

"Hell, I know who you are," said the deputy, dropping the smart tone now. "So does the sheriff. And I'm sure he'll want to see you. Hold on just a minute while I get him." The deputy went inside where the sheriff was having a conversation with the two other deputies.

"Uh...Sheriff?" asked the deputy.

"What the hell do you want?" hollered the sheriff. "Can't you see I'm trying to talk to these other two idiots who are supposed to be doing something for their pay?"

"Sorry, Sheriff, but there's a young man outside who wants to talk to you."

"Like I give a shit," retorted the sheriff. "Tell him to go tell his mama about his problems."

"But, Sheriff...he says his name is Jess Williams," said the nervous deputy. "You know, that kid we heard about? The one who took down Ben Grady up in Timber?"

"Well, that's different," said the sheriff, his attitude changing completely. "I'd sure like to meet that boy. Send him on in here. And as for you two dumb-asses, we'll finish this later!"

Jess could hear loud talking and then the deputy was at the door again and waving Jess in. Jess looked at each of the three deputies and they all seemed nervous, but he could see a look of respect in their eyes. Jess's gaze settled on the man sitting behind a large desk. On top of the desk lay a shotgun and a .45 pistol. Jess remembered what Earl the stable man had said and Jess could tell that Earl had told the truth. This man was just plain ornery right down to the bone. Jess knew from the moment he locked eyes with the sheriff that he would have to tread carefully. Then the sheriff did something he rarely did. He smiled at Jess. This did not unnerve Jess, but it sure startled the deputies. Each one of them could count on one hand the number of times the sheriff had smiled and it was usually when he had run someone out of town or shot someone. Even then, he rarely smiled.

"So, you're the Jess Williams we keep hearing so much about. You've got quite a reputation already for such a young man. I hear you've killed a dozen men and you don't look like you've made seventeen years old yet. Now, that's pretty impressive, even in these here parts." The sheriff stood up and reached out and shook Jess's hand. "Welcome to Largo, Texas, Mr. Williams. My name is A. J. Rubel. I'm the sheriff here in this godforsaken town. What can I do for you?"

"I'm looking for a man by the name of Blake Taggert," replied Jess. "He's one of three men who murdered my family back in Black Creek, Kansas. Here is a sketch of him. My last lead said he was still in Red Rock, but I thought I'd check in and see if you knew anything about him while I was here." The sheriff took the sketch and shook his head no and then handed the sketch to the deputies and they passed it around to each other. None of them recognized Taggert.

"If he had been around here, we would have known about it," the sheriff said. "Murdered your family, you say?"

"Both my parents," he replied. "Then they raped and shot my little seven-year-old sister."

"Bastards ought to be shot down like dogs," replied the sheriff, shaking his head in disgust.

"Two of them have been already. I just need to find the last one of them and finish the job."

"Good for you, son. I've always believed in an eye for an eye."

One of the three deputies who had been standing quietly walked over closer to the sheriff's desk. "Sheriff, I was just reading over some papers and there was a murder real similar in Red Rock recently. Seems some son of a bitch robbed and murdered a family there. I remember it 'cause it sounded so bad. The young girl was raped on the bed between her dead parents lying in their blood. Then the bastard who did it stuck his pistol up her…well, you know. They say it was awful, but they don't have any suspects yet. If your man is supposed to be in Red Rock, then maybe he did it."

"Well," said the sheriff sharply, "I'm going to send a wire to the sheriff of Red Rock and let him know about this Taggert fellow. It sounds like he could be the guy who did the killings over there, too."

"Sheriff, could I ask you a favor?" asked Jess.

"Sure," he replied.

"When you send the message to the sheriff in Red Rock, could you just inquire about Taggert's whereabouts? I'd like to deal with him myself. If they catch on to him, he will probably be hanging from a tree before I get there, and that would be too good a way for Taggert to die."

"I agree. All right, I'll just make an inquiry as if an old friend was looking for him. Anything else I can do?"

"Yes, one more thing if you could. Can I look through your wanted posters? I'm looking for men who have a bounty on their heads, but only the worst of the lot. I'm not looking for horse thieves or bank robbers, only the ones guilty of murder or rape and wanted dead or alive."

"So you're going into the bounty-hunting business, huh?" asked the sheriff.

"I guess I came by it naturally. Seems like it's what I was born to do, Sheriff," Jess stated plainly.

"Sure. But I don't think you'll find any of what you're looking for here. Most of my posters are for small offenses."

"Thanks, Sheriff. I'll stick around a few days until you get a response from Red Rock, if that's okay with you?"

"You're welcome to stay as long as you want. You watch your back," warned the sheriff.

"Why's that, Sheriff?"

"Your reputation with that gun of yours is spreading like a wild-fire. There are some real tough guys that come into town from time to time. They'd like nothing better than to be the one to take you down, if you get my meaning."

"Thanks for the warning, Sheriff. I know exactly what you mean."

Jess left the sheriff's office and stopped in at the first hotel he found. Then, he found Bridger's Café. Earl was right. The food was excellent and the biscuits were even better. Jess sent a dollar back to Earl's wife, Becca, for baking him the biscuits. After a great dinner, Jess decided to turn in for the night early. He found the room quite comfortable and clean. He dozed off thinking about Blake Taggert. He wondered if he was the one responsible for the murders in Red Rock the deputy had spoken about. It sounded so similar. Especially about the young girl being raped and then shot. Jess decided that even if Taggert didn't do the killings in Red Rock, he would hunt down the man responsible for doing it, but not before he got Taggert. Nothing would stand in his way or distract him, or so he thought.

CHAPTER SEVENTEEN

Jess rose early, ate a good breakfast and took a leisurely walk around town to check things out, things like back alleys, escape routes and ambush points. After he finished, he stopped in to see Gray and then decided to take a seat outside the hotel and just watch the town.

Largo was busier than most towns he had been in. People were all around, talking to one another. He caught many of them glancing at him and even a few of the men stared. One thing was constant though. Whenever he looked back, they quickly looked away, except for the women. The young ones smiled and the old ones glared. This was something he figured he was going to have to get used to now that he was quickly gaining a reputation with a gun. He had been sitting there for about an hour when he noticed something different about the townsfolk's expressions. Many of them began to break up conversations and go into stores and buildings. He thought that odd and wondered if it had something to do with him. Then, out of the corner of his eye, he saw Sheriff Rubel walking toward him.

"Morning, Sheriff," said Jess, as the sheriff sat down next to him. The sheriff didn't return the greeting. He just watched everyone quickly scatter into shops. Within minutes there weren't many townsfolk left on the street, except for some of the older women and they just glared at the sheriff.

"Yep," the sheriff stated plainly, "these people hate my guts. They want a safe town and a tough sheriff, but they can't put up with anyone mean enough like me to get the job done."

"Well, Sheriff, each of us carries our own burdens in life," he offered. "I suppose some are worse than others."

"One of my burdens is I worry that one day these people will have me shot. It will probably be in the back, since not one of them would face me straight on. But hell, that's my problem. Yesterday you asked about any men with a bounty on them. Well, I just got a message from a little town about thirty miles from here. It seems a drifter stole a horse from some rancher there."

"Sheriff, I appreciate you bringing me this, but as I told you, I'm not interested in chasing horse thieves," refuted Jess.

"What if I told you that this rancher wasn't about to give up a good horse so willingly and the drifter shot him dead?" the sheriff responded.

"Okay. Now you have my attention."

"And then, what if I told you that his twelve-year-old son went in the house and got his pa's rifle and took a shot at the drifter and the drifter plugged that poor kid right in the chest?"

"Now I'm definitely interested. Tell me more," he said leaning forward in his chair.

"Now, there ain't any law in this little shit-hole of a town, so the Texas Rangers have been assigned to go get the bastard. The only problem is there are no Rangers within at least a week's ride of the town. You could get there easily in two days. Since there's no law in town, he might stay for a day or so. Plus, there is a reward of five hundred dollars for his return, dead or alive. So, you want the job?"

"Sheriff, why not send one of your deputies?"

"Hell, they'd probably get lost and never come back. Besides, I hear this drifter is pretty fast with a leg iron. My deputies are tough as nails, but none of them is that fast with a pistol. From what you told me, this is exactly what you've been looking for," he said, smiling and raising his eyebrows.

Jess sat up straight and thought a second or two about Blake Taggert. He'd never been this close to catching him, but he'd been waiting to catch him for two years now. What were another few days? Besides, it might take that long before Sheriff Rubel got any information on Taggert. Jess looked at Sheriff Rubel and asked, "You said the boy was twelve?"

"Yep."

"Sheriff, tell me where this town is."

"So, am I to assume that you will be bringing him in dead?" asked the sheriff.

"Yes, but not on the horse he stole. That will be returned to the rancher's wife. I'll drag him here with my horse if I need to."

"The more I get to know you, the more I like you," said the sheriff perceptively. "And I don't like most people." Jess headed straight for the stable and told Earl to saddle up Gray.

"Boy, I thought I'd never stop hearing about this nice young man who gave my wife a dollar tip last night," said a happy Earl. "She must've talked about you for an hour. Couldn't hardly get a word in edgewise, not that I usually get one in anyway. That was mighty nice of you, Mr. Williams. Yes, sir, mighty nice."

"Her biscuits were worth the dollar all by themselves. Of course, I did take into account that she's a whole lot better looking than you are, Earl."

Earl let out one of those huge belly laughs. "Man, you're right about that, too!" he exclaimed.

"I'll be gone for about four or five days, Earl. Save me a good spot for Gray when I get back and you'll still get a dollar a day just for holding it."

"You're a damn right nice feller, Mr. Williams," he boasted. "Yes, sir. Where you headed?"

"Some little town called Jonesville east of here. Got a man there with a bounty on his head. He killed a rancher and his twelve-year-old son."

"Sounds like a man who needs to see a hanging rope."

"I don't think he'll make it that far," he said boldly, as he swung into the saddle.

"Well, you make sure you come back now," said Earl. "I'll need that money for sure. Got three kids of my own to feed and they never seem to stop eating."

"Don't worry, I'll be back. Most likely with some dead weight."

Sheriff A. J. Rubel was sitting behind his desk reading a newspaper when one of his deputies came in and poured himself a cup of coffee. He, like the other two deputies, never knew for sure whether to bother the sheriff. Sheriff Rubel's temper was erratic as hell. They had been quite surprised by his friendly tone with Jess Williams.

"Uh…Sheriff, could I talk to you a minute?" asked the deputy.

Sheriff Rubel slowly put his paper down on the desk and looked up at the deputy. "I suppose so, as long as you can answer me one question," the sheriff said, looking at the deputy.

"Sure, Sheriff, what is it?" the deputy asked, feeling pretty good that he hadn't pissed the sheriff off.

The sheriff said, "I just want to know if there is a sign on my forehead that says, 'Will the first dumb-ass that walks in here please interrupt me?' " The deputy hung his head, realizing he had screwed up again with the sheriff, which was pretty much normal.

"Sorry, Sheriff, I guess I should've known better," he said soberly. "I know you like to read your paper in silence."

"Well, go on already," said Sheriff Rubel. "You've done interrupted me now. But the next time you see me reading my paper just turn your sorry ass back out the door. Understand? Now what is it?"

"I was just wondering what you thought about that kid, Jess Williams?" asked the deputy. "You seemed awful friendly to him."

"And you, who finished all the way up to the fifth grade all by your lonesome, can't seem to figure that out, eh?"

"But…if I could do that why would I be asking?"

The sheriff just shook his head, thinking to himself how hard it was to get good help these days. His deputies were tough, but they weren't the brightest bunch. He got up and walked to the table where the coffeepot was and poured himself a fresh cup. Then he walked back to his desk and sat down again.

"Well," the sheriff said, pausing for a moment and looking as if he was thinking real deep about what he was about to say. "I've seen a lot of different men in my lifetime: brave ones, cowards, braggarts, idiots, crazy ones, liars and a few stone-cold fearless types. But this kid, Jess Williams, is something I ain't seen before. When you look into that kid's eyes you can see that there is a good side to the boy, but it's buried way back in there behind all that rage and hatred for the men who murdered his family and men like them. That boy's going to hunt men for a living and he's going to be damn good at it. Now some people are destined to be just normal, average people and some are destined to be something special, something completely out of the ordinary. That kid's one of those destined to be special. I just think that it's a privilege to have had a chance in our lifetime to know someone like that. It don't happen all that often."

The deputy had listened to all of this and he took a minute to ponder all that the sheriff had said. "And you could see all of that in his eyes?" asked the deputy.

"You can read a man's life history in his eyes if you know how to look for it."

"Damn. I wish I could do that."

"And I just wish I could get back to reading my damn paper!" countered the sheriff, getting back to his normal grumpy self.

"Sure thing, Sheriff, and thanks," replied the deputy, as he walked out and sat in the chair outside the office and thought about Jess. He wondered what he would have done if his family hd been murdered like that. He suddenly felt glad that he wasn't that drifter over in Jonesville.

Jess hit the trail hard. It only took him a day and a half to reach Jonesville. The sheriff was right; there wasn't much to the town: no law, no bank, just a saloon, general store and a livery, along with a few houses scattered around the area.

He stabled Gray and asked the boy working the livery to brush him down and give him some extra grain. He had ridden him hard the last day and a half. He headed for the saloon. There was no name on the building and there weren't any doors either. Jess walked in and stopped just inside the entrance. There were four men in the place, not counting the barkeep. Jess walked up to the barkeep and asked for a beer. The barkeep brought Jess his beer and set it down, but not before wiping up the bar in front of him. The barkeep was a short fellow, but he looked like the kind of man who didn't take crap from anyone. Jess figured he might know about the drifter he was looking for.

"What's your name, barkeep?" he asked.

"Who's asking?"

"Jess Williams, and I'm looking for a drifter."

"Information costs money here, mister. Hell, you don't think I make any money serving drinks in this hell-hole of a place, do ya?" Jess took out a five-dollar gold piece and placed it on top of the bar.

The barkeep took it, smiled and said, "Whatcha wanna know?"

"I'm looking for the drifter who shot that rancher and his son. You know who that might be or where I might find him?" The barkeep's eyes turned cold. He reached into the pocket where he had put the five-dollar gold piece and threw it back on the counter. The gold piece spun around and then fell flat on the top of the bar.

"Mister, that information ain't for sale," he said bluntly. "You can have it for free, especially if you're here to make him pay for what he did. Hell, I knew that rancher and his kid. They were real nice folks. Now, if you tell me you're a friend of his, you can take your ass back out of here."

"I'm no friend of his," he replied sharply. "I'm here to take him back for the bounty."

"I thought you might be a bounty hunter, what with all them guns you're wearing. Not only is the information free, but so is the beer. That sumbitch has been hanging around here and he'll most likely be back tonight. How are you with that fancy shootin' iron you got there?"

"Good enough."

"You'd better be, 'cause that drifter is slicker than shit with a pistol."

"You let me worry about that," said Jess with a knowing look in his eyes.

The barkeep brought Jess another beer. Jess hadn't realized how fast he had downed the first one. It had been a dusty and windy ride the last two days. Now that he thought about it, it seemed like it was always dusty and windy in Texas. The other four men in the saloon just sat there and drank. They listened to the conversation between Jess and the barkeep and decided they would wait and see what happened. They all knew the rancher and his son, too, but they weren't gunslingers. They were ranchers and farmers. And since there was no law in town, they had long ago learned to mind their own business. Jess didn't have long to wait. He had just put his glass down on the bar when the barkeep gave him a look and nodded toward the door. Jess moved back into the corner at the far end of the bar. The drifter slowly walked into the bar as if he owned it. He stopped at the table where the four men were sitting. He stared at them until each one of them lowered his eyes, humiliating them without even saying a word.

The drifter was about six feet tall with a little meat on his bones, not heavy, but stocky. He wore two six-shooters low on his hips, but it wasn't a double holster; it was two separate holsters, one strapped over the other. The right hand gun was lower than the left. The left gun was backward and slightly forward. Jess figured he used the second gun as a backup gun since it was designed to be drawn with the right hand.

"You boys gonna buy me another beer tonight?" the drifter asked.

"Uh, sure, mister. No problem," said one of the four men sitting at the table.

"Why, that's mighty nice of you fellows, mighty nice indeed," replied the drifter, as he walked up to the bar, but not before noticing Jess. He stopped at the bar and ordered a beer. He took a long, slow sip and set his glass back down on the bar, all while never taking his eyes off Jess. He noticed the shotgun behind Jess, but he had not noticed Jess's pistol yet since Jess was still facing the bar, watching the drifter carefully out of his side vision.

"Well, well, seems we have a newcomer to town," announced the drifter. "What's your name, boy?" Jess didn't respond right away. He just looked at the barkeep who had a look of foreboding in his eyes.

"Barkeep," asked Jess, "you got any grub in the back?"

The barkeep was somewhat surprised by the question. "Sure, mister, we got some stew left over. I can get a plate of it for you if you want some."

"That would be mighty nice of you," said Jess. "I'd like to eat a bite before I leave town tonight." Jess finally turned to the drifter, exposing his gun and looking the drifter straight in the eyes.

The drifter was obviously not used to someone treating him so casually. "I asked you what your name is, son," demanded the drifter.

"You're really not going to need to know that, actually."

"Really?" replied the drifter sarcastically. "I always like to know the name of the man who's going to buy me my next beer."

"I'm not buying you a beer. Matter of fact, you're not having another beer. At least not if you are who I think you are."

The drifter changed his stance a little. "You tell me, since you seem to know so much."

"You're the drifter who shot the rancher and his son. Isn't that right?"

"What if I am? What the hell are you gonna do about it?"

"Well, there's a bounty on your head in the amount of five hundred dollars if you're the man who did it, and I intend to collect the money."

The drifter laughed out loud. "So, I guess this means you ain't gonna buy me that beer, eh?"

"No, not likely. I will buy those four men a beer though, to make up for all the beer they've obviously bought you."

The barkeep came back out from the back of the bar with a big plate of hot stew and set it down in front of Jess. Jess didn't look at it, but he could smell it. "Sure hope it tastes as good as it smells," he observed.

"It does," bragged the barkeep. "And the answer to your question is yes. That's the rotten bastard who shot the rancher and his son!"

"Shut the hell up, barkeep!" hollered the drifter. "I hear one more word coming out of your pie hole and I'll come back there and shove that sawed-off shotgun you want to reach for straight up your ass!" While the drifter was yelling at the barkeep, Jess had ever so slightly lowered his gun hand closer to his pistol.

"Seems like another mystery has been solved," said Jess. "Well, mister, seems like there is only one thing left to do."

"And just what is that, smart-ass?" demanded the drifter.

"I'm here to make you pay for what you've done, so why don't you go ahead and show these men just how tough you really are?"

"You've got a real smart mouth on you, boy."

"Maybe."

"You know who the hell you're messing with?"

"Not really."

"I'm J. J. Johnson," the drifter said, as if his name should put fear into another man.

"Never heard of you."

"You should have. I've got a reputation."

"For what? Making other men pay for your beer?" he asked, knowing it would piss him off some more.

"Hell, no!" retorted Johnson angrily. "For being quick at skin-nin' leather!"

"Really?"

"Ain't that what I just said?"

"Show me."

"Show you what?"

"How fast you really are."

"I'll kill ya for sure."

"Really?"

"You're really pissing me off."

"I'll tell you what. If you beat me, you can have my stew here."

That was the last straw. Johnson tried a sleight of hand on Jess. He moved his left hand on the bar just a few inches. It was enough to get Jess's attention for a split second. It was a trick that had worked often for Johnson and it had cost many a cowboy gunslinger his life, but not today. Jess caught the hand movement and thought it was pretty slick; it was something he would remember.

Johnson's right hand reached for his pistol a split second after he had moved his left hand on the bar and actually got it out of the holster completely, but not up far enough to point it at Jess when he felt a hard thump on his chest. He looked down at his chest as he dropped his pistol to the floor. He saw the blood streaming from the hole in his shirt and he looked up at Jess. He never thought the last sight he would see in his life would be of a young man taking a bite of stew while watching him slump to the floor.

"Barkeep," said Jess, "this stew is wonderful. Do you think I could get another plate of it after I finish this one?"

The barkeep put the sawed-off back down under the bar. "Damn," he exclaimed. "How the hell did you learn to shoot like that and where the hell did you get that shootin' iron?"

"My pa taught me, and I found it," he said, not really elaborating.

Jess finished the first plate of stew and while the barkeep was getting another plate for him, he walked over to the drifter and took off both his guns and checked his pockets. He found three hundred forty dollars. Jess assumed it was probably stolen money. Jess gave the barkeep forty dollars of the drifter's money and told him it was to clean up the saloon and buy the four men beer until the money ran out to make up for the money they had spent buying beer for the drifter. They all thanked him. That left Jess with three hundred dollars of the drifter's money.

"Barkeep, is that the horse that was stolen from the rancher?" asked Jess.

The barkeeper looked outside at the horse. "Sure is."

"I want you to take that horse and saddle to the wife of the rancher tomorrow. I also want you to take the rest of this money and give it to her," said Jess, as he handed the money to the barkeep. "I know it won't replace her husband or her son, but it ought to help her some."

"That's mighty generous of you, mister," the barkeep said thoughtfully. "Whatcha gonna do with his guns?"

"I plan on trading them for a mule I saw at the stables to haul his carcass back to Largo for the bounty on his head."

Jess had the four men drag the body to the stables. The stable owner was more than happy with his trade. He could sell the two guns for twice what the mule was worth. Jess decided to leave in the morning and asked the man running the stable if he could bunk down there for the night. The owner had no problem with that.

Jess got settled in and started to nod off to sleep. His thoughts that night were thinking he was finally close to finding Blake Taggert. He just had to make this delivery back to Largo and collect his five hundred dollars. And as sleep finally found him, his last thought that night was that bounty hunting sure paid well.

CHAPTER EIGHTEEN

J ess headed out of Jonesville at first light. It took two full days to get back to Largo since he was dragging a stubborn mule with two hundred pounds of dead weight on it. The weather didn't help much either. The first day was a nice sunny day, but with a strong wind hitting him straight in the face. On the second day, it started to rain just after the noon hour, not a hard rain, just enough to make him put his slicker on and make the ride uncomfortable. It was still raining when he got to Largo just before dusk. He stopped at the sheriff's office and one of the deputies was sitting on the porch in front of the jail. Jess handed the reins from the mule to the deputy and told him he would send Earl over for the mule later and he would check in with the sheriff in the morning about the bounty. He was tired, wet and cold and he needed sleep. He walked Gray over to the stable and told Earl about the mule.

"He's yours to keep, Earl, that is, if you want him. He's a stubborn cuss though. I had to drag his ass all the way here."

"Never met a mule that wasn't stubborn, Mr. Williams," replied Earl. " 'Sides, if I can't put him to work, I can sure put him on the table. I got hungry mouths to feed."

"You know, Earl, I never thought of that; but as stubborn as he is, I can just see you cutting into a thick, tough steak," laughed Jess.

Jess was tired enough that he passed up going to Bridger's Café for some late supper. All he wanted was a good night's sleep. He got himself a hot bath and turned in for the night. He rose early and had a huge breakfast. Becca was definitely the best cook he had ever met, except for his ma of course. He left her two dollars for a tip this time. He could tell that Becca and Earl were just simple folk working a hard life to make ends meet, like most people. Yet, here he was, getting ready to collect five hundred dollars for less than one week's work. He decided that as long as he had the money, he wouldn't be greedy with it. He felt good about leaving the three hundred dollars with the rancher's wife back in Jonesville.

He finished breakfast and walked down to the sheriff's office. The usual deputy was sitting on the porch and he greeted Jess and told him to go on in. The deputy thought again about what the sheriff had said about Jess and he looked at him with a newfound look of respect. Jess returned the greeting and found the sheriff sitting behind his desk, reading a telegraph message.

"Well, good morning, son. That's a good piece of work you did there," said Sheriff Rubel. "Five hundred dollars ain't bad for less than a week's work. Your money is at the bank right next to the hotel you're staying at. They can pay you cash or wire the money wherever you want. By the way, I knew that fella and he was damn fast with a gun. He's one sorry cuss who won't be missed."

"Can't argue with you about that, Sheriff. Did you get any word about Blake Taggert while I was gone?"

"Matter of fact, I was just reading the message now. It seems Mr. Taggert has been in Red Rock for quite a while now. I have a hunch they don't suspect him of any wrongdoing."

"Well, whether he had anything to do with the killings in Red Rock or not, he sure is guilty of murder and he's going to pay for it," Jess said with intent.

"I have no doubt about that, Jess."

Jess spent the rest of the afternoon walking around town. He stopped in and talked to Earl. He had already sold the mule to a farmer and he offered half the money to Jess, but Jess refused to take it.

"I have all the money I need, Earl," he said. "Now, you might give a little of that money to your pretty wife. She just might want to buy a new dress or something."

Earl laughed that loud belly laugh again. "Hell, she done already got it all, Mr. Williams," laughed Earl. "Every last penny of it."

Jess grinned at Earl and said, "I'm going to have dinner tonight and when I see her, I just might suggest that dress thing, especially since she's already got your money."

"You tell her old Earl says she can have whatever she wants. She deserves it just for putting up with me, not to mention all the hard work she does to help out. She's a keeper, that's for sure. You be sure to tell her I said that."

"I will, Earl. I surely will."

Jess stopped in at the bank and wired half the reward money to his bank in Black Creek and took the other half in cash. He decided to have an early dinner. He headed for the café and was laughing to himself about what Earl had said about his wife. Jess figured he would throw in a real nice tip for her. The café was almost empty, with only a half dozen people eating. Becca saw him come in and nodded to him to sit at a table. She came out from the kitchen a minute later and walked over to a table behind him, delivering two heaping plates of hot food. Then, she turned around to Jess's table.

"How you doin' today, Mr. Williams?" she asked.

"I'm doing just fine, Becca. I had a nice talk with Earl today," he said with a slight grin on his face.

"Did you now?"

"Yes. He told me to tell you what a wonderful wife you've been and to make sure that you rewarded yourself with a nice new dress with the money from the mule."

"That's a right nice thing for him to say, but we can't afford any new dresses. We still got kids to feed and lots of repairs to the house. New dresses are for those who got more money than we do."

"I think you deserve a new dress. Consider it found money."

"I'll think about it," she said, trying to get him off the subject. "Would you like something to eat?"

"Absolutely. I'm hungry as a bear coming out from a long winter."

Jess ordered and Becca had his meal out to him with a load of fresh biscuits in about fifteen minutes. During that time, several more people wandered into the café, including two men who looked like they had been on the trail for a while. They obviously had not stopped in for a bath before supper. They sat down at a table to Jess's left. Both of them were packing pistols, but one look-over told Jess they weren't anything to worry about. After Becca delivered his supper to him, she turned to the table where the two men were sitting and asked them if they wanted to have something to eat.

"Damn right! What the hell you think we came in here for?" one of them said. The other one laughed, revealing the four teeth he had left.

The other man spoke in a sarcastic tone and said, "We came in for a drink, so why don't you go get us two whiskeys?"

"We don't serve drinks in here, just food," she replied nervously.

"If we wanted whiskey, we would have gone to the saloon. But we wanted something to eat, so we came in here; and you ask us if we came in here to get something to eat. See how dumb a question that is? That's why they shouldn't let people like you work in public places. Now, get us two plates of grub and hurry it up, bitch!" barked the first man.

Becca was standing there speechless. She was just about to open her mouth when Jess, without looking up from his meal or even looking over at the two men said in a soft voice, "Becca, why don't you go wait on a different table, since it seems these two men don't seem to know what they want yet."

Becca gave the men a look of contempt as she walked over to another table and continued to stare at them just like everyone else in the place. Jess kept eating slowly and the two men were so surprised they were dumbfounded for a few seconds. They looked at each other and figured the odds were two against one so they felt somewhat daring.

"Mister, this ain't your business," said the first man nastily.

"Yeah, you'd be better off if you just kept eating your grub and kept your nose out of other people's business," said the second man. Jess still did not look up at either of the two men. He reached in his pocket and pulled out a silver dollar. He threw it over onto their table, still not looking up at them and continuing to eat as if nothing was happening. The silver dollar spun around for a few seconds, both of the men watching it spin, and then it fell flat on the table.

"What the hell is this for?" asked the second man.

"You said you wanted two whiskeys, didn't you?" replied Jess, still not looking up.

"No, you dumb-ass!" hollered the second man. "What we said was we wanted something to eat. Mister, you're as dumb as that woman over there."

Still not looking up at the men, Jess said in a firm, quite voice, "That very nice lady over there happens to be a friend of mine. She has a name and it's not what you've called her. Now, I suggest you pick up that dollar and go buy yourselves some whiskey at one of the local saloons while you still can. I'm not going to spoil my meal by eating in the same room as you two idiots." The two men stood up and they were pissed. Jess watched them out of the corner of his eye. He knew from the start these two were just talkers and he wasn't one bit worried.

"And just who the hell are you to tell us what we will or won't do, mister?" hollered the first man.

"The name is Jess Williams," he stated bluntly. Both men stiffened like oak trees on a windless day because they had heard of Jess Williams when they arrived in town that morning. Neither of them spoke for what seemed like a whole minute. Jess still never looked up from his meal.

"Uh…we're sorry, Mr. Williams," said the second man. "We didn't mean no harm. We…we ain't looking for no trouble, especially with you."

The second man picked up the silver dollar and put it in his pocket. "Thanks for the whiskey," he said. Both men started to walk out when they stopped dead in their tracks as they heard Jess speak up again.

"You two forget something?" They knew exactly what Jess meant without asking. They both looked over at Becca and with their eyes down to the floor they apologized sincerely. "We're mighty sorry, ma'am. We won't ever bother you again," the first man said.

Becca said nothing. She simply looked at the two men with disgust. She was satisfied enough at the fact Jess had stuck up for her. No one, except her husband, had ever done that before. She walked over to Jess and put her hand on his shoulder as the two men left the café.

"I can't tell you what that meant to me, Mr. Williams," said a sincere Becca. "No one has ever done something like that for me before. Being a black woman ain't easy."

Jess quickly looked up at Becca with a surprised look on his face. "Earl is a black man?" he asked in a serious voice. Becca was startled for a moment until she saw Jess give her a big smile.

She slapped Jess on his shoulder and laughed. "So you do have a sense of humor under all that hatred you got bottled up inside you," laughed Becca. "You had me going for a second or two."

"Well, I don't see black or white when I look at you, Becca. What I see is a friend and a nice person. I like you and that's all that counts."

"You sure ain't like most people I ever met, Mr. Williams."

"Judging by the likes of those two idiots who just left here, I hope not," he said, as he finished his plate of food. "Now, what are the chances of me getting a second helping?"

"For you, all you want, any time you want," she replied with a proud look. "And thank you again."

Jess finished his second helping of food while everyone else in the place seemed to be watching him. When he finished, he placed two ten-dollar gold pieces next to his plate and left before Becca got back to his table. He knew she would refuse to accept the money from him. Jess went back to the hotel and got a pretty good night's rest. In the morning he stopped in to thank the sheriff one more time and headed for the livery to get Gray. Earl had him all saddled up and ready to go.

"Mr. Williams, I sure do want to thank you for what you did for my Becca yesterday," said Earl with a thankful look on his face. "She told me all about it."

"I don't stand for any man picking on a woman. It makes my blood boil."

"All the same, you sure made some friends here and that's a fact," he said with meaning. "You ever need something, you call on old Earl, you hear?"

"I'll certainly remember that."

"Oh, and Becca said to stop by the café on your way out," he added. "She's got something that she wants to show you."

Jess climbed up in the saddle and headed out of town for Red Rock. As he came up to the café, there was Becca in the most beautiful yellow flowered dress. She was standing in front of the door of the café and just beaming at him.

"I wanted you to see what I bought with some of that money you left me yesterday," she said, a wide smile washing across her face. "You sure didn't have to do that. You already did enough for us."

"Becca, just seeing how lovely you look in that dress was worth it all," Jess said smiling. "You take care of yourself and my friend, Earl."

"I sure will, Mr. Williams, and thank you so much for everything. You are surely one person we will never forget."

Jess nodded to her and turned his horse around. As he rode past the sheriff's office, Sheriff Rubel was standing there and had a look of respect on his face. That was a rare thing to see. There weren't many men he had respect for, but Jess Williams was undeniably one of them. The usual deputy was sitting in the chair next to the sheriff and Jess thought the deputy had a strange look on his face. It was as if he was trying to figure out something about Jess. He shrugged it off, not giving it any more thought.

The trail along the way to Red Rock was lonely, but Jess didn't mind it at all. It gave him plenty of time to think about things and to practice his shooting skills. He stopped in a few towns to get supplies; but whenever he did, he arrived in the morning, got what he needed, and headed straight back out. Usually he spent no more than an hour or two in town, depending on whether or not he wanted a hot bath badly enough. It was a long haul to Red Rock from Largo, and after about six days of riding, he finally arrived at the outskirts of town. As usual, he camped outside of town, planning to go into Red Rock in the morning. He fried some potatoes, cooked some beans and then made some pan bread. He got out his bedroll. As he lay there, sipping hot coffee, he thought about all that had happened up to now. He thought about Taggert and hoped that he was still in Red Rock. He finally dozed off, thinking about just how he would kill him. He wanted to make him suffer for what he did to his family, especially Samantha. He was sure now that he was the one who raped and killed her. He was sure in his mind that he was the one who committed the murders in Red Rock. Taggert was about to finally pay for his crimes, and the cost would be a slow, painful death. Jess fell asleep with a slight smile on his face.

CHAPTER NINETEEN

Jess woke a little before daybreak. He was anxious to get to town so all he had was coffee and a piece of leftover pan bread. He figured he could get a good meal once he reached Red Rock. He arrived about half an hour after daybreak and the place was already bustling with activity. He found the first livery and met the stable owner, a young man who seemed to have a permanent smile on his face.

"Morning, mister, need to stable your horse?" asked the man. "I got plenty of room and you won't find a cheaper price in town. I brush each horse down once a day and they get good feed here, not that cheap crap you find at some of the other liveries in town."

Jess noticed that the man was wearing a pistol, which was kind of odd for a stable hand. "Sounds like this is the place for my horse to be. I like to make sure he gets the best feed. If you make sure he gets a little extra feed each day, I'll throw in an extra dollar every day."

"You've got yourself a deal, mister. I can sure use the extra money," the man said. "I just bought this place last month. Trying to build up the business isn't as easy as I thought it was going to be."

"I've never seen a stable man wear a six-shooter before. You use that thing often?" asked Jess.

"No, not really. You need to carry a gun around here though, what with all the outlaws and drifters coming in and out of town every day. This place just seems to attract the worst of the lot. Hell, we have a shoot-out just about every night in one of the saloons. I'm pretty good with a pistol 'cause I practice and all, but I'm no gunslinger. Just figured it might save my life one day as long as I don't have to go up against someone really fast. Are you a gunslinger? Because if you're not, you sure got a nice pistol," the stable owner said, as he looked closer at Jess's odd-looking pistol and holster.

"What's your name?" asked Jess.

"Name is Ted Watkins. Nice to meet you," he said as he stuck out his hand to shake.

"Nice to meet you, Ted. My name is Jess Williams."

"You don't say? Why, hell, I've heard of you. They say you're like greased lightning with that pistol of yours. Are you one of them bounty hunters?"

"I guess that's what I seem to be doing so far," he replied, with somewhat of a puzzled look on his face.

"Man, I sure wouldn't want you hunting me. Who are you looking for here in Red Rock?"

"The man I'm hunting is the last of three men who killed my family," he replied in a serious tone. "The man's name is Blake Taggert."

Ted had a look of surprise on his face. "Hell, I know Blake. He stables his horse here sometimes. He always seemed like a pretty nice fellow. His family was murdered when he was just a kid and he took off, scared to death when it happened. Now, he's damn fast with a leg iron. If you plan on taking him on, you'd better be real good with that pistol."

"I am. Is Taggert still in town?"

"Actually, he left about a week ago with another man. He should be back any day now. I didn't like the guy he was riding with though. He seemed like trouble. He weren't exactly a nice fella, if you get my drift. Real young too, like you. As a matter of fact, he kind of looked like you and always had something smart to say. Quick with a gun though. I heard he taught Taggert a thing or two and from what I hear he's quicker than Taggert, if you can believe that."

"What was his name?" asked Jess.

"Don't know. He came into town and only stayed one night. Then, he and Taggert took off and Taggert said he would be back in about a week."

"I can wait. Now, how about pointing me in the direction of the sheriff's office and telling me the best place to get a good meal and a room," he asked.

Ted gave him the information he asked for and Jess headed for the hotel first. He figured that since Taggert wasn't in town right at the moment, he might as well get his room and a meal before paying a visit to the sheriff's office. He got a room at a place called the Boardman Hotel and a meal at Little's Eats, which was a perfect name for the place. It only had four tables, but the food was good, hot and served quickly. While he was eating, a young boy who looked to be about ten years old ran in and went back to the kitchen area. He could hear the kid talking really quick. He ran back out the door without even giving Jess more than a quick glance.

Jess finished his meal and headed for the sheriff's office. The door was open and Jess knocked on the outside wall before entering. He found Sheriff Clancy, a man who looked tired. He was in his sixties, with more lines in his face than a piece of crumpled paper, sitting behind a rickety old desk. He looked up at Jess, but said nothing.

"Afternoon, Sheriff. My name is Jess Williams. I'm looking for a man by the name of Blake Taggert. I hear he's out of town at the moment, but I understand he'll be back soon. I was wondering if you could tell me anything about him."

"So, you're that young shooter everyone's been talking about," said Sheriff Clancy. "What do you want with Blake Taggert? There isn't any bounty on his head as far as I know and you sure look like a bounty hunter."

"He's got a bounty on his head, but I'm not worried about it, although I'll collect it anyway. I'm just looking to kill him. He's the last one left of three men who killed my family back in Black Creek, Kansas."

"What happened to the other two?" the sheriff asked, already guessing the answer.

"They died."

"Well, he's not wanted for any crimes here and he has friends all over Red Rock," said the sheriff. "They're not about to just let you shoot him down like a dog."

"Any of his friends who get in my way will go down with him," warned Jess. "That will be their choice, not mine."

"Well good luck, son," he said. "I think you're making a huge mistake, but a man has to make his own decisions. If I were you, I'd make sure you've made your peace with the man upstairs. If Taggert don't kill you, one of the other gunslingers who run through here might. There sure ain't been any shortage of them lately."

"Sheriff, I'd like to know where you stand on this matter. Are you planning on getting between me and Taggert?"

"Hell, no," he said flatly. "You think I got this old by getting in the middle of gunmen hell-bent on killing each other? Not me. I just drag out the bodies after it's over. If it isn't a fair fight and someone back shoots someone, I try to arrest him. I'm not getting shot over wearing this tin star. I can tell you that for sure. If they want better law than that, they can get someone else for the job. I've told the mayor exactly that more than a dozen times myself."

"I appreciate the honesty, Sheriff."

"Just watch your back here."

"Don't worry about me, Sheriff. I can take care of myself, but luck doesn't have anything to do with it." Jess turned to walk out and stopped at the door and turned back around to the sheriff.

"Sheriff, the man at the stables said Taggert rode out of town with another man. "You know who he is or if you think he'll throw in with Taggert?"

"That sumbitch is one big heap of trouble," replied Sheriff Clancy. "Don't be messing with him if you can avoid it. He was only here one night and killed one of the locals over a card game. I was in the saloon when it happened. It was a fair fight, but almost didn't seem so. That Sloan fella is mighty quick with a pistol, and meaner than a rabid dog." Jess stiffened a little at the name of Sloan.

"Sheriff, did you say his name was Sloan?" he asked probingly. "Is that his last name?"

"I believe so."

"Did he say what his first name was?" asked Jess in a serious tone.

"Jim or Tim, something like that; I can't remember for sure. Glad he's gone and I hope he never comes back this way. Don't know what his business with Taggert is."

Jess felt like he had just been hit in the chest with a ten-pound hammer. Could this be the twin brother he had been told about before he left Black Creek? If so, was he the kind of man that Jess would hunt? What would he do if that were the case? What was he doing with Taggert, and if he was Jess's brother, did he know that he was riding with one of the men responsible for murdering their mother?

Jess calmed himself down. It was too much to think about right now. He would just have to play whatever cards were dealt him. If Sloan was his brother, and he came back to town with Taggert, Jess figured he would have to face him and get at the truth. Jess's subconscious was trying to tell him something, but he wouldn't let it through. It was too awful a thought. Jess didn't say another word. He turned back around and walked out of the sheriff's office.

Jess realized that the sheriff would be of no help, but at least he wouldn't get in the middle of things. He didn't want to kill a sheriff, but he might if he were forced into it. He headed down the street to one of the saloons. He found a place called Little's Drinks. He wondered if the same person who owned the small café where he had eaten earlier owned the saloon, too. Jess pushed through the swinging doors and looked around. Even though it was early in the afternoon, the place was quite busy. There were people playing cards, some sitting at tables and drinking and several men bellied up to the bar.

He picked out the two or three men in the place who might be trouble. One was playing at one of the card tables and there were two others at the bar that he figured for gunmen. One of the two men standing up at the bar seemed dressed too nicely to be a gunman and he seemed to project a friendly attitude. Jess wasn't sure about him, but his gut told him to treat the man with caution. A young kid was sweeping the floor and Jess noticed it was the same kid who had run in and out of the café earlier. Jess found that his preferred place at the right end of the bar was occupied by this neatly dressed man. He was forced to take the far left of the bar. He ordered a beer and took a long pull from it. He noticed that the barkeep's head wasn't much above the bar, which made Jess lean over the bar to look. He found a raised platform behind the bar that was about a foot high off the floor.

The barkeep, whose name was Paul Little, watched him do this. When Jess was done looking the barkeep gave him a stern gaze. "One smart-ass word from you about me being short and you'll not get another drink from me. I don't care who the hell you are," warned the barkeep.

"Sorry. I wasn't planning on making any remarks. I was just curious."

"Yeah, well you can be curious about something else."

"Sorry, I meant no offense," he added as he took another sip of his beer.

Jess glanced down at the nicely dressed man at the other end of the bar and the man held up his glass of whiskey as if to salute Jess. The man was tall and muscular. He was dressed in all black and wearing a very nice black holster tied down low and tight. Jess noticed the man's hammer strap was removed. When he had first walked into the bar, it had still been over the hammer. Jess smiled to himself thinking that that was exactly why he always took the right end of the bar. It could hide such movement from most men, but Jess wasn't like most men. Jess had already removed his hammer strap before he walked into the bar.

He took another glance around the room and he could tell trouble was about to find him. He could tell from the changed expressions on the faces of the men in the bar. Jess finished his beer and ordered another one.

"Barkeep," the man at the opposite end of the bar said, "put that beer on my bill. I'd be honored to buy Mr. Williams a drink." The barkeep just grunted and got Jess another beer.

189

Jess took a long sip of his beer and then turned to the man. "Thanks for the beer. Do I know you?"

"Thought maybe you might," said the man. "They call me Nevada Jackson. I'm a bounty hunter myself. Just finished a job in a small town east of here and stopped off to see if there was some money to be made here in Red Rock."

"Well, it's nice to meet you, but I don't have any bounty on my head. Well, at least not yet, if that's what's on your mind."

"You sure?" he asked, tipping his head down a little at Jess.

"Pretty sure."

"I'm going to take your word on it. I always believe a man until he lies to me. I figure that's the right way to go about it. Don't you?"

"I couldn't agree more, Nevada."

"Well, I'd still like to make a little money today. I like a good challenge and haven't had a serious one lately," stated Nevada. "Fact is I'm getting bored. I think I have a way to combine both needs into one." Jess didn't respond. He simply stood there, looking at the man and sipping his beer.

"Don't you want to know what it is I'm talking about, Mr. Williams?" asked Nevada.

"The way I figure it, you're going to tell me all about it sooner or later anyway. My hunch is whatever I say won't matter much."

Nevada laughed a little and smiled back at him. "Well, at least you have a sense of humor," he said smiling. "I have to say, I'm quite impressed with you. You're a cool one for being so young. I like that in a man. Now, here's what I propose. Let's each put five hundred dollars down on the bar and then we face each other. The man standing after the smoke clears gets to keep all the money. What do you think about that?"

Jess thought about it for a moment. "You know what, Nevada? I've learned that things happen and sometimes you just don't have any real control over them. Things like this: Here you are, and I don't even know you, and yet you're going to force me to kill you in a gunfight that I don't want any part of. One day I hope to understand why; but for now, I'd be satisfied with one simple answer."

"I'd be glad to answer any question you've a mind to ask, Mr. Williams," replied Nevada. Jess took another pull from his beer.

"Have you ever killed someone in cold blood for no good reason?" asked Jess.

"I've killed more than my share of men, but they all deserved dying and they all had a fair chance to defend themselves. Why?"

"Well, if the answer had been different, it would have been a lot easier to kill you. Now, I don't really want to square off with you, but I suppose you're going to push me on the matter anyway."

"Well, I guess so, unless you decide to walk out and refuse to face me. I never shoot a man who refuses to draw in a fair fight."

"Of course, you and I both know I won't do that."

"Of course," he agreed quickly. "I've heard all about you and that fancy pistol you've got there. I heard all about you taking down that drifter up in Jonesville who shot that rancher and his boy. As a matter of fact, I was heading up there to collect that bounty when I heard you already took him down. You cost me five hundred dollars on that deal. I guess this would make me whole, so to speak."

Nevada pulled a wad of money out of his front pocket, counted out five hundred dollars and placed it on the bar. "Barkeep," he said, "you hold the money. Mr. Williams, do you have the five hundred?"

"I've got three hundred on me, but I can put up my gun and holster for the rest. If you win, I guess I wouldn't need it anymore anyway. Agreed?"

"Agreed on both counts!" exclaimed Nevada quickly. "I'd love to have that pistol of yours. It's worth the five hundred all by itself."

The barkeep took the eight hundred dollars and put a bottle of whiskey on top of the money. Jess took another sip of his beer and turned to face Nevada when everyone in the bar was startled by the words that came from the batwing doors of the saloon.

"Get ready to die, mister!"

CHAPTER TWENTY

The man standing in the doorway to the saloon looked to be about fifty. He had a bushy beard and a mustache and looked like he hadn't had a bath or a new set of clothes in several years. Jess didn't recognize him, but he knew for sure the man was talking to him and not Nevada or anyone else in the bar.

"I said get ready to die!" the man repeated, as he walked into the center of the saloon. Jess saw the man had a gun tucked in his belt in the front of his belly. The gun looked as if it was used more for pounding nails than for shooting. He glanced at Nevada and then turned to face the old man. Neither Jess nor Nevada saw this man as any threat.

"Mister, I don't know who you are and I have no quarrel with you," said Jess. "What's your beef with me?"

"I ain't got no beef with ya! I just need the money!" hollered the man.

"What money?"

"The three thousand dollars that old man Carter put up for your head, dead or alive. I need it. I ain't had a good meal or a new set of clothes in three years. I've been riding a sorry sack of a mule 'cause I lost my horse and whatever few nuggets of gold I had left from years of prospecting work to some damn thieves. I figure I ain't got much to live for anyway. I heard about the money Carter had on your head and figured that I might as well go for it. Either way, my suffering will be over with. And right about now, I don't much care which way it ends."

"How are you going to collect the money when you don't have a gun?" asked Jess, somewhat sarcastically.

"I got me a gun," the man said defensively.

"Where?"

"Right here," he said pointing at the shabby-looking pistol in his front waist. "What the hell you think this here is?"

"That thing?" said Jess, with a look of amusement. "It looks more like a hammer. What are you going to do, throw it at me?"

"Sir," Nevada politely said to the old prospector, "Mr. Williams and I have a business proposition to complete first. You've interrupted us and I would suggest you wait until we are finished."

The prospector kept his gaze on Jess, but now he recognized Nevada Jackson and he knew of his reputation. He began to have a sinking feeling. He took a few steps back and began to rethink his plan. He knew he was outgunned by both of these two. His senses began to return and he sat down at a table. When he did, the old pistol slipped out of his belt and fell onto the wooden floor with a thud. They all watched as one side of the grips fell off the gun. The old prospector just gazed up at Jess with a sorrowful look.

Nevada turned to the barkeep and told him to get the old man a drink on him. The prospector asked for beer. The barkeep handed it to the kid who worked there and the kid took it over to his table.

Nevada then turned back to Jess. "Well, it seems that if I win this thing, I can collect the money on the bar, your fancy pistol and holster and three thousand dollars from this Carter fellow," said an enthusiastic Nevada. "It seems to be my lucky day."

"Only if you win," claimed Jess. "And that three thousand dollars is just blood money Carter put up to have me murdered. It's not an official bounty. He's just pissed off because I killed his only son in a fair fight."

"That don't matter; if I win, I might as well collect it. If I didn't, it wouldn't make you any less dead."

"Well, I guess talking you out of this is out of the question?"

"Hell, I was ready to face you for the three hundred dollars and your pistol and holster. Now with three thousand dollars added to the pot, I mean, who could walk away from that?"

"Someone who wants to live."

"You're assuming that you'll beat me."

"I'm not assuming anything."

"So, you're saying I might beat you?"

"Well, I might drop my gun or something like that," replied Jess, smiling.

"A man with a sense of humor," said Nevada with a grin. "I like that in a man."

"Then why push this?"

"Did you forget about the three thousand dollars?"

"I didn't forget."

"Well, neither did I."

"So, you're still going to push this?"

"I would say you have a good grasp of the obvious. Now, since I made the challenge, I think it's only fair that you get the chance to draw first."

"I never draw first. Besides, this isn't my choice. If you want this fight, you'll have to start it."

What happened next was another lesson that Jess would never forget. Nevada feigned a move so slight that only Jess saw it. It was so slight that it couldn't really be called a movement. Jess realized in that small fraction of a second that Nevada was attempting to get Jess to draw first. Jess couldn't figure if it was out of some sense of fairness or some way to trick him into stalling his draw so that Nevada had an advantage. When it happened, Jess almost fell for it.

Instead, he turned the tables on Nevada and did the same to him, feigning a draw and when Nevada saw it, he went for his gun. Nevada was fast. He had outdrawn a dozen men and had never taken a bullet yet. Some of the men he had outdrawn were seasoned gunslingers who were fast, which was why Nevada was so shocked at what happened next. After he felt the thud in his chest and looked down at the bloodstain beginning to form on his shirt, he noticed he had his hand on the butt of his pistol, but it had not moved out from the holster.

He turned his gaze to Jess with a look of disbelief in his eyes. "Damn. I didn't even have a chance, did I?" he asked.

"Now it's you who has a good grasp of the obvious. I guess things just don't always work out the way you plan them."

"I guess not," replied Nevada, a hint of a smile on his lips. He took his right hand off his pistol and went to pick up his whiskey for one last drink. He never tasted that last drop. Nevada slumped to the floor, dead.

Paul, the barkeep, who never had much to say and was not easily impressed, spoke up. "I've seen lots of men go at it in here and I've seen a few dozen gunfights in my lifetime, but I've never seen anything like that. You ain't normal." He went back to cleaning glasses.

One of the men sitting by the bar was the town's preacher. He turned to Jess with a dreadful look in his eyes. "I seen it, too, and I don't believe it neither, son," the preacher said, looking right at Jess, "I don't know who you are, but Paul here is right. You ain't normal. Maybe you're a soul incarnate who's been brought back to this world by God Almighty himself or maybe you've been sent here by the devil to do his dirty work. Whichever it is, you're not welcome in my church."

The preacher stood up, picked up his Bible and walked out, not saying another word. Jess said nothing to the preacher. Instead, he turned his attention to the prospector who was still sitting down, holding his glass with both hands so that Jess would see he wasn't even thinking about going for his gun, which was still lying on the floor under the table.

"I hope you're still not going to try to collect that blood money, old man," said Jess.

"No way in hell," replied the prospector. "I saw what I saw, and my mama, whoever she was, didn't bear no fool. I was just desperate and on my last straw when I came in here. I'll be glad to leave here the same way, if'n you'll let me."

"Well, I have to think about that for a minute," he said curiously.

The prospector moaned a little. "Damn it," he exclaimed. "I just knew when I opened my eyes this morning that it was going to be a bad day."

"Really? Why is that?" asked Jess.

"Because I was able to open my eyes."

"Well, maybe it won't be such a bad day after all," said Jess. The prospector looked somewhat confused. He still wasn't sure what Jess was going to do. Jess picked up the eight hundred dollars from the bar and counted out three hundred dollars. He walked over to the old prospector, who wouldn't move his hands from his glass, and sat down at the table with him. "What's your name?" he asked.

"My name is Dusty Slim. I got that name 'cause I don't particularly like baths and I get kinda dusty. I also don't have a chance to eat very often, as I ain't never got any money." He finally took his hands from his glass and patted his chest a little and some dust flew off the old man's clothes.

"Well, Dusty, I want you to take this three hundred dollars and use it to get yourself a new start." Jess threw the money on the table. "And, I want you to promise me you won't try anything that stupid again. Otherwise, I'm making a bad investment in you. "Besides," he said, glancing down at the sorry-looking pistol on the floor, "that thing would probably backfire and blow your damn head off even if you did get off a shot. You best let the barkeep sweep it up and get rid of it."

Dusty wasn't quite sure what to say. He had come into the saloon to try to kill Jess for the money and now Jess was giving him money for a new start. This was not a normal day for Dusty Slim. It seemed his never-ending bad luck might have finally changed for the better.

"Mr. Williams, no one's ever done anything like this for me before. I don't rightly know how to thank ya. I need the money real bad so I'll take it, but I promise to pay you back every penny and more. I know a secret place that I'm sure still has some gold in it. Not enough to get rich, but enough to pay you back and let me finally quit mining. I'm right thankful, Mr. Williams, mighty thankful."

"You're welcome, Dusty. You tell the man at the livery down the street that I said to give you Nevada's horse, saddle and rifle. That is if he had one, and I'm sure he did. Leave the saddlebags or any other belongings though. Tell the stable man I'll be along to claim those later. Anyone gives you a problem, you let me know about it."

"Yes, sir, Mr. Williams, yes, sir," Dusty happily agreed as he headed out the door before Jess could change his mind.

"You're gonna claim Nevada's belongings? You sure that's right?" asked the barkeep.

Jess looked at the very dead Nevada and pursed his lips. "He sure ain't going to need them anymore. And besides, that man lying there was going to kill me just as dead as he is right now," explained Jess. "If that had happened, what do you think would've happened to my belongings? You think all my things would just disappear? The way I look at it, his things belong to me now, his money, his horse, his gun and anything else of value he's got. Hell, if right had anything to do with it, I wouldn't be here today, and I wouldn't have had to kill this man. I imagine there is some right in the world, but it hasn't been hanging around me for quite some time now."

"Fine by me," replied the barkeep, "but Nevada had a lot of friends and a brother who just might not agree with your way of thinking, if you know what I mean."

"I'll deal with that when it happens."

Jess removed Nevada's gun from his body and found another two hundred dollars in his pockets. He also removed a beautiful gold pocket watch from his front pocket. Jess didn't have a watch—he never had much use for one—but this one was beautifully engraved on the front. He decided it was time to have one.

Sheriff Clancy walked into the saloon and looked at the dead body. "Damn," he said. "You took down Nevada Jackson."

"He sure did," interjected the barkeep. "Nevada never even got his gun out."

The sheriff got his two deputies to take Nevada's body over to the undertaker. Sheriff Clancy looked at Jess. "You know he's got a brother," he said in a cautionary tone.

"So I've heard."

"He's not going to be happy about this. And he taught Nevada everything he knew about slinging lead."

"Evidently not enough."

"Well, there's no bounty on him, at least not that I know of," said Clancy.

"Sheriff, I tried to talk him out of this. It was his decision, not mine."

"Hey, I got no problem with it. As far as I'm concerned, it was a fair fight. I guess it won't be the last one today."

"Why's that, Sheriff?"

"Several new toughs came into town a little bit ago," he replied miserably. "Looked like trouble for sure. They went over to Jake's saloon down the street, but they'll end up in here before long, especially once they find out you're here. Sure as shit, at least one of them will be looking to add to his status by taking you down. You have time to ride out if you want to."

"You know I can't do that, Sheriff. Taggert didn't happen to be one of them, did he?"

"Nope. Never seen any of these fellows, but I've sure seen their kind before. I aim to check my wanted posters for their faces. I wouldn't be surprised to see at least one of them on one."

The sheriff walked out and Jess finished his beer. He thanked the barkeep, gave him a nice tip, slung Nevada's gun and holster over his left shoulder and walked down to the stables. Jess actually felt a little bad about killing Nevada even though he had forced him into the fight. Nevada wasn't a cold-blooded killer; he was just another bounty hunter out to make some money and a name for himself.

He walked into the stables and called out Ted's name. There was no answer. Jess was about to turn around when he heard some moaning coming from the back of the stable. He walked over to where the sound was coming from and saw Ted Watkins lying flat on his back in a pile of hay. He had been severely beaten. Jess grabbed a water pail and took it over to him. He dipped a rag into the water and placed it on his forehead. After a minute or so, Ted came around and was startled at seeing someone leaning over him.

"Easy, Ted," said Jess. "Just stay down there for a minute and get your wits about you before you try to stand up." Jess saw several knots on his forehead and at least a dozen cuts and bruises, along with a really bad gash just below the hairline over the right eye. Someone had really worked him over good.

"Who the hell did this to you?" he asked, after Ted seemed to have shaken some of the fog from his brain.

"That damn bunch that came into town a little bit ago. I told them it was extra for the good grain for their horses and they started to argue with me. They were just looking for a reason and before I knew it, one of them hit me with the grain bucket. I punched the bastard square in the nose and he started bleeding like a stuck pig and that pissed off his friends. They all jumped me and beat the tar out of me. I could've taken the one guy, but I didn't have a chance against all of them," he explained.

"Well, at least you were smart enough not to try using that pistol."

"Hell, I'm not afraid of any fight, but I'm no fool either. They'd have shot me down like a dog. I've been there. I've seen their kind before. They make a life out of looking for trouble and trying to find a reason to kill someone."

"Well maybe this will make you feel better," said Jess, as he gave Nevada's pistol and holster to him.

"What's this for?"

"I took this off Nevada Jackson. I figure I don't really need another gun and since you seem to want to wear one, you might as well have a nice one."

"I can't keep this. Nevada will..." Ted's words cut off as his brain began to fire on all cylinders and he remembered the old prospector coming in to claim Nevada's horse and rifle, but not before telling him about the gunfight.

Ted stood up and shook the cobwebs out of his head. "So, you really did outdraw Nevada Jackson?"

"You're holding his pistol and holster," Jess replied clearly.

"Damn," replied Ted, rubbing his forehead.

"I'm going to head back to the saloon, but I wanted to ask you for a favor," said Jess.

"Name it. I figure I owe you one."

"Let me know when Blake Taggert comes back to town."

"You got it, Jess. And thanks a lot for the pistol and holster. They're mighty nice," he said examining them.

"You're welcome. I think it's one of the nicest ones I've seen, except for mine, that is. Now go see someone about that bad cut over your eye."

Ted nodded and walked out right behind Jess, but not before putting on Nevada's gun and holster. Jess walked back into Little's Drinks. As soon as he stepped inside the door, he saw trouble in the form of five men standing at the bar drinking and slamming their glasses down on the counter. All five of them were wearing guns, but only two of the men had them tied down low and tight on their legs. Jess wondered if these were the men who had beaten Ted Watkins earlier.

He walked up to the far right end of the bar and ordered a beer. Four of the five men didn't pay Jess any attention at first, but one of the men in the group did. The man had watched Jess walk into the saloon and he was still watching him. Jess didn't return the stare, but was well aware of it and had already taken his hammer strap off. The man turned back to his other four friends and they suddenly became quiet. Then they all seemed to turn so they could see Jess. They drank quietly and spoke among themselves for a while, all the time glancing over at Jess. The five men were distracted when Ted Watkins walked into the saloon. The men smiled at Ted as he walked over to the bar and stood next to Jess.

"Well, lookee here," one of them said. "It's the little stable boy. You come to tell us you done raised the boardin' fee on our horses?"

"Naw," said another one of the men, "he just likes the beatin' we gave him and he's come back for another."

Ted ordered a beer and was just about to respond when the one who had been carefully watching Jess spoke.

This man was the leader of the group and his name was Ike. "Now, boys, we done gave the stable boy here enough exercise for the day, don't ya think?" he asked. "I mean, look at that big ole bandage on his forehead. I bet he's got a real nice cut under that thing." The other four men laughed at that.

"Besides," Ike continued, "I'd like to know more about his friend there at the end of the bar. He's been ignoring us since he came in here and I don't think I like that. Are you shy and hiding behind the stable boy there?"

Ted looked at Jess, who gave him a look that Ted understood. He motioned his head to tell Ted to move away from the bar, which he did. Ted moved about ten feet and stood next to a table.

Jess took another sip of his beer and slowly turned to the men and responded to the question very simply. "Neither," he said.

The response from Jess took the man a little by surprise. He wasn't used to getting a simple one-word answer from someone and it riled him a little, although it didn't show on the man's face.

"You ain't one for carrying on much of a conversation, are ya?" asked Ike.

"Nope."

"So is it that you don't like to carry on a conversation or is it that you just don't want to carry on a conversation with me?"

"Neither," replied Jess. The man laughed for a moment until he finally realized what Jess had answered. That really riled him up and this time it showed in his facial expression.

"You smart-ass punk!" hollered Ike. "Don't you know who you're talking to?"

"Nope, and I really don't care either."

"You'd best care, mister," Ike spat angrily.

"Why?"

"Because I'm Ike Hardy. I was puttin' men in their graves before you were a twinkle in the eyes of the half dozen men you call your daddy! Besides, you ain't even a man yet, just a young punk who thinks he is."

Ike's face had turned two shades rosier now and the other four men spread out. The one man who had his gun tied down low and tight was looking right at Ted Watkins. Jess knew that he would have to hit that man if he wanted to save Ted.

Ike took a step forward. "Well, smart-ass, why don't we find out how good you are with that fancy shootin' iron you got there?"

"If you want to find out, all you have to do is grab for yours," said Jess. "That should be about the last thing you'll remember."

Ike went for his gun. The first thing he felt was his thumb beginning to put pressure on the hammer of his Colt Peacemaker as he went to jerk the gun from his holster. The second thing he felt was a heavy thump in the middle of his chest from Jess's first shot. Before he fell to the floor of the saloon, he saw three flashes from Jess's gun barrel. It seemed as if it was one continuous blast, but it wasn't. Jess's second shot hit the man who was eyeing Watkins and his third shot hit the man to Ike's left. Ted Watkins had just drawn his gun and had it cocked when the other two men in the group raised their hands high in the air. "We give! Don't shoot! Don't shoot!"

Ted Watkins was standing there in disbelief at what he had just witnessed. He had watched in the blink of an eye as Jess had taken out three men and was ready to shoot a fourth one and not one of the men had cleared leather yet. His mouth was open, but he couldn't speak. He slowly put his gun down at his side, but didn't holster it.

Jess continued to keep his gun cocked and ready. "You men take those gun belts off," demanded Jess.

"Okay. Sure, mister, whatever you say. Just don't shoot," one of the two men said. Both men unbuckled their gun belts and let them drop to the floor. "Okay, now what?"

"Well, I would suggest you men leave town immediately. Don't bother taking your friends' horses with you. I'll be taking care of them since they're mine now." Jess stated plainly.

"You gonna keep their horses?" asked the other man incredulously.

"Shut the hell up, you fool," replied the first man. "Let's get our asses out of town while we still have them."

The two men almost ran over to the stables and got on their horses and rode out of town at a dead run. Ted Watkins finally put his gun in the holster and sat down. Jess got two beers from the bar, sat down at Ted's table and slid one of the beers across the table toward him. Ted gulped it down and Jess noticed his hand was shaking a little.

"Mr. Williams, I don't know what to say. I'd be dead right now if it weren't for you. Are you for real?" Ted asked, still somewhat shocked at what he had just witnessed.

"I guess so, at least the last time I checked anyway. What the hell did you come in here for? You must've known these men were in here. Are you trying to get yourself killed?"

Ted shook his head, still stunned a little by what had happened. "No, I wasn't even thinking of that," he replied eagerly. "I was just doing what you asked me to do."

"What do you mean?" asked Jess with a confused look on his face.

"Blake Taggert is back in town and he's already heard there was someone looking for him," he explained. "He's down at Harry's Place right now and he's got a friend with him. I was just coming to let you know he was back, like you asked me to do."

Jess's eyes turned darker as he slowly stood up. "Well, I guess I'll have to go have me a drink over at Harry's. Ted, get these men's guns and whatever money they have on them and take it over to your place for me, okay?" Ted nodded.

Jess left Paul a tip and started to walk out. He was at the doorway when Ted stopped him with a question. "Jess, I got a hunch that Blake Taggert is in a whole heap of trouble, ain't he?"

"You are absolutely right about that," said Jess, as he walked out. Ted turned to the barkeep and asked for another beer. The barkeep poured him another beer and walked it over to the table.

"Well, Paul, I guess you got some cleaning up to do here," said Ted, looking at the three bodies lying on the floor.

"I guess so. I figure Harry's going to be doing some mop work in a few minutes himself."

"Yeah, but I got a real strong hunch that it won't be any of Jess Williams' blood on the floor once it's over."

"If I didn't know any better, I'd think you were one of them mind readers," said the barkeep.

Jess stood there in the street for a moment thinking about everything that had happened so far. He looked up at the sky. It was a beautiful afternoon. The sun was shining and the sky was a deep, rich blue with just a hint of clouds here and there. He reloaded his pistol as he began walking toward Harry's Place. Yes, he said to himself, this is a good day to finish it. He slowly walked straight down the middle of the street. His thoughts turned to his little sister Samantha and what Blake Taggert had done to her. Blake Taggert's final destiny was finally coming to him and it had a name—Jess Williams.

CHAPTER TWENTY-ONE

As Jess walked down to Harry's Place, he saw a few men run-ning for Little's Drinks. He figured they must've heard the gunshots and wanted to see what happened. He saw Sheriff Clancy heading toward him from the direction of Harry's.

"Jess, I heard gunshots," said Sheriff Clancy. "I suppose there's some more business for the undertaker back at Little's?" Clancy fell in step with Jess, heading back toward Harry's.

"You're an observant man, Sheriff," Jess replied. "Three men down and for no real reason other than they thought they had to prove something."

"Prove what?"

"That they were tough, but now they're dead," he replied matter-of-factly, as he continued walking while keeping his eyes straight down the street, looking directly at Harry's.

"I suppose you're headin' down to Harry's?"

"You're staying right up with my way of thinking, Sheriff."

"Guess you know that Taggert is down there, huh?" the sheriff, asked already knowing the answer.

"I heard."

"I guess there ain't much chance of talking you outa this, is there?"

"Not a chance, Sheriff."

"Well, you watch yourself. He's got a friend with him and he's a mean one. Don't trust him. He'll draw on you when you ain't lookin'."

Jess stopped suddenly and looked at the sheriff. "Is this the man you said left with Taggert?" asked Jess intensely. "The man you called Sloan?"

"No, I know this man. His name is Winn Deets. He's a hired killer and a no-good sumbitch."

"Thanks for the warning, Sheriff. I assume that you aren't going to involve yourself in this?"

"Now you're staying up with my way of thinking," responded Sheriff Clancy. The sheriff let out a little chuckle that he quickly suppressed. "You be careful, Jess." The sheriff headed back toward Little's Drinks and Jess started back toward Harry's Place.

Jess reached Harry's, stopped outside the saloon and stood in the street looking at the place. He wondered why the place was called Harry's. He understood why Little's Drinks was called Little's because the owner was short and his last name was Little. He thought about calling Taggert out into the street to face him, but decided instead to go ahead and walk right in. He knew they were waiting for him and might be setting him up for an ambush. Jess stepped up onto the boardwalk and before entering the saloon, he pulled the sawed-off shotgun from his back sling. He used the barrel of the shotgun to push the batwing doors open.

He walked in and stopped just two feet past the doorway. He noticed there was quite a crowd in the place. At least twenty locals were sitting around at tables and standing at the bar. The half dozen or so men at the bar were in two groups. Four of them were standing in the middle of the bar and two men were standing at the far left end of the bar. The two men at the left end of the bar were the men he had to deal with. They slowly turned around to look at who had come in. Taggert and Jess locked eyes from the instant they looked at one another. Jess couldn't forget that face, even if he had wanted to.

Taggert did not recognize Jess and had no idea who he was or what he wanted with him. All he knew was that someone in town was looking for him and this must be the man. Jess continued to keep an eye on everyone in the room, but his gaze never left

Taggert. The place was almost silent, with just a whisper here and there. Everyone had noticed the double-barreled shotgun and no one in the place wanted a taste of that. Jess very slowly worked himself around and behind several tables, keeping the wall at his backside, making his way to the far right end of the bar. The barkeep walked over to him. The barkeep's face was covered with thick hair. His hair hung down to his shoulders and his beard almost reached down to his waist. The only part of the barkeep's face that showed was two openings for his eyes. Even his eyebrows were unusually bushy. Another mystery solved, Jess thought to himself.

"Welcome to Harry's, Mr. Williams," said the barkeep. "I own this place. I'd like to buy you your first drink. What'll you have?" Jess carefully placed the shotgun on top of the bar, making sure that it was still pointed in the direction of Taggert and the other man with him. Jess asked for a beer, which Harry quickly poured. A few of the other locals who were close to the bar slowly moved away. That left Jess looking straight down the now empty bar at Blake Taggert and Winn Deets.

Jess took a few sips of his beer and stared at Taggert, remembering that day they'd first met. Jess wondered how any man could be as evil as he was. He was certain in his mind that Taggert was the one responsible for the grisly murders recently in Red Rock. Taggert said nothing for several minutes. He wasn't really worried, but he wondered who this kid was who was gunning for him with a shotgun on the bar and a strange-looking pistol and holster. Taggert knew he had committed many crimes. Maybe he had done something to this kid. The only way to find out was to ask.

"I understand you've been waiting for me," said Taggert. "Do I know you?"

Jess didn't respond right away. He wasn't sure if it was because he wanted to savor the moment now that he finally found the last of the three men who killed his family, or if he wanted Taggert to remember who he was. Here he was, his life changed forever in such a dramatic way, and this man couldn't even remember him.

"You don't remember me, do you?" asked Jess.

"I can't say I do," replied Taggert. "What's your name?"

"Jess Williams."

Taggert still had a puzzled look on his face. "Sorry, I don't know any Jess Williams."

"Maybe you remember a farm back in Black Creek, Kansas," said Jess.

Taggert's body language changed slightly and Jess immediately picked up on it. "Never been to Black Creek, Kansas," replied Taggert, knowing he wasn't telling the truth.

"Maybe you remember a woman hanging from a doorway, all cut up," Jess pushed, his voice getting slightly louder.

"I still have no idea about what you're talking about," Taggert lied.

"Remember a man shot several times behind a plow out in a field? Do you remember that?" he asked as the anger started to well up inside him. Winn Deets had not said a word up to now, but he was getting aggravated and it showed.

"Hey, kid," snapped Deets. "I don't know who you are and I don't much give a shit. Why don't you just haul your ass out of here while you're still walking upright?"

"Mister, I'm not walking out of here until that man standing next to you is dead. If you want to die with him, that's your decision. I don't much care either way." Jess knew Deets was pissed. He also knew Deets was ready to draw, just as soon as he felt Jess wasn't watching him closely enough.

Jess turned his attention back to Taggert while keeping a close watch on Deets. "Maybe you might remember a little seven-year-old girl who you raped and murdered by shooting her in the forehead," Jess pushed further. "Do you remember her? Remember a young boy you met out on the road about an hour before you murdered an entire family? That boy was me and the family you murdered was my family. Surely any man who could commit such brutal acts would remember them. I know that I can still see it in my mind like it was yesterday."

Taggert remembered very well what Jess was talking about. He just wasn't going to admit to any of it. He especially remembered the little girl. He had enjoyed that. "You've got me mixed up with someone else," said Taggert.

"You're a damn liar, but I guess that shouldn't surprise me," Jess countered angrily. "I suppose you ain't going to admit to murdering that family outside of town right here either. That was you, wasn't it?"

"Maybe the man who murdered your family is the same man who murdered that family here in Red Rock," replied Taggert, smiling to himself inside at the thought of the young girl he had so brutally raped and murdered.

"You're finally getting it right. That same man is you."

"I'm telling you, you've got it all wrong, kid," contested Taggert. "I never murdered anyone, ever, especially in this town." Taggert was getting a little nervous now as some of the men in the saloon started whispering between themselves about the murdered family.

"I've got a message from two friends of yours," said Jess.

"Who might that be?" Taggert asked, quizzically.

"Your two friends Randy Hastings and Hank Beard."

"What was the message?"

"That they'd see you in hell."

"Hell?"

"Yeah, that's where I sent them and that's where you're going next," he replied bluntly.

"And who's going to send me there?" asked Taggert, a contemptuous look washing across his face.

"You're looking at him."

"You?" he said sarcastically.

"Do I have to repeat myself?"

"And you think you're good enough?"

"You're about to find out."

"Kid, I've been drawing a pistol damn near as long as you've been breathing air," spat Taggert. "What makes you think you can take me?"

ROBERT J. THOMAS

"Only one way to find out for sure," Jess said threateningly.

Deets had been listening to all of this and he was getting more and more agitated by the moment. He finally spoke up. "You might think you can take Taggert, but you can't take the both of us at the same time," he claimed boldly.

Jess glanced at Deets. "You throwing in with him?"

"Damn right."

"Then you'll die right next to him."

"You gonna use that damn fire breather you got on the bar?" asked Deets, nervously looking at the double-barreled shotgun on the bar.

Jess smiled. "Naw, I don't need it," he said, cocking his head a little and grinning somewhat evilly.

Jess knew that Deets would draw first. He watched Deets moving his right hand closer to the butt of his pistol. He could see a bead of sweat dripping down Deets' left temple. Taggert began to move his left hand down to the butt of his pistol and he was watching Deets, trying to time it so they both drew at the same time. As soon as Taggert knew Deets was moving, Taggert's left hand went for his gun. Jess's first shot hit Deets in the stomach. Jess fanned his second shot and hit Taggert in the right shoulder, spinning him around a full turn, throwing him down on a table flat on his back, his gun flying across the room. Jess's third shot hit Deets in the chest, punching a hole in his heart and putting him down for good. Jess wanted Deets down and out of the picture so that he could put his full attention toward killing Taggert, slowly.

Jess watched the room to make sure no one else was going to be involved. He saw Taggert still lying on the table, but on his side now, holding his right shoulder with his left hand. Jess noticed two things simultaneously: a little dust falling from the upstairs railing and a gunshot going off in the direction of the swinging doors of the saloon. He quickly looked over and saw Ted Watkins. He was holding Nevada Jackson's still smoking pistol in his hand. He heard a thud against the floor upstairs and realized that Taggert had hidden a third man in a room upstairs to ambush Jess. He nodded to Ted.

"Figured I owed you as much," said Ted. "Besides, I had to try it out."

Jess looked at Taggert. He was now standing upright, his buttocks leaning against the edge of the table he had fallen on. He was bleeding, but he wasn't dying, at least not yet. Jess put a slug into Taggert's left kneecap. Taggert fell away from the table, hit the ground and rolled over holding himself up with his left hand and his right knee facing away from Jess.

"Damn it! I ain't got no gun! You can't shoot an unarmed man!" he hollered.

"Is that right? Let's see about that." Jess fired another round, this one ripping into Taggert's right buttock, the force rolling him over onto his back. Taggert pushed and wiggled himself up against the wall.

"You bastard!" Taggert exclaimed. "You can't just kill me in cold blood."

"You and your dead friend both reached for iron before I did."

"Yeah, but this ain't right!"

"Maybe you should have been thinking that way when you were raping and killing my little sister," refuted Jess. "Besides, who's going to stop me?"

"I know a lot of people in this town," spat Taggert, as he looked at some of the men in the saloon "You can't just let him kill me! Stop him! Go get the sheriff!"

Surprisingly, no one moved. Maybe they were too afraid of Jess or maybe they were beginning to believe Taggert might be guilty of what Jess was accusing him of. Jess had one more round in his pistol. He put that round into Taggert's left elbow, tearing it up so badly that his left arm just dangled to the floor. He was bleeding profusely. Jess quickly reloaded his pistol and put it back in his holster. He reached behind and pulled out his knife. He flipped it in the air and grabbed it by the blade and threw it right at Taggert, hitting him in the groin, pinning his gonads to the floor of the saloon. Taggert let out another scream and had an excruciating look of pain contorted on his face. "You ain't supposed to hit a man in his privates!"

"Now, where have I heard that before?" asked Jess curiously. "Oh, yeah, your friend who helped you murder my family. Now you'll have even more in common to talk about while you're in hell together. That one was for my mother," Jess said, coldly.

He walked over to Taggert's gun and picked it up. "I figure this is the pistol you used to put a bullet into my little sister's head," Jess said with disgust. "I think it's only fair to finish you off with the same gun, don't you?"

"Just do it, you bastard! I can't take any more! Finish me!" screamed Taggert, writhing in pain.

"Oh, I'll finish you, of that you can be sure," he promised. "But you know all this gun fighting and excitement has made me a little thirsty. I think I need a nice sip of my beer."

"You go to hell, you bastard!" Taggert yelled, as he watched Jess walk back to the bar where Harry had set down a fresh glass of beer. Jess, keeping his eyes on Taggert, set Taggert's gun on the bar and picked up the glass and took a nice, long sip. He wanted Taggert to suffer as much as he could. Taggert tried to remove the knife that had his gonads pinned to the floor, but he was losing what little strength he had from the loss of blood. Jess walked back to Taggert and just looked at him moaning in pain. It would make most men feel a little bad, but Jess felt no pity for him, not after what he had done to his family.

"You ready to meet your friends, Beard and Hastings?"

"Kiss my ass, you son of a whore!" shrieked Taggert, bloody spittle flying from his lips.

"Just make sure that you give Beard and Hastings my regards," whispered Jess, as he placed the barrel of Taggert's gun about two inches from his forehead, just above his nose.

As Jess pulled the trigger, he closed his eyes and all the events leading up to this point flashed through his brain. When he opened his eyes, Taggert was lying against a fallen chair, his head half blown off. It's over, Jess thought to himself, it's finally over.

Jess hung his head and closed his eyes for what seemed an eternity, but in reality, it was only about ten seconds. He threw the gun down on the floor in front of him and retrieved his knife, wiping the blood off on Taggert's pants. Then, he walked back over to the bar, picked up his shotgun and put it back in its sling over his shoulder and downed his beer. Harry refilled it quickly and Jess took a long pull from it. Ted Watkins walked over to him and ordered a beer and took a drink.

"Well, I guess you finished what you came here to do," Ted remarked, looking at the dead body.

"I guess so. It seems strange though, as if it's not really finished. What do you think that means, Ted?"

"I don't think you're finished, Mr. Williams."

"What do you mean?"

"There are a lot more Blake Taggerts out there."

"Yeah, and someone has to deal with them," he said, realizing his calling. "I suppose it might as well be me."

"I can't think of anyone better suited for the job," said Ted confidently.

Jess finished his beer and thanked Ted for his help. He told Ted to take the guns and holsters back to the stables. Jess checked both men for any money. To his surprise, he found over one thousand dollars between the two. He thought that odd. Most men were lucky to walk around with ten dollars in their pockets. He headed over to the sheriff's office to check on any bounty that might be available on any of the men he had killed that day. Five men, he thought to himself, I've killed five men today and it's not even dark out yet.

Sheriff Clancy was sitting outside his office. He had heard the shots and had already gotten word of how Jess had killed Taggert and Deets. Word traveled fast in this town. "I was hoping to see you again, Jess," the sheriff said, standing up.

"You had doubts?"

"No, not really," he replied. "Come on in."

Jess followed him into his office and the sheriff picked up a wanted poster he had on his desk. "Seems that one of those three you killed over at Little's had a bounty of two hundred dollars on his head."

"Well, I'll sure take it, Sheriff. This bounty-hunting business pays pretty well."

"It does for the ones who stay alive, but not too many of them do," cautioned Clancy.

"Sheriff, I found over a thousand dollars on Blake Taggert and that Deets fellow. It's been a highly profitable day, that's for sure."

"A thousand dollars? Really?"

"Well, it's about fifty dollars more than a thousand, why?"

"I just got a wire from a small town about a three-day ride from here. It seems two brothers who ran a ranch together along with their wives were murdered last week. Both women were raped and killed. Luckily, their two children were staying with relatives and not home when it happened. The brothers kept their earnings at the ranch. One of the brother's uncles says they had almost a thousand dollars saved up to buy some more cattle. I wonder if it was Taggert and Deets who took the money and killed those poor folks," the sheriff stated.

"That would be my guess, Sheriff. I'll make sure the money gets returned to the two children. I'll have Ted Watkins take the money to them personally, along with a message that the men most likely responsible for it are dead," he said pensively.

"That's mighty generous of you, Mr. Williams. I don't believe I've met a nicer fella or one who killed five men in one day either."

Jess thought about what Sheriff Clancy had just said. He didn't know what to say in response so he just nodded to the sheriff and walked out. He walked to the livery and told Ted what to do with the thousand dollars. Ted promised to deliver the money right away. He sold the horses to Ted and the guns to a local gunsmith that Ted knew. He shook Ted's hand and said goodbye. He climbed up in the saddle and nudged his horse into a walk. As he rode out of Red Rock, he thought about the men he had killed and how much money he had collected in return. The way he figured it, he was a little richer and he had a pretty nice watch to boot. Not bad, he thought.

As he turned Gray's head back toward Black Creek, Kansas, his thoughts turned to the three men who had murdered his family.

August of 1878 was coming to a close and it had been over two years since that horrible day. He could still remember all the details vividly, too vividly. He also remembered killing each one of the three men responsible just as strongly. His thoughts turned to Blake Taggert lying on the floor of Harry's Place in a pool of blood, all shot up with Jess's knife sticking out of his groin. Anyone who looked really closely at Jess would almost catch a slight hint of a smile.

The ride back to Black Creek, Kansas, was a long and somber one. Jess stopped only a few times in some small towns to get supplies. His visits were short and for the most part uneventful. He finally arrived back at his family's ranch about an hour before sundown. He sat down by the grave markers under the big oak tree and told his ma, pa and sister they could rest in peace now because the men who had murdered them were all dead. He noticed someone had been putting flowers on the graves, probably Sara and Jim, he thought. He would go into town to visit them in the morning. It would be nice to see them again. He couldn't bring himself to sleep in the house, although he took a stroll through it. He peeked inside each of the bedrooms and tried to imagine his folks sleeping quietly. He glanced at the floor where his ma was hanging that day and could still see the fading dark spot from all the blood. He cried silently, tears running down his face. It was the first time he cried since he had left home. He swore it would be his last time.

He bunked down next to the gravesites that night with the big oak tree at his back. There was a slight chill in the night air and he pulled a light blanket over himself. As he lay there, his thoughts turned to his brother, Tim Sloan. He needed to find him and ask him how he knew Blake Taggert. He needed to find out if his brother knew what Taggert had done. If his brother was a killer and a bad man like Taggert, Jess would deal with him in the same way he dealt with other bad men, brother or not. He decided that would be his next mission in life: find his brother and talk with him. He would start out by talking some more with Sara and Jim, but that was for tomorrow. Tonight, he would again sleep with the family he loved so dearly and wished he could be with once more. He would lie here next to their graves. Somehow he hoped that his dreams would take him to them so he could see and talk to them once more.

As he fell off to sleep, he imagined he was a sheriff in a small town and he was facing off with two bad guys and...

That night, Jess had good dreams.

EPILOGUE

It had been four years since Dave Walters' new pistol and holster had mysteriously vanished from his locked gun safe. He had continued to compete in fast draw competitions and he was finally in the high twenties, but he still hadn't won the elusive title of Fast Draw Champion. He had continued to use his old pistol and holster, not even thinking about saving up enough money to have Bob Graham build him another one. Truth be known, he was almost afraid to. He sometimes felt that it was some kind of omen having the gun vanish the way it did. It had scared the living hell out of him. The night it vanished he hardly slept. For months afterward, he just kept looking at the gun locker as if some evil spirit would come out of it and take him next. Of course, with the way his wife had been carrying on about how he'd lost a two-thousand-dollar gun and holster and she still hadn't gotten any furniture, maybe that wouldn't be such a bad thing.

He didn't really think about it all that much now, only when he had idle time on his hands, like right now. He was traveling with his wife, Jean, heading for Yellowstone National Park. After coming out of Granite Pass, the road to Cody, Wyoming, was a little boring compared to the drive through the pass and that gave him some time to start thinking about that day. He still couldn't figure out how it could've happened. After all, he was sitting right in the next room watching television and he could see the gun cabinet through the bedroom door. Sure, he had gotten up a few times to get another beer and to use the bathroom, but those things took all of sixty seconds. Someone would've had to enter the bedroom from the window, break into the gun locker, remove the gun and holster, close the locker and make it out of the bedroom in one minute. Even with the combination to the safe it would take at least fifteen seconds just to spin the dial. There had been no marks or any signs of forced entry on the locker. No, it had to have just vanished into thin air, taken by some means not known to Dave, and he wasn't sure he wanted to know. He never reported it to the police. When he told his shooting partner Pat about it, Pat just looked at him like he was crazy.

They pulled up to a local motel in Cody and checked into a small but clean room. They had planned to go to the Wild Bill Hickok Museum the next day, but in the morning, they slept in too late and decided to continue on their trip. They headed out on highway 14/16 and when they reached Wapiti, they came to a sign that caught Dave's attention: "Old Guns of the Old West."

The sign was in the yard of a big white house just off the highway. On the sign it also said "five bucks." He decided to stop in and check it out. Jean stayed in the car. Dave knocked on the door and a small man who looked to be in his sixties opened the door with a big smile on his face.

"You here to see the gun collection?" asked the man.

"If that's okay," replied Dave. "I always love to see old guns, especially from the Old West."

"Well, come on in. My name is Steve. I have some really neat stuff, but it'll cost you five bucks to see it." Dave paid him five dollars, which the man put in his front pocket.

"I got the stuff in my basement. I collected some of it myself, but a lot of it came from my Uncle Henry who collected guns right up until his last heart attack several years ago."

Dave followed him down to the basement and he was quite impressed. Steve had several tables set up and covered with white cotton material. Next to each item was an index card with a description of the item. There were three saddles sitting on homemade wooden stands and the sign next to one said "Last Saddle used by Jesse James." Dave wondered about that one. There were several old rifles, a dozen pistols dating back to the 1800s and several holsters. Dave took a few pictures. Then, he noticed a stand in one corner of the basement with a fairly long glass case.

Steve noticed Dave's eyes focusing on it. "That's my best piece. Never saw anything like it before. My Uncle Henry said it was given to him by his lifelong friend, Jess Williams, Jr., who passed away several years before Uncle Henry.

Dave walked over to the case and when he looked inside, he froze as stiff as a tree. "Oh my God!" he exclaimed, his voice trembling.

"I know," said Steve. "It don't look like any pistol from the 1800s, but my Uncle Henry said he first seen it way back in 1925 when he first met Jess Williams, Jr." There was no response from Dave so Steve walked up next to him and looked at him. Dave was just staring down at the gun and holster. The holster was laid out lengthwise and the pistol was lying flat between the belt of the holster and the strap for the leg. It was the holster that had mysteriously disappeared from his locked gun safe. He was certain of it.

He looked at the pistol very closely, almost placing his face on the glass. He could just make out the stamping on the side of the gun. RUGER BLACKHAWK .41 MAGNUM CALIBER. The custom, hand-carved staghorn handles were a little beat up, but they were as beautiful as the day he had picked up the gun from Bob Graham four years earlier.

There was no logical explanation for what he was looking at, but there it was right before his eyes. The gun and holster both showed signs of wear and looked old, but they were the same gun and holster. There was no doubt about it. Dave must have stood there for five minutes, thinking about how they had disappeared that fateful day. He looked up from the case and into Steve's eyes.

Steve had a worried look about him. "Are you all right, mister?" he asked.

"I'm not really sure," replied a visibly shaken Dave. "Steve, you're not going to believe this."

"Believe what?"

"This gun and holster you have in this case are the gun and holster I bought four years ago. They disappeared on the same day I bought them. This is the first time I've seen them since."

"You mean you purchased one just like it?"

"No, Steve. This gun and this holster," replied Dave emphatically. "I had this gun built by a custom gun builder by the name of Bob Graham. This holster was made for me by Bob Mernickle, of Mernickle Custom Holsters. I know it sounds crazy, but it's true."

"It can't be. I first saw this gun back in 1967 when my Uncle Henry showed it to me and told me he would give it to me for my collection when he passed on, which was in 1969. I've had the gun ever since, right here in my basement in that glass case."

"You said your Uncle Henry got the gun from a Jess Williams, Jr.?" asked Dave.

"Yeah, he got the gun from him back in 1959 when Jess Williams, Jr. passed away. Jess Williams, Jr. was given the gun and his holster on the day his father, Jess Williams, passed away back in 1921. That's an interesting story all in itself, the way my Uncle Henry told me."

"What was the story your Uncle Henry told you?" asked Dave.

"Well, as the story goes, Jess Williams Junior's father found the gun mysteriously hanging up in the barn way back in 1876 when Junior's father was only fourteen. He never figured out how it had gotten there; it just seemed to appear out of nowhere. The strange thing is, this happened just after the murders."

"What murders?" asked Dave.

"Back in 1876, Jess Williams' entire family was brutally murdered when he was just a boy. I guess it was quite horrific. They tied his ma up in a doorway and raped her and cut her up so bad you wouldn't believe it. They even gouged one of her eyes out. They shot his pa out in the field. The story is they ambushed him and he never had a chance. The worst part though, is the little girl, Samantha. I guess one of the guys who did the killings took her in the barn and did things to her that you wouldn't think any man would do to a little seven-year-old girl. When he finished with her, he beat her up and shot her in the head.

"Well, Jess was crazy with hate and revenge for the men who killed his family and he went hunting for them. Jess had gotten pretty good with his pa's gun, but when he used this gun and holster he found in the barn, he found they gave him an advantage that no other man had. He had a gun and holster that seemed to be designed for a quick draw. That, combined with plenty of practice and a burning desire to hunt the men down, made him truly the fastest man on the draw in the Old West, although the history books don't even mention him. As a matter of fact, Jess Williams turned to bounty hunting and was never beaten on the draw, ever. He finally settled down in 1899 and Jess Williams, Jr. was born in 1902. Jess Williams, Jr. and my Uncle Henry became friends early on in his life and that's how Uncle Henry got the gun and holster. So you see, this can't be the gun and holster you had four years ago. This gun has been in my family for over forty years and I've had it here in the display case since 1969."

Dave had listened to this whole story. In a strange sort of way, it made some sense to him. This Jess Williams had somehow found his gun back in 1876 in the same mysterious fashion that the gun and holster disappeared in 2002. And Jess Williams had a burning need for the gun, more than Dave Walters needed it, although they both needed it for the same reason, to be the fastest man at drawing and shooting a pistol. It was almost as if, in some unexplainable and unimaginable way, Dave had done something to help Jess Williams find justice in a land and time that didn't see much of either. Yes, in a strange surreal sort of way, it made perfect sense. He had lost an expensive gun and holster, but something good had come of it. He wished he could have met Jess Williams.

"Steve, I'll bet you five bucks that I know the serial number stamped on the other side of the gun, as well as the serial number on the back side of the holster," Dave challenged.

"How could you possibly know that? I've never met you before and you've never been in this basement before."

"What if I told you that the serial number on the gun is 40-01079?" Steve had a strange look on his face. He reached inside his front pocket and got a set of keys. He unlocked the case and picked up the gun and turned it over. He read the numbers off, not believing what he was seeing. 40-01079.

"I don't understand," exclaimed Steve. "How can this be? How could you possibly know that? This gun has been locked in this case since I put it in there in 1969."

"Now, turn over the holster and you'll find the serial number stamped in the leather. It will be SN020679 and it will also have the name BOB MERNICKLE CUSTOM HOLSTERS and MADE IN CANADA stamped on it," Dave challenged.

Steve turned over the holster and it was exactly as Dave said it was. The serial number was exact.

Steve was absolutely and totally dumbfounded. "I just don't understand," he muttered. "How could you possibly have known that? I've never met you before and I'm sure you've never seen this pistol and holster before. My Uncle Henry never displayed it or showed it to anyone except family as far as I know."

"Steve, do you believe in destiny and fate and all that?"

"I sure do, always have."

"So do I."

"Well, what do we do now?" asked Steve, a little worried.

Dave simply put his hand out. "I guess you owe me five bucks."

Steve took the same five-dollar bill that Dave had paid him to see the guns and gave it back to him. "Are you going to make a claim for the gun?" asked Steve, a worried look forming on his face.

Dave didn't have to even think about it for even one second. "No. I believe things happen for a reason. I think Jess Williams was destined to have this gun and I simply played a small part in his calling. Some things that happen in our lives, no matter how unexplainable, are best left unchanged, don't you think?"

"Yes, I believe that's true," replied Steve, with a look of relief.

Dave thanked Steve again and headed up the stairs. As he walked down the driveway to the car he thought about how destiny had intertwined the fate of both his life and Jess Williams' life together in such a strange way. He got in the car and closed the door.

His wife Jean looked up at him. "Dave, are you okay?" she asked, a worried look on her face. "You look like you've seen a ghost or something."

He let out a sigh and decided right then and there that he wouldn't tell his wife what he had just seen. She probably wouldn't believe him anyway. She still often wondered about his sanity after his claim that the gun simply vanished into thin air.

"I'm fine," replied Dave. "Maybe it's the altitude. I'll be fine."

"Well, was it worth the five bucks?"

"Oh, yes. I would have paid five hundred bucks to see what I just saw." Jean looked at him, puzzled. He offered no explanation. He knew better than to try.

Dave started the car and drove down the driveway and back onto highway 14/16. As he drove, his thoughts turned to Jess Williams, the bounty hunter and fastest draw in the West. He could picture him wearing his gun and holster and beating the bad guys to the draw. Then he pictured himself there in Jess Williams' place, back in the old days, shooting it out with the best, and always the man standing in the end. As Dave hit the first hill going into Yellowstone Park, his wife looked over at him and noticed he had a strange smile on his face.

Dave was imagining he was facing down some bad guys in the Old West, and he had Jess Williams' gun and holster and...

The End

BROTHER'S KEEPER

A JESS WILLIAMS WESTERN

SECOND IN THE SERIES

In memory of Bernice V. Dopkowski (October 28, 1913 – August 29, 1993). In this book, I have depicted Bernice as Wanda Dopkowski, a Polish immigrant who came out west and worked as a cook in the town of Baxter, Texas. She had a huge impact on my wife's life.

CHAPTER ONE

J ess woke at daylight and ate a breakfast of salt pork and pan bread. He had learned to make it several different ways. Sometimes he made it with just flour and water, mixing it well and pouring it into the skillet after frying the salt pork. Sometimes he added a little corn meal. He had even taken to adding some beef or salt pork crumpled up in it. He would make extra so that he could eat it on the trail during the afternoon when he got hungry.

He ate breakfast right there under the big oak tree that graciously shaded the family cemetery. He had spent last night sleeping under the tree after returning from a long and very bloody hunt to track down and dispense justice to the three men who had viciously murdered his entire family. His hunt had been very successful. As he ate, he looked around the old homestead and wondered what might have been if his family were still alive. He tried to imagine that nothing had happened and he was still working the ranch with his pa. He took a deep breath and he could smell the richness of the soil that had led his pa to this land. He tried to imagine sitting down to supper with his family and enjoying a good meal that his ma had prepared. He tried to imagine his sister Samantha. He wondered if she would ever have quit causing him more work and trouble. He tried, but he couldn't. His life had changed so drastically that there was no going back, even if just for a moment in his thoughts. He had seen too many bad things and killed too many bad men to think much of anything else.

He finished his breakfast, washing it down with a final cup of hot coffee and said another good-bye to his family in their graves.

He saddled Gray and headed toward Black Creek, Kansas. As he rode down the trail to the main road leading to town, he felt a slight twinge of sorrow slowly creeping into him. The sorrow was like a weight on his shoulders. It was the sorrow of knowing that he would miss most of what people would consider a normal life. A tear started to puddle in the corner of his eye but he brushed it away defiantly.

Much, but not all of the rage that still burned deeply within his heart had been tempered by the knowledge that he had brutally killed all three of the men responsible for the brutal deaths of his family. He also felt the burden of the awareness that he had killed many men, even though most of them were bad men. Nevada Jackson had not been a bad man. He was simply a bounty hunter who was very fast with a pistol but had also made a deadly miscalculation. Nevada believed that he was faster with a pistol than Jess and that cost him his life. Jess couldn't feel bad about it; it had not been his decision to draw against Nevada. Yet, knowing all of this, something deep within him knew that some of the rage would never leave him. He would take some of it to his grave. That was probably a good thing.

The thought of crying for his family didn't enter his mind now. He had promised himself that he had cried for the last time last night. From now on, he would do what he could do to right any wrong or injustice that he came across. He would bring justice to the killers and rapists of innocents just as he had brought justice to the three men responsible for the murder of his entire family. It was his own brutal style of justice and he had learned it at such an early age from dealing with other brutal men.

It had not been his choice in the beginning but he now fully accepted it. In many cases, he would get paid for dispensing such justice. That would be his life's work, and he was already quite good at it. He was now a hunter of men, or as some people called it, a man killer. He had the right tool to help him in his quest. That tool was the unique pistol and holster that had somehow found its way to him a few years ago. He never figured out where it came from or why it came to him. He was simply grateful for it.

He had spent the last several months using that unique pistol and holster to kill the three men responsible for the murder of his family and quite a few more who made the fatal mistake of getting in his way. He had not wanted to kill those other men but they had forced him to and he could not, or more so, would not allow himself to feel any remorse for it. It had been their choice and he had tried to talk some of them out of it, but he had learned very quickly that mean and stupid seemed to go together hand in hand most of the time for hard cases and gunslingers on the prowl.

Jess had not quite turned seventeen yet and he had killed more men than most would kill in a lifetime. He was now a professional bounty hunter with a rapidly rising reputation. A reputation that would cause other men to track him down just to challenge his skill with a pistol and he knew he had to live with that. He would keep his promise to himself. He would not hunt men for crimes like bank robbery or cattle rustling. He would leave such things to men like Frank Reedy and Sheriff Mark Steele. He would not hire his gun out to some rich rancher to enforce his will on others. He would only hunt men who were responsible for the killing of innocent men, women and children. He would come to the defense of those less able to protect themselves or their families against the brutal treatment that some men inflicted on others.

He stopped at the big boulder in the bend of the creek where he had met those three men that fateful day. He let Gray drink his fill as he thought of his trips into town. He remembered how he used to stop at the boulder, strip down, and jump into the creek. Those were good memories. He would not have many of those in his lifetime and he would have to hold onto them. He would keep those memories right next to the place where he kept the rage inside of him to call on when he needed to.

Gray finished his long drink and Jess gently nudged him toward town. He hadn't been back to Black Creek in quite a while, and the last time he had been there, he killed his first man, in his first gunfight. That man was Red Carter and as far as Jess was concerned, Red deserved to die that day. He knew that Dick Carter, Red's father, was still offering a three thousand dollar blood bounty on his head for killing his son. He had second thoughts about riding into Black Creek knowing that Dick Carter was still after him, but he had friends there and it was his home, after all. Dick Carter could make his own decisions and he would make his. He decided that whatever happened, he would deal with it when it happened. That was one lesson Jess had learned from his pa. There were times when a man had no control over events and he simply had to play the cards that life dealt him.

As he rode into Black Creek, the town looked as if it hadn't changed much except for a new building, but he could sense that something was different. He couldn't put his finger on it, but there it was nonetheless. He had developed somewhat of a sixth sense about such things. There were people milling about on the street and the boardwalk, but there was something different about them. He reined up in front of Smythe's General Store and wrapped the reins around the post a few times. It had been a long time since he had seen Jim or Sara Smythe and he was anxious to see a friend. He walked into the store and when he saw that there was no one behind the counter, he called out.

"Hey, doesn't anybody work here anymore." Jess heard some footsteps and a few seconds later Jim Smythe came out from the back. When he reached the counter, he stood there a moment or two with his mouth agape.

"Oh my Lord! Jess? Is that really you? By the love of God, it is you."

Jim came around the counter and gave him a big bear hug. He was somewhat startled by it and wasn't sure how to react. On one hand, he was unsure about letting any man that close to his gun, but this was someone he trusted entirely. Jim finally let him go and took a step back.

"Damn good to see you, Jess," he said, as he turned his head in the direction of the door going into the kitchen and hollered for Sara. "Sara, you won't believe who's here. Come on out here and see who finally dragged his sorry ass back to see us." Sara came shuffling quickly out of the back. She almost screamed when she saw Jess standing there.

"Jess," was all she could say as she ran to him and gave him a hug and a kiss on the cheek. Jess was much more comfortable with that. As she hugged him, she could see the butt of the shotgun strapped to his back. Jim finally intervened.

"Come on into the kitchen, Jess. Sara will put on a pot of coffee and I'll bet she can whip up a few biscuits for you."

"That's sounds mighty good right about now."

They walked into the kitchen, Sara still clutching Jess's right arm as if she would never let it go. She couldn't help but notice the same unique gun and holster he had been wearing the last time he had left town. She wondered to herself how many men he might have killed with it. He sat down with Jim while Sara hastily went about making coffee, along with some fresh biscuits. She threw in some milk gravy for good measure. Sara served the coffee and biscuits and they sat around talking small talk for a few minutes before the conversation turned in the direction that he knew it eventually would.

"Well, Jess," asked Jim, "did you finally make things right and finish the job you set out to do? Did you catch up with all three of those bastards you were looking for?" Jim already knew the answer; it was simply a question to get the conversation on the matter started.

Jess took another long drink of coffee and set his cup down. He looked at Jim for a moment before he answered. He noticed that Sara had stopped what she was doing and turned to hear the answer. He wondered if they would think less of him for what he had done. He needed to be truthful with them since that's how it's supposed to be with good friends. Good friends stick through thick and thin, good or bad. His answer was slow and deliberate.

"I hunted every one of them down and made sure they paid with their lives for what they did. I don't feel bad about it either. Those men deserved to die and any others like them." Sara hung her head slightly as she fetched some more butter. Jim nodded at Jess as if he understood and agreed.

"You're already getting quite a reputation, Jess. We've heard about some of it back here. Most people know about some of your gunfights, especially the gunfights with Blake Taggert and Nevada Jackson. Those two were as fast as they come. People also heard about Blake Taggert being the one who murdered that family just outside of Red Rock. Most people like what you did about it."

Sara was watching Jess all the time Jim was talking to him. She could see the dramatic change in him. He looked ten years older even though she knew he hadn't been gone that long. She could see the coldness and the darkness that loomed just below the surface of his eyes. It was a strange look. It was a cold, hard unnerving look and yet she could still see the good deep down, almost hidden unless you looked for it. She could also see the death in his eyes. He knew she was looking him over. He knew that she was sad about the change in his life, but there was nothing he could do about it. He wasn't sure he even wanted to do anything about it. He was what he was, a man killer. In his mind, someone had to do it. In his mind, it was right.

"Jess," Sara asked, "how many men have you killed so far?"

At first, he thought that to be a strange question, but the more he thought about it, he realized it was a question she had to ask. There was no point in dodging it, but he decided there was no point in giving exact numbers or details.

"Let's just say I've killed more men than most men twice my age. I will tell you that every single one of them deserved to die. I never started a fight except for Red Carter and two of the three who murdered my family. I never drew first on anyone except for Hank Beard and that was because he tried to ambush me in my room like a coward in the middle of the night."

Sara put her head down and looked at her plate. She had prayed that Jess might be able to have some kind of normal life and she knew now that it would never happen. Jim broke the awkward silence in the room.

"We heard you went into the bounty hunting business. Is that true?"

"Yes. A man has to make a living somehow and it seems to be what I'm good at. I found out that it pays pretty well too. Besides that, I promised myself that I would only hunt the worst of the lot. I will only hunt down men who have murdered and raped innocent people who have done nothing to deserve it. I won't stand for that. If I ran into a man who had done something as terrible as the three men who murdered my family, I would call him out and kill him whether there's a bounty on him or not. Men like that don't deserve to live among the rest of us."

"It's hard to argue that one," Jim said, darting his eyes at Sara, seeing the uneasiness in her.

"Well, enough about me," Jess said, trying to change the subject. "How are you two doing? How has business been? I noticed no one has come in since I arrived. Is it a slow day or what?" Jim shook his head in disgust.

"Every day is a slow day since that jackass of a new sheriff took over."

"I'm glad to hear that you finally got a new sheriff in town but what does he have to do with your business?"

Jim acted as if he didn't want to explain.

Sara looked at Jim with that look that most men should understand right away but never do. "You might as well tell him. He's going to find out anyway and he's going to need to know," she said in a motherly fashion.

"Need to know what?"

"Oh hell, Sara's right. I might as well tell you. I don't guess that it will come as any surprise that Dick Carter is still after you for killing his son Red. When that one bounty hunter came back... what was his name...oh yeah, Frank Reedy. Well, he came back, gave Carter his money back, and told him he wouldn't have anything more to do with hunting you down. Carter was madder than a peeled rattler and I don't think he's cooled off one bit yet."

"I already know that," replied Jess. "What I don't know is what all that has to do with your business?"

"Well, I'm-a-gettin' to that part if you'll let me finish," said Jim. Jess smiled and picked up his coffee cup and let him continue.

"Now, Dick Carter, being the rich son of a bitch that he is, puts up a new general store right down the street. Then he uses his money and influence to get a new mayor elected here in town. Then, after he has the mayor in his pocket, he tells him who he wants for the new sheriff and it just happens to be one of Carter's men. Now Carter has threatened everyone in town to use the new general store and he's using the sheriff to enforce it. Anytime one of my old customers comes in here, the sheriff comes in and scares them off. Hell, Carter has the whole town terrified and as nervous as a whore in church. The worst part of it is I think he likes it. And, to make matters worse, Carter is using his money to discount everything below my cost just to put me out of business. Hell, he doesn't care about losing a few dollars."

"But why? What does Dick Carter have against the two of you? You've never done anything to him that I'm aware of."

"It's because we're friends of yours," announced Jim. "He knows we're like family and when he tried to get us to say something bad about you when he first came into the store after what happened, we refused. Well, that pissed him off and I told him to get the hell out of my store. The rest is history and damn if we ain't just about done in. I don't think we can hold out much longer. He's a mean old cuss, that Carter." Jess set his cup down and looked at the coffee in the cup as if he were looking for some answer, but he already knew what the answer would be.

"The apple doesn't fall far from the tree," said Jess. "His son, Red, was the same way. If anyone is at fault in his son's death, it's Dick Carter himself. Sure, I shot Red, but he deserved it. Dick Carter raised him to be a bad one."

"Jess," said Sara, "why don't you leave town now before Carter finds out you've come back. He has a gang of hired killers and as soon as he knows you're here, they will surely be coming after you. Some of his hired guns are in town right now and I'll bet they already know. You have nothing to prove here. Why not ride out of here while you still can?"

Jess thought about what Sara had just said, but he didn't have to think about it long. He knew what he had to do and he made his decision quickly. That's the way it was with him. Once he set his mind to something, there was no changing it after the decision was made.

"I'm not here to prove anything, Sara. Neither of you abandoned me when times got tough and I don't plan to abandon you either. You both took me in and helped me at a time that I needed it the most. You fed me and left food on my doorstep while I was learning how to fend for myself. You helped bury my family and stuck with me through some tough times. My pa taught me never to forget such things. You were there for me, and now I'm here for you. Jim, you always told me that you always find out who your real friends are when the chips are down and you've always practiced what you preach. Well, so do I. Here's what we're going to do. First, I have more money in the bank already than I need with my simple lifestyle. I'm going to have Mr. Jameson deposit two hundred dollars into your bank account today."

Jim quickly interrupted. "No, Jess. We don't want you handing out money for our problems."

"Well, who's not letting someone finish what they're trying to say now?"

"Sorry," Jim replied, sheepishly.

"As I was saying, after I have the money deposited into your account, I will pay a visit to the new sheriff and let him know that I won't stand for any more interference with your business from this day forward, from him or anyone else."

"You know he's going to ride out and tell Carter five minutes after you see him, don't you?" Jim asked. Jess smiled a slight but devious smile.

"Hell, I wouldn't have it any other way." Jess gave Sara another hug and shook Jim's hand, giving Jim a serious expression. "You should have sent for me before it got this far."

"I figured you were a little busy," replied Jim.

"Well, I was, but I have plenty of time now." Jess walked out, heading straight for the sheriff's office.

"Oh God, Jim," said Sara, shaking her head fretfully, "he's going to get himself killed for sure and we're going to be the cause of it." Now Jim had the devious smile beginning to form across his lips.

"Better men than Dick Carter and his bunch have tried and failed."

The new sheriff was a man by the name of Dan Newcomb. He was one of Carter's hired guns, but he certainly wasn't the best of the lot. He was fast, but not that fast. Those who really knew him though, knew he had a yellow streak down his back wide enough to fill the space between two fence posts. He would face off with someone, but only if he was fairly certain that he could win. Newcomb did what he was paid to do, which was whatever Dick Carter told him. When Jess reached the sheriff's office, the sheriff was walking down the boardwalk from the opposite direction. He noticed Jess standing in front of the office, staring at him.

"Looking for someone?" asked Newcomb, nonchalantly.

"Actually, I think I just found him, unless you're going to tell me that you found that sheriff's badge and pinned it on for fun."

"No, it's my badge, and I'm the sheriff here. Now, who the hell are you?"

"My name is Jess Williams."

The name struck Newcomb like a dagger. The truth was, there wasn't one man on Dick Carter's payroll who didn't know the whole story about Jess Williams and how he had killed Dick's only son, Red. Newcomb knew all about Jess and his reputation. He tried to stay calm but Jess was reading Newcomb like a book and he could tell that he was as nervous as a titmouse watching a circling hawk.

"So you're the Jess Williams everyone is talking about. You have quite a reputation for such a young man. Did you also know that Mr. Carter still has a personal bounty on your head in the amount of three thousand dollars?"

"You plan on trying to collect it?" asked Jess, staring deep into Newcomb's eyes, unnerving him even more.

"Well, I am the sheriff. I suppose I should lock you up and let Judge Hollingsworth decide what to do with you." Newcomb hadn't said it with very much conviction, and even if he had, it wouldn't have meant much to Jess anyway. He took a step closer to Newcomb, slipping his hammer strap off, a dark look in his eyes now.

"Let's get something straight right up front, Newcomb. You're no sheriff regardless of what that badge you've got pinned on your shirt says. You're nothing more than a hired gun for Carter and that's exactly how I plan to treat you. Now, if you're going to do anything more than flap your gums together, let's get on with it. If not, get the crack of your sorry ass up on your horse and run on out and tell Dick Carter that Jess Williams is back in town and that he doesn't plan on leaving anytime soon."

Newcomb thought about going for his gun. It would be such a feather in his hat to take out Jess Williams. He would be considered a deadly gunslinger if he did. He thought about that for a half a second and then his senses rushed back to him. He touched the brim of his hat and nodded.

"Well then, I'll let Mr. Carter know that you're in town. Any other message you want me to give to him?"

"As a matter of fact, yes. Tell him the next person that does anything to hurt Jim or Sara Smythe, or their business for that matter, will answer to me, and that includes you." Newcomb tipped his hat as he walked away.

"I'll be sure to give him your message. I don't think he's going to like it though."

"I don't suppose he will," replied Jess, with that same devious smile.

Jess knew the challenge was in place now and he was smart enough to know that it meant war. He knew Carter would come to town in a day or so, but not before having some of his hired guns take a crack at him first. It was the way rich men did things and he understood it, even though he didn't agree with it. He knew that when Carter finally did come to town, all hell would break loose and he had to be ready for it. He knew many of the townsfolk in Black Creek and many of them had helped him in his time of need. He was not about to walk away from them now, any more than he could walk away from Jim and Sara. Besides, it just wasn't right for one man to run a town like it was his own private domain. People had rights and no one man had the right to take them away. He would take on Carter and everyone else Carter threw at him. He couldn't help himself. It was his nature.

Jess walked over to the new general store. As he did, he noticed Newcomb riding out of town. He didn't have to wonder for a minute as to where he was headed, but he did wonder to himself where the comment, "crack of your sorry ass" had come from. Maybe he had heard it somewhere and it just stuck in his head, waiting for the right moment to come out. He shook his head and smiled inwardly. What he didn't know was that Newcomb had already spread the word to some of Carter's hired guns who were in town. Newcomb knew that before he reached the Carter 'D' ranch, every gunslinger and hired gun working for Carter would know that a young man by the name of Jess Williams was in town and that Carter would pay the sum of three thousand dollars to the man who killed him.

The new general store was the finest he had ever seen. And of course, it was called Carter's General Store. He noticed that it was quite busy with several people inside. Some were buying; others were looking around at things. He looked at all of them. He recognized some of the people in the store. He was sure a few of them recognized him, but if they did, they were afraid to say anything or even acknowledge him. Jess walked right up to the counter and picked up a hammer that was on it and pounded the counter three times.

"I'd like everyone's attention for a moment please."

"Hey, hold on there, mister," said the clerk behind the counter. "You can't come in here and bang on my counter like that. What the hell d'ya think you're doing?"

"I'm just trying to make an announcement."

"Well, you can't do that."

"Why not?"

"Well, 'cause I say so."

"Really? Well, I say I can."

"Yeah, well, who the hell are you anyway? You work for Carter?"

"No, I don't work for anyone and I wouldn't work for Carter for any amount of money. Now listen up everyone," said Jess, turning his back on the clerk as if he didn't even exist. All the customers were just standing around in surprise, shocked at what was taking place, but they were paying attention.

"I know some of you people and I know you used to be loyal customers of Jim and Sara Smythe. I'm here to tell you that Jim will match Carter's prices, and his service is much better, but you all know that. As for being intimidated by the sheriff or Dick Carter, you don't have to put up with that anymore. Most of you people used to get credit from Jim back when you couldn't afford what you needed and he let you pay him back whenever you could. You don't turn your backs on a man like that. Those are the kind of people who make a town what it is. If anyone bothers you for shopping at Smythe's General Store, they'll have to answer directly to me."

There was an awkward moment of silence as all the customers looked at one another and then back at Jess. Then a strange thing happened. Every single one of them quickly walked straight out of the store as if they really hadn't wanted to be in there in the first place. As they were walking out, one older woman spoke very quietly as she walked past Jess.

"It sure is nice to see you again, young Mr. Williams." Most of the customers walked into other establishments but three of them went straight over to Smythe's General Store. Jess threw the hammer back down on the counter. The clerk stared at Jess as if somehow it would bore a hole in him.

"Mr. Carter ain't going to like this one damn bit. You're in a whole heap of trouble, mister. You'll be lucky to still be alive by tomorrow night. What name shall I tell the undertaker to put on your headstone?"

"Jess Williams is the name but I wouldn't be ordering any head-stones yet, unless you want to order one for Carter ahead of time. I have a hunch he might need one soon." Jess walked out of the store and the only thing he heard from the clerk was; "Holy shit, things are gonna get wild around here."

Newcomb's horse was plumb tuckered out when he arrived at the Carter 'D' ranch. He reined up in front of the huge ranch house and quickly scurried inside. He found Carter sitting in the dining room with four of his best hired guns. Carter motioned for him to take a seat and have something to eat. Newcomb sat, picked a warm roll out of a basket on the table and started to pinch off little pieces one at a time, chewing very slowly. Carter watched him for a minute and knew from his sly expression that he was just busting at the seams to tell him something, but Newcomb knew better than to say anything until he was called upon. That was the way it was with Carter. You just didn't run in and start talking to him. He would call you down hard for that. You had to wait patiently, act like you had something to tell him, and then wait for him to ask. That was the way Carter liked it. He liked to control the situation every time. Carter finally put down the chicken leg that he was gnawing on and began to wipe his hands with a white cotton napkin.

"All right, Newcomb. You look like you've swallowed a cat and waiting to spit out a hair ball, so tell me what the hell you rode out here to tell me. It had better be good since you interrupted my lunch here with my best men."

"Sorry, Mr. Carter, but I knew that you would want to know right away."

"Know what?"

"That kid you been looking for, Jess Williams? Well, he rode into town this morning."

Carter fell silent and he stayed that way for almost a full minute. He looked down at his plate of food, which he had lost all interest in now. His mind wasn't on the food anymore. He was thinking about his only son, Red, and how Jess Williams had killed him in a gunfight. It may have been a fair fight but that didn't matter at all to

Carter. Red was just as dead, fair or not. He thought about the discussion that he had had last week with his friend, Cal Hardin, who owned the ranch abutting his. He thought about the note he had written out and sealed in an envelope that he was going to give to a rider tomorrow. He thought about how he had put up three thousand dollars and offered to pay the money to anyone who killed Jess Williams. He remembered how he had sent Frank Reedy and Todd Spicer to hunt Jess down and how Spicer had gotten himself killed. He remembered how Reedy had come back to the ranch and returned the money to Carter, refusing to go after Jess. And now, here he was, right back in town not more than five miles away. An evil grin began to form on Carter's face and it didn't go unnoticed by anyone in the room.

"Did you see him yourself? You're certain it's him?"

"Yes sir. I talked to him personal like."

"You talked to him? What the hell did he have to say?"

"He said to tell you he was back in town and he didn't plan on leaving anytime soon. He also said he wasn't going to put up with anyone bothering Jim or Sara Smythe or their store." Carter mumbled something as he hung his head but no one in the room could make out what it was and then he looked back up at Newcomb.

"He said that?"

"Yes, sir."

"Well, you go back to town and you tell that no good son of a bitch that he's a dead man whether he stays in town or travels to the far ends of the earth. I'm going to see him dead one way or another. You tell him when it's over I'll drag his carcass back here and bury him next to my son's grave so my son can watch me piss on his grave every damned morning! You tell him he can count on that and tell him that I swear by it on my only son's grave!"

"Yes, sir. I'll tell him." Newcomb stood up and almost made it to the doorway to leave when Carter stopped him.

"Tell me something, Newcomb. Why didn't you kill him when you had the chance? Three thousand dollars ain't enough money for you?" Newcomb shrank from Carter's cold stare and he put his eyes to the floor as he spoke. He did it partially out of shame but mostly out of fear for Carter's wrath.

"Mr. Carter, you know I ain't that good with a pistol. I wouldn't stand a chance against that kid and you know it. I ain't half as fast as any of these men in the room with a gun, sir. I figured I'd just get plugged trying and decided instead to ride out here pronto and let you know."

Normally, Carter would have stood up and punched Newcomb for failing him, but all he could think about now was the fact that Jess was right here under his nose. He was within his grasp. Newcomb sidled out of the room and left Carter with his four best men. He looked at the four of them, who had been silent.

"Well, boys, seems like it's time to earn your pay."

All four of them nodded, still not saying one word. These four were professionals and the best that Carter's money could buy. They understood what that meant and while not one of them was in a hurry to die, every one of them was in a hurry to collect the three thousand. They went back to finishing their meals, except for Dick Carter. He was thinking about Jess Williams. He felt like the cat that had chased a mouse around the room and finally had it cornered. He was, however, forgetting one small fact. Not all cats have nine lives.

CHAPTER TWO

Terrence Hanley was a run-of-the-mill ranch hand and his pistol skills were definitely short of spectacular, which is exactly why Dick Carter picked him. Carter knew he would need his best hired guns with him when he went into town, which would most likely be tomorrow or the next day. He had something else he had to attend to in case everything that could go wrong did, and that's why he had sent for Hanley.

Hanley was grumbling to himself as he strolled up to the ranch house to see Carter. He worried that maybe he was getting fired for losing a few extra head of cattle to rustlers the last few weeks or even worse. Maybe Carter had picked him for one of several men who would ride into town tomorrow and kill this kid named Jess Williams. Hanley had heard the story about how Red was killed, especially about how fast the kid was who shot him with a strange-looking pistol and holster. He didn't want any part of it. Truth was, neither did most of the men at Carter's ranch, except for the crazy ones. That's exactly what Hanley called men who stood out in the middle of a street, skinned leather, and shot it out for something as little as a cheap whore or a two-bit poker hand.

Carter was waiting for him in the large room that he always thought of as his study. It was the room where Carter did all his heavy thinking about such things as which rancher he would run off next week or which ranch he would buy out or force out if his offer was rejected. Those were big decisions and he needed a place of solitude to do such planning. It was a large room with heavy wood trim all stained in a dark mahogany. He probably chose that color because it matched his mood most of the time, which was usually dark and brooding. He was pouring himself some expensive brandy into a nice crystal glass when Hanley tapped ever so slightly on the door to the study, which was partially open.

"Mr. Carter, sir? You sent for me?"

Hanley was nervous and Carter could sense that right away. Knowing what he was going to ask him to do, he wanted to put him at ease right away.

"Yes I did, and don't worry, you're not in any trouble. I've lost cattle before and I'll lose cattle again. Some of the other boys are taking care of that little problem." Hanley knew exactly what that meant and he suddenly had a vision of men hanging from tall oak trees with their tongues all swollen and hanging out. "Anyway," continued Carter, "that ain't why I called you in here. Would you like a glass of this fine brandy? It's really quite good." Hanley felt the tension leaving him.

"Yes, I would, sir, and thanks for letting me know right away about not being in trouble. I need this job and I was worried that maybe I might have lost it. I appreciate you going easy on me." Carter poured him a full glass of brandy and Hanley took a sip of it. It went down smooth.

"Damn, I don't get this kind of stuff often. I think this is just about the best brandy I've ever had the pleasure of sipping."

"I have that stuff shipped in by the case all the way from New York City. It's expensive brandy for sure but it's worth every damn penny."

"Well, I sure appreciate your sharing this with me," said Hanley, taking another slow sip.

Carter smiled. He always enjoyed showing off that he had more money than most men could count. Hanley sat there for a minute or two slowly sipping the fine brandy and then his curiosity finally got the better of him.

"So, why did you call me in here, sir?"

Carter sat down in a plush leather chair and motioned for Hanley to do the same. Hanley sat in another chair and the leather seemed to wrap itself around him with a comfort he had not felt before. Carter eyed him for a few moments.

"I have a very important job I'd like you to do for me," said Carter, his smile now turning to a more serious look. "It pays a nice bonus, along with your normal pay, and it's easier work than busting your ass herding cattle all day."

"Sounds interesting, but will I live through it to get my bonus?" he asked, wondering if Carter was going to ask him to go into Black Creek for the big showdown.

"Hell, yes, you'll live through it. I'm not talking about when I kill that little no-good son of a bitch who murdered my only boy. I'm talking about you delivering a letter personally to a man for me."

"What letter, and who do I deliver it to?"

"It's a sealed letter and it's only to be read by the person you're going to deliver it to. Only he can open the letter, is that understood?"

"What if I can't find this man you're talking about?"

"Then bring the message back here to me. If for some reason you can't do that, I want you to destroy the message. Burn it."

"Who is this person you want me to deliver it to?"

Carter poured them both another glass of the fine brandy. "His name is Tim Sloan." Hanley looked at Carter as though he recognized the name.

"Did you say his last name was Sloan?"

"Yes. Why, do you know him?"

"I've heard of Eddie Sloan. He's one mean son of a bitch and they say he's damn quick with a side iron. I heard he outdrew two men at the same time in a bar over in Abilene. The way I hear it, he's one of the best."

"You're right on both counts, but the man I'm sending you to see is his son, Tim Sloan. They say he's just as fast as his old man, and probably faster since he's got youth on his side."

"Never knew Sloan had a kid. Where do I find this Tim Sloan?"

"The last place he was seen was in a town called Holten, about three days' ride south of here. That was about two weeks ago. I wired the sheriff there and asked him if Sloan was still in town, to give him a message to wait there and that a man was coming to personally deliver him a letter."

"What makes you think that this Tim Sloan will wait around that long?"

"Because I told the sheriff to tell Sloan that the man coming to see him would pay him five hundred dollars just to wait."

"Not bad pay just for waiting around."

"That's why I figure he'll still be there when you show up."

"So, how much do I get paid for delivering the letter?"

"Same as I'm paying him to wait, five hundred dollars. That's on top of your normal pay. But you have to make sure you give the letter to him personally and no one else, and you make sure that he reads it before you give him the money, understand?"

"Sir, for five hundred dollars, a man can understand a whole lot."

"Good. I knew I picked the right man for this job."

Carter walked over to the counter where the brandy was and picked up a small envelope, which was sealed in wax with Carter's personal stamp on it. He walked over to Hanley and handed him the envelope. Then Carter pulled another envelope out of his back pocket.

"The sealed envelope is the one you hand to Tim Sloan. The other envelope has one thousand dollars in it, five hundred for you and the other five hundred for Sloan. Give him the five hundred, but only after he reads the letter."

"I don't suppose you're going to tell me what the letter says, are you?"

"No, but it's very important to me. I trust you to make sure that you get it to him." Hanley finished his brandy and stood up with a smile on his lips.

"Consider it done, Mr. Carter."

"I already did."

Hanley walked out and headed for the barn to get his things and saddle his horse. It was a liver chestnut color, which was close to the same color of the wood in Carter's study. He took exceptional care of the horse and the truth was, he liked him more than he liked most people. Hanley knew that a good horse could mean the difference between life and death sometimes, especially on the trail.

It was early in the day yet so Hanley figured he might as well get a head start to Holten. He didn't really care what was in the envelope he was to give to Tim Sloan. Hanley was a simple man and he knew how to follow orders. He had a job to do and he would simply do it without question. He did, however, believe it must be important since Carter was paying a whole lot of money just to have it delivered. And paying a man five hundred dollars just to wait around for a letter was pretty much unheard of. Hanley saddled up and rode out.

Carter sat down in one of his big leather chairs and sipped his fine brandy. He had a grin forming across his lips that only he and his innermost dark side could really understand. He hadn't told Hanley what the letter to Tim Sloan said, although he could remember it word for word by heart. He recited it again in his head and the evil grin grew a little wider.

⚞ ⚟

Jess left Carter's store and walked back to Smythe's General Store. Jim had just finished waiting on the customers that he had steered over to him. Jim had a smile on his face for the customers, but as soon as they left, the smile quickly evaporated.

"Are you out of your mind? Carter's going to be pissin' blood an' shittin' nails when he hears about this."

"You leave Carter to me."

"And how about his two dozen or so hired guns?"

"I'll deal with them also. Here's all you need to worry about. Have Tony from the livery come over and get my horse and tell him to take good care of him." Jim nodded.

"Good. Now, I need to buy some shotgun shells and I want a couple boxes of .45 cartridges. I have a feeling that I'm going to need them before this is all over."

"I've got lots of ammo. I haven't been selling much lately."

"I'm going to take a little look around town and maybe pay a visit to the saloon." Jess pulled the shotgun out of its back sling, checking to make sure both barrels were loaded. He checked his pa's Colt .45 Peacemaker that was tucked in the front of his holster by his left hip along with his unique pistol. Then he spun on his heels and headed for the door.

"You watch your back, Jess," warned Jim, "they'll be gunnin' for you and before this day is over, Carter will know you're here, if he doesn't already."

Jess looked back at Jim with a sly grin. "I'm counting on it."

Jess walked out and stayed on the boardwalk. He walked the entire length of the town on both sides of the street and looked behind every building. He checked for any ambush points including ones that he himself might need to use. He stopped in at Tony's Livery. Tony was a big strapping hunk of a man. Some said he was so strong that he could bend the shoes for horses with his bare hands. Yet he was a gentle man. It was hard to rile him but once you did, you'd wish you had riled a grizzly bear watching over a new cub instead.

Tony had been the one who had made the grave markers for Jess's family and checked all the stock at the ranch the day his family had been buried. Jess had worked for Tony before leaving Black Creek the last time and he taught him some hand-to-hand fighting techniques, which Jess had not forgotten. Tony was a good man. Jess considered him a good friend and more importantly, a man you could count on when things got tough.

"Well, well, look who comes to visit me," Tony said as he looked up and saw Jess standing in his doorway. Jess shook his hand and Tony's grip was like a vise.

"Hello, Tony. How have you been?"

"Just fine, but we sure have missed you, Jess. I know it's been a while now but not a day goes by that I don't think about..." Tony's voice trailed off after seeing the look on his face. "I really miss your pa. He used to stop by and talk some with me whenever he came to town."

"He told me you were the best smithy he'd ever met. He said you could do things with metal that most men couldn't."

"Well, I've heard that you can do things with that fancy pistol of yours that most men can't," acknowledged Tony, glancing down at Jess's pistol. "Sure is a pretty thing."

"I'm not sure yet whether it's a blessing or a curse though."

"The way things are shaping up here in town, I'd start calling it a blessing."

"I guess so. I trust you'll take good care of Gray?"

"I'll take care of him like he was my own. Jim brought him over to me. I already brushed him down and put him in a stall with some of my best feed. That's one damn fine horse. I'm the one who sold him to your pa."

Jess thanked Tony again and headed for the saloon. He had noticed several men watching him when he strolled around town earlier. He knew they were trouble and knew that before the day ended he would be facing some of them and it wouldn't be over a deck of cards in a friendly game of poker. He figured that he might as well get things started. He knew that most of these men wondered about his reputation and his plan was to capitalize on that. They wanted to test him and he was going to give them the chance to do exactly that. Afterward, either he would be dead or they would fear him more than the grim reaper himself.

It might even cause some of Carter's hired guns to leave town rather than have to face him. It was one thing to walk away from a challenge. It was quite another to simply get on your horse for no particular reason and head out to the next town. Jess's real problem though was that the best of the lot would stay. Those would be the gunmen who were being paid the most and you get what you pay for. Jess figured that he would deal with that later. For now, it was time to thin out the herd.

Two men were standing across from the saloon when Jess walked through the doors. They stood there silently, watching him. He knew they were there and that they were watching every move he made. He was watching them also, although he wasn't sure they realized it. He had already made a mental note of what they were carrying. Each of the two men wore a single pistol tied down tight and both had a full cartridge belt. The man on the left had a small knife tucked in his left boot. Jess had learned to notice such things quickly. The name of the saloon was Andy's and there were at least a dozen men inside. Jess sized up the room quickly and decided there were four men that he might have to deal with. Two of them were at the far right end of the bar and two more were sitting in a corner table with a bottle of whiskey and two glasses in front of them on the table.

The place went silent for a moment when Jess walked in. He had already pulled the double-barreled 12-gauge out from his back sling and had it in his left hand. He walked to the left end of the bar, placed the shotgun on the top of it, and ordered a beer. The chatter in the saloon slowly began to pick up again. He had the barrel of the shotgun pointed straight down the length of the bar toward the two men and he still had his left hand on it. He decided that if he needed to, he could use his left hand to trigger the shotgun in their direction and still leave his right hand free to use his pistol on the two men at the table. The bartender, Andy, knew Jess, got him a glass of beer, and placed it on the bar in front of him. Jess placed a dollar on the bar and Andy refused to take it.

"Beer's on me, Jess. I used to serve your pa whenever he came in. He was a damn good man. He stood up for me one time when a couple of cowboys tried to give me a beatin'. I don't forget things like that. I wasn't here the day ya shot Red, but I'm glad ya did it. I liked Sheriff Diggs. He was a fair man."

"Thanks, Andy. I appreciate it, especially what you said about my pa. So, how much trouble do you think I'm really in here?" Andy shook his head slowly.

"A lot more trouble than I'd care to be in. Old man Carter wants you dead real bad and the hired guns he's got working for him want a piece of that reputation you seem to be building up so early in your life. I'd say that you've got at least six men in town right now who would plug you if they got the chance. A couple of them are in here right now, and there's at least eight or ten more out at Carter's place that will eventually come for you. Hell, you give them half a chance and some of them would shoot you in the back when ya ain't lookin'. If you've got a lick of sense in you, you'd get on your horse and ride out of town now while you're still standing upright."

"Can't."

"Why not?"

"My horse is tired."

"Well, I'd shoot the damn horse and get me a new one," chastised Andy, a disgusted and yet somewhat proud look on his face. "But since you're stayin', I'll back ya with my shotgun I keep down here under the bar. And if I can serve you a cup of coffee in the morning, I'll consider you a lucky man."

"Luck's got nothing to do with it." Jess leaned toward Andy.

"I'll tell you what, Andy, I have the two at the end of the bar and the two over in the corner covered. If you need to use that sawed-off, cover anyone else in the place that has a mind to throw in, but I don't think anyone else will."

"You got it, my friend."

Jess sipped his beer and waited, knowing he wouldn't have to wait very long. The two men at the opposite end of the bar were staring at him, talking quietly back and forth and laughing. He figured this was as good a time as any to get the show started and that's exactly what this was going to be. He turned and looked directly at the two men at the bar. They were both grungy-looking men who looked like they had been on the trail for a while, but neither of them looked to be real gunslingers. Jess still had the scattergun lying on the bar pointed in their direction and set for his left hand to grab and trigger it, if needed.

"You boys sure seem to be having a good time over there. Why don't you let me in on the joke?" Both men turned to face Jess.

"Hell, kid, you are the joke," the larger of the two men said.

"Really? Me? Why, whatever do you mean?" Jess asked, feigning innocence.

"Hell," the larger man spoke again, "Carter's put up three thousand dollars on your head. Shit, my maggot-riddled grandma would crawl her ugly ass out of her grave and back shoot you to collect that kind of money. If that ain't enough, there's a few men in town who would shoot you just for your reputation. And, there's about a dozen more getting paid to shoot you and the first one to do it still gets the three thousand dollars of bounty on top of that. Now, I don't know about you, mister, but I find that kind of funny. You're going to be lucky to live through the night."

Jess took another sip of his beer and purposely took a minute before he replied, and when he did, he used his left hand to cock both barrels of the shotgun and looked straight into the eyes of the two men, who stopped smiling now.

"I have a question for the two of you. Do either of you want to try to collect that money?"

Everyone in the room stiffened. Jess figured that there was not a man alive who liked the sound of a scattergun being cocked and they liked it even less when it was being pointed in their direction. The two men certainly didn't like it and the looks on their faces told Jess everything he needed to know. They didn't want any part of this. One of the two men who were sitting at the table slammed his glass down on the table. Not because he was done with it, and not because he wanted the bartender's attention, he did it to attract Jess's attention. Jess had been watching both of them out of the corner of his eyes. They didn't want to be left out. After all, three thousand dollars was a whole lot of money to kill one man.

"I know you two are there," said Jess not even looking directly at them, which was somewhat of an insult in itself. "And if you want in, that's entirely up to you."

One of the two men sitting at the table stood up. The other man stayed in his seat. He was quiet and never looked up at Jess. Jess knew that this man was the more dangerous of the two and the one he had to worry about if he threw in. The way a man acted spoke the loudest and always said more than mere words ever could. He calmly, but coldly raised his eyes and met Jess's.

"Just because you're Jess Williams and have that fancy pistol, you think you can take four men at once?"

"The only thing better than killing two assholes at once is killing four assholes at the same time. And by the way, it wouldn't be the first time."

Jess could see the nervousness heighten in the two men at the bar. They could see that Jess was as calm as ever. The looks on their faces screamed that they didn't want any part of this, no matter how much money it paid. They had heard of Jess's reputation and while they weren't the smartest two men in town, they were smart enough to know that dead men couldn't spend money. Andy had his sawed-off already cocked under the bar. He would throw in with Jess if it came to that.

"We ain't having anything to do with this, mister. You can count us out. We'll be leaving town as soon as we finish our beers." Two men out, Jess thought to himself.

That left the two men at the table. The one was still standing and the other one, who was still sitting, was now glaring at Jess. He seemed a little agitated at Jess's remarks.

"Mister, did you just call me an asshole?" he probed. Jess took a drink of his beer and turned to face them directly. He let go of the shotgun on the bar.

"I guess I did. Of course, if you're not trying to collect the blood money on my head, then maybe I'm wrong."

The man slowly stood up. He was a gunslinger for sure. He had a Colt in a low-cut holster, tied down tight and low. Jess could sense this man was a killer. He spoke softly and sounded sure of himself. He exhibited an air of confidence, which made him a very dangerous man.

"I guess that makes me an asshole then, but I'll be the one with half of three thousand dollars."

"No, you'll be the one with half of nothing," Jess replied with sarcasm.

"How do you figure that?"

"Because you'll be dead."

"You sound awfully sure of yourself for such a young punk."

"You're about to find out if you plan on pulling that pistol."

"You planning on using that shotgun you got there?" asked the man at the table who had stood up first. Jess darted his eyes over at the shotgun. He had heard Andy cocking his sawed-off while he was talking with the other two men who were still standing at the bar, watching and listening.

"No, I only use that when I'm dealing with four assholes. For two assholes I only need this," he replied as he motioned his head down toward his pistol. "So, which one of you want to be first?"

Jess had barely gotten the words out of his mouth when both men went for their guns almost simultaneously. The one on Jess's right, the second man to stand up, was faster and Jess hit him with the first shot, square in the middle of the chest. He stumbled backward and dropped to the floor. Jess fanned the second shot, which found the other man's stomach not more than a fraction of a second later. He bent over and then slumped down in a chair, his gun dropping to the floor.

"You son of a bitch! You gut shot me! I swear I'm gonna kill you for that!" Jess cocked his head slightly and smiled at the man. Then he walked over and picked up the man's gun. "You're going to need this, aren't you?"

Jess handed the gun back to him. The man was literally thunderstruck by this. Jess walked a few steps backward from the man and slowly put his pistol back in its holster. Andy and the two men at the bar were watching, but they couldn't believe what Jess was doing. Andy raised the shotgun above the bar just in case.

"Well," said Jess, "I guess all you have to do is cock that hammer back and shoot me. That's what you wanted, wasn't it?" The man's eyes went crazy with hate.

"You son of a bitch," the man yelled as he thumbed the hammer back. He never had a chance to pull the trigger and he never heard the gunshot that killed him. Jess fanned the shot and hit the man right between the eyes. The man's brains sprayed over onto the next table behind him and then he fell backward in the chair.

"Holy shit!" one of the two men at the bar said. "It's time to get the hell out of this town." The two men hurried out of the bar and headed for the livery. They got on their horses and rode out, but not until they told a few men about what they had just witnessed. Jess walked back to the bar, replacing his spent cartridges as he did. Andy got him a fresh beer.

"Well, that ought to slow them down a bit, now that they know you won't hesitate. Those two were good at skinnin' leather. It won't be more than an hour before everyone in town knows what happened in here."

"That's the plan, Andy," replied Jess as he took a long sip of his beer. "That's the plan."

CHAPTER THREE

The two men who had been watching Jess from across the street had seen what had taken place in the saloon. They had been thinking about trying to collect the blood money on Jess, but now they had some serious reservations about it. The other two men, who had left the saloon after witnessing the gunfight between Jess and the men at the table, stopped and talked to them before leaving. The fellas from across the street headed for the livery and mounted their horses. When they rode up to the saloon, they stopped for a moment. Jess was still standing at the bar, watching them through the swinging doors. One of the two men stared at Jess, and for a moment, he thought the man was going to dismount and challenge him. Then Jess saw a change in the man's eyes and knew that there would be no challenge. The man looked at his partner. They both had the same look in their eyes. It was the look of fear. They both heeled their horses and rode out of town.

Jess felt certain his plan was working so far. Two men down and at least four men run out of town. That in itself didn't even the odds, but it certainly made them better. Hopefully, before the night was over, a few more men would value their lives more than money or their reputation and leave town while they could still ride a horse sitting upright. At least he hoped so.

"Well," said Andy, "seems like you scared off a few of 'em."

"Looks like it."

"Don't get your britches all bunched up in the crack of your ass," cautioned Andy. "There's sure to be more of them coming into town tonight. You'll have more trouble than a pack mule tryin' to peel a potato in a few hours. Tomorrow will be even worse for sure."

"Boy, you sure do know how to light up a man's life, Andy."

"I'm just tellin' the truth."

"Well, thanks for being ready with that scattergun back there. I appreciate the help."

"Hell, you didn't need my help. I reckon you coulda taken all four of 'em by yourself."

"Yeah, but I'm still thankful you were ready," Jess said with a slight grin.

He finished his beer and headed to the livery, which also served as a blacksmith shop. He asked Tony if he could sleep in the top of the livery tonight and Tony told him he could have anything he needed. Jess did want to stay with Jim and Sara since that might put them in danger. He fully expected some of Carter's men to come for him in the middle of the night and he didn't want to risk the lives of his friends. He set himself up in the loft, placing his bedroll on some hay on the floor. Then, he visited Jim again over at the store.

"How has business been?" asked Jess, as he found Jim stocking some ammo behind the counter.

"Business still ain't what it used to be, but for sure a damn sight better. Some of my old customers are trickling in, one by one. The sheriff came by right after I saw him ride back into town, probably from visiting Carter and informing him that you were in town, but he didn't come in like he used to. He just stood around outside and watched."

"I warned him not to bother you or your store ever again. He obviously didn't take me seriously," said Jess. "Maybe he needs a little reminder." Jess started for the door but Jim spun around with a worried look on his face.

"Jess, don't go fooling around with him," he pleaded. "It's not worth it. He didn't say anything or bother the customers; he just stood outside and watched." Jess stopped outside the doorway and turned back to Jim.

"It doesn't matter. When I say something, I mean it and he understood exactly what I warned him about. He's obviously decided to test me to see how far he can push me and he's about to find out right now."

Jess walked straight from the store to the sheriff's office. He walked in and found the sheriff sitting at his desk with his feet propped up on it. There was another man sitting in the office. Jess figured him to be one of Carter's men.

"Sheriff, are you a patient of Doc Johnson?" asked Jess.

"Well, he is the only pill-roller in town, so I guess so. Why?"

"Because you obviously have a hearing problem and since it's going to start affecting your health, maybe the doc can help you out with it."

"Whatever do you mean, Mr. Williams? Is there some kind of problem?" asked the sheriff in a nervous but sarcastic tone of voice. He seemed a little braver since he had another man in the room with him. "And how would bad hearing, if I had bad hearing, affect my health anyway?"

The other man in the room began to stand up but before he got his rump off the chair, which was to the left of the sheriff's desk, Jess glared at him with eyes that could bore a hole through a chunk of granite.

"You sit your ass back down in that chair unless you're ready to be fitted for a pine box. And I won't say it again."

That riled the man, who was probably in his early forties and not used to being talked to by a young man who didn't even look like he was past twenty yet, but he did, however, sit back down in the chair.

"Now see here," protested Newcomb. "This is my office and I'm the sheriff of this town unless you've forgotten that already." Jess walked up and shoved Newcomb's feet off the desk, his boot heels slamming on the floor.

"You're no sheriff. You're another hired gun with a tainted badge pinned on you by a mayor who works for a man who thinks he owns the town. If you think for one minute that I'll respect that badge as long as it's pinned on you, you're making a bad assumption and one that could cost you your life. I don't give a shit about you, your badge, the mayor who pinned it on you, or the piece of crap paying you both."

When Jess walked over to the desk, he partially turned away from Carter's man in the chair. He could still see him out of the corner of his eye. He heard, more than saw, the man reaching for his gun. Jess pulled his gun, squeezing the trigger as he brought it across his belly and fanned a shot that hit the man in the chest. The barrel of Jess's gun was only a few inches past his left elbow and he could feel the heat from the blast. The man fell back onto the chair, breaking one of the chair's legs and sending him to the floor. He was dead when he hit the floor. Newcomb stood up. Jess used his left hand to slap Newcomb across the face so hard it put him against the wall. Not a punch, but open handed, which was much more insulting and exactly why Jess did it. Newcomb never tried to reach for his gun. He knew better after seeing Jess draw. Jess grabbed Newcomb by the neck with his left hand and rammed him harder against the wall. He put his pistol back in its holster and pulled Newcomb's gun out. Newcomb froze in absolute terror.

"Oh shit, you're not going to shoot me, are you?"

"Not yet, but I will guarantee you this; if you ever go within one hundred feet of Jim and Sara Smythe or their store, you'll need an undertaker instead of something for the pain."

"I won't ever bother them again. You have my word. But, what did you say about pain?"

Jess didn't bother to explain what he meant. He took Newcomb's gun and cracked him hard across the nose with the butt of the pistol. Jess could hear the bone snap and the blood came gushing out of Newcomb's nose so fast that Jess had to quickly step back so as not to get any blood on his shirt. Newcomb grabbed a white cloth out of his front pocket and held it to his nose with both hands. The cloth quickly turned red from the blood.

"Damn it! You broke my nose! You're a crazy man!"

"Maybe I am, but when you need something for the pain, you be sure to go to the new general store to get it, understand? If I so much as see you walk in front of Smythe's General Store, you'll be seeing the front end of my pistol instead of the butt end of yours. And don't give me a reason to warn you again. If I have to, it'll be your last day on Carter's payroll and your first day in hell."

Jess spun on his heels and walked out, leaving Newcomb cussing and hollering about his nose. He had blood all over his face and his shirt. That sure was messy, Jess thought to himself.

He still had Newcomb's gun in his hand. He unloaded it and threw it in the dirt. It landed about a second before a bullet hit the ground not more than two inches from Jess's left boot. Jess reacted with pure instinct. He knew that the bullet had come from high up and to his left from the way the dirt sprayed up from the impact. He quickly moved to his right a step and as he did, he saw two figures on a roof across the street about ten feet apart. Jess fanned two shots and hit both men dead on. One of the men fell forward off the roof, bounced off the short overhang and fell onto the boardwalk while the other man stumbled backward, out of sight on the roof. Jess ducked down and made a full turn around, scanning everything he could to see if there were any more threats. He saw none. One of the townsfolk who had watched the failed ambush walked over to the body that had fallen onto the boardwalk. Jess quickly reloaded his empty chambers before holstering his pistol and strolled cautiously over to the body.

"That's old Ned Cullen. He won't be missed much," the man said, spitting some tobacco in the dirt.

"Is he one of Carter's men?" asked Jess.

"He was, but I guess he's off the payroll now."

"Do me a favor and go up to the roof and see who the other man is."

"What if he ain't dead yet?"

"Don't worry, he's a goner. I caught him square in the chest. If he's not dead yet, he's not long from a meeting with his maker."

The man walked through an opening between two buildings and over to the back of the building where the men had been shot. He went up the back steps and onto the roof. The man Jess had shot in the chest was lying face down, dead in a pool of his own blood. The man went back down and back over to Jess, who was standing under the overhang and looking around.

"He's dead for certain. I know he works for Carter, but I don't know his name."

"Thanks for the help, mister."

"No problem. Most of us here in town understand what's going on. You're fighting for us and we sure appreciate it. We ain't gun-fighters but we'll do what we can to help. Carter's had an iron grip on this town since you left and it's high time someone did some-thing about it. Sure can't count on the new sheriff. Carter owns him lock, stock and barrel, just like he owns the mayor."

"I have a hunch the sheriff might back off a little."

Just as the man was giving Jess a look of puzzlement, the sher-iff came storming out of his office with a blood-soaked rag against his face. Newcomb was heading straight for Doc Johnson's office, cursing to himself. They watched Newcomb for a few seconds and turned to give Jess a curious look.

"What the hell happened to him?"

"I gave him something else to do to occupy his time other than bothering Jim or Sara Smythe."

The man chuckled. "I think it's gonna work," he said.

Jess noticed that the blacksmith, Tony, and the barkeep, Andy, had appeared in front of their doors. Tony had his Winchester rifle in his hands and Andy had his shotgun. They nodded their heads to him as if to say that they were watching his back and he could count on them when the time came. It gave Jess a comfort level he wasn't used to. He nodded back and they knew exactly what he meant. They went back into their establishments.

Normally, Jess would apply for any bounty that these two men might have on their heads, but he knew that he couldn't rely on

Newcomb to assist in that, so he figured to hell with it. He did, however, remove a very nice pistol and holster from the very dead Ned
Cullen, along with fifty dollars that he found in his front pocket. He
decided he would give the pistol and holster to Jim Smythe to sell.
He climbed up the back steps to the roof where the other man lay
dead and he picked up a very nice model 1876 Winchester rifle and
another thirty dollars. The dead man's pistol and holster weren't
worth taking.

He was certain that the attempted ambush was a result of
Newcomb's trip out to see Carter earlier. He also realized that this
was a personal war between himself and Dick Carter, but it was also
a fight for the town and the people. His pa had been friends with
most of the longtime residents in Black Creek. His pa would have
wanted him to help these people and that's exactly what he was
going to do. Even if it cost him his life, which was entirely possible
the way things were going so far. Two more down, he thought to
himself. The odds were still bad, but they were getting better by the
hour. He knew that he would have more trouble tonight and he'd
be prepared for it, as always.

Jess decided to go back to the saloon and get something to eat.
Andy's daughter, LeAnn, was an attractive woman, with medium
brown hair and brown eyes. She had a nice shape but you could
tell she was a sturdy woman and quite a talker. Andy had once com-
mented that she could talk a man right out of his passions. LeAnn
did most of the cooking and serving at the saloon. Simple meals like
stew, beans, cornbread or steaks and not much else. Jess took a seat
at a corner table and Andy brought him a beer.

"Andy, you'd better bring me some coffee and make it strong. I
think I'm going to need to be awake most of the night."

Andy nodded, knowing exactly what he meant and went back
and got Jess a hot cup of coffee. "Can I get ya anything else?"

"Well, I am sort of hungry. How about a plate of whatever smells
so good back there?" Jess said, nodding in the direction of the
kitchen. "And thanks for earlier, Andy."

"It was my pleasure, Jess. It weren't nothin' compared to what you're doin' for the town and all of us."

About five minutes later LeAnn came out from the kitchen carrying a huge plate of stew and homemade bread. It smelled wonderful. She put the plate down in front of Jess and poured him another cup of coffee.

"My, my, my, Jess Williams, you sure look as cute as you did when you left here a few years ago," she started, speaking briskly. "I remember you coming to town and picking up supplies for your pa. Don't you remember me? I used to see you over at Smythe's store picking out candy. Didn't you see me in there? I used to go there every time you came to town. How have you been? I heard you shot a lot of men already and that you're faster than a rattlesnake. Do you have a girlfriend or a woman you're partial to and..."

"Damn it, LeAnn, let the man alone to eat his meal," hollered Andy. "He don't need to listen to you jack your jaw all day long. Get your ass back there in the kitchen where it belongs!"

Jess never said a word, not that he would get one in anyway. He had just looked at LeAnn and smiled while she talked. Now, he watched her as she threw her head back and stormed back into the kitchen.

Just as she got to the door, Jess spoke. "Yes and no." LeAnn turned around with a look of puzzlement on her face.

"Yes, I do remember you at the general store, and no, I have no woman that I'm partial to." LeAnn smiled one of those devious smiles.

"Well, maybe we need to change that." Jess didn't respond; he just looked at her, now regretting the answers he had given. I sure have to learn when to keep my mouth shut, Jess thought to himself.

"I told ya to get yer ass back in the kitchen and I mean now." Andy yelled. LeAnn threw her father a kiss and went back to cooking. Jess looked at Andy who had this strange look of frustration and hopefulness all wrapped up in one bewildering look.

"I shouldn't have said that, huh, Andy?"

"No, you shouldn't have but I'm sure glad ya did." Now Jess had a strange look on his face. He shook his head and went back to eating.

"No chance in hell, Andy." Andy's head hung a little low, his hopes dashed.

"Damn women, you can't live with 'em and you can't shoot 'em."

Jess chuckled as he began to eat the heaping plate of pork stew. The bread was as good as any biscuits he had ever eaten, almost. He finished his meal, went back to the livery, and asked Tony if he would keep watch while he took a little nap up in the top of the barn. Jess knew he wouldn't get much sleep tonight and he wanted to rest while he had the chance to do so without someone ambushing him. The way he figured it, the next ambush would take place in the late hours of the night.

"You go on up and make yourself comfy, Jess. I'll wake you before I leave, which won't be for another three hours or so," Tony told him.

"Thanks, but make sure you holler up to me, even if you leave for five minutes."

"I will. Don't you worry none about it."

Jess felt comfortable that he could nod off and finally get some rest. He knew he was going to need it later. He could hear Tony downstairs and could tell that Tony had started doing work that caused the least bit of noise. Jess thought that awfully nice of him. Tony was a good man and one that he figured he could count on when the going got tough. He finally fell off to sleep with his left hand on his shotgun lying across his stomach. He woke to gunfire and Tony hollering up to him.

"Jess! Jess! You better come on down here!" He quickly scrambled to his feet and climbed down to the bottom level.

"There's shooting over at the saloon. Been about three shots so far. I was heading over there with my rifle, but wanted to wake you first."

"Thanks," he said, shaking the cobwebs of sleep off as he slung his shotgun into its back sling. "But why don't you let me handle it and you wait here with your rifle. You keep a watch on the tops of the buildings just in case they try that little trick they pulled earlier again. This might be another set-up for me."

"Alright, but I'll come a runnin' if you need me."

Jess headed for the saloon, slipping his hammer strap as he did. He kept a close watch on the buildings in case this was another ambush. Tony also watched the tops of the buildings but saw nothing going on. Jess walked up to the front door of the saloon and peered inside. He saw LeAnn holding a rag to Andy's shoulder, which was bleeding quite profusely from what was obviously a bullet wound. Andy was sitting down at one of the tables and he looked like he was in more pain than a dog walking on rocky ground with a nail in his paw.

He saw two men at the bar and they both looked like they had been drinking more than their share of whiskey. Neither of them looked like gunslingers to Jess, but one of them still had his pistol on the bar. He was obviously the one who had shot Andy. The other man was short and paunchy and he looked like he didn't want to be there. Jess knew he would not be the problem. When he parted the batwings and strolled in, both men immediately took notice. The one who had his pistol on the bar placed his hand on the butt of it, but he didn't pick it up. He saw a look in Jess's eyes that prevented him from doing so, but he still kept his hand on the butt of his pistol and his thumb on the hammer. The other man stared at Jess, but said nothing. He simply put both of his hands on the bar as if to say he wasn't going to be part of any gunplay. Both men were looking at Jess, who walked to his left a little closer to Andy and LeAnn but not so close as to put them in the line of fire. The man holding the butt of his pistol finally spoke. "And who might you be?"

Jess didn't answer. Without ever taking his eyes off the two men, he asked Andy how he was doing.

"How the hell ya think I'm doin'! I've been shot, damn it! I'm bleedin' like a stuck pig and that bastard right over there is the one who shot me," hollered Andy, glaring at the man at the bar.

"Well, I wouldna had to if'n you hadn't reached for that damn shotgun back behind the bar."

"And I wouldn't a had to if you'd have shut yer yap like I warned ya." Andy said, moaning in pain. The man ogled LeAnn again.

"Well, she does have a nice shape to her. A little extra meat on it, but that's how I like my women, strong and meaty," the man said as he spat some of the liquid from his chaw onto the floor. Andy started to say something but LeAnn beat him to it.

"You ain't gettin' any of this shape or anything else for that matter, mister."

"You know you want it. You're just playin' hard to get. I like that too."

"You are nothing but a filthy pig. You get the hell outta here," hollered LeAnn.

"And who's gonna make me?" the man said in a leering voice. LeAnn started to answer but Jess cut her off mid-sentence, which in itself, was quite an accomplishment.

"I guess that would be me," said Jess.

The man, who had been eyeing LeAnn up and down, looked at Jess. "Let me tell ya somethin', boy. I been eatin' younguns like you fer breakfast the last twenty years. You ain't makin' me do nothin' unless I want to."

"I hope you're hungry, then, because you'll be eating something in about one minute, which is just about all the time you have to leave."

"I'm real scared. Ain't you scared, Barry?" he said, nodding back to his partner behind him at the bar, who had not moved or said a word during all of this.

"Cole, I think we oughtta leave," Barry said, still not moving his hands from the bar.

"I ain't goin' nowhere! This little shit ain't makin' us do nothin'!"

"You've got about another thirty seconds or so left. I advise you to use them wisely," Jess warned the man.

"You go to hell, boy! Case you missed it, I got my hand on the butt of my pistol and yours is still stuck in your holster. I think you're the one who oughtta get whilst ya can!"

"You're down to about fifteen seconds," Jess replied, calm as a cat curled up on a blanket.

"And what do you plan on doin' after that, boy?"

"I plan on putting a little lead in your ass."

"You ain't got the gumption for it, boy."

"Five seconds," Jess said, his right hand at the ready. Andy moaned again.

Cole's face turned three shades redder. Cole Parker wasn't the smartest man you would ever meet, which is probably why he didn't see in Jess what his partner, Barry Jacobs, had seen. If he had, he would have left while he had the chance. Jess saw Cole tighten his grip on the butt of his pistol. Cole figured all he had to do was cock and fire it. In his mind, he thought he had the advantage over this young man standing him down. He figured he'd shoot him and then get his hands on LeAnn. He figured dead wrong.

He actually got to lift the pistol off the bar but he never got to finish thumbing the hammer back before the slug from Jess's pistol found his chest. The man looked surprised and tried to speak but nothing came out except a little spittle with some blood and tobacco mixed in with it. He fell forward and landed facedown on the wooden floor with a heavy thud. His partner, Barry, never moved a muscle, which is the only thing that saved his life. Jess's pistol was still out, the barrel smoking and pointed straight at Barry Jacobs. His left hand was ready to fan another round.

"I ain't pullin' on ya, mister," Barry said, keeping his hands on the bar. "I know who ya are and my momma didn't raise no fool. I'll be leavin' if'n that's okay."

"I think that's a wise decision, Barry. When you leave, keep on leaving, right out of town and don't come back, ever."

"I'll be gone quicker than it took Cole to die; you can be sure of that."

Barry took one look at his pal on the floor on his way out. He never put his hands down by his side until he got outside the saloon. He was taking no chance that Jess would consider him a threat. He wanted to live another day and find a new pal. Maybe one with a little more sense. Jess reloaded and holstered his gun and looked back over at Andy who was still bleeding. He started to speak but LeAnn beat him to it.

"Why, Jess Williams, I've never seen anyone draw a pistol that fast before. That man never had a chance. You sure are something and…"

"Would you just shut yer everlovin' jaws, woman, and go and get the doc before I bleed to death right here in this damn chair!" LeAnn huffed and headed out the door to go get Doctor Johnson. Before she got to the door, Andy hollered out again.

"I swear by God that the next man that comes in here and wants ya, I'll let him take ya!" LeAnn stopped for a moment and looked at her father through expectant eyes.

"Well, Jess was the next man in here." She looked at Jess and headed out the door for the doctor. Andy looked up at Jess with a look like a hungry dog begging for some scraps.

"Don't look at me like that, Andy," he said vigorously. Andy lowered his head and moaned. Not from the bullet wound in his shoulder though.

CHAPTER FOUR

Doctor Johnson and LeAnn both came running into the saloon and the doctor immediately went to look at Andy's wound.

"Well, you're lucky, Andy," said the doctor. "The bullet went clean through the flesh and it doesn't look like it did that much damage. Come on over to the office and I'll fix you right up."

"Lucky? Since when is it lucky a man gets shot?"

"I'd say you're a damn sight luckier than this fellow lying here," the doctor said, nodding at the dead man lying on the floor of the saloon. Andy moaned and let the doctor help him out of his chair. LeAnn helped too and she started walking out of the saloon with Andy and the doctor.

"Where the hell do ya think you're goin', woman?" Andy asked LeAnn, groaning in pain.

"I'm going over to the doctor's office with you."

"Like hell you are! You gotta run this damn place till I git back from the doc's. He don't need any help causing me any more pain than I already got!" Doctor Johnson had a look of indignation on his face.

"On second thought," he said as he examined Andy's shoulder again, "maybe I should explore around a little just to make sure there are no pieces of bone or lead floating around in there." Andy moaned some more, knowing that he would pay for his remark. He looked over at Jess,

"I shouldn't have said that, huh, Jess?"

Jess shook his head in sympathy. "Nope, you sure shouldn't have."

The doctor took him out and walked him over to his office. That left Jess inside the saloon with a dead man and LeAnn. Suddenly, he wished he hadn't shot the man, or at the very most just wounded him.

"Well, Jess Williams, I guess I should give you a great big kiss for saving Daddy and me," she said, smiling expectantly at him. "What do you think about that?" Jess felt strangely uncomfortable. It was a feeling he hadn't experienced before and he didn't like it. Tony from the livery came walking in before Jess could respond. He looked at the dead man on the floor and looked back up at Jess.

"You sure are having a busy day, ain't ya?" asked Tony.

"Yeah, and I don't see it slowing down much either. Tony, could you get some men over here and get this body over to the under-taker? I have to go see Jim and Sara."

"Sure thing, Jess, I'll tend to it right now."

Jess nodded at LeAnn and before she could say anything to stop him, he quickly pushed through the doors of the saloon. The fact that he got out before she spoke was nothing short of a miracle. He hadn't really planned on visiting Jim and Sara; he had used it as an excuse to get out of LeAnn's sight. She looked a little too much like a starving cat eyeing a big bowl of milk. He decided that he would visit the general store and have a cup of coffee with Jim and Sara anyway. He always enjoyed that. Jess found Jim stocking some shelves since business was picking up. Sara put on a pot of coffee and the three of them sat down.

"Business must be pretty good if you're restocking shelves already," said Jess.

"Sure is, thanks to you," admitted Jim, a cautious tone in his voice. "I'm still not sure it was the right decision for you though."

"How's that?"

"Carter's not going to stop until he gets you," warned Jim. "He ain't the type that likes losing. He's already tried to have you killed and I hear tell he's coming into town tomorrow to make sure you don't get out alive. He's a mean cuss and won't stop until one of you are dead."

"I figure you're right about that, Jim," agreed Jess. "This will never be over until one of us is maggot food and there is no getting around that. That's why there's no sense trying to get out of this. He'll hunt me down even if I leave town. I might as well end it here, right now, one way or another."

Jim lowered his head a little. "Well, I feel kind of responsible for it," he said. "Hell, Sara and I could've retired and let that old cuss get his way."

"You know as well as I do that would never have satisfied him anyway," countered Jess. "Men like Carter are used to pushing people around and making them do what he wants them to do. That's going to end right here and soon. You have a right to run your business and the only reason you're being punished is because the two of you are my friends. I won't stand for that."

Sara grabbed the coffee pot and poured three cups. She got out some cornbread and put it on the table.

"You know, Jess," Sara piped in, "Jim's right. We could survive okay with the way things were. It's not worth you getting killed over it. I'd rather burn this place to the ground and leave town with what we could carry in a wagon before seeing anything happen to you."

"That's exactly why I won't leave. You two are good people and my friends. I won't abandon you and leave town. I could never live with myself. That blood bounty will follow me around until he's dead and can't pay it. Besides, Carter is the kind of man who needs to learn that he doesn't own the world."

"What are you going to do when he comes to town tomorrow?" asked Jim.

"I'm more concerned with getting through the night, right now. As for tomorrow, I'll deal with it when it gets here. I can tell you this though. If Carter comes to town, I'll kill him for sure. His hired guns may get me before the smoke clears, but he will be the first one to go down. He's the one who caused all this grief and he's the one who's going to pay for it. And not with all his money. He's going to pay for it with his life."

Jim and Sara looked at one another and knew there was no way they could talk Jess out of any of it. They also knew deep down in their hearts that he was right. Even though they didn't agree with the path in life that he had chosen, they knew that men like Carter would just push and push the common people until they gave in, and when that finally happened, he would push some more until he had everything they owned. They both knew that Carter would never leave the town alone, even if he did succeed in having Jess killed. He had the town under his thumb now and he would never give it up. That was the way it was with most rich and powerful men. Once they had the taste of power, the only way they would give it up is when you pried it from their cold dead fingers.

Jess picked up a nice slab of warm cornbread and buttered it heavily. He began to eat it, but his mind wasn't really on the cornbread even though it tasted wonderful. He was deep in thought about something else. Not about Carter or the fact that there were as many as a dozen men who would shoot him on sight for the money or the reputation. He was thinking about his twin brother, Tim Sloan. He knew that once he settled things in town, if he survived it, he would have to turn his attention to his brother. He would have to find him and find out how and why his brother had come to know Blake Taggert, one of the murderers of his family. However, he couldn't think about it much right now. He had to stay focused on his immediate problem, trying to keep from getting killed by one of Carter's thugs or even Carter himself. While Jess steadfastly refused to stay overnight at Jim and Sara's, he did agree to take a short nap. He figured he would head to Andy's Saloon shortly after dusk. He had two good hours of sleep before Sara woke him. He grabbed a quick swallow of coffee and headed down to the saloon.

Jess watched carefully while he walked over to Andy's. He noticed Tony sitting slightly inside the door of his livery, with his Winchester across his lap. Jess nodded to him and felt very fortunate to have a friend who would stick by him in a time like this. Men like that, in fact, were not that common. Most men would have gone home, had

their supper and been resting between some cool sheets, but not
Tony. Here he was, watching the rooftops and any other ambush
points he could see from his vantage point. Jess stopped outside of
Andy's, looking in to see who was inside. From behind the bar Andy
gave him a look that said it was okay to enter. Jess walked in and
surveyed the room. There were over a dozen men in the saloon and
Jess quickly sized them up. Only two men inside looked like they
might be a problem. The rest were there for the show, if there was
one. Andy brought Jess a hot cup of coffee and he sipped it slowly.

"Didn't plan on seeing you back here so soon," said Jess.

"I wouldn't want to miss any fireworks," said Andy, smiling.

"You might get shot again."

"They'd just put me out of my misery."

"Misery?" Jess asked, with a grin. "You've got it made. You've got
a great saloon to run here and a wonderful daughter by your side."

"Who the hell you think I was talkin' about when I said misery?"
Jess shook his head and smiled. LeAnn came out of the back room
with a few plates of food.

"Why Jess Williams, the way you ran out of here today, I didn't
think I would ever see you back in here," she said, obviously a little
miffed by his quick departure earlier.

"I missed Andy," he replied sarcastically. LeAnn threw her head
back and stormed back into the kitchen.

"I think I understand," Jess told Andy.

"Huh? 'Bout what?" Andy asked, somewhat confused.

"That thing you said about misery."

Andy nodded, finally catching on.

Jess stayed at the saloon for the next several hours expecting
something to happen, but surprisingly, nothing did. A few men had
given him more than a few glances, but they were just curious and
he could tell they would not be a problem. About two o'clock in the
morning, the place was almost empty. There was one man at the bar
who was very drunk and Andy kept trying to get him to go home.
LeAnn had left already. Two men were deadlocked in a poker game,
neither one of them wanting to give up.

Jess thanked Andy and headed to the livery to get what little rest he could. Tony was gone from his spot when he reached the doors. Jess climbed up to the top and pulled the ladder up with him. He figured there was no sense in making it easy if someone decided to pay him a visit in the middle of the night. He checked the floor for squeaks and found a quiet spot in a dark area. Then he found a small chunk of wood on the floor and placed it close to where he was going to sleep. Jess hung the back sling with the shotgun on a nail within easy reach and lay down with his pistol in his hand, resting on his stomach.

Men like Jess never really slept soundly. They couldn't take the chance. They could, however, sleep through certain natural sounds. Sounds like frogs croaking or crickets chirping. They could sleep while owls hooted and coyotes howled. But certain noises, noises that didn't seem to fit or belong to the natural order of things, would suddenly startle a man like Jess and wake him. It was just that sort of unnatural noise that the ambusher in the bottom of the livery made that sentenced him to a certain death. He had brushed his left elbow against a wall where some bits were hanging up and the metal on one of them bumped the wall ever so slightly. Jess's subconscious woke him. He wasn't sure what he had heard, only that he had heard something out of the ordinary, something that didn't quite fit, and that meant danger.

He slowly rose from his bedroll and stood quietly, backing himself against the wall where it was pitch black next to his shotgun and waited, watching for any movement. There were two men. One was standing just inside the front door of the livery, a pistol exposed in his right hand. Jess couldn't see the other man but he could tell he was below him by watching the face of the man in the doorway nodding in the direction below Jess. The man at the door was pointing his pistol up to the top of the livery. Jess knew he had only seconds to act before they would spot him. He picked up the small chunk of wood he had found on the floor earlier. Then he very quietly holstered his pistol, tightened the hammer strap, and quietly pulled the shotgun out of its sling.

Jess threw the piece of wood to the right of the man in the doorway. At the exact same instant that the wood hit the floor, he cocked both barrels. Just as the man in the doorway shifted his attention to the sound of the wood hitting the floor, Jess let him have the first shot and the back of the man's head exploded like a melon. Before the man fell, Jess turned and stepped off the top and jumped straight down to the floor. As he descended, he looked for the other man. Before Jess's feet hit the ground, he spotted him and let him have the second barrel just as the man's shot went wild, missing Jess by at least five feet. The shotgun blast hit the man full force in the middle of his chest. The force slammed him against the wall and he hit the ground, never to move again.

Tony lived behind the livery. Jess heard him running up the short trail and saw him enter the back door. He had his Winchester and an oil lamp in his hands. Tony glanced at the two men and looked at Jess who appeared no worse for wear.

"You okay, Jess?" asked Tony, putting his rifle across his left arm and setting the lamp down on a worktable.

"Better than these two boys."

"Can't argue with you on that."

"You know these two? Are they working for Carter?"

"That one by the front door is one of Carter's men. Never seen that one though," Tony said, nodding in the direction of the other dead man lying in a pile of hay. "Must be one of the many fans you've gained since you came to town."

"I do seem to have a lot of people interested in me, don't I?"

"You are becoming right popular, and that's a fact. Hell, you ought to run for mayor. You would win hands down."

Just then, Andy came running up to the front of the livery, his shotgun in his left hand. He was breathing heavy and moaning from the pain in his shoulder.

"Holy shit," blurted Andy, "don't ya ever take a break?"

"Only when they let me, Andy."

"Well, the odds are gettin' better. Hell, you must've killed damn near a dozen men today alone," said Andy.

"That's how those rumors get started. Actually, it's closer to a half dozen," Jess replied.

Andy cocked his head and gave Jess a sarcastic look. "Like it really matters."

"Well," said Tony, "I'll take care of the bodies. Jess, why don't you go on back up and get some rest. I'll stand guard again so you can get some sleep. You're going to need all you can get for tomorrow."

"Yeah," agreed Andy, "I'm sure you're gonna have quite a day tomorrow. Probably worse than today, if that's at all possible."

"Andy, you're just a little ball full of good news," replied Jess as he used a rake to pull the ladder back down so he could climb back up to the top.

"Don't get me riled up or I'll send LeAnn over here for ya."

"Hell no, I'd rather deal with a few more ambushers," Jess replied. Andy and Tony both laughed at that.

Tony took care of the bodies. Andy went back home after having a cup of coffee with Tony. Jess had listened to the two of them chat back and forth before he finally fell off to sleep. Jess remembered shuddering a little just before he did. He thought it might have been from the chill of the night air, but he realized it was really from the thought of Andy sending LeAnn over as he had threatened. Tony sat guard until five in the morning.

Tony woke Jess before the sun rose and he climbed down from the loft. He had a few cups of strong hot coffee with Tony. They sat there and watched the town come to life. People were slowly coming out and moving around. Jess smiled when he saw two people walk into Smythe's General Store inside of a half hour. He smiled mostly because not one person had yet entered Carter's General Store except for the clerk that Jess had met when he went into the store yesterday. Jess spotted Sheriff Newcomb opening his office, his nose still bandaged from his encounter with the butt of his own pistol.

"Nice piece of work on the sheriff by the way, Jess," chuckled Tony.

Jess nodded. "Yeah, maybe he'll keep his nose out of Jim and Sara's business."

Tony and Jess watched two men walk out of Andy's Saloon and stretch. They were the same two men who had been deadlocked in the poker game last night. They either played all night or had fallen asleep at the table. The sun was up and the night chill was slowly dissipating. It seemed like such a peaceful day and yet Jess knew that this day would be anything but.

᠊᠊᠊ 🙐 🙑

While Jess and Tony sat there watching the town come alive, Dick Carter was sitting in a chair on the front porch of his huge ranch home, deep in thought about Red, his only son. Red had been a pain in his ass most of the time, but like any father, Dick had still loved his son and Jess had taken Red from him. Red had been such a pain in the ass growing up that Carter's wife wouldn't have anything to do with him after a while. Carter raised the boy the best he could and of course, Red had picked up a few of his father's bad habits. The worst one was Carter's bad temper. He had wanted Red to inherit the sprawling ranch that he had built from the ground up and now there would be no one to leave it to except his wife, and he wasn't happy about that. Their marriage had been a sour one right from the start and it only got worse with each passing day.

He thought about drawing up an agreement with his friend Cal Hardin, who owned the ranch next to him. The agreement would specify how much Hardin would pay for Carter's ranch and everything that went with it in the case of Carter's demise. That would make Hardin the largest ranch owner in the area but that wouldn't matter to Carter since he would be dead anyway. He thought of how Hardin had reluctantly agreed to hold the ten thousand dollars in bounty money to be paid to a man by the name of Tim Sloan when he could bring the dead body of Jess Williams to Hardin to identify. Hardin thought the idea was wrong but he owed Carter a favor. Carter had helped him get rid of some rustlers when Hardin's men couldn't seem to handle the situation on their own. Carter's men took care of the problem hastily, eliminating the rustlers within a week's time.

Then Carter's thoughts turned to Jess Williams. He was obsessed with the thought of killing him. His mind was crazy with revenge. He wasn't thinking straight and he realized that, but there was nothing he could do to stop himself; it was simply his nature. He planned to ride into town today with six of his best hired guns, but not until the late part of the afternoon. He already had a few men in town and a few more riding out today to try to kill Jess, and if they failed, he would see to it himself. As he stood to stretch, he watched as two of his hired guns rode out toward Black Creek. He knew what their mission was. To find and kill Jess, anyway they chose. They could ambush him, shoot him in the back or shoot him while he slept. Carter had two more men who would leave in a few hours and their mission was the same in case the first two failed. He didn't care about the morality or the right or wrong of it. He just wanted Jess dead, like his son.

⌖ ⌖

After several strong cups of Tony's coffee, Jess borrowed a razor from him, shaved his little fuzz of youthful stubble, and washed up a bit. Then he walked over to Smythe's General Store, sat with Jim and Sara, and had some breakfast with them. Jess could see the worried look on Sara's face; she was on the verge of tears. She knew what was coming today and she was deathly afraid for Jess. It was about nine in the morning when they finished a meal of eggs, bacon, ham, fresh biscuits, and apple pie.

"Sara," said Jess, "you sure can cook. That was surely one of the best meals I've had in a long time."

"I'm glad you enjoyed it. I hope it won't be your last, though."

"Ah...come on now," Jim piped in, "Jess can handle himself. He's pretty damn good with that pistol of his."

"Maybe, but he's facing a dozen hired guns, not just one man in the street," said Sara.

"I have a hunch that Jess will have more help than he thinks before this thing is over," Jim added.

"What do you mean by that?" asked Sara.

"I've heard some of the other men talking and they say they're thankful that Jess is here trying to help the town. I heard that when trouble starts today, there'll be more guns than Jess's talking. I know that Tony over at the livery will throw in and Andy over at the saloon will be ready with his scattergun. I heard a few other men say that they'll be keeping their rifles handy for the next few days. Jess, you ain't in this alone. I aim to throw in with my shotgun too when trouble starts."

"Oh my Lord!" exclaimed Sara. "You wouldn't know which end is the barrel. You'd just shoot your foot off or something. Are you out of your mind?"

"If Jess is willing to risk his life for our problems, the least we can do is back him up and help him fight our battle. If that means losing a foot, then so be it." Jim said it so proudly, as if he were a politician making a speech and running for office. Jess sat there watching them go back and forth and his smile finally turned to a quiet laugh. Both of them turned to look at him, Jim smiling and Sara looking concerned.

"Listen," cautioned Jess, "I appreciate the help, but don't risk your life unless you have to. I can handle Carter and his men with a little help from Tony and maybe even Andy. I didn't ask anyone to throw in with me, but if they want to, I can't stop them and I'm not sure I would want to. I reckon there's nothing wrong with people fighting for their own town."

Jess got up, hugged Sara, thanked Jim, and walked out into the street. It was a little after nine in the morning and it was indeed a beautiful day. The sun was shining brightly, quickly warming the air. The sky was a bright blue with no clouds in sight. Jess almost laughed at the irony of it. It was such a beautiful day. A beautiful day that he knew would soon turn bloody and deadly. Jess wondered how many men would lie dead before the day was over. He knew one thing for sure though. Dick Carter would hit the ground dead before Jess would and he made that a vow to himself.

CHAPTER FIVE

The two men took their time to saddle up. They were in no particular hurry even though they had a very important and deadly task. Blaine Roth was as tough as nails. One look at his face would tell you that: a scar on his left cheek, his face tanned and leathery. He had received the scar from a bar fight with another hard case several years back over a woman. It wasn't the only scar on his body. He had been in more fights than he could remember over his forty plus years, including several gunfights. He wasn't considered fast with a gun but he wasn't the type to get too easily rattled. He had once faced off with two men in a gunfight and stood his ground like an oak tree. He hit the first man square in the chest and even though he knew the other man had already fired his first shot, burning a hole in the soft flesh of his left side just below his ribcage, he took careful aim and hit the other man with his second shot. Both men had been faster, but both ended up on the street in a pool of their own blood. Roth went back into the saloon, ordered a bottle of fine whiskey and told the barkeep to collect the money for it off the two dead men outside.

Gene Horn was nothing like Blaine Roth. He was always clean-shaven and neatly dressed and he wasn't one to get into fistfights. Some of his friends had even taken to calling him Pretty Boy for a nickname. He was, however, very quick with a pistol. He had killed several men and never been hit. Horn seldom drank or frequented saloons. He had reached the age of twenty-two a few weeks back and he was somewhat of a loner, spending much of his off time reading or practicing his pistol skills.

Both men did have one thing in common though. They both wanted to collect their share of the three thousand dollars of blood bounty on Jess Williams' head. Carter had ordered them into town first this morning with another two to follow a few hours later. If Jess survived that, Carter would lead a group of six of his best hired guns into town and personally see to his death, one way or another. Both men mounted their horses and headed out to Black Creek. They rode in silence for about fifteen minutes before either one of them spoke.

"What are you going to do with your half of the money?" Horn asked.

"Ain't you getting a little ahead of yourself?"

"What do you mean?"

"Hell, boy, we ain't even got to town yet, much less killed this Williams fella."

"Well, there's two of us and one of him and I am pretty damn good with a pistol. You have that shotgun. Hell, I'd say he's pretty much finished when we get there."

"Listen up, Pretty Boy. You should never assume that you have the upper hand when facing down another man. That will kill you quicker than a chunk of lead in your chest."

"You're not rattled about going after this kid, are you? I mean, yeah, he's fast and all and he has that fancy pistol of his, but he's too young to be that fast. Hell, I've probably been practicing with a pistol longer than he's been able to hold one in his hands."

"I ain't rattled. I'm just saying you never really know what's going to happen when it comes right down to it. I plan on finding him and killing him. The truth is, either he'll get me or I'll get him. It's that simple."

"Well, don't you worry, Blain, I'll be there to make sure that it's him that goes down." Blaine Roth looked back over at Horn.

"Just remember, we ain't playing fair. I don't plan on back shootin' him, but I don't plan on giving him any quarter either. We face him together and we shoot first. If I don't get him with my scattergun, you make sure you put some lead in him with that hog leg of yours, you got that?"

"Don't you worry about me. I'll have two chunks of lead in that kid before you can cock the barrels on that shotgun. You can count on that and when it's done, I'm going to take that fancy pistol and holster of his for myself."

"I ain't countin' on anything," replied Roth, still trying to make his point.

Roth knew that Horn was indeed fast with a pistol and the truth was it did give him a small level of comfort. On the other hand, Roth was twice as old as Horn and that gave him twice the life experience. Enough experience to know the reputation of some of the men that Jess had already killed. Roth knew they were all men who were fast with a pistol and probably faster than the young gunslinger riding next to him at this very moment. For a brief moment his common sense told him to ride past Black Creek and head for Texas. The only thing stopping him from doing that was the thought of three thousand dollars. That was an awful lot of money even if he did have to split it with his partner. They rode the rest of the way in silence.

Jess decided it was a nice day to visit the mayor of Black Creek. He had already warned Sheriff Newcomb and since the sheriff worked for the mayor, Jess figured it was only fair to give the same warning to him. That way there would be no misunderstanding about Jess's intentions.

Nigel York was not a gunslinger. He didn't even carry a pistol and if he did, he would probably shoot himself with it. He was in his late thirties. He was a man who liked to dress neatly and chase the women. He had worked for Carter over the years, running errands for him in Black Creek. Things like running supplies out to the Carter 'D' ranch or taking messages to other ranch owners. He was a coward but more importantly, a yes man for Carter, which is why Carter ran him for the position of mayor.

It wasn't much of a race though. Carter had everybody in town so scared that no one would run against his man. Even the incumbent mayor decided it was time to retire instead of challenging Carter. York had a small office in town. He was sitting behind a desk reading a newspaper and enjoying some hot coffee when Jess knocked on his open door.

"Yeah, who is it?" asked York, not bothering to look up from his paper.

"I thought I would pay a visit to the mayor and introduce myself," replied Jess as he walked inside the room. York finally looked up from his paper. His startled expression told Jess that he recognized him immediately and he had a look of fear in his eyes. He stood up and backed away from his desk until his back hit the wall.

"No need to introduce yourself, Mr. Williams. I know who you are and I saw what you did to Sheriff Newcomb. You can't run around assaulting people whenever you feel like it, especially officials of the town."

"Really, why not?"

York looked down at the floor for a moment as if he would somehow find an answer written on the floorboards and not quite sure how to respond. He looked back up at Jess.

"Because it's against the law," York replied, a small hint of defiance in his voice.

"Whose law?"

"The town's law."

"Don't you mean Carter's law? The law he bought and paid for?"

"I am the legal and duly elected mayor of this town. I won the election honestly. If you don't believe me, go ask Judge Hollingsworth. He'll tell you."

"Of course you won. No one ran against you. What a stroke of luck for you, don't you think?"

"Maybe, but I'm still the mayor, and Newcomb is still the sheriff and you're going to have to abide by the laws of this town and its officials." Jess shook his head, amazed at how men could fool themselves into such a false sense of reality.

"Listen up, York. Let's get something straight. I don't have to live with anything. I don't have to respect your or the sheriff's positions.

Both of you are bought and paid for by the same man and neither of you are working for the benefit of this town. You're both working for the man who is paying your salary. The same man who is trying to have me killed and the same man who is trying to run my good friends out of business."

"There's nothing against the law about Carter starting up a new store in town," York interjected, before Jess could continue.

"Shut up and let me finish because I'm not going to say it again. You and your pal, Newcomb, are nothing but hired gunmen to me. I have no respect for your authority or Newcomb's since it was bought and paid for with the same money that's trying to have me killed. Which, by the way, is against the law, but I don't suppose you're going to do anything about that, are you? I'm going to give you the same warning I gave Newcomb and I'm not going to repeat it. If I have to, you won't have to worry about your next reelection. You stay out of this and you leave Jim and Sara Smythe alone, understand? If I find out you have even so much as looked in the direction of their store, I swear to you that I will come back here and blow one of your kneecaps clean off. Now, did you understand exactly what I said, or do you need me to repeat it for you?"

York's eyes darted to the floor. He was terrified and his knees were getting so weak he thought he might collapse at any moment. "I understand. I won't bother the Smythes again, ever."

"Good. I'm glad to hear it. You can pass on a message for Judge Hollingsworth too. He used to be on good terms with my pa but that was before Dick Carter put him on his payroll. Tell him if he stays out of my way, he'll live, but if he gets in the middle of this, I'll treat him the same as any of Carter's hired guns. Have a nice day, Mayor."

Jess turned around and walked out of York's office. He thought about Judge Hollingsworth. Hollingsworth had been a good man in years past. His penchant for women and whiskey, along with his love for money, had been his downfall. The fact that Dick Carter could supply him with all three was the reason that Carter now owned Judge Hollingsworth. Jess remembered how his pa had helped him one time when some cowboys were trying to rough him up before he had become a judge. Hollingsworth had never forgotten that and always told his pa that if he ever needed anything, all he had to do was ask. Jess didn't want to hurt Hollingsworth, but he would if forced to. He also figured that there would be no need for a judge in this whole situation. It wasn't like Carter was trying to have him arrested and put on trial for killing his son Red. He was trying to have Jess murdered and he was willing to pay well for the deed.

He noticed Tony down the street sitting there like a rock, just inside the large door of his livery with his rifle across his lap. Again, he felt good that someone was watching his back, but he noticed that Tony was now looking down toward the sheriff's office. Jess saw what he was looking at and he knew immediately what it was—more trouble. Blaine Roth and Gene Horn had already tied their horses to a post and were walking into Newcomb's office. Jess strode quickly across the street to where Tony was now standing.

"What do you think those boys are up to, Tony?" asked Jess, already knowing the answer.

"You're joshin' me, right?" Tony answered.

"I suppose things are about to heat up again."

"I'd have to say you are right about that. I know one of those men who went into Newcomb's office. He works for Carter. He is one mean son of a bitch and he ain't gonna come at you fair. He will shoot you on sight when he sees you and he's carrying a shotgun with him. My guess is that Newcomb's already told those boys where you are."

"No sense in hiding then, wouldn't you say?"

"Guess not," replied Tony, a grim look on his face.

Jess pulled the shotgun out of his back sling and removed the strap from his pistol. He peeked out around the large open door and saw that both men were still in Newcomb's office as he cocked both barrels. Jess glanced back at Tony and with a nod of his head, he was out the door and walking briskly across the street, his hand on the butt of his pistol. He went behind one building and worked his way between Andy's Saloon and Jackson's Hardware, which was the smallest hardware store Jess had ever seen. He was standing in the middle of the opening looking across the road when both men came out of Newcomb's office. Jess could see Newcomb standing in the doorway pointing at Jess. The instant that Blaine Roth saw Jess, he opened up with both barrels on his shotgun. Jess had barely gotten his back to the wall enough to get some cover when Roth's blast took out one of the windows of the hardware store as well as a few chunks of wood from the corner of both buildings. Jess could hear the pellets hitting the wall opposite him.

Jess knew that the slightest hesitation would cost him his life. A half second after the shotgun blast peppered the buildings he was between, he crouched down and moved to the left just enough to see the two men and then he opened up with both barrels. He saw instantly that the man with the shotgun was hit. As Roth spun around and hit the dirt, the spent shotgun shells he was trying to remove went flying in the air. Jess didn't know for sure if it was a fatal shot or not, but he figured it was good enough for the moment.

He saw the other man, who had already started running off toward the right of the man with the shotgun. Jess heard Tony's rifle crack and the man went down like a sack, but not before the man got off two shots from his pistol. One of them took another chunk of wood out of the hardware store about four inches above Jess's head and the second one hit the dirt not more than two feet from Jess. Jess quickly reloaded the shotgun, put it back in the sling, and walked quickly across the street, his pistol in his hand now, his eyes scanning the street thoroughly.

"Tony, cover me!" he hollered out.

"Got your back, Jess," Tony yelled, as he walked out into the middle of the street.

Jess walked toward the first man, who was moaning and wriggling around on the ground. The shotgun was well out of reach and the man's right hand was missing a few fingers. Jess looked over at the younger man, who was lying on his back in the middle of the street not moving, his gun also out of reach. Andy had come out from the saloon with his sawed off and Jess nodded to him to watch the younger man. Jess walked up to the man who was still moaning loudly. He glared down at the man who was defiantly looking back at him. Roth was bleeding from several areas including both of his legs. Jess reached down, jerked Roth's pistol out of his holster, and threw it away.

"Do I know you?" asked Jess.

"Go to hell, kid," replied Roth.

"I suppose you were after the money, right?"

"Yeah, but I guess it don't matter now, does it?"

"Nope, sure don't," he replied bluntly. "Looks like you're hit badly. I figure you'll bleed out in a few minutes or so."

"Maybe not, if you get me to a doctor."

"Doctor?" Jess responded with a hint of anger in his voice. "You just opened up on me with that scattergun with no warning in an attempt to murder me in cold blood for money and now you want a doctor?" Jess shook his head. "Not today, mister. What you're getting today is a hot seat in hell. I'm not going to let the doctor patch you up so you can come after me again, and you and I know that's exactly what you would do. I don't play it that way. I have to go check on your partner over there." Jess turned and walked toward the other man.

"You bastard. You can't just let me die here in the middle of the street!" hollered Roth.

"I'm afraid you're dead wrong about that," replied Jess, not even turning his head back to the man as he said it.

"Well, Andy, how's his partner?" Jess asked as he walked over to the younger man lying on his back in the street. The front of the man's shirt was covered in blood and a large pool of blood was slowly being sucked up by the dirt.

"He's a goner. He just passed on while you were havin' that delightful little conversation with his partner over there. You ain't really going to let him lay there and bleed to death, are you?"

"Absolutely," he said, looking back at Roth who wasn't moaning as loudly now. "That man is a cold-blooded murderer who has killed before and will kill again. I'm not giving him a chance to kill anyone else, especially me."

"All right then, I guess it's your show. Can't argue with ya anyway. He sure woulda come back at ya the first chance he got. That's Blaine Roth. He's sure enough a hard case and that's a fact."

A few people were now gathering in the street and that gave Newcomb enough courage to come out of his doorway and onto the porch, but not enough courage to step down into the street. "You can't just let him lay there and die. Someone should go and get the doctor," Newcomb said, his voice trembling in fear.

Jess glared at him and noticed a sign that was hanging above Newcomb's head that said "Sheriff's Office" on it. It was hanging with a small chain on each end of the sign and two hooks that fastened to the porch ceiling. Jess never said a word as he snapped off a shot from his pistol. The slug cut one of the chains in half, causing Newcomb to duck and then look up. His face tilted up just as the sign swung downward, striking Newcomb square in his broken nose. He let out a scream and a few curse words, grabbed his nose, and began running over to the doctor's office. Doctor Johnson had been standing in the doorway to his office, watching the entire incident. Jess looked at Andy and Andy just shook his head.

"What?" asked Jess.

"I think you're beginning to get a mean streak in ya."

"Maybe, but he did deserve it. He's the one who pointed me out to these two."

"Like they weren't gonna find ya anyhow?"

"Well, they didn't need any help and besides, I did warn him." Jess reloaded and holstered his pistol.

"Looks like Roth is just about done in. He ain't breathin' regular," said Andy, nodding in Roth's direction. Roth was in his final death throes. Blood was beginning to wet his lips and he was barely breathing. Jess and Andy watched him take his final breath.

"Two more down, and who knows how many more to go," said Jess.

"Too many," said Andy. "It's gonna be a long day."

"I believe it," he agreed. He knew he was in for more trouble today. He didn't know when or where it would come from, but he knew for certain it was coming. Andy went back to the saloon and Jess turned to Tony who had walked up, still holding his rifle, still watching the rooftops.

"Thanks, Tony. I appreciate the help."

"No problem. I ain't the only one who will throw in with you when you need it."

"That's a little comfort. I have a hunch that by the end of the day, I'm going to need the help. I figure Carter's coming to town later today but not until a few more of his men try to take me out."

"I see it that way too."

"Tony, will you do me one more favor?"

"Sure, you name it."

"When Carter does come to town, leave him for me."

Tony smiled an evil smile. "No problem."

Jess decided to take another stroll around town. As he started down the street, the undertaker was walking toward the two dead men who lay in the street. As the undertaker passed Jess, he smiled and nodded as if to say thanks for the business. Jess nodded back and then smiled at the irony of the thought that while he and the undertaker were in two completely different occupations, they both profited from the same thing, the death of men. He thought about all that had happened since his return to Black Creek. He had hoped that his visit would have been a pleasant one, but instead it had turned deadly with this battle for his life because of Dick Carter. He hated men like Carter almost as much as he hated the men who had brutally murdered his family. He hated him for what he represented and what he stood for: power, money, and the willingness to use it for all the wrong reasons. That was about to change—and Dick Carter wasn't going to like it.

CHAPTER SIX

It had been a hard three days' ride to the town of Holten from Black Creek, Kansas for Terrence Hanley. He stopped only once in a small town along the way. Just long enough for a quick bath, a few shots of whiskey at the saloon and a stop at the general store for a few supplies. He arrived in Holten late in the afternoon. He stabled his horse, got himself a room for the night, and headed for the sheriff's office to see what he could find out about Tim Sloan.

Russ Mathers had been the sheriff of Holten for about a year. He wasn't what you call a tough sheriff, but he did okay for a man in his late fifties. He let a lot of things slide, only getting involved in the most serious of affairs. If a gunfight happened between two men, he would let it go on as long as it was a fair fight. Mathers was walking out of his office heading for some supper when Terrence Hanley walked up to him.

"Afternoon, Sheriff. My name is Terrence Hanley and I wonder if I could have a quick word with you?"

Mathers stuck his hand out and smiled. "Nice to meet you, Mr. Hanley. What can I do for you?"

"I'm looking for a man by the name of Tim Sloan. I've been told you know him and could probably point him out to me."

"Oh yeah, you must be the man with the message. I remember getting a wire from a man by the name of Dick Carter asking me to ask Sloan to wait for someone who would be bringing him a letter. I only remember it because this man Carter said he would pay Sloan five hundred dollars just to wait for you. That true?"

"Sure is, Sheriff. I have the money on me right now and I'm ready to deliver it to Sloan after he reads the letter."

"Well, all right then. You can find Sloan at the saloon, which is where he spends most of his time. He's a damn good card player, even though he's a young one. He and his father ran a successful poker game here the last few weeks or so. His father left yesterday and Tim stayed around waiting to see if someone really would show up and pay him the money, and of course, to try and squeeze a few more dollars out of the gamblers here in town. I hope you ain't looking for any trouble with him though. He may be young but he's damn fast with a pistol and he ain't real friendly, if'n you know what I mean. He's killed one man so far and riled up quite a few more since he's been here."

"Not me, Sheriff. I'm no gunslinger. I'm just here to deliver a letter. After that, I plan to ride out tomorrow and head straight back to Carter's ranch."

"That's a good plan. Anyway, there's the saloon down the street where he hangs out. I'm sure you'll find him down there, probably locked in another poker game. Food's pretty good too. I'm heading down there if you want to walk with me."

"Thanks, Sheriff. To tell you the truth, I am mighty hungry and I would appreciate it if you would introduce me to Sloan."

Both the sheriff and Hanley walked to the saloon. The place was a little on the shabby side but at least it was clean. Hanley walked into the saloon behind the sheriff, went straight to the bar, and ordered a whiskey. The place was busy, with several people at the bar and two or three tables occupied. Six men, who were obviously long into a poker game, occupied one table. The sheriff walked over by that table and waited. Five of the men were probably in their mid-twenties to mid-thirties, and one looked young enough to be a kid. That man was Tim Sloan. He was dealing the cards. When he finished dealing, the sheriff spoke up.

"Sloan, I got a fellow who wants to talk to you." Sloan looked up at the sheriff with a nasty look of disgust on his face.

"Can't you see that I'm in a damn card game here, Sheriff? I ain't got time to meet someone right now. Tell him to come back later."

The sheriff smiled. "It's the man who was supposed to bring you a message, remember? He's got the five hundred dollars with him, so he says."

That piqued Sloan's interest immediately. He had been waiting for the messenger and had decided recently that the man wasn't going to show up. Sloan pushed himself away from the table and told the other five men to deal him out for a while. A few of them complained but they started a new deal as Sloan stood up.

"So, where is this man with the money and the message?"

"Right there at the bar, sipping a whiskey," replied the sheriff, pointing directly at Hanley. Sloan looked him over carefully and then walked over to the bar next to Hanley and ordered a whiskey.

"So you're the man who has a message for me and five hundred dollars just to read it, is that right?"

"Yes I am, and yes I do. My name is Terrence Hanley and I'm bringing a message from Dick Carter." Hanley put his hand out to shake hands with Sloan, but Sloan didn't offer his hand. Hanley felt strangely uncomfortable and he took another sip of his whiskey. This young man he was facing seemed to have an empty look in his eyes. It was a look that said a lot, and yet nothing, all at the same time.

"Where's my money? Do you have the five hundred?"

"I have it, but you have to read the letter before I give you the money. Those were my instructions."

"Well then give me the damn letter," growled Sloan, another nasty look on his face.

Hanley was getting a little perturbed at Sloan's nasty disposition and for a moment, he thought about walking out and going back to Black Creek and telling Carter he couldn't find him. He knew it would cause him problems either from Sloan or from Carter and right now, he didn't know which was worse. Something about this young man scared Hanley. He reached into his back pocket and pulled out the letter, which had Carter's seal on it. Sloan grabbed the letter from him and sat down at a table, leaving Hanley at the bar. That was fine with Hanley. He wanted to get this over with and get away from Sloan. Hanley had met his share of mean and nasty men in his lifetime, but this young man was one of the worst. Sloan sat down and opened the letter. He looked at it and the letter read as follows:

This letter is to be read only by Tim Sloan.

Mr. Sloan,

My name is Dick Carter. After you read the contents of this letter, the man who delivered it to you will pay you the sum of five hundred dollars whether or not you agree to the terms of my offer. The five hundred is yours simply for waiting and reading my letter. Here is my offer to you.

You have a twin brother by the name of Jess Williams. I don't know if your father told you about him, but I can assure you that I am telling the truth. I will pay you the sum of ten thousand dollars if you kill your brother, Jess Williams, who killed my only son. I know what I am asking you to do is out of the ordinary, but ten thousand dollars is a lot of money. I will be truthful and tell you that your brother is very quick with a gun and will not be easy to kill. If you agree to my terms, make your way to Black Creek, Kansas as quickly as you can. There are men here who are trying to collect a bounty I have placed on his head as you read this letter. If he is still alive when you get here, that will mean that I am already dead and you must contact a man by the name of Cal Hardin. He has the ten thousand dollars and instructions to pay you the money as soon as you bring the dead body of Jess Williams to him to identify. I hope you will take the job. Nothing would please me more, even in my death, than to know that Jess Williams' own brother would collect the money to kill him.

Godspeed. Dick Carter

Sloan folded the letter back up and sat there thinking about its contents. He knew about his twin brother. His father had told him all about what had happened. Of course, by that time, Tim had as bad a disposition as his father and he really didn't care. Sloan smiled at the evilness of Carter's proposal. It was something that he himself would have thought up. Sloan looked back over at Hanley, who was sipping another whiskey at the bar.

"I'll take my five hundred now."

Hanley slugged down his drink, turned around, walked to Sloan's table, and placed an envelope on it. Sloan opened it and counted out five hundred dollars. He smiled. He liked money and the things it could buy him: expensive whiskey, the best whores, and a stake in another poker game.

"Any message you want me to take back to Mr. Carter?" asked Hanley, after Sloan finished counting the money. Sloan glanced up at Hanley with a look that ran a chill up Hanley's spine and caused the hair on the back of his neck to stand straight up.

"Yeah, tell him I'll be collecting my ten thousand as soon as I can get to Black Creek."

Hanley's curiosity got the best of him when Sloan mentioned ten thousand dollars. "Ten thousand dollars? What in the hell would Dick Carter want you to do that he would pay you ten thousand dollars for?"

Sloan sneered at Hanley. "Well, I guess if he had wanted you to know that, he would have let you read the letter."

Hanley nodded, not wanting to pry any further. He had done what he had been assigned to do, and as far as he was concerned, his part in this matter was over with. He did, however, still wonder what his boss had written in the letter, but it was not his business. Hanley walked over to another table where Sheriff Mathers was sitting, eating what looked like a tasty steak and a large helping of potatoes.

"Looks mighty good, Sheriff. Mind if I join you?"

"Grab yourself a chair and sit down. The food is real good. I'm sure they have another steak in the back."

Hanley ate his supper and chatted with the sheriff for about an hour and then the sheriff left to make his rounds for the evening. He thanked the sheriff and told him he would pay for his meal. After all, he had just earned five hundred dollars. The sheriff thanked him and walked out of the saloon. It was dark outside now and a little chill was creeping into the saloon. The bartender put some more wood in the stove and it didn't take long for Hanley to feel the warmth.

Hanley decided to sit at the table and order a bottle of good whiskey. He had nothing else to do and he wasn't ready to turn in yet. Sloan had gone back to his card game. He was winning hand after hand, which was evident by the remarks from the other players. Hanley wondered how things were going back in Black Creek. He figured that Jess Williams was probably dead by now, already gunned down by Carter and his hired guns.

His thoughts were interrupted by some commotion at the card game. One of the players was getting angrier about Sloan's uncanny luck. The man who was getting upset was Cobb White. He was in his mid-thirties and had had a little too much to drink, which is what gave him the courage to start complaining about Sloan's gambling skills.

"I'm telling you no one is that lucky," hollered White. No man can win that many hands without cheating somehow."

"Now settle down, Cobb," warned Sloan. "I can't help that you keep losing your money. Maybe you should just take what you have left and go on home. Maybe your luck will change tomorrow."

"I ain't got any damn money left! I started this game with two hundred and now all I have is twenty dollars."

"Well, that's why they call it gambling," said Sloan, smiling sarcastically.

"I've about had it with your smart aleck remarks too," hollered White.

"Now, I already told you to take your money and go home. I think that's the best thing you could do right now, before you get yourself into something you can't get out of."

"You go to hell, kid. I ain't scared of you!"

"Maybe you should be."

"Maybe you should show us the cards you got stuck up your sleeve," White accused, as he stood up, shoving his chair backward.

Sloan remained unusually calm and placed his cards on the table. Then he slowly pushed his chair back and stood up, glaring at White. Hanley noticed that Sloan had already removed his hammer strap from his pistol. You could sense that White had a momentary lapse of courage, which is normal for a man to have just before an impending gunfight. A sober man with common sense usually backed down about now. However, when you've had one too many whiskeys, common sense seems to take a holiday. Pile that onto the fact that most men are more afraid to back out of a gunfight than to continue it. For both these reasons, Cobb White stood his ground, even when he knew he shouldn't.

Sloan slowly unbuttoned his sleeves one at a time and rolled each one of them up for everyone to see. There were no cards. The truth was, Sloan was cheating, but he didn't need to hide cards in his sleeves. He would just palm whatever cards he needed from the deck. Sometimes it didn't work, but more often than not it did, and he won the majority of hands. His father had always told him that you never want to win every hand and you never want to be caught with cards up your sleeves or in your pockets. Walking away with a smaller profit after a night's work is better than lying dead under a large pile of money. It was good advice and he had heeded it, most of the time.

Tim Sloan's father, Eddie Sloan, had only taught him to do a few things in life very well. How to gamble, lie, and cheat were some of those things. More importantly though, he had taught him how to draw a pistol, and he had taught him very well. Sloan was an accomplished poker player by the age of eight and an expert gunslinger by the time he was twelve years old. Both professions went together perfectly. It was times like this that proved it. Sloan's father had bought him a beautiful pistol and holster for his tenth birthday. The pistol was a beautifully engraved, silver-plated Colt

.45 Peacemaker with a black left-handed holster made in Mexico by a man who was an artist with leather. The holster was cut lower in the front and the barrel of the pistol was slightly shorter than most, with the front sight removed, which allowed it to clear the holster quicker.

"Well now, Cobb. Did you see any cards up my sleeves?"

Cobb's gaze went to each of the other four men at the table, looking for any help or encouragement. He found none.

"I didn't see any, but you were cheating just the same," complained Cobb. "Maybe I can't figure out how you did it, but I know that you did."

"So, what do you want to do now?" asked Sloan, the sarcastic tone turning more serious now.

"I want my damn money back. I'll go play it in a fair game."

"Listen, Cobb. I ain't giving you your money back. Like I told you, take what you have left and go on home. If you don't, you might be making a bad mistake."

"Just give my money back to me and I'll leave."

"You don't seem to be listening and I'm getting tired of talking. Now what's it going to be?"

Cobb White had a few beads of sweat on his forehead now. He had looked at the other four men, who were still sitting at the table, chairs pushed back. He knew that he wasn't going to get any help from any of them. None of them had uttered a word since the argument had begun between the two. Cobb knew that he should take what he had left and go home but he just couldn't make himself do what he knew he should do. He couldn't bring himself to back down now. Then, he made a fatal error. He drew on Sloan.

Cobb went for his gun but he never had the slightest chance. He had only gotten a grip on the butt of his pistol when Sloan's gun seemingly flashed out of its holster. The slug blew a hole straight through Cobb's heart. He stumbled backward, tripped over his chair, and collapsed on the floor, never to complain about a card game again. Sloan whirled his gun around with his left hand and slipped it back in its holster as slick as silk. Then, he simply sat back down in his chair and picked his cards up as if nothing had happened. The other four men looked stunned but slid their chairs back in and continued the game. They didn't care if they went home broke; they simply wanted to make it home alive.

Hanley watched all of this from his table. He had seen a few gunfights before. Men would kill each other over the smallest of things. Things certainly not worth dying for, at least in his mind. He was, however, surprised by three things. The incredible hand speed of this young man by the name of Tim Sloan was the first. The second was the calm that he had displayed during a gunfight. Those two things were uncommon in most men and probably the reason that Carter had sent a message to Sloan. The third thing, and probably the most important, was the pistol and holster combination that Sloan was wearing. The holster was a lot fancier than most men had and the pistol was a silver engraved Colt .45 Peacemaker. He still didn't know what the letter to Sloan had said, but he had pretty much figured out now what Carter wanted from Sloan. Carter wanted Sloan for his pistol skills. Hanley downed another shot of whiskey, paid the bartender, and walked out of the saloon without saying a word or even looking over at Sloan. All Hanley wanted to do now was get away from him.

As Hanley walked down the street toward his hotel, he met the sheriff who was heading down toward the saloon.

"Turning in for the night, Mr. Hanley?"

"Yeah, I'm tired and need a good night's sleep. Besides, I'm getting itchy to get out of town, if you know what I mean."

The sheriff grinned. "I know exactly what you mean. I suppose it ain't Sloan lying on the floor over at the saloon, is it?" The sheriff had a wishful look on his face.

Hanley knew what he was hoping for. "No, it ain't Sloan, but I figured you knew that already, Sheriff."

"Yeah, suppose I did. Can't blame a man for hoping though," said the sheriff.

"I suppose not, but if it's any consolation, I believe you'll be rid of Sloan first thing in the morning."

The sheriff smiled cleverly. "I guess good things do come to those who wait."

"I suppose so," agreed Hanley. The sheriff headed down for the saloon and Hanley went to his room and turned in.

It was early sunrise and Hanley was splashing some cold water on his face in his room when he heard a horse galloping below his window. He looked out and saw Sloan riding out of town seemingly in a hurry. He wasn't surprised. Even though he didn't know what the money was for, he knew that ten thousand dollars would make men do things they wouldn't usually do. He decided that maybe he would stay in town another day. He would rather ride behind Sloan than catch up to him or even worse, have Sloan follow him out on the trail.

Dick Carter watched the second team of men ride out from the Carter 'D' ranch. He didn't know whether the first two men out this morning, Gene Horn and Blaine Roth, had been successful in killing Jess or not, but that didn't matter. If they had, they would meet the second team on their way back and then notify Carter that the job was finished. If not, Carter would ride out with his best six hired guns and finish the job himself, one way or another. He didn't care if he got killed in the process. The only thing that would bring him comfort now was the death of Jess Williams.

The two men on the second team were Woody Hampton and Flynn Dugan. Both men were hard cases and good with a gun. Woody was especially good with a rifle and used it whenever possible. Flynn fancied himself as an expert with a pistol. Neither of them had any problem with ambushing a man and killing him, even if it meant shooting a man in the back. They were simply well-paid gunmen who didn't play by any set of rules.

It was early afternoon back in Black Creek, Kansas. Jess was sitting with Andy at the saloon making small talk. As they sat there, two men rode into town and hitched their horses across the street at the sheriff's office. It was Woody Hampton and Flynn Dugan. Jess and Andy watched them and they knew they were watching trouble.

"Well," Andy said, "seems like ya got more problems, Jess."

"You're always so quick to spread the good news, Andy. Anybody ever tell you that?"

"Yeah, seems like I heard that once before from a young smart aleck"

"Wonder who that might be."

Andy cocked his head again in that "You know what I'm talking about" look. Andy got up, walked behind the bar and grabbed his shotgun while Jess sat at the table, waiting for the inevitable. A few minutes later, Jess got up and walked to the bar.

"Do you think maybe they're not involved in this?" he asked Andy.

"Not a chance. I recognized both of those two. That's Woody Hampton and Flynn Dugan. My guess is they plan to ambush you the second they spot you."

Jess carefully walked over to the window, peeked out, and looked around as best he could so as not to make himself a target. He saw nothing, but they had to have gone somewhere. He wondered if the men knew where he was yet. He couldn't see from his position whether or not Tony was watching what was going on, but he had to hope that he was. He looked back at Andy, who was standing at the bar keeping an eye on the back door.

"Well, Andy, it seems like I've got more work to do."

"I'm beginnin' to think you're one of them real smart fellers."

CHAPTER SEVEN

Jess was still peeking out the front window from time to time and Andy was standing guard behind the bar, keeping an eye on the back door just in case the two men knew that Jess was in the saloon. Andy's nerves were getting frayed. He didn't like waiting for something to happen.

"What the hell are they waitin' for?" asked Andy, not really looking for an answer.

Jess was standing to the right of the front window and looked over at Andy. "Maybe they're waiting for you to show your pretty face."

"I don't think it's me they're waitin' for. Besides, this face ain't been pretty in a hell of a long time."

"You'll get no argument from me on that one." Andy glared at Jess and mumbled something that Jess couldn't quite understand.

"You in a hurry to get shot again?" asked Jess.

"It ain't gettin' shot that's bothering me so much. It's the waitin' fer it."

"I'm getting tired of waiting too. I might as well try to get things moving. Those two boys have had too much time to think about what they're planning. I'm going out the back door to take a look around and see if I can spot them."

"Okay, but be careful."

"I'm always careful. You watch your back."

Jess slowly walked to the back door. The screen door had a tension spring on it. Jess grabbed a broom and pushed it out a little and let it spring back. It made some noise, but didn't draw any fire, which is what he wanted to know. He walked over to the screen door, peeked out, and looked around to see if he could spot any ambush. What he did see was a lot of junk and debris in the back of the saloon.

"Hey, Andy," he quietly called down the hallway.

Andy poked his head around the corner. "What?"

"When this is over, how about cleaning up the mess you've got back here?"

"Give me a break, for Christ's sake. We got more important things to worry about right now, like gettin' shot," griped Andy with a look of frustration on his face.

Jess stepped out the screen door and down the two steps. He pulled his shotgun out of the back sling and checked it to make sure it was loaded. He knew it was, but it was just an automatic thing he did. He worked his way along the back wall until he got to the opening between Andy's Saloon and Jackson's Hardware. He decided he was too close to Andy's Saloon. If they knew he had been in there, they would spot him too easily in that opening. He made his was along the back of the hardware store to the next opening and began to work his way along the walls while looking up at the rooftops and the windows of the two buildings, looking for the two men he knew were looking for him. He had almost made it to the opening when he heard someone speak.

"Hey, mister," a soft voice said. Jess spun around with the shotgun and just as he lined up with the voice he had heard, he spotted a head darting back into a window of the one building.

"Don't shoot. I'm not armed," the voice said from behind the window.

"Okay, but you come out of that window with a gun and I'll blow you and half of that window apart."

"I'm just trying to help. I know where those two men are that are after you."

"Where are they?"

"One of them is up on the roof of the sheriff's office with a rifle, and the other one is on the roof of the building next to mine. I saw him climb the back steps of the hardware store right after they came to town. I think he's still up there because I heard some noise a minute ago."

"Thanks, mister. I appreciate it."

"No problem. I know what you're trying to do to help the town out. I don't like that damn Carter one bit either."

"Keep your head down when the shooting starts."

"You ain't talking to no fool."

Jess worked his way to the back again. He found the steps that led to the roof of the hardware store. He waited for a moment to decide what he was going to do. He looked at the steps, which looked old and dried out. He decided what his plan would be. The only problem was that half of the plan relied on Tony being at the ready from his vantage point at the livery. Jess had to hope that Tony had already spotted the other man who was across the street or that he would spot him when he came out of hiding, which is exactly what the man would do when he heard the gunshots that were about to happen. Jess slowly climbed the back steps, keeping his feet to the outer edges of the steps. There were a few creaks and noises as he climbed the steps but they were so slight that Jess was sure that the man on the roof wouldn't hear.

As he got to the top, he removed his hat, slowly raised his head, and peeked over the top. He found what he was looking for. There was a man standing behind the fake front of the building holding a rifle. He was peeking around the edge and looking around the street. With the other man on the other side and down several buildings, they would have him in a crossfire. It was a good plan but one that was about to go bad for the two men who had planned it, although they didn't know it yet. Jess put his hat back on, stepped onto the roof staying low, and very deliberately walked toward one side of the rooftop so that he could keep himself out of sight from the man across the street on the roof of the sheriff's office.

He couldn't go much farther forward for fear that he would expose himself to the other man. A ledge about a foot or so high ran all around the roof so Jess figured that he could hit the ground for cover if the man across the street opened up on him. So far, so good, Jess thought to himself. He decided it was time to have a little conversation with the man. The man looked to be in his thirties and fairly well dressed. He was Flynn Dugan, but Jess didn't know him. Dugan was watching the street and the buildings across from his ambush point. For some reason, he never thought he would have to watch his back. That was about to be a fatal mistake that the man would never make again.

Jess had him in his sights with the shotgun and decided to warn the man first. He wasn't quite sure in his mind why he should have to, since the man standing there was surely going to shoot him on sight with no warning. Jess wasn't able to do that, although he internally fought himself over it. Why not just pull the trigger on this man? He would do it to me. Why play fair with a man who doesn't? Why not treat this man exactly the same way he was about to treat me? It was the same running argument that he was having more and more often with himself. There was still something in him, some sense of fairness that was embedded in his mind that just wouldn't allow him to shoot a man without the man at least having a warning. He decided to call out to him.

"Hey," he said softly. "Have you seen him yet?"

The man made the slightest movement, as if he were going to turn. Then, he froze in place and Jess could sense that for a moment, the man was trying to process what was happening. It took Dugan only about three seconds to figure it out and then it took him another two seconds to decide what he would do about it. Jess saw it coming. Dugan had both hands on his rifle but he slowly shifted the rifle to his left hand, still with his back to Jess. He knew there was no chance that he could get off a shot with the rifle while spinning around. That left Dugan's right gun hand free and it was slowly moving toward his pistol. Jess knew exactly what he was going to do and simply watched and waited for it.

Dugan thought he was fast. The truth was, he was fast. Just not fast enough for a man who was holding a shotgun cocked and pointed at him and just waiting to pull the trigger. Flynn dropped the rifle with his left hand and spun around, jerking his pistol out. The pistol had just cleared the holster when Jess opened up with both barrels. The blast of death hit Dugan so hard that he flew backward, fell over the edge and bounced off the short roof over the wooden walk below the building. Before Dugan hit the walk a rifle cracked and a bullet whizzed past Jess, missing his head by inches. He dropped down flat on the rooftop, his pistol now in his right hand. Then he heard another rifle crack, but it didn't seem to be coming from across the street on the roof of the sheriff's office.

Jess slowly crawled to the front of the rooftop he was on and peeked over the edge. He looked across the street in the direction that the rifle fire had come from and saw nothing. Then, he noticed Tony walking out into the middle of the street, his rifle still trained on the roof where the other man, Woody Hampton was.

"Jess, I'm sure I hit him!" Tony hollered out. "I'll keep the rooftop covered while you go check on him." Jess holstered his pistol, reloaded the shotgun and put it back in its sling, and quickly climbed down the steps, grabbing his hat as he did. He ran between the buildings and across the street. He ran behind the sheriff's office and climbed the steps slowly. He peeked over the top of the roof half expecting another rifle shot, but what he saw was Woody Hampton. He was leaning up against the front ledge of the building holding his chest, his rifle lying about six feet from him. Jess walked up to him, his pistol now in his hand. He picked up the rifle and threw it off the roof.

"I found him, Tony," Jess called down. "You hit him for sure, but he's not dead yet."

"Me and Andy are keeping an eye on everything down here. You be careful up there. Don't give that snake a chance, Jess. He'll bite you for sure." Jess simply stared at the man, who was bleeding profusely. He hadn't said a word; he was occupied with trying to stop the blood from flowing from the hole in his chest.

"You don't look too good, mister. I don't think you've got long to live."

The man glared up at Jess with a face full of hate. "Just be thankful you threw my rifle off the roof, else I'd plug you for sure."

"Mister, about the only thing you're going to do is plug a hole in the ground when they bury you."

"Yeah, well…Carter will be putting you in the ground before this day is over. He's coming for you and there is nothing you can do to stop him."

The man coughed and let out his last breath. Jess simply watched him die.

If Hampton had lived another few seconds, he would have heard Jess's response. Jess knew he was speaking to a dead man but it didn't really matter. What he said was more for himself than anyone else. His voice was low, firm, and deliberate. "I wouldn't have it any other way."

Jess made his way back to Andy's Saloon. He passed the undertaker again and he still had that strange smile on his face as he walked by Jess and nodded to him. Jess, Andy, and Tony sat down at a table. Andy brought out a good bottle of whiskey.

"I didn't know you had any good stuff here," said Tony.

Andy had a hurt look on his face. "I do if you got the money to pay for it."

"I can't afford that stuff," said Tony.

"It's on me," offered Jess. "Actually, it's probably on Carter. I found fifty dollars in the front pocket of the man you plugged earlier. Besides, it's the least I can do after you just saved my life."

"I don't know about that, but I will drink this fine whiskey," said Tony as he picked up the glass.

They sat there for what seemed an eternity, but in reality, was only about fifteen minutes. It was a strange thing about time. It seemed to slow down after an event such as men shooting it out with one another, some living, and some dying. Maybe it was because the ones who survived savored the few minutes following their brush with death. It wasn't something they thought about; it was something they felt and yet couldn't put a finger on. They slowly sipped the fine whiskey and savored it.

"Well," Andy broke the silence, "since I'm the one who always points out the good news, I think things are about to get a whole lot worse in a few hours."

Tony didn't say anything and Jess looked at Andy, shaking his head. "You just can't let a man have a good moment, can you?"

"Well, someone had to say it," grumbled Andy. "What do ya think Carter's gonna do? Let us sit here all day and drink this fine whiskey? I'll tell ya what he's doing. He's probably on his way into town right now with a bunch of professional killers and they ain't coming to town to thank ya for killin' all their friends. They're coming to kill you, me, Tony, and anyone else who will throw in with ya."

"Well then, I guess we'd better have a plan," declared Jess. "Taking on two men is one thing. Taking on six or eight is quite another. Tony, if you still want in, I'll need you up on a rooftop with your Winchester where you can see them coming and warn us."

"No problem. I'm with you all the way," agreed Tony.

Jess turned to Andy. "Andy, I'll need you with that shotgun. As a matter of fact, go see Jim Smythe and borrow two more so you have three of them loaded and ready. You can do a hell of a lot of damage with three scatterguns. Don't fire off both barrels at once though. Make sure you get six separate shots out of them before you have to reload."

"Okay," replied Andy.

"All right, then. In the meantime, if you know anyone else who wants to help, tell them to stay in their houses or their stores and cover us with rifle fire or whatever they have. If they can keep Carter's men ducking, it will give us the edge to take them out as quickly as we can."

"Sounds like a good plan," admitted Tony, trying to smile.

"It's the only one we've got right now," said Jess, as he got up and started walking out of the saloon.

"Where are you going?" asked Andy.

"I got something I need to tend to right now. Oh, and by the way, don't let Carter or his men get off their horses. Understand?

I figure they'll ride right into town as if they own it. If they get a chance to dismount and run for cover, that's bad for us. If they try to do that, just open fire on them and don't stop until every last man is down."

"So, we don't give them any warning? We just plug them even if they haven't fired a shot?" asked Tony, not caring much about it, but wanting to be clear on the matter.

"Don't worry. They'll have a warning, but only one and it won't last long. I'll see to that." Andy and Tony nodded and Jess walked out and headed for the mayor's office, slipping his hammer strap off. He found Nigel York at his desk writing a letter.

"Afternoon, Mayor. How is your day going? Better than mine, I hope."

"Well...uh...I suppose my day is going okay so far. What do you want?"

"I'm here to inform you that your day just got worse."

York was terrified of Jess. Of course, he was a coward and was terrified of most men. "What do you mean? What do you want with me? I'm not the one shooting at you."

"No, but you have played a part in the overall plan to have me killed and I'm not going to give you any opportunity to help again in any way."

"What are you going to do? You're not going to shoot me, are you?" York asked, afraid of the answer.

"I should plug your sorry ass right now or maybe save the cost of a bullet and just beat you to death with a big stick. But for now, I'm at least going to make sure you can't do anything to help your boss. Now get up."

"Where are we going?"

"Down to visit your friend, the sheriff."

"What for?"

"You'll see. Now get up and don't make me say it again or I swear I'll just plug you right there in your chair. That would save me a lot of aggravation."

York got up and walked out of his office and Jess pushed him toward Sheriff Newcomb's office. York walked in first with Jess right behind him. Newcomb was getting himself a cup of coffee when he heard them come in and turned around. His smile quickly turned to a frown when he saw Jess.

"I didn't have anything to do with those men who tried to kill you today," said Newcomb, immediately trying to put up a defense.

"You sure were quick to point me out though, weren't you?"

"They already knew who you were, honest," Newcomb replied, nervously.

"It doesn't matter now anyway. Get your keys and pick a cell for the mayor here."

"You're going to lock up the mayor? You can't do that."

"I'm getting awfully tired of you telling me what I can or can't do. The way I see it, I can do anything I want to do as long as I'm willing to die for it. Now get the keys and pick a cell before I start to work on that nose of yours again."

Newcomb put his hand over his still bandaged nose. Knowing there was no point in arguing with Jess, he got his keys, picked out a clean cell, and opened the door. Jess pushed York into it and York sat down on the bed in the cell.

"You're next," said Jess, as he removed Newcomb's pistol from his holster.

"Huh, what...you're locking me up too?"

"You catch on real quick. Now get in there with your partner. I don't have any time to fool around with the two of you and I'm not going to give you the chance to help Carter when he gets here."

Newcomb got into the cell with the mayor and closed the cell door. Jess made sure it was locked. Then he took Newcomb's gun and broke the key off in the lock. He looked at both men.

"The next time I lay eyes on either of you, one of two things will happen. One, you'll both be on a horse riding out of town, or two, and don't ever doubt this for a second, the undertaker will be fitting you both for a pine box. Understand?" Both Newcomb and

York nodded in the affirmative, Newcomb still with his hand over his nose as if somehow shielding it.

Jess walked out and stood in the middle of the street. He looked up at the sky and smiled. He spotted Tony up on the roof of the livery and Andy in the window of the saloon. He looked over at Smythe's General Store and saw Jim Smythe sitting on the porch with a shotgun on his lap. I sure hope he doesn't shoot his foot off, he thought to himself, after remembering what Sara had said.

"Well," Jess said to himself, "it's a good day to die...for Dick Carter."

CHAPTER EIGHT

It was one of those peaceful days that made people feel good to be alive. The sky was a beautiful blue color with just a hint of clouds to dress it up without blocking any of the sunshine from the large yellow orb. It was all lost on Dick Carter, though. He didn't see any of the sunlight. He didn't see any of the blue sky. All he saw was dark looming clouds and all he could feel was hatred deep in his dark brooding soul. A seething hatred that caused his head to slump slightly lower than normal and made his eyes look into some strange beyond that no one else could see because it wasn't really there. He realized that the four men he had sent into town today had failed and were most likely dead.

Dick Carter was sitting on the front porch of his sprawling ranch home. Deke Moore was sitting on a chair opposite the front screen door, carefully watching his boss slink into that strange beyond that Deke could not see and yet he knew was there; at least it was for Dick Carter. Deke was waiting for what he knew was inevitable, and he knew he wouldn't have to wait much longer. He tried not to stare at Carter, but instead he glanced over to his left every few minutes and tried to read the look on his face. Carter was so deep into his dark thoughts that he never noticed Deke glancing at him, even though he knew he was there on the porch with him.

Deke was never too far from Carter. He was the best man Carter had with a gun. He was easily twice as fast at pulling a leg iron as any of the other five men Carter had picked to go into town with him this afternoon. Deke's job was to keep Carter alive. Beyond that, he would kill anyone Carter told him to kill. It didn't matter to him if it was an unarmed man, woman, or even a child. Deke was simply a hired killer with no conscience. The consequences of his actions had long ago been lost on him. He just didn't care anymore.

The other five men who would ride into town with Carter today were all good with a gun and quite experienced at killing. They were men who would not hesitate to shoot and would give no quarter to any man. Homer Densley and Butch Ramsey had come to work for Carter recently. They'd heard that Carter was hiring gunslingers and paying well. They had been working together as bounty hunters for a few years before coming to work for Carter about two months ago. They were both looking forward to their share of the three thousand dollars.

Vic Nalley had been with Carter the longest. He had been a field hand at the Carter 'D' for about five years and had honed his skills with a pistol to the point that Carter decided to pay him as a hired gun. The pay was much better and there wasn't much labor involved. Most of the time was spent sitting around waiting to run off the next rancher or possibly killing some poor soul who was either brave enough or dumb enough to defy Dick Carter's wishes. Nalley had welcomed the move.

Nick Priestly was the oldest of the bunch. He wasn't the fastest with a pistol, but he was probably the most dangerous of the lot. Some said he was so mean that he already had a seat reserved in hell. He had killed his share of men and raped his share of women. One of the most talked-about stories around the ranch regarding Priestly was the one about the whore he had pleasures with one night. At the end of the night, he beat her to death with the butt of his rifle just for charging him more than what he thought he should pay.

Warren Malarky was a young Irish lad who had worked as a gunman for the last two years. He had a good sense of humor and was always telling jokes around the campfire. He had traveled from the east to escape murder charges after killing a man in his brother's pub.

All five of them were waiting in the bunkhouse for the order they knew was coming. They had all cleaned and oiled their weapons, making sure they were loaded and had extra ammunition for them. It was a ritual they performed often. A hired gunman relied on his tools of the trade and if he failed to keep them in proper working order and at the ready all the time, it could cost him his life. All that was left to do now was to mount up and ride.

Dick Carter slowly rose his head from where it had been hanging. He looked straight out in the direction of Black Creek. He stared out that way for a long two minutes. Then, he slowly turned and looked straight into Deke Moore's eyes with a cold hard stare.

"Deke, tell the boys to saddle up and get my horse ready."

Deke didn't have to respond. It wasn't necessary. He simply got up from his chair and slowly walked over to the bunkhouse where the other five men were waiting. He walked in to find the men sitting around and chatting. Deke stood just inside the door looking the five men over. He felt comfortable with them.

Warren Malarky was the first to speak. "Is the boss man ready for his little ride into town?" he asked.

"As a matter of fact, he is. Mount up, boys, and get the big man's horse for him. It's time to earn our pay and maybe a big bonus."

"I like the sound of that," replied Warren.

"Especially that bonus thing," said Densley.

"Just remember, this Williams kid is one tough hombre," warned Deke with a serious look on his face. "He might be young, but he has put down some mighty fast gunmen already. You boys, don't give him any quarter at all. Just plug him when you get him in your sights."

Deke turned and walked back out toward the house. He saw Dick Carter, who was standing now, checking his pistol. Deke couldn't shake the ominous feeling that would not leave him today. He wanted to try to talk Carter out of this whole business, but he knew there wasn't the slightest chance of that. There was something that just didn't feel right, but he couldn't quite put his finger on what it was. The one thing he did know for sure is that whenever he had that feeling, things usually went bad.

But he was loyal to the bone to Carter and he would take a bullet for him. Carter had been very good to Deke over the years and he wasn't the kind of man who would walk away from someone just because the going got tough. He walked up to the front of the house and looked at his boss. Carter holstered his pistol and walked down the two steps and over to him. He stared deep into Deke's eyes as if trying to read what he was thinking. He could sense his uneasiness about the whole matter, and the truth was he felt it too. Yet, all he saw in Deke's eyes was loyalty.

"Deke, let's go kill that bastard who killed my boy."

"You're the boss," said Deke. "The boys are ready and so is your horse."

Without turning away from Carter, Deke waved his hand. The other five men mounted their horses and walked them over to where Deke and Carter were standing. Carter and Deke mounted their horses and Carter led the way into town. He had a strange look about him. It wasn't so much a look of someone who was going to avenge a death, but more like someone who was going to his own death. The other five men could feel it and they too wondered about it, but the thought of three thousand dollars pushed it from their minds.

᚜ ᚛

Jess made one final check around the town. Tony was up on the rooftop of the livery with his rifle. Andy was sitting just inside the doorway of the saloon and had placed a heavy wooden table against the wall next to a window. He figured that would give him a little extra protection. Jim Smythe was standing behind his counter and had his shotgun leaning up against the wall next to the open door. On a table next to it lay at least a dozen shotgun shells in a bowl.

Jess also noticed another man up on the rooftop of Smythe's General Store. He had a rifle and waved at Jess. It identified him as the man who had directed him to Ned Cullen. That made two rifles and two shotguns on his side. Even though he wasn't sure how much help Jim or the man on his roof would be, the extra fire would distract Carter's men nonetheless. He felt more comfortable, at least as comfortable as any man who was facing down a bunch of murderous hired guns could be.

⌐ ¬

The ride to Black Creek started out as a slow and somber one. As they neared Black Creek though, Dick Carter's ears got redder and redder and then his face began to take on a slight tinge of color. There was a slow crescendo of hatred building up inside Carter, driving him forward. Deke, who was riding next to him, noticed the change as well as the change in Carter's pace. He was slowly pushing his horse faster until the horse was in a slow gallop. Then, as the buildings in Black Creek became visible around the last bend, Carter pushed his horse even faster. The seven horses stirred up quite a dust cloud. In town, Tony had stood up to stretch a little when he noticed the dust.

"Rider's coming in," hollered Tony, loud enough for everyone to hear. "I count seven riders."

Jess was on the opposite end of the main street from where Carter and his men were riding in. He was heading toward the spot he had picked out between Andy's Saloon and Jackson's Hardware. He heard Tony's call and saw the dust at the other end of town. There wasn't enough time to reach the spot he was heading for and he quickly looked for any other cover. For a split second, he began to head for the first building on his left. Then he looked back down the main street and saw seven men riding abreast along the street as if they owned it. He could see that Dick Carter was in the middle of the men and he knew that they were all there for only one reason, to kill him.

For some reason, and he didn't quite know why, a sudden change washed over him. He stopped in his tracks and turned to face the seven riders slowly coming toward him. He realized that he was putting himself in an extremely dangerous position and yet he simply didn't care. Rage began to surge in him as he thought about the unfairness of life. Here he was, guilty of nothing but killing Carter's son for the cold-blooded murder of the previous sheriff of the town. And now, seven men, six of whom he had never met, were getting ready to kill him for money. He stood there in the middle of the street, staring at the seven men, not moving one inch. If anyone had been close enough to him, you would have heard him say to no one but himself, "I wouldn't have it any other way." His strap was off his pistol and he had already picked out his first target, Dick Carter.

Tony had quickly ducked out of sight but he had watched Jess turn to face down Carter's men. He wondered if Jess hadn't all of a sudden gone plumb loco. He remembered what Jess had said earlier about Carter, so Tony trained his rifle on one of the other six men. Andy had moved to his spot next to the window and had his shotgun trained on the men who had just ridden slightly past him. Jim Smythe was shaking in his boots, but he had his shotgun sticking out the front window. He had never killed a man before, but he would if it meant saving Jess. The man up on Smythe's roof had his rifle trained on the men also.

All of a sudden, Carter and his men stopped dead thirty feet from where Jess now stood like a statue. Everybody tensed and Tony put a slight bit of pressure on the trigger of his rifle. He had it aimed at the side of Homer Densley, although he had no idea who the man was and didn't really care. No one moved. It was as if for a moment or two, time stood still.

Dick Carter was staring straight at Jess, his face the color of a red apple. Deke was looking around a little, but they had already ridden slightly past the other men who were helping Jess, so he didn't see them. Homer Densley leaned over to his pal Butch Ramsey.

"Kid's kind of stupid to just stand there and make it easy for us."

"Ain't no kid that stands down seven men in the middle of the street," replied Ramsey as he spat on the ground, a nervous twitch in the corner of his eye.

"I ain't ever seen anything like this before," declared Malarky. "That boy sure has gumption."

"What do you think he plans on doing, Butch?" asked Densley.

"Making us all rich," replied Ramsey.

"I think you boys are right about that," agreed Malarky.

Deke was listening to the chatter of the men and watching the expression on Carter's face. He didn't like the feeling he was getting and he leaned over to Carter and whispered to him.

"Mr. Carter, are you sure you still want to go through with this?" he asked nervously. "We could turn around and go back to the ranch. We've already lost enough men to this kid. He just ain't worth it."

Deke had said it soft enough that none of the other men heard him, but Carter never heard a word. He was in his own little reality, where all he saw was Jess Williams' body lying in the street riddled with bullet holes. All he could hear was Jess Williams screaming out in pain as he lay dying. A chill ran up Deke's spine as Carter began to move his horse forward at a slow walk. Carter had pulled a few feet ahead of the other men and they followed along. They all had their weapons ready, hands on butts of pistols, thumbs on the hammers of rifles.

"Look alive, boys," ordered Deke with a cautious expression. "I don't like the feeling I'm getting."

"Let's just shoot this little bastard and go have a drink," complained Nick Priestly.

"We follow the boss man's lead and you know that, Nick," barked Deke in a scolding voice.

Carter walked his horse straight at Jess and stopped within ten feet of where he was still standing, his feet seemingly rooted to the ground like an oak tree. Everyone tensed again, waiting for the fireworks to happen. Deke and the other five men moved up to where Carter was. Jess stared straight into Carter's eyes, but he still kept the other six men in his view. He had already spotted Deke Moore to Carter's immediate left and he figured him for a quick draw by the looks of him. He also sensed that this man was the leader of the other hired guns. He decided that this man was his second target, with Carter being his first. For the second time in a few minutes, time seemed to stand eerily still. Carter leaned a little forward in the saddle, the leather creaking in the absolute silence. He glared at Jess with as much hatred as any one man could muster.

"You killed my boy, Jess Williams," said Carter, his voice actually shaking from the seething hatred he felt in his heart.

Jess didn't respond right away. Instead, he shifted his glance to the three men on the right, and then to the three on the left, making sure his eyes locked on each one of them for just a second. Then, he shifted his eyes back to Carter and Carter saw something that surprised even him. He saw more hatred in Jess's eyes than he himself had ever felt, even at this moment. It was then that Carter realized that this young man standing defiantly before him was no kid, but a hardened killer of men. Yet, Carter could not turn back now; he had to finish this even if it cost him his own life.

"Mr. Carter," warned Jess with a firm look of resolve on his face. "You have exactly one minute to turn around with your men, head back to the ranch, and end this thing once and for all and I mean everything. That includes trying to have me killed, the bounty on my head, and your grip on this town. If you don't, I will surely kill you right there on your horse."

Carter glared back at Jess. "Like you killed my boy? Well, I ain't going to be so easy. I'm not going anywhere until your sorry ass is lying in a pool of your own blood right here in the middle of this street."

Jess cocked his head ever so slightly and you could see what looked like a hint of a slight smile beginning to form on his lips. "You know what, Mr. Carter? I wouldn't have it any other way," he said in a firm voice. Dick Carter started moving off his horse. What stopped him was what Jess had to say next.

"By the way, Mr. Carter...I'm afraid you're out of time."

Then Jess did something that was out of the ordinary, even for him. Maybe he was just plumb tired of playing by someone else's unwritten rules or tired of playing fair with men who didn't know the meaning of the word. Maybe it was the fact that he was facing off with six professional killers hired and paid for by Carter or maybe it was a combination of all of these things, but whatever it was, he had simply had enough.

Carter had no sooner righted himself in the saddle and was getting ready to make one more comment to Jess and then go for his pistol when Jess's right hand moved in a blurring motion. His first slug found Carter square in the middle of his chest. Jess fanned his second shot at Deke Moore but Deke's horse was startled by the gunshot. He moved ever so slightly and the slug hit Deke in the left shoulder, knocking him out of the saddle. As soon as Jess had fanned his second shot, he began running to his right. He wanted to avoid catching a bullet from one of Carter's men. He also wanted to stay clear of the lead and buckshot from the fire that was beginning to rain down on the group of men still on their horses.

The shots were coming from both directions as well as from above and from ground level. Deke hit the ground about the same time that Carter's dead body landed. Shots were ricocheting everywhere. Tony had hit Homer Densley in the neck with a rifle slug. Butch Ramsey had taken a shot at Jess, barely missing him, when Andy's shotgun barked and blew him clean off his horse. Vic Nalley threw a shot at Andy and took a chunk out of the wood wall as the slug went through it. It stuck solidly in the wooden table Andy had placed in front of him. Jess fanned a third shot and hit Nalley in the chest and he hit the dirt, dead.

Nick Priestly had taken a few pellets from both Andy and Jim Smythe's shotguns, but not enough to put him down. He threw himself off his horse just as a rifle slug from the man on Jim Smythe's roof sizzled past his head. As he hit the dirt, he looked through the legs of the moving horses, searching for Jess's legs. He took a wild shot and the slug poked a hole in Jess's left pant leg. The horses were scattering now and there was dust, lead and blood flying everywhere.

As soon as Jess found an opening between the horses, he fanned two shots at Priestley. The first one hit him in the shoulder and the other one hit him in the top of his head, killing him instantly.

Warren Malarky took a few pieces of buckshot, but hadn't fired one shot yet. Slugs were whizzing past him in rapid succession and he realized he was in a hopeless situation. He quickly decided he might have a chance if he made a run for it. He spurred his horse and headed out at a full gallop away from the bloody carnage that was going on in the street. With his left hand, Jess grabbed the rifle in the scabbard on Priestley's horse as it began to move away from the commotion. He holstered his pistol and then levered a cartridge into the chamber of the rifle. He quickly glanced at the other six men lying in the street to make sure they weren't able to take a shot at him.

Andy was running out of the saloon with a shotgun and Jess hollered at him to cover the six men. Then he lifted the rifle up and sighted it on the back of Warren Malarky, who was now heading past Jim Smythe's store, blasting away with his pistol. Jim was trying to get behind the front wall when one of Malarky's shots hit him in the leg. Jess fired and the .45-70 slug from the Winchester hit Malarky in the middle of his back, exiting out the middle of his chest and then hitting his horse in the back of the head.

The horse's front legs buckled and the forward momentum caused the horse to roll forward and flip onto his back, pinning the now dead rider underneath. Neither of them moved again. Jess threw the rifle down, pulled his pistol back out of his holster, and hollered out to Tony who was now standing on the roof watching everything.

"Tony, go and see if Jim's okay!"

Tony didn't respond, he took off, headed down off the roof and over to check on Jim.

Jess began replacing the spent shells in his pistol as he turned back toward the bloody mess in the street. He looked at Andy who was watching the only one left alive. Deke Moore had been dazed by his fall off his horse and the slug in his shoulder, but he was still very much alive. Jess looked over at Carter who now lay motionless in a pool of dark blood, which was already seeping into the dry dirt of the street. He looked at the other four men who lay dead in various grotesque positions scattered around the street, each in his own pool of blood. Then he looked back down the street at the dead man pinned under a very dead horse.

"One hell of a shot there," remarked Andy, as he too, looked down the street at the dead horse and rider. Jess said nothing, but simply nodded at Andy.

It was then that Andy noticed something different in Jess's eyes. A darkness seemed to loom behind them that Andy had not seen before. It actually made him a little uncomfortable. Jess holstered his pistol and Andy noticed that he didn't put the hammer strap back on. Jess turned his attention to Deke, who was sitting up, holding his shoulder. The fog in Deke Moore's brain was beginning to clear now and he was beginning to feel the pain more. Jess stared deep into Deke Moore's eyes as if trying to read something in the man. He found what he was looking for.

"What's your name, mister?" asked Jess.

"Deke Moore, not that it matters."

"It matters."

"To you maybe, not to me."

"I usually like to know the names of the men who try to kill me."

"So now you know it and now you can go to hell."

"I'll pass on that." Jess looked around at the dead bodies again. So did Deke.

"Those were all good friends of mine you killed," Deke remarked angrily.

"Maybe I killed them, but I'm not the one responsible for their deaths. Your boss Carter over there is the one responsible for every bit of this. I didn't ask for any of it," replied Jess, anger rising in his voice now.

"Well, I guess that don't matter now," said Deke. "There are six men dead, just the same."

"Actually, I count seven," countered Jess, his jaw tightening.

"Kid," Deke replied sarcastically, "you sure are good with that pistol, but your mama obviously never taught you how to count."

"Actually, she taught me how to count to ten before I was five years old. Could you count to ten when you were five?"

It took a full five seconds before Deke finally figured out what Jess was getting at. He looked over at his pistol lying in the street where Andy had thrown it. "I'll tell you what, kid. You give me my pistol and then we can face each other in the street like men, fair and square. My right arm still works fine. What do you say?"

"Well, Mr. Moore, It seems the bad news is fair got chased clean out of town when you seven men rode into town today to kill me. I got a hunch that fair won't be back until sometime tomorrow."

"Well, you ain't gonna' just shoot me, are you?" asked Deke. Jess looked at Deke square in the eyes and that's when Deke saw it.

"What do you think?" replied Jess. Deke lurched for his gun but it was too far away. Jess drew his pistol and put two slugs solidly into Deke Moore's chest. Deke fell back into the dirt on his side.

"Gawdalmighty!" Andy blurted. "You can't just plug a wounded and unarmed man like that!"

Jess replaced the spent shells and holstered his pistol. "It seems as though I can...because I just did."

"And you don't feel even a little bit bad about it?" probed Andy, a concerned look on his face.

Jess looked down the street where Warren Malarky lay dead pinned underneath his dead horse. "Well, I do feel bad about the horse," he said frankly.

Andy cocked his head and gave him one of those strange looks.

"Well, I do. I like horses," said Jess defensively.

"You remember that thing I said before about thinkin' you're gettin' a mean streak in ya?" asked Andy.

"Yeah?"

"Well, just so ya know, I ain't wonderin' about it anymore."

Tony had been walking up to Andy and Jess when he watched Jess plug Deke Moore in the street. Tony stopped for a moment, hung his head, and said "Damn" in a whisper that only he could hear. He continued toward the bloody carnage in the street until he was standing in front of Jess and Andy.

"Damn shame this had to happen like this but then again, we didn't ask for it either," said Tony.

"How's Jim?" asked Jess.

"He's fine. He took one in the leg but it went clean through. The doc is with him now."

"That's good. Don't either of you two feel sorry for any of this," he said. "These men all came in here to kill me along with anyone else who got in their way. They got exactly what they deserved. You can be sure of one thing; I wouldn't have been the last person these men would've killed. You probably saved a dozen innocent lives that would've been taken by these murderers over the years if they had ridden back out of here. Carter there would've owned this town lock, stock, and barrel and would have run it the way he wanted. That's what you need to think of."

Both Tony and Andy looked at the seven dead men. As they did, they realized that what Jess said made sense, even though it didn't seem to fit the normal way a man would think. They knew that these were hardened killers, who had killed before and surely would have killed again. You could see the expressions on both men slowly change.

"Andy," said Tony, "I think maybe we did a good thing today, even though it might not feel like it right now."

"I'm beginnin' to think so, too," Andy replied, still shaking his head. "But I do think our boy here is gettin' a little loco."

Jess looked down at the dead bodies and looked at Andy. "Well, I might be a little loco, but we're alive and they ain't. Now, I'm going over to check on Jim. Tony, strip these men of all their guns and money and give it all to Jim. It will make up for the money he lost due to Carter's new store. You can keep all of the horses."

"Hey, what the hell do I get?" retorted Andy, "I coulda got shot again, ya know."

"Well, Andy, you can have that poor horse I shot over there," answered Jess, as he looked down at the horse still lying on Warren Malarky's dead body.

"What the hell am I goin' to do with a damn dead horse?"

"You serve steaks in your saloon, don't you?" Jess asked as he turned and headed for Smythe's General Store.

Andy gave Jess another one of his looks and then he glanced down at the dead horse. "Well, I guess they probably won't know the difference anyway. What do ya think, Tony?"

Now it was Tony's turn to give Andy a comical look. "Have you eaten one of your steaks lately?"

Andy had a hurt look on his face. Then they both turned to watch Jess as he walked over to check on Jim.

"Did you see what he did to that last fella?" asked Andy, never taking his eyes off Jess.

"Yeah, I sure did. I guess I can't blame him, but it ain't something I could've done."

"I don't think I could've either," admitted Andy. "That boy's gettin' hard as nails. One thing is for sure, ain't no one in this town gonna mess with that boy now, after what he did today. I guess we might as well start cleanin' up the mess." Tony nodded and they both started to strip the men of their valuables. The undertaker showed up with his usual smile and loaded the bodies on a wagon, never saying a word.

As Jess walked over to check on Jim and Sara, he wasn't thinking about the dead men lying in the street. That was over with and there was no reason in his mind to waste any more time thinking about it. Besides, his thoughts were somewhere else. His thoughts were on his brother. He wondered how he was going to find him and what he might do when he did.

CHAPTER NINE

Jess finally got a full night of sleep. With a little prodding, he had agreed to stay at Jim and Sara's. He slept in the same room he had stayed in the night his family was murdered. When he woke, he dressed and washed his face with water out of the same bowl he had used on that fateful night. When he looked at himself in the mirror, which was something he didn't care to do very often, he noticed how much older he looked. It was then that he realized how much older he actually felt. He thought about his brother, wondering if he looked like him. He wondered what his brother was doing right now. Where did he live and what kind of life did he have? Too many questions and not enough answers, he thought to himself.

He strapped on his gun belt, checked his pistol, and walked down the stairs. He could smell the food all the way down. Jim was sitting at the table stuffing his mouth and Sara was busy at the stove as usual.

"I see that bullet in the leg didn't slow down your appetite any," said Jess as he pulled out a seat and sat down.

"Hell no, a man's got to eat, especially when he's trying to heal up. Dig in, Jess, you got to be hungry after yesterday."

"As a matter of fact, I am starved for sure. It smells good, Sara."

"It's always good," she bragged. "Dig in because I'm making more eggs and bacon right now and I have more fresh biscuits in the oven."

"You don't have to tell me twice," said Jess, as he filled his plate.

Jim and Jess ate without saying a word for about five minutes and Sara thought they sounded like two men eating their last meal before being hanged. Sara put some more food on the table and finally sat down to join them. She fixed herself a plate and after she took a bite, she turned to Jess.

"Jess, maybe I shouldn't ask but...doesn't it bother you at all after killing those men yesterday, especially that last man? The man you shot while he was unarmed and helpless?"

Jess put down his fork, picked up his coffee cup, and took a long swallow before answering.

"Sara, I don't expect you to understand some of the things I do. I suppose I look at things in a different way than most folks. It's not like I came to town yesterday and shot a few of the townspeople for no reason. With the exception of Carter, the men I killed yesterday were all hired killers who kill innocent people for money. I didn't know any of those six men and yet they came into town yesterday to murder me. They're no better than the men who murdered my family. I live by a few simple rules. If a man tries to kill me, I will brace him, and I won't stop until he is dead. I certainly won't let a man who has tried to kill me for no good reason get patched up and come at me again. That's why I shot the man sitting in the street yesterday. He would have been hunting for me as soon as he was well enough to ride a horse. What sense would that make when it was him that tried to kill me for the money simply because Carter told him to? I won't apologize for what I did, even if you can't understand it."

There was a long and awkward moment of silence at the table while Sara and Jim thought about everything that he had said. Jim understood it plainly and the truth was he agreed with what Jess had done, even though it somehow seemed wrong at the time it was happening. Sara was having a much harder time understanding how men could kill one another. She did, however, have to agree that it was better that Carter and his men died than to have Jess shot down dead in the middle of the street, leaving Dick Carter running the town under his iron rule. Sara put her hand out, touched Jess's face, and smiled at him. She gave him a look that told him that she was trying to understand it all.

"Well, no matter what, we love you and I'm glad you're here with us today," she said thoughtfully. "I'll just have to try to understand the rest of it. It may take some time, but I'll try."

"That's all I ask for," he told her.

Jim interrupted with a big smile. "Okay, now let's all dig in before this great food gets cold." Jess agreed and cleaned his plate and then asked for a second helping.

Andy was wiping down the bar when Tony walked in. Andy grabbed the pot of coffee from the iron stove and two cups and they sat down at a table.

"You don't make a half-bad cup of coffee, Andy."

"It's always good when it's free."

Tony took another sip. "You know, it does taste better now that you mentioned that. Andy, have you seen Newcomb or York anywhere yet today?"

"Nope, but I sure saw 'em last night. It wasn't long after Jess let them out of jail that I saw the two of 'em hightailin' it outta here. I guess they figured they was both plumb out of a job."

"Lucky for them they left. I heard some of the men talking about getting a rope and giving them what they deserved."

"I don't think we'll be seeing their sorry asses here in this town again," said Andy.

Tony smiled. "I think you might be right about that. Of course, we don't have a sheriff anymore. I was thinking about asking Jess if he wanted the job. I already talked to some of the other men in town and they said it was fine with them. What do you think, Andy?"

"Hell, I'd love to have him as our sheriff but I don't think there's a damn chance in hell that he'd take the job."

"Why not? We could pay him good and maybe it'll settle him down some. It might be good for him."

Andy gave Tony one of his comical grins. "Hell, in case you haven't picked up on it yet, that boy's on a mission in life and the last thing he's planning on doing is settlin' down."

"Well, I'm gonna ask him anyway, just in case."

"Good luck. If you're successful with that, maybe you could talk to him about my LeAnn."

Now it was Tony's turn to grin. "I may be good, but I ain't no miracle worker."

Andy groaned and lowered his head.

Tony got up and headed for the door. As he reached it, he turned back Andy. "What's the special for tonight?"

Andy cocked his head. "What do ya think?"

Tony just shook his head and walked out, heading to Smythe's General Store where he knew Jess was. Sara welcomed him in and escorted him to the kitchen. Jim and Jess had finished with breakfast and were chatting and sipping hot coffee. They both greeted Tony and Sara fixed him a plate over his feeble objections.

"Tony, thanks for throwing in with me yesterday. I appreciate it."

"Couldn't do no less," said Tony. It wouldn't be right to let you take on all our problems by yourself. Jess, how would you like to be our new sheriff?"

Jess almost choked on his coffee. "Well, don't you just get right to the point?"

Tony smiled a wide smile. "I've already talked to several of the men and they agree. I know you could have the job just for the asking. We can pay you well and it might be a good move for you."

Jess didn't have to think long about it. "Tony, I appreciate the fact that you would offer me the job of sheriff and I'm thankful that the town would have me, but my interests are elsewhere. I'm a bounty hunter now and there are a lot of bad men out there to hunt down."

"I understand that, Jess," replied Tony. "But some of them are bound to turn up here from time to time and when they do, I'd sure like to know that you were here to protect the town."

"I understand that Tony, but I think after yesterday, this town can protect itself pretty well. And if anything does happen, you get in touch with me and I'll be here as fast as a horse can carry me. You have my word on that. Besides, I have to find my brother now. I found out that he knows one of the men who murdered my family.

I need to know why, and I need to know if my brother knew about any of it. I'll be leaving soon to look for him."

"Jess, you never told us anything about your brother knowing any of the men who murdered your family," Sara said.

"Actually, we haven't had much time to talk since I got to town."

"Ain't that the truth," said Jim, shaking his head.

"When I was in Red Rock, Texas, Sheriff Clancy told me that when Taggert left town before I got there, he left with a man by the name of Jim or Tim Sloan. I'm not positive that it was my brother but I'm guessing it probably was," Jess said.

"So, where are you headed for?" asked Tony.

"I suppose I'll start out by heading back down to Red Rock. That's where he was spotted last as far as I know. Maybe I'll pick up some information or a lead on him there."

"Well, good luck, and if you change your mind, the job's still open," replied Tony, as he dug into the plate of food Sara had put in front of him.

"I see you changed your mind about eating," Sara said with a smile.

"I decided it was a good idea since I might miss supper tonight."

"Why is that?" asked Sara. Tony looked at Jim, Jim looked at Jess, and then they all laughed, which left Sara wondering what was so funny.

"I don't think you'd want to know," Tony said as he dug in again.

Sara realized this was one of those discussions she would not get to share in, so she simply gave up trying.

"Jess, are you sure you won't stay for another day or so?" Sara asked with expectant eyes.

"I'd love to Sara, but I can't. I have to find my brother and find out what he knows. After that, maybe I can find out about my father. I need to know who and what kind of men they are, especially after hearing about my brother riding with Blake Taggert over in Red Rock."

"If he's anything like your real father, you might not like what you find," Sara cautioned.

"I realize that, but I need to find out, especially now that I know he might have had something to do with one of the men who murdered my family. I have to find out how he knew Blake Taggert and more importantly, if he knew about what Taggert had done."

"I still wish you would stay, at least for a day," Sara pleaded.

"I can't, Sara. But I promise to visit with you and Jim as soon as I can."

"Well, I guess that's all I can hope for," Sara said with disappointment evident her face.

"I rounded up those supplies you asked for, Jess," Jim said briskly, changing the conversation.

"I'll stop by and pack my saddlebags on my way out. What do I owe you?"

"Not a damn penny and don't you argue with me on this one. You've already done enough for me and Sara, as well as the whole town. I threw in some extra ammo for you too."

Jess could tell by the tone of finality in Jim's voice that there was no point in arguing with him. "All right, I'll let you get away with it this time."

Jim let out a grunt and nodded.

Jess went to the livery and saddled up Gray. He thanked Tony for everything and then he stopped by the saloon to say goodbye to Andy, who was busy wiping down some tables.

"So, ya didn't take the sheriff's job, eh?" probed Andy.

"No, I appreciate the offer, but I have to find my brother."

"You know, it gets mighty lonely out on the trail. You just might want some company."

Jess knew exactly what Andy meant as he looked over at the swinging door to the kitchen. "Not a chance, Andy, not a chance in hell."

"Well ya can't blame a man for tryin'."

"Thanks for everything, Andy. I'll be back before you know it."

Jess was almost out the door when LeAnn came running out of the back.

"Why, Jess Williams! Are you trying to run out without even saying goodbye to me or letting me thank you proper for everything you done for us?"

"I'm kind of in a hurry, LeAnn. You're welcome and goodbye."

Jess said it as fast as he could and then he nearly ran down the steps and grabbed the reins of his horse. He could hear Andy laughing in the background, along with what sounded like LeAnn throwing another one of her tantrums. He walked Gray over to Jim's and loaded everything he needed, hugged Sara, thanked Jim again, and rode out, heading for Red Rock. He hoped he would find a lead on his brother there.

He had gotten a late start leaving Black Creek, but he was in no hurry, so he didn't make it too far south the first day. He stopped a little early and cooked a rabbit he had shot along the trail. He fried some pan bread and cooked some beans to go with it. He drank several cups of coffee and turned in for the night.

He made better time on the second day. He found a nice spot to make camp on top of a small hill with a rock ledge on one side. A small creek ran along the bottom of the hill less than two hundred yards from where he made camp. The wind was blowing strong and the ledge would protect him from the chilly air and retain a little more heat from the fire. The nights were getting quite cold this time of year. He unpacked an extra blanket Sara had given him and he was thankful for it. He wondered about maybe picking up a packhorse to carry more supplies since he would probably spend more of his time on the trail than in towns.

He ate his meal and was finishing the coffee that was left when, off in the distance, he could see the glow from another campfire. He stood up and tried to estimate the distance but it was hard to do in the dark. It was far enough away though, that he didn't figure on any trouble. Even though it was quite a distance, he could see that the other fire was a small one and Jess decided it was just another lone man on the trail. He was not one to take chances though, so he looked around his area. He noticed that the ground was quite rocky and gravelly coming up the small hill where he was camped. A lot of scrub brush was scattered about.

He took out the ball of string that he had bought from Jim at the store and tied a piece of it to the end of one bush. Then he attached a can to the other end and placed the can gently into another bush. That left the string dangling about six inches above the ground so if someone tried walking up the hill, he would hit the string and pull the can out of the bush, which would make enough noise to wake him. He only had one empty can, but he decided that he would save more cans and have enough of them to cover a larger area. Of course, he could always count on Gray to give him a heads-up, but this contraption would give him an extra level of comfort. He leaned back on his saddle and laid the shotgun next to his left leg in case he would have the need for it.

He woke a few times during the night but not from someone tripping the string. He always woke at any unusual sound that didn't seem to belong. He rose at dawn and made some breakfast and coffee. He rolled the string around the can and packed it in his saddlebags. He saddled Gray and headed south again.

As he rode along the trail, he wondered who it had been across the way last night. Maybe it was a traveling salesman with a wagon full of snake oil and products to sell. Maybe it was a lawman on the trail of someone or maybe it was that someone the lawman was trailing. He decided he would buy one of those spyglasses he had seen in Jim's hardware store. It didn't matter though; he had something more important on his mind: Find his brother Tim Sloan and confront him. That was his mission and he would not be diverted from it.

CHAPTER TEN

It was a three-day ride to Black Creek, Kansas from Holten for Tim Sloan. He didn't mind the ride though. He liked to be out on the trail and the truth was, he liked to be alone most of the time. He liked playing poker, stealing other men's money, and he liked the company of whores and dance hall girls, but he was a loner deep inside. He had packed enough supplies for the ride before he left Holten because he didn't want to stop in any towns along the way. He couldn't afford to get distracted now. He had a mission and his mind was on the big payday. Ten thousand dollars was a huge amount of money for killing one man. Sloan had killed men for as little as a twenty-dollar bet in a poker hand, so for ten thousand dollars, he would kill a dozen men. But he only had to kill one, and even though that one man was his only brother, as far as he knew, it didn't bother him in the slightest.

His father, Eddie Sloan, had told him about his brother and how he had separated them. His father hadn't told him the whole truth, however. He hadn't told him about the whore by the name of Sally who took care of him until he was four. He hadn't told him he beat Sally nearly to death, leaving her in a little town without a penny when he decided that he didn't need her help anymore. Tim vaguely remembered someone holding him. It was a woman with soft skin and the smell of lilac, but that was about all he could remember.

His father had told him about his real mother, a worthless woman by the name of Becky. He had told him how she was a filthy whore and didn't want anything to do with Tim or his brother Jess after giving birth to them. He told him about how Becky had run off three days after their births and threatened to throw the two babies into the creek to drown rather than have to raise them. He told him about how he had found someone to raise his brother and that he had taken Tim to raise by himself along with the help of a woman by the name of Sally. He told him that his real mom, Becky, had died from a beating a man had given her while she was working in a whorehouse in a small town somewhere in Texas. Tim hated his real mother for what she had done to him and he grew up hating pretty much everything else in life.

Of course, what Tim didn't know was that his father lied about all of it except for the fact that his real mother's name was Becky, but that didn't matter. He believed what his father had told him mostly because no one had told him otherwise and because he grew up with his father going from one whorehouse to another and from one gambling house to another. He grew up among thieves, murderers, and whores. Before he had a chance to form any of his own opinions about life, he was already tainted. He simply ended up being a product of his environment. It was not the life he had chosen; it was simply the life he had been handed.

Sloan had killed his first man when he was twelve years old. He hadn't started the fight. The other man had seen him sitting outside a gambling establishment where his father was deadlocked in a high-stakes poker game. The man decided that the pistol and holster Tim was wearing were too nice for a young kid to have and he wanted them for himself. He demanded that Tim take the gun off and give it to him. When Tim told him to go to hell, the man challenged him. Tim obliged and shot the man straight through the heart before he got his gun out of his holster. From that day on, no one considered him a twelve-year-old kid anymore. Everyone considered him a killer who had a lightning-fast left hand.

Now he was a young man just a few months shy of seventeen, one who had already killed several men and was now on the trail of his twin brother. When he found him, he would kill him for the ten thousand dollars of blood money that Dick Carter had promised him. He would not hesitate or feel bad about it; he would just do it for the money. He didn't think about the morality or the fairness of it. He hadn't learned those lessons from his father. He had only learned to cheat, lie, steal, and especially how to kill men. Yes, he was a product of his environment and quite a bad one at that.

Tim made camp by a small creek the first night after leaving Holten. He ate a simple meal consisting of bread and coffee. He was just about to turn in after putting a few more pieces of wood on the fire when he caught a slight glare from a distant fire. It was up higher like it was on the top of a hill. For a moment, he thought about going to see who it was. Maybe it was someone he could rob; but then again, it might be a law dog on the trail and that would put a dent in his plan. He decided not to tempt fate. He had more important things to do and one thing especially that would pay him a lot more money than whoever was at the other campfire could. All he had to do was find and kill one man.

In the morning, he made coffee, ate cornbread with fried bacon, and broke camp. He always traveled light and never really ate much, only what he needed to sustain himself. As he rode north, his thoughts turned to the campfire he had spotted last night. He wondered who it was, but not because he cared. He was simply occupying his time. Then his mind turned to the idea of having ten thousand dollars in his pocket. He began to think of all the things that the money would buy him, he fine whiskey and the best whores, especially the good-looking ones that weren't scarred up or ugly as an old mule's ass. He thought about a new set of clothes, a new hat, and even a stake in a high-dollar poker game. Then he thought about how he was going to get all these things and that led him to think about his brother again. If anyone could have been there to see it, he would have seen an evil grin beginning to form on his face.

⌐◄ ►

Jess hadn't been riding very long since breaking camp. He was following a creek, which ran almost straight south. He stopped and filled both of his canteens with water. It was starting to warm up with the sun out and it felt good on his face. He loved the open range. It was lonely, but at the same time, so peaceful. The quiet always helped him gather his thoughts. He thought about what he had done back in Black Creek. He thought about the man sitting in the street that he had simply shot and sent on to meet his maker, whoever that was. He wondered if he should have kicked him his gun and given him a chance to face off with him, but he couldn't think of a good reason to have done so.

The man was a murderer and hired gun. He had come to town with Carter and the rest to kill him and who knows how many others before it ended. Jess was not afraid of a fair fight, but seven against one simply wasn't fair. Sure, he had help from some of the townspeople, but the seven men riding up to him while he stood his ground in the middle of the street didn't know that. They had intended to shoot him down like a dog. Of course, he did have to wonder to himself about the sanity of standing down seven men in the middle of the street. That might have been just slightly on the edge of crazy. Of course, he really did feel bad about killing the horse. He thought about how lucky he was to have survived the showdown with Carter and his men. Then again, he wondered if it was fate playing a role in his life again. He mounted Gray and continued along the creek.

The creek suddenly made a sharp turn to the west and Jess decided to cross at a shallow part. He let Gray get his fill of water. He took his hat off, stroked his hair back, and looked around. He looked down the creek and way off in the distance, he could barely make out what looked like a man stooped down at the creek next to a horse. He wondered who it might be. For a moment, he wondered if it could be his brother but after he entertained the thought, he figured the odds of that were slim. It didn't warrant checking. Gray finished drinking and Jess climbed back up in the saddle. He crossed the creek and continued south.

Terrence Hanley finished filling his canteen and started northward again back to Black Creek. He wondered if he would still have a job when he got back to Carter's ranch. Not because he thought

Carter might fire him, but because he wondered if Carter was still alive. He kept his horse at a slow pace, not wanting to run into Sloan on the trail. He wondered more than once on his trip back to Black Creek if he should just take the five hundred he had in his pocket, head out farther west, and find himself another ranch to work at, but he couldn't bring himself to do it. He had started a job and he needed to finish it. That was his way. He wondered who the man was he had seen off in a distance at the creek. He knew it wasn't Sloan since the man was heading south and Hanley had been following Sloan's trail all the way back to Black Creek. Probably just another drifter, Hanley thought to himself.

⌐ ⌐

Tim Sloan could see the town of Black Creek, Kansas from the trail. It was still a mile or so away, but he could see most of the buildings. He had passed a few farms along the way and now he was coming up to a house on the outskirts of town. He saw a man who was working on replacing some old weathered fence posts. He decided to stop and talk to him. The man working on the posts noticed Sloan approaching. He stopped his work and stood up. He took a rag from his back pocket, wiped his hands off, and looked up at Sloan as he reined up by the man.

"Howdym mister," the man said, putting the rag back in his pocket. "Can I help you with something?"

"Do you know a man by the name of Jess Williams?"

The old man's eyes twinkled. "Yeah, but he left town already."

"So, he's still alive?"

"He was when he rode out, and I'd have to believe he still is."

"Why do you say that?"

"Because he done killed off all of Dick Carter's hired guns along with Carter himself."

"Dick Carter is dead?"

"Yep, that young man is one tough hombre," the man said almost proudly.

Sloan sat in the saddle for a few moments thinking, while he rubbed his stubbly chin. He thought about the letter again. "Do you know where I can find a man by the name of Cal Hardin?" Sloan asked.

"I sure do. The Hardin ranch is down the road the same way you're heading. It's about four miles past the town and on your right side. You can't miss it. The Hardin ranch is one of the largest in the area. He has a big gate area and a big sign atop the gate rails that says "HARDIN" on it. He's not a bad fellow for a rich man. I do some work for him now and again. He always pays well and he's never treated me bad either. You tell him Charlie says howdy."

"Thanks, mister, I appreciate it," Sloan replied, trying to be friendly, which wasn't easy for him. Sloan continued down the road and passed the turn into the town. He wanted to get to the Hardin ranch, speak to Cal Hardin, and get as much information as he could about the job he was being paid to do.

He finally reached the gate of the Hardin ranch and turned down the road. He could see the house, which was about five hundred feet back from the gate. He noticed several men sitting on horseback in front of the house. They seemed to be in some discussion about something, probably about who was going to do what for the next day or something like that. Sloan thought about the everyday drudgery of being a ranch hand and the thought repulsed him. They spotted Sloan and two of them broke from the group. They rode over to meet him. They reined their horses up in front of him, putting themselves between Sloan and the Hardin house. Sloan did not excite easily. He simply stopped and waited for the men to do exactly what he knew they would do. Art Wheye and Newton Cash were the two men.

Art was the first to speak. "Can we help you with something, mister?"

Tim, always cold and deliberate with his actions, took a moment to look the two men over. They both wore pistols and looked tough enough, but they were not gunslingers and Tim knew it with one glance. Sloan looked over at the other men who were now all facing in his direction and watching to see what would happen next. He was certain he could take these two in front of him but that was not what he was here for, at least not at the moment.

"I'm looking to speak with a man by the name of Cal Hardin. I was told to look him up by a man named Dick Carter." Wheye and Cash both knew that Carter was dead, which is why they both looked at one another oddly.

Cal Hardin had just finished his supper and was looking out the window to see what was going on. His wife, Ruth was peeking over his shoulder.

"Is that Jess Williams? What do you suppose he wants with you? I thought this whole damn mess was over with," she said with more than a hint of worry in her voice.

"It damn sure looks like him, but it ain't," Cal replied, after looking at the young man who sat on his horse out on the ranch road.

Cal moved back from the window to go to the front door. When he did, he stepped on his wife's left foot. She let out a howl that sounded somewhat unnatural and Cal, stumbling to get his footing back, glared at her.

"Damn it, woman," he scolded her. "How many times have I told you not to stand behind me like that? Finish up cleaning the dishes instead of worrying about things that don't concern you." Ruth huffed and went back to cleaning.

Cal walked outside onto the porch and waved at the two men in front of Sloan. "Let him come on in," Cal said. The two men backed up their horses just enough to allow Sloan to pass. Sloan, not one to be friendly, didn't even nod at the men as he moved past them. He acted as if they no longer existed. He kept his gaze on the man on the porch waiting for him.

"Sure enough not the friendliest guy I've met," said Cash.

"You ain't wrong 'bout that," replied Wheye.

"You know what else I noticed?" added Cash.

"What?"

"He looks a lot like that Jess Williams kid."

"Damn if you ain't right about that too, Cash," he replied. "But I wouldn't call Jess Williams a kid anymore."

"Why not? Hell, I'm more than twice his age."

"Yeah, but he's already killed more men than any other one man I know. And after what he did to Deke Moore the other day, well...he ain't no kid anymore."

"Yeah, that was pretty cold, even though Deke most likely had it coming. He sure enough killed his share of men up to then." They both started their horses over to the house. They knew that their boss would want some company close.

"You know what?" asked Wheye. Cash looked at him, but didn't answer.

"I'm thinking maybe you might be more like three times his age," laughed Wheye.

"Damn that's cold, Wheye. I thought we was friends and all."

"Hell, I never did like your sorry ass."

They both laughed as they dismounted their horses and wrapped the reins around the rail on the front porch. Sloan had already tied his horse. He walked up the steps, stood in front of Cal Hardin, and took a moment to size him up.

Cal spoke first. "I'm Cal Hardin and my guess is you're Tim Sloan."

"You guessed right. I would like a minute to speak with you...in private," Sloan said, as he looked over at Cash and Wheye, who were not about to let Sloan out of their sight just yet.

Hardin nodded at the two men. "You boys wait out here on the porch. Mr. Sloan and I have something to discuss inside." Both Cash and Wheye nodded and took a seat on the porch. The other men dispersed, heading to their assigned duties. Hardin went inside, followed by Sloan. Hardin offered him a seat at the table.

"Can I offer you some coffee or a drink?" Hardin asked.

"Coffee would be just fine."

"Ruth, pour the man a cup and I'll have one too."

Ruth did as she was told. She thought about limping on her foot a little to get her husband's attention. She always liked to get in a dig whenever and however she could. Sometimes it was simply a breath exhaled too loudly and sometimes it was stomping her feet and slamming doors. Her favorite was when she would slam his plate or coffee cup down hard on the table. Cal Hardin dominated the household and ran roughshod over his wife most of the time. Ruth thought about it, but she didn't act on it. She was a little too distracted by the striking resemblance that Sloan had to Jess Williams. When she finished serving the coffee, one look from Cal was all she needed to know that she was to leave the room. When she did, that left Cal Hardin and Tim Sloan in the room alone.

Hardin knew that his men were right outside on the porch, but he still felt uncomfortable. He knew Jess Williams had killed a lot of men already, including Dick Carter and most of his hired guns and yet, if Jess Williams were here sitting where his brother Tim Sloan was, he would not feel uncomfortable. The truth was, Hardin still liked Jess and felt sorry for what had happened to him and especially to his family. However, he did not like this young man sitting here before him, but mostly, he did not like what he was here for. They both looked each other over.

Tim took a sip of his coffee and set his cup down ever so slowly as he kept his cold stare on Cal. "Well, Mr. Hardin, I understand that you are holding the sum of ten thousand dollars for me, is that right?"

Cal shifted in his seat and leaned forward slightly. "Do you have a letter that you would like to show me first?" asked Cal.

Tim dug into the front pocket of his shirt and pulled out the letter. He handed it to Cal. He read it and looked at Dick Carter's signature. It was his handwriting; Cal was sure of it.

"Damn you, Carter," Cal growled. He wasn't speaking to anyone. He was speaking to an unseen entity that may or may not have been able to hear him. "The dirt on your grave hasn't even begun to settle yet and you're still causing people grief."

Cal hung his head for a moment before he looked back up at Sloan. He did not like what he was doing, but he would do it because he had promised he would. A man's word was one of the most important things in life and once it was given, it was given.

"That's Carter's signature on the letter but you don't get the ten thousand until you..." Cal's voice broke off for a second "...finish the job."

"Oh, I'll finish it; you can count on that."

"You'd really kill your own flesh and blood, your own brother, for money?"

"Mr. Hardin, I've killed men over a poker bet for a twenty-dollar gold piece and I've killed men just for calling me a cheat. I ain't got no brother as far as I'm concerned. The only flesh and blood I have is my father, and I'd even kill him for that kind of money."

"Jess Williams is your brother. I can assure you of that."

"I don't need your assurance, Mr. Hardin. All I need right now is for you to tell me that if I bring his dead body strapped over his horse to you for identification that you will pay me the ten thousand Carter promised."

"Just so we understand one another, I don't like you or what you are here to do. But I did agree to do what Carter asked. So yes, I'll pay you the money if you are able to do what Carter is paying you to do." Sloan took another swallow of his coffee and slowly stood up.

Hardin looked at Sloan's pistol and holster. "You know, your brother has a pretty fancy pistol and holster himself. He's damn fast with it too. You might want to think this thing over."

An evil grin formed on Sloan's lips. "I've already thought about it. Just be ready to hand me my money when I deliver his corpse to you."

Sloan turned around and walked back outside. Cash and Wheye were still sitting on the porch. Tim walked past them as if they still didn't exist and walked down the steps of the porch. He grabbed the reins of his horse and mounted himself into the saddle with an easy fluid movement. Cal came out onto the porch and both men stood up. All three of them were facing Sloan.

"I don't suppose you know where I could start looking for Jess Williams?" asked Sloan.

Hardin lowered his head for a second. He was thinking about what he had promised Dick Carter and that didn't include helping Sloan find Jess Williams. He slowly looked back up at Sloan.

"Actually, I have no idea of his whereabouts."

Sloan smiled that evil grin again. "That's what I thought," replied Sloan, as he slowly turned his horse toward the main road heading into town.

"Not a very friendly feller, huh, boss?" asked Wheye.

"Nope. That young man is a lot of things, but friendly sure ain't one of 'em."

"I know one thing he is," Cash said. Hardin and Wheye both looked at him with interest. "He's a damn sight better-looking than Wheye here," Cash chuckled, getting his dig back at Wheye.

"Guess I had that one coming for sure," laughed Wheye.

"That and a damn sight more, too," said Cash.

"Now who's being cold?" complained Wheye as he and Cash headed back to some of the other ranch hands, who were now standing around at the side of the house.

Cal Hardin watched Tim Sloan until he was out of sight. The feeling in his gut that had started with uneasiness had now turned to something more like someone slamming him in the gut with a ten-pound hammer. He didn't like what he was being a part of. He wondered about his loyalty to a dead man but then again, loyalty was loyalty, even in death. He had made a promise and no matter how much he disliked the matter, he would keep it. He hung his head again as he recalled his conversation the day that Carter had come to visit him with the envelope with ten thousand dollars in it. Then, he remembered another thing that he hadn't promised Carter as he slowly raised his head back up. As he looked out at the road where he had finally lost sight of Tim Sloan, a slight smile came to his lips.

CHAPTER ELEVEN

Tim Sloan knew that Cal Hardin had lied about the whereabouts of Jess Williams. It mattered little to him though. He knew that he would find him eventually. Sooner would be better, but later would be just fine with him. He decided the town of Black Creek was the best place to start. The sun was just about to go down when he finally rode into town.

Tony, the blacksmith, was just finishing filing the left front hoof of a beautiful palomino mare when he looked up and saw Jess riding back into town. He stopped what he was doing and grabbed a rag to wipe his hands as he walked outside of the livery.

"Well, well, well, I guess that job offer sounded better than he first thought," he muttered softly.

He kept looking at Jess, who was riding his horse slowly toward the livery. The horse was the first thing he noticed. It wasn't Jess's horse, Gray. Tony knew that horse. He had sold it to Jess's father, John Williams. Then, Tony realized that the young man on top of the horse wasn't Jess. It was someone who looked an awful lot like him, but the way he sat on the saddle was all wrong.

Tim Sloan rode right up to the large man who was standing outside the livery wiping his hands. Actually, the man looked more like a huge bear standing there. Sloan dismounted and handed the reins of his horse to the man. Sloan stared into Tony's eyes. He could read a lot from a man's eyes. It was something that he had learned from working the poker tables. He could usually tell if a man was lying or cheating just by staring into his eyes for a moment. He saw something, but he wasn't sure what it was. He logged it in the back of his mind. Tony took the reins but said nothing, still staring at the close resemblance this young man had to Jess Williams.

"I'm looking for a room. I assume you can take care of my horse," Sloan said.

"Uh…sure thing, mister, you can find a room at the hotel right there," said Tony, pointing in the direction of the Creek Hotel. "I'll take care of your horse for you." Tim noticed the odd behavior of the blacksmith but he simply nodded and headed to the hotel to get a room. He figured he would settle in and then start asking some questions about the man he was looking for. Tony went about stabling the man's horse and as soon as he was finished, he headed straight over to Jim and Sara Smythe's place. He knew that Jess was looking for the brother he never knew he had. While Tony wasn't the smartest guy in town, he knew that there might be something to what he had just seen.

When he arrived at Smythe's General Store, Jim was on a step stool stocking the top shelf and Sara was holding a box. She was handing Jim small bottles of some elixir that probably delivered an unpleasant reaction to whoever was dumb enough to drink the stuff.

"Well, hello Tony. What do you need?" asked Sara.

"I need to talk to the both of you about what I just saw," Tony replied with enough anxiousness in his voice to cause both Jim and Sara to stop what they were doing. Jim came off the stool, wincing in pain every time he put pressure on his wounded leg. Sara put the box on the counter.

"What did you see that has you so rattled, Tony?" asked Jim.

"You know that brother that Jess is looking for?"

"Yeah," replied Jim.

"Well, I think I just stabled his horse. I thought it was Jess coming back to town at first until he got right up close to me. Then I realized it wasn't Jess but someone who looked a lot like him. I think it might be his brother."

Sara had a worried look in her eyes. "Oh Lord, Jim. What if it is his brother? What are we going to do?" Sara asked nervously.

"We ain't going to do anything until we find out who this man is," replied Jim. "Hell, maybe he's just someone who looks a lot like Jess. I mean, what are the odds that he would show up here in Black Creek now? Let's not get too excited until we know for sure. Besides, Jess ain't here anyway."

"What do you want me to do?" probed Tony.

"Keep an eye on him, but don't talk to him or tell him anything," decided Jim. "Especially anything about Jess. Make sure you warn Andy too."

"I'll go see Andy right now." Tony quickly headed out for Andy's.

Sara put both her hands on her face. "My Lord, Jim, I'm worried," she declared. "I don't want any more trouble. I don't know that I can take it. I want it all to just go away."

"Now Sara, stay calm and don't you worry. Things will all work out the way they are going to work out no matter how much you worry about it. Jess ain't here and all we have to do is keep quiet and not let on about Jess. Maybe this guy just looks like him."

Andy was busy wiping down the bar when Tony came in. Andy could see that Tony was excited about something. "What's up, Tony?" asked Andy.

"Well, we ain't sure yet, but a young man came into town a few minutes ago and I have a hunch he might be that brother that Jess is looking for."

"You gotta be kiddin' me," declared Andy, with one of those strange looks he gives when he tilts his head slightly.

"I ain't kidding. I thought it was Jess coming back to town when I first saw him ride in. If it ain't his brother, he sure could pass for him."

Just then, the swinging doors to the saloon parted. A young man stepped inside and stopped, the doors swinging a few times behind him. His eyes swept the room completely and when he was seemingly satisfied that he was aware of his surroundings, his eyes fixed on Andy.

Andy looked him over for a minute. The man wore a very nice black left-handed holster with a silver engraved Colt .45 in it. The holster was tied down and you could tell by his demeanor that he was skilled in the use of it. There was a dark and foreboding look about the young man. His eyes were cold and his expression was one of contempt for anyone but himself.

Andy couldn't believe the resemblance. Tony turned away from Sloan and said in a low voice that only Andy could hear, "I told ya."

Sloan slowly walked up to the bar and Tony turned around again. Sloan could tell that Tony was concerned by something, but he felt no threat from him. He sauntered up to the bar and stared coldly into Andy's eyes.

"Well, barkeep, do you sell whiskey in here or not?"

Andy didn't move for a second. He was staring strangely back at Sloan. "Uh...yeah, we got whiskey," he answered. "You want the good stuff or the rotgut?"

"I'll take the good stuff." Andy got a bottle from the back shelf and poured Sloan a shot. Sloan downed it and Andy refilled the glass. Sloan looked over at a table where two men were engaged in a poker game. He looked back over at Andy.

"Do you mind if I get a table started later on?"

Andy looked at Tony and then back at Sloan.

"I don't suppose so, as long as it's a clean game."

Sloan smiled at that. "What makes you think it would be anything other than a clean game?" replied Sloan, a hint of agitation in his voice now.

Andy paused for a moment. "I'm just lettin' ya know, that's all," Andy replied, a little attitude beginning to show.

"Also," Sloan said, as he turned to look back over at the men at the poker table, "I'm looking for someone. I was told he was here in town lately. His name is Jess Williams. Either of you two men know anything about him or where he might be?"

Well, there it was. It was the one question that neither Tony nor Andy wanted to hear and the fact that Sloan asked the question told them the whole story. This young man was surely Jess's brother and he was looking for him. Andy and Tony looked slightly uncomfortable and delayed their answer.

Andy replied first. "We don't know any Jess Williams, mister," replied Andy. Tony nodded as if to say the same thing when Sloan's eyes turned to look at him. Sloan looked at them both and he knew that they were both acting strangely.

"Really?" Sloan asked, not sure they were being honest.

"That's right, mister," replied Andy, "but if we was to run into a man by that name, who should we say is lookin' for him?"

Sloan smiled deviously and downed his drink. "You can tell him that his brother Tim Sloan is looking for him."

Tony turned back toward the bar and looked at Andy. Both had a look of dread on their faces. Sloan threw a few dollars on the bar, walked over to the two men playing poker, and asked if he could join the game. They nodded and Sloan sat down, pulled out a few hundred dollars, and placed it on the table. Both men looked at the pile of money and began thinking how they were going to spend it once they won it. About an hour later, both of them left the bar with empty pockets.

※ ☞

Cal Hardin walked out to the front porch with a cup of hot coffee in his hand and called over to Newton Cash. He walked over to the porch.

"Morning boss, what do you need?"

"Newton, do you know Terrence Hanley? He was one of the men who worked for Dick Carter."

"Not personally, but I'd know him if I saw him. I've seen him a few times in Andy's Saloon. Seemed to be a nice enough fellow, not like those other men that worked for Carter. They were mighty mean. Those rustlers were breaking the law sure enough, but what those men did to them...well, I would have done it a little differently."

"So would I, but that's over now and we can't do anything about it. I know I owed Dick Carter a favor and I am a man of my word, but maybe we can do one good thing about this whole damn mess." Cash didn't know about everything or about Hardin's role in identifying Jess and holding the ten thousand dollars for Sloan, so he looked a little confused.

"Cash, I want you to go and find Terrence Hanley for me. I would think that he is still at Carter's ranch. I believe Carter's widow would have kept a few of the hands that survived to help out on the ranch and Hanley was one of the best ranch hands they had. I want to hire him to do something for me. Tell him that I will pay him very well."

"I'll be on my way in five minutes, boss."

Hardin nodded and walked back into the kitchen of the house. His wife was busy making some breakfast and she had overheard his discussion with Cash. She was one of those women who tried very hard not to say something or to interfere with her husband's affairs, but sometimes she just couldn't help herself. She knew all about the money Cal was holding and she didn't like the whole matter one bit. She liked Jess Williams even though she was fearful of him, although if you asked her, she didn't really know why.

"So, what do you want to talk to Terrence Hanley about?" she asked, somewhat sheepishly.

Cal didn't even look up from his coffee cup. "That ain't any of your business, woman," Cal replied firmly.

"I know about the money you're holding and I know why you're holding it too. I don't like it," she replied, gaining a little courage.

Cal looked up at her and handed her his coffee cup. "You get me another cup of coffee and let me handle the affairs around here. Do you understand me, woman?" he hollered.

Ruth had a look of indignation on her face. It was one that Cal had seen many times before. She grabbed his cup, refilled it, slammed it down in front of him, and stormed out of the kitchen.

Cal sat there and said in a low voice that no one else could hear, "What a pain in the ass." He looked up to see Cash heading out toward the Carter ranch. He smiled, knowing that he was about to try to do something to right things a little.

Jess was making good time on his journey to Red Rock, Texas. He was looking for a spot to make camp along a creek he had been following for the last few hours when he thought he heard voices. He reined up and listened. He heard them again and though the voices were far off, he could tell that they were loud and angry. He figured there were at least two men. He dismounted and tied Gray to a branch and worked his way toward the voices, his hammer-strap already off his pistol. He worked his way through some trees until he could see the men. There were two men and they were sitting on boulders across from each other. They were obviously engaged in a loud argument. Jess didn't see any horses and the men had nothing but one canteen and a sidearm each. Neither of them noticed Jess and he decided to wait and listen for a minute before announcing himself.

"Dammit, Carl, I can't believe you did this to us."

"Oh, it's always my fault. It's never your fault, is it Murry? No, never your fault."

"I'm not the one who forgot to check him to see if he had a knife on him."

"Oh, so I don't check the man's boots and that's my fault?"

"If I would have checked him I would have looked at his boots."

"You say that now, but you didn't say it when I was checking him over. What...you forgot then, but you remember now? Oh, that's good...that's real good, Murry."

"Well, what do we do now?"

"Now you want me to figure things out? You trust me to do that?"

"Quit your bellyaching, Carl. I can't help it if you screwed up... again."

"Again! What do you mean again?"

"Just like last time, Carl. You let the last man get the drop on us and he robbed us just like this man did. How are we going to make any money at this business if we keep letting our prisoners get the drop on us? We're supposed to be making money at this, not losing money."

"So now it's my fault we're losing money? Sure, let's blame everything on Carl. That's the easy thing to do. Just blame me. You're really starting to piss me off, Murry. It isn't all my fault. You had a hand in this too."

"I didn't let the man keep a knife in his boot, Carl. You did that. Remember?"

"Yeah, yeah, yeah, it's all my fault. I'll take the blame so you can feel better, okay."

"Okay."

"Oh, just like that? It's okay? You're something else, Murry, I'll give you that."

"Well, what are we going to do?"

Carl put his hands up in the air with a look of exasperation on his face. "I told you. You figure it out. You're such a damn genius. It's your turn to screw up. I'm all done screwing up for the day. You're not going to blame me again today, that's for sure."

Murry stood up and started waving his hands in the air. "For Christ's sake, quit complaining about everything and start thinking about what we're going to do next."

"I already told you," hollered Carl, "I ain't doing anything!"

It was then that Jess decided he would announce himself. He put his hand down by his gun and stepped around the big pine tree he had been standing behind.

"Afternoon, gentlemen." Carl jumped to his feet and Murry's hands shot up straight in the air, followed by Carl's a half second later.

"Easy, men. I don't mean you any harm. Put your hands down and relax, but don't be reaching for those pistols," Jess said, in a calm and reassuring voice. "My name is Jess Williams. Who might you two be? And how did you get way out here without any horses?" Murry and Carl both looked down at the ground for a moment. Then Murry looked over at Carl.

"Well, we had horses until Carl here gave them away along with our money and everything else we had except one canteen and our six-shooters."

Carl shook his head with a look of disgust. "We got robbed, mister. I didn't give anything away. And yeah, it's all my fault, according to Murry here."

"I'm just telling him the truth, that's all," quipped Murry.

Jess didn't want to hear the whole argument again so he suggested that they have a cup of coffee with him. Jess retrieved Gray and got out the coffee and the pan. Carl and Murry collected some dry firewood and got a small fire going. Soon they were all sitting on some big boulders and enjoying a good cup of coffee. Jess decided to find out a little more about the two men who seemed to have been robbed and left stranded miles from any town.

"So, what are you two men doing out here?" probed Jess. "I got the drift from your argument that you got robbed, but who robbed you?" Carl and Murry looked at one another and quickly looked away as if disgusted with each other.

"We got robbed by our prisoner," admitted Carl contritely. "We took him into custody in a small town about fifteen miles east of here and we were taking him to Abilene for the reward money."

"So, you two men are bounty hunters?"

"Yeah, that's what we are, but we don't seem to be very good at it yet," replied Murry. "We've arrested two wanted men so far and we've been robbed by both of them. Not too good, eh?"

"Doesn't sound like it," agreed Jess, holding in a laugh.

"Well, we have to get better at it if we want to make enough money to start up our business back east," said Carl, throwing a harsh look at Murry. Murry started to wave his hands in the air again.

"Don't look at me like that, Carl. This whole thing about coming out west and making a fortune as bounty hunters was all your idea, not mine."

"Don't give me that," griped Carl. "You thought it was a great idea and you even said so." Murry was about to reply when Jess decided he would have to either cut in or listen to another protracted debate between the two.

"Where back east?" asked Jess. Both Murry and Carl looked at Jess and forgot about their argument for the moment.

"We're from the city of New York," answered Carl. "We were partners in the supply business."

"What kind of supplies?" Carl started to answer but Murry cut in first.

"Anything you need. We would supply almost anything any place of business could want. If someone needed dishes for an eatery, we would get them and resell them to him. If a man needed lumber, we would get it and resell it. Pots, pans, clothing, whatever any business needed, we would go out, acquire it, and then resell it for a profit. Hell, there's about a million people who live in New York City and that's a lot of customers." Murry said it as if he were proud of being able to make a profit running a business.

"So, let me get this straight," said Jess. "You two men left a profitable business back east to come out west and make a fortune at bounty hunting?" Jess asked the question with a hint of humor in his voice.

Murry looked over at Carl when he answered. "Well, Carl thought we could make a fortune. I wasn't so sure, but hey, he's my partner and I thought I should come out here with him and make a go of it." Carl was going to respond but he gave up and just waved his hand at Murry as if to shoo him away.

"So, how much money have you lost so far?" asked Jess.

"As far as we can tell, about five hundred dollars," answered Murry. "That's counting the four horses and saddles, four rifles, miscellaneous supplies, and about a hundred in cash." Jess shook his head and tried to contain his amazement.

"What? You think that's funny?" Murry demanded.

"I'm sorry," replied Jess, trying to be polite, "but yes, it is kind of funny. You two left a perfectly good business back east to come out here and make a fortune at something neither of you knew anything about. Since then, you've been robbed twice by the very same men that you were trying to collect a bounty on and lost about five hundred dollars' worth of stuff in the process. You don't think maybe that's a little bit funny?"

Carl and Murry looked at one another and both conjured up a smile as they thought about it for a moment.

"You are lucky in one respect though," said Jess. Both Murry and Carl lost their smile.

"Lucky?" replied Murry, a surprised look on his face.

"Yeah, what do you mean lucky? How the hell can this be lucky?" asked Carl, the same look of surprise on his face. Jess shook his head, wondering about the sanity of these two men who obviously had no idea of what they had gotten themselves involved in.

"Yes. You two are lucky to be alive. I'm a bounty hunter myself of sorts and it is a very dangerous business. Most of the men out west that have a bounty on their heads are very dangerous men…killers most of them. You men are lucky you haven't been shot dead and left as feed for the vultures. You might want to think about giving this line of work up, going back east, and making your fortune in the supply business you were in."

"We can't do that," Carl said, his head shaking, regret showing on his face.

"Why not?"

"We did a lot of bragging when we left," admitted Carl. "Some of our friends said we was crazy and that we would come back broke riding a mule together. They laughed at us and…well…we just can't go back broke. It would be too humiliating."

Carl hung his head as Murry chimed in. "I told you not to go bragging now, didn't I?" admonished Murry. "You just couldn't keep your mouth shut, could you?" Carl just waved his hand at Murry, too disheartened to reply.

"He is right, though," Murry told Jess. "We can't go back as failures. We have to make enough to go back and start up our new place of business. If we go back broke, we can never live it down."

Jess felt bad for the two men. They obviously were in a bad situation even though it was a result of their own actions. He gave both men a curious look. "So, what kind of business are you going to start if you do go back?"

Both Carl and Murry sat up straight and a look of excitement replaced their look of failure. They seemed like they wanted to talk at the same time, but Murry was first.

"We are going to open up 'Murry and Carl's'. It will be a place where men with money can come, drink only the finest liquors, and smoke only the finest cigars available from around the world." Murry said it proudly as if he had said it a hundred times before, which wasn't far from the truth.

"I say we call it 'Carl and Murry's' but we can talk about that later," added Carl, shooting a prickly look at Murry as he continued. "It will be a small, but beautifully decorated establishment with dark wood and large mirrors on the walls. It will have nice paintings and the finest rugs on the floor. We will have wine too, and waiters to serve the customers while they remain seated in plush leather chairs. It will be a place for any men of money to patronize and have their favorite liquor and cigars. We can make a fortune with it. There are a lot of rich men in New York City and they will spend it at our place."

"It seems like you two finally agree on one thing, except for the name of the place," said Jess.

"We'll work that out by the time we get back home to open it," replied Carl.

"Well," said Jess, as he looked up at the sun, which was slowly going down, "it's too late to do anything tonight so I suggest we make camp. We can eat and tomorrow we can figure out how to get you two some new horses."

"That's mighty nice of you," said Murry. "We can wire for more money if we can get to that town back that way where we captured that man."

Jess unloaded some supplies and made enough beans and pan bread for the three of them. Usually he made the pan bread with just flour and water but this time he made the pan bread by mixing some cornmeal, flour and water together and frying it in some bacon grease. They made more coffee, sat around, and talked for hours.

They asked Jess about his strange-looking pistol. He explained how he had found it hanging on the peg under his pa's hat. It was the most conversation he had had with strangers in a long time and he was enjoying it.

Carl and Murry cleaned up and gathered some firewood for the night. Murry was dropping off a few pieces of wood when he saw Jess with a can and a string wrapped around it. He watched as Jess unrolled the string from the can and placed it in a bush about twenty-five yards from the campfire. He watched with interest as Jess tied the string to another bush about six feet away. Jess put a few small rocks in the can. Then, Jess got out three more cans with string wrapped around them and started placing them around the area.

"What the heck are you doing with those cans?" quizzed Murry.

"I put them around my camp every night. I figure if anyone tries to ambush me, it might give me enough warning to prevent it from happening. I've been trying to think up more ways to guard my camp at night and I thought about another one while we were eating. I'm going to place a few medium-sized rocks along the area where I would walk if I were trying to sneak up on this camp. That way, if it's dark enough, someone might not see them and step on one. That would make noise or make them stumble enough to give me a warning."

Murry smiled cagily. "You're mighty smart for a young fellow. You want to be partners?"

Now it was Jess's turn to smile. "Thanks, but no. I work alone. I figure a partner could get me killed. I might start relying on him and that might cause me to let my guard down just enough to get myself killed. I like the fact that the only one I have to rely on is myself. That's what keeps me on guard all the time. Besides, you already have a partner."

"Yeah, but he's not as smart as you, and he's getting dumber by the day."

Jess smiled as he looked over as Carl was walking up to the camp area. Carl didn't see the string and as he pulled the can out of the bush, he was startled by the noise. He tripped over a rock, spilling the firewood and landing on his hands and knees, cursing up a storm. Murry just shook his head with an embarrassed expression.

"Well, he's all yours, Murry," chuckled Jess, as he continued to place the cans and rocks around the camp.

"I think the cans and rocks work just fine," admitted Murry as he walked over to help his partner up, still shaking his head in frustration.

"Damn it," complained Carl. "Where the hell did that can come from? It wasn't there a minute ago." Carl began to pick a sliver out of his hand.

"I'll tell you all about it later," said Murry. "Now, go and get some more firewood and watch where you're walking. Jess has these cans all around the area."

Jess finished up with the cans and Carl found some more wood. They settled in for one last cup of coffee and then they lay down for the night. Jess gave them his extra blanket for some warmth and they thanked him repeatedly. Jess didn't get much sleep though. He spent most of the night watching Carl and Murry wrestle the blanket back and forth all night.

CHAPTER TWELVE

Newton Cash rode up to the Carter ranch house. It was the biggest house in the area, probably twice the size of Hardin's house. One of the ranch hands took the reins from his horse as he dismounted.

"What can I do for you, mister?" asked the ranch hand.

"I'm looking for Terrence Hanley. Is he still working for the Carter spread?"

"Yep, he's one of the few hands that Mrs. Carter kept after... well...you know."

Newton nodded. "Yeah, I know all about what happened. Quite a thing, don't you think?" asked Newton.

"I was there and saw it. I never seen anything like it afore in my life. I was in the hotel sleeping off a hangover. By the time I got up and saw what was happening, it was over, except for when that kid shot Deke Moore right there in the middle of the street. He didn't even give Deke a chance. That boy's meaner than a basket of rattlers and twice as fast, I'll say that."

"Yeah, but he did have reason. You've got to give him that," allowed Cash.

"I guess I have to agree with you on that. Anyway, Hanley is over in the barn working. I'll tie up your horse for ya." Cash thanked the hand and walked over to the barn. He found Terrence Hanley working on one of the stalls that had some loose boards. He was pounding away and didn't hear Cash enter the barn. He waited for Hanley to stop and when he did, he spoke.

"Mr. Hanley?"

He turned around and looked at Cash. "I'm Hanley. What can I do for you, mister?"

"I'm delivering a message from Cal Hardin. He'd like to talk with you."

Hanley narrowed his eyes. "What in the hell does Cal Hardin want with me?"

"He wants to ask you to do a job for him."

"Hell, I'm trying to keep the job I still have. At least, I hope I still have it. Don't know whether or not I'll have a job tomorrow. Carter's widow ain't happy with most of us and she's fired most of what's left of Carter's old crew, at least the ones who are still alive. What kind of job?" Hanley asked, his curiosity getting the better of him.

"He wants you to go and look for a man and take a message to him."

Hanley put his hammer down and looked Cash over real good. "I've seen you before in Andy's Saloon, haven't I?"

"Yeah, I've seen you in there a few times. We've never had any words, but I know who you are," replied Cash.

"Cal Hardin seems to be a fairly nice fellow. I've never heard a bad word about him. Who does he want me to find?"

"He wants you to find that young man, Jess Williams, who killed Carter and his men. He wants you to take a message to him."

Hanley took off his hat and looked at Cash in amazement. "Do I look stupid? Do I look like a crazy man? I only ask because only a stupid man who is crazy in the head would go looking for that kid who took down Carter and that bunch that went into town looking for him. I knew those men and they were all damn fast with a pistol. That kid, if you can call him a kid, took out four of them and Dick Carter all by himself. And now, Cal Hardin wants me to go and have a chat with him? There's no way that's going to happen. You go find him. Go back and tell your boss I ain't interested in getting dead just yet."

"He said he will pay you well."

Hanley look frustrated. "Why me? Why would he ask me to do it?"

"He said you would know how to find the kid."

"I don't know the kid. Don't think I ever saw him."

"You were the man Carter sent to find Tim Sloan, weren't you?"

"Yeah, but what does that have to do with Jess Williams?"

"From what I gather, they look an awful lot alike. I guess they're brothers."

Hanley looked at the ground and shook his head thinking. "Carter, you mean old son of a bitch, you," Hanley said softly, finally realizing why Carter had sent him to find Tim Sloan. He thought for another moment and then he looked up at Cash with a grin. "Tell Mr. Hardin I'll be there to see him first thing in the morning."

"I'll tell him."

"Good. And when you do, make sure you remind him about the part about paying me really well."

Cash laughed. "Does this mean you're stupid and crazy?"

"I'm sure beginning to see it that way lately," replied Hanley, almost smiling.

Cash retrieved his horse and headed back to the Hardin ranch.

Hanley went back to working on the stall and wondering about the crazy notion that he was going out to find the very same man who Dick Carter had tried to kill. Now Hanley realized that he had found Jess Williams' brother and given him a message from Dick Carter and he figured out what the message had probably said. Now he was seriously considering going back out and finding Jess Williams? I must be crazy, Hanley thought to himself.

⚑

Whump!

"What the hell!"

Murry jumped up from the ground, throwing the blanket down and trying to catch his hat, which had been covering his face. His hat hit the ground and he reached for his pistol and found his holster empty. He spun around to where he thought he heard the cursing. He was trying to get his head out from the fog of sleep. He looked back to the campfire and saw Jess lying comfortably still.

"Don't worry," said Jess, without even opening his eyes. "It's Carl. He must've tripped over one of the rocks I placed around the camp."

It all suddenly came back to Murry as the fog of sleep began to lift. "Dammit, Carl. I told you to watch out for the rocks and cans," scolded Murry.

"Well I can't see 'em in the dark," he hollered back, finally getting up and dusting himself off.

"That's the whole idea, you idiot!"

Carl released a string of cuss words that neither Murry nor Jess could hear. He came back into the light of the fire. He looked down at the ground at Murry's pistol.

"Well, at least I know how to keep my gun in my holster," teased Carl, very happy to point out one of Murry's flaws. Murry picked up his pistol and dusted it off before placing it back in his holster.

"I might need it now since you've alerted anyone within five miles of us as to where we are."

"Well, a man has to piss sometime," he grumbled as he lay back down.

Jess leaned up on one elbow and looked at the two of them. "Why don't you go back to sleep and finish your argument in the morning. It's only a few hours until daylight."

Murry lay back down and tried to pry some of the blanket out of Carl's grip. Jess closed his eyes and nodded back to sleep.

"Rise and shine, men." Both Murry and Carl woke up to the aroma of fresh coffee, bacon, and potatoes frying in a pan.

"That smells damn good," Carl said, as he filled his cup with hot coffee. Murry poured himself a cup and the three of them devoured the breakfast. Jess poured himself another cup of coffee and sat down on a boulder. Carl stood up, filled his cup again, and looked back and forth at Jess and Murry.

When neither of them spoke, Carl did. "Well...what's the plan?"

Murry looked at Jess and then back to Carl.

Jess could sense that another argument was about to begin and he didn't want to hear it. He cut in before either of them could get a word out. "I passed a small ranch back that way about three miles before I ran into you two yesterday. I plan to ride back there and see if I can buy me a packhorse. Then, you two can ride the packhorse into that town you told me about and we can all supply up. How does that sound?"

"That's sounds great," Murry said smiling.

"Yeah, that would be mighty nice of you," added Carl. "We'd even be glad to pay you back for everything."

"That's not necessary. Just the pleasure of your charming company has been rewarding enough. You two stay here and I should be back in a few hours."

Carl and Murry both nodded in agreement and began making another pot of coffee while Jess saddled up Gray and rode out the way he had come yesterday.

He found the ranch. The man who owned it was more than willing to sell one of his horses. Jess picked out what he thought was the strongest of the lot. Luckily, the rancher had a used saddle and saddlebags and Jess bought those too. He paid the rancher and headed back to the camp to pick up Murry and Carl. On the way, he thought about what supplies he would need for the packhorse. The more he thought about it, the more he liked the idea. The packhorse would allow him to carry a lot more supplies as well as a being an extra horse in case something happened to Gray. He would be able to carry more ammunition, more weapons, water, and even a dead body now and then. He got to camp and picked up Carl and Murry. They headed for the town where Carl and Murry had captured the man who had robbed them.

⌐ ¬

Terrence Hanley reined his horse up in front of the Hardin ranch. Newton Cash was sitting on the front porch having a cup of coffee with Cal Hardin. He wrapped the reins around the post and walked up on the porch. Hardin and Cash stood up and Hanley shook hands with both men. Hardin called into the house and had Ruth bring out a cup of coffee for Hanley, which he gladly accepted. Hanley took a sip of the coffee and set the cup down.

"I understand you want me to go and find this Jess Williams kid?" Hanley asked Hardin.

"Yes. I asked for you because I knew that Dick Carter sent you to find Tim Sloan."

"I took a letter to Sloan from Carter. I never read the letter but I have a hunch about what it said."

"I'll tell you what it said," Hardin replied. "It was an offer to pay Tim Sloan ten thousand dollars to kill his own brother, Jess Williams. The letter told Sloan to contact me because I'm holding the money for him and I'm the one who is to identify the body of Jess Williams if Sloan does, in fact, kill him. Carter asked me to do this for him because I owed him, which I did. I didn't like the whole matter but when you owe a man for helping you out when you need it, you have to repay the favor, no matter what the favor is."

"Has Sloan showed up here yet to see you?" asked Hanley.

"He was here yesterday. He showed me the letter and asked me if I would pay him the money I'm holding. I told him I would. I don't like it, but I will do what I promised."

"And yet, you want me to find Jess Williams and what, warn him?"

"That's exactly what I want you to do."

"Doesn't that go against the promise you made to Dick Carter?" Hardin smiled.

"I promised Dick Carter that I would identify the body and that I would pay the money to Sloan. I didn't promise anything else."

"How will I know who this Jess Williams is when I see him?"

"Just look for a young man who looks an awful lot like Tim Sloan. They aren't identical twins but they look enough alike that you should be able to pick him out. He rode out south, heading for a town called Red Rock, in Texas. That's where he heard his brother was seen last. He has no idea that his brother was in Holten, Texas, and he has no idea that his brother is here in Black Creek right now, looking for him. That's what I want you to tell Jess Williams if you can find him."

"It won't be easy. He's already got a good head start on me. How do we know he didn't make a change in plans by now?"

"We don't, but he is dead set on finding his brother and I don't think he would let anything deter him. Just keep after him and try your best to find him and tell him what is going on. If you fail, I'll understand. If you succeed, I'll pay you a bonus along with your pay."

"Exactly what is the pay?" asked Hanley, wondering whether or not the job was worth it. After all, Hardin was talking about more than just a few days. Finding Jess Williams could take weeks or even months and he might never find him at all.

"I said I would pay you well and I meant it. I will pay you five hundred up front, another ten dollars a day plus all your expenses."

"What is the bonus if I'm able to find him?"

"Another five hundred dollars, paid upon your return." Hanley took a moment to think about it.

"That's mighty tempting. I might lose my job, however. Mrs. Carter ain't going to like me taking off for who knows how long to do this job for you. Hell, she'll probably fire me as soon as I tell her about this. She ain't exactly a forgivin' woman, if you know what I mean."

Hardin smiled. "I know exactly what you mean. Old man Carter wasn't the easiest man to live with and she sure wasn't the happiest woman I've ever met, even on her best days. Don't worry about a job though. If she fires you, you come here to work for me as soon as you get back if you want. Does that take care of all of your concerns?"

"I guess you know how to make it easy for a man to say yes, Mr. Hardin."

Hardin shook hands with Hanley to seal the deal. "I have two of my best long horses picked out for you. That will give you the edge and help you catch up with him. I expect you to ride long and hard each day. I have all your supplies and they will be packed up and ready for you at first light."

Hanley nodded. "I'll ride back to Carter's ranch, pick up a few things, and be back here tonight. I might as well bunk here and get an early start."

"Cash will see to your needs. Thank you, Mr. Hanley, for doing this for me. I will owe you a favor if you are successful."

Terrence Hanley rode out of the Hardin ranch at first light, heading south. Jess had quite a head start on him but Hanley figured Jess would be riding at a normal pace. Hanley, however, would be pushing the trail hard to close the gap. The two horses that Hardin had provided were two of the most magnificent long horses Hanley had ever laid eyes on. They were fast and they had endurance to spare. He would switch from one horse to the other every few hours. He figured that he would ride from dawn to dusk every day until he either got to Red Rock, Texas or found a lead on the trail. He wasn't sure that he would meet up with Jess on the trail, but if he headed as straight as he could to Red Rock, he might get lucky. If not, he would try to find out whatever he could once he arrived in Red Rock. Hanley estimated that as hard as he was riding, he might get there about the same time as Jess. He began watching the trail for any signs of a camp. He found one by a creek and hoped it might have been Jess's camp but there was no way to know for sure. He made a mental note of the hoof prints at the camp and he at least knew that it was a single rider. He pushed on hard until he couldn't see anymore and made camp.

CHAPTER THIRTEEN

Baxter was a small town and somewhat off the beaten path. And, like many other small towns, it had only one hotel, one saloon, and a few various rundown buildings on the main street. Jess, Murry, and Carl arrived in town in late afternoon and Jess stabled Gray and his newly acquired packhorse. They all got rooms at the hotel after making a quick stop at the bank to wire for money. They agreed to meet at the saloon for something to eat in a few hours. Murry and Carl headed for the general store for supplies and Jess went to pay a visit to the sheriff. Jess found the jail, which was extremely small. It had a desk and one cell that could hold maybe five people, if they could sleep standing up.

Ollie Bannick was a drunk. He started drinking whiskey after his first cup of coffee in the morning and didn't stop until he passed out each night. He couldn't handle a six-shooter anymore and had even quit wearing one a few years back, most likely because he had shot himself in the foot the last time he tried to use one. He was, however, the only person who would take the job of sheriff in Baxter. Jess found him sweeping up the small jail cell in the sheriff's office. It looked like he was doing more leaning on the broom handle than sweeping but then again, he was on no schedule. He looked up at Jess standing in the doorway. He just stared at him for a moment and then he let out a belch that must've lasted a whole five seconds. When he was done he worked his tongue around his mouth as if he was trying to dislodge a ball of cotton and couldn't quite get it out.

"What…what can I do for you, mister?" asked Bannick through bleary bloodshot eyes.

"I'm looking for the sheriff."

"You found 'im."

"You're the sheriff? I don't see any badge."

"Damn town don't pay me enough to wear it and I don't even know where it is. I don't like advertising it anyway."

"Why'd you take the job, then?"

"I get free whiskey over at the saloon. Other than that, I get to sleep in the cell here and they pay me ten dollars a month to boot. Ain't much, but it's better than sleeping on the ground."

Jess remembered about what Sheriff Diggs had told him about the lawmen in some of the small towns and how they didn't amount to much. He shook his head.

"I came in to see if you had any wanted posters in your office."

Bannick put his broom against a wall and took a good look at Jess. He focused on the shotgun behind him and then his eyes rolled down to Jess's pistol. Jess could see Bannick's gaze linger on it.

"Where the hell did ya get that?" Jess had tired of answering that question and he assumed it would be lost on Bannick anyway.

"Sheriff, do you have any wanted posters?" he asked again, acting as if he never heard Bannick's question.

Bannick grunted and reluctantly went to his desk. He fiddled with some papers and found what he was looking for. "Here," said Bannick, as he handed Jess a piece of paper.

He looked at the wanted poster. The man on it looked to be in his thirties, with a full head of hair, a bushy beard, and a mustache. He was wanted dead or alive for five thousand dollars for robbery and murder. His name was Lloyd Aker. Jess paid extra attention to the words at the bottom of the wanted poster: "Preferably Dead!" That was a little unusual and he asked the sheriff about it.

"Way I heard it was that he shot a woman while robbin' a train," explained Bannick. "Only problem was the woman he killed was the wife of one of the owners of the train. That's why the bounty is so high and that's why they put Preferably Dead on there."

Jess smiled. "Well, that's the way I usually bring them in anyway. Do you have any idea where he might be?"

"Rumor has it he was possibly in a little town less than a day's ride from here called Holten. Don't know if that's true, but that's all I know." Jess borrowed a scrap of paper from the sheriff's desk to write down the name from the poster.

"Hell, take the poster if'n you want," said Bannick.

"This the only one you have?"

"Yeah, but that don't matter none. I ain't gonna bother him if he comes around here. I don't even want to know where he is. Ten dollars and some whiskey don't buy a good sheriff, just one who keeps the cell cleaned out and locks up a few drunks once in a while, including myself."

Jess wondered about such people, but he simply put the poster in his pocket and thanked Bannick. He went back to sweeping the floor and Jess headed over to the general store to get some supplies. He packed them in the oversized saddlebags he had purchased for his new packhorse. He wondered why he hadn't thought about a packhorse earlier. He bought extra pans, canteens, beans, flour, cornmeal, rice, and other such things a man needed to survive on the trail. Then, he went to the saloon to get a bite to eat. The saloon wasn't much. He found Murry and Carl sitting at a table and they were sharing a bottle of whiskey. Jess sat down with them.

"How are you two doing?"

"This stuff tastes like a dirty sock was soaked in it," stated Carl, after taking another swallow of the whiskey, his face scrunching up.

"Yeah," added Murry, "and they said this was their good stuff. I wonder what the bad stuff tastes like."

Jess smiled. "In these little towns out here, they don't get much call for any good whiskey. People out this way don't have the money to pay for it and the ones that do don't come here to drink anyway," he told them.

"I don't blame them," admitted Carl. "By the way, we hope you don't mind but we told the barkeep that you would be paying for the drinks since we can't get any money till tomorrow," Carl said sheepishly.

"We will pay you back tomorrow. You have our word on that," said Murry.

"I figure you two are good for it. I'll even buy you both a good meal, providing we can get one here."

"They got food. We saw some of the plates coming out of the back and the food didn't look too bad," said Carl. "You want some of this…stuff?"

"No thanks. I could use a beer though."

Jess called over to the barkeep and asked for a beer. The barkeep poured him one and brought it over to the table. They ordered three meals and the barkeep went back into the kitchen area and told the cook. A few minutes later, he went back into the kitchen and brought out three heaping plates of food. It was beef stew with two big biscuits lying on top of it. They all dug in and devoured their meals. They leaned back in their chairs and let the food settle in. Carl and Murry poured themselves another shot. They winced as they swallowed the cheap whiskey.

"I want to take a bottle of this back home with us," said Carl, examining the bottle.

Murry looked at him with a confused look. "What the hell you want to do that for? This stuff tastes awful. Why the hell would you take any of this stuff back home with us?"

Carl smiled knowingly. "I just want to make sure we place it on our shelves with a sign that says: 'We don't serve cheap whiskey like this in our establishment.' "

Murry's frown quickly turned into a smile. "You bet your ass we won't. Only the finest whiskey will be poured at our establishment. We won't serve any of this rotgut."

"I think you two have a real good idea with the place you want to open up," said Jess. "That is, if you actually make it back to New York City. I just hope you two stay alive long enough to make it back." Murry and Carl both had a hurt look on their faces.

"What do you mean, if?" asked Carl.

"It's like I tried to tell you the other day. This isn't the city of New York or back east. This is the west and the men out here, especially the bad ones who are wanted by the law, don't have any sense of fair play or reason. They would simply put a bullet in you and they usually don't care if it's the front or the back or if you are awake or sleeping soundly. They'll simply kill you unless you kill them first. And I don't think you boys are good enough with a gun to make sure it's them first."

"We know how to shoot a pistol," said Murry, almost indignantly.

Jess looked at him with one of the looks Andy usually gave him when trying to make a point. "Yeah, when you can keep it in your holster so you can find it, that is," said Jess, grinning.

"That was an accident," Murry replied defensively, "and it was only because of Carl here tripping around like an old blind woman."

"Hey, I told you it was a mistake! I forgot about the rocks and the cans. Don't blame that one on me, Murry," argued Carl.

Murry was about to reply again when Jess cut him off. "That's what I'm trying to tell you two. That one mistake would have cost you your lives." Jess took out the wanted poster from his pocket and unfolded it. He placed it on the table and put his finger on the face of the man on it.

"Take a look at this man," Jess told them. "He shot and killed a woman while robbing a train. What do you think he would have done if it had been him sneaking up on our camp the other night? I'll tell you. He would have shot the both of you before you had a chance to pick up your pistol. Then he would have drunk your coffee, took everything you had, and left your bodies for the scavengers to eat. And he wouldn't feel bad about it either." Jess looked back and forth at Carl and Murry who didn't seem to be listening now. They were both looking at each other and back at the poster again.

"Five thousand dollars," Carl blurted excitedly. "That's enough to start our business when we get back."

"Yeah," added Murry keenly. "Five thousand would be enough to get started. Maybe we lighten the inventory a little in the beginning and we don't put the rugs down right away and…"

"Haven't you two been listening to what I'm trying to tell you?" demanded Jess, a look of frustration beginning to form on his face.

Murry and Carl looked up at him as if they didn't know what he was talking about. All they could think of was the five thousand dollars and how that could start their establishment.

"This is enough money to go back east with," replied Carl.

"Yeah," added Murry.

"You don't plan on going after this man, do you?" inquired Jess, afraid he already knew the answer.

"Well...yeah. Ain't that what bounty hunters do?" asked Carl.

Jess shook his head in amazement. "I'm sorry I even showed you this poster. I was just trying to make you understand how dangerous this business is. This man is a born killer and if you two go after him the both of you will wind up with dirt for a blanket."

Jess called over for another beer. Carl and Murry looked at the poster some more and they began talking to each other, planning on how they would sneak up on him and capture him, then turn him in for the reward money, go back east, and operate their drinking establishment. Jess was amazed at how naïve some men could be about certain things in life. He had thought about taking a few days to look for Lloyd Aker and collecting the bounty. Five thousand dollars was, in fact, a very large reward.

He was certain though, that these two men were going to end up dead trying to collect the bounty on Aker. He was frustrated with these two, but for some reason unknown to him, he liked Murry and Carl. Maybe he liked the fact that they were naïve. Maybe he liked the fact that these two men came from a different place where men weren't as ruthless and cold-blooded as some of the men he dealt with. Maybe it was the fact that Murry and Carl had hopes and dreams of what they wanted to do with their lives and it was a far better picture of what Jess had in store for him. He was destined for a life of killing. Maybe he was jealous of that, but he wasn't really sure that he would change it even if he could. Then, an idea came to him. He took the wanted poster, folded it back up, and placed it back in his pocket.

Murry looked at him beseechingly. "Can we have that poster?" requested Murry.

"No," he replied, staring at the two of them.

Carl placed both his hands on the table. "So, are you going after that man?" asked Carl, hoping the answer was no.

"Yes."

"Dammit! I knew it!" blurted Carl. "I knew it was too good to be true. The one time we could've gotten enough money to go back east and we ain't going to get a chance to collect it."

"Carl, he did find the poster first," replied Murry. "It's only fair that he gets the first chance at the man. After all, he has treated us with kindness and respect."

Jess took another long sip of his beer and put his glass down on the table ever so slowly, looking at the glass as if he were reading something that wasn't there. "I'll make you two a deal," said Jess, looking up at the two of them.

"What deal?" Carl asked impatiently.

"We will go after this man together. If we find him, we collect the bounty. If I let you keep most of the reward, will you promise me you will get on a train and go back to New York City?"

Murry and Carl looked at each other and then nodded in agreement.

"Okay, it's a deal," agreed Murry. "It will mean we have to start smaller, but we can make it work."

"Yeah," added Carl. "We can even wait on the padded leather chairs and maybe the wood work won't be so nice but it will still be Carl and Murry's, a place where gentlemen will want to come and drink the finest whiskey in all of New York City."

"You said it, partner," agreed Murry as he patted Carl on the shoulder, "Murry and Carl's will be the place for gentlemen to go, even if we have to cut back a little bit on the opening expenses."

Carl was about to argue the point of the name of their establishment again and Jess was slowly lowering his head in anticipation of another drawn-out debate. What stopped him was what, or rather who, pushed through the batwing doors of the saloon.

The man was tall and slender and dressed quite nicely. What stood out to Jess was the fact that he was dressed too nice for his demeanor. Jess could size men up in an instant. This man was nothing but trouble and his clothing didn't fit in with what he represented. He wore a six-shooter tied down low. He walked to the bar and ordered a drink. When the barkeep tried to take the bottle back, the man grabbed it and slammed it back down in front of him. "I'll be keeping this."

The barkeep, a little man, thought better about making it a big deal, so he left the bottle and waited on a few of the other men standing at the bar. Carl and Murry had been chatting excitedly while this was going on and Jess was amazed at how little they paid attention to their surroundings. Jess scanned the saloon looking for any other men who might be with this one or might be a problem.

"So, you two still want to be bounty hunters, eh?" asked Jess.

"Of course," replied Murry.

"Yeah," Carl added.

"So when are you going to start acting like bounty hunters?"

"What are you talking about?" Carl asked. Just then, Murry took a good look at the man at the bar. He focused on the man for a minute while Jess talked to Carl.

"How are you planning to stay alive when you don't even know what's going on around you, especially now?" Carl looked frustrated and Murry kept staring at the man at the bar.

"I still don't get what you mean," Carl stammered.

"I'll tell you exactly what I mean. The man who, a moment ago, walked past the both of you? The man who is standing over at the bar right now? I noticed him the second he walked through the door and I noticed a few odd things about him. One, he is dressed too nice for the way he acts. Two, I'm guessing he's wanted by the law. Three, he is going to be involved in some kind of trouble before he leaves this saloon. Now, I don't know these things absolutely. But I sure have a gut hunch that I'm right on all three counts."

"Now how could you figure all that out when you don't even know who the man is?" Carl asked cynically.

Jess glared at Carl. "Because if you plan to hunt men, you need to learn real fast how to spot trouble or things that don't seem to add up."

Murry, who had been watching the man at the bar all the while Jess and Carl were talking, finally spoke. "Actually, we do know that man."

Carl looked over at the man at the bar. He noticed the clothing. "Son of a bitch," grumbled Carl. "That man's wearing my shirt."

Murry shot Carl a glaring look. "No shit, Carl. He's wearing your shirt, and those are my pants. I can tell you why too. That's the man who robbed us the other day. You know, the one you let get away by letting him keep a knife in his boot."

"When are you going to quit blaming me about him getting loose? I thought we were supposed to share in everything? That means it's half your fault he got the drop on us," Carl complained, a little too loudly. Before Murry was able to respond, the man at the bar, who was obviously disturbed by the loud outburst, turned around and glared at Carl.

"Why don't you shut yer yap and let a man drink in peace?" the man barked.

Carl and Murry looked at each other, trying to decipher from each other's look as to what to say. The man set his glass down and poured himself another drink without taking his glare off both of them. He put the bottle down next to the glass. Carl and Murry were both standing now and shuffling back and forth. They hardly noticed that Jess had slowly risen and walked up to the bar about ten feet from where the man was standing. The man had noticed it, but seemed too focused on Carl and Murry to be distracted. Carl and Murry had both noticed it, however, and they looked over at Jess with confusion on their faces.

The man, Curley Simms, noticed them looking at Jess. It was then that Curley Simms recognized the two men. "Hey, I remember you two eye-ballers," said Simms, smiling now. "I thought I left you two for the buzzards to pick your bones."

Carl looked at Jess again and Jess simply smiled back at them. Carl looked at Murry. Murry looked at Jess and saw the same funny smile. Then, Carl and Murry looked at each other seemingly trying to figure out what the other one was thinking. They both looked at Curley who had downed his whiskey and refilled his glass again. He took off his hat and slowly set it down on the bar as if that was a sign that he was about to get serious.

Then Carl said what Jess thought was about the dumbest thing he had ever heard. When Carl said it, Jess shook his head slowly. "Curley Simms, we are taking you into custody...again," intoned Carl as if he had practiced it in his sleep. "Give us your gun so we can tie you up and take you in for the reward money. And, we ain't letting you rob us again either."

Carl tried to say it with all the conviction he could muster but he would not have convinced even the most cowardly man in the saloon. Curley paused for a moment and then he burst out laughing. Murry shot Carl a glare that would have stopped a freight train on a downhill run.

Carl glared back at him. "Well...you weren't saying anything!" Carl stammered.

"I sure would have come up with something better than give us your gun so we can tie you up! Where in the hell did that come from?" Murry looked back at Jess and then he looked at Curley Simms who had now finished laughing and was now glaring at Carl.

"I'll tell you what," snarled Simms. "Why don't you boys come on over here and see if you can tie me up again?" Carl looked at Jess again.

"Why do you keep looking over at him?" asked Simms, pointing at Jess. "Ain't anybody in this bar going to mess with Curley Simms. It would take a man to try me on, not some kid. Besides, I owe you one. I got rope burns on my wrists from you tying me up. Lucky for me I always keep a knife in my boot. I can't believe you was dumb enough not to look for it."

Curley looked at his right wrist, examining the rope burns. "I don't think it's bad enough to slow me down any on the draw though. Why don't we find out for sure? Why don't you see if you can outdraw Curley Simms? Then, after that, I can try your partner there, if he's a mind to," said Curley in a sneering voice.

Jess decided this confrontation had gone on long enough to teach Carl and Murry a lesson…maybe. It was one thing to talk about taking down a man in a gunfight but it was quite another thing to go through with it.

"That won't be necessary, Curley. My two partners have asked that you give up your gun and I think you should listen to them," advised Jess as he stood away from the bar and looked straight down at Curley. "Murry, what did you say the bounty on Mr. Simms was?" Jess didn't take his eyes off Curley, who seemed agitated by this interruption.

"The bounty was supposed to be five hundred dollars for cattle rustling and horse thievery. We tried to collect it from the sheriff in town here, but he wouldn't even take Mr. Simms into custody," answered Murry.

"I met the sheriff earlier and I don't think he will be of much help in this matter."

"Well, we could still take him to Abilene like we were trying to do before."

"Yeah, but I bet he won't get the drop on you again," replied Jess knowingly, with a tone to his voice that he knew something that Carl and Murry didn't.

Curley had been listening to this conversation between this young man and Murry and he was getting more agitated by the moment. "Ain't nobody taking me anywhere for anything! You two tenderfoots couldn't keep me before and this young pup ain't gonna help you none. I'm Curley Simms and I'm meaner than all three of you put together." Curley was now paying more attention to Jess than Carl or Murry.

Jess kept his stare straight at Curley. "Murry, did the poster say dead or alive?" Jess asked him.

"I think so. Let me look. I kept the poster in my back pocket." Murry took out the piece of paper and unfolded it. He read it aloud.

"Yep, it says right here. Wanted, dead or alive, Curley Simms, cattle rustler and horse thief. Reward is five hundred dollars."

Jess smiled strangely. "Mr. Simms, I usually don't shoot horse thieves or cattle rustlers so I will ask you to give up your gun willingly and allow my two partners to take you into custody to be taken to Abilene for the bounty on your head. I will warn you though, I won't ask you twice."

Curley's anger heightened instantly. "You think you and that fancy-lookin' shootin' iron is enough to take on Curley Simms? I'll send you hoppin' over hot coals in hell if'n you try me!"

"I'm going to give you about ten seconds to drop that gun belt," cautioned Jess.

Murry and Carl were sweating now and neither one of them knew what they should do. They just stood there, Carl looking back and forth between Curley and Jess. Murry still held the piece of paper in his shaky hand. Jess scanned the room again and saw no other threat except for Curley.

"You're down to five seconds," warned Jess, in a calm and nonchalant voice.

"I'm gonna' fill you so full o' holes you won't float in brine," Curley threatened with a snicker on his lips. "Then, I'm gonna take care of your two partners."

"Time's up," Jess said ominously.

Curley went for his gun. Curley was indeed fast with a pistol. He actually got to pull his pistol halfway out of its holster. He was thinking how good he was going to feel when he stood over the dead body of this young man who had the nerve to challenge him. What he felt though, was a burning sensation in his chest as Jess's slug hit its mark. The force made Curley stagger back and lean against the bar, his gun in his hand, which was now down at his side, but not cocked yet. Curley placed his left hand over the oozing wound in his chest, trying to stop the flow of blood. He looked down at his chest as if he couldn't believe what had happened. His look changed from one of surprise to one of utter contempt as he glared at Jess.

"You son of a…" He never got to finish his words. He cocked his pistol and began to raise it but he never got it high enough to shoot anything but the floor. Jess fanned two more shots into Curley and he hit the floor with a loud thud. No one in the saloon moved, not even Murry or Carl. They both kept looking at Curley's body and the growing pool of crimson red blood on the floor. After a moment or two, Murry looked over at Jess.

"I…I don't think I even saw you draw. How can anyone be that fast?"

"Practice, Murry, lots and lots of practice," replied Jess.

"Hell," Carl said, "we wouldn't have been any help to you, that's for sure." Jess pursed his lips as he looked at both of them.

"I don't suppose so, especially since neither one of you removed your hammer straps from your pistols," he said, almost sarcastically. Carl and Murry both checked their pistols at the same time and then simultaneously hung their heads in shame.

"You two sure are something else and that's a fact," noted Jess as he replaced the spent shells in his pistol. "Well, the least you can do is haul him down to the undertaker until we can leave town. His dead carcass is worth five hundred dollars."

"Yeah," replied Carl, "and we'll be glad to split it with you."

Murry shook his head and Jess simply smiled. "That's mighty nice of you, Carl, since I did all the work," he said shaking his head as he holstered his pistol. "I'll meet you two back here in the morning for some breakfast."

"Sorry," Carl replied, realizing what he had said.

"I swear, Carl, I'm going to have your mouth stitched shut," Murry proclaimed.

"What? I said I was sorry. Why is it always me?"

"Because it is always you, you sorry ass!" Carl put his hands up in the air in frustration. Then they carried Curley Simms' body down to the undertaker. Jess finished his beer and headed to the hotel for the night.

CHAPTER FOURTEEN

Jess woke before daylight, headed to the livery, and checked on Gray and his packhorse. He tried to think of a name for the new packhorse but couldn't come up with one yet. He began to think about all the extra things he could carry now and that gave him another idea. He went to meet his two new partners for breakfast at the saloon. Carl and Murry had already ordered food. They were about halfway finished when Jess entered the saloon. There weren't many people inside. Jess ordered and sat down to a hot cup of strong coffee.

"You two sleep good last night?"

"Pretty good," replied Carl. Murry simply nodded, not able to answer because of the wad of biscuit he had stuffed in his jaws.

"Good. Listen up, here is the plan," started Jess. "As soon as you can get the money from the bank, go to the livery. I spotted a good mule there this morning and we can use him to carry Mr. Simms' carcass with us since it's worth five hundred dollars. Then, we will head over to the town of Holten and look for this Lloyd Aker. If we find him, I'll put him down and then we can collect the reward. Then, I can send you two on the train back home, alive I hope. That sound okay with you two?"

Murry finally swallowed his mouthful of biscuits. "When you say, put him down, do you mean like what you did last night?"

"Yes."

"Don't you ever take one in alive?" asked Carl.

"No."

"Well, we ain't going to question your methods, since they seem to work quite well," added Carl.

"You can be sure of one thing," said Jess with an experienced look, "Curley Simms won't be robbing you or anyone again."

"I don't suppose so," added Murry. "We found most of our money still on Mr. Simms last night. That should pay for the mule and more supplies we might need. I found my horse and saddle in the livery last night also but he must have sold Carl's horse or let him go."

"I'll buy another one tomorrow morning," said Carl.

"My guess is he let him go," said Jess. "Men like that travel light and keep only what they need. Anything else they need, they usually steal. Anyway, I have to go and get a few more supplies at the general store and I'll meet you two at the livery. Make sure you strap Simms down good enough. Once that body starts to stink, you won't want to pick it back up and tie it down on the mule again." Jess headed over to the general store. He walked in. Behind the counter was a pencil-thin man wearing spectacles.

"Morning, young man. What can I get for you today?"

"I need another skillet and five pounds of coffee and I'll take a few dozen twelve-gauge shotgun shells." The old man went to getting what Jess wanted and Jess was looking behind the counter when he spotted a heavy-looking, long-barreled rifle. The man came back to the counter with the things Jess ordered.

"Could I take a look at that rifle you have back there?"

The man looked over his shoulder. "Oh, I bet you're talking 'bout the Sharps. That's one damn good rifle. I don't sell very many of them though, in this godforsaken town. I get buffalo hunters now and then who buy 'em. They call it the 'Big Fifty' and some say it's the straightest shooting rifle ever made." The old man handed the rifle to Jess.

He looked it over for a few minutes. The rifle was much heavier than his Winchester. The rifle had long-range sights on it. "What kind of ammunition does this thing use?"

The man reached down below the counter, brought up a box of cartridges, and placed it on the counter. "This one shoots the .50-caliber cartridge. Some of the hunters I've talked to claim it can kill a buffalo at a thousand yards, although that would be a small miracle if you ask me. It does shoot pretty far though. I took it out back once just to see for myself. I shot it straight out and the dust it kicked up when it finally hit the ground was a good distance off. The buffalo hunters I talked to say that for long distance shots, you have to learn to use those sights on it and you have to cut a tree branch with a fork in it to rest the rifle on. One of 'em showed me how he tied up three sticks with leather to make a rest for the rifle."

"How many cartridges do you have for it?"

The clerk looked under the counter and brought up three boxes of ammo for the rifle. "This is all I have right now. I don't get that much call for them. I can order you more but it would take about a week to get here."

"Don't order them on my account. I'm leaving this morning for Holten. Add the rifle and the ammunition to my bill."

The clerk figured out the bill and Jess paid the man. The clerk informed Jess about the general store in Holten and said they would carry a lot more ammunition for his new rifle. He also told him what direction to head in to get to Holten. Jess also purchased a nice leather scabbard for the rifle. When he met Carl and Murry at the livery, they were sitting around the front with the man who ran it.

"What the hell do you have there?" queried Carl.

"A new Sharps long gun that buffalo hunters use for long shots."

"You going to start buffalo hunting?" asked Murry.

"No."

"Then what are you going to use it for?" asked Carl.

"To shoot men," he replied as he tied it down to his packhorse. As he was doing so, a thought came to him. "I got it," he said to himself aloud.

"Got what?" asked Murry.

"The name for my packhorse. I've been trying to think of a name for him and I've decided to call him Sharps."

Neither Carl nor Murry understood why there was any need to name a horse but they simply nodded and walked their horses out of the livery. Jess had fixed a long line to his packhorse with a heavy rope. As they mounted their horses, Jess asked Carl and Murry which way to head out for Holten. Carl and Murry looked at each other and then at Jess with a dumb look on their faces. Jess simply shook his head and grinned. He gave Gray a little prod and headed into the street.

"Come on, you two bounty hunters," Jess said, sarcastically. "Holten is this way." Carl and Murry fell in behind Jess, quietly arguing about who should have found out how to get to Holten.

It took two days for them to get to Holten. On the first day, Jess stopped at noon and tried out his new Sharps rifle. They were in a large flat area. Jess fired off about a dozen rounds straight out and he was surprised to see how far off the round hit in the dusty ground. Then, he tried a few rounds with the barrel raised up about six inches and again, he was surprised. He made a decision to begin practicing on long distance shots once he was finished with his business with Carl and Murry.

Holten, while certainly a larger town than Baxter had been, wasn't all that big, but the railroad ran through it, and that made it a busier town than some. There were a couple of hotels, several saloons, and a few supply stores. The livery in town was large and the man who met the three of them when they arrived was a large rotund man with a smile that seemed to be planted permanently on his face.

"Welcome to Holten, men. My name is Rusty and I'd be glad to take care of your horses for you. They will get the best feed and care right here. I have a man who works the place until the wee hours of the night so there is usually someone here. That mule with the stinker on it will have to stay outside though."

Jess, Carl, and Murry all dismounted and the man led their horses into the livery. He helped the three of them take off the saddles and stable the four horses. Carl went around back and tied up the mule.

"So, what you boys in town for? You cattlemen, or maybe buffalo hunters?" he asked, as he watched Jess remove the new Sharps rifle from its scabbard.

"Actually, we are bounty hunters looking for a man," replied Carl proudly.

"Really?" the man replied, as he changed his glance from Carl to Murry and then to Jess. "Now that young man looks like a bounty hunter but you two...well...you don't seem like the type to hunt men. Are you men looking for someone particular?"

Carl and Murry both seemed hurt by Rusty's comment so Jess took over the conversation. "I'm...we're looking for a man by the name of Lloyd Aker. He's wanted for several crimes but mostly for murdering some woman on a train that he robbed." Jess showed Rusty the poster with the sketch of Aker on it.

Rusty looked at it. "I wouldn't know his face because I never saw him before, but I sure know about the son of a bitch. The woman he murdered was Lee Connor. She was one of the nicest women I ever met. She lived in the house down at the end of the street with Mr. Heath Connor. He's part owner of the train that comes through town here. He hasn't been out much since it happened. He took it real hard when she was killed. He put up most of the reward for Akers. He wants him dead bad. Says that if someone brings him in alive, he will personally pay any man another thousand dollars to hang him. That man really loved that woman. It's a hard thing to lose someone that you love that much."

Jess hung his head a little. "I know exactly how he feels. If you see him, tell him that we will try to make it right for him."

"The only way to make it right for Mr. Connor is to either bring that murderer in strapped over a mule just like this one or alive so he can watch him swing," replied Rusty, nodding at Curley Simms' corpse. Jess looked Rusty straight in the eyes. "You tell him for me that if we find him, we will bring him in exactly like this one."

"What is your name so that I can tell him who said that?"

"You tell him that Jess Williams said it."

Rusty looked at Jess, then looked down at his pistol and then back up to Jess. "So you're that young man people are beginning to talk about. I should've known by that fancy pistol you got there. You're the one who put down Nevada Jackson and Blake Taggert and a few more. I'll be damned. I thought you were just a made-up story and didn't really exist."

"I'm real. I can promise you that."

"You have to go and see Mr. Connor yourself. I know that he would want to talk to you personally about finding Lloyd Aker."

"We heard from someone in Baxter that he was last seen here around Holten."

"That was partially true. They figured that he hid out in the hills for a few days or so, but they never found him even though they had thirty men combing those hills. They found one campsite but never saw so much as a shadow of Aker. He robbed the train just a few miles out of town to the east and that's where he killed Mrs. Connor. The train came back to town and Mr. Connor sent out the posse immediately, but they never found him." Murry and Carl had been listening to all of this in silence.

"Show me where Mr. Connor lives," said Jess.

"Well, if you go down the main street, it's the third house on the left after the barber shop. It's a big white house with a large porch. Most likely Mr. Connor will be sitting on the porch." Jess thanked Rusty and motioned to Carl and Murry to follow him.

"We going to see Mr. Connor?" asked Murry.

"You're pretty sharp for an easterner."

"We didn't know you was famous and all," added Carl.

"That comes as much of a surprise to me as you two. I guess talk travels pretty fast, especially when it's about one man killing another."

"So, all those men you killed, they were all pretty fast?"

"Not fast enough," he replied.

They walked down the street until they came to the big white house. No one was sitting on the porch so Jess walked up the three steps and knocked on the door. He heard some rustling around in the house and then a tall lanky man dressed in a light blue suit came to the door.

"I've already told everyone in town that I'm not hiring any men right now."

"We're not looking for a job."

"Then what are you here for?"

"We're here to talk to you about Lloyd Aker. Rusty over at the livery told us we should speak with you," replied Jess.

Connor's demeanor changed at once. He opened the door and let the three men in. He motioned for them to sit down in the dining area. He got out a bottle of brandy, placed four glasses on the table, and filled them. Then he sat down.

"I want Aker dead and I will pay good money to any man who does the job. There is already a five thousand dollar reward on his head. I put up three of that and the train company put up the other two. I will personally pay another thousand dollars to the man who brings me his body dead so that I can actually see it. Better yet, bring him in alive so I can watch his eyes bug out as he hangs slowly."

"That's a lot of money for one man," said Carl excitedly.

"I got a lot of hate for that man. He took the one thing that meant the world to me. I'm a rich man in the sense of money and power, but none of that matters each day when I get up in the morning knowing that murderer is still breathing the same air I am. I will not rest until he is dead."

"We will try to see that you get your wish, Mr. Connor," Jess told him thoughtfully.

"I hope you men are good. Aker is fast with a pistol and meaner than a rattler who's been cornered. He doesn't play by any rules either. If he don't like you, he'll plug you and without so much as a warning. You sure you can take him?"

Jess looked him square in the eyes with a look that made him believe. "If I can find him, I can kill him."

Connor looked into Jess's eyes and saw something there. It was something that you couldn't put a finger on, but something that you could feel. It was a feeling of confidence and a complete lack of fear. He also saw the dark side to Jess and that made him wonder about the young man and who he was.

"What is your name?" asked Connor with interest.

"My name is Jess Williams and this is Carl and…"

Connor cut Jess off in mid-sentence. "Did you say Jess Williams?"

"Yes."

"I know of you. You were that kid who had his family murdered. You hunted the men down and killed all three of them. They say you can't be beat on the draw and that you give no quarter in a fight. They say you're the bounty hunter who never brings his man in alive."

"Most of that is true. If a man tries to kill me, I put him down. If he is wanted for murder, I bring him in dead."

Heath Connor felt as though destiny had thrown him a miracle when he needed it the most. The only thing he wanted in life anymore was to see the killer of his beloved wife brought to justice and that didn't mean a trial. Now, here he was, sitting in his dining room with the one bounty hunter that could make sure his wish came true. Finally, a spark of hope engulfed him.

"Mr. Williams, if you can bring me the dead body of Lloyd Aker right here to my front door, I will be indebted to you for life. I would give you everything I own if you could do that for me."

"Mr. Connor, that won't be necessary. The reward and the bonus you offered is enough payment for one man. The truth is I would do it even if there weren't a reward for him. This Aker is just like the men who killed my family and I've made a vow to myself that I would hunt down and kill such men, reward or not."

"You'll get the reward, and as a matter of fact, I'm going to throw in an extra thousand dollars bonus just for you."

"That's mighty generous of you, but you don't have to do that." Carl and Murry shot a look over at Jess. He shot a look back at them, and they both picked up their glasses and took another sip of the fine brandy.

"I know, but I want to give you every incentive to find Aker and kill him."

"Finding him will be the only problem. Any idea of where he might be?"

"I've had men searching for him since it happened. I keep trying to think of where he might be hiding. That's what I do for most of my day now, sit on my front porch and try to think of where he might be. I don't think he will be in any town around here since he knows I have men in every town watching for him. I have a hunch he's still hiding in the hills not far from where it happened."

"Seems like you know a lot about the man."

Connor took another sip of his brandy. "I should. He worked for me for over a year."

Jess looked surprised as Connor continued. "That's why I know he's fast with a pistol. That's why I hired him. He used to work security on the train when I was transferring money back cast. That's how he figured out how to rob the train and when I would have the most money on it."

"Did he do the robbery alone?"

"No, he had one of the other men who worked for me helping him, a man by the name of Adair Kemp. We found his dead body about two miles from the tracks where the robbery occurred. Aker must have figured he didn't want to share the money and gold."

"Well, we've taken enough of your time. I'd like to speak with the sheriff in town. Maybe he could take us out to where the robbery happened. We might as well start there. Maybe we might spot something that everyone else missed."

"I hope so. Anyway, Sheriff Mathers' office is right down the street. He can take you out to where the robbery and murder happened."

Carl and Murry shook Mr. Connor's hand and thanked him. Connor shook Jess's hand and held it for a moment, as he looked into his eyes. "Please find him and kill him for me...please."

"Like I said, Mr. Connor, if I find him, I will put him down for sure."

The three of them headed for the sheriff's office. As they got close to it, Jess spotted an older man with a full head of gray hair sitting on the porch in front of the jail. As they approached, the man stood up. He was wearing a sheriff's badge. Then, the sheriff's smile turned to a frown.

"I thought you left town for good, Sloan. What in the hell are you doing back here so soon?"

Jess stopped in his tracks. Carl and Murry, who had been following right behind him, saw the change in him immediately. Murry almost bumped into him. Jess looked as though someone had slammed him in the stomach with a ten-pound hammer. He looked at the sheriff with a growing look of confusion.

"Did you call me…Sloan?"

Sheriff Mathers walked down the two steps and looked at Jess a little closer. "I'll be damned. I thought you was that Sloan fellow. You look an awful lot like him, but now I can see that you ain't him. These damned old eyes are gettin' worse every day. You sure could pass for his brother, that's for sure."

Jess's brain began to churn out all kinds of thoughts. He had just promised a man who had lost his wife to a killer that he would hunt the man down and kill him. Further, he had two newly acquired friends that he knew would most certainly get themselves killed if they were to go after Aker without him. Yet, here he was, talking to the sheriff of this town that he had come to because of unknown circumstances, and the sheriff obviously knew his brother, the man he was searching for. His brother had been here in this town recently and yet Jess had been drawn to it by accident, or so it seemed. Then again, was it really an accident or was it destiny playing a role in his life again, as it had with the pistol and holster?

"Are you all right, son?" the sheriff asked, after Jess didn't respond for a moment. He finally got a hold of himself.

"Yeah, I'm okay," stammered Jess. "Sheriff, we came to ask you to take us out to the site of the robbery where Mrs. Connor was murdered."

"Have you talked to Heath Connor yet?"

"We just came from there and we told him that we would try to find the man who murdered his wife."

"Good luck. Every man in town and a few dozen more have been trying to do the same thing. Nobody's had any luck so far. I think Aker dug a hole, buried himself with all that money and gold, and he's simply waiting it out."

"Maybe a few new sets of eyes might make a difference," said Jess.

"Well, I'll be glad to show you where it happened. By the way, I noticed a mule at the livery with a stinker strapped onto it. Is that your work?"

"Yes sir, it is. The body is that of Curley Simms. He has a reward of five hundred on him and these two men are taking him to Abilene for the reward."

"That won't be necessary. I know Mr. Connor is willing to do anything to make sure Mr. Aker pays for what he done. You can turn the body over to me and I'll take care of everything and make sure you get the reward money."

"Thank you, Sheriff," said Carl. "We appreciate that."

"Sheriff," added Jess, "what can you tell me about Tim Sloan?"

The sheriff cocked his head with a quizzical look. "I never mentioned his first name. How do you know Sloan?"

"You said I look a lot like him."

"At first glance, I thought you were Sloan."

"I'm his brother and I've been looking for him."

"I guess that explains the likeness between the two of you. You only missed him by a few days. A man came to town and paid him five hundred dollars to read a letter."

"What did the letter say?"

"Don't have any idea. The only thing I know is that he left at daylight and he looked like he was in a hurry."

"Who sent him the letter?"

"The letter came from a man in Black Creek, Kansas." Jess felt another punch in the stomach. "A man by the name of Dick Carter wired me and requested I ask Sloan to wait for a rider who was bringing him the letter and five hundred dollars in cash to read it. The only reason I know that much is that I had supper with the man who brought Sloan the letter. I think his name was Hanley or something like that. Nice man though. Bought my supper for me. Can you imagine? What kind of man would pay someone five hundred dollars just to read a letter?"

"A dead man," replied Jess. "Sheriff, where do you think Sloan was in a hurry to go to?"

"I don't know for sure, but my guess would be he was heading to Black Creek." Another slam to the stomach. "That's where the letter came from and that's where the rider who delivered it came from and he worked for the man who sent the letter. It would only make sense that he would head there. Sloan did ride out in that direction."

A worried look came over Jess as he thought about it. "Sheriff, what kind of man is my brother?"

The sheriff looked at Jess as if he were wondering why he would ask. "You don't know?"

"I've never met him. I just found out recently that I had a brother."

"You're about to find out something else. Sloan was running a poker game with his father, Eddie Sloan. So, if Tim Sloan is your brother, Eddie Sloan is your father, I would guess."

Jess's stomach took another blow. He didn't know what to think. His thoughts were spinning around in his head so fast he couldn't grab hold of any of them.

"Sheriff, do you know where Eddie Sloan headed off to?" Jess couldn't bring himself to call Eddie Sloan his father.

"Don't know for sure but he headed out southwest of here. Rumor has it that he runs off to a small town in Mexico to hide out for a while when things get too hot for him. That man has many enemies who would like nothing better than to plug him. He's one mean curse of a man, that's for sure. Your brother ain't any better. He's a gambler, a liar, a thief, a killer, and not much else."

Another punch to his stomach as Jess hung his head a little. He had hoped that his brother might be someone he could call family, but based on the fact that he had been seen with one of the killers of Jess's family and what Sheriff Mathers had just told him, that was probably not going to happen. Moreover, if the sheriff was telling the truth, and Jess had no reason to doubt him, his father was rotten to the core also. He felt somewhat sad, as if he had just lost the one piece of hope for something normal in his life.

"Thanks, Sheriff. I guess we're ready to take a little ride with you out to the site of the robbery and murder," said Jess, looking as if his mind was elsewhere, which was entirely true.

The sheriff nodded as they all walked to the livery in silence. Murry and Carl could see the pain on Jess's face. Jess wanted very much to head straight back to Black Creek, but he had made a commitment to Heath Connor and had to honor it. They mounted their horses and started to head out of town. The sheriff had been watching Jess, thinking about what he had told him. As they turned down the main street out of town the sheriff asked Jess one more question.

"So, what are you going to do when you finally meet up with your brother?"

Jess thought about it for a moment. He didn't look at the sheriff or at Murry or Carl. He kept his gaze straight ahead. "Most likely, I'll have to kill him. After that, I'll be looking for Eddie Sloan."

Carl and Murry exchanged glances at one another, but said nothing. They rode out to the site of the robbery and murder in complete silence.

CHAPTER FIFTEEN

Sara brought some more bacon to the table. Jim, Tony, and Andy had been stuffing themselves for the last half hour as if this would be their last meal.

"You men will be able to eat again later, you know," she said as she plopped down the plate of bacon.

"A man has to eat when he can," declared Jim.

"Besides," added Tony, "our next meal might be over at Andy's place."

Andy had a hurt look on his face. "What the hell does that mean?" demanded Andy.

Tony smiled at him. "You still serving those big steaks over there?" Andy and Jim knew what Tony was talking about, but they hadn't told Sara about the horse.

Andy smiled as if he was proud of something when he responded. "Just sold the last of my weekly special last night. Those two-pound steaks went right quick at the price I was charging," bragged Andy.

Tony smiled with a twinkle in his eyes. "I'll just bet they did." Jim grunted and kept eating.

Sara shook her head at the three of them. "What do you think Tim Sloan is up to today?" asked Sara, a worried tone to her voice.

They stopped eating and looked at each other. Sloan had been in town for three days now. Tony, Andy, Jim and a few other men in town that they could trust had been taking turns watching him. Sloan had started up a daily poker game at Andy's Saloon and had emptied more than a few pockets and bank accounts of the local townsfolk. Luckily though, he had not killed anyone yet, although there had been a few shouting matches over his uncanny luck with cards. Sloan always opted to settle the argument with words concerning his poker skills when he could. Not because he had any problem killing someone over a card game. It was simply good business. Once you start shooting the losers at your poker table, people quit playing.

Sloan had spent some time walking around town talking to various people, but most didn't offer much in the way of useful information. After all, Jess had saved their town from the harsh domination of Dick Carter and his hired guns. He had wandered into Jim and Sara's general store, but he had no idea of their connection to Jess.

"So far, he seems to be satisfied with winning all the money he can at the card table at my place," answered Andy. "He's been down to Dixie's place. I heard he spends most of his afternoons with a woman by the name of Vivian. She's new at Dixie's and no one knows much about her."

"I've heard him ask a few people about Jess, but so far, no one has said anything or admitted they know who he is, but I'm pretty sure that he knows that most people are hiding something," added Tony.

"Why do you say that Tony?" Sara asked.

"It's just a hunch," he replied. "It's something about his way of asking and his response. I think he knows everyone is lying to him. I think he's just biding his time, trying to see how many people will lie to him. I'm not positive but that's how I see it."

"He's a slick one and that's a fact," said Andy. "I think he knew that me and Tony lied to him the first time he asked us and yet he never let on that he knew. I think he's playing with all of us and simply waiting for someone to slip up or to say something, or maybe he's waitin' to see if Jess shows up back in town."

"That might happen," cautioned Jim, a worried tone in his voice.

"All we can do is keep doing what we have been the last few days and hope that he just goes away," Sara said hopefully.

"No man walks away from ten thousand dollars just for killing one man. At least not men like Tim Sloan," countered Andy.

"What the hell are you talking about?" demanded Jim. "What ten thousand dollars?" Andy and Tony looked at each other and Tony decided they might as well tell Jim and Sara what they had heard about the money.

"Yeah," Tony said, hanging his head. "It seems that Dick Carter agreed to pay Tim Sloan ten thousand dollars to kill Jess."

"We heard a couple of the ranch hands from the Carter 'D' talkin' about it yesterday in the saloon," confessed Andy.

"Damn that Dick Carter," bellyached Jim. "That son of a bitch is still causing us grief even after his death."

"I say we all go out there and piss on his grave," Andy said, defiantly.

"That won't solve anything," Sara remarked. "Let's all keep our heads and hope for the best." All three men nodded in agreement.

"And you should have told us about the ten thousand dollars before," complained Sara, a cutting tone in her voice. Tony and Andy said nothing, but simply hung their heads, knowing that they should have told Jim and Sara as soon as they had heard about the money.

They finished with their meals. Andy went back to the saloon and Tony went back to the livery. Tony watched as Sloan left his hotel room and headed over to Dixie's place, probably to see Vivian again. He put his hand on the barrel of his Winchester rifle that he always kept near, especially after the Dick Carter affair, as it was now being called. I should just plug him with my rifle and save everyone the trouble that's coming, Tony thought to himself. The only thing that really stopped him from doing so was that human trait most men called being civilized. He leaned his Winchester back against his worktable and went back to work.

Sheriff Mathers finally reached the spot where the train robbery and murder of Conner's wife had happened. He looked at Jess, who still had a conflicted expression on his face.

"Well, this is where it happened," he started. "Not much to tell though. Aker stopped the train here and his partner was waiting by the tracks with three extra horses to carry the money and gold away. I talked to the people on the train after it happened. They said that after Aker had a few of the passengers load all the money and gold onto the horses, he came into the passenger car and looked for Mrs. Connor. He told her to thank her husband for the pay raise. She stood up and called him a traitor and a thief and he shot her. She fell into the aisle between the seats and tried to sit up and he shot her two more times. There just wasn't any good reason to do that except for plain meanness. People couldn't believe a man could do that to a woman. I knew Mrs. Connor and she was a real fine lady. If anyone brings that son of a bitch in alive, I guarantee I will hang his sorry ass the very same day and there won't be any trial before I do it."

"Sheriff, if I catch him, you won't have to waste any good rope on a hanging," said Jess, the rising anger beginning to show on his face. "I know this type of man, and I know only one way to deal with him."

"Well, I have to get back to town. Good luck in your hunt."

"Luck doesn't have much to do with it, but thanks anyway, Sheriff."

Sheriff Mathers turned his horse and headed back to town. He hadn't ridden ten feet when he stopped and turned around. He reached down into one of his saddlebags and pulled out what looked to be some nice spyglasses.

"These might come in handy. If he's hiding out in these hills, you might have better luck finding him with these." He handed them to Murry who had walked his horse over to the sheriff.

"Thanks, Sheriff. I'll return them to you when we come back to town," said Jess.

The sheriff nodded and again turned back to town. Murry handed one of the spyglasses to Jess. He pulled it open, extending it all the way and looked through it. It made quite a difference.

"This works really good. I'm going to have to get me one of these after this is over. It brings things up a lot closer than you can see without it," said Jess.

Murry looked through one. "Yeah, this makes a big difference." Carl tried one and was just as impressed.

"Well," Carl asked, "what's our plan?" Jess looked around. They were in a small valley surrounded by hills. Not tall or steep hills, but rather low rolling ones.

"First, we have to get on high ground," he said. "We'll stay on top of the hills and start in a small circle and work our way out. Murry, your job will be to keep track of which hills we've been on. Mark each hill with a stick and a piece of white cloth so we know which ones we've been on. Carl, your job will be to use your spyglass to see down in the valleys and the hillsides." Carl and Murry nodded in agreement.

"What are you going to do?" asked Carl. Jess looked around at the hills again. Then he slid from the saddle and walked to his pack-horse. He took the Sharps rifle out of its scabbard and checked it. He took out a box of cartridges and placed some cartridges into a small leather pouch he usually kept tied to the horn on his saddle. Jess had picked up some extra rounds for the Sharps while in Holten. He swung back up in the saddle.

"I think I'll do some target shooting with my new rifle," replied Jess. Carl and Murry looked at each other somewhat confused.

"We're looking for a killer in these hills and you plan on target shooting?" Carl asked.

"That's right. Let's start up there," he suggested, as he headed up the first hill.

"You're the boss, Jess. We'll follow your lead," agreed Murry.

Jess smiled at Carl and Murry and headed up the first hill, the Sharps rifle across Jess's lap. When they reached the top of the hill, they dismounted. Both Carl and Murry were wondering exactly what Jess had in mind but they had no real idea. Jess sat down on a big rock for a moment, checked the rifle, and made sure it was loaded. Carl looked around with the spyglass, while Murry found a stiff branch to tie a white cloth to it.

"See anything, Carl?" asked Jess.

"Nothing yet, but what am I looking for? I know we're looking for Aker, but everyone has already looked for him in these hills. Do you think he will be sitting on a rock down in the valley sipping some coffee and waiting for us?"

"No, I don't think that, but if the sheriff is right, and everyone has combed these hills since the robbery happened, how could he have gotten out?" Jess asked.

"Maybe he hightailed out of here before anybody got here," Carl answered.

"Let's think about it," said Jess. "He had three other horses besides his. He had a partner with him. No one said he saw Aker kill his partner, so he had to do it after the train backed up into town. That had to take a little time, even if he shot his partner in the back."

"Yeah?" replied Murry, trying to follow Jess's thought.

"So, after he kills his partner, he still has three horses and a whole lot of gold and money," continued Jess.

"Okay," added Carl, "so he takes his gold and heads straight out."

"How much do you think that gold weighed, Carl?" asked Jess.

"Hell, I don't know. I guess it depends on just how much gold there was."

"According to the sheriff, it was quite a lot, which is why Aker needed a partner and the extra horses," continued Jess. "I don't think Aker could have gotten far enough away with all those horses and extra weight. Think about the dust three horses loaded with gold makes. Someone would have spotted him before he could have gotten out of these hills and the area around them is flat land for miles. Aker also knows how Heath Connor loved his wife since he worked for him for almost a year. He knows that Connor would have him hanged for killing his wife. I might be wrong, but I think he's still here, hiding out in these hills."

Carl and Murry shook their heads in agreement as if what Jess had said made sense. Then, Murry stopped pounding the branch in the ground and looked over at Jess, the rock still in his hand.

"But…even if he is somewhere in these hills, how are we going to find him? Dozens of men have already looked and no one has seen a trace of him except for some of his tracks he left at the railroad. That ain't worth anything since everyone else in the area had trodden through here looking for him."

Jess stared down into the valley to his right. "Well, I guess we have to think a little different from all those others," replied Jess, a smile forming on his lips. "Carl, look down in this valley and let me know if you see anything that looks out of place."

Carl looked dumbfounded. "What the hell are you talking about? It's all the same shit—rocks, bushes, and a few small trees."

"I know that. But look for something different. Something out of the ordinary, like too many bushes together or maybe trees lying sideways as if someone put them there to hide themselves."

Carl was getting the idea now and his eyes lit up. "Oh…I get it now. Like maybe he made himself some cover that looks like everything else around him," Carl said, as if he had come to a sudden realization.

Jess smiled some more and shook his head, which was becoming an all too often occurrence lately. Murry sat on a rock and just glared at Carl.

"What? What did I say? Don't start on me, Murry, I swear."

"Carl, just keep looking and let me know if you spot anything out of the ordinary, anything at all," said Jess, before the two of them could start their all too familiar banter.

Carl looked around with the spyglass. He saw some clumps of bushes and a few extra rocks in piles but nothing that looked suspicious. Then Carl spotted a larger section of brush that looked like it was two or three bushes put together.

"Jess, look down to my left, just above that large boulder with the single piece of wood on top of it. There's a large clump of bushes," said Carl. "It looks bigger than the other bushes in the area."

Jess laid the rifle on a boulder that was about four feet tall and looked down the barrel in the direction Carl was pointing to. "I believe I see it."

Jess took aim at the small piece of wood on the boulder and slowly squeezed the trigger on the Sharps. The rifle exploded with a thunderous boom and the shot echoed throughout the hills. He missed the small piece of wood by only a few inches, the fifty-caliber round smashing into the hillside, pieces of rocks scattering in all directions.

"See anything moving, Carl?" asked Jess. Carl stared through the spyglass.

"Nothing."

"Keep looking," said Jess, inserting another round.

A few minutes later Carl spotted something else.

"Okay. I spotted an extra-large shadow next to a few large boulders over that way." Jess spotted the area and fired off another round as Carl looked through the spyglass.

"Nothing, Jess," said Carl, still looking through the spyglass.

Carl spotted a few other areas that might mean something and Jess threw a round at them, but they came up empty.

They went to the next hill and did the same, Carl looking for anything that seemed out of the ordinary and Jess firing a round from the Sharps at it. Jess was getting better with the rifle and whenever Carl couldn't find anything unusual to shoot at, Jess would simply fire off a half dozen rounds into the hills at nothing but rocks and shadows. That's the way the remainder of the day went and they made camp and turned in for the night. The three of them took turns at watch on the top of the hill they planned to start from in the morning. They woke before daylight and started the entire process again. Five different hillsides and almost a hundred rounds later, they were all getting discouraged.

"Maybe this ain't gonna work, Jess," said Murry, a discouraged expression on his face.

"Besides, you're going to be out of ammo for that rifle soon," added Carl.

Jess looked at them and they could see that even he was getting disheartened. "Okay, maybe you two are right, but let's finish out the day and turn in and see how we feel in the morning."

The three agreed and they moved on to the next hill. Carl was spotting and Jess was firing off shots at the hills. Murry was pounding a stick into the ground when he looked off into the direction of one of the hills they had started on the first day. Something wasn't right but he couldn't put his finger on it immediately. Then it hit him. He couldn't see the stick he had pounded in on the top of the hill. It was gone.

"Hey, Jess?"

"Yeah, Murry, did you see something?"

"It's what I don't see that's interesting."

"What does that mean?" asked Carl.

"The first marker I put on the first hill is missing."

"It probably just fell over," said Carl, dismissing it. Jess, however, did not dismiss anything that seemed out of the ordinary.

"Murry, are you sure you pounded it in far enough?" asked Jess.

"Are you kidding? I haven't had anything to do except pound these sticks into the ground and I pounded them in good. And there hasn't been even a hint of a breeze since we started," replied Murry. Jess sat down and took a few swallows of water from a canteen.

"Here's what we are going to do," Jess told them. "Let's act like we don't know the stake is missing. We make camp tonight and start out in the morning, following the same pattern we have the last few days. When we head over the next hill, we backtrack to the first hill and come at it from the south. If it's our man who took the stake down, he's probably on the other side of the hill from us."

"But why would he take the stake down?" probed Carl. "How does he know we wouldn't think that we hadn't checked out that valley and go there later?"

"Because if it is him, he's been watching. Maybe he thinks we might forget where the stakes were or that we didn't even start there and might get frustrated and not go back. Maybe he's just pissed off and ripped the stake out. Who knows for sure," replied Jess. "We have an hour before dusk so let's keep on like nothing has changed. That way, if it is Aker, he will think that in the morning, we'll be one more hillside away from him."

"You're the boss," replied Murry. They continued and then made camp. Supper consisted of two rabbits that Jess had plugged with his Sharps earlier while he was pounding the hillsides with lead. He had taken the heads clean off, leaving all the good meat. Murry was cutting a few sticks to cook the rabbits on and Jess was cutting a large forked stick.

"What are you going to do with that?" asked Carl.

"The man at the general store back in Baxter told me the buffalo hunters use a support stick similar to this to balance their rifles on when they're shooting long distances."

"After seeing you take the heads off those two rabbits, I don't think you need it," said Carl.

"I'll take any edge I can get."

Carl smiled and the three of them ate a full meal. They turned in, each taking their turn at watch. At dawn, they ate a simple meal of pan bread and some bacon, along with a pot of coffee. Then, they slowly made their way atop the next hill and went down the hill just enough to be out of the line of sight from the first hill that they had started on. They immediately turned south and worked themselves around the area until they reached the bottom of the first hill. They made their way up to the top. They found the spot where Murry had pounded the stake in. The hole was still evident. Someone had removed it. Jess could sense the danger even though the other two men couldn't.

"Stay low and be careful. I think he's watching us right now," cautioned Jess. "Carl, take a look at that large clump of bushes where we started the other day, remember? That small stick is still sitting on the large boulder just below the clump of bushes."

He peered through the spyglass. "Yeah, I see it. That little piece of wood is still there. You missed it the other day."

"Well, let's see if I've gotten better with this thing," said Jess, as he found two bushes with an opening between them. He stuck the forked stick into the ground deeply enough to support the rifle. He lay down flat and placed the barrel on the forked piece of wood. Then, he found his target, the small piece of wood lying on the boulder. It was probably a hundred and fifty yards away and there was no breeze at all.

"Carl, watch those bushes closely. I'm going to fire a few shots off. Murry, let us know if you see any movement around that area." The two nodded and Jess took careful aim. The Sharps barked, belching flames, smoke, and lead. The piece of wood shattered into splinters.

"I guess you have gotten better with that thing," said Carl, not taking his eye away from the spyglass, which was still trained on the large clump of bushes. The Sharps barked a second time and then a third, one shot into the boulder, shattering chips of stone into the bushes. One slug flew straight into the middle of the bushes. Still, there was no movement. Jess fired a fourth round.

Carl leaned forward a little, as if that could somehow let him see better, when a bullet ripped through his left arm, causing him to drop the spyglass and scream like a cat grabbed by the tail. He spun around and hit the ground behind the large rock he was sitting on. A volley of shots kept coming at a steady pace. Jess rolled over to the large rock he was next to and Murry lay flat just behind the edge of the hill, out of sight of the shooter. Jess counted at least a dozen shots. They sounded like they came from a rifle.

"Carl, how bad are you hit?" Jess asked him.

"It hurts like hell, but it went right through the flesh and missed the bone."

"That's good; wrap it up tight with some cloth. Tear off your sleeve and use that."

"Nothing good about being shot," complained Carl, as he began to tear off his sleeve.

"Quit complaining and give me the spyglass," growled Murry. Carl threw the spyglass over to Murry, who rose up slightly to catch it and when he did, a bullet smacked into his forearm.

"Dammit," he hollered. "That son of a bitch shot me!" He crouched back down and began ripping off his shirtsleeve to wrap his arm. Jess looked back and forth at the two of them and shook his head.

Murry looked at him, anger showing on his face. "That bastard shot me!" complained Murry.

"What did you think he would do, invite you down for lunch?" Jess asked sarcastically.

"Yeah, well he shot me first," grumbled Carl. "And mine is worse!" A dozen more shots pounded the rocks and edge of the hill all around the three of them.

"I told you two to be careful. Now stay down. At least we know where he is and he can't come out because he would be too exposed. There is no other cover for him except for that clump of bushes. Can you two still handle your Winchesters?"

"Hell, yes," replied Carl, angrily, "I'll put some lead in that bastard for shooting me."

"Murry, how about you?" asked Jess.

"Just say the word; I'm ready to start shooting."

"Carl, you start firing first. Murry, you take over when he's empty and keep a steady but slow firing pattern to give him time to reload before you're empty. Carl, you start reloading as soon as your rifle is empty. That should keep our man below busy while I try to get a shot at him." They both nodded as if they understood what Jess wanted.

"Hold on just a minute. I guess we should ask if it's really Aker down there." Jess hollered out as load as he could. "Mister, we're looking for Lloyd Aker. If you're not him, now would be a great time to let us know." There was a moment of silence, as if the man was deciding what to do. Then a loud voice boomed back.

"You tell Heath Connor I'll see him in hell with that bitch of a wife of his!"

"Well, I guess we have our answer," said Jess. "If it isn't Aker, the man down there just made his last mistake. Okay, men, start shooting."

"I guess we're really bounty hunters now, huh, Murry," bragged Carl, as he began firing his Winchester steadily.

"Hell, yes, I damn well guess we are," replied Murry.

"Shut up and keep throwing lead," Jess told them, as he rolled back over and propped his Sharps back into the forked branch. He kept looking at the bushes above the large boulder and he could see some lingering powder smoke rising from the left side of the bushes. Carl's shots were hitting all around the area. As soon as Carl's Winchester emptied, Murry started firing a few seconds later. Before he did, a few rounds came back at them from the bushes, one hitting the rock that Carl was now crouching behind, feverishly reloading.

Jess saw a muzzle flash coming from the left of the bushes. He picked out the spot where he had seen the flash. He figured Aker would fire off a few rounds again when Murry was finished. He figured right. As soon as Murry stopped firing, Jess spotted the muzzle flash again and at the very same instant, the Sharps barked, aimed directly at the muzzle flash coming from the bushes. Jess heard a howl and saw the bushes move. A few seconds later, he saw a rifle clatter down out of the bushes. He held up his hand to stop Carl from shooting. They waited for a few minutes.

"I think I might have hit him. I'm going to go down there and I need you two to cover me. Split up a little more so you both have a sharper angle at the bushes. That way there will be less of a chance of hitting me with a stray bullet if you two have to open up. Murry, take my extra Winchester and make sure both of yours are loaded. If he starts shooting again, I want both of you to open up at the same time from both angles."

Jess left the Sharps rifle on the hill. He grabbed his Winchester and slowly worked his way down the hill toward the other side. The bushes where the shots had come from were on the other side about twenty feet above the valley. Jess approached cautiously and used whatever cover he could find, which wasn't much. He finally made his way to the boulder and stopped there for a moment.

"Aker, are you in there?" asked Jess. No answer.

"I have two men with Winchesters on the hill across from you. If you so much as fart, they'll open up on you." Still no answer. Then, Jess heard a horse. He worked his way around the large boulder, which was the size of a small cabin and then he saw it. Aker lay dead at the mouth of a cave. He had a few wounds from the Winchesters, but it was the Sharps heavy caliber slug that had obviously put the large hole in his chest. He was in a sitting position against the wall of the cave, his head tilted to one side. Jess made sure he was dead and then he waved for Carl and Murry.

"Leave the horses up there and come on down."

Jess walked into the cave, which opened up after the first twenty feet or so. It was a steep drop and it led into a large cavern with a small waterfall pouring down from one side of the cavern into a large deep pool of pristine water. Four horses were tied up to a small log that was lying by the pool of water. There were remnants of piles of hay by the pool. Jess heard Murry holler loudly outside the cave opening.

"Son of a bitch!"

"I told you to be careful," Carl yelled.

"Dang rocks," shouted Murry. The two of them came into the cave, looking at Aker's dead body. Murry was limping and Carl looked in amazement at the cavern.

"What happened?" Jess asked. Murry just groaned.

"Clumsy idiot tripped over a rock and sprained his ankle," Carl answered, smiling because it wasn't him this time.

"Sprained hell, I think it's broken!"

"Aw, quit your grumbling. We got Aker and now we have enough money to open our place back east," Carl said grinning widely. Murry smiled at that and then went back to moaning. Carl looked around and spotted a large pile of gold bars with some saddlebags next to them. He walked over to the saddlebags and sure enough, they were plumb full of cash. There were empty saddlebags lying by the gold bars.

"Guess he had to keep handling it," said Carl.

"I've heard that gold will do strange things to a man," added Jess. "I hear it can make a man go crazy. He probably had to handle it every night before turning in."

"Looks like they planned this thing well," said Murry.

"It sure looks like it," agreed Jess. "They hauled enough hay in here for the horses and they stashed enough food for a month.

There's plenty of water available. They placed enough extra bushes around the opening that no one would have seen it unless they walked right up to it. Pretty slick."

"He almost got away with it," said Carl, looking out at Aker's dead body.

"Yeah, but he didn't know he was going to be hunted by the best bounty hunters in the business," Murry said proudly.

"Let's get the gold loaded up into the saddlebags and get these horses out of here. We have a bounty to collect, and a good one at that," Jess told them

Both Carl and Murry agreed and went to work as Jess busied himself with tying Aker's body tightly on one of the horses. They loaded up the gold and cash on the other horses and Carl and Jess walked them up the hill. Murry had to ride because of his ankle. They collected their things and headed back into town.

CHAPTER SIXTEEN

They arrived back in Holten in the late afternoon. Sheriff Mathers had seen them come in from the east end of town where the livery was. He noticed it because there were three men with a string of horses following, and one of them had a body strapped across it. He walked into the livery as Jess was handing Gray over to the liveryman.

"I'll be damned. How in the hell did you find him?" asked Mathers.

"I thought about what you said about him having dug himself a hole and buried himself, so I took a guess that he must have had a cave that he was hiding in," answered Jess.

"Yeah, but how did you ever find it? We combed those hills several times."

"You would've never found it, even if you passed within ten feet of it. It was hidden real well behind some bushes."

"Jess here decided to do some practice shooting with that new Sharps rifle of his," added Carl. "He kept pounding those hills until we finally got a response from Aker."

Mathers chuckled as he turned to Jess. "You mean you kept shooting at the hillsides waiting to see if something would happen?"

"I figured we had to do something different. No one had any luck any other way. Besides, I needed the practice with the Sharps and I got good with it. Sheriff, let's go over to Heath Connor's house and personally deliver this piece of dead flesh along with his gold and money."

The sheriff grabbed the reins of the horse carrying Aker's body and Carl and Murry held the reins of the horses carrying the gold and the cash. They headed down the street toward the Connor house. Heath Connor was waiting on the front porch. He had already heard that some bounty hunters with a dead body had come into town and the truth was, Connor pretty much knew whatever happened in town as soon as it happened. He stood as he watched Jess, Sheriff Mathers, and two more men walking horses toward his house. He looked directly at Jess through watery eyes.

"Is...is it Aker?" he asked, his voice breaking up with raw hatred.

"Yes it is," replied Jess, grabbing Aker's hair and lifting his head so that Connor could see the face. "I told you if I found him, I would kill him. I wanted to deliver his carcass to you personally."

Connor hung his head in silence for a moment as if in deep thought. His head rose slowly. "Mr. Williams. I don't know how I can thank you. I will be indebted to you forever for what you have done for me. You, sir, can have anything from me that you wish, any time."

"Thank you, Mr. Connor, but the reward will do just fine for us."

"Sheriff," said Connor as he shifted his gaze. "I want you to take this piece of crap out to the edge of town and place his body spread eagle and face up. I want to be able to watch the vultures and coyotes pick his bones clean."

Mathers shook his head. "That's pretty cold, Mr. Connor. You sure you don't want me to just bury him?"

"There is no way that bastard will ever get a decent burial. He doesn't deserve it or anything else meant for a decent human being."

Mathers had long ago learned better than to argue with Heath Connor when his mind was made up. "If that's what you want, that is exactly what you'll get, Mr. Connor." The sheriff headed back toward the east end of town, towing Aker's body behind him.

"Mr. Connor, we got all your gold and money here in these saddlebags," said Carl. "It took us damn near an hour to load it all up."

Connor nodded, and that's when he noticed that the two men had been wounded. "You men should see the doctor and tend to those wounds."

"We will as soon as we get your money in the house. Besides, we ain't hurt all that bad," said Murry, almost proud of his flesh wound.

"Bring all of it into the house," said Connor. Jess followed Mr. Connor into the house and Carl and Murry started carrying the saddlebags in behind them. It took them several trips, especially with Murry limping with every step.

"That's all of it," Carl said, as he dropped the last of the saddlebags on the floor. "Jess, we're going over to see the doctor and then get cleaned up at the hotel. How about we meet for some supper in the hotel café at five?"

"That sounds good to me. You two did real good out there, by the way," Jess added.

"Well, we did have you to lead us, that's for sure," said Murry.

"Yeah, but you still did well. Some men would have jumped on their horses and run for the hills at the first shot. You two stayed at it, even after you each took a bullet. That counts for something."

"I guess that we really are bounty hunters then?" asked Carl.

"Yeah, retired bounty hunters," stated Jess, with finality in his voice that both Carl and Murry understood. Both of them headed out to see the doctor and get a good hot bath. Connor motioned for Jess to take a seat.

"Would you like a brandy, Mr. Williams?"

"I don't drink much of the hard stuff, but yes, I think I will."

"So, are you retiring after this job?"

"Oh no, those two are, but not me," Jess said frankly. "It was a deal I made with them. I would help them get the reward for Aker and they promised me they would go back east before they ended up dead."

Jess explained the story about how they were going to make enough money to open up their establishment and how they had come out here to make quick money at bounty hunting to do it.

411

Connor laughed at that. It was the first time he had laughed in quite a while. Then, he looked at Jess with a serious expression.

"I have a business suggestion for you, Mr. Williams." He told Jess what he was thinking about and Jess did, in fact, like the idea. He finished his drink and as he stood up, he told Connor he needed one more favor.

"Anything. All you have to do is ask," replied Connor with a smile.

Jess went back to the livery, took care of Gray and Sharps, and got a few of his belongings. He went to the hotel, had a nice hot bath, and headed down to the café to meet with Carl and Murry. The two of them were already seated and sharing a fine bottle of whiskey. Jess joined them.

"I figured we could afford the good stuff now," bragged Carl.

"Well, this isn't what I would call the finest whiskey, but it sure is better than that rotgut we drank before," remarked Murry. "Jess, do you want a shot of this?"

"No, but I will have a beer." Murry motioned over to the barkeep and he brought Jess a beer.

"This has been an exciting day for me," declared Carl. "I can't believe we actually did it."

"Of course, we couldn't have done it without you," admitted Murry. "I don't think we can thank you enough."

"The good thing is that you have enough to start your business back in New York City, and better yet, you're both still alive to see it happen." Carl and Murry looked at each other.

"Well," Murry said, somewhat sheepishly, "we are a little short of what we had planned. We wondered if we might try one more job before we go back." Carl said nothing; he just kept his head down.

"Not a chance in hell," Jess said firmly. "You two made a deal with me and you're going to keep it."

"But Jess...we..."

Jess cut Carl off in mid-sentence. "Nope, we made a deal and that is the end of it. I won't hear any of it. You two are going back to New York City or I swear I'll shoot you both myself and get it over with."

"We did make a deal," Murry agreed, "and we'll stick by it. We just thought…"

"I have another deal for you," said Jess, cutting Murry off in mid-sentence.

"Oh yeah, what might that be?" Carl asked, getting excited.

"I want you two to take the entire six thousand dollars of the reward money. I'll keep the five hundred reward from Curley Simms."

"Now who is backing out of a deal? We were supposed to share the money," said Murry.

"We are, but I want to invest my share in your business. I figure it should buy me a ten-percent share of the profits since you two will be doing all the work. Sound like an okay deal with you two?"

"Consider it done, my friend," said Carl.

"Yeah," added Murry, both men shaking hands with Jess to seal the deal.

"Maybe we can get those padded leather chairs right away after all," said Murry.

"And maybe the rug too. I think we can cut back on the crystal glasses and some of the fancy woodwork," remarked Carl, looking up at the ceiling, picturing it in his head. Jess kept shaking his head as he spent the rest of his meal listening to the two of them bantering back and forth about their business. They finished eating and had one more drink.

Carl leaned back in his chair. "I guess all we have to do next is collect our money and get some tickets for the train," he said as he sat back in his chair with another shot of whiskey in his hand.

Jess smiled as he reached into his back pocket. "No need for that, said Jess. "I already have you two booked on the train to New York City. I also have your bank draft for the six thousand dollars and I will personally put the two of you on the train leaving tomorrow."

"I heard the train to New York City didn't leave until the day after tomorrow," Carl said, looking confused.

"Mr. Connor was nice enough to change the schedule for me. It leaves tomorrow and your two sorry asses will be on it," Jess said with that same finality in his voice.

"Sounds like our friend here has been busy," Murry said to Carl.

"I didn't know you wanted to get rid of us so fast," protested Carl.

"The faster, the better," replied Jess. "I need to protect my investment." They all laughed at that.

CHAPTER SEVENTEEN

Carl, Murry, and Jess had their morning meal at Heath Connor's house. He had left a message at the hotel for them. As they arrived at the Connor residence, he was sitting on his porch with his chair turned toward the end of the main street. They could see why. As instructed, the sheriff had placed Aker's corpse spread eagle just outside the end of town. Far enough to keep the smell from bothering anybody and yet close enough to allow Heath Connor to watch the vultures and coyotes pick his bones clean. Connor was actually looking through a spyglass when the three of them walked up to the porch. Carl and Murry had a strange look on their faces but Jess smiled as if he understood in some strange way. As soon as Connor noticed them he put the spyglass down and stood up to greet them.

"Good morning, gentlemen," he said smiling. "I'm so glad you agreed to accept my invitation to join me for breakfast. I have the best cook in town in my house and she has whipped up some mighty fine food. The dining table is already set and I believe she is ready to serve it anytime we're ready." The four men went inside and sat down at the dining room table. They had no sooner taken off their hats when a woman with a smile as wide as the Mississippi waltzed into the room with a hot pot of coffee.

"Good morning," she said in a somewhat melodious tone. "Anyone want coffee?" They all nodded in the affirmative and she went about pouring the coffee.

"There's cream and sugar as well as some honey on the table if you want it," she added as she swept back into the kitchen.

"That is Wanda Dopkowski," bragged Connor, "and she is probably the best cook in town. She is a Polish immigrant who showed up here about five years ago and has been working at a little café just around the corner from the hotel. You are going to love her cooking."

"It sure smells mighty fine," Carl said, sniffing the air.

Before Jess and Murry could add their opinions, she came bustling back into the dining room with a huge plate of flapjacks in one hand and a heaping pile of bacon in the other. She plopped those down and returned a few seconds later with a pot full of scrambled eggs along with a large plate of freshly baked biscuits and cornbread. That was followed by a large plate of ham along with some eggs done over easy and one of her Polish dishes called potato pancakes. The butter, syrup, and all the other fixings were already on the table. Murry, Carl, and Jess were so overwhelmed by all of the wonderful food they simply stared at it. Wanda put both of her hands on her hips and looked at them as if trying to break the spell.

"I cooked it, but I ain't gonna put it on your plates, gentlemen. Now, dig in, I have a nice chocolate cake waiting its turn on the table for dessert.

They all dug in as instructed. Plates were passed around to one another and they ate more than their share of the food. As soon as they finished, each one of them made the claim that he couldn't eat one more bite. Wanda came in with four plates, each with a large slab of chocolate cake with some type of chocolate syrup on it. One look from Wanda and every man picked up his fork and dug in. It was delicious.

"I have never had cake this good before," said Carl. Murry stopped cramming the cake in his mouth and lifted his head, which was about two inches from the plate.

"This is one time I have to agree with my partner. This is wonderful. Wanda, do you want to go back east with us? We can set up a little shop and you can make cakes and whatever else you make. We can sell them to all the restaurants in the area around where our establishment will be." Wanda put her hands back on her hips, which was what she always did when she was trying to make a point.

"That's a nice offer, gents, but there are too many people back there in the east. I like it fine out here. Some of the people out east are a little too fussy for me. I want people to appreciate the food I cook, and out here, they really appreciate a fine meal when they can get one."

"Well, that is exactly what we had here," admitted Jess, as he finished his last morsel of cake off the plate. "I hate to admit it, Wanda, but this was every bit as good as my ma used to cook." Heath Connor had told Wanda about Jess and how he had lost his family, so Wanda understood how meaningful the comment was. She gave him her best smile and looked him in the eyes with a motherly look.

"That's about the best compliment any woman could get, Mr. Williams. I'm glad you enjoyed it. It's too bad you gentlemen can't stay for supper. I could make you some of my p\Polish dishes. You would love them, I'm sure."

Heath Connor broke in. "Thank you, Wanda, for another fine meal. As for the supper offer, that would be wonderful, but these men have to leave this morning. Okay, men, the train is waiting for you. It was scheduled to leave an hour ago, but I told them to sit still until we get there."

The four men got up, headed out toward the north end of town and arrived at the train station. Jess was almost laughing at the sight of Carl and Murry. Both of them had bandages wrapped around their arms and Murry was still limping from his sprained ankle. They loaded up the few things that Carl and Murry had to take back to New York City. The most important thing was the large bank draft from Mr. Connor. Murry had that in his shirt pocket. He wasn't about to let it out of his sight.

"Well, I guess this is it," said Murry, as he shook hands with Jess and Connor. "I appreciate everything you did for us, Jess, and we won't forget it. You will have to come out east and see your invest-ment sometime. We discussed it last night and we are going to have a wooden J hand carved out of the finest wood and hang it over the door of Murry and Carl's. When people ask what it stands for, we'll tell them all about you. And, once a week, everybody in the place will get a free drink and we'll tell them it's from our partner, Jess Williams."

"That's right, Jess," Carl added, as he too shook hands with both men. "Everyone who comes into Carl and Murry's will know all about you and what you did for us. We were lucky to have run into you and that's a fact." The train whistle blew loudly.

"Time to board the train, you two," said Connor. Carl was helping Murry step up into the train and Murry was moaning about the pain in his ankle.

"Quit pushing me," snapped Murry.

"Well get your ass up the step before the train leaves without us," argued Carl.

"It ain't leaving without us. I thought we agreed to call our place Murry and Carl's?"

"I never agreed to that; you just kept saying it. Besides, Carl and Murry's sounds real nice to me. It kind of rolls off the tongue right nice, don't you think?"

"I'll roll your sorry ass off this train once it gets going a little faster and you can walk back to New York City!"

"If I get off this train, that bank draft is going with me," Carl blurted snappily.

Murry finally got on the top step and they entered the train. Jess and Connor watched as they walked back and sat down at a table by the window facing them. The window was open and Connor and Jess could hear the argument still going on. As the train pulled out all Jess could see was Murry and Carl locked in another heated debate with each other. Jess shook his head.

"I'm glad we got them on the train. I don't think I could've taken much more of that. I think I would've had to shoot at least one of them." They both laughed.

"They sure do argue a lot, that's a fact," said Connor. The two men walked in silence back toward the livery. Jess retrieved Gray and the newly named packhorse, Sharps, and then they walked back to Connor's house.

"Thanks again, Mr. Connor," said Jess, as he shook his hand one last time.

"No, I'm the one doing the thanking here," said Connor, as he looked out at the now half-eaten body of Lloyd Akers. "You gave me what I needed and I will never forget it. You have a friend for life, Mr. Williams. You ever need anything, you let me know." Jess got up in the saddle and tipped his hat at Connor.

"You think those two will make it to New York City alive?" questioned Connor.

"Yeah, but not before they drive a few people to jump off your train though," he replied as he turned Gray toward the end of town. Connor watched as Jess headed out and then turned north, heading back in the direction of Black Creek, Kansas. He watched as a few vultures flew off when Jess went by. He smiled as they returned to continue picking at Aker's body again.

"Keep eating till it's all gone," he said, to no one but himself. He sat back down in the chair on his porch and continued watching the vultures with what could only be described as a look of satisfaction on his face.

❧

Jess headed west first, looking for the trail he had come south on since he knew there were a few good creeks along the way. He found a nice spot to take a break around the middle of the afternoon. He started a fire, made some coffee, and started eating one of the biscuits that he had willingly taken from Wanda before he left Heath Connor's house. He saw a dust cloud off to the north, probably a mile or so away. He got out the spyglass he had bought in Holten and opened it up. He saw a single rider coming at a good pace and a saddled horse behind him. Someone's in a hurry to get somewhere, he thought to himself. He removed his shotgun from his sling and set it down on the boulder next to him. He didn't know if the man meant trouble or not but he would be prepared for it anyway.

Jess was only about twenty feet off the trail so unless the rider took a turn east or west, he would ride right by Jess. He stood as the rider approached and slowed after seeing him. He waved as if to let Jess know he was friendly but that did not make him relax yet. The rider dismounted about fifty yards from Jess and walked his horses the rest of the way.

"Howdy, mister, mind if I sit a spell and take a break?"

"Not at all. Help yourself to some coffee and a biscuit if you like."

"That sounds good. Mighty nice of you." Hanley went about tying his horses to a branch on a tree and got out his coffee cup. He walked to the fire, filled his cup, and grabbed one of the large biscuits. He sat on a rock and noticed the shotgun on the boulder next to Jess.

"You expecting trouble?" asked Hanley.

"Not really, but if it shows up, I'll be here to greet it."

"Well, just so you know, I ain't it."

"I figured as much, once I got a look at you." Hanley was about to take a large bite out of the biscuit when he finally noticed it. He took one look at the pistol Jess was wearing and that caused Hanley to look at Jess a little more closely.

"I'll be damned. I was hoping to get lucky, but not this lucky," admitted Hanley as he stood up. Jess looked at him curiously, wondering what he meant.

"Might your name be Jess Williams?"

Jess stiffened a little at the question. He had gained a reputation as a fast draw and he knew that men would begin to seek him out simply to try to outdraw him and prove that they were faster. For all he knew, this man was one of them. Jess slowly rose up and stood. It was then that Hanley noticed that the hammer strap was off Jess's pistol.

"Who might you be and why are you asking?"

Hanley could immediately sense the danger. "Hold on, mister, I ain't no threat to you," he stammered nervously. "I'm not a gunfighter looking to call you out. If you are who I think you are, I've been sent to find you and bring you a message."

Jess relaxed and took another sip of coffee. He looked Hanley over for a moment. "Who sent you to find me?"

"So you are Jess Williams?"

"Yes."

"Well, I'm Terrence Hanley and it's an honor to share a cup of coffee with you."

"It's a pleasure to meet you too, but let's get back to that part about who sent you to find me and bring me a message."

Hanley filled his cup again and sat back down. "Cal Hardin, back in Black Creek, sent me to find you. He wants me to tell you that your brother, Tim Sloan, is back in Black Creek waiting for you." Jess didn't respond; he calmly listened as Hanley continued.

"It seems that Dick Carter, before his untimely death by your hand, sent a message to your brother. In the message was the offer to pay your brother the sum of ten thousand dollars to kill you. Carter gave the money to Cal Hardin to hold. Hardin promised Carter that he would pay the money to your brother once he brought your dead body to him to identify."

"I thought the bounty Carter had on my head was three thousand dollars," replied Jess.

"There's still that too, but Carter must've figured that hiring your own brother to kill you was worth a whole lot more money. Hell, Carter was crazy with hate for you. He probably would have paid anything to see you dead by your own brother's hand."

Jess thought for a moment about what Hanley had said before responding. "So, if Hardin is supposed to pay off my brother for killing me, why did he send you to find me and warn me?"

"Because Hardin don't like any of this one bit. He figured he owed Carter and he made a promise, but he will only keep the promise he made to Carter and he never promised not to warn you."

"Why did he pick you to find me? I've never met you before. How would you even know what I look like?"

Hanley went silent for a moment and swallowed hard. "I'll tell you, if you promise to keep that pistol holstered." Jess grinned and nodded in agreement.

"I work, well…did work for Carter. Now I work for his widow, at least I did when I left. I'm not sure I'll be working for her by the time I get back, but that don't matter none since Hardin offered me a job. Anyway, I was the one that Carter sent to find your brother. Since you and your brother look a lot alike, Hardin figured I might be able to pick you out. I want you to know that I never read the letter that I delivered to your brother but I knew that it involved money and that your brother would collect it back in Black Creek. By the time I got back to the Carter ranch, you had already killed Carter so I thought the whole mess was done with. When I accepted this job with Hardin, he told me the whole story. I guess that's the whole of it, in a nutshell."

Jess didn't respond right away. He sat there, thinking about what Hanley told him. He thought about the evilness of Dick Carter's plan to have his own brother attempt to kill him. Again, destiny seemed to be playing a role in his life. It was almost too much to take in and grab hold of. Here he was, looking for his brother when his brother was looking for him. He wondered if some unknown force was at work, pushing the two of them together or if it was simply the way things were supposed to work out. Less than six months ago he had learned about the brother he never knew he had and then he found out that his brother had been spotted with one of the killers of his family, Blake Taggert. Now, his brother was being paid to kill him for no other reason than money. Then he remembered the lesson that his pa had taught him. You have to play the cards life deals you. You can't change it, and you can't run away from it.

Hanley watched as Jess was thinking about all that he had told him. He watched the expressions on his face moving from puzzlement to anger and finally to a look of determination. He could see darkness looming in his eyes. He had never seen a darkness quite like it in a man's eyes before. It was something that you could actually feel, if that was at all possible. It sent a chill down Hanley's spine. Then, in an instant, Hanley could see calmness come over Jess as he got up to fill his coffee cup again.

"Well, it seems I finally have something in common with my brother."

"What would that be?"

"It seems that we are both out to do the same thing, except he's being paid a lot of money to do it."

"Ten thousand dollars is a whole lot of money," admitted Hanley.

"Yeah," agreed Jess, "but he won't be collecting it, you can be sure of that."

"I saw your brother kill a man back in Holten over a card game. He's pretty fast with that left hand of his."

"He'll need all the speed he can muster when he faces me," Jess said bluntly.

"I'm thinkin' you might be right about that, and thanks by the way."

"Thanks for what?"

"For not shooting me like you did Deke Moore."

"Deke Moore got exactly what he deserved. Besides, you're just the messenger. And I guess Cal Hardin is trying to make something wrong a little more right, I have to give him that much and I'll tell him so when I see him."

"He'll appreciate that. I know it for a fact. He ain't like Carter, I can tell you that."

"Well, seems like you will have some company on your ride back to Black Creek, Mr. Hanley," said Jess.

"Terrence will do just fine, Jess," he replied, "and I can't think of any man I'd rather have riding next to me."

They broke camp, mounted up, and started their ride back to Black Creek. It was a quiet trip, neither man talking much. Terrence Hanley was thinking about what was going to happen when they got back to town. He would glance over at Jess occasionally. He felt sorry for the horrible turn of events that had changed this young

423

man's life so dramatically. Yet, he seemed to have taken it all in stride, dealt with it, survived to be a honed man-killer even though he was young enough to be Hanley's son.

Jess's thoughts were on something else though. He was asking himself one question repeatedly in his head. Why had Tim Sloan been riding with Blake Taggert?

CHAPTER EIGHTEEN

"How damn lucky can one man get," bellowed Trent Holt. "You ain't lost a hand in over an hour."

"I guess I'm just lucky today," said Tim Sloan.

"Yeah, you've been lucky every day since you came to town," added Tom Otto, who had been locked in a poker game with Trent Holt and Tim Sloan. Sloan had been taking their money, winning pot after pot over the last few hours. He had cheated on a few hands when he needed to win, but in most of the hands, he simply had outplayed the two. Trent Holt went to the bar and got another bottle of whiskey. Andy handed him the bottle.

"Why don't ya quit while you still have a few dollars left, Trent?" asked Andy.

"Hell no, I'm gonna win all my money back from that snake. I know he's cheatin', but I can't spot it. He's one slick player for sure."

"Well, don't go gettin' him riled and get yourself a dirt blanket."

"Yeah, yeah, yeah," Trent murmured as he sauntered back to the table and poured himself another drink. It was Otto's turn to deal and he dealt all three of them another hand.

"Them boys ain't got sense enough to quit," Tony said, shaking his head. He had been sitting at the bar drinking some coffee with Andy for the last few hours. He was doing what he was supposed to do, keeping an eye on Sloan.

"Nope," Andy agreed, "and they both been drinkin' too much. I got a bad feelin' that one of 'em is gonna do somethin' stupid sooner or later."

"That's what usually happens when you mix whiskey, poker, and one man winning too much money hand after hand," quipped Tony. Just then, Jim Smythe came into the saloon and walked up to the bar next to Tony.

"I got some bad news, boys," he said.

"I was wondering when it would happen," groaned Andy.

"I just talked to one of the ranch hands from the Hardin spread. He told me that Cal Hardin sent a rider out to find Jess and tell him about his brother being here looking for him."

"Damn," said Tony, "I was hoping Jess wouldn't come back for a while and this brother of his would get tired of waiting and leave town. Guess that was hoping for a little too much, huh?"

"Hell, he ain't goin' anywhere 'cept right here," replied Andy. "Ten thousand dollars will plant roots on a man. Besides, he's been making a pretty good living at the table the last few days. Damn kid is as good at the card game as any I've seen."

"Well, what the hell are we going to do now?" asked Jim.

"What the hell can we do," Andy asked bluntly.

Tony looked back and forth between Andy and Jim. "Well, maybe we should just plug him out in the middle of the street with no warning, like Jess did to that Deke fellow."

"We can't do that, Tony," Jim said shaking his head. "That would be considered murder and we ain't like that."

"Maybe not, but I'll tell you this. If that snake Sloan doesn't face Jess in a fair fight, I'll put a few chunks of lead in him with my Winchester and I won't warn him before I do it. I promise you both that." They all nodded in agreement.

"I've got to get back to the store. Tony, keep an eye on Sloan and we'll just have to wait it out and see what happens."

Jim walked out of Andy's, heading back to the general store. Tony was about to get up and go out back to relieve himself when the argument at the table flared up again. Trent Holt was standing up now and weaving back and forth, the effects of the liquor working on him.

"I know you've been cheatin' but I can't figure out how," shouted Trent. Tom Otto was trying to grab Trent's left hand and pull him back down in his seat but Trent kept pulling his arm away, which caused him to weave even more. While that was going on, Sloan's left hand dropped below the table.

"Come on, Trent. Let's just quit and go get something to eat and sober up before you do something stupid," advised Otto.

"I ain't hungry and I ain't goin' nowhere till this cheatin' snake tells me how he's doin' it."

"I told you I don't need to cheat against you boys," replied Sloan, sarcastically. "You two just ain't good enough at the game."

"I've been playin' poker longer than you been breathin' air, boy. I could win you any day in a fair game. If you ain't tellin' me how you're cheatin', I want my money back from the last dozen hands."

"Now, don't get yourself into something you can't get out of mister," warned Sloan. "If you handle that side iron as well as you play poker, your losing streak is about to get worse."

Otto had given up trying to get Holt back down in his seat and could only watch now. Holt stood there, weaving back and forth, glaring at Sloan. The whiskey had clouded his brain as well as his judgment. Then he did what deep down he knew he shouldn't do. He reached for his pistol and before he got it out of his holster, Sloan's gun barked loud from under the table. The slug ripped into Holt's right thigh, knocking him down to the floor. Sloan stood up slowly, his pistol still pointed at Trent Holt lying on the floor. Holt was still holding onto his pistol, which was yet another bad decision for Holt. If he had been thinking clearly, he would have dropped the gun, but he wasn't able to think clearly. Too many shots of whiskey and too many poker hands lost were all too common ways for a man to get killed. This was no exception. Holt tried what he normally knew he shouldn't. He tried to take another shot at Sloan, who was all too happy to finish what Holt had started by putting another slug square in the middle of his chest, ending the game, along with

Holt's life. Andy had reached for his shotgun under the counter but Tony spotted his move and grabbed Andy by the arm with a grip that made Andy's mouth tighten up like a spinster woman holding her pocket book.

"Don't you even try that, Andy," Tony said quietly. "That boy will plug you before you can get that thing above the counter." Andy grunted to himself, knowing that Tony was right and had probably saved his life.

Tom Otto hadn't moved an inch during all of this. He sat right there with both hands on the table. Sloan, seeing no other threats in the saloon, whirled his gun and dropped it ever so gently back in the holster. He sat back down at the table and started collecting the cards. He looked over at Tom Otto, who had that same look Sloan had seen before after taking a player out of a poker game... permanently.

"I suppose you don't want to be dealt back into the game, huh?"

Otto nervously looked over at Sloan. "Well, uh...I suppose I best be gettin' back to the missus, if you don't mind, Mr. Sloan."

"Go on and get home to your woman," sneered Sloan, a look of disgust on his face. Otto wasted no time in leaving. Andy walked around the bar and over to Trent Holt's body.

"You didn't have to do that. You already had him wounded and on the floor," grumbled Andy.

Sloan glared at him. "Man pulls on me, I kill him. It's that simple. You all saw it. I tried to get him to give it up but he wouldn't let it go."

Andy sent Tony out to get the doctor and the undertaker. "I saw it, just like everyone saw it, but you didn't have to plug him that second time," countered Andy. "You coulda shot him in the arm and just wounded him again; you're good enough with that side iron to have done that."

"I don't see it that way. Man should've walked away and gone home to his woman like the other man did."

Andy shook his head. "I don't think I want you playin' in my saloon anymore. It's bad for business."

Sloan glared at Andy with a hateful look. "No man tells me where I can or can't go. If you want to go back and try for that shotgun again, I'll let you get it above the counter before I put a slug or two in you."

"You saw that, did ya?" Andy was almost smiling.

"I saw you go for it and I saw your friend save your life. You were one second away from blazing a trail straight to hell."

Andy stopped smiling and Tony returned with the doctor and the undertaker. Two men helped haul the body off and Doctor Johnson and Tony had a drink with Andy at the bar. Sloan, true to his word, sat back down at the table and kept shuffling the cards and folding them one handed. Doctor Johnson finished his drink and turned to head out of the saloon. He stopped at Sloan's table. He looked him straight in the eyes.

"Trent Holt was a friend of mine, Mr. Sloan. You best hope you don't get shot in this town because if you do, you'll have to ride to the next town to find a doctor to fix you." Doctor Johnson walked out.

"You tell him, Doc," added Andy, not one to leave well enough alone.

"Shut up, old man, before I come over there and yank that pile of fur you call a beard right off your face," threatened Sloan. Andy gave Sloan one of his looks and turned back to Tony, who gave him a warning look.

"You're going to get yourself shot for sure if you keep needling him."

Sloan hung around the saloon for another half hour hoping to get another game going, but no one showed up, at least to play poker anyway. He asked a few of the men who had come in for a drink or a meal if they wanted to play, but none of them would sit at his table. They had already heard about Trent Holt's demise and no one wanted to be next. Sloan finally got bored, walked out, and headed down to Dixie's place. He was probably going to see Vivian again. She was his favorite and they had become more comfortable with each other with each visit.

Sloan walked into Dixie's and was met by Dixie herself. She had no last name; none of the women working there used last names. Dixie was older than she looked but she had long ago stopped peddling her flesh in a cathouse in Dodge City, Kansas. She had saved all her money and several years ago she moved to Black Creek, Kansas. She purchased a nice little boarding house with four rooms upstairs. She hung out a sign and opened her establishment. She started out with two of the girls she used to work with in Dodge City and she was now a businessperson, and quite a successful one at that.

"Where is my little woman, Vivian?" Sloan asked.

Dixie smiled. "She's right upstairs in room four, like always. She's been whining about you not showing up yet today. I think she has taken a liking to you."

"Most women do once they find out about my wonderful personality," Sloan said, as he patted Dixie on the rear.

"I don't think it's your personality she is fond of."

Sloan smiled and headed up the stairs. He knocked on the door of room four and heard footsteps shuffling quickly. His hand was on the butt of his pistol with the hammer strap off. It was just something he did without even thinking about it. Vivian opened the door and smiled at him.

"I thought maybe you weren't coming by to see me today."

"I've been a little busy."

Vivian frowned, her lips pouting slightly. "I heard the gunshots over at Andy's Saloon and I heard about Trent Holt." Sloan took off his gun belt and carefully placed it on a chair, which was next to the bed. It was within easy reach if he were to need it.

"He shouldn't have called me a cheat. I tried to warn him, but he decided to do something stupid when he shouldn't have."

Vivian started undressing. "I heard one of the other girls just this morning say something about you looking for your brother, Jess Williams. You know, he was just here not too long ago."

Sloan stopped all movement. "What, you know about Jess? Why didn't you tell me?"

Vivian blushed. "I just found out about it this morning. I was waiting for you to come to visit me so that I could tell you."

"Tell me what?"

"A lot of people in town know Jess. Jim and Sara Smythe over at the general store know your brother very well. He stays there when he comes to visit. That's all I know." Sloan picked his gun belt back up and began strapping it on again and Vivian was now stark naked. She could tell Sloan was furious.

"You're not leaving yet, are you? We haven't even kissed. Don't you want a little of this before you rush off."

"Not right now. There is something I have to do and it can't wait. Thanks for the information." Sloan threw ten dollars on the bed and headed out the door.

"Where are you going off to in such a hurry?" asked Vivian.

"To pay a visit to the Smythes, and it won't be a pleasant one, I promise you that."

Sloan headed down the stairs and straight out the front door of Dixie's. He looked straight down at Smythe's General Store. He walked off the boardwalk and headed for it. Tony was sitting in his chair just inside the livery. He watched as Sloan headed toward Smythe's General Store. What caught Tony's attention was the way Sloan was acting. He looked mad and hell-bent for trouble.

As soon as Sloan walked into the store and found no one behind the counter, he banged his fist on the counter.

"Doesn't anyone work in this damn store?" Jim came running out of the back room to see what all the commotion was. Sara was one step behind him.

"I'm going to ask you a question," growled Sloan, "and I better get the right answer the first time because there won't be a second. Do you two know Jess Williams and where he is?" Jim and Sara exchanged nervous glances.

"Don't be looking at your whore, just answer the question!"

"Now see here, mister, you can't call my wife...."

Sloan cut him off before he could finish. "I can damn well say whatever I want!"

Jim reached down to where he kept his shotgun, but the cocking back of a hammer stopped him. Sloan had slicked his pistol out before Jim's hand moved one inch.

"Yeah, you go ahead and grab that scattergun and see how fast you can get a glimpse of your next life." Jim stopped and put his hands on the counter.

"Sara, go into the back room." Sara didn't move, mostly because she was frozen in fear. She knew this young man would not hesitate to pull the trigger. She began to think about what Jess had told her about how ruthless some men could be.

"She ain't going anywhere," Sloan said with a sneer. "I want her right where I can see her. Now, you've got about one second to answer my question and then I'm going to put a bullet right through your skull. Then, I'm going to ask your whore there the same question and if she don't answer, I've got no problem with putting a bullet in her head. If you doubt me, you will surely be sorry. I've had it with this two-bit town. Now, what's it going to be?" Sara was even more terrified now and she couldn't move or hardly even breathe.

Jim, knowing he had no choice now, answered the question. "Yes, we know him," Jim answered slowly.

"That's a start. Now where the hell is he?"

"I don't know for sure, but he is on his way back here now."

"Really? How did you find that out?"

"One of the men who works out at the Hardin ranch told me that Cal Hardin had sent a man to find your brother and tell him that you were here."

Sloan looked a little puzzled. "Now, why do you suppose he went and did that?"

"You'd have to ask Cal Hardin that question."

"I think I might, but not before I finish what I came here to do."

"And just what did you come here to do?" asked Jim, afraid of the answer.

"Why, to make ten thousand dollars...and kill my brother," Sloan answered, speaking as if what he had said was nothing more than going down to the creek for an afternoon of fishing. He holstered his pistol in his customary fashion and turned to walk out when Jim spoke again.

"You didn't ask me why your brother left town." Sloan stopped and turned back to Jim.

"All right, I'll ask. Why did he leave town?"

Jim smiled what could've only been considered an evil smile when he answered. "He's looking for you."

CHAPTER NINETEEN

Tim Sloan walked out of Jim and Sara's store and headed for the saloon again. He never knew that Tony had had the sights of his Winchester square in the middle of Sloan's back all the while he was talking to Jim and Sara. Tony kept the Winchester on him as he walked to the saloon. He wanted to pull the trigger, but something inside him, something that he could not understand, refused to let him do it.

"Dammit," he said to himself as he put the Winchester down. As soon as Sloan was inside the saloon, he walked over to Jim and Sara. When he walked in, Jim was holding Sara, who was sobbing in his arms.

"I had my Winchester aimed square in the middle of his back all the time he was here. If he'd have shot either of you, I would've plugged him," said Tony.

Jim was angrier than he had ever been in his life. "Hell, you should've plugged him anyway."

Tony shook his head. "He had that pistol trained on you. How was I to know it wouldn't go off and kill you anyway? I thought it best to wait it out and see. What the hell did he want?"

"He wanted to know if we knew Jess and where he was."

"You didn't tell him, did you?"

"Hell yes, I had to tell him," Jim replied guiltily. "He threatened to kill me and then Sara after that. I had no idea you had him covered. I swear, if I had known, I would've refused and let him shoot me just so you could kill him. It would've been worth it."

Sara lifted her head from his chest. "No, I wouldn't want that and Jess wouldn't either and you know it. Besides, Jess wants to face his brother and it's going to happen sooner or later. If it's later, someone else will die by that young man's hands."

Tony grunted and looked knowingly at Jim. "You know what? She's right. We've all been trying to keep Jess's brother from finding him when that's what Jess wants in the worst way. We should've told Sloan about it when he first hit town. Maybe Trent Holt would still be alive."

"I doubt it," refuted Jim. "That boy has a lot more killing inside of him."

"I reckon you're right about that. Let's hope he can keep that smoke wagon of his in the holster until Jess gets back to town. I'll go over and fill Andy in. Sloan is over there again, probably trying to get another poker game started." Tony headed over to the saloon.

Sara placed her head back on Jim's chest again and sobbed some more. "Jim, I have never been so scared in my life. I was sure he was going to kill the both of us," she sobbed. "I think I understand now."

"Understand what, Sara?"

Her head slowly lifted up. "I think I understand why Jess is hunting down men like that. I've been having a hard time trying to justify it, but when I felt for that one moment that I was going to lose you for no reason and maybe lose my life, too…well…I think it finally hit home with me. Jess is right. Men like that don't deserve to walk the same streets as the rest of us. Men like that don't deserve to live. I think that if I had the courage to do it, I would kill that young man myself. I would shoot him down in the street like the dog he is."

Jim put her head back on his chest and held her firmly. "Now, now, calm down. We're not like that, but we sure know someone who is…and he's on his way back here, I hope."

Tony walked into Andy's Saloon and sauntered up to the bar. Andy was wiping off some glasses and exchanging glares with Sloan, who was sitting at a table, shuffling cards.

"Well, the secret's out," said Tony.

"What do ya mean by that?" asked Andy. Tony told him about all that had just taken place over at Jim and Sara's.

"That little bastard needs killin'," said Andy in a low enough voice that Sloan couldn't hear him. "I say we grab my shotgun and blow his sorry ass outta that chair the first time he ain't lookin'. Maybe you should distract him somehow so I can get the drop on him."

Tony shook his head. "In case you've forgotten, we ain't professional gunmen like him. I don't think he misses much. He'd probably get at least one of us before it was over. I say we let our boy Jess handle it. I think he would want it that way."

"You're probably right about that."

Just then, LeAnn walked out of the back, but Andy stopped her dead in her tracks. "Get yer ass back in that kitchen, woman!"

LeAnn huffed and spun around and went back in the kitchen. Andy wanted to keep her out of sight from Sloan, figuring that nothing good could come from it.

"That damn woman's got a memory shorter than my pecker," Andy complained.

"I thought you wanted to marry her off?"

"Not to that piece of crap."

There was a moment of silence and then Tony smiled. "That short, huh?"

"Go to hell," grumbled Andy as he looked over at Sloan, who now looked agitated.

"A man can't think with you hollering like some old woman," blurted Sloan.

"What you gonna do, shoot me like you did Trent?" snarled Andy.

"You know the only reason I don't, you old cuss?"

"No, why don't ya tell me?"

" 'Cause you look like the ass end of a mule I once had," retorted Sloan, smiling at Andy. Andy almost replied, but common sense finally got a grip on him. He kept his mouth shut and went back to wiping glasses.

⁂

Terrence Hanley woke up to what he thought was cannon fire. He jumped from his bedroll, trying to shake the cobwebs from his head. He was reaching for his pistol when he saw Jess lying flat on his stomach, the Sharps rifle propped on his saddle. Smoke was still coming from the end of the barrel and the smell of gunpowder still lingered heavily in the air. Hanley then realized that he was making himself quite a nice target. Now that his brain was starting to come out of the fog, he dropped back down on the ground behind his saddle.

"What the hell is going on? Are we being shot at or what?"

Jess smiled and stood up, propping the rifle against his saddle. "No, I don't think that rabbit's got a gun or a head anymore. Figured we could use some fresh meat today and when I woke up, I spotted that rabbit out about one hundred and fifty yards. I decided there was no sense in missing out on the opportunity for a good meal later on."

"You hit that rabbit a hundred and fifty yards out?"

"Yep, that Sharps is one fine long gun. I like it more every time I shoot it."

"You might want to warn a man who's in a sleep before you fire up that thing."

"Sorry about that. I'm so used to being alone on the trail I guess I didn't think much about it."

Jess walked out to pick up the rabbit. He gutted it and tied it on the packhorse. It would make a good meal later in the day. They made some coffee, bacon, and pan bread and broke camp, but not before Jess cleaned the Sharps rifle. He always kept his weapons in good order.

They had been riding for a few hours when Hanley finally broke the silence when they were walking the horses to rest them. "You don't talk much," said Hanley.

Jess glanced over at him and smiled. "I do when I have something to say."

"Mind if I ask you a question?"

"Don't mind at all."

"When you finally meet up with your brother and face him, do you think you will actually be able to...well...kill him?"

Jess thought about it, but only for a few seconds. "If he is what I think he is, yes, I'll kill him for sure, brother or not. I still have some hope that maybe he's nothing more than a liar, a thief, and a man who cheats other men out of their money at the poker table. I can live with that although I wouldn't want any part of him. If he turns out to be a killer of innocent men and women, then he's no better than the men who murdered my family and that puts him on my bad list. I only know one way to deal with people on my bad list."

Hanley didn't have to wonder what that meant. "Remind me not to ever get on your bad list."

Jess smiled at him. "You know, I was looking over your horses this morning. They are two of the finest horses I've seen in a long while. You wouldn't want to part with one of them, would you?"

"Not mine to part with," admitted Hanley. "Cal Hardin loaned them to me to catch up with you. They are mighty fine animals and they can run long and hard too. Maybe Hardin will sell you one if you ask him."

"I might do that. Gray here has been a great horse but he's getting a little on in years. He's going to deserve a long rest soon."

Hanley looked at Gray and then at the packhorse. "Where'd you pick the packhorse up at?"

"I bought him from some rancher along the trail. I ran into two men who had been robbed and stranded and needed a ride."

"How'd they get robbed?"

Jess thought about the whole thing with Carl and Murry for a moment. He shook his head and laughed. "I don't think I want to tell you."

"Why not? Hell, we ain't doing nothing else but riding."

"It's too long of a story."

"Come on, the way you're smiling it must be a good one."

"It is."

"Then tell me."

Jess smiled at him again. "Remember that thing about reminding you not to get on my bad list," cautioned Jess, still smiling.

Hanley frowned. "I think I just lost all interest in that story. I'll be shuttin' up now."

They rode in silence for the next several hours. They decided they wouldn't make it to Black Creek until the next day, so they made camp and fixed a nice meal with the rabbit. They picked the bones clean and both finished off a good plate of beans. That was followed by a few pots of hot coffee and some casual conversation before they finally turned in for the night.

Randolph Jackson had been on the trail for months now. He was hell-bent on finding and killing the man who shot his brother Nevada. He knew who shot his brother; he just didn't know where the young man was, at least, not until recently. He had started his search in Red Rock, Texas, after he heard the news that his brother had been killed in a gunfight. By the time he heard the news and made arrangements to hit the trail to Red Rock, Texas, Jess Williams was long gone.

Randolph traveled from one small town to another, asking questions about the young man, Jess Williams. He finally ended up in a small town called Baxter and it was there that he found out Jess Williams was from Black Creek, Kansas. He had also come to the realization from the information he had gathered about

Jess Williams that he was very fast with a pistol. When he had first learned of the demise of his brother, his first thought was that there must have been some trickery involved or that his brother had no warning and was murdered, even though he was told that it was a fair fight. He thought that because he knew how fast his brother Nevada was at shucking a pistol out. He knew because he had taught him how to draw. The only one who could beat Nevada Jackson in a fair showdown was Randolph himself, or so he thought.

But he had finally come to the realization that it probably had been a fair fight between his brother and Jess Williams. Of course, it didn't matter to him now. He was hell-bent on finding the man who killed his brother and, as usual, reason or common sense would have nothing to do with the matter. That was the way it was as far as he was concerned. He would avenge his brother's death and that was that. It was his sworn duty to do so.

He rode into Black Creek in the later part of the afternoon. He stopped at the first place most men did, the first saloon he could find. He tied his horse and walked into Andy's Saloon. Randolph dressed much like his brother Nevada, mostly black, with a black leather holster with some silver studs and a very nice Colt .45 Peacemaker in the holster. The holster was tied down low and tight to his thigh. Randolph could sense the tension in the saloon immediately and he could sense where most of the tension was coming from. It was emanating from a young man sitting alone at a table, shuffling and dealing cards to himself and an imaginary player that wasn't there. Randolph walked up to the bar.

"What can I get ya?" asked Andy.

"Whiskey, and make it the good stuff."

Andy grabbed a bottle of his good whiskey from under the bar. He poured him a shot, which he downed with one quick motion and motioned for Andy to pour him another one.

"Where ya from, mister?"

"Hell, I'm not sure anymore. I've hit every damn shit-hole of a town over the last several weeks. Can't remember half the names and don't want to anyway," answered Randolph, downing the second shot and asking for a third.

"Lookin' for work or just riding the trail?" asked Andy.

"Naw, I'm hunting for the young man who killed my brother."

Andy had a smile on his face and an idea in his brain, which didn't happen all that often.

"Might the young man who killed yer brother go by the name of Tim Sloan?"

"No, why do you ask?"

"Cause that's Tim Sloan sittin' right over there at the card table. He's killed his share of men, that's fer sure."

Randolph glanced at Sloan and then back to Andy. "He fits the description, but not the name. I guess the only way to find out for sure is to ask," Randolph said, downing his third whiskey. He turned to face Sloan who had already sensed something going on. He decided to see if the man at the bar was interested in a game of cards.

"How 'bout a game, mister?" asked Sloan.

"I'm not looking to get into a card game; I'm looking for the young man who killed my brother, Nevada Jackson."

Andy, who had been leaning on the bar, hoping to see a gunfight ensue between these two, heard the name Nevada Jackson and that made him stand straight up. He remembered about Jess telling him about his gunfight with him. Damn it, he thought to himself. He listened intently now at the conversation as it continued.

"You fit the description but the barkeep says your name is Tim Sloan. That right?"

Sloan shot a glare at Andy, knowing that Andy obviously had something to do with this. "That's right, I'm Tim Sloan, but I didn't kill anybody by the name of Nevada Jackson, at least, not that I know of. What's the name of the man you're looking for?"

"They told me his name was Jess Williams."

That got Sloan's attention real fast. Andy, now that what he feared was confirmed, shook his head. Here was yet another gunslinger looking for Jess to kill him for revenge. Sloan was thinking hard now about how to continue with the conversation. He didn't want this man to get a crack at his brother before him and lose the ten thousand dollars he had already been spending in his head. He slowly stood up and pushed his chair back, his hammer strap already removed.

"Mister, what is your name?"

"Randolph Jackson, brother of Nevada Jackson," he answered, slowly removing his hammer strap.

"Well, Randolph, it seems that we have a little problem."

"What might that be?"

"Jess Williams is my brother."

Randolph stiffened a little at that. "Is that so? I guess that's why you fit the description so well. You're wrong about that little problem thing, 'cause if you're taking his side in this matter, we have a big problem. So if that's the case, let's get this over with right now and then I'll take care of that no good brother of yours as soon as our paths cross."

Sloan was trying to keep some information from coming forth until he could decide how to handle the whole matter, but he couldn't let the threat go unchallenged. It was simply his nature. His mood changed toward a darker side and his words now held a sarcastic tone as he spoke.

"Listen, Randolph, I ain't taking my brother's side in this matter or anything else, but if you want to challenge me, I suggest you go meet with the undertaker first to get measured up real nice for the pine box you'll need when this is over."

Randolph smiled so hard he almost laughed. "Hell kid, I've taken down more men already than you will if you live to be an old man, which ain't likely. What makes you think I can't take you? Hell, I've been slinging iron longer than you've been breathing air."

Sloan glared at Randolph, trying to decide whether to chance outdrawing this man. Normally, he would have gone through with it without a thought, but that ten thousand dollars was nagging at him like an itch that couldn't be scratched, and that altered his way of thinking, temporarily at least. It was then that the idea came to him.

"So, you want my brother dead in order to avenge the death of your brother, correct?"

"That's exactly what I want, and I don't care how I get it either."

Sloan smiled an evil grin. "Well, what if I told you that I am here waiting for my brother's return so that I can kill him myself?"

Randolph was taken aback by that. He had had such a close relationship with his brother Nevada that he couldn't fathom one brother killing another, yet he had heard of such things. "You're going to kill your own flesh and blood, your own brother?" Randolph asked, not believing what he was hearing.

"Yes sir, that is exactly why I've been sitting here waiting around for the last few days."

Randolph was still trying to wrap his brain around this idea. He was thinking about it all when Andy broke the silence.

"The only reason he's here to kill his brother is that he's being paid ten thousand dollars to do it," Andy hollered.

Sloan shot a harsh glare over at Andy. "I swear, old man, I'm going to put a bullet square in your ass before this is over," threatened Sloan.

"Why my ass and not my head?" Andy asked, sarcastically.

"Because every time you sit down, I want you to think of me."

"Yeah, well...when your brother gets back to town, you won't be gettin' a chance to shoot anyone else," boasted Andy.

Randolph interrupted. "Ten thousand dollars, eh? That's a lot of money for killing one man. I suppose if I'm the man who kills your brother, I could collect the money myself."

Sloan was beginning to lose his patience when he came up with another angle. He did not want to lose the money and even though he thought he could take Randolph, he didn't want to take the chance now. He was a poker player and was always trying to assess the odds.

"Okay, I'll make you a proposition."

"I'm listening."

"If you and I go at it right now, one of us is going to die; that we know for sure. If it's you who is shot, you'll go to your grave never having the satisfaction of knowing that the man who killed your brother is dead. Who knows? He might just beat me to the draw. Unlikely, but you never know. Now, if it's me who goes down, you'll get your chance at my brother, but he is fast and he might kill you, in which case, you still don't get your revenge."

"That's a whole lot of fancy talk but what the hell are you getting at?" asked Randolph, trying to follow Sloan.

"Here is what I propose. You wait here until my brother gets back and let me face him down first. If I kill him, I will give you one thousand dollars just for letting me get the first chance at him. If for some reason, he gets me, then you still have the opportunity to face him and collect the entire ten thousand dollars yourself. Don't you see? You have nothing to lose in the venture. Plus, you will have the satisfaction of watching Jess Williams' own brother kill him. What could be better than that?"

Randolph went back to the bar, poured himself another shot of whiskey, and downed it. He thought about the proposal for a few minutes. Andy was staring at him the whole time. Randolph slammed his shot glass down on the bar and turned back around to face Sloan.

"You know what, kid? I have to agree with you. I wanted to be the one to kill him, but to be able to watch you kill him in front of me, well, that's even better. And, I'll make a thousand dollars to watch him die. I couldn't think of a better deal in a hundred years."

Sloan relaxed and sat back down at his table. Andy went back to cleaning up and shaking his head in disgust. Sloan shuffled the cards again. "Randolph, would you like to play a few hands of poker?"

Randolph grabbed the shot glass and bottle from the bar and walked to the table. "Hell, I might as well. I have to keep an eye on you anyway. I don't want to miss the big showdown."

Sloan smiled and dealt the cards.

CHAPTER TWENTY

Hanley and Jess woke to a cool breeze and a light rain. Jess had to work to get the fire going. He scrounged around some trees to get some kindling that wasn't wet from the rain yet. They made a nice meal and some hot coffee.

"Damn, it's getting too close to winter for me," said Hanley.

"I agree. I think once this is all over, I'll head south until it gets warm enough."

"Hell, you might have to go into Mexico to do that."

"If that's where it's warm, then that's where I'm going."

Hanley laughed. "If I had a lick of sense, I'd join you."

Jess thought about that for a moment. He liked Hanley, but he liked to ride alone most of the time. He didn't want to start relying on someone else. He was in a very dangerous business and the only person he could fully trust was himself. He hoped Hanley wasn't serious and didn't think he should say anything unless it came up again. He threw what was left of his coffee into the fire.

"I suppose it's time to break camp and head into town. No sense in putting off what is going to happen eventually, right?"

Hanley nodded in agreement. "I guess not, not that I want this to happen. I wish you would just ride on down to Mexico and enjoy the weather and the women, but I know you ain't going to do that until this thing between you and your brother is finished."

"You are right about that, except for the women part," Jess replied.

"What, you don't like women?"

Jess thought for a moment as he finished saddling Gray. "I guess I probably would, but there is no place in my life or line of work for women. They will surely take your mind off other matters and that's when someone will put a bullet in you. That's not going to happen to me. I'll leave the women to you."

"Hell, I like that idea even better."

They mounted up and headed toward the town of Black Creek, Kansas. Hanley was riding to the right side of Jess. He kept looking at the pistol that was firmly held in its holster by a leather strap. Hanley noticed that the hammer went straight up instead of curving back like most pistols and the strap had to be tight. He had also noticed that Jess, in what he believed to be a somewhat unconscious move, was always testing the strap and making sure it was firmly on the hammer. If not, it would fall out too easily since it didn't hold the gun in like most holsters. Of course, what Hanley had noticed most of all was when Jess would walk away from camp every night and spend some time practicing.

"That sure is an unusual pistol and holster, that's for sure," observed Hanley.

Jess looked down and checked the leather strap again. "It sure is, and I'm lucky to have it. I can't explain it, but the gun almost forces you to draw it differently. Because of the way it was put together, you can do things with it you couldn't do with any other gun I've seen. I don't know who made this thing but whoever it was sure knew what he was doing."

"I know one thing for sure," said Hanley. "You can snake that thing out of the holster quicker than anything I've ever seen, and I've seen some fast gunmen."

Jess smiled. "So, you've been watching me practice?" he asked, knowing all along that Hanley watched when he spent his practice time, usually right after supper.

"It's hard not to watch a master at his trade."

Jess actually laughed aloud at that. "I don't think anyone has ever called me a master yet. I'm not sure that's true but I am pretty good with it."

"You can call it what you want, Mr. Williams, a shootist, an expert, a gunslinger, or whatever description you want to use to describe your ability with that thing. Maybe unnatural would be the best description for it, but you are most likely the fastest man alive on the draw. And not just that either; that thing you do with thumbing that first shot and then fanning the next few shots is… well, unnatural. I saw it, but if I told someone about it, I believe they would call me a liar right to my face."

"Well, I did once have a preacher say something like that to me. Maybe it is unnatural, but whatever it is, I'm thankful for it. It will help me accomplish what I want to do with my life."

"And that is?"

"Kill as many bad men as I can."

Hanley shook his head, but not in a bad way. "Bounty hunting is a dangerous business, but I think you've taken it to a whole different level than most men."

"You are most likely right about that."

"You know what else I'm right about?" asked Hanley.

"What?"

"I think your brother is in a whole heap of trouble."

Jess didn't respond right away. Hanley could see that he was thinking something through in his head. When he did respond, his voice had a tone of determination in it. "I do believe you are right, Mr. Hanley." They rode the rest of the way in silence.

Hanley suggested that since the Hardin ranch was right along their trail they stop there to freshen up and get any information on what was going on with Sloan. Jess agreed. They rode up to the Hardin ranch and were greeted by a few of the ranch hands. Cal Hardin walked out of the ranch house and motioned for them to come inside. Both Jess and Hanley walked up onto the large porch that surrounded three sides of the house. They all exchanged handshakes, went into the house, and sat down at a large wooden table.

Cal Hardin was the first to speak. "Woman, get some coffee poured for these men."

Cal's wife got busy, not in any mood for another argument with her husband. She kept staring at Jess though, trying to figure out how to feel about this young man. She feared him and yet she still could not understand why. Maybe it was simply because she knew that he had killed so many men at such an early age or maybe it was because he looked so similar to his brother, Tim Sloan. She did not like Sloan one bit. She could sense that he was an evil man and maybe she believed since they were brothers, that they both had some evil in them. Yet, she could sense no evil in this young man sitting at her table. She could see hardness in his eyes, but she also sensed good in him at the same time. She placed some cornbread and butter on the table and filled their cups with coffee.

"That will do," said Cal. "Leave us alone for now and if we need anything else, I'll let you know." She walked out of the kitchen and went upstairs.

Jess was the first to speak. "Mr. Hardin, is my brother in town right now?"

Hardin hung his head a little, still somewhat ashamed of his part in this whole thing, although he was trying to make it as right as he could. "Yes. I've had men watching him around the clock. I felt it was the least I could do since I'm the one who agreed to hold the blood money on your head. I hope you can accept my apology for it, but when a man owes another man a favor, I believe in granting it."

"Yet you sent Mr. Hanley out to find me and warn me. Doesn't that kind of go against what you promised Carter you would do?"

"I suppose so, to some degree. I'm trying to justify that myself, but I simply could not stand by and let it happen without trying to warn you. Maybe I was wrong to agree to hold the money in the first place, but that's behind us now. I think what's important is what happens next."

"What happens next is I go into town and face my brother. I have a few questions I want to ask him."

"Your brother ain't here to answer any questions. He just wants to kill you and come and collect the ten thousand dollars I'm holding."

"I know that, but first things first. Besides, it's not him who is going to control the event."

"You think you're that good with that pistol you have?" Hardin asked, nodding at Jess's pistol.

It was then that Hanley, who had been silent so far, entered the conversation. "Oh yeah, he's that good and a whole lot more. I've had the pleasure of watching him work with that thing. I can tell you that he can draw faster than anyone I've ever seen and he doesn't miss what he's aiming at either. I watched Sloan draw on a man and he ain't half as fast as Jess here is." Hanley said it as if he was proud to be the one to say it.

"Well, you'll have to be good," said Hardin. "One of my men watched him kill a man in Andy's Saloon. Your brother is quick with a gun, but the worst thing is that he has no regard for another man's life. In my book, that makes him a very dangerous man."

"Mr. Hardin, I know one thing for sure. If my brother is what I think he is, even if he gets me, he is going to die doing it," Jess said bluntly. Hardin and Hanley both believed him.

Hardin figured this was a good time to give Jess some more bad news. "You have another problem facing you when you get to town."

"What is that?"

"There is a man by the name of Randolph Jackson in town. He's looking for you too."

"He wouldn't happen to be the brother of Nevada Jackson, would he?"

"I don't know."

"I kind of thought that was going to happen sooner or later, but I didn't know when."

"The way I heard it, Jackson is going to let you and your brother go at it, and if your brother doesn't take you, Jackson will step in next."

"Yes, and he ain't forgot who shot his only brother."

"The timing sure could be better but I'll just have to deal with it," said Jess, almost casually. "I do have a question for you though. I'd like to ask you about those two very fine horses you own out there. What is the chance I could buy one of them from you?" asked Jess.

"Not a chance in hell," replied Hardin. "But I would be honored if you would accept them both as a peace offering for my involvement in this matter."

Jess's frown quickly turned to a grin. "I guess that makes us even then, but I only asked for one."

Hardin looked at him through experienced eyes. "Hell, that packhorse outside would never survive the run either of those two long horses would give him. He'd drop dead in his tracks and either of those two horses would keep on running long and hard. If you plan to stick with a packhorse, you'll need the both of them. I won't change my mind and that's the end of it."

Jess reached out and shook Cal Hardin's hand. "I'll take good care of them, you can be sure of that."

Hardin finally began to feel a little better about things.

"Well," said Jess, "no sense putting it off any longer." He stood up and shook hands with Cal Hardin and thanked him for the horses again. "I'll come back and get them after this is all over."

"You won't have to. I want Hanley to ride to town with you. That way he can report to me. He can leave both horses at the livery for you."

"That's mighty nice of you, Mr. Hardin. Hanley was right about you when he told me you were a fair man."

"One more thing," said Hardin, as he handed Jess an envelope filled with money. "Here is the ten thousand dollars from Carter that I've been holding. My deal with the devil is over. I guess if your brother's good enough, he can take the money off you himself. If not, I believe the money belongs to you."

Jess took the envelope and looked at Hardin with a new look of respect. "I don't think I could ask anything more of you, Mr. Hardin, and that's a fact."

Jess and Hanley mounted up and headed into Black Creek. Hanley could sense the change in Jess as they rode. He could feel the impending doom that was about to happen. Two brothers would be facing one another and one would surely kill the other. Hanley was sure who was going to be lying in the dirt when it was over.

Tony was working on the front hoof of a horse when he noticed two riders coming into town. He stopped what he was doing and was wiping his hands off when he noticed who one of the riders was. It was Jess. He felt good and bad all at the same time. Jess and Hanley rode up to Tony and dismounted. Tony gave Jess a firm handshake.

"I'm usually glad to see you come back to town, but I'm not so sure this time."

"Under the circumstances, I can understand why," agreed Jess.

"So, you know your brother is here and looking to put a bullet in you for money?"

"Yes, I know the whole story now, even the part about Nevada Jackson's brother being in town also."

"You just seem to draw the worst of the lot, don't you?"

"I think it's my wonderful personality that does it."

Tony laughed and looked at Jess's pistol. "I think it's that thing you got strapped around your waist that does most of it," Tony said, as he looked at the two fine horses that Hanley had brought to town.

"Damn fine animals," said Tony, as he looked them over, running his hands up and down them, checking their teeth and hoofs. Must be long horses, I suspect?"

"They belonged to Cal Hardin until today," said Hanley. "He gave them to Jess as a peace offering."

Tony frowned at the mention of Cal Hardin's name and looked over at Jess. "Is that his way of saying he's sorry?"

"Maybe," Jess replied, "but he really didn't cause this. Carter did. I don't have any problems with Hardin. My problem is with my brother and I'm about to deal with that shortly. Tony, will you take care of my two new fine horses?"

"I'll be glad to. What are you going to do with Gray? He's still a good horse although he ain't g'tting' any younger."

"I was hoping that you would take him for me. Ride him occasionally to work him, but mostly let him relax. I trust you won't sell him to anyone?"

"I'll keep him right here. Anytime you come back to town, he'll be here waitin' for a visit. What about the packhorse?"

Jess looked at the packhorse. He was a good horse but nothing compared to the two that Hardin had given him. "You can sell him and put it toward my livery fees, which you seem to keep forgetting to collect from me."

Tony grinned. "I guess that's fair enough."

Jess nodded as if they had an unwritten agreement. Then his mood changed as he gave the look that Tony had seen all too often before.

"Tony, I suppose my brother is over at Andy's?"

Tony frowned, knowing that something was about to happen and he knew from experience that it would not be something good. "Yep, and I'm going over there with you. Andy and I will make sure things go fairly for you, I promise you that."

Jess checked both his pistol and his pa's Peacemaker. "How are Jim and Sara, Tony?"

"Fine, but scared clean out of their wits. They ain't been outside the store since yesterday."

"Why, what happened?"

"That damn brother of yours pulled a gun on Jim and threatened to shoot him and then Sara next if they didn't tell him what he wanted to know about you. I damn near plugged him with my Winchester, but I didn't." Tony could see Jess's face harden some more.

"He shouldn't have done that."

"Don't I know that for sure," replied Tony, knowing what it meant.

Jim and Sara were the closest thing to family that Jess had and he would not allow anyone to harm them in any way. If someone did, they would answer to him for it. Everyone in town still remembered the Sheriff Newcomb event.

"Well, let's go over and visit with Andy and have a little talk with my brother," said Jess, as he removed the hammer strap from his pistol. Tony and Hanley walked about two steps back from Jess as they headed for the saloon. They hadn't walked more than a hundred feet when Tim Sloan walked out of Andy's and stood on the porch, watching as Jess and the other two men approached. Their eyes locked on one another. Life was ironic sometimes. Two brothers separated at birth, never knowing one another, and now they were going to engage in a gunfight where one was sure to kill the other.

"Well, well, well, I finally get to meet my brother, the great Jess Williams. They say you're fast with that side iron of yours."

"I've heard the same about you."

"I guess it runs in the family."

"Speaking of family, where is my so-called father who abandoned our mother?"

Tim Sloan slowly walked down the few steps and into the street. "My guess would be that he is already down in Mexico somewhere where it's warm. Then again, you never know with him. He's a wanderer for sure. Why do you care? He won't have anything to do with you anyway."

"You are wrong about that. I intend to find him just like I found you and face him."

"What makes you think you'll get the chance?"

"Oh, I'll get the chance. You can count on that."

"But, that would mean I'd be dead."

"You might be able to count on that too," said Jess, a hardness forming on his face.

"You sure are a cocky little bastard. I'll give you that. I like confidence in a man."

"I have another question for you."

"Go ahead. I believe in granting a man his last wishes, especially my own kin."

"What were you doing riding with Blake Taggert?"

"Why would you want to know that?" asked Sloan, puzzled by the question.

"I'm asking because he was one of the three men who murdered my family, including your real mother."

"What do you mean 'was'?"

"Yeah, he seems to have gotten himself killed."

"Taggert was pretty fast with a pistol. Who took him down?"

"That would be me."

"Taggert was a good friend of mine. We worked together on a few card games and shared some whores. I didn't know he was involved in your family's demise but why the hell should that matter to me anyway? I ain't got a mother, just a father."

"You have a mother who gave birth to you. She's buried out at the ranch right beside my pa and my little sister Samantha. She would have raised you and taken care of you if our father, if you can call him that, hadn't taken you away. Now you tell me that one of the men who did it was a good friend of yours?"

"Hey, I don't give two shits about your mama or your little sister. I'm only here for one reason. I'm getting paid ten thousand dollars to put a slug in your chest. What do you think about that?"

"I'll tell you what I know for sure. Cal Hardin gave me the ten thousand dollars and I have it on me right now. If you want it, you'll have to take it from me."

Sloan sneered at Jess. "I don't think that will be a problem."

"I hope you haven't spent any of the money yet."

"Not yet, but I'm thinking about buying Dixie's. I like the women there and I wouldn't mind coming back to town from time to time and causing all your friends here in town a little grief."

Jess realized now that his brother was no better than the Blake Taggerts of the world. He was just one more killer who needed to be put down, brother or not. Tim Sloan would go through life causing innocent people nothing but grief. He would continue to kill, rape, lie, cheat, and steal. Maybe it wasn't ultimately his fault and he was simply a product of his environment, but that didn't matter. In the end, no matter how you try to reason it out, Tim Sloan was a bad man and had to suffer the same fate that many others already had and many more to come, if Jess had his way.

Just then, Randolph Jackson walked out of Andy's and stopped on the porch. He had a shot of whiskey in his left hand, leaving his right hand free. "I just want you to know that I'm here to finish things if your brother can't."

Jess spoke to Randolph without taking his eyes off Tim Sloan. "You must be Nevada Jackson's brother, I take it?"

"That's right, and you're the little bastard who killed him."

"You know it was a fair fight. I didn't want to draw on your brother. The truth is, he forced it."

"That don't mean squat now. He's still dead and as his only brother it's my job to avenge his death."

"That'll be your choice but I'm going to warn you not to make even the slightest move until this is over. If you do, Andy, who is right behind you with that scattergun pointed at your back will blow you off the porch. If that don't kill you, I'll put a bullet in you without even thinking about it, understand?"

"I don't mind waiting my turn. I've been looking forward to it," replied Randolph, finishing his whiskey and throwing the shot glass out in the street. Jess's eyes turned to ice and Sloan saw something that he hadn't noticed until now. There was a sense of seething rage emanating from him. It made Sloan wonder for just a second or two, but nothing mattered now except the ten thousand dollars. He sneered at Jess.

"I suppose it's time to find out which one of us is faster," declared Sloan.

"I wouldn't have it any other way..." Jess had barely finished his last few words when Sloan went for his gun. Sloan got it partially out of the holster when Jess's first slug hit him square in the chest. He staggered back a few steps and dropped his gun, his hands trying to stop the flow of blood that was now making a large red stain on the front of his shirt. He stood there wobbling back and forth with a look of amazement on his face. He coughed, a little spittle of blood forming on his lips. He wheezed when he spoke.

"I guess we found out who was faster, huh?"

Jess still had his gun trained on his brother. "I guess we did."

"I suppose there's no sense in getting the doc either, huh?"

"Nope," he replied, the hardness showing on his face. "I wouldn't let him save you anyway, even if he could. I will do you one last favor though. I like your idea about granting a dying man his last wish."

"And what might that be?"

"I can put you out of your misery right now."

Sloan's knees were beginning to buckle a little now. He knew he didn't have much more than a minute left and it just didn't matter anymore.

"Go on and finish it now and let me die in the street standing with my boots on," Sloan replied, only a second away from collapsing.

Jess didn't hesitate. No sooner than Sloan had gotten the words out of his mouth, Jess fanned two shots. The first blew out Sloan's heart and the second hit him just above his eyes. He flew back and hit the dirt with a thud. Jess stood there for what was probably a whole minute looking at what he had done.

He had killed his own flesh and blood, his own brother. He had taken a big step over that imaginary line that most men won't cross under any circumstances, and yet, he was okay with it. He searched his heart to find some remorse for killing him, but he could only find pity. He felt sorrow for the fact that his brother never got the chance to turn out to be something else, someone better, but that was not Jess's doing.

He had kept an eye on Randolph who seemed to be acting somewhat different now. He hadn't moved during all of this. Probably because Andy was aiming his scattergun at his back and Tony had his Winchester trained on him at the same time so Jess knew he was covered. Of course, the main reason he hadn't moved a muscle was that he had witnessed the incredible hand speed that Jess had just demonstrated. He slowly began to empty the three spent cartridges from his pistol and reload it. He looked up at Randolph with a look that could make most men shudder.

"Well, Mr. Jackson, it seems it's your turn now," advised Jess, his voice low, but firm. He could see that Randolph was visibly shaken and still wouldn't move.

"I...I think I might have changed my mind about it. I mean, my brother is dead and this won't bring him back, so I'd be willing to call it off if that's okay with you."

Jess holstered his pistol and looked at Tony. Tony saw the look; he had seen it before and he knew it wasn't anything good for Randolph.

"I don't think so," said Jess, almost nonchalantly.

Randolph looked puzzled, as if he hadn't expected that answer. "So, you don't agree with me getting on my horse and riding out of town and forgetting this whole matter?"

"No, I surely don't."

"I don't understand. You know I can't beat you. Hell, even I know it now after I saw you draw that thing."

"Let me explain it to you so you do understand," said Jess. "You came here to kill me because I killed your brother, even though you knew it was a fair fight between Nevada and me. Now, you've seen me draw and you don't want to face me at this time. What you will do for sure though, is wait to see me somewhere in another little town or maybe follow my trail and shoot me in the back like a coward. I know men like you. You won't give up until you kill me. Since you know you can't do it fair, you'll do it any way you can, but you will try to do it, of that I'm sure. So, you're going to do it right here and right now. Get down off that porch and face me."

"What if I refuse?" exclaimed Randolph, still nervous, but now agitated.

"Then I'll just plug you right there on the porch where you stand. If you don't want to draw, that will be your choice and I won't take any blame in it. Don't make the mistake of thinking I won't do it, because I surely will." Jess heard Andy's voice holler out from inside the Saloon.

"He'll damn sure do it. I saw him do it before myself," hollered Andy.

Randolph was beside himself now, but he was smart enough to know he had run out of time. He had just watched this young man kill his own brother and that made him a man who would do the unthinkable. He knew he was doomed, but there was no way out of it now. And, he had his pride to think of. He would rather go out in a blaze of glory than be known as a coward who ran from a fight. He walked down the steps and into the street.

"Well, at least I'll be remembered as one of the many men who braced Jess Williams," said Randolph, mustering all the courage he could.

"Yes you will, and you will have something in common with your brother Nevada."

"Yeah, both murdered by the same man," replied Randolph, a hint of defiance in his voice. His eyes narrowed as he stared into Jess's eyes, seeing nothing but a darkness lurking in them. He slowly lowered his hand to the butt of his pistol. He steadied himself, waiting to feel the exact moment to draw.

Randolph went for his gun and when he did, Jess hesitated for a fraction of a second. Randolph saw it but he didn't stop his motion, hoping he might have a chance now. He didn't. Jess had given him that fraction of a second, but no more. Jess drew and fired two rounds into Randolph's chest. Randolph staggered back and fell right next to Sloan's body. He was dead before he hit the ground. Jess holstered his pistol after reloading it and Tony walked up next to him.

"Jess, why did you hesitate like that?" asked Tony.

Jess looked at him oddly. "You know, I'm not really sure. Maybe it was because I didn't give him any choice I felt I owed it to him, but I don't quite know for sure. It just seemed to happen. Maybe something in the back of my brain was trying to stop me from killing

Randolph and let him ride out of town and that made me hesitate. I'm not sure I'll ever know for certain."

"Maybe there's hope for you yet."

Jess looked at Tony, not quite sure of what he meant. "I do know one thing for certain."

"What's that?"

"I think I'm always going to have a long list of men to watch for over my shoulder, but these two won't be on it."

Andy came out of the saloon, his shotgun slung over his shoulder. He looked at Jess with frustration. The onlookers all started to go back to their shops and homes.

"Are ya finished fer jest a little while now?" asked Andy. "I'd like ta have a little peace and quiet for maybe a day or two."

Jess put his hand on Andy's shoulder. "I think that's a great idea, Andy."

"Might as well. You done killed everybody what needed killin', 'cept for that man, Randolph," said Andy. "I'm not sure you shoulda done that."

"Yeah, but it wouldn't have been you he would have been looking for tomorrow or the next day, it would have been me."

"I suppose I can't argue with ya on that one."

The undertaker came and took the bodies away, but not before Jess removed his brother's gun belt from him. He took Randolph's pistol and holster. He kept his brother's but gave Randolph's to Tony.

Tony took it and smiled. "I suppose this is your way of building up some credit at the livery?"

Jess smiled back at him. "You could say that."

"Let's go have a drink and relax for a bit," suggested Tony.

"Damn good idea," exclaimed Andy, "and I'm a buyin'."

"You sure are getting generous lately, Andy," declared Jess.

"Well, I figure I gotta stay on your good side. I seen what you do to people on yer bad side," he said keenly.

Jess grabbed the envelope that Hardin had given him and showed it to both Andy and Tony.

"I have a better idea, Andy. I think it's only fair that Tim Sloan pay for the drinks since he won't be having any use for this money now." Both Andy and Tony nodded in silent agreement. Both also noticed that Jess had not referred to Tim Sloan as his brother.

EPILOGUE

Andy, Jess, and Tony headed to the saloon and were met by Jim Smythe along the way. The four of them sat at a table and drank a bottle of Andy's best whiskey. They all shared their thoughts about everything that had happened over the last several months. They talked about how Carter had taken over the town and how Jess had come back to Black Creek to release the town from his greedy claws. Carter and his bunch of hired killers were gone, never to cause the town any trouble again. They talked about Jess's brother and how that had all played out. Jim, Andy, and Tony did most of the talking, Jess adding a comment now and then.

"Well, Jess, what now for you?" probed Tony. "You want to reconsider that sheriff's badge?"

"No thanks, Tony. I've got to move on in a few days. I think I'll head south toward Mexico and warmer weather."

"Might that have a little something to do with your father?" Jim asked.

"I suppose so."

"Well, ya don't need to be in no hurry," submitted Andy. "You should stay in town a few days and relax."

"Actually, I'm going to do that, believe it or not. I need to take care of a few things. In fact, you boys can help me with some of it. Tony, I need you to make me a new leather sling for my scattergun and knife."

"I'll make it look real nice for you," agreed Tony.

"Jim," Jess said as he turned to him, "I need that new double-barreled twelve-gauge I saw behind your counter. I'm going to have

Tony here cut it down a little more and then shave off the stock some to make it more like a pistol handle like this." He took Andy's scattergun and showed Tony how he wanted it cut down and the handle shaved.

"Consider it done, my friend," said Tony, still looking over the scattergun and mentally making notes as to how he would do it. The four of them all raised their glasses and tapped them together in friendship.

Over the next few days, Jess relaxed and wandered around town, spending time with Jim and Sara, along with Tony and Andy. Most of the townsfolk were friendly although some would not even exchange glances with him. He sensed it wasn't because they didn't like him; it was more that they were fearful of what he had become. The preacher in town tried to give him a spiritual lesson on the evils of killing, but he politely told him to work his words on someone who was listening. He knew there was no way he could make any preacher understand what he was doing.

"You do your work, and I'll do mine," Jess told him.

He paid a visit to the gunsmith in town and had him load some ammo for him. He had him make some special loads for his pistol. He had the gunsmith reduce the powder slightly as well as the slug. That would reduce the kick a little, but still deliver deadly results. He thought it would help when fanning the pistol. He switched out Gray and the packhorse for the two long horses. He got supplies for his trip south. He purchased extra stock ammo from Jim along with the best spyglass Jim had in stock.

He stayed with Jim and Sara, in the same spare room upstairs where he had stayed the day his family was murdered. He remembered that day as if it were yesterday and mostly because he made sure to remember it every day. It was those thoughts that gave him the strength and drive that made him the man he had become. It was the hatred he felt for the men who had murdered his family that allowed him to do things most men couldn't. Like shooting Deke Moore, wounded and sitting in the middle of the street unarmed, or forcing Randolph Jackson to brace him in the middle of the street.

He knew that most people couldn't understand the way he looked at things. Maybe that was because they couldn't feel the rage that he felt. It didn't matter to him that some people would never accept his way of dealing with bad men. All that really mattered is that he believed in what he was doing.

He was looking at himself in the same mirror he had looked into that very day that his life had changed from normal to something very different and dangerous. He could see it in his own face: the loneliness, the sadness, and the coldness underneath his eyes, hidden deep until someone made the fatal mistake of bringing it forward. He finished washing his face and went down for breakfast with Jim and Sara.

Jess was leaving today and Jim and Sara were sad about that, but they were grateful that they had at least been able to keep him with them for a few days. They talked, ate, and simply enjoyed each other's conversation, but it was time to say goodbye, for now.

"Are you certain you won't stay for one more day?" Sara asked.

"I'd like to, but I have to get moving. It's going to get cold soon and I've discovered that I don't like it much, especially when I'm riding the trail most of the time," he replied.

"Well, it was sure nice to have you around for a little, especially when you ain't shooting someone," laughed Jim. "Hell, it's been almost three days now since you shot someone."

Jess grinned. "I don't really take much joy in shooting someone, but if it needs doing, I don't mind it much either." He stood up and put his hat on.

Sara gave him a long hug and kissed him on his cheek. Jim did the same, but left out the kissing part. Jess turned, walked out and headed for the livery where he knew Tony had been getting his horses and his things ready. He had told Tony he would be leaving today. As he walked into the livery, Tony was sitting with Andy, waiting for him.

"Morning, you two," Jess said. "Time for me to move on." Tony and Andy stood up and both shook his hand.

"You goin' lookin' for yer father, eh," asked Andy.

Jess looked at Andy and then over to Tony. "Tony, I think Andy might just be getting a little smarter each day."

"Yeah," chuckled Tony, "but still not smart enough to keep his yap shut when he should." They all laughed at that.

"You sure you don't want to take LeAnn with ya?" asked Andy, his hopes dangling on a thin string.

"Not a chance in hell, Andy. But you knew that already," replied Jess, smiling.

"Well, ya can't blame a man for tryin'."

"That's exactly what I was talking about," Tony said, laughing. "The man can't keep his yap shut."

Jess walked his horses out of the livery and swung up in the saddle. He had decided to call his new horses the same names, Gray and Sharps. He liked to keep things simple. He nodded his head to Tony and Andy and turned his horse toward the end of the street.

As he walked his horse out of town, some of the townsfolk waved at him as if to say thank you. He felt good about that. As he got to the end of the street, he saw an old woman sitting on her porch in a rocking chair. She stood up as he reached her place. She was the old woman who had spoken to him back in Carter's Hardware store the day he chased all the customers out and over to Jim's store. He halted his horses and turned to look directly at her.

"You take good care of yourself, young Mr. Williams. Some of the people in town won't say it, but most of them are grateful for what you did. As for me, you keep doing it. There are a lot of people out there who need someone like you even though they might not know it."

He smiled at her and removed his hat in respect. "Why ma'am, I think that's probably the nicest thing anyone has ever said to me," he said. "Thank you. I promise you that I will continue doing what seems to have turned out to be my life's work. You take care of your-self, ma'am," he said and he turned his horses and rode out of town.

As he rode that first day, he thought a lot about what had happened. He thought about his father and where he might find him and when. It didn't matter, just so long as he finally did. When that day arrived, he would deal with him in the same manner as he had his brother. He smiled at the irony of being the one to collect the ten thousand that Carter had paid to have him killed.

It was a cold, but sunny day with just a slight hint of a breeze. He shuddered a little, not from the cold though. It was because he remembered Andy asking him to take LeAnn with him.

The End

SINS OF THE FATHER

A JESS WILLIAMS WESTERN
THIRD IN THE SERIES

This book is dedicated to my brother, Tony, who fought the good fight against lung cancer. He is an inspiration to us all. He showed more bravery than I thought possible and I am very proud of him. His walk through life was a tough one from the day he was born and yet he faced every complication that was thrown his way and he did it with a stern determination that he would overcome any and all obstacles put in his path. He was a better person for it and a better man than any other I know. Tony, we all love you and are truly proud to have been blessed to have you as a brother and a part of all of our lives.

ACKNOWLEDGEMENTS

Thanks to Dave Hile from Hile Illustrations for the magnificent artwork on the front cover. He did the holster and all the artwork within the holster. His talent for detail is remarkable.

Thanks to Barb Gunia from Sans Serif for the rest of the cover design. She is responsible for everything on the cover outside the holster and is always a pleasure to work with.

Thanks to my wonderful, beautiful and talented wife, Jill.

Thanks again to Ted Williams Jr., who is once again depicted on the cover as Jess Williams. He never fails to amaze me.

Thanks to Michael J. Reddy, Sr., who is depicted on the front cover as Frank Reedy, a bounty hunter turned U.S. Marshal. Mike is also a Publisher with Immortal Investments Publishing. He has published many famous sports celebrities' books.

Thanks to Mark Neal who is depicted on the front cover as Eddie Sloan.

CHAPTER ONE

Spring of 1880

"Mister, I don't even know your name. You don't have to do this."
"You don't need to know my name; all you need to know is
that I'm going to be the one who can brag that I took down Jess
Williams."

"Mister, dead men don't brag, and if you plan on pulling that
smoke wagon, that's exactly what you're going to be. Why don't you
let me buy you a drink and forget about this whole thing? I don't
have any beef with you."

"What you think don't matter to me. Everyone keeps talking
about how fast you are with that fancy pistol of yours and I don't
believe it. I ain't been beat on the draw yet and you ain't gonna be
any different. I know I can beat you."

Jess found himself in yet another confrontation with a gunslinger that he had no desire to brace but he would have no choice
in the matter. If he didn't draw on the man, the man would simply
go for his pistol and shoot Jess. The only other option for Jess was
to admit that the other man was faster and walk out of the saloon
and be considered yellow. That was not an option that Jess was ever
going to choose. He had been on the trail of his father for almost
two years now and he had been in more saloons in little towns than
he could remember. The confrontations had become all too familiar and all too often. His reputation as a man with a lightning-fast
hand had spread widely, and he couldn't go anywhere now without
some gunslinger recognizing him and of course, challenging him.

He didn't like it and he didn't want it, but there wasn't much he could do about it. The results were always the same. Another gunslinger would lie dead on the floor or in the middle of the street. Then the reputation would grow even more and attract more men who would search him out just to challenge him.

That's exactly what Bear Deever was doing right now. He had spotted Jess as soon as Jess had walked into the little saloon and stepped up to the bar. He wanted to claim the reputation of beating Jess Williams and he wanted it bad enough to put his life on the line to get it.

Jess put his beer down on the bar and turned slightly to face Deever, who was standing next to the table he had been sitting at when Jess had walked into the saloon. "Well, Mister, if I can't talk you out of this, then we might as well get it over with. I don't understand why a man would want to end his life over nothing, but if that's what you want to do, I reckon it's not my place to keep you from doing something stupid."

Deever gave Jess a sarcastic look. "Ain't you getting a little ahead of yourself? We ain't even drawn yet, and you're already predicting the outcome. You ain't one of them mind readers, are you?"

"Nope, I've just seen this too many times before."

"Well, you're going to see something else today. You ain't been braced by Bear Deever yet."

"Yeah, and I have a hunch that it won't ever happen again."

That pushed Bear Deever over the edge. He had been talking long enough to get up the courage to pull on Jess. He went for his gun and his hand got the Colt halfway out of the holster when the slug from Jess's pistol hit Bear Deever straight through the heart, dropping him instantly. Jess looked around the saloon. Seeing no other threat, he put his pistol back in the holster, but not before reloading the one spent cartridge. He turned back to the bar and the bartender brought him another beer.

"That son of a bitch has been itching for a fight since he came to town yesterday," the bartender said, setting the beer down in front of Jess.

"That's the way it is with men like him," replied Jess. "They have no regard for any life including their own. He would have gotten himself shot sooner or later, and if it hadn't been me, it would have been someone else."

The bartender smiled. "Well, I'm glad it was here, and I'm glad it was you."

"Really? Why is that?"

"Because I've heard a lot about you and that fancy pistol of yours and I always hoped that I would see it in action for myself. It was hard to believe that any man could draw a pistol that fast."

"Well, now you've seen it."

"Yeah, but I'm still having a hard time believing it," said the bartender, as he began to walk away to wait on another man who had walked up to the bar.

Jess picked up his beer and took a long drink of it. It tasted good. He had been on the trail of his father, Eddie Sloan, since the fall of 1878. It was now early spring and he had come up from Mexico to this little town of Kern in the southwestern corner of Texas. It was just another one-street town with one hotel, one saloon and a few other small shops. Kern didn't even have a town sheriff. The only law here was a gun and any man brave or stupid enough to use it.

He had found his father's trail more than a dozen times, but each time he lost the trail or got distracted from his hunt due to the profession he was in. Bounty hunting was an unpredictable business and you never knew when the next large bounty would come up. He would travel to some small town where he heard that Eddie Sloan had taken money, and sometimes the lives of the men who thought they could beat Sloan at poker, only to find a wanted poster of some low life murderer with a bounty on his head. He would go on the hunt for the man and after he brought the dead body in and collected the bounty, he would start his hunt for his father again. The trail would be cold but that did not deter Jess. He would simply keep looking for his father until he finally caught up with him and it didn't really matter when it would happen, just as long as it did.

A couple of cowboys helped the bartender drag the body of Bear Deever out of the saloon. The bartender came back in and refilled Jess's glass. "Well, Mr. Williams, what were you asking me about before Deever interrupted with his request to get a look at his next life?"

Jess took another long sip on his beer. "I'm looking for a man by the name of Eddie Sloan. I heard he was here working a poker game recently."

The bartender, whose name was Nash, raised his eyebrows. "He was here about a month ago. He set up his game right over there at that table. Game ran about a week and he drained every dollar from every man who tried to beat him. A couple of the men who lost their money to him claimed he was cheating somehow, but no one could see it. He is a slick one, that's for sure. What do you want with him?"

"I just need him to answer a few questions."

"Well, he ain't the friendly type, if you know what I mean."

"I've heard that about him before. Any idea of where he might have headed to?"

"Seems like I remember him saying something about a big game up in Abilene, Kansas. Lots of players with lots of money the way I heard it."

Jess finished his beer and put some money on the bar. "Well, I'm sure that's where he's headed so I guess that's where I'm going next."

The bartender smiled when he saw the five dollars Jess had left on the bar. "Why thanks, Mr. Williams. This is the biggest tip I've ever had."

"You're welcome. And thanks for the information. I'm going to turn in early tonight and get a fresh start in the morning," said Jess, as he turned to walk out of the saloon.

"Hey, you sure you don't want to hang around and play with a few of the other local hot heads in town? There's a few more need plugging, if you know what I mean."

Jess turned back and smiled. "No thanks. I'm no lawman, but if you know of someone who has a bounty on his head, you let me know."

Jess walked out and headed for the only hotel in town. There was no name on the hotel, just a sign that read "rooms for rent." He paid for one night and went up to his room and turned in.

~ ~

Jed ducked just in time to hear two shots ring out so close together that they sounded as one. The first slug was from Harlan Woolsey's pistol and it shattered a bottle of cheap tequila on a shelf behind the bar. The second slug was from Sheriff Mark Steele's Colt .45 Peacemaker and it made its way straight through the heart of Harlan Woolsey, dropping him like a sack of potatoes. There were several other men in the saloon but they were not going to be involved in any further gunplay against Steele.

Two of the men in the saloon had come in with Harlan Woolsey. Mike Winters and Jeramiah Paxton were hired guns of Rance Madden, but not quite the caliber that Harlan Woolsey was. They had come to town to watch Woolsey brace Sheriff Steele and then go back to the Double 'M' ranch and brag to Rance Madden that Sheriff Steele was now officially out of the way. Instead, they would have to go back to the Double 'M' carting the dead body of one of Madden's best hired guns.

Steele reloaded his Peacemaker. "You boys go back and tell your boss that this has got to stop. There has been enough killing the last few months to last a lifetime. Tell Madden that I want to set a meeting between him and Henry Thornton in a few days to see if we can settle this war once and for all. I'm sending the same message to Thornton. We will meet here at Jed's Saloon, Wednesday at noon."

Mike Winters sneered at Steele. "Yeah? And what if he don't want to meet with Thornton?"

"You tell him whoever doesn't show for the meeting will be the one I'll hold more responsible for this whole damn mess and the full weight of the law will come down hard on him. I'm sending for a U.S. marshal along with some deputies to straighten this thing out."

It was Jeramiah's turn to sneer. "Rance Madden will just hire some more guns. He's got more money than Thornton and the whole town combined. You can get all the marshals and deputies you like. It won't make any difference."

"Just make sure he gets the message."

"We'll tell him, but he ain't gonna be happy about it."

Now it was Steele's turn to sneer. "If that man has ever had a day when he was happy, I sure as hell missed it. Now get that dead weight out of here before it starts to stink the place up."

Winters and Paxton carried out Woolsey's body and tied it to his horse. Steele turned back to the bar to face Jed, who had a shot of good whiskey waiting for him. Steele downed it quickly and Jed filled the shot glass again.

"Sheriff, you can't keep taking on all these hired guns. Sooner or later, Madden will hire one faster than you and one that can aim better than this last one. Woolsey outdrew you but he missed. I hope you weren't kidding when you said you were sending for a U.S. marshal and some more deputies."

Steele slammed the second shot down as quickly as the first. "I wasn't kidding. I'm going to send the message out right now. A good man knows his limitations and I've reached mine. I hate to admit it, but this thing is just too big for one sheriff and a few local deputies to handle."

"So, who are you sending for?"

"A good friend of mine by the name of Frank Reedy. He went and pinned on a U.S. marshal's badge recently. I guess he got tired of the bounty hunting business. We've called on one another over the years and I guess it's his turn again."

"Well, he'd better be damn good and just as tough. You got a war brewing and I don't think it will be over until a lot more men get killed."

"Oh, he's good, and tougher than most men you would meet. He doesn't rattle in a fight. I'm going to ask him to bring at least two deputies with him. With my deputies here in town that will give us six good men. That's not an army, but it might get the job done."

"Well, you're more optimistic than I am. I think it's going to take more than that to put this problem to rest. Hell, I ain't made a profit since I bought this damn bar. I can't afford to replace the mirror behind the bar again and I've lost dozens of bottles of whiskey. My damn floor is drunker than any cowboy who leaves here, as much as been spilled on it."

Steele thanked Jed for the whiskey and headed straight for the telegraph office. He jotted down a note and handed it to the telegraph operator. "Send this message to these fifteen towns I have listed at the bottom of the message."

"Yes, sir, Sheriff. I'll get to it right away."

Steele walked back to his office. On the way, he stopped one of Thornton's men and gave him the same message he had sent to Madden. He hoped that Frank Reedy would get the message soon. He had bought himself a few more days with the meeting he was setting up between Rance Madden and Henry Thornton. The two ranch owners had been deadlocked in a bitter dispute over water rights to the one small river that ran through the area. Thornton had built a few retention ponds on his land to give his cattle enough water through the dry times. When the dry times hit, there was hardly enough water for the old Mason spread, which was now owned by Rance Madden.

Mason was bad enough when he owned the spread, but Rance Madden was much worse. He cared little for any other human beings or their needs and he would not hesitate to send his hired guns out to run out or kill another rancher who might get in his way. His plan was to eventually own everything in this area, but Henry Thornton had grown his cattle ranch from less than one hundred head over twenty years ago to over three thousand head today. Madden had offered Thornton twice what the Triple 'D' was worth but Thornton wasn't about to sell. Thornton's ranch had been established long before Rance Madden came to this valley and Thornton swore that he would be put in his grave before he sold out to the likes of Rance Madden. The possibility of that happening was growing with each passing day unless Sheriff Steele could somehow resolve what he was beginning to think was an impossible problem.

It mattered little to Madden that Thornton had refused his offer. He would simply use the money he offered Thornton to hire the best gunmen that money could buy. His overall plan was to drive Thornton off the property or eventually kill Thornton and every one of his men. Madden already had at least a dozen fairly good gunmen and he had sent a few of them, along with Harlen Woolsey, to get rid of the one problem still standing in his way of settling his dispute with Thornton. That problem was Sheriff Mark Steele. Now that Steele had taken down Harlen Woolsey, Madden's best man, Madden would have to send for another fast gun for hire. It would cost him a lot of money, but it would still be cheaper than buying Thornton out.

Mark Steele pondered all of this as he sat in his little office. He knew that he was running out of time and cheating death every day. Steele was fast with a gun, but he was smart enough to know that someone out there was faster and all Madden had to do was to find him and hire him. His message to Frank Reedy was:

> *Frank,*
> *Make your way to Timber, Texas, as fast as a horse will carry you. This is of the utmost urgency. Bring two deputies with you.*
> *Your friend,*
> *Mark Steele*

Steele knew that as soon as the message found Frank Reedy, he would drop whatever he was doing and head to Timber to help. He just hoped that it wouldn't be too late.

CHAPTER TWO

Mike Winters and Jeramiah Paxton arrived back at the Double 'M' with Harlen Woolsey's body draped over his horse. They dismounted and handed the reins of Woolsey's horse to one of the other hired guns. "Here, go and bury him out back by the others," said Paxton. Sheriff Steele had already killed three men so far and they were buried out on a hillside behind Madden's large house. Harlan Woolsey would be the fourth. Winters and Paxton went inside to talk to Rance, which was something they were not looking forward to. They knew their boss would be in an unusually foul mood over losing Woolsey. They found Madden sitting at the large dining table. The glare on his face told them that he had seen the dead body already.

Madden glanced up at them with a disappointed look. "I thought you two said Woolsey was the best. I guess you were wrong about that."

Paxton and Winters sat down after pouring themselves cups of hot coffee. Paxton was the first to speak. "Well, boss, we said he was one of the best."

"Oh, and that's supposed to make me feel better?"

"I know you're upset but we can get another fast gun. Hell, there are plenty of them out there."

Winters broke in. "Boss, I know of another man we could send for. Actually, he works with a partner most of the time and I bet you could hire them both. They are both fast and meaner than a basket of snakes."

"All right, tell me who they are and where they might be. I'll send for them both."

"They won't be cheap. You'll have to pay more than you did for Harlen."

"Well, Harlen obviously wasn't a good investment. I don't care what it costs; I need Sheriff Steele dead before I can run off Henry Thornton."

Paxton spoke again. "We have a message from Sheriff Steele for you about Thornton."

"What message?"

"The sheriff has set a meeting up between you and Henry Thornton for Wednesday at Jed's Saloon."

"Screw Sheriff Steele! I'm not going to any meeting with Thornton."

"The sheriff said whoever didn't show up at the meeting would be held responsible for this whole matter. If you don't go, he'll side with Thornton. You know that Thornton will go to the meeting. He would love to have Steele on his side in this thing."

Madden shook his head in disgust. "That sheriff is beginning to be a huge pain in my back side. He keeps killing my men and now he's going to try to force an agreement between me and Thornton. I guess I'll have to go to the meeting, but the only thing I'm going to agree on is that Thornton sells out to me. Now, who are these two men you mentioned?"

Winters finished his coffee and set his cup down on the table. "Quentin Unger and Gregory Timmons. Last I heard, they were up in Wichita. You want me to send for them?"

"Hell yes, and the sooner the better. I want the two of you to go into town right now and send a message to them. Tell them what the job is and that they'll be compensated very well for it. Tell them I'll pay each one of them one thousand dollars if either of them kills Steele."

Paxton and Winters both stood up and started for the door. "I'll bet that'll get them here sooner rather than later," replied Paxton. "That's a lot of money."

"I just hope they're as good as you say they are."

"Oh, they are. I can promise you that either of them is twice as fast as Harlen was," replied Winters.

Paxton and Winters mounted up and headed into town to the telegraph office to send the message to Unger and Timmons. Rance Madden watched them until they were out of sight. He thought about the meeting on Wednesday and a hateful look came over his face. "I'll have something to tell the sheriff at the meeting, that's for sure," he said to no one but himself.

Sheriff Steele woke up to a gloomy Wednesday morning. The sky was heavy with dark clouds and he could smell rain in the air. He walked briskly through the damp cool air over to the only saloon in town where he knew Pattie was cooking up breakfast. He sat down at a table and watched the bartender, Jed, rearrange some bottles behind the bar. There were only a few men in the saloon and they were concentrating on their plates of food as if they were on a mission.

Pattie Nate came through the door from the kitchen with two more plates of food and set them down at a table where a man sat alone. He began shoving food into his mouth before she let go of the plates. She had smiled at Steele as she walked past him and now she sat down at the table with him.

"Well, Sheriff Mark Steele, how is this day starting out for you?"

"No better than the last several days have gone. I have a meeting set up with Madden and Thornton this afternoon and I'm not looking forward to it one bit."

"I guess not. Those two men are going to ruin this town before their feud is over with."

"I'm not going to let that happen."

"How are you going to stop it? Between the two of them, they have a small army. Every time one of them hires another gunman, the other goes out and hires two more. You can't handle this with the few deputies you have and no one else will let you pin a badge on him. You're lucky to still be alive."

"I sent for some help a few days ago."

"I'm glad to see you finally got some sense. Who did you send for?"

"My old pal, Frank Reedy, and I told him to bring some help."

"I thought he was in the bounty hunting business."

"He was, but he done got himself a U.S. marshal's badge. I guess that whole thing between him, Spicer, and that Williams kid soured him and he decided to get back into the law business."

"That's who you should send for."

"That's what I just said."

"No, I'm not talking about Frank Reedy; I'm talking about that nice young man, Jess Williams."

Steele shook his head. "No, that boy has had to face some tough things for a young man of his age. You know, he finally found his brother."

"And what happened?"

"He killed him and then he forced Nevada Jackson's brother, Randolph, into a gunfight and killed him, too. Hell, I guess it ain't his fault but he is a man-killer of a different sort from what I've ever seen in my entire life. If I called him here he would probably go and just shoot Madden and Thornton and get it over with."

"Maybe that's exactly what needs to happen."

"Pattie, I'm a lawman. I believe in the law and I have to abide by its rules."

"Even if it gets you killed?"

"Yes, now go and fetch me some of what you gave those other men. It sure looks and smells awfully good."

"It's always good. You should think some more about what I said."

Sheriff Steele shook his head again and Pattie headed back into the kitchen to get him some breakfast. He thought about what she had said but he withdrew the idea from his head. I'm trying to stop a war, not start one, he thought to himself. Pattie brought the food out and he began to eat.

Quentin Unger and Gregory Timmons were locked in a hot game of poker with several other men in a saloon in Wichita, called Jake's Place. Unger was winning and Timmons was losing. A young boy ran into the saloon and stood next to Quentin Unger with a piece of paper in his hand.

"What the hell you want, boy?" Unger demanded. The boy said nothing but simply handed the message to Unger and ran off. Unger unfolded it and read it. A smile came to his lips. He looked over at his partner Timmons, who was now getting curious.

"What does it say?" Timmons asked.

"It seems we have a paying job if we want to ride on down to Timber, Texas," replied Unger.

"What kind of job?"

"It looks like we're being hired to kill a sheriff."

Timmons smiled. "Well, as long as we get paid a lot of money for doing it. Killing a law-dog puts a mark on a man for life."

"It says here that we will each be paid the sum of one thousand dollars no matter which one of us kills the sheriff."

"One thousand dollars? Well, that is a lot of money for one man, even if he is a sheriff. When do we leave, partner?"

"I'd say first thing in the morning. Why don't you stay here and try to win some of your money back while I go over to the supply store and provision us for the ride. I'll send a message back to this Mr. Madden and tell him that we'll take the job."

"That sounds good to me, partner. Let's meet back here for supper tonight. Unless I win some of my money back, you're buying."

Unger smirked at Timmons. "Some things never change."

Quentin Unger headed for the mercantile to get the supplies they would need for their ride to Timber. Unger was usually a cool-headed man but he also had a mean temper just below the surface, and if you riled him, he could instantly turn dark and ugly. He had killed his first man when he was seventeen. The man was drunk and insulting everyone in the saloon they were in and eventually he got around to insulting Quentin who was minding his own business. Unger ignored the first insult and the man hurled another insult at

Unger and that's when Quentin Unger's temper flared up and he invited the drunken fool out to the street. He shot the man straight through the chest. Unger's temper was so bad, he actually went over to the dead man and began kicking his dead body in the street until a few men pulled him away. Unger finally cooled down and went back into the saloon. He had killed quite a few men since that day and he would hire out his gun to anyone who paid the most money. He didn't have any conscience and thought nothing of shooting a man in the front or in the back. He finished packing up the supplies at the livery and headed back to the saloon to have dinner with Timmons.

Gregory Timmons had won all of his money back along with some more. He wore a big smile when Unger walked back into the saloon. "Hey, partner, 1 guess supper is on me tonight since I won some money while you've been gone."

"About damn time," replied Unger.

They moved to another table and ordered two huge steaks with potatoes and carrots. "I think our luck might be changing for the better," said Timmons. "I finally won some money and we have a job that will pay quite handsomely, and all in one day."

"Yeah, well, don't get too excited. You'll probably lose your money in the next card game and we can't be certain about this job, either. We won't know until we get to Timber and meet up with this Rance Madden fellow."

"Hell, you always try to take all the fun out of things, partner."

"And you take things a little too lightly," replied Unger. "Let's turn in early tonight and get started first thing in the morning."

Timmons nodded in agreement and they finished their meals in silence. They turned in and rode out of town the next morning just as soon as it was light enough to see.

CHAPTER THREE

Jess rode out of Kern, Texas at daylight with a fresh load of supplies. It would be a long ride up to Abilene, Kansas. He knew the nights would get colder as he went north since it was early spring so he had purchased an extra blanket for warmth before leaving Kern. He always enjoyed being out on the open range. He didn't mind staying in towns and getting a hot bath once in a while, but he felt more at home on the trail. He had become quite an expert shot with the Sharps rifle over the last couple years. It was high noon and the sun was shining through a slight hint of high thin clouds. The quiet on the trail felt comfortable to Jess. He was coming to the top of a hill when the silence was broken by the sound of gunshots. He prodded Gray and stopped just below the top of the hill. He ground-reined Gray knowing he would not move even in the presence of gunfire. He grabbed his telescope, climbed to the top of the ridge, and placed himself on the ground between two rocks.

He did not like what he saw. There was a lone wagon at the bottom of the hillside, angled so that he could see inside the back of the tent covering. He saw a man, a young boy and a woman firing rifles in the opposite direction. Jess raised his gaze to the top of the opposite hillside and spotted three men, one by one. They were spread apart by about fifteen feet each and were firing rifles down at the wagon. They had already killed both horses that had been pulling the wagon so the people inside were helplessly trapped. The family inside had only the wood sides of the wagon and a few boxes of supplies that they had piled up on that side of the wagon to protect themselves. They were at a bad angle for the rifle fire coming from the top of the hill.

Jess had looked at each man and figured them for robbers or worse. Jess didn't know for sure about the facts of what was taking place but he did know that any men firing on a woman and a young boy were bad men and needed to be dealt with. Then he saw her, a young girl about the same age as his sister Samantha was when she had been raped and killed. Jess knew what he had to do.

He immediately went into action. He grabbed the Sharps, the forked stick and a leather pouch that he had made to carry the rounds for the Sharps. The pouch had an extra-long flap so Jess could set rounds on the flap and keep them out of the dirt. He also grabbed his Winchester. Jess checked for wind. There was only a slight breeze going left to right. He sighted in on his first target. He was an older-looking man with a beard and wearing a red bandana. Jess figured the distance to be about three hundred yards. He aimed a little high and to the left of the man. The Sharps barked loudly creating echoes around the hillsides. A second later, the man on the other hillside slumped over and rolled down the hill.

All the shooting stopped for a few seconds. Everyone was trying to find out where this new firing was coming from. Jess had counted on that and he used it to his advantage. He took careful aim and hit the second target, a younger man who looked to be about in his twenties. This man flew back and landed solidly. The 50-caliber bullet had blown most of his brains out the back of his head. The third man now had located Jess and started firing at Jess's location but the family in the wagon peppered him with so many rounds that he ran off behind the hillside before Jess could get off another shot. Jess knew exactly what he had to do.

He untied the packhorse, Sharps, and tied him to a small tree and mounted Gray with the Sharps gun and the ammo pouch. He headed Gray down the hillside to the right and up the other hillside, allowing Gray to go as fast as he could on the rocky terrain. He only hoped he would get there in time. He got to where the three men had been. Two horses were still tied up to a tree. A cloud of dust was settling on the trail below the hill. Luckily for Jess, that side of the hill was quite rocky and had slowed the man's escape, but now the man had hit flat ground and was at a full run. Jess found a good boulder, placed the Sharps on it and sighted the man in. He was going to lose him so he did what he had to do, even though he didn't want to. He shot the man's horse out from under him. The horse tumbled forward, throwing the man about ten feet into the air and he landed in a cloud of dust. "I'm sorry," he said to the horse, knowing the horse couldn't hear him.

The man crawled upright and was trying to run, but he was slowed down by his right leg, which had either been broken or badly injured by the fall. "Well, you're not going to get too far," Jess said to no one but himself. Jess took careful aim and his first shot landed just to the right of the man and about six feet in front of him. He turned around and was screaming back at the top of the hillside where Jess was. "Yeah, that's it. Stand real still for me," said Jess as he fired off his second shot, which hit the man right in the middle of his chest. He fell back flat on the ground. Jess didn't see the man move, but he couldn't be sure that he was really dead. He took careful aim and put two more shots into the man, making sure he would never get up again and saving Jess from having to walk Gray down the steep slope of the rocky hillside to make sure the man was truly dead.

Jess retrieved his packhorse and rode down the hillside toward the wagon. He had put the Sharps back in the scabbard, but he had his Winchester across his lap, just in case. The people were still in the wagon, probably afraid to come out and wondering if Jess was a savior or just a new robber. Jess hit flat ground but stayed about a hundred feet from the wagon. "Hey in there, I don't mean you any harm. I'll put my Winchester away. My pistol is already holstered. I'll walk up slowly."

"You're damn right you will; we ain't taking any chances right now," the man in the wagon replied.

"I don't blame you one bit. Just be careful with those rifles." All three of them in the wagon had their rifles aimed directly at Jess.

"You don't have to worry anymore about the three men up on the hillside; they're all dead."

"What about the one that got away?" the man in the wagon asked.

"He didn't get away. He's lying on the ground over on the other side of the hill with three fifty-caliber slugs in him." Jess finally reached the back of the wagon and the man, woman and the boy looked him over real good.

"What's your name?" asked the woman.

"My name is Jess Williams, ma'am."

The woman put her rifle down and looked over at her husband. "Hadley, I think he means us no harm. After all, he shot those other men and he could have just kept shooting from the hillside at us if had wanted to. I think we have found a friend in this godforsaken place."

Hadley nodded in agreement and put his rifle down. "Put your rifle down, son."

The young boy did as he was told. As he did, a little girl's head slowly rose up from behind the back of the wagon. "Hi. My name is Jessica," she said as she reached her hand out to shake hands with Jess. Jess took her hand and helped her out of the wagon and the other three jumped out as well.

"Father," said the woman, "I think introductions are in order."

Hadley nodded as he put his hand out and shook hands with Jess. "Mighty grateful you were passing by and saved us. We would never have survived if you hadn't. I would hate to think of what would have happened to the women. Anyway, my name is Hadley Brown and this is my wife, Jane, my son, Harold, and my youngest, Jessica."

"Well, I'm mighty pleased to meet you and I'm glad I happened to come along at the right time. You sure were in a whole heap of trouble."

"You're not wrong about that. What in the hell's the matter with people out here? Hell, we didn't do anything to those men. We was just passing through on our way to a new homestead outside of Abilene, up in Kansas. We came through these two hillsides and they just opened fire, killing my horses right off."

"Where are you folks from?"

"We're from back East where people don't shoot at each other, unless they have a good reason."

"Well, Mr. Brown, men out here don't need any reason to start shooting. Sometimes they want your money and sometimes they just need to kill someone to make their day go a little better. It doesn't make any sense to me either, but I see it all the time."

Jane looked at her husband and Jess. "Well, I might as well start a camp and get a fire going and feed everyone. All this excitement has sure got me hungry."

Jess looked back up at the hillsides. "I don't think you want to make camp here, ma'am. I suggest we find some better surroundings first. This is a great ambush spot for any other men who might be looking for someone to rob."

"Well, how do you suggest we move the wagon? Both of our horses are dead. Can we use your two horses?"

Jess grinned. "No, ma'am. Those are two of the finest long horses you'll ever see. They won't be pulling any wagons, now or ever."

"Well, then what do you suggest we do, pull the wagon ourselves?" Jane asked, sounding a little agitated.

"There are two horses tied up behind the top of that hill over there. I have a hunch the men that owned them won't be using them any longer. Hadley, unhook your wagon from your dead horses. I'm going up there and retrieve them."

"Don't you want me to go up and help you?" Hadley asked.

"I think I can handle retrieving two tied up horses."

"No, I mean burying those three men?"

Jess grinned at Hadley. "Hell, those men don't deserve it and besides, the vultures have to eat, too."

"Well, I can't argue with you on that, but that isn't the way things are done back East."

Jess mounted Gray. "Hadley, you are going to find that most things are done a whole lot differently than back East. You might as well start learning to adjust to it."

Jess retrieved the two horses and a couple of brand new Winchester rifles from the dead men. He looked over and the vultures had already found the third dead man down in the flat land. He felt no remorse for killing the man, but he shook his head in sorrow for shooting the horse. He went back and helped Hadley hook up the two horses to the wagon and they traveled a few hours until they found a nice stream with a rocky ridge close by. Jess had them set up so that the ridge protected them from one angle.

Jess started to unpack some of his things and as he did, he watched the Brown family unpack the wagon. Each one of them had their tasks to do and they all went about it like little ants scurrying around and moving past each other as they did their assigned duties. Harold immediately started gathering firewood. He looked to be about ten and had a thick head of dark curly hair. Jessica, who looked to Jess to be about seven or eight, used two buckets to refill the water barrels on the wagon. She had long blond hair and seemed to always be smiling. Jane got some food out and got ready to cook supper. Jess figured her to be in her late twenties. She had short blond hair and was very pretty and petite. She had piercing deep blue eyes that had not gone unnoticed by Jess. Hadley took care of the horses and checked the wagon for damage from the onslaught earlier. Hadley was probably in his early thirties and was of a slight build and not very physically strong. Jess noticed all of these things but did not say anything; he kept such things to himself. Jess unpacked his bedroll, removed the saddles from both of his horses and got out some coffee. He started the fire with the wood that Harold had piled up neatly next to a small hole he had dug with a shovel.

Jane had four boxes sitting around the campfire that held all the cooking supplies. They used them for seats. She was setting up to cook and looked at Jess apologetically. "We only have four boxes but we can have Harold sit on the ground so that you can have a seat, Mr. Williams."

"No need for that, ma'am. I always sit against my saddle, or on it. Hell, a seat would spoil me."

"I'll have to apologize for the meal, too," said Jane. "I don't have any meat left at all. Just potatoes and some carrots, I'm afraid. We usually take time each day to hunt for meat but today was not our ordinary day."

Jess smiled at her and walked over to his pile of stuff on the ground. He retrieved two large rabbits he had shot in the morning. "Well, I just happen to have these two rabbits I shot this morning. I'm sure it will be enough to make a pretty good stew."

Jane almost cried. "Mr. Williams, you are certainly a savior. I don't know how to thank you."

"Can you whip up some biscuits?"

Jane smiled. "I certainly can."

"That will be all the thanks I need, and call me Jess."

Jane took the rabbits and immediately started cleaning them, cutting them up and making the stew. She let it cook a long time while they all sat there and talked about what had happened that day. Jess made more coffee and realized he was really enjoying the company. It made him feel like he was part of a normal life to some degree. Jane finally served the stew and some wonderful biscuits just as she had promised Jess. They all ate in silence and devoured every bit of stew and every biscuit, the last one going to Jess at Jane's insistence. Jess made another pot of coffee and Jane and Jessica went to the stream to clean the pans. When that was done, they all sat back down around the fire, which Harold had replenished with some fresh dry wood.

Jane put Jessica and Harold to bed in the wagon and came back to the fire where Jess and Hadley were sipping hot coffee. "So, Jess, where are you bound for?"

"Actually, as luck would have it, I'm heading for Abilene myself. I figure I might ride along with you, if you don't mind?"

You could see a relief come over Jane's face. "Jess, I would feel so much better if you would. I mean my husband here is no coward and will fight when forced to, but the way you handled those men today, well, I've never seen anything like that before."

"You should be proud of your whole family, Jane. You were putting up a good fight in the face of insurmountable odds today. Most people would have just given up, which always ends up being a mistake. Those kind of men have no respect for human life, or anything else for that matter."

Hadley looked over at Jess's pile of things, the Sharps propped up on the other saddle. "What the hell kind of rifle is that? Sure shoots a hell of a long way and it sounds like cannon."

"That's a Sharps rifle. Some of the buffalo hunters use them. It shoots straight and quite a long distance. I used it to kill those rabbits today."

"They didn't have any heads on them," responded Jane.

"No sense messing up the meat, and besides, it's good practice for me."

"Practice for what?"

"I'm a bounty hunter. I track down the worst of men and collect the reward money on their heads."

"I've heard stories of such things but I've never met a real bounty hunter before," said Hadley.

"So, you hunt men for money?" Jane asked.

"Yes."

"How many men have you killed so far?"

"I've lost count."

"You are such a young man. What could have possibly happened to you that would make you hunt men for a living?"

"It's kind of a long story and one that I don't often like to talk about since it's not a very happy one. Let's just say I have my reasons. And I don't hunt down horse thieves or cattle rustlers or even bank robbers unless they kill some innocent people in the process. I only hunt down the murderers and the men who would rape or kill innocent women."

Jane laughed a confused laugh. "So, you kill men for money, but you actually have standards and a set of rules that you go by?"

"I've never thought of it that way, but, yes, I guess I do."

"Well, Jess, I'm just thankful that you showed up today when you did. I'm afraid of what would have happened if you hadn't. I was really worried about the children."

Jess lowered his head for a moment and then looked back up at her. "You should always be worried about them out here. Some men on the trail don't make any distinction between little girls and grown women, and the worst of them can't even make a distinction between little boys and grown women if you grasp my meaning."

Jane looked at her husband and nodded back at Jess. They all turned in and Jess slept extra lightly during the night. He didn't want to see any harm come to these people. They were a nice family. He was in a protective frame of mind.

CHAPTER FOUR

The ride to Abilene was slow and uneventful. The wagon broke down a few times. On one rainy day, it got stuck and they tried to push it out and couldn't. Jess tied Gray and Sharps to the team and that finally got them moving again. Jess shot a few rabbits each day and a pretty nice deer on one day. They feasted on the venison until they couldn't eat any more. Jess had noticed Jane looking at him quite a bit with those piercing blue eyes. He felt somewhat uncomfortable about it, although he didn't want to feel that way. He had already decided that he would not allow himself to get distracted by any woman, but she was hard not to look at. He simply kept pushing it from his mind. His only thought was to get this family to Abilene alive and safe.

They made camp about four hours from Abilene. That way, they could arrive in town by noon, which would allow Hadley to supply up and then get to their homestead, about two hours out of Abilene. Jess watched as the family went about their respective duties exactly as they did every day when they made camp. After supper, they sat around, sipped hot coffee and talked about their new life in the West.

"We'll have to live in the wagon until we get the house built. I figure we'll start with just one room to get a roof over our heads and then we can add on two more rooms as we get the time," said Hadley.

"Yeah, and I'll start collecting the stones and rocks we need for the fireplace so Mother can cook," added Harold, seemingly excited about the idea of a new home.

"And I'll help Mother keep the house clean and wash the pots and pans," said Jessica, not wanting to be left out. She looked over at Jess. "Are you going to come and live with us, too?"

Jess almost choked on his mouthful of hot coffee. There wasn't a time that Jess looked at Jessica that he didn't think about his little sister Samantha. Jess was tongue-tied and couldn't think of what to say, when Jane came to his rescue.

"Mr. Williams is always welcome to stay with us for a while if he needs to but he won't be living with us, Jessica. I'm sure he has more important things to do than to keep looking after us."

Jessica frowned for a moment but then that smile came back. "Well, you visit us then."

Jess finally got his composure back. "Jessica, I have a hunch that might happen." Jess turned to her father. "Hadley, if you need help loading up a supply wagon with lumber for the house, I'll be glad to help you load and unload it."

"That's mighty nice of you to offer, Jess. I might take you up on that. By the way, you never said why you were heading to Abilene."

Jess didn't know whether or not to tell them the whole story. He didn't want to burden this family with his horrible story about his family and his life. "I'm just looking for someone," he answered.

"Would this someone have a bounty on his head?" Hadley asked.

"I'm not sure, but it's possible. That's not why I'm looking for him, though."

"Then why are you looking for him?"

"Let's just say that it's personal."

"I'll not ask any more about it. I know when to keep my mouth shut," said Hadley, knowing that Jess didn't want to talk about the matter. "Well, I suppose it's about time to turn in for the night."

Jess nodded and told Hadley that he would finish another cup of coffee before turning in. Jane and Hadley left the fire. Jess sat there and watched them go through the same motions they did every night. They moved the children around to make room for them to sleep. Jess had come to like this family. He had really enjoyed his time with them and he considered them friends. Jane looked out at Jess one more time and said goodnight. Jess replied with the same.

Then his thoughts turned in another direction. He wondered if he would find his father in town tomorrow. He decided he would help Hadley out with the lumber and make sure they were out of town before he looked for his father. He didn't want the children to see what might take place if they were nearby when he found him. He dumped his cup out, threw a few small pieces of dry wood on the fire for a little warmth and then turned in for the night.

Four days earlier in Abilene...

There were five men left at the poker table. Probably ten thousand dollars or more was on the table to be won by the last man in the game. The game had started out with eight men and every one of them had come to the table with a thick stack of money. Each of the eight men who started had agreed on the rules. There would be no limit on the bet size and they all agreed to play until all their money was lost. Each man had to have at least one thousand dollars to get into the game. Eddie Sloan had anteed his thousand when he sat down and now that the game was down to five players, he was up to about three thousand. That, and his cheating skills, gave him the upper hand. He had just won the last three hands in a row.

The other four left at the table with Eddie Sloan were Stan Nobel, Will Morton, Gabby Hunt and Willie Hodges. They were all well-to-do men and business owners in Abilene and didn't need to worry about where their next meal was coming from. Willie Hodges had been consistently losing; you could see the agitation on his face.

"You sure seem to be having a run of good luck today, Sloan," Hodges remarked, a hint of sarcasm in his voice.

Sloan never looked up from his hand, which was a good one, especially since he had palmed a pair of aces when he had dealt the hand. "Luck has nothing to do with it, Hodges. I'm just too damn good. Of course, you knew that when you sat down at the game, so why complain about it now?"

"Because I'm losing all my money, that's why."

"Then maybe you shouldn't have joined the game today. Every man who sits down knows he is either going to win or lose. It's that simple."

"Yeah, well you seem to be doing a lot of winning, especially when you deal the cards."

Sloan looked up at Hodges. "Now, don't go making accusations you can't prove or it might get you into a spot you can't get out of," said Sloan, with a hint of a threat in his voice. Hodges knew of Sloan's reputation at poker, but more importantly, he also knew about his reputation with a gun. The glaring look in Sloan's eyes made Hodges shut up, and he returned his attention to his hand again. None of the other three men spoke during the banter between Hodges and Sloan because they knew better than to do so.

Five hands later, a slim built, neatly dressed man walked into the Blue Diamond Gambling House. He looked around for a moment and then walked up to the bar and ordered a whiskey. Sloan had noticed that the man had a nice pistol and holster worn low and tied down, the mark of a gunslinger. Sloan did not recognize the man but he made a mental note to keep an eye on him anyway. Willie Hodges had won a few hands now, but Will Morton and Stan Nobel both had folded, losing all of their money. Sloan had about six thousand dollars, Willie Hodges had about three thousand dollars and Gabby Hunt had almost two thousand. They decided to take a break and the saloon owner had two men with scatterguns watch the table so that no one would get the idea of trying to grab the money. Willie Hodges and Gabby Hunt sat at a table together and ordered some drinks and something to eat. They had known each other for a long time. Sloan went up to the bar and ordered the best brandy the saloon had. He figured he could afford it, especially with his winnings today. The game wasn't over yet, but Sloan knew what the outcome would be in the end.

The man who had walked in earlier was Jack Stone. He hadn't recognized Eddie Sloan when he arrived but he knew who he was now as he leaned on the bar, five other men separating them. He put his drink down after he had it almost to his lips.

"Well, I'll be damned, if it ain't the one and only card shark, Eddie Sloan. I didn't even notice you when I walked in, even though I saw a poker game going on. I should've known if there was a high stakes game going on, you'd be in it."

Sloan looked over at the man and then recognized him. "Jack Stone?"

"Yeah, that's right. Remember? You took all my money in that high stakes game over in Dodge City last year. You shot a friend of mine a few months after that. I didn't have a problem with you taking my money but killing my friend, well, that wasn't right."

"You know, now that you mention it, I do remember killing a man a few months after that big game in Dodge City. It was in some small town. I don't even remember the name of the town, but I do remember why I killed him. He called me a cheat and then he drew on me. He shouldn't have done either of the two. Now, do you still have a problem with that?"

Jack Stone took another shot of whiskey, set his shot glass down ever so gently and then looked up at Sloan. "I guess I do."

"Well, if we're going to settle a problem, let's get to it. I have a poker game to return to and more money to win. I hope you're better with that smoke wagon then you were at playing cards."

"As a matter of fact, I am better drawing a six-gun than cards."

"Well," said Sloan, "do you want to do it here, or outside?"

"I like it fine right here. I can pour myself another shot right after I plug your sorry ass."

The other men at the bar had already moved away, as well as anyone behind Sloan or Stone, who both had their hammer straps off and their right hands near the butts of their pistols.

"You're a betting man, ain't you, Sloan?" Stone asked.

"You know the answer to that question already, so why ask?"

"Because I'd like to make a bet between you and me, Sloan. I have two hundred dollars in my pocket that says I can outdraw you. I'm willing to put it on the bar if you match it. We have witnesses, so whoever is standing when it's over can collect the four hundred. What do you think?"

"I'll take that bet. I don't mind taking your money along with your life, if you insist." Sloan and Stone each put their two hundred dollars on the bar. The bartender took the money, counted it and placed it back on the bar in the middle between the two men. Sloan and Stone were both staring at each other now, one trying to read the other.

"You ready, Sloan?"

"Go ahead and slick that thing out."

Stone was the first to reach for his pistol. He was pretty fast and had almost leveled his pistol at Sloan's chest. He wasn't quite fast enough, though, and Sloan's first shot hit him dead center in the chest. Sloan fanned a second shot before Stone fell. The shot hit him in the stomach. Stone turned to his left and fell to the floor. He gasped a few breaths and twitched twice before he finally passed on. Sloan had his gun trained on him just in case. Once Stone expired, Sloan collected the four hundred dollars from the bar and ordered another fine brandy. The banter started back up in the saloon and Sloan felt comfortable in his element. The fact that he had just killed another man did not bother him in the slightest.

CHAPTER FIVE

Jess and the Brown family arrived in Abilene, Kansas just before noon. Abilene was established in 1857 and had grown to be a large cow town at the end of the Chisholm Trail. Over the years there had been a lot of trouble between the Texas cowboys and the local cowboys. It was still a rowdy and wild town, but not the likes of what it was when the cattle drives were at their peak and Wild Bill Hickok was present. The sheriff of Abilene was fairly new since the last one had been shot by an unknown drifter who came through town.

Bad Axe McCoy was the new sheriff. He had gotten that nickname because of his prowess with throwing an axe; he won every axe-throwing contest he had ever entered. His father had nicknamed him "Axe" when he was about five, when he first picked up an axe and began chopping wood. At age six, he began throwing the axe at trees and just had a natural ability. After a while, and nobody remembers who it was, someone called him Bad Axe McCoy and the name stuck from that point on. He was a no-nonsense sheriff with a short fuse for anyone dumb enough to light it. He watched as Jess rode in with the Brown family and headed for the first mercantile store they came to, which was right across the street from the sheriff's office. The sheriff was sitting in a rocking chair and watched the new family carry supplies out and pile them into their wagon. Bad Axe McCoy got up and walked across the street and found Jess standing behind the wagon, pushing boxes full of food and other necessities needed to start a homestead. Jess turned to face the sheriff.

"Afternoon, Sheriff," said Jess, as he stuck out his hand for a handshake.

The sheriff hesitated for a second and then slowly brought his hand up and shook hands with Jess, but he did not let go of Jess's right hand, which made Jess feel very uneasy. The sheriff looked down at Jess's gun and then back up at Jess. "Am I going to have any trouble with you, young man?" Sheriff McCoy asked.

"No sir, I'm not looking for any trouble. I don't run from any either, though," said Jess, as he slowly pulled his hand free from the sheriff's iron grip.

"You drifting through or planning on staying in town?"

"I'm going to help these people haul their supplies out to their homestead and then I plan on coming back to town later today."

"What are you here for?"

"Sheriff, why do you ask? I haven't done anything wrong. I just rode in not ten minutes ago and you came over. I offered my hand as a friendly gesture and you act as if I've done something wrong."

This little conversation had gotten the attention of both Hadley and Jane, who had now come out of the mercantile with their hands full.

"Sheriff, is there a problem?" Hadley asked.

"That's what I'm trying to find out."

"Jess here hasn't done anything since we got here, so what is the problem?"

"The problem is that I know who he is. Jess Williams, the famous bounty hunter, although some have begun to refer to him as a natural born man-killer. You hunting someone here in my town, Mr. Williams?"

"No, Sheriff, but I am looking for someone."

"Might I ask who that might be?"

Jess thought about it for a moment. "Sheriff, why don't you let me finish up what I'm doing here and as soon as I get back to town, I will come and see you first and explain."

The sheriff seemed satisfied with that answer. "Okay, that seems fair to me. I expect you to follow your word on the matter."

"You have my word on it, Sheriff."

Sheriff McCoy turned away and that left Hadley and Jane staring at Jess. "We knew you were a bounty hunter, but not a famous one. What did he mean by that man-killer thing?" Hadley asked.

Jess could feel those piercing blue eyes of Jane on him. "Well, it's probably because I have a reputation of always bringing my man in dead."

Hadley looked down at the ground for a moment and then looked back up at Jess. "You mean to say that you never bring a man in alive?"

"Nope."

"Never?"

Jess looked at Hadley and just shook his head negatively.

Jane looked uneasy at first, but then her look turned friendly. "Jess, I don't care how many bad men you have killed. All I know is that if it weren't for you, we would all be dead or worse by now."

"Thanks for not thinking badly of me. There is a long story behind all of this. Maybe one day I'll tell you all about it, but for now, let's get that lumber loaded up."

"The store owner says they're short on lumber in town at the moment. Says there will be a shipment in a few days, so you can stay in town if you want. We can unload all of these supplies ourselves, Jess."

"Are you sure?"

"Yes, you go ahead and see the sheriff and take care of your business in town. Come and see us before you leave, though. Our place is straight west out of town about two hours by wagon."

"I'll probably do just that, Hadley. Jane, it was nice meeting you and your family, although I wish it would have been under different circumstances." He shook hands with Harold and when he tried to shake hands with Jessica, she jumped up into Jess's arms and gave him a long hug.

"You make sure you come and visit me, Jess, promise?" Jessica asked.

"I promise," replied Jess, as he put her back down. "Well, I'm off to see the sheriff."

Hadley loaded up his family and headed out of town to their new homestead. Jess watched until the wagon was out of sight. He was still trying to deal with the feelings he had for this family. His stomach had knotted up when Jessica had hugged him. It made him feel normal for just a moment and it brought back memories of his own sister, Samantha. He looked across the street and the sheriff was sitting in his rocker, watching Jess. Jess walked over to talk with him.

"Sheriff, I'm here in town looking for a man by the name of Eddie Sloan."

The mention of Eddie Sloan's name made the sheriff sit forward in his rocker. "What's your business with Eddie Sloan?"

"It's kind of personal."

"Well, I'm making it personal and I'm making it my business."

"He's my father, although I don't like to admit it, and I've been on his trail for a long time. I've never actually met him. I found out a few years back that he was my natural father."

The sheriff leaned back in his rocker again. "Well, Eddie Sloan left town three days ago on the train. Who knows where he is by now? He cleaned up on a poker game here in town over at the Blue Diamond Gambling House. He won about eleven thousand dollars in that game. He also managed to kill a drifter who came through in the middle of the game. He shot the man twice and went back to his poker game as if he had stepped on a cow chip. If Eddie Sloan is your father, I feel sorry for you, young man."

"Don't feel sorry for me, Sheriff. I didn't say I liked the man, only that he was my natural father."

"What are you going to do when you finally catch up with him?"

"I don't know for sure, but I don't think that anything good will come of it."

"I think you might be right about that. I know all about you, Jess Williams. I know about you killing your own brother. Why did you go and do something like that?"

"Because he was a bad man."

"And you always go around killing bad men, don't you." It was a statement, not a question.

"That's right."

"There are a few bad men in town right now. If you stick around, I'm sure you'll run into one of them before long. Are you going to shoot them, too?"

"Only if they start a fight or if they have a bounty on their heads."

"If there was someone in my town with a bounty on his head, I would have already collected it myself."

Jess smiled. "Sheriff, can you point me to the best hotel in town and the best place to get a meal?"

The sheriff gave Jess the information he had asked about. He found the Star Hotel and got himself a room. Then he treated himself to an extra long hot bath. He then headed for Jensen's Café, where the sheriff had told him he would find the best meals in town. One smell and a few looks at the plates of food on the tables when Jess walked into the café assured him that the sheriff had given him the right tip. He sat down at a small table. It wasn't even a minute when a young woman with dark hair and brown eyes walked up to his table.

"Hello, my name is Candice," she said. She handed him a menu and explained what the special of the day was. "Can I get you something to drink while you decide?"

"Hot coffee will be fine, but I've already decided to take your special, Candice."

"Good choice. My mom does most of the cooking in the back and she makes the best fried chicken anywhere in town."

Jess looked around the café. There were several people eating and most of them Jess figured for locals. Only one man was wearing a pistol. He was dressed nicely, and Jess didn't figure him for any trouble. Probably only carried a gun for protection. He liked the place. It was clean and there were even white tablecloths on the tables. He was not accustomed to eating in such a decent place, but it was nice for a change and he liked it.

Candice had refilled Jess's coffee cup a few times before she finally came out of the back with his platter of food. She placed it on the table and delivered silverware along with salt and pepper and a plate of warm rolls with a slab of butter. Everything looked and smelled absolutely wonderful.

"I'd wait a few minutes before you bite into that chicken because it's fresh out of the pan and very hot. Can I get you anything else?" Candice asked.

"I'll take your advice," Jess said, as he touched the chicken. "If you keep the coffee coming, I'll be just fine. This really smells wonderful."

"I assure you that it will taste even better. If you need anything at all, you just call for me."

Jess finished his meal and was stuffed. He ate all four large pieces of chicken, a huge helping of mashed potatoes and gravy, a bowl of carrots and two rolls, along with several cups of coffee. He usually didn't eat that much, but it was so good he couldn't bring himself to leave anything on the plate. He left enough money on the table for the meal and a very nice tip for Candice.

He walked around town for about an hour trying to work off all the food, but also to check things out. There were plenty of saloons, mercantile shops and gambling houses. Some of the saloons and gambling houses were quiet and some were quite rowdy. He found the Blue Diamond Gambling House and went inside to see if he could find out anything about his father and maybe where he was headed. He walked in and checked his surroundings. There were two games going on and the faro table was busy. Three men stood at the bar, all of them wearing six-shooters. It was early in the afternoon and Jess figured this place would be busy in the evening. Jess ordered a beer and the bartender poured it and placed it in front of him.

"Can I get you anything else, mister?"

"What's your name?" asked Jess.

"My name is Jonathan. What's your name?"

"Jess Williams." One of the three men at the bar turned around at the mention of Jess's name.

"Jonathan, I'm looking for any information on a man by the name of Eddie Sloan. I know he was in a poker game here a few days ago and the sheriff said he left town on the train. Is there anything you can tell me about Sloan or where he might be headed?"

"I can tell you he's a real bad one, that's for sure. He killed a man by the name of Jack Stone right where you're standing in the middle of a poker game. Sloan went right back to the game, like he had just stepped on a cockroach. Mean son of a bitch, that one."

"Did he say anything about where he was going?"

"Not that I heard. It's pretty noisy here at night. Why don't you come back later? Some of the men who were at his table will be here tonight. Maybe they can tell you something more."

"I'll do that. Who should I be asking for?"

"Gabby Hunt and Willie Hodges. They play here every night and they were both at the table with Sloan. Willie and Sloan had words, but Willie was smart enough to shut his mouth."

Jess thanked the bartender, paid for his beer, and left Jonathan a nice tip for the information. As he walked out of the gambling house, the one man who had turned around at the mention of Jess's name watched Jess as he left. None of this was missed by Jess. He simply chose to act as if he didn't notice. He didn't know the man, but that didn't mean that he would not have a confrontation with him before he left town. He went to his hotel room and took a short nap before going back to the gambling house to speak with Willie Hodges and Gabby Hunt.

CHAPTER SIX

Wednesday came too quick for Sheriff Mark Steele. The meeting he had set up between Rance Madden and Henry Thornton had, in fact, bought him a few days of peace. There had been no shootings or attempts on Steele's life in the last two days. Both of Steele's deputies, Buck Hern and Tex, had not reported anything out of the ordinary. Sure, a few fights had occurred and a few drunks had been locked up, but that was normal. Neither Madden's nor Thornton's men had come to town since Steele told them about the meeting that was to take place today. Steele was in the office when Buck and Tex showed up. Tex had no last name and knew nothing of his family. He had been abandoned in Mexico when he was three years old and was raised by a Mexican family for a few years, but he ran away when he was only eight and lived on the range by himself, going from town to town taking on odd jobs for enough money to eat. Then, he ended up in Timber and Sheriff Steele offered him a job as a deputy. He had been there ever since.

"Morning, Sheriff," Tex said as he headed for the coffee.

"Good morning, men, I hope you two are ready for today."

"Hell," replied Buck, as he filled his cup with coffee, "no one is ready for today. We'll be damn lucky to get through this meeting without at least one man going down. I just hope it ain't one of us."

"Well, it's a last chance meeting," replied Steele. "After today, we're going to have to take a tough stand against all of this or maybe even take sides in the matter."

"Taking sides never seems to work," replied Buck.

"If I were to take sides, I would side with Thornton. He didn't start this war; Madden did," said Tex.

"True," added Steele, "but he did send out for hired guns when he could have let us handle the whole thing."

"Sheriff, the three of us can't be everywhere watching every hired gun those two have. Hell, they had shoot-outs we don't even know about out on the range. We don't have enough men to handle this problem. Did you ever hear back from Frank Reedy?" asked Buck.

"No, but I sure hope I do. I sent messages out to the fifteen most likely towns he would be in or stop at. I told the telegraph office to notify me the second they get a response from Reedy. Let's just pray we're alive to read it."

The three men sat in the office drinking coffee and talking small talk to pass the time until noon. They all tried to act like things were normal, but they all felt an ominous feeling of doom slowly coming over them.

Steele and his two deputies were waiting in Jed's Saloon when Henry Thornton and his two hired guns reined up, tied their horses to the rail and walked in. Steele had warned both Thornton and Madden to bring only two men each. Steele figured that would help to keep any problems from getting out of control. Thornton's two hired guns, Mack Packard and Toby Hewett, walked up to the bar and Thornton sat down at the table with Steele. Buck and Tex were on opposite sides of the saloon, both with scatterguns.

"Sheriff, I hope this meeting will resolve this matter, but I'm not betting on it," said Thornton.

"I'm not betting on it either, Henry, but I don't know what else to do. You two sure haven't given me many options so far, I have to tell you."

"I didn't start this war. Madden did. I never had any problem with Mason over water. It wasn't until Madden bought the Mason spread that we had problems."

"Yes, but Mason didn't have as many cattle as Madden has and your herd has grown considerably too. You could have worked this out in the beginning but you both have let this matter go too far."

"Well, let's see what Madden has to say. At least I haven't sent hired guns into town to kill you."

"I will give you that, and I appreciate it."

Just then, Rance Madden reined up with three hired guns. They got off their horses and started to walk into the saloon. Buck and Tex exchanged glances. Tex nodded to Buck to go to the door and Tex shifted his attention to Thornton's two men at the bar. They were looking straight into the two barrels of the scattergun and neither of them moved an inch.

Madden was coming through the door and his three men were on his heels. Buck stopped Madden before the swinging doors closed behind him. "Mr. Madden, you knew the rules of the meeting. Only two men apiece and I count three."

"Kiss my ass, Buck. No one tells me what to do."

Sheriff Steele spoke without even getting out of his chair. "Mr. Madden, if you don't order one of your men to ride out of town in the next ten seconds, I'm going to order my deputy to blow a hole in your chest large enough for a watermelon to fit through, and you damn well know that I'll do it."

Buck had a wide grin on his face as he cocked back both barrels of the scattergun and placed it one foot from Madden's chest. Madden's face was contorted with anger, but he knew Steele did not make threats he didn't intend to carry out, so he motioned for one of his men to leave. Only after the man was out of sight did Buck go back to his position, letting Rance Madden take a seat at the table with Steele and Thornton. Madden's two hired guns, Vernon Foster and Leonard Sand, took a seat at a table in a corner.

"Hell of a way to start this meeting, Sheriff," complained Madden.

"You knew the rules and you're the one who decided to break them. You caused the problem, not me or Thornton here."

Madden ignored Steele and glared at Thornton. "Why don't you just sell out and move your herd somewhere else and settle all of this?"

"I've told you a hundred times, I'm not leaving. I was here years before you got here, and I plan to be here years after you're gone."

"Well," said Steele, "at least we're talking. That's a start." They both just glared at Steele.

"Listen, Thornton," said Madden, "I've offered you almost twice what your place is worth. Only an idiot would turn that offer down."

"Insults won't help resolve our problem. I at least came with something to offer to help resolve our dispute."

Madden sat back in his chair. "Let's hear it and it better be good."

"If you build another retention pond, a really big one that can feed your smaller ponds, I'll increase the flow from my last pond by at least one quarter in the summer and by half in the winter. Plus, we both agree to dig a few more wells to help fill the ponds. That way, you will start out in the spring with twice the water you have this spring."

"That sounds like a pretty good offer, Madden," said Steele. "I think you should take it."

"Hell, that won't solve my long-term problem. I plan on doubling my herd in the next five years. Plus, what if a drought hits? Also, I'll lose too much to evaporation and I'll lose too much to ground seepage. You know there ain't any clay anywhere on my property."

"Then use all that extra money you were going to pay me to ship clay in or build holding tanks. I'm willing to give you more water. It's your job to figure out how to store it. I can't solve all your problems. I have my own."

"Yeah, and I'm your biggest problem right now. Why don't you just finally take my offer and that will solve our problem for good," responded Madden, getting madder by the moment.

"I'm not going to ever say it again, Madden. Hell will have to freeze over before I'll sell to you. I plan on dying on my own property."

"Yeah, and I'm going to make sure that happens and it will be sooner rather than later!" hollered Madden.

"Calm down, Madden," interjected the sheriff. "I think what Thornton offered was far more than most men would offer. I think you're being unreasonable about this."

"Kiss my ass, Sheriff. I ain't calming down or backing down. My spread will be the largest in Kansas before this is over. I'm going to need that water and I need all of it. I intend to get it one way or another."

Thornton sat back in his chair and let out a deep sigh. "Well, Sheriff, I tried my best. This offer leaves with me after this meeting. He'll have to take it now or forget about it."

Steele turned to Madden. "Madden, you're not leaving me much choice in this matter. If you're not willing to compromise, what do you expect me to do?"

"Stay out of our business and let us settle this thing ourselves, that's what I expect you to do."

"You know I can't do that. I'm the law here and it's my job to keep the peace."

"You're going to have one hell of a job then, because peace ain't what's coming. Its war that's coming and I can promise you that it will be a bloody one."

"Madden, you leave me no choice then. I'm going to side with Mr. Thornton here in this matter."

"Sheriff, that's your last mistake. I think you should reconsider your thinking," replied Madden.

"You've left me no other option. You've started this war, and now that Thornton has made a reasonable offer to help with the water dispute, that you have rejected, I can't blame him for the problem. The responsibility sits dead on your shoulders now."

Madden sneered at Steele. "There will certainly be some men lying dead in the street before this is over, Sheriff, and you just might be one of them."

"Is that a threat, Madden?"

"Make of it what you will."

ROBERT J. THOMAS

Steele looked over at Buck. "Buck, would you please take Mr. Madden over to the jail and lock him up. Maybe a few days behind bars might change his way of thinking."

Buck and Tex exchanged glances with the unspoken language that they both understood. Tex would watch Madden's hired guns while Buck locked up Madden.

"Are you out of your mind, Sheriff!" exclaimed Madden. "You can't lock me up!"

"Yes I can, and I will. I don't take to threats very lightly and you know it."

Buck came over and prodded Madden with the scattergun, which still had both barrels cocked. Madden stood up with an unbelievable rage in his eyes and he glared at both Steele and Thornton. He looked over at his men. "Boys, if he don't let me out in a couple of days, come and get me and when you do, you can burn this town to the ground!"

"Let's get going, Madden, before your mouth gets you into more trouble than you're already in," said Buck.

"We'll keep Madden's men company here until you get him locked up. If Madden even speaks on the way to the jail cell, shoot him on the spot. Consider that an order," added Steele.

Vernon Foster and Leonard Sand knew better than to try anything at this point. They knew Steele would have their boss shot if they did. Besides, they were outnumbered with Tex and his scattergun and Thornton's two hired guns in the room, not counting Steele, who was a formidable foe all by himself. Madden walked out and headed straight for the jail. He never said a word or made a move. He knew Buck was praying that he would so that he could pull the trigger on the scattergun. He would wait his time and he knew his men would know what to do. Plus, he knew something that Steele didn't know; he still had Quentin Unger and Gregory Timmons coming to kill Sheriff Steele.

Madden's men left shortly after Buck had Madden locked up. They rode out of town. Thornton and his men left and that left Sheriff Steele and Tex in the saloon. Pattie Nate was in the back and had been listening to the meeting while peeling potatoes and preparing food for the few customers who would show up for supper. She came out of the kitchen with a fresh pot of coffee. She set it down with three cups.

"Well, that went really well," said Pattie.

Steele let out a big sigh as he filled his cup with the hot coffee. "Damn, I really hoped we could avoid this war, but it doesn't seem likely now."

Tex filled a cup with coffee. "You know, Sheriff, it's been bad enough so far, but it's going to get really bloody from here on in. We'd better get us some help and fast. I've been through one of these wars before and it never ends up right for the good guys."

"Got any suggestions?"

"I sure do. I'll go over to the jail cell and shoot Madden right between the eyes if you just give me the order. That will end the problem. You know what they say about a snake. Cut his head off and he will still keep moving, but he can't see and won't know which direction to go in. The body eventually dies off."

"You would do it too, wouldn't you?" Steele asked.

"Damn straight, and I wouldn't feel a bit bad about it either."

"Tex, as long as we wear these badges, we have to follow the law the same way we expect others to follow it."

"I can let this badge fall off on my way to the jail, if you know what I mean."

"I know what you mean, but I can't let you do it, even though I want you to," Steele said, frustration taking hold of him.

"Sheriff, I can tell you this. If we handle this and follow the letter of the law exactly, we'll all end up dead for sure. This ain't just two hot-headed cowboys liquored up and ready to shoot it out. That we can handle all day long. We're dealing with two rich ranch owners who have already hired at least a dozen hired guns each and I'm betting they will hire some more, and you, me and Buck are right in the middle of it. We don't have a prayer if we follow the rules of the law."

"You know he's right," added Pattie. "Even if Frank Reedy and his deputies show up, you still won't have enough men to settle this.

You've got to bend the rules if you plan on surviving this situation. I still think you should send for Jess."

"He would be my last resort. If we brought him into this war, who knows how many men would die?"

"Probably quite a few, but at least they would be the right ones," replied Pattie.

Steele took a sip of his coffee. "I'll think about it, but only if Reedy doesn't show up in the next day or two. Locking Madden up in jail probably buys us a few more days."

"That's a start, anyway," said Tex.

"Tex, I'm going over to check on Buck and try to talk some sense into Madden again."

"All right, but it's hard to talk sense to a man who ain't got any."

After the sheriff left, Tex poured himself and Pattie another cup of coffee. "I've heard the sheriff speak about this Jess kid before and I've heard stories about him. Is he really that good?"

"Yes, he is. He's just the kind of man you need to resolve a problem like this. He doesn't play by any other man's rules. He plays by his own set of rules and he just kills any man who needs killing. I've seen him in action before myself, and I can tell you there ain't any man faster on the draw or more deadly than Jess Williams."

"I can attest to that, too," said Jed from behind the bar. "I seen him shoot a man, but I swear I couldn't see him draw. One second, he was facing down a man and the next second his gun was in his hand and smoke coming from the barrel. Never saw anything like it before or since."

Tex took another sip of his coffee. "Sounds like the man we need on our side."

"Yeah," replied Pattie, "now if you can just convince your boss about that."

"Well, I never claimed to be no miracle worker."

CHAPTER SEVEN

Jess had a nice long nap. He got up, washed his face with some fresh cold water, and dried off with a clean white towel. He headed down to the Blue Diamond Gambling House to see if he could find Gabby Hunt or Willie Hodges. When he walked into the Blue Diamond, he noticed the same man who had turned around at the bar earlier. He was standing at one end of the bar with the two pals he had been with earlier. The Blue Diamond was noisy and rowdy, men throughout the place engaged in all sorts of gambling. Whores were walking around offering their services to the men. The room was heavy with smoke. Jess walked up to the bar and ordered a beer. Jonathan brought him a beer and set it down in front of Jess. Jonathan had to almost yell for Jess to hear him over the noise in the place.

"That's Gabby Hunt and Willie Hodges over at that table there. They're the two I told you about earlier."

"Thanks, I appreciate it," Jess yelled back.

Jonathan motioned for Jess to come closer as if he had something to say that he didn't want others to hear. Jess moved his ear closer to Jonathan.

Jonathan spoke just loud enough for Jess to hear. "That man at the end of the bar was asking about you after you left today. I just thought that you should know."

"Thank you. I did notice him today and I appreciate you telling me," replied Jess.

"He knows who you are," said Jonathan.

"That tells me all I need to know," replied Jess. "Thanks again."

Jess walked to the table where Hodges and Hunt were sitting, playing a game of stud poker. "Which two of you are Hodges and Hunt?"

The six men at the table all looked up at Jess. Two of them raised their hands like kids in a classroom not sure if they were in trouble or not.

"Can I speak with both of you men for a moment?" asked Jess.

"We're kind of busy right now and on a winning streak," replied Hodges.

"It'll only take five minutes and I'll put twenty dollars toward each of your pots if you'll oblige me."

"Well, now you're talking," said Hunt. "With my luck tonight, I'll turn that twenty into a hundred."

The three of them walked to a table in the corner trying to get away from the noise. Jess motioned for Jonathan to bring drinks for them and Jonathan delivered three shots of brandy.

"So, what can we do for you?" Hodges asked.

"I understand you two played in a high-stakes poker game with a man by the name of Eddie Sloan recently."

"Yeah, that son of a bitch took all our money. We know he had to be cheating, but no one could catch him. He is one slick player and that's a fact," replied Hunt. "Willie here got into an argument with him about it, but it didn't seem to matter to Sloan one bit."

"He shot a man during one of our breaks. I mean, the man challenged him so he didn't start the fight. It was just the way he handled it that was kind of unusual," added Hodges.

"What do you mean?"

"He didn't seem concerned at all about the gunfight. He acted more like a man who was picking out a new hat or something, not like a man about to shoot it out with another man. He was very cool and after he killed the man, he acted like it was something he did every day, like it was nothing. He sat back down at the game like it never happened."

"Did he say anything about where he was heading next?"

"He said something about how he was going to use the eleven thousand he collected here to play in another high-stakes poker game in Missouri somewhere. I don't think he said what city, but it most likely would be one of the larger ones like St. Louis."

"Thanks, men. I really appreciate the information. Here is the twenty each I promised for your pots."

Jess handed them the money and they thanked him and went straight back to their game. Jess sat at the table and thought about things for a minute. He had missed his father by only a few days again. Now he would have to head to Missouri and see if he could catch up with him there or get another lead on him. It was getting frustrating but he would never give up. Jonathan showed up at the table with a fresh beer.

"That man that I told you was asking about you wanted to buy you a beer," said Jonathan, as he set the beer down.

Jess looked over at the man, who tipped his hat in response. He had already figured this man for a gunslinger. The fact that he was here again tonight had certainly alerted Jess the moment he stepped in the door tonight. He would have normally accepted the drink as a friendly gesture, but Jess knew a confrontation was coming and there was no reason to put it off.

"Tell the man, no thanks. I'll pay for my own beer."

"I figured that's what you were going to say."

Jonathan took the beer back to the bar and served it to someone else. He walked over to the man who had sent the drink to Jess and gave him Jess's message. The man looked over at Jess and tipped his hat again, but he did not come to Jess's table right away. He stayed at the bar talking with his two friends and had two more shots. Jess figured he was either getting up enough courage or maybe deciding whether or not it was worth dying for a reputation. The answer to the question mattered little to Jess. He simply waited to see what decision the man would make.

Finally, the man walked to Jess's table and stood about five feet away. "You too damn good to have a drink on me?"

519

Jess looked up at him. "And you are?"

"Name's Max Hall. Heard of me before?"

"Can't say that I have. I'd ask, but I already know what you want."

"Figured as much. I hear you're the fastest, but I think I'm faster."

"And let me guess. You picked today to prove it, right?"

"Like you said, you already knew that."

"Yes, I did say that, didn't I?"

"Yep."

"Well, I suppose I can't talk you out of this, can I?"

"Not a chance. I've been waiting for over a year to come across your trail and I ain't waiting any longer."

"Where do you want to do this?"

"The middle of the street would do just fine."

"I always figure a man deserves to pick the place he wants to die."

Jess followed Max out into the street. He knew that Max's two friends were close behind. He wasn't sure whether or not they would involve themselves in the matter but he would be ready just in case. Max's two pals positioned themselves about ten feet apart just outside the door to the Blue Diamond. Jess walked into the middle of the street and Max walked about fifty feet away and turned to face Jess.

"How many men have you killed so far?"

"I've actually lost count, not that I was trying to keep track of it."

"So, if I outdraw you, I'll have one hell of a reputation, won't I?"

"I suppose so, but it's overrated."

"What do you mean by that?"

"Having that kind of reputation just means that every young gunslinger trying to build his own reputation will be hunting you down for the rest of your natural life. They will never stop coming at you and eventually, you will get older and slower and one of them will take you down."

"Yeah, but I bet I'll take a lot of them with me before that happens."

"Then, I'm probably doing you a favor today."

"How do you figure?"

"I'm going to shorten the process and end your misery today and get it over with."

"Mighty sure of yourself, I'll give you that."

"Are your two friends going to be involved in this?"

"I guess that's your problem to worry about now, ain't it?"

"It's no problem, I'll deal with it. Go ahead; make your play because this warm little conversation is definitely over with."

Max went for his gun. He never had a chance. The surprised look on his face showed that, but Jess never got to see it. He had turned instantly to see Max's friends going for their pistols. Jess fanned his next two shots, hitting both of them square in the chest. One went down immediately, but the other was still standing and trying to raise his hand to get off a shot. Jess was about to put another round into him when the sound of a rifle cracked and the man went down. Jess spun around to his right only to see Sheriff McCoy walking toward him, holding a rifle, smoke still lingering at the end of the barrel. Jess relaxed a little due to the fact that the rifle barrel was not pointed at him.

At the sound of the first shot, the Blue Diamond went totally silent. Then, when the shooting was over, dozens of men came out and stood on the boardwalk to see what had happened.

"Easy, Jess. I saw it and I know it wasn't your call. I don't tolerate any unfair fights in my town."

"Thanks, Sheriff, but I had it under control."

"I know, but I have a reputation to uphold just like you."

"I understand, Sheriff, and thanks for seeing things right."

"You're pretty damn fast with that smoke wagon of yours. I've never seen anyone that fast before. How would you like a job as my deputy?"

Jess smiled at the sheriff. "No thanks, Sheriff. I have more important work to do in life."

"I kind of thought so, but I just had to ask."

The boy from the telegraph office was on a dead run toward Sheriff Steele's office. He had a piece of paper folded up and clenched in his right hand. He ran inside the sheriff's office and stood in front of Steele's desk.

Steele leaned forward in his chair. "Son, if that's the message I'm hoping for, I have a shiny new one dollar coin for you." The boy smiled but said nothing as he handed over the folded piece of paper. Steele opened it and read the message aloud.

I'm on my way to Timber with two deputies as fast as our horses will carry us.

Your friend,

Frank Reedy

Steele smiled as he tossed a silver dollar to the boy who took it and ran back out as fast as he had come in.

Steele headed over to Jed's Saloon where he knew his two deputies were having lunch. He set the message down on the table and Buck and Tex both read it as Jed brought Steele a cup of coffee.

"That's damn good news," said Buck.

"Yeah, I was beginning to worry we wouldn't hear from him," added Tex.

"At least it gives us a chance to get through this," replied Steele.

"Great, now we have probably a thirty percent chance instead of a ten percent chance," said Tex, sarcastically. "Sheriff, why don't you send for that young man, Jess Williams?"

"I won't do that until we absolutely have to. I thought I made that clear to the both of you."

"You did, but we need all the help we can get. From what I heard about that kid, he's exactly what we need here," replied Tex.

"Hey, you don't kill a rabbit with a cannon and that's exactly what that kid is," said Steele.

"You're the boss, Sheriff. I'm just bringing it up for discussion."

"We have help on the way. Let's hope for the best. When Reedy gets here, we'll let Madden out of jail. When he sees a U.S. marshal's badge in his face, he might think twice about continuing this war with Thornton."

"I hope you're right, boss," Buck said, skeptically.

Steele ordered some lunch and felt more comfortable that help was on the way. What he didn't know was that more trouble was on the way at the same time. Quentin Unger and Gregory Timmons had arrived at the Madden ranch and were awaiting Madden's return along with the order to go to town and kill Sheriff Steele.

CHAPTER EIGHT

Frank Reedy arrived the next day in the late afternoon. He brought two of his best deputies with him, Torrey Abel and Hal Banks. Both were seasoned lawmen and tough as nails. Sheriff Steele met them on the front steps of the sheriff's office.

"Frank Reedy, you are a sight for sorry eyes. I thought you'd never show up," Steele said, as he grabbed Reedy's hand and shook it.

"Damn good to see you too, Mark. I'm sorry I didn't get here sooner but we were chasing some bank robbers and we were out on the trail for a few days before hitting a town. As soon as I got the message, I grabbed my two best men and headed straight here. Let me introduce them. These are Torrey Abel and Hal Banks." Steele shook hands with both men.

"Why don't we go get something to eat over at the saloon and I can tell you all about it," suggested Steele.

"Both me and my men could eat the ass end out of a skunk right about now," replied Reedy.

The four of them walked to Jed's Saloon and sat at a table facing the front window. Jed was busy with stocking the shelves, so Pattie came out of the back with a pot of coffee and four cups, along with some cream and sugar. Sheriff Steele introduced Reedy and his two deputies to Pattie.

"It's nice to see you again, Mr. Reedy. You didn't have a U.S. marshal's badge on the last time you were here. Here's some hot coffee, men. Can I get you all something to eat?"

Frank Reedy sniffed the aroma coming from the kitchen. "Is that ham I smell back there?"

"You've got a good nose, Mr. Reedy. Yes, it is. I have two large hams cooking and a big pot of bean and ham soup going. Would you men like me to fix you some plates and some bowls of soup?"

"You were reading my mind, ma'am. Bring four servings and make them big."

Pattie headed back into the kitchen. While she was getting the plates of food ready, she overheard Mark Steele explain all about the situation that he and the town were in. She had to make three trips to bring out all the food. "I'm sure glad you're here, Marshal Reedy. Mark here is going to need all the help he can get, but I'm not sure the three of you will be enough."

"Between me and my deputies and the sheriff and his two deputies, that gives us six experienced lawmen, and all six are good gun handlers. I think we'll be okay and if not, we can send for more help."

"I'll be praying for all of you," Pattie said, as she headed back to the kitchen. They all dug in like starving animals.

"Sheriff, I gather she doesn't seem to think we can handle it," said Reedy.

"It won't be easy. I'm hoping that U.S. marshal's badge you're wearing will be enough to slow Rance Madden down a little. By the way, what made you pin a badge back on again?"

Reedy thought about it for a minute. "I suppose I kind of got tired of the bounty hunting business and not having steady pay. Hell, that young friend of yours, Jess Williams, pretty much put some of us out of business."

"Yeah, and I hear he's still at it. Tough little hombre and not afraid of anything," replied Steele.

"He needs to watch himself, though; I keep waiting for a wanted poster on him to come across my desk. I sure don't want to have to go after that boy."

"Why do you say that?" Steele asked.

"Well, he comes darn close to breaking the law sometimes. He shot Deeke Moore in the middle of the street when he was unarmed. On another occasion, he forced Randolph Jackson into a gunfight even though Jackson wanted to walk away. I mean, they all asked for trouble and he didn't start any of it, but he's coming closer and closer to crossing that line, if you know what I mean."

"I think the thing that counts is that he hasn't shot anyone who didn't deserve to die," replied Steele.

"I think that's the only reason no one has sworn out a warrant on him yet. Well, let's go and have a little talk with this Rance Madden fellow," said Reedy. "Fine cooking," he hollered toward the kitchen as they left Jed's Saloon.

They walked to Sheriff Steele's office. Rance Madden, who had been lying on the hard bed, sat up when he heard them. Buck was sitting in a chair in the corner; Tex was doing rounds around town. Frank Reedy walked up to the cell.

"You must be Mr. Rance Madden?" asked Reedy.

"That's right. Are you here to let me the hell out of here? Steele had no reason to lock me up, I didn't break any laws, and he's the one who should be behind these bars."

"Shut the hell up and listen to me, Madden, because I'm only going to say it once. I'm a U.S. marshal and I'm here to help the sheriff keep the peace here. I've heard all about your little war with Henry Thornton and I don't particularly give two shits about your problem with water. I know the law and it's on Thornton's side. He was here first and you knew the water situation before you bought your spread. If you didn't, that's your fault, not Henry Thornton's. Now, I'm letting you out of jail, but if you continue with the dispute you started, you're going to have the full weight of the U.S. marshal's office rain down on you like hellfire. Do I make myself clear on the matter?"

Rance Madden was madder than hell but he stood up and looked over at Steele. "I'm not making any promises to any of you. Now let me out of here before I get me a lawyer and sue the sheriff."

Steele unlocked the cell door and handed Madden all of his things along with his gun and holster. "Consider yourself warned, for the last time, Madden."

"Kiss my ass, Sheriff," replied Madden, as he stormed out of the jail and headed for the livery.

Reedy looked at Steele. "I got a hunch we're going to see that hunk of trouble again."

"Yeah, he won't stop. It's just not within his nature to do so. We'd better get ready because I think trouble's coming to town, and soon."

Rance Madden headed straight for his ranch. One of his men grabbed the reins of his horse. As soon as Madden's feet hit the ground, he asked, "Did my new men show up yet?"

"Yes sir, they are in the bunkhouse right now. Do you want me to send them into the house?"

"Give me enough time to take a hot bath and get the cook to prepare a big meal. We've got plans to figure out and I want all the best men at the table."

About an hour or so later, Rance Madden was sitting at a large dining table when Mike Winters walked into the large room with Quentin Unger, Gregory Timmons, Vernon Foster and Leonard Sands following behind him. "Boss, this here is Quentin Unger and this is Gregory Timmons."

Madden stood up, shook hands with both men, and motioned for them to take a seat. "So, are you two as good as Winters told me?"

"Yes, sir, Mr. Madden," replied Quentin Unger, "Gregory and me have worked together for a long time now. We started out working on bounty hunting and still do some of that, but mostly we hire our guns out to whoever is paying the most. We have no problem with killing whoever you want killed, and that includes a sheriff."

"Can we assume that the offer of one thousand dollars is still the price for killing the sheriff?" asked Gregory Timmons.

"Yes," replied Madden, "but there's a new complication. Sheriff Steele sent for a U.S. marshal and he showed up today with two deputies."

"Do you know who the U.S. marshal is?" asked Quentin.

"Said his name was Frank Reedy."

Quentin looked over at his partner and then back to Madden. "Reedy is one tough hombre and not one to go messing around with. He doesn't take any shit and he won't hesitate to do whatever is necessary to get a job done. That does complicate things a little."

"Does that mean that you won't take the job?"

"No, but the price will have to be double," said Quentin.

"I don't care. I'll pay you two thousand dollars each. I just want the son of a bitch dead," replied Madden.

"What about Frank Reedy?"

Madden thought about it for a moment. "Take care of the sheriff first and if Frank Reedy becomes a problem, I'll pay you to kill him and his deputies too."

"Frank Reedy will cost you triple what you're paying for a sheriff. Killing a U.S. marshal is big trouble. If we did that, we would have to leave the country, head for southern Mexico and hide out for quite a while and maybe never come back," added Timmons.

"How are you going to go after Steele?" asked Madden.

Quentin looked over at his partner and never said a word. They had worked together long enough to have an unwritten language between the two of them.

"We'll have to ambush him at night and ride straight out of town and fast. We'll need two extra horses so we can switch back and forth. That should give us a lead on the posse that I'm sure Frank Reedy will put together within ten minutes of us killing Steele. You'll have to pay us up front because we can't stop back here to get paid."

Madden stood up and shook hands again with both men. "I guess we have a deal. Mike, pick them out two of our best horses.

I'll have the money ready for you in a few minutes. I suppose you're going to do the deed tonight?"

"No sense putting off the inevitable is what I say," replied Unger.

꿩 ꛷

Sheriff Mark Steele was sitting in the jail with his two deputies along with Frank Reedy and his two deputies. They were talking small talk and just passing the time waiting for something to happen. It had been quiet for the last few hours since Rance Madden had stormed out of the jail.

"Well, Sheriff," asked Reedy, "do you think maybe Madden has changed his mind about this whole matter after seeing this U.S. marshal's badge?"

Steele shook his head negatively. "After seeing his reaction today after we let him out of jail, I don't see a chance of that. That old cuss is too mean to know when to quit. He might wait a while but he will definitely start more trouble with Thornton. He might wait a day or two but you can be sure he will eventually do something stupid."

"I figured as much. I've seen a whole lot of Rance Maddens in my days and they're all just about the same."

Tex broke into the conversation. "I just hope it's me who gets to plug his sorry ass when it comes time for it. I'd like nothing better than to screw that mean bastard into the ground. That's the only way to bury that man, he's so damn crooked."

Reedy laughed at that. "I don't think I've ever heard it put quite that way before, but you do have a point, that's for sure. You know what, Sheriff?" Reedy said as he turned his attention back to Steele. "Maybe I should go out and meet this Thornton fellow and give him the same warning as I did Madden. It might help if he finds out that a U.S. marshal is in town."

Steele thought about it for a minute. "It sure can't hurt. Why don't you take Buck out with you and your deputies?"

"Me and my two deputies here can handle it. After all, we're just going out to talk and you told me that Thornton is the more reasonable of the two."

"Yeah, but I like the idea of showing more force. Four badges are better than three. I'll keep Tex here with me. I don't think Madden will try anything tonight. He's probably back at his ranch plotting with his hired guns, and I figure that will take him a day or so to actually do something."

"You're probably right. I'll take Buck along with me, but he has to understand that he must follow my orders when he's with me," he said, as he looked at Buck.

"I understand, Marshal. I have no problem with following the orders of a U.S. marshal," said Buck, before Steele could even reply.

"Well, let's saddle up and take a little ride out to the Thornton ranch," said Reedy, as he and everyone else stood up.

Reedy, Torrey Abel, Hal Banks and Buck Hern all walked out and over to the livery. It wasn't more than five minutes before they rode out of town heading for the Thornton ranch. Steele and Tex took a stroll around town, checking for any signs of trouble. Finding none, they decided to have an early supper and sample some more of Pattie Nate's fine cooking.

CHAPTER NINE

"That was one mighty fine meal," remarked Sheriff Steele, as he patted his stomach as if he were testing a watermelon for ripeness.

"Yep," added Tex, "it was good and tasty, and that bean and ham soup was the best, and that's a fact."

Pattie Nate was collecting the plates from the table. "You two sure ate enough. You'd think you both believed this was your last meal or something," said Pattie. "You want some more hot coffee?"

"Yeah, that sounds good," answered Steele. "Me and Tex here are going to sit a spell and then go make a round after dark."

Pattie fetched a fresh pot of coffee and brought it out and left it on the table with some fresh cream and sugar. "Where is your friend, Mr. Reedy?" asked Pattie, as she sat down with them for a minute.

"Reedy took his two deputies and Buck out to the Thornton ranch to give the same warning to him as he did to Madden."

"Thornton ain't your problem. That no good Rance Madden is your problem," replied Pattie.

"To a certain degree, I suppose that's true, but Thornton has used his share of hired guns."

"He was forced to by Madden. Thornton never caused any trouble the last ten years he's been here. It wasn't until Madden bought the old Mason spread and started all the trouble over water."

"I agree, but we have to try to treat them both as fair as we can. That's the law and I'm sworn to uphold it."

"Well, I think you should just go out and arrest Madden and keep him in jail until he rots," said Pattie sternly, as she got up from the table and went back into the kitchen before Steele could reply.

"I just love hearing you two going at it," said Tex, filling his coffee cup.

"I'm glad you find it amusing."

"Well, what else do we have for entertainment? Things haven't been a whole heap of fun since this all started and if you ask me, she's right."

"About what?"

"About locking Madden up and letting him rot in jail."

"You know we can't do that. We have to have a reason or else the judge will just let him go free and then it will be us who'll be in hot water."

Tex grinned. "Well, then why don't you let me go and plug that sorry ass from a hilltop and get this whole thing over with before any other good men get killed, and that includes anyone wearing a badge?"

"I can't let you do that, either."

"Well, I had to ask. Consider it an open offer."

"I'll keep that under my hat," Steele replied as he picked up his coffee.

"You know what else?" asked Tex with that wide grin.

"What?"

"I think Pattie is sweet on you."

"Don't start on me about that again. She just ain't ready quite yet."

"Yeah, well, maybe she's saving herself for old River Bend Bill," Tex said sheepishly, knowing that would get immediately under Steele's skin.

"You just had to go and spoil this fine meal by bringing that old codger up, didn't you."

"Well, I'm just trying to encourage you," Tex replied.

"I can just tell that this is going to be one long night with you. Now shut up and drink your coffee."

᠊᠊᠊᠊᠊᠊

Frank Reedy and the three deputies arrived at the Thornton ranch just before dusk. They never got off their horses. They waited out in front of the house until Thornton came out, followed by six other men, all hired guns, Reedy figured.

Thornton knew Buck but he had never seen the other three before. He didn't miss the fact that one of the three men was wearing a U.S. marshal's badge, and the other two were wearing deputy U.S. marshal's badges. "Why am I being visited by a U.S. marshal today?" asked Henry Thornton.

"I'm here to deliver the same message I delivered to Rance Madden this afternoon," answered Reedy.

"And what message is that, Marshal?"

"I'm here to stop the war brewing between you and Madden. From this moment on, anyone breaking the law will have the full weight of the U.S. marshal's office on their shoulders. This will be the only warning you will get, so heed it carefully. Have I made myself clear?"

"I'm not the one who's starting this war. Rance Madden is. Arrest him and all the problems will stop. I've only hired these men to protect my life and my property from that greedy bastard. Keep him off my property and away from my water and you'll have no problem from me. I will, however, protect what is rightfully mine and will do so by force. You know I have that right, Marshal."

"I understand the law, Mr. Thornton. I'm not here to get a lesson. I'm here to give one to anyone who breaks the law from here on in. I have two deputies with me and I can have a dozen more here in a matter of days. I'll leave you to enjoy the rest of your evening, gentlemen," said Reedy, as he turned his horse around, all three deputies following his lead.

Thornton and his men stood on the front porch of the house until Frank Reedy and his men were out of sight. One of Thornton's men, Toby Hewett, was the first to speak. "I know that marshal. He used to be a bounty hunter and he ain't someone to be messing with. He don't take no for an answer and once he's on the trail of a man, he don't quit until he gets him."

Thornton didn't respond right away. He kept looking out toward the trail leaving the ranch as if he could somehow still see the marshal and the three deputies. "Well," said Thornton, "I'm glad that he's here. Maybe he can finally convince Rance Madden to back off."

"I wouldn't bet on it," replied Hewett, "Madden is as stubborn as they come."

"I say we try to stay out of the way and see if the marshal and Sheriff Steele can handle the problem. If not, we'll hire some more guns to protect this ranch and the water."

Frank Reedy and the three deputies rode in silence for the first mile or so back to town. Reedy was trying to size Thornton up and figure out what kind of man he was. His conclusion was that Thornton wasn't the problem, but that Thornton would fight back with everything he had if cornered. There was no doubt in Reedy's mind that Rance Madden would be the problem.

"What are you thinking about, Frank?" Banks asked.

"I've just been thinking about Henry Thornton and what he might do to protect his water rights."

"The way I see it, Thornton will fight when pushed too far," replied Banks.

"That's the way I see it, too."

"Me too," added Abel, as he turned to Buck who was bringing up the rear. "Buck, what's your take on this? You've known Thornton for some time. Are we right?"

"I've known Thornton as a decent man who never started a fight. I agree, though, that he will fight when forced to and he will go to great lengths to protect that water and his land. If this war gets started, it will be a bloody one, and that's a fact," answered Buck.

"I'm afraid you're exactly right about that," said Reedy. "We might as well start planning for the worst."

⌐¬ ⌐¬

Quentin Unger and Gregory Timmons rode into Timber just before dusk. They went into Jed's Saloon to get a drink. As luck would have it, they found the sheriff and one of his deputies sitting at a table drinking coffee. Now that they could identify the sheriff, they could move along with their plan. This included starting a fire in a small vacant shack at the end of town. That would cause a distraction and would most definitely bring the sheriff out into the open.

"What about the deputy?" Unger asked.

"What about him? We've been paid to kill Steele, not the deputy."

"Yeah, I know that, but once we shoot the sheriff, we'll have his deputy on our trail before we can put some distance between us. I say we shoot the deputy, too. I didn't see any sign of that U.S. marshal or his deputies in town."

"Maybe you're right. If we shoot them both, we can probably get a good head start. I'll take the sheriff and you take the deputy," said Timmons.

Sheriff Steele and Tex were still relaxing and drinking hot coffee when one of the townsmen ran into the saloon. "Sheriff, that old shack down at the end of the street is on fire."

"Well," said Tex, "so much for a relaxing night. Next thing you know, we'll have a gunfight and who knows what else."

"I'm sure glad you look on the bright side of things, Tex."

"Trouble always comes in pairs, the way I see it."

Sheriff Steele and Tex walked out and headed down toward the fire. Men were already throwing buckets of water on the shack, but they were quickly losing the battle. Steele and Tex were about two hundred feet from the fire when a bullet hit Steele from behind, whirling him around from the impact, a second bullet slamming into him before he hit the dirt. A fraction of a second after the first bullet hit Steele, two bullets slammed into Tex, the first one in his left shoulder and the second one in the right leg, just below the hip. The two men fell into the dirt at the same time. Quentin Unger and Gregory Timmons were on their horses not more than five seconds after that and making a full run south of town, both dragging an extra horse.

With all the commotion and yelling about the fire, it took a full minute or so before anyone came to the realization that shots had been fired. Jed, who was still in the saloon, had heard them. When he ran outside, he spotted Sheriff Steele and Tex lying in the dirt. He yelled over to the dozen or so men who were still valiantly fighting the fire. "Hey, forget about that fire. The sheriff and Tex have been ambushed!" he hollered.

The men who had been fighting the fire stopped and one of them ran for the doctor while the rest of them ran to where Steele and Tex were. Steele was unconscious and Tex was moaning and groaning, holding his left shoulder. Doctor George Hammond came running, carrying a big black bag. He checked out the sheriff first.

"How bad is he, Doc?" Jed asked.

"He's been hit pretty badly. He took one shot in the back just above the right shoulder blade and the second bullet went straight through his left side, just below the lung, I hope. You men get him on my table right away while I check on Tex."

Four men picked up Steele and headed for the doctor's office. When they went past, Pattie Nate came running out of Jed's Saloon and let out a scream at the sight of Steele being carried into the doctor's office.

"What happened to him?" Pattie asked, visibly shaken.

"Someone ambushed the sheriff and Tex while we were trying to put out the fire," one of the men answered.

"Who did it? Who shot him?"

"No one knows. Everyone's attention was on the fire. We didn't even hear the shots above all the commotion over the fire. It was Jed who heard them."

"Is he still alive?"

"Well, he's still breathing, but he's unconscious. He's been hit twice and the doctor said it was pretty bad."

Pattie had tears running down her face as she watched the four men gently place Steele on one of the two tables in the middle of the room. They left and headed back to where Doctor Hammond was still checking out Tex. Pattie gently cradled Steele's face in her hands, some of her tears falling onto the sheriff's face. She kissed him on his forehead. "Damn it, don't you die on me Mark Steele. You hang on, you hear me?"

There was no response from Steele. Pattie knew that the doctor would need plenty of boiling water and cloths, so she immediately began the chore. She was putting the cloths into the pots of water when the doctor and Jed came into the room with four men carrying Tex who was moaning from the pain. They laid Tex onto the other table.

"Well," said Doctor Hammond, "I've got to work on the sheriff first since he's bleeding so badly. Pattie, get those cloths boiling as quickly as you can. One of you men go out back, get some extra firewood for the stove, and stoke it hot. It's going to be a long night."

The bullet that hit Steele in the back just above his right shoulder blade had bounced off the bone and exited out of the top of his shoulder. Doctor Hammond probed around, removed some bone fragments, and cleaned the wound. All the while he was doing this, Pattie was holding bandages on Steele's left side, trying to stop the bleeding as much as she could.

The doctor finished up with the first wound and started working on Steele's side. "Looks like a straight through and through. I don't think it hit any vital organs or bones, but one more inch and it would have hit the lower part of the lung, and that would not have been a good thing."

Doctor Hammond thoroughly cleaned out the wound from both the entry and exit points, stitched it up, and bandaged it. "That's all I can do for him now, Pattie. He's lost a lot of blood and I think he might be in a coma. I've got to work on Tex now." Pattie nodded, tears still streaming from her now blood-red eyes. She held onto Steele's left hand.

The doctor moved on to Tex, who was still moaning and groaning with pain. The doctor gave him some laudanum for the pain, but he knew it wouldn't help all that much. He started on the shoulder wound and that's when he noticed it. The bullet had bounced off the deputy's badge before entering his shoulder. Two men had to hold Tex down while the doctor dug around and found the bullet and a chunk of metal from the badge. He cleaned the wound and bandaged it up, and then he went to work on Tex' right leg. The bullet had bounced off the bone and exited out the side of the leg. The doctor dug out several bone fragments, cleaned the wound, and bandaged it.

"Well, he'll live, but he won't be able to walk on that leg for a while. He didn't lose as much blood as the sheriff did, so that is certainly in his favor. Damn sure will be sore for some time. I'm worried about the sheriff though," he said, as he turned back toward the table that Steele was lying on. He checked on his bandage job and was satisfied with it. "He's lost a lot of blood, and I'm going to have to change those bandages every day and clean the wounds. I'm worried about infection setting in. With the weakened condition he's in from the loss of blood, it might kill him."

Pattie looked up at Doctor Hammond with a determined look. "We are not going to let that happen, Doctor. I'll stay with him night and day and tend to him if I have to, but we can't let him die."

"We'll do all we can, but I can't guarantee that he'll make it, especially if he doesn't wake up in the next few days. He's going to need nourishment to get his strength back. I believe he's in a coma and that might last a few days or weeks. There is no way to know for sure."

"I'm staying here for the night, Doctor. I want to help as much as I can."

Doctor Hammond nodded in agreement. Pattie got herself a chair and sat there holding Steele's left hand. She could hear Tex moan once in a while, but he didn't say anything.

CHAPTER TEN

Frank Reedy and the three deputies rode into town about an hour after the doctor had finished up working on the sheriff and Tex. The doctor walked over to the livery to give the news to Reedy.

"Marshal, something terrible has happened."

"What happened?"

"Someone ambushed the sheriff and Tex. They both were shot twice. Tex is going to make it, but I'm a little worried about the sheriff."

"Who did the shooting?"

"We don't know; someone started a fire in a little shack at the end of the street, and everyone was distracted by it, and that's when it happened."

Reedy turned to his two deputies. "You two saddle up again and find a few other men who will volunteer for a posse. I'm going over to see Steele for a minute and then we'll go after those bastards who ambushed the sheriff and his deputy."

"I want to go too," added Buck.

"Don't you think you should stay in town?"

"Normally, I would agree with you, but I want to be there when you catch these men. I might just hang them from the nearest tree when we catch them."

"All right, if you feel that strongly about coming with us. I will tell you though, that there will be no hanging. If we catch them, we bring them into town and lock them up, legally, understand?"

"I suppose you're right. Let's go see the sheriff and Tex."

Reedy and Buck walked into the doctor's office to find two motionless bodies, Doctor Hammond and one sobbing woman. Pattie Nate looked up at the marshal. "I want you to get the men who did this, Marshal."

"I'll do my best, Pattie, you can be sure of that. Mark Steele was not only a fellow lawman to me; he was a personal friend," replied Reedy. "I have a posse waiting and I have to go now. You take good care of my friend, Doctor."

Doctor Hammond nodded affirmatively. Frank Reedy walked back to the livery and met up with his two deputies and three other men who volunteered to join the posse.

"Anybody find their tracks yet?" Reedy asked.

"I found them," said Banks. "They headed south. By the looks of the tracks, they both have an extra horse and it's been a couple of hours since the shooting. I don't know if we can catch up with them, especially at night. It will be slow going following the tracks."

"Well, we'll damn sure try anyway. At least we can get a start," replied Reedy, as he mounted his horse. "Let's go, men. Hal, you're the best tracker so you take the lead."

All six men headed south. The three men who had volunteered for the posse were Roland Johnston, Al Calahan and Marsh Carsen. It was painfully slow going with Hal having to dismount and light a match to see the hoof prints. Twice they had to double back to find the tracks again after losing them. Reedy finally decided that they should make camp and wait until morning to continue.

They headed out at daybreak riding as fast as they could with Hal in the lead, tracking. The tracks led them around a large hill that opened up to a large flat area that had to be ten or fifteen miles across. Reedy reined in his horse at the edge of the clearing and the rest on the men followed suit.

Reedy took off his hat and wiped his forehead. "Damn it. The tracks go straight across that flat land and that gives them a hell of a lead. I guess we'll have to ride a little harder."

"Hell, my horse is plumb tuckered out already," replied Roland. "He'll be damn near dead once we get to the other side."

"We have to give it a try anyway. Any of you three men who volunteered can drop out if you want. The rest of us are still going after them," replied Reedy.

They all looked at one another. Roland Johnston was the first to speak. "I guess I might as well find out how far this old horse can go."

"I'm in too, Marshal," added Al Calahan.

"Don't leave me out," said Marsh Carsen.

"All right," replied Reedy. "Let's ride," he said as he spurred his horse.

They rode at a pretty fast pace straight across the open land. They slowed the pace the last few miles as the horses started showing the stress they were under. By the time they got to the end of the open stretch they were at a walk. The tracks led them to a heavily wooded area. They got off their horses, letting them rest for a few minutes.

"Marshal, we've got to find some water for these horses," said Banks.

"Yeah, they won't get much farther without some."

"I don't think you'll have to worry about water for too long, Marshal," said Carsen, as he pointed to the sky. "Those clouds are full of water and it looks like they're going to dump it right on us any minute now.

Frank Reedy looked up. The storm clouds were coming at them from the same direction that the tracks went, which meant that the men they were tracking were probably already in the rain. "What do you think, Hal?" asked Reedy.

"I could follow their tracks just fine through the woods even with the rain. I can spot broken branches and trampled weeds and brush. The problem will be once they get out into a clearing again. The rain will wash the tracks enough that we'll most likely lose their trail."

"Damn it! I hate to give it up, but I reckon you're right."

The rain started slowly and picked up speed quickly. Within a minute, it was pouring down in buckets. They all took their hats off and let the clean water rinse the dust off their faces. Then they all used their hats to gather water and made sure each horse had enough to drink.

"Men, mount up and let's head back to Timber. We'll have to put this off until later, but make damn sure that we are going to find out who those two are and put them on our wanted list," Reedy said.

Pattie had not left Sheriff Steele's side for the last twelve hours since he had been shot. He was still unconscious, but Tex had woken in severe pain along with a severe appetite. Doctor Hammond sent for some food and propped Tex up so that he could eat. He was watching Pattie as he ate some soup. She smiled at him but didn't say anything. She kept staring at Steele as if he were going to open his eyes any minute.

"Pattie," said Tex, "go on and get some sleep. I'm awake now and I'll watch over him. The doctor will send for you as soon and he wakes up, I promise."

"Do you promise?"

"I promise."

"The second he wakes up?"

"Yes, the second he wakes up, I promise. Now go get some sleep. Besides, we've got to get Jed out of that kitchen," Tex said, as he put his half-eaten bowl of soup down.

Pattie smiled a little and squeezed Steele's hand one more time.

"Go on and get some rest and go cook something eatable over there, 'cause I'm going to be mighty hungry later on."

"I guess you're right. Jed never did learn to cook much. I'll get a few winks and go back to the kitchen. Don't you forget to call me. I mean it."

"I promised I would and I always keep my promises," said Tex.

Pattie walked out and headed for her room, which was upstairs over Jed's Saloon. Jed had given her the room in order to keep her working there. She washed up and put her face in her hands, shaking her head. She got into her bed, placing her face on the very soft pillow. She thought about Mark Steele as she slowly fell off to sleep, but just before she fell into darkness, she thought of another man. She was thinking about Jess Williams and what she might have to do.

The explosion from the large bundle of dynamite was deafening. Seconds after the smoke cleared, thousands of gallons of water came rushing out of Henry Thornton's last retention pond and down the river. Rance Madden had an evil smile on his face as he watched the water head down the river, going exactly where he wanted it to go. Into his four water storage basins, which were almost empty. This would be enough water to completely fill his four basins. He had brought out ten of his men with him. Not because it took ten men to dynamite the basin, but because he knew that Thornton's men would be close by and would come running to the explosion site. That was exactly what he wanted. It didn't take long.

Four of Henry Thornton's men came riding their horses as fast as they could. As soon as they reined up their horses to examine the damage from the explosion, Rance Madden's men, who had been hiding in the brush, opened fire with their Winchesters, knocking all four riders out of their saddles. They never had a chance to draw their weapons. Three more of Thornton's men came over a slight rise and rode straight into the gunfire, firing Winchesters as they rode. They were able to pick off two of Madden's men before all three of them took slugs and hit the ground, their horses circling off, back toward the ranch.

Madden looked over the carnage and the damage he had just caused and smiled with an evil satisfaction. He had gotten the water he needed and killed seven of Thornton's men in the process. That left him with more men than Thornton and that gave him the edge, for now. He had taken Sheriff Steele out of the equation and Marshal Reedy was on the trail of Quentin Unger and Gregory

Timmons. On top of all that, Madden had sent for at least six more hired guns who would be arriving over the next few weeks. He had a plan and he was going to carry it out, and it didn't matter to him how many men had to die before he accomplished it.

Madden gathered up the eight men he had left and headed for Timber to execute the next part of his plan. As they rode into town, his men were firing off rounds into the air, whooping, and hollering. Doctor Hammond came out to the front of his office and one of Madden's men shot out the window to his left. Hammond went back into his office. The bullet went right over Tex's head.

"Doc, get my gun over there and help me off this table," demanded Tex.

"Are you out of your mind? If you get off that table, you'll bleed to death in five minutes when those wounds open up."

"Yeah, but I'll get a few of them before that happens."

"I won't do it; you just lie still and let's see what happens. Maybe they'll get drunk and leave."

"That's Madden's bunch. They ain't just going to get drunk and leave. I can promise you that."

"It doesn't really matter; you can't get off that table. If you do, you'll die for sure."

Madden's men reined up in front of Jed's Saloon and tied up their horses. Madden took two of his best men with him as he walked over to the doctor's office. Murphy Monroe and Taylor Stowe were hard men with honed pistol skills. Madden walked into Doctor Hammond's office and found Hammond sitting sheepishly behind his desk. Steele was still unconscious but Madden looked at Tex who was sneering back at him in defiance.

"Madden, you get your men out of town right now, before I have you all arrested and locked up," Tex exclaimed.

Madden laughed and his men smiled. "I don't think you or your boss is in any position to give orders anymore. I have control of this town now and I'm giving the orders. Would you like to know what my first order is?"

"You kiss my ass, Madden. You ain't in control of anything."

"We'll see about that," replied Madden, as he nodded at Monroe and Stowe. "Men, take Tex and go lock him up in the jail.

"You can't do that," pleaded Doctor Hammond, who had now stood up. "If you move him you'll open up his wounds and he'll bleed to death."

"I don't give a shit if he bleeds to death or not. If you want, I can have him shot right now and save you all the worry, Doctor."

Hammond shut his mouth and Monroe and Stowe grabbed Tex and pulled him off the table. They began to drag him over to the jail cell. Pattie Nate intercepted them and stopped them in the middle of the street.

"What in the hell are you two men doing? You can't move him. He'll bleed to death."

Monroe took the back of his hand and hit Pattie so hard that she fell into the street, almost unconscious. Then the two men went over to the jail, threw Tex into a cell, and locked it. Tex was bleeding pretty badly now and he fell unconscious from the weakness and loss of blood.

Rance Madden was standing over Steele, who was still in an unconscious state. "What about the sheriff, Doc? Is he going to come around or not?"

"He's in bad shape. He's lost a lot of blood and he's so weak that he won't be a problem to you even if he does wake up. Just leave him with me," pleaded Hammond.

"All right. But if he gets off that table, I'll not only kill him, I'll kill you too. You hear me?"

"I hear you."

Pattie Nate came rushing in, blood running down her cheek from her right eye. "Rance Madden, you get away from him!" she screamed.

Madden grabbed Pattie by the neck and pushed her down into a chair. "You shut your mouth, woman. If I have any more trouble from you, I just might decide to let a few of my men have a private moment alone with you, if you get my drift. Remember what I said, Doc," added Madden as he walked out and headed for the saloon. A minute later, one of Madden's men walked into the doctor's office and stood guard with a rifle. He smiled at Pattie as if he had known what Madden had said to her.

Madden walked into the saloon and had a drink with his men. They were all drinking whiskey and had already shot the place up pretty bad. Madden walked behind the bar and grabbed the best bottle of whiskey he could find and nodded for Murphy Monroe and Taylor Stowe to join him at a table. The three of them sat down and Madden poured them all a drink.

"Monroe, I want you to go out to the ranch and bring back four more men. Stowe, I want you to pick out four good men, go out of town, and figure out where that damn marshal will come into town. I want you and your men to ambush them and either kill them or capture them. I don't care which."

Both men finished their drinks and went about their assigned duties. They were loyal to Madden and were paid well for their work. Madden sat there sipping the fine whiskey and feeling pretty satisfied with his accomplishments today. He had Steele and Tex out of commission and Frank Reedy on the trail of the ambushers and about to be ambushed himself. And he had total control of the town. That along with killing seven of Henry Thornton's men and draining his water basins was pretty satisfying to him indeed. Yes, he had finally gotten what he had wished for, or so he thought.

CHAPTER ELEVEN

J ess got an early start from Abilene. He tipped his hat as he went past Bad Axe McCoy who was sitting in his rocker with a hot cup of coffee. Jess could see the steam coming from the cup, caused by the cool morning air. He decided that he might as well stop in Black Creek on his way to St. Louis, since it wasn't really that far out of the way. He would only stay one night and then head back out in the morning, just enough time to have a meal with Jim and Sara and see Tony and Andy. It took him a day and a half to get to Black Creek. He reined up in front of Tony's Livery and Tony came out from inside to greet him.

"Jess, it's about time you came back here for a visit. Did you find your father?"

"No, and don't call him my father. Call him Eddie Sloan. From what I've learned about him, I wouldn't want him for a father."

"I hear you, and I'll do as you ask."

"I'm on his trail again, though. He's on a train heading for St. Louis right now. It seems like every time I catch up to him, he's gone and I have to start all over again. I figured I might as well stop by for one night and visit since I was going close by Black Creek anyway."

"Well, I'm sure glad you did. Jim, Sara and Andy will be mighty glad to see you."

"I trust you've taken good care of Gray?"

"He's out back sunning himself as we speak."

Jess looked out back and saw Gray. "He does look mighty happy."

"He should be. He gets the best feed and plenty of rest. I ride him once in a while, like you asked."

"You're a good man, and a good friend, Tony."

"Hey, I got good news for you."

"I need some good news for a change. What is it?"

"Old Andy finally got LeAnn married off to a young man here in town. He's the new preacher who showed up about a year or so ago."

"A preacher?"

"Yeah, they fell in love the minute they laid eyes on each other. Andy is in his glory. He's hired himself a new cook and she's pretty good at it."

"I'll make sure to stop and congratulate Andy after I stop and see Jim and Sara."

Jess walked over to Smythe's General Store. He walked in on Jim stocking shelves, as usual. "I see that you're still doing a good business, Jim."

Jim turned around and almost fell off the footstool. "Why, I'll be damned. It's about time you came back home. Sara, come out and see who's come back home for a visit."

Sara came out and a wide smile spread across her face. "Jess, I'm so glad to see you again," she said, as she gave him a strong hug. "Come on into the kitchen for some coffee and a bite to eat."

"I won't argue with you about that."

The three of them went into the kitchen. Jim poured Jess a cup of coffee and then one for himself and Sara. Sara cut three pieces of chocolate cake that she had baked the morning before. It was rich and heavy, just the way Jess liked it.

"So, how have you two been?" asked Jess.

"Things have been pretty quiet since you cleaned up the town. Cal Hardin bought out the Carter spread and the new hardware store. He's been good to the townsfolk, too. He helped build a new schoolhouse and he got us a good man for our sheriff. We've got a new mayor and town council, and everyone is working together to make Black Creek a nice little town."

"I'm glad to hear all that. How about the other general store that Hardin bought? Is it hurting your business very much?"

Sara spoke up before Jim could answer. "Not at all, Jess. He's carrying different merchandise than what we carry. He came over to meet with us, he made a list of the things we carry, and he assured us that he would carry different things. He sells a lot of woman's clothing and things that we can't afford to stock. He's been really nice about the whole thing. He speaks very highly about you, too. He said he wouldn't do anything to hurt any of your friends."

"I guess there really are some good men in the world after all," said Jess.

"Seems like it," replied Jim.

"Well," said Sara, "how long are you planning to stay?"

"Actually, I was on my way to St. Louis, but I decided to stop by on my way and stay overnight."

"What's in St. Louis, Jess?" Sara asked.

"Eddie Sloan is on a train heading there. I almost caught up with him in Abilene but just missed him again. That seems to happen most of the time so I might as well stay overnight and visit. If he ain't in St. Louis when I get there, I'll get another lead and follow him wherever he goes."

"Well, we're glad to have you stay, even if it is for only one night."

"Thanks, Sara. I'm going to go over to Andy's to see him. I assume I can stay in the room upstairs?"

"You don't even have to ask about that. It's always available to you."

Jess walked out and headed over to Andy's Saloon. He walked in and Andy was behind the bar with his back to Jess, trying to put some bottles of whiskey on a shelf that was almost out of reach.

"You old cuss, how are you?" asked Jess.

"Huh?" Andy turned around to see who was talking. "Why, I'll be damned. "It's about time ya came around to visit. Where the hell have ya been the last few years?"

"All over the country, chasing my tail around in a big circle."

"Did ya find Eddie Sloan yet?"

"No, he keeps one step ahead of me all the time. Every time I think I'm going to catch up with him, he moves again. He is one slick fellow, I'll give him that."

"He ain't headed here, is he?" asked Andy, with a worried look on his face.

"No, he's headed for St. Louis for a high stakes poker game. Why the worrisome look?"

"I ain't had my place shot up for a while and I'd kinda like to keep it that way. Anytime you come around, trouble seems to follow right behind."

"Yeah, that does seem to be the case, doesn't it?"

"Yep, it sure does. Hey, did ya hear the good news?"

"Are you talking about getting LeAnn married off?"

"Hell, yes. It's been so much quieter around here since she gone off and married that new preacher, Elmer Nevans. They live in a room up above the church. I got me a new cook and a damn good one, too. You know the best part?"

"What?"

"She does what she's told and don't talk back none."

"I'm real glad to hear it, especially the part about LeAnn getting married. That's one thing less I have to worry about. Andy, since you have this great cook, how about I have supper with Jim and Sara here tonight? Why don't you and Tony join us, too?"

"Damn if that don't sound mighty nice. I'll have her whip up something real nice."

"Who is the new sheriff?"

"Albert Eaves is his name. He went to work for Hardin after you left and when Hardin found out that he had been a sheriff before, Hardin told the town council if they would hire Eaves on as sheriff, he would pay the wages for the sheriff for the first year. He's been a pretty good sheriff so far. Ain't nobody tested him yet though, if ya know what I mean."

"Well, I suppose I should go and announce my presence in town."

"He'll be glad to finally meet ya. We all been talkin' 'bout ya."

"Okay, then. I'll see you back here for supper, say about six?"

"I'll have a table ready for ya."

Jess walked out and headed for the sheriff's office. Albert Eaves was sitting behind a small desk, reading the newspaper when Jess walked into his office.

"Good afternoon, Sheriff Eaves. I'm Jess Williams," Jess said, as he extended his hand out.

Eaves jumped up and shook hands with Jess. Eaves had a big smile. "I'm glad to finally meet the man everyone has told me about since taking this job. What brings you back to Black Creek? Thinking about settling down again?"

"Not me, Sheriff. I'm just here for an overnight stay to visit with some old friends. Just figured I should let you know I was in town."

"Hell, I knew that before your horses were stabled. Everyone noticed you the moment you rode into town."

"I get that a lot."

"I bet you do. Well, if you need anything, let me know. I hope your stay will be a good and uneventful one."

"I know exactly what you mean. Sheriff, do you have any wanted posters? I figured I might as well check as long as I'm here."

"Let me look. I know I've got a few of them." Eaves looked around his desk shuffling papers from one pile to the next. "Here's one. A three hundred dollar bounty for robbing a bank." He shuffled some more papers. "Here's another one. A five hundred dollar bounty for cattle rustling. That's all I have at the moment. You want them?"

"No. I only chase the worst of them."

"I heard that about you."

"Thanks again, Sheriff. I'm going to head to the telegraph office to check for any messages."

Jess shook hands with the sheriff again and walked to the telegraph office to see if he had any messages. He always did that when he hit any town. The telegraph operator informed him that there were no messages for a Jess Williams. Jess tossed him a dollar for his efforts and the operator thanked him. Jess told the operator that if any message came in before he left town to have someone deliver it to him. The operator said that he would do that. Then, Jess went back to Jim and Sara's and took a nice afternoon nap.

Jess woke and headed for the livery to check on his horses and tell Tony about supper. Tony was pounding metal when Jess arrived. "Tony, I'm having supper over at Andy's at six with Andy, Jim and Sara and I would like you to join us."

"I'd be more than happy to oblige you. I like the new cooking over there."

Tony looked past Jess at the same time that Jess heard it. Jess turned around to see who the rider coming into town was. The minute Jess laid eyes on the man, he knew it meant trouble. The man's name was Bill Langsten, but Jess didn't know that yet. What he did know was that the man had the unmistakable look of a gunslinger. The rider looked at Jess as he slowly rode past and headed for Andy's Saloon. He locked eyes with Jess only for a moment but that was all that was needed.

"Looks like trouble to me," said Tony.

"You're quite right about that."

"Does he look familiar to you?"

"Nope. I've never laid eyes on him before, but I'm betting I'm going to meet him before long."

"Do you think he knows who you are?"

"I don't know if he knows who I am, but I'm certain that he knows what I am, and that's all the reason a man like that needs. Let's hope he's just passing through."

"I knew it was too quiet around here."

Jess went back to Smythe's General Store and picked up the supplies he had asked Jim to gather for him. He took them to the livery and loaded them into his saddlebags. Then they all met at Andy's for supper. Andy had a nice tablecloth for the table.

Tony was the last to arrive in the saloon. "Well, ain't this fancy, a tablecloth and all," Tony said, somewhat sarcastically, the comment meant for Andy.

"Don't you git smart with me or you'll git no supper," retorted Andy.

"A smart man knows when to shut his yap," replied Tony.

Tony and Andy were on one side of the large table with Jim and Sara sitting across from them. The one end of the table was empty. Jess had done that on purpose. The empty end was closest to the bar and the other end, where Jess was seated, allowed him a full view of the saloon, including Langston, who was still bellied up to the bar. Langsten would glance over at Jess once in a while but Jess did not look directly at Langsten; he simply kept him within his peripheral vision. Andy's new cook, Marianne Beals, began bringing large plates of food to the table. She brought fried chicken, steaks, boiled potatoes, carrots and fresh baked rolls. It was all delicious.

They all sat there and ate for over an hour, making small talk about nothing in general. Jess was enjoying the company of good friends and decided that he needed to do this on a regular basis. He did, however, keep an eye on Langsten, not letting his guard down, even at a time like this.

"Well, that was one mighty fine meal, Andy," said Jim.

"You'll get no argument from me on that one," Tony said, holding his rock hard stomach, as if to keep it from bursting.

"I'm glad you all enjoyed it," said Jess. "We have to do this more often."

"That would be nice," added Sara. "You should make it a habit to stop back in town once in a while and have a good meal with good friends. I have really enjoyed myself tonight. Now, I have to go and finish up some paperwork at the store. Jim," Sara said, as she stood up, "why don't you stay here and have a drink with these three while I do that?"

All four men stood up in respect when Sara got up from her chair. Jim had a wide smile. "I'll be delighted to stay and have a drink with my friends here. You sure you can handle all that paperwork by yourself?"

"You'd just get in the way, like always," Sara said, as she turned to leave. "Jess, I'll have your room ready for you for tonight."

"Thank you, Sara. I enjoyed myself tonight," replied Jess. He ordered a fine bottle of brandy for the four of them. They sat there and enjoyed the bottle and talking about all sorts of things. Langsten never made a move or even acted like he would. Jess thought that odd and hoped that Langsten would ride out of town without incident. Jess and Jim walked back to the store, Andy went back to work, and Tony went back to his place and went to sleep. Not one of the four slept comfortably.

CHAPTER TWELVE

Jess woke to the smell of eggs and bacon frying. He quickly got dressed, headed downstairs, and had a huge breakfast. He hugged Sara and shook hands with Jim and walked to the livery. Tony, knowing Jess, had already saddled up Gray and Sharps and had them ready for Jess before he got there.

"Thanks, Tony. I guess that gunslinger left town?"

"I don't know. I didn't see him leave. Andy came in a few minutes ago and told me that he left the saloon at closing time but that he didn't actually see him leave town. Probably did though. He would've done something by now, don't you think?"

"I would've thought so. Well, I've got to hit the trail. Thanks again for everything, Tony."

Jess climbed up in the saddle and walked Gray toward the east end of town. That's when it happened. Langsten walked out from the side of the last building on the trail out of town. He walked out into the middle of the street and waited for Jess. Jess rode to within fifty feet of Langsten, got off Gray, and handed the reins to Tony, who had seen what happened and had already walked over to Jess. Tony took the horses off to the side and tied them to a rail.

Jess's hammer strap was already off. He noticed that the other man's hammer strap was also off. They stared at each other for almost a minute before Jess spoke.

"What's your name, Mister?"

"My name is Bill Langsten and I already know who you are. It took me a while to figure it out but that pistol and holster are a dead giveaway."

"It usually is. Normally I would ask why, but I already know. You're here for the reputation, aren't you?"

"Fast on the draw and smart too," said Langsten. "Yep, I aim to be the one who finally outdraws the famous Jess Williams."

"I do have one question for you though. Why didn't you make a move last night in the saloon?"

"I may be a gunslinger trying to make a name for myself, but that don't make me rude. I saw you were having a nice supper with your friends, so I decided to let you finish it in peace. There is always time later for gunplay."

"Mr. Langsten, you seem to be a nice enough fellow. Why don't you just forget this and go on about your business. The reputation just ain't worth dying for."

"That's where you're wrong. Every gunslinger I know worth his salt would take a crack at you if he had the chance."

"Okay, it's your play. I'm ready when you are."

Langsten continued to stare at Jess for almost another whole minute. Jess thought for a moment that Langsten was going to change his mind and ride out, but then he saw it. It was that revealing look that Jess had seen in every gunslinger's eyes a fraction of a second before he went for his gun. Langsten had snaked his pistol almost out of the holster when Jess's first slug hit him in the chest. Langsten stumbled backward a few steps and dropped his pistol in the dirt. He never looked at his wound even though he felt the warm blood running down his chest under his clean white shirt. He just kept staring at Jess until his legs gave out. He collapsed to the ground on his knees and then fell face forward into the dirt. Jess shook his head, wondering again about the idea of a man dying just so he could claim he was faster than another man.

The gunfire had woken the town. Andy was running up the street with his scattergun and the sheriff was running out of his office, buckling his gun belt as he did so. The sheriff checked to see if Langsten had a pulse. There was none. He looked up at Jess, who had holstered his pistol but had not yet replaced the hammer strap. He didn't know Sheriff Eaves that well and would take no chances.

"It was his call, Sheriff," said Jess, "I didn't want any part of it. He forced my hand."

"Jess is telling it right," added Tony. "I saw the whole thing. Jess was riding out when that man walked out into the middle of the street and stopped him."

Sheriff Eaves looked back and forth at Tony and Jess and then back down to Langston's body. "I figured he might be trouble before he left town. I thought he rode out last night."

Jim and Sara came running down the street. "Jess, are you all right?" asked Sara, as she gave him a hug.

"I'm fine, Sara. Sorry this had to happen but I tried to talk him out of it," replied Jess.

"Well," said the sheriff, "you might as well continue on your journey, Mr. Williams. "I don't see where you have any wrongdoing in this matter. Tony, go fetch the undertaker."

Just as Tony was going for the undertaker, a young man was running past him and toward Jess. "Mr. Williams…Mr. Williams…I have a telegraph message for you."

The young man handed Jess a piece of folded paper and Jess handed the young man a silver dollar. "Thanks, Mister," he said, as he ran back to the telegraph office.

Jess unfolded the message and read it to himself. Sara, Jim, Tony, Andy and the sheriff watched the change come over Jess's face as he read it. They could tell it wasn't anything good. The message was as follows…

Dear Jess,

Sheriff Steele was ambushed and is on his deathbed. Rance Madden has taken over the town. Marshal Reedy is on the trail of the men who shot the sheriff. A war between two ranches is taking place and we are all in the middle of it. Please make your way here as fast as possible. If this message doesn't reach you soon, I'm afraid of how many will die.

Your friend,
Pattie Nate

"What is it, Jess," Sara asked.

"A change in plans. Looks like it's another lucky day for Eddie Sloan."

"What happened?" asked Tony.

"A good friend of mine, Sheriff Steele down in Timber, Texas has been ambushed and shot. It seems that a ranch war has erupted between two ranch owners and my friends in Timber are square in the middle of it."

"I know Sheriff Steele," said Sheriff Eaves, "and I know Marshal Reedy. Reedy can handle it."

"Maybe he can, but he's about to get some help," replied Jess, as he swung up into the saddle. "It was a nice visit but I have to ride fast and hard."

Jess nodded to everyone as he took off out the east end of town and headed in the direction of Timber, Texas. He figured it would take him at least three days of hard riding to get there. It was times like this that he appreciated the two fine long horses that Cal Hardin had given him.

❧ ❧

Frank Reedy and the three deputies, along with Marsh Carsen, Alfred Calahan and Roland Johnston, were drenched from the rain that had not let up on their way back to Timber. The three men who had volunteered for the posse split off from Reedy and the three deputies about a mile out of town and headed for their respective homesteads. Reedy and the three deputies all had their slickers pulled up tight around their collars and their hats tilted down. That's probably the only reason why Marshal Reedy or the other three deputies didn't see what they normally would have noticed. They were only about three hundred feet from the single main street of Timber when they were stopped by four men, each of them wielding a scattergun. The four men were Treat Knudsen, Richard Braun, Fred McAllister and Lester Kennedy.

"Hold up there, Marshal. Don't any of you try for your weapons or we'll open up on you with these here scatterguns," said Treat Knudsen.

Reedy knew a bad situation when he was in one, and four scatterguns going off all at once would definitely be as bad as it gets. He knew that they had no chance. Their slickers were in the way of getting to their pistols.

"Men," Reedy said to the deputies, "don't try anything. They've got the drop on us. We'll have to wait for another time."

"Shut up and get off those horses, one at a time," said Knudsen. "McAllister, grab their reins." McAllister took the reins of each horse as Reedy and his deputies dismounted. Then, they walked Reedy, Banks, Abel and Buck right down the middle of the street and through the mud and up the two steps to the jail. Two men armed with scatterguns were guarding the front of the jail. Dale Tombs and Gus Gilroy had been sitting in rocking chairs and stood up as Reedy and his men got to the wooden walk under the overhang of the jail.

"Well, I'll be damned. Marshal Frank Reedy himself, come to pay us a visit in our new jail cell. What do you think of that, Gus?" asked Tombs.

"I think it's mighty nice of the marshal here to come and stay a night or two. The food's real good, Marshal. All the bread and water you boys can choke down."

Knudsen prodded Reedy with the barrel of the scattergun and Gus Gilroy opened the door. Reedy and his three men walked into the small office. There were two more armed men inside. Vernon Foster and Leonard Sand had been playing poker before Reedy and his men had been walked down the street, but they were now standing up and holding rifles. They were not taking any chances with Reedy and his men. Foster opened up a jail cell and Knudsen pushed all four of them into the one cell. Vernon Foster locked the cell door.

Reedy took off his hat. "This cell ain't big enough for four men. Why don't you put two of us in the other cell?"

"Because we don't have to do anything you say, Marshal. You ain't running things around here any more than Sheriff Steele is," responded Knudsen.

"Where is the sheriff?"

"Why, he's all laid up over at the doc's place. He's taking a slow walk to hell."

"You men will hang for this, I can promise you that," said Reedy. "There will be more marshals looking for me if I don't check in regular."

"Oh, we'll be checking in for you over at the telegraph office since you'll be unavailable. We'll make sure your message says that everything is just fine and that you don't need any more help."

Tex, who had been sleeping in the other cell, was now awake and moaning. Buck walked over to look at Tex who was lying on the floor, wounded in two places and still bleeding.

"Tex, it's Buck. Can you hear me?" Buck asked.

Tex just moaned once more, not opening his eyes. He moved a little and then fell off to sleep again. Reedy and the four men took off their slickers. Two of them sat on the bunk and two sat on the floor. Knudsen and the other three men with him left, leaving Vernon Foster and Leonard Sand in the jail. Vernon locked the door after they left.

"Me and my men could use some hot coffee," said Reedy. "We've been riding in that downpour all day."

Vernon and Leonard looked at each other as if the other one was supposed to decide what to do. Vernon sat back down, leaving it up to Leonard to decide whether or not to make a pot of coffee for the four wet men. "I guess I can make a pot of coffee for you. I'd be wantin' a hot cup right about now if I was you boys. Just make sure you sit still and don't give us any reason to shoot you 'cause those are our orders."

"Orders from who?" Reedy asked.

"Orders from the new boss in town, Mr. Rance Madden."

"So now he owns the town?"

Leonard looked over at Reedy with a glare. "You want this coffee or not?"

Reedy knew that if he pressed it, his men wouldn't get any coffee. Quite frankly, they needed something to warm them up and so did he. They were shivering badly from the damp cold.

꙰ ꙮ

Rance Madden had made Jed's Saloon his new office. He stayed there with several of his men planning his next move. He had been informed that Marshal Reedy and his two deputies along with Buck were locked behind bars at the jail. That left Madden with an open hand to do whatever he was willing to do without interference from the law. Pattie had spent most of her time cooking for Madden and his men, and Jed, a timid man, kept serving them whiskey. Once in a while Pattie would say something to Madden, but whenever she did, one of Madden's men would shove her back into the kitchen. One time they shoved her so hard she fell to the floor and banged her head on the corner of a cabinet, leaving her with a large knot on the top of her head. The knot had gone down somewhat but not her temper. She was still furious about what Madden had done to Sheriff Steele and she would never forgive Madden for it. Sometimes her temper would flare and she thought that she would lose complete control and get herself shot or even worse, raped and shot.

The only thing that kept her in check was the thought that she had been lucky enough to get the telegraph message sent to Jess before Madden had taken complete control of the town. She prayed that Jess would get the message and she knew that if he did, he would come and help. She also knew that it meant a lot of men would die, but she didn't care anymore. As far as she was concerned, Madden and every one of his men deserved to die. She would shoot them herself if given a gun and the opportunity to carry it out. But that would not happen. She had to rely solely on Jess Williams receiving her plea for help.

Madden was sitting at a large table with Knudsen, Braun, McAllister and Kennedy. Madden was a smart man and he knew that he needed to strike again while Thornton was down.

"Men, I think that tomorrow morning we go out to the Thornton ranch and attack. Have the men stay as far back as possible and use rifle fire and try to pick off some more of his men. If we get two or three, that will put him way down in force. We have him outnumbered at this point and I want to keep it that way. I've sent for several more men who should arrive at different times in the next several days. The more men we have, the better off we will be."

"That sounds like a good plan, boss," replied Knudsen. "How many men do you want me to take out there?"

"Take seven men and be careful. Be out there before first light and get your men hunkered down. Wait for any movement in the morning. Once you see two or more men visible, open fire and get as many of them as you can. Then ride out fast and hard. I don't think Thornton will send any men to chase after you. They will want to regroup and wait for more help."

"I see it that way too," said Knudsen. "We'll outsmart them and before long, we'll burn the place to the ground. Okay, boys, let's go and find four more men. We have our orders and we need to bunk down on the trail to Thornton's tonight so we can hit him at first light."

The four men walked out of the saloon. Jed brought Madden another whiskey. Pattie was glaring at him from behind the doorway of the kitchen.

"Get your ass back to cooking, woman, before I come over there and give you another knot on that thick skull of yours," exclaimed Madden.

"And why don't you take your men and leave town now, before something even more terrible happens? You can't escape the law forever. Do you really think that no one will ever find out what you've done? Do you think no one will ever come through this town again? Maybe that someone will be a marshal or a lawman. What will you do, kill them all? Don't you think someone will get suspicious eventually? My God, man, are you crazy?"

Madden's face got beet red and he threw the coffee cup at her. She ducked into the kitchen, the cup shattering on the wall. "Keep your ass back there, woman! I swear, if you keep pissing me off, I'll let my men have a go at you!"

CHAPTER THIRTEEN

The Thornton ranch was just coming alive at first light. Henry Thornton was waiting for the hot coffee to finish and he could hear a few of his men stirring slowing. One of them, James Malloy, went out to use the outhouse. Mack Packerd had been heading for the outhouse, but Malloy had beaten him to it so he decided to just roll a smoke on the front porch while waiting for Malloy to finish his morning constitution.

Treat Knudsen nodded at his men to spread the signal. The other seven men knew not to shoot until Knudsen fired first. Knudsen took careful aim at Packerd and fired. The slug hit Packerd right in the middle of his gut. Within seconds, dozens of rifle rounds were being fired at the Thornton ranch. Packerd was hit with two more slugs, finishing him off for good. Several slugs splintered the wood of the outhouse and Malloy stumbled out, firing his pistol with his right hand and holding up his pants with his left. He took three slugs, two to the chest and one in the leg.

Ezra Black was running from the bunkhouse and trying to get to the house to protect Thornton. He made it to the porch but was gunned down—four rifle slugs slamming into his back. Henry Thornton ran upstairs, grabbed his Winchester, and fired from the upstairs window. Three more of his men were in the ranch house and they were returning fire now. But then, all of a sudden, the firing that had been raining down on them ceased immediately. A few of Thornton's men were still firing and Thornton ordered them to stop. Once they did, Thornton could barely hear the noise of horses running. He couldn't see anything because the horses were running away back behind a rise and into the woods.

Thornton went down and outside to check on his men. Ezra Black lay on the porch next to Mack Packerd, and James Malloy lay dead just outside the outhouse. Amazingly, none of his other men were hit but that now left him with only seven good men. Certainly not enough to hold off any more attacks from Madden's men; he knew this was Madden's work.

Toby Hewitt walked out of the ranch house with his rifle across his arm, smoke still coming from the barrel. "Boss, do you want us to go after those men out there?"

Thornton didn't have to think long about his answer. "No. You'd probably be outnumbered and you'd probably never catch up to them. They planned this well, using rifles from a distance to pick off a few of us and then running like hell knowing that we wouldn't be able to mount up and ride fast enough to catch up with them."

"You figure it was Madden's men?"

"Who else would it be? I'm sure it was Madden who ordered this attack. For now, we'll have to hunker down here at the ranch and post guards twenty-four hours a day. We can't afford to lose anyone else. I'm going to have to send for more men but I have a hunch that if we go into town, we'll end up like Ezra and the other two we lost here."

"Boss, why don't you let me sneak into town tonight and see just what's going on? After I get back, if you don't think it's safe to go into Timber, we can send a rider to Red Rock to send for more men."

"That sounds like a good plan, but you be real careful. Don't take the normal trail into town. If any of Madden's men see you, they'll shoot you on sight and I can't afford to lose you."

"I'll be real careful, boss. I'll arrange for the guards and head out at dusk tonight."

"All right, but I suppose we need to dig some more graves. Bury these three out back next to the other seven we lost the other day.

That's ten good men dead in only a few days and all because of one greedy bastard."

Toby Hewitt, who was now the lead boss over the other six remaining men, ordered Stumpy Watson and Victor King to do the first round of guard duty. He took the other four and they dug the graves and buried the three dead men. Henry Thornton slowly walked back into the house and made coffee, his head hung low as he mourned the loss of his men.

⌐⌐

Treat Knudsen and the other seven men rode into Timber about an hour after sunrise. They stabled their horses and headed for the saloon. When they got there, the seven men headed straight for the bar, but Knudsen walked over to where Madden was sitting, eating bacon and eggs, all cooked up grudgingly by Pattie Nate.

Madden washed his mouthful of food down with some coffee. "Well, by the look on your face, Treat, I take it the attack went well?"

"It was perfect. We took out three of Thornton's men and all without a scratch on any of our own. The way I count it, Thornton should have only about seven or eight men left about now, unless he's gotten some more men that we don't know about."

"I doubt it, since some of them would have come through town to get to his ranch and we haven't seen anyone pass by. I'd say that Thornton is finished. Even if he does hire some more men, by then, we'll have burned down his place and killed Thornton and the rest. I say we let him worry himself sick for a few days and then go out and finish him off."

Pattie Nate, who had been listening to all of this, came out of the kitchen with a new pot of coffee and slammed it down on Madden's table. "You won't stop until you kill everyone you don't like, won't you?" Pattie asked, tears welling up in her eyes.

"This ain't none of your damn business, woman. Now get your ass back in that kitchen and start cooking up some more grub for these men."

566

Pattie walked back into the kitchen feeling helpless. She didn't like it one bit, but she did cook some more food for Madden's men. There was nothing else she could do. At least Madden had let her go and sit with Steele a few times each day. Steele had not regained consciousness yet and Pattie was worried sick. Doctor Hammond had told her that the longer he stayed in a coma, the less likely he would come out of it alive. At least Tex had regained some strength and was now sitting up in the jail cell. Madden had allowed her to take some soup to him. As for Frank Reedy and the other three deputies, it was still bread and water only. Things were not good, to say the least.

⚞⚟

Toby Hewitt had taken the long way into town, staying along the edge of the woods as much as possible. He knew that if he was caught, he would be shot on sight. He left his horse about a half mile outside of town and slowly and painstakingly made his way to the edge of town. He crawled most of the way to keep out of sight. He had made his way behind the first few buildings and had to dart between them a few times when anyone was around. Madden had so many men in town that he couldn't trust anyone. He figured he might try the doctor's office. When he finally made it there, one peek in the back window showed him an armed guard and Sheriff Steele, badly wounded and lying very still on a table. He was sitting on the ground trying to think about what he might do next. He wondered about Steele's deputies, Buck and Tex, and about Marshal Reedy and his two deputies. Just when he decided to try to make it to the jail and see what he could find out, he heard a woman's voice in the doctor's office.

Pattie Nate had finished feeding Madden's men and Madden had allowed her to go and see Steele before she went to her little room above the saloon that Jed had let her use. She walked in past the man sitting in the chair with a rifle across his lap and sat on a chair next to Steele. She held his hand. Doctor Hammond was sitting behind his desk reading some medical books.

"Doctor, is he ever going to come out of this?" Pattie asked, with new tears forming in her eyes.

"I won't lie to you Pattie; it doesn't look good for him. He hasn't moved a muscle yet. If he doesn't come out of that coma in the next few days or so, I don't think he ever will. He needs nourishment badly and he's getting weaker by the hour. The bleeding has stopped but he's lost a lot of blood. I'm afraid all we can do now is pray for a miracle."

Pattie sobbed quietly and kissed Mark Steele on his hand. "Please open your eyes, Mark, please," she begged quietly. There was no response. After about twenty minutes, she got up to leave and thanked the doctor again. She slowly walked over to the saloon, climbed the stairway on the side of the building, and opened the door to her little room. It wasn't much, only a ten by ten room with a single bed and one dresser with a small mirror on the wall. She didn't need much more than that. Of course, she had dreamed of having her own house one day, with Mark Steele.

Toby Hewitt had watched her and followed along the backs of the buildings slowly until he reached the bottom of the stairway leading up to Pattie's room. He quickly climbed the stairs as quietly as he could. There was a small window in the door and it was covered with a simple white piece of cotton cloth. He couldn't see inside and he didn't know if she was in there alone, but he needed to do something before someone spotted him at the top of the stairs. He decided to tap lightly on the window. A few seconds later, the cloth covering the window moved aside and Pattie's face appeared. Pattie was startled and a little scared. She figured maybe Rance Madden sent this man to carry out his threat of having his men teach her a lesson. Pattie started to say something and Toby put his finger on his lips, signifying for her to be silent.

He talked as quietly as he could through the glass pane. "Ma'am, I work for Henry Thornton. I need to speak with you about Madden. Please let me come in before one of Madden's men spot me up here."

Pattie closed the cloth and placed her back against the door, her heart thumping with fear. The man didn't look familiar to Pattie. She hadn't seen him around Madden or any of the other men, but then again, Madden had men arriving at different times so maybe this was a new hired gun. If this was one of Thornton's men though, he would be shot on sight if any of Madden's men spotted him, and they would surely take it out on her for having one of Thornton's men at her door. She had to let him in. She unlocked the door and let him enter.

"Thank you, ma'am. I was getting worried you weren't going to let me in. I was an open target out there. My name is Toby Hewitt."

"My name is Pattie Nate. You can call me Pattie."

Toby noticed a small chair by the dresser. "Ma'am, do you mind if I sit and talk to you about what has happened in town the last few days?"

Pattie motioned for him to sit and she sat down on the edge of her bed. "How about you tell me what you're doing here first? You said you work for Thornton. He's not completely innocent in all of this."

"Well, he's sure not as guilty as Madden. The marshal came to visit Thornton at the ranch and warned Thornton to let the law take care of the problem. That's exactly what Thornton was doing. Then, Madden sent men out to the Thornton ranch at daybreak and they opened fire on us with rifles while we was half asleep. They killed three of our men. Madden blew our water basins the other day with dynamite and killed seven more of our men in the process. That leaves us with only seven men left, including me. Now I come into town and find the sheriff lying almost dead over at Doc Hammond's and no sign of the marshal or any deputies."

"I can tell you where the marshal and the deputies are," interjected Pattie. "Madden has them all locked up over at the jail."

Toby lowered his head. "Damn, this is not good. That means we got no law left in town. Tell me everything that happened."

Pattie took in a deep breath. "Sheriff Steele and Tex were doing rounds after Marshal Reedy took his two deputies and Buck out to talk to Henry Thornton. Two men set fire to a small shack out at the end of town and during all the commotion, some men ambushed the sheriff and Tex. They shot them down in the street and took off out of town like cowards. Tex is conscious now, but the sheriff is still in a coma. When Marshal Reedy came back later that night and found out what had happened, he got a small posse together and headed out of town to try to catch them. When they came back, Madden had a trap set for them and he locked them up in the jail. I heard them planning to blow the water basins but I didn't know about the attack this morning.

Now, Madden has the town under his rule and he's sent for several more hired guns. He'll have more than twenty men when the rest arrive. You won't have a chance against that many men and I don't see any law coming to town. Even if they do, Madden will have them shot on sight. I'm telling you, the man has gone absolutely crazy with greed and hatred."

"That's the way it is with men like Madden. They're like mad dogs. Once they get a taste of greed and power, they need more and more and never seem to get enough of either. He won't stop until he gets everything, Thornton's spread and the town included."

"Well, Mr. Hewitt, I suggest that you stay here until late tonight and leave once some of Madden's men are asleep. You'll have a better chance of getting out of town alive that way. Once you get out of here, I suggest you tell your boss to get out while he can or send for help, and lots of it."

"Thank you, Pattie. That's exactly what I intend to do. How'd you get those bruises around your neck?" asked Hewitt, pointing to her neck.

"That's Madden's work. He grabbed me by the neck and shoved me. I got a knot on my head from one of his men who pushed me so hard I fell down and hit my head. I got bruises on other places that you can't see from his men pushing me around. He's threatened to send some of his men to have their way with me. I thought you might have been one of his men coming to carry out the threat. That's why I was so afraid to open the door."

Hewitt looked apologetic. "I'm right sorry, Pattie. I don't like to see women get slapped or pushed around by men. It just ain't right."

"Rance Madden is not a man; he's an animal," said Pattie, with anger in her voice.

"I can't argue with you on that fact."

The two of them sat there for another two hours before they decided it was probably safe for Hewitt to sneak away. "I guess it's a good time to leave," said Pattie.

"I agree. Madden will still have a few men on guard but I figure most of them will be asleep by now. Thanks again, Pattie. Let's pray we live long enough to get to speak to one another again."

Pattie thought about it for a minute but then decided that she would tell Hewitt. "Well, we might have one chance left, maybe."

"What are you talking about? What chance could we have against Madden's army of hired guns?

"Before Madden took control of the town, I was able to send off a message from the telegraph office."

"Who did you send the message to?"

"A young man by the name of Jess Williams."

"With all due respect, Pattie, we're in a war with a man who has an army of hired guns and you sent for one man? Pattie, you should have sent for the cavalry instead."

Pattie looked at Hewitt with a strange smile. "Why, Mr. Hewitt, you may not realize it but that is exactly what I did do."

CHAPTER FOURTEEN

Toby Hewitt made his way back out of town and to his horse. He again stayed off the main trail and traveled along the edge of the woods as much as he could. He made it back to the Thornton ranch just as the sun was trying to light up the sky with a soft orange glow. He handed the reins of his horse to the man who was standing guard on the front porch and headed inside to inform Henry Thornton of everything that he had learned from his trip into town and his discussion with Pattie Nate. Thornton sat there sipping hot coffee while Hewitt explained everything from Sheriff Steele and Tex being shot to Marshal Reedy and his deputies being jailed.

Thornton put his cup down and looked into the dregs, deep in thought. Stumpy Watson, who did most of the cooking for Thornton, refilled the two coffee cups in front of Hewitt and Thornton. Stumpy had a bushy beard that was a salt and pepper color and a full round face. Then he went back to making up a mess of flapjacks.

Thornton had a serious and worried look on his face. "We're in a whole heap of trouble, Toby. It looks like Madden's got the upper hand and there isn't anything we can do to change it."

"This is one time I hate to agree with you, boss. All we can do now is send for help and hunker down and try to survive until relief arrives. That might be a few days or even a few weeks. We can send for help to the U.S. marshal's office and tell them that one of their marshals has been ambushed and jailed. Maybe that will put a burr under their asses and make them send someone right away."

"Well, that might work, but how many can they send? Madden's already got a small army and sending for more. They'll have to bring thirty men with them or call out the cavalry to help."

The word cavalry made Hewitt remember what else Pattie had said. "Boss, I forgot about one thing that Pattie Nate told me when I was holed up in her room."

"What else did she tell you?"

"She told me that before Madden took control of the town, she sent for help."

"You don't sound too pleased about it. Who did she send for?"

"Well, that's the part I'm not pleased about. She said she sent for only one man, a young man by the name of Jess Williams."

"Do you mean to tell me that she only sent for one man?" asked Thornton, a look of concern on his face.

"That's exactly what I'm telling you, boss. She only sent for one man. I know, I can't believe it either, but I suppose she was just trying to help."

"What in the hell does she think one man will be able to do in this situation? Does she think he's just going to ride straight into town and ask Madden to surrender and give up? Madden will have him shot before he gets halfway down the street. Damn woman probably just got that young man a certain death."

Stumpy, who had been listening to the entire conversation, had stopped what he was doing and turned around to face Hewitt and Thornton at the mention of Jess Williams. "Maybe not, boss," said Stumpy.

Thornton and Hewitt both looked up at Stumpy Watson. "What the hell do you mean?" Thornton asked. "Do you know about this young man, Jess Williams?"

"Yep, I sure suppose I do, Boss. I saw him shoot Curley Simms over in Baxter. That boy snaked his pistol out of his holster quicker than the eye could see. It was a strange thing to witness. One second, he was bracing old Curley and then, in the blink of an eye, his pistol was out and smoke was coming from the end of the barrel. I talked to some of the other men later on and they said he was a bounty hunter and a damn good one at that. He has a strange-looking pistol like I've not seen before. They told me that he's killed more men than any other bounty hunter alive."

Thornton wanted to believe that this was good news, but he just couldn't see what any one man could do, no matter how good or how deadly the man was. "Well, maybe he might get a few of Madden's men, but that won't solve the problem."

"Maybe," replied Stumpy, "but they told me something else about this Williams kid."

"And what was that?" Thornton asked.

"That he doesn't usually do things…well, usual."

Thornton and Hewitt looked at one another and a glimpse of hope came and vanished as they looked at one another. Both of them knew the dire predicament that they were in and they both knew that one man wouldn't change the outcome.

"Stumpy," said Thornton, "as soon as you finish up with feeding the men, I want you to ride over to Baxter and use their telegraph office. I'll write one message that I want you to send to the marshal's office and another message I want you to send to some more hired guns. While you're in Baxter, let every man who can shoot straight know that I'm paying twenty-five dollars per day per man along with a fifty dollar bonus the minute they show up."

"Okay, boss, I'll ride out as soon as I can, but that's a lot of money for regular men though."

"We don't have time to think about money. If we don't get help soon, money won't be necessary. We'll all be planted out back with the others before long."

Stumpy went back to flipping flapjacks and frying salt pork. The other men came into the house and ate their fill in shifts so as to keep at least two men on watch at all times. About an hour later, Stumpy saddled his horse and rode out toward Baxter. He figured it would take him most of the day to get there if he pushed his horse hard.

Jess had ridden hard the last few days. It was a little past noon and he decided to stop and have something to eat. He built a quick fire out of some small dry branches and made a pot of coffee. He ate a chunk of pan bread after he warmed it by the fire and was finishing his first cup of coffee when he heard a rider approaching. He calmly removed his scattergun from his back holster and laid it across his lap after refilling his cup. The rider, who looked to be in his fifties with a large bushy beard, was just topping the rise as Jess took a swallow from his tin coffee cup.

Stumpy had seen the smoke at the top of the hill, which is why he detoured off the trail. He didn't know who it was, but it might be someone he could hire and send off to Henry Thornton. What he found was a young man, sitting on a boulder, sipping coffee. Stumpy was not lost on the fact that the young man had a scattergun across his lap. He reined up his horse about thirty feet from the young man.

"Mister, might I sit a spell and share a cup of coffee with you?"

Jess looked him over and decided that he would not pose any real threat. He propped his scattergun against the boulder. "I guess I can spare a cup or two. Tie up your horse and join me."

Stumpy tied his horse to a small tree by the campfire. He dug around in his saddlebags and retrieved a coffee cup. He was pouring coffee into his cup when it hit him. "Well I'll be damned; you're that Williams fellow, ain't you?"

Jess looked at Stumpy, who noticed that somehow Jess had removed his hammer strap without Stumpy even seeing it. "I'm Jess Williams, and who are you?"

Stumpy stood up and stuck out his hand, slowly. "I'm Stumpy Watson and I work for Henry Thornton. I'm on my way to Baxter to send off some telegrams for help. I don't usually speak for Mr. Thornton, but I'll bet he'd pay you any amount of money for your talent with that thing," he said, pointing to Jess's pistol.

"I don't hire my gun out to anyone. Tell me, why is this Henry Thornton looking for more hired guns?"

Stumpy filled his coffee cup again and told Jess the whole story just like he had heard it from Toby Hewitt this morning. Jess heard about Steele getting shot and Reedy being locked up in the jail. Stumpy could feel the tension coming from Jess as he told the story.

When Stumpy was finished, Jess got another pot of coffee going. "Stumpy, it seems like me and your boss have something in common."

"What's that?"

"Rance Madden. I received a telegraph a few days ago from a friend of mine in Timber. I know Sheriff Steele and Marshal Reedy. The telegraph was sent by Pattie Nate telling me to get to Timber as soon as a horse could carry me."

The name Pattie Nate jogged Stumpy's memory. "Oh, yeah, I forgot about Pattie Nate. When Hewitt was filling Mr. Thornton in this morning, he mentioned that a woman by that name had sent that telegraph to you. I tried to tell Mr. Thornton that you might be able to help but they said that one man couldn't do enough to make a difference in this situation. Besides, no one knew if you had even gotten the message. Who'd have guessed that I would've run into you on the trail?"

"Is Pattie Nate okay? Has Madden harmed her in any way?"

"I guess he and his men have shoved her around some. Hewitt said she had bruises on her neck and a knot on her head. At least she's still alive, which is lucky if you knew Rance Madden."

"I know one thing for sure."

"What's that?" Stumpy asked.

"Rance Madden is going to know me before this is over."

"So, you are going into Timber to see this Pattie Nate?"

"That is the plan."

"Well, I might make a little suggestion."

"I'm listening."

"I wouldn't go into town right now. Rance Madden has about twenty hired guns and at least a dozen are holding the town under Madden's rule. You'd never get to the livery before they'd shoot you. You'll have to sneak in at night and try to get her out of town. That

U.S. marshal is locked up and there are always at least two armed men inside the jail. There is no law in town except for Madden's, and he ain't too forgiving, if you know what I mean."

"I know exactly what you mean; I've dealt with the likes of him before, but thanks for the information. I guess I'll have to take a little different approach to this situation."

"Might I make another suggestion?"

"I'm still listening."

"You should stop by and talk with Henry Thornton before you do anything. He can fill you in on what has happened since this morning. You best approach the ranch house carefully 'cause those boys are trigger happy and you can't blame them none. They won't take any chances with any strangers."

"I think that's good advice and I will do just that. Well, I better get going."

"Me too, I still have to get to Baxter."

"Stumpy, might I make a suggestion to you?"

"I'm all ears."

"You tell anyone who comes to work for Thornton that if he runs into anyone on the trails leading into town, that he informs that someone who he's working for."

"Why would you say that?" asked Stumpy, not quite sure why Jess would make such a request.

"You just make sure to tell them. It might save their lives."

"I don't understand why, but I will tell them."

"Thanks, Stumpy. Enjoy your ride into Baxter."

Jess swung up onto Gray and headed toward Timber. Stumpy had told him that the Thornton ranch was about ten miles west of Timber. Jess was already formulating a plan for dealing with this Rance Madden and his hired guns and he hoped that Stumpy would not forget the warning that Jess had told him about. He finally spotted a large house in the distance. He got out his telescope and extended it to look the place over. He had a side view of the Thornton house. There were two men on the front porch, two in the back and one man atop a large barn. He followed along the trail going out. About a half-mile out from the house, he spotted a man sitting on a horse. Jess figured this man was positioned to see anyone coming from a distance and ride back to the house to warn the other men. Stumpy was right; these men were not taking any chances. Jess knew what to do.

Jess slowly walked his horse toward the house. Before he got too far, he heard the man on top of the barn hollering and a few seconds later three riders were coming straight at him. He stopped and kept his hands on the horn of the saddle. He had removed his hammer strap just in case. The three men who were riding out to meet Jess were Toby Hewitt, Dana Stevens and Lindsey Stanton. They were all holding rifles in their right hands. As they approached Jess, two of the men veered off about a hundred feet from the man in the center. That split them up and made it harder for one man to take down all three of them. They really aren't taking any chances, Jess thought to himself.

Toby Hewitt reined up in front of Jess. The other two men stayed back about twenty feet and they both had their rifles trained on Jess.

"Who are you, and what do you want here?" asked Hewitt.

"My name is Jess Williams, and I'll only ask you once to tell your men to put those rifles down."

Hewitt looked surprised and Jess could tell that Hewitt knew the name. "Dana, Lindsey, put those rifles down. I think we have a friend here." Both men lowered their rifles.

"Thank you," said Jess. "I'd like to speak with Henry Thornton."

"I'm sure he would like to speak with you, too," answered Hewitt. "Follow me, Mr. Williams."

Jess followed the three men to the Thornton house. Henry Thornton was standing on the front porch with a rifle in his hands when Jess reined up and tied off Gray and Sharps. He walked up the two steps and onto the porch and extended his hand out to Thornton.

"Mr. Thornton, I'm Jess Williams and I'm here to help out my friends in town."

Thornton shook his hand and motioned for him to come into the house. Toby Hewitt stayed with Thornton but Dana Stevens and Lindsey Stanton went back to their guard duties. The three men sat down at the kitchen table and Thornton put a pot of coffee and three cups on the table.

"Mr. Thornton, I ran into one of your men this afternoon, a man by the name of Stumpy. He told me to stop and talk with you before I do anything or go into town."

"Stumpy works for me and he gave you some good advice. You don't want to go riding right down the main street of Timber, that's for sure. I'm not sure what you think you can do for your friends. Sheriff Steele is near death, one of his deputies is shot, and the other one is locked up in the jail along with Marshal Reedy and his two deputies. Just what do you think that you can do?"

"You let me worry about that. I just need to make sure that your men don't go back into town, and that if you get any more hired guns arriving at your place, that you keep them here and not go into town or try to attack Madden or his men."

Thornton laughed out loud. "That's an awful lot to ask a man who has lost ten of his men to Madden's hired killers the last few days."

"It may be a lot to ask, but it's for your own protection."

"Really? And why is that?" Thornton questioned with a somewhat threatening tone in his voice.

"Because after today, it's not going to be safe out there."

Henry Thornton leaned forward, put his elbows on the table, and folded his hands together. "Let me understand this correctly. You want me and my men, and any other men I can hire, to sit here at my ranch and do nothing about what has happened up to this point. Is that correct?"

"That is exactly what I'm asking."

"And you are telling me that it's not going to be safe out there."

"That's correct."

"So, tell me again why it's not going to be safe out there?"

"Because, Mr. Thornton, I'm going to be out there."

CHAPTER FIFTEEN

Jess woke at daybreak and headed out from Thornton's. He had \
gotten Henry Thornton to agree to keep his men at the ranch
and to keep any other hired guns who showed up with him. Jess
had finally convinced him by telling him it was better to wait until
he had enough men to try anything. Thornton realized that since
he only had seven men left, waiting was about all he could do anyway. He probably couldn't hold off an attack from Madden's men
as it was. Thornton would be lucky if Stumpy could hire more than
a few men with such short notice, and they probably wouldn't be
hardened gunslingers.

Jess figured that it was good advice not to go into town. He
wanted to in the worst way, but he was smart enough to know better.
He came up with another plan. He knew that Sheriff Steele would
never agree with his plan, nor would Marshal Reedy, but they were
unable to do anything about it anyway. Steele was near death and
Reedy was locked up with his deputies. There was no law in town,
except for Madden's law, enforced by the end of a gun barrel. Jess
was about to change that.

Jess spent the entire day checking out everything from a distance. The main street of Timber ran pretty much east and west. On
the north side of town was a high ridge facing south that was too
steep for a horse to climb. The other side of the ridge had a gentler
slope and was easy to climb. There was a thick forest at the base of
the slope. Jess had found what he was looking for. There was an
opening that he remembered from a trip he took with his pa when
he was a kid. The opening was just barely large enough for him to

fit into. Once he got into the hole, it opened up into a cave that ran to the other side of the ridge. Jess peeked out of the opening and it looked right down on the town of Timber. Jess figured it was probably over six hundred yards away. That would be a long shot for the Sharps but he would have gravity working in his favor. It was a steep drop to the main street.

Jess left the cave and rode to the south side of town. He tied Sharps up to a tree in the forest, deep enough so that no one would see or hear him. He took the small shovel from the packhorse and tied it to the back of the saddle on Gray. A heavy forest started about eight hundred feet out from town. The trees ran all along the trail leading into and out of Timber. That would give him some good cover and hiding places. He used his telescope and spotted several men in town. They were all heavily armed and he figured them for Madden's men. He could see the jail but he could not see inside well enough to see if Reedy was still there.

He rode out toward the east to see Madden's ranch. He stayed way back in the heavy trees and used his telescope to check things out. He counted seven men outside. He could see a few men inside the house and a few in the bunkhouse. Every man was armed with pistols and either a rifle or a shotgun. What in the hell have I gotten myself into this time? Jess thought to himself.

He left the Madden ranch and headed back toward town, always staying along the edge of the woods. He found a spot where the trees came within a hundred yards of the main trail leading into town. He took Gray and tied him to a tree about a hundred feet inside the tree line. Then he walked out to the edge and started digging about ten feet past the tree line. It took him almost three hours of heavy digging before he finished. When he was done, he was looking at a hole that was four feet deep and four feet long and three feet wide. Then, he cut a bunch of branches and wove them together to make a top for the hole he had just dug. He tore enough tall grass to cover the top he had made and placed it on top of the hole. He stepped back and checked his work. You could spot it if you were right on top of it, but from the trail, no one would ever know it was there. Then he heard horses coming down the trail from the Madden ranch. He ducked into the woods and watched.

There were five men in all. He grabbed his telescope and extended it. All five men were armed to the teeth. One man stuck out though. Jess could tell that this man was a gunslinger for sure. He was wearing a double holster and was dressed in black with a very nice black hat. You could see the confidence in this man even by the way he sat in the saddle. Jess finally recognized him. It was Galt Dixon. Dixon was a gunslinger with a reputation, and a bad one at that. Madden had obviously hired Dixon; he would be someone to be reckoned with. Jess knew that if Dixon made it to town, someone would most likely die before the day was over.

I guess now is as good a time as any to start working my plan, Jess thought to himself. He ran over to Gray and grabbed his Winchester. He ran back to the edge of the tree line just as the five men were coming closer. It was over a hundred yards. Jess waited until the men were less than one hundred yards. He put his sights on Galt Dixon's chest and pulled the trigger. The slug hit its mark and Dixon fell from his horse, dead. Jess didn't hesitate even for a split second. He began firing at the other four men who were confused and trying to see where the shots were coming from. Jess took out two more men before the other two spotted him. One of the men spurred his horse back toward the Madden ranch and the other man pointed his horse toward Jess, firing his pistol at Jess as he did. Jess fired again, hitting the man in the neck. Jess immediately ran back to Gray and grabbed the Sharps out of the scabbard. He ran at a full pace toward the trail with the Sharps in one hand and two rounds in the other. As soon as he had the man in sight, he dropped to the ground on his belly and sighted the man in. The man was still within range for the Sharps, but he was not a stationary target. Jess took careful aim and slowly pulled the trigger back. The Sharps exploded and the round missed the man but it had surprised him to the point that he made a deadly mistake. He stopped and turned his horse to look back, figuring whoever was shooting at him was close behind him. That's when Jess's second round hit him square in the chest, knocking him off his horse. The horse took off down the trail back in the direction of the Madden ranch.

Jess ran back and put the Sharps in the scabbard. He mounted Gray and stopped to check the four men. They were all dead, including Galt Dixon. Jess then rode out to the man who was lying in the trail. The man was still alive, but fading fast. Jess got off his horse and walked up to the man, his Winchester at the ready.

The man was holding his chest with both hands but the blood was running out quickly. His face was a pale white and he was breathing hard. He looked up at Jess barely able to lift his head. "Do I know you, Mister?"

"No, and I guess you never will, either."

The man put his head back down in the sand. "What the hell did you shoot me for? I was running away. I didn't shoot at you."

"Do you work for Rance Madden?"

"Yeah, I work for him."

"Then that's all the reason I need."

The man gasped his last breath as Jess watched. He had watched many men die and it didn't bother him. "Well, that's five men down and who knows how many more to go," Jess said to the dead man.

Jess swung back up into the saddle and headed toward town. He didn't try to hide the bodies. He wanted them to stay where they were, as if to send a message. Besides, the horse running back to the Madden ranch would alert the other men who would come out and check. Taking out Galt Dixon was a real bonus since Dixon was, indeed, fast with a gun.

Jess made his way around town and back up to the cave on the north ridge. It was just about dusk and he wanted to get at least one shot off before it got too dark. He placed himself back in the cave far enough that no one would be able to see the muzzle flash or the smoke from the Sharps. He was looking through the telescope and he found his target. A man walked out of the jail holding a scattergun. He didn't have a badge on so Jess figured him for one of Madden's men. He got the man in the sights of the Sharps, which was propped up on the tall forked branch that Jess had cut off a tree in the woods where his packhorse Sharps was still tied up. He fired, and the slug hit the man in his right side, throwing him to the ground. Jess took his telescope and watched. Three men came out of the saloon and ran over to the man. Before long, a dozen men were standing over the dead man and they were all trying to see where the shot had come from. Jess studied their faces, placing them in the back of his head so that he would remember them later. A few of them looked up at the ridge but no one thought that the shot could have come from that far off. One man was giving all the orders to the other men. Jess didn't know if this man was Madden, but he figured it must be. If he wasn't, he must be one of Madden's top men because all the other men listened to him. He sent them running all around the town trying to find out who had shot the man down in the street. They found no one.

Then, Jess spotted Pattie Nate standing on the porch of the saloon. The man who had been yelling out all the orders walked back to the saloon and was waving his hands around hollering at Pattie Nate. Then the man slapped Pattie so hard that she fell back onto the porch against the wall of the saloon. Jess's temper spiked instantly, but there was nothing he could do about it at the moment without possibly giving his cover away. He looked at the man again through the telescope and said to no one but himself: "Mister, I don't care if you are Madden or not. You just earned a death sentence for that."

About a half hour passed and it began to get dark, so Jess rode down the slope, retrieved Sharps, and went back into the forest about three miles. He made camp next to a small stream and opened a can of cold beans. There would be no fire tonight. No hot coffee and no hot food. He did not remove the saddles or saddlebags from either horse. He had to be ready to mount up and ride quickly. He put out a few strings with cans, leaned back against a tree, and fell off to a restless sleep.

Clyde Tustin was the man Jess had shot while he was trying to run away from the ambush. His horse came strolling back to the barn at the Madden ranch. Grant Hull and Denzel Matheny were in the barn when the horse walked in and nickered. The two men turned around to see Tustin's horse standing in the doorway.

"Hey, ain't that Tustin's horse?" asked Matheny.

Hull walked over and took the reins of the horse. "Hell yeah it is. I wonder what the hell happened to Clyde. He rode out of here escorting Galt Dixon to town to meet the boss. Something ain't right. We'd better get a few men and go looking for Clyde."

Hull and Matheny rounded up two more men and rode out toward town. About a half hour out, they found Clyde in the middle of the trail, lying there as though he was taking a nap. He had both hands on his chest and when Hull moved his hands, they exposed a large hole in Clyde's chest.

"Hey," hollered Matheny, "I see there are more bodies up here."

They rode over to the other bodies. Galt Dixon and two men lay dead on the trail and another dead man was about a hundred feet off the trail in the tall grass.

"Who the hell do you think did this?" Matheny asked.

Hull was standing over the body of Galt Dixon. "I don't know, but the boss is sure going to be pissed about it. He was paying Dixon here a whole lot of money."

"Yeah, and he'll want to know right away," replied Matheny, as he looked over at one of the other two men who had ridden out with him. "Clevis, you go into town and tell the boss what's happened."

"Yes sir, I'm already moving," said Clevis Danville, as he spurred his horse and headed in the direction of town.

"Who in the hell could have taken down four men along with Galt Dixon?" asked Rory Clement.

"It couldn't have been just one man," answered Matheny.

"I bet it was Henry Thornton's men. They're trying to repay us for our attack the other day," replied Grant Hull.

"Well, maybe old Thornton needs another licking," said Rory Clement.

"I have a hunch you might be right," replied Matheny. "Rory, go back to the ranch and bring out the wagon. We have to bury these men."

Rory headed back to get the wagon. While Matheny and Hull waited with the bodies, they each rolled a cigarette and smoked them.

Clevis Danville had ridden fast to town. When he arrived, he headed straight for Jed's Saloon where he knew he would find his boss. Madden was sitting at a table with Treat Knudsen. He sat down at the table and poured himself a whiskey from the bottle on the table. "Boss, I got some bad news to tell you."

"It wouldn't be the first bad news today."

"Why? What happened?" Clevis asked, almost afraid to tell Madden about Galt Dixon.

"Someone took out one of our men today. Shot him down in the street and we don't know where the shot came from. I've had men looking all over and around town, but they haven't found who did it."

"Well, my news is a whole lot worse. We lost five men today on the trail into town, and one of them was that Galt Dixon feller."

Madden stood up so fast the chair went flying back and toppled over. "Jesus Christ! Galt Dixon was my best man and I never even got to use him! Henry Thornton will pay for this," he said as he grabbed his chair, slammed it to the floor, and sat back down. "Treat, get together another group of men and go back out to Thornton's place and burn it to the ground!"

"I'll round them up and go out late tonight. I can't think of a better way to spend an evening, Boss."

Treat Knudsen went to round up some men. Rory poured himself another whiskey while Madden just sat there and steamed in his thoughts.

CHAPTER SIXTEEN

Stumpy Watson had sent four men to the Thornton ranch. None of them were gunslingers, but they all knew how to fire a rifle and they didn't have a problem with getting paid to throw lead. That gave Thornton a better chance at protecting his property and his men. Thornton was in bed asleep, but he had men posted in all four directions watching for an ambush.

One clump of trees on the north side was only about fifty feet from the house. Lindsey Stanton was sitting in the middle of the clump of trees, affording him a good spot to watch from. He heard something and he kept squinting his eyes and looking in the direction it was coming from. He finally spotted someone crawling on his straight for the clump of trees. He didn't know who he was, but he knew he was trouble. He waited until the man came within fifty feet of where he was. Then, the man who had been crawling suddenly stood up and began running toward the clump of trees. Lindsey Stanton never even warned him. He fired his Winchester and the man fell forward with a heavy thump.

Victor King, who had been on guard in the barn, had also spotted someone crawling on the ground. As soon as Stanton fired his Winchester, this man stood up and started to light a large stick with cloth wrapped around it. It had just barely ignited when Victor fired his Winchester and the man fell backward, the grass catching on fire from the stick.

Gunfire was now coming from all four directions, slugs hitting the house and the barn. Earlier in the day Thornton had ordered his men to reinforce the areas that they would be firing from. They had nailed four-inch lumber on the inside, below and around the sides of the windows of the ranch house. That way his men would only take a slug if they were exposed in a window. Thornton had one window in each direction manned, each man had at least two rifles and one shotgun with him, and they were putting down some heavy fire at Madden's men.

All of a sudden the gunfire stopped. Thornton could hear horses running off in the distance. Thornton and his men waited for a full five minutes before coming out to assess the casualties. Lindsey Stanton lay dead in the clump of trees, a bullet to his head. One of Madden's men had seen the muzzle flash coming from the clump of trees and saw a shadowy figure of a man. He fired off several rounds; one of them hit its mark. Victor King lay dead just inside the large door of the barn. Thornton sent his men around the house to locate Madden's men. They found four dead men. Thornton ordered his men to strip them of their weapons and ammunition and bury the bodies in the morning in one grave. Thornton figured there would not be another attack that night, so he let a few extra men get some sleep. He was hoping that Stumpy would be sending more men soon.

Dana Stevens came into the ranch house after they were done cleaning up and had guards in place again. "Boss, they were trying to burn us out. Both men we found close to the house had torches and were trying to throw them at the house and barn. One of them caught the grass on fire, but we put that out. Lucky we were on guard and ready for them this time."

"It wasn't luck; we planned to be ready. Reinforcing the windows and doors with lumber saved some men today. There's a dozen slugs stuck in the boards of all four windows."

"Well, I hope Stumpy sends a few more men. We took out four of Madden's men and lost only two, so that gives us an advantage, but not much of one."

"Hell, Madden's probably hired a dozen more men by now. We don't have any advantage. We just have to wait it out and hope for a miracle."

"Go ahead and get some sleep, Boss. I'll make sure everything is taken care of tonight."

Henry Thornton went up to his room and got into bed. It took him a while to fall asleep. He kept thinking about the dire predicament he was in. He wasn't sure that he would survive it. He had worked so hard for so many years to build up his herd of cattle, and now he was on the verge of losing it all, because of one greedy man with a lot of money. He had no idea that Jess Williams had already taken out six of Madden's men today and that's why the attack took place tonight. For all he knew, Jess Williams had left and would not come back or even worse, had been hired by Madden. He finally fell off to a restless night of sleep.

Jess woke up to gunfire off in the distance. He was sure that the gunfire was coming from the direction of Henry Thornton's ranch. That gave him an idea. He figured that if it was Madden's men who were attacking Thornton's ranch again, they would be riding back into town along the trail. He swung up in the saddle and turned Gray in the direction of the trail going into the west end of town. He hid inside the trees just off the path. Then he spotted four riders. They were riding slow and talking back and forth among each other. As they neared the spot where Jess was, he stepped out from behind a large tree. They didn't even notice him until he spoke.

"Hey, you men work for Madden?" asked Jess.

The four men, obviously surprised, stopped and turned their horses toward Jess.

Treat Knudsen was the first to speak. "Who the hell wants to know?" Knudsen asked sarcastically.

"I asked you first and I expect an answer. If not, I'll have to assume that you do work for Madden."

"And what the hell are you going to do about it if we do work for Madden? In case you can't count, it's four against one."

"I can count just fine."

Jess slicked his pistol out, thumbed his first shot, and fanned the next three. Jess's first shot caught Phillip Ryan in the chest. His second shot found its mark knocking Fred McAllister out of his saddle. Jess's third shot caught Lester Kennedy in the face, entering just below his left eye. Treat Knudsen was the only man out of the four who got off a shot, which came so close to Jess's head he swore he could feel the heat from it; but then Jess's fourth shot caught Knudsen in his left side as Knudsen spurred his horse at a dead run. He fired back at Jess, causing him to duck behind a tree. Jess fired off two more rounds but in the darkness and with a target that was moving away quickly, he missed with both shots. He had thought about going to get his Winchester, but he figured that the man would be out of sight before he could get it.

He had tied Gray up about a hundred feet inside the woods. Jess thought for a moment about waiting here to see if more of Madden's men came along the trail, but he figured he would stick to his original plan. He would hit and run, moving each time after he met up with any of Madden's men. That way, they would not be able to pick up on any pattern. He would keep Madden and his men guessing and wondering about where the next attack would come from. Nine men down and one man wounded in one day, Jess thought to himself. Not a bad day's work. He headed back to his camp and still kept Gray and Sharps saddled and ready to ride.

Jess woke before the sun came up. He moved Sharps to a new location with some fresh grass to feed on near the same small stream. He gave Sharps an extra twenty feet of rope so that he could eat plenty of grass. He rode Gray slowly through the trees around town, keeping himself well out of sight of any of Madden's men. About two hours after daylight, he found himself on the trail heading east from Madden's ranch. He rode about five miles out and made a small camp just off the trail. He used small pieces of dried branches so that no one would be able to spot the smoke from the small fire. He cooked some coffee, warmed another chunk of pan bread, and opened another can of cold beans as he waited.

Treat Knudsen had ridden into town in the middle of the night. He was wounded badly but he would live. As Doctor Hammond was cleaning out the wound, which had gone straight through, Rance Madden walked in.

"What the hell happened out there?" Madden asked.

"They was waitin' for us, Boss. We lost four men during the attack, and as near as I could tell, Thornton only lost two men."

"Damn it, that's bad."

"It gets worse," replied Knudsen.

"Worse? How the hell can it get worse?"

"Well, we were riding back to town and got stopped by a man who came out from the woods. He asked us if we worked for you. We had words back and forth, but he just skinned leather and starting shootin'. He killed Phillip Ryan, Fred McAllister, and Lester Kennedy and shot me after I took a shot at him. I ain't never seen anyone draw a pistol and shoot so fast, Boss. He had three of our men shot before I even got my gun out of its holster, and he shot me a split second after I got off a shot. I rode like hell and I'm lucky to be alive."

"Did you get a good look at him? Did he say who he was?"

"No on both accounts, Boss." His voice sounded young but he stood his ground. "I don't know if he's working for Thornton, but if he is, we've got a serious problem. Any man who faces down four men has got to have gonads the size of a bull and no fear about dying. That's a dangerous man."

"I'll bet you that whoever this man is, he's the same one who shot Galt Dixon and the four men who were escorting him into town this morning. And I bet he's the one who shot our man out in the street. Doctor Hammond said that the bullet he removed was a large caliber, probably from a buffalo gun."

Knudsen was wincing in pain from the stitching he was getting from Doctor Hammond. "Well, whoever he is, we've got to take him down before he gets any more of our men. We've lost thirteen men today by my count. I hope you have more men on the way and quickly, Boss."

"You can count on it. Finish getting patched up and get some rest."

Madden walked back to Jed's Saloon. He sat at a table with Vernon Foster and Leonard Sand. They were sharing a bottle of whiskey and Pattie was serving them some steaks. Pattie's left side of her face was black and blue from Vernon Foster's right hand, which he had used earlier to slap her. Foster smiled at his work as she served him his steak. She wanted to say something but she knew better. Foster would just slap her again.

"Why don't you take one of them steaks and put it on your face," said Foster, grinning, "Might make an improvement on your looks."

Pattie said nothing. She simply returned to the kitchen and they could hear her crying. Jed started to head to the kitchen to console Pattie, but when Madden saw him going toward the kitchen, he stopped him.

"Jed, you leave that bitch cry until she can't no more. She deserved what she got and a whole lot more."

"Yeah," added Vernon Foster, "she's lucky we ain't used her for a pin cushion, if you get my drift."

"All right, enough of that," said Madden. "Vernon, you were supposed to hire me some more men. Tell me some good news."

"Boss, I got good news and then I got better news for you."

"Keep talking."

"Well, I got six men coming in from Holten. Seems they were on their way to a job down by the Mexican border, but when they found out how much you were paying, they decided to come here. They should be here either tomorrow or the next day. Then, I got four more men coming in from Dodge City, all tough men. I told them to bring any more men they can find along the way, too. They won't get here for at least three more days. I saved the best for last, though." Vernon Foster waited and smiled at Madden, knowing how impatient he could get, but he knew that the news would earn him some extra points with his boss.

"What the hell are you waiting for, man. Spit it out!"

"All right, take it easy, Boss. Have you ever heard of a man they call the Reaper?"

"I can't say that I have. Who the hell is he?"

Leonard Sand sat straight up at the mention of the Reaper. "I know about him. They say he's one of the best in his field. I hear he's a gun tipper."

"What the hell is a gun tipper?" Madden asked.

"I've only seen it once before, but some men fix up their holster so that the holster swivels on the belt. That way, they don't have to pull the gun out of the holster; they just swivel it and fire. It's kind of tricky at first but they say that if a man practices with it long enough, he gets mighty fast."

"He is mighty fast, and fearless, too. They say he's not playing with a full deck," said Vernon. "It seems that he used to work for one of them gun companies back East for a long time. He designed guns and learned how to shoot them. The story goes that he wanted to design a pistol and the owner of the gun company didn't want him to. The owner said the design was too expensive to manufacture and sell. Well, the Reaper, whose real name is Jake Morgan, went behind the owner's back and made up one of his guns based on his design. Well, the owner fired him and Morgan paid for the gun. Then, he had a special holster designed for the gun and went about practicing with it. He tried to sell the design off to a few other gun makers, but no one wanted it. It bothered him so much that he headed out West to become a hired gun. He is one of the best and he's worth every penny."

Madden was smiling now. "How much does he want?"

"He charges one thousand dollars to kill a man. He doesn't care how you want the job done, as long as you pay."

"That's a hell of a lot of money for killing one man," replied Madden.

"Well, you paid four thousand to have Sheriff Steele and Tex shot and they didn't even finish the job. Now you've got this new man who killed nine of our men today. Maybe you might want this Reaper fellow to find and kill him, whoever he is."

"Maybe you're right, if we can find out who he is. He's a ruthless one, that's for sure. So, when will this Reaper fellow get here?"

"He said he'd be here in about four days or so."

"I wish it was sooner, but at least by that time we might know who this new man is that we're dealing with and if he's working for Thornton. We'll have some more men in a few days. I have the word out all over the area, so I expect a few more to show up on top of what you have coming. In the next three days, we should be back up in force enough to finish Thornton off."

"Boss, when all this is over, what are you planning to do with Marshal Reedy and his deputies?" asked Leonard Sand.

Madden thought about that for a minute. "Well, if we let them go, they'll just go and get a small army of U.S. marshals and deputies and come after us. I say we use them as hostages for now, but in the end, we take them out of town, shoot the whole bunch of them, and bury the bodies deep. We'll do it at night so that no one in town knows what happened to them. They'll never find the bodies."

"Yeah, but what about Sheriff Steele and his deputies?"

"Looks like Reedy and his deputies will have some company when they cross over to their next lives," said Madden, with an evil smile on his face.

Pattie Nate was in the kitchen and heard what Madden was planning to do with Reedy and Steele. She almost panicked but one thing helped keep her from losing her wits. She had also heard about a new man who had been attacking Madden's men. She knew of only one man capable of killing nine men in one day and not getting caught. That man was Jess Williams. He must have gotten her message and was here to help. She prayed that Jess could stop this madness before Madden murdered the man she loved.

CHAPTER SEVENTEEN

J ess had been waiting for five hours before he spotted a rider off in the distance. He put his small fire out, swung up into the saddle, walked Gray out to the trail, and just waited. He took the scattergun out of its sling and laid it across his lap. He turned Gray at a ninety-degree angle across the path so that the barrels of the scattergun faced the trail in the direction of the rider, who was still about a mile off. As the rider came closer, Jess cocked both barrels. The man, Clint Underwood, finally spotted Jess blocking the trail.

Underwood was a hired gun. He had heard that a man by the name of Rance Madden was paying well, so he decided to quit cattle rustling and go and work for Madden. He wondered if the man sitting in the middle of the trail was there to greet him or if he was trouble. As Underwood got closer, he saw the scattergun and removed the hammer strap from his pistol. He stopped about twenty feet or so from Jess.

"Mister, unless you own this trail, I expect you to move and let me pass on through," said Underwood.

"What's your name?" Jess asked.

"Clint Underwood, not that it's any of your business."

"I'm making it my business."

Underwood looked Jess over, trying to pick his memory to see if he knew this bold young man blocking the trail. He didn't know who he was, but that mattered little. Underwood had a bad temper, with a disposition to match. "And just what business is that?"

"Rance Madden's business."

"Are you one of Madden's men?"

"No. Are you?"

"What the hell business is it of yours if I am? Didn't you hear my name the first time, boy? The name is Clint Underwood, and if you haven't heard of me before, you should have."

"I don't know your name and I don't really care. I'm only going to tell you one more time. Like I said, I'm making it my business. Now answer the question."

Underwood's temper was starting to show now. "You might have that scattergun pointed at me but you can still kiss my ass, boy. I ain't telling you shit. What the hell do you think you're going to do? Are you just going to open up with that scattergun without even giving a man a fair chance?"

Jess's face hardened and Underwood could see the change. "Mister, I'm only going to ask you one more time and if you don't answer, I'm going to assume that you're a hired gun and heading for the Madden ranch to join up with the rest of them. Now, for the last time, are you working for Rance Madden?"

"Like I said, I ain't telling you shit."

"Actually, you just did."

Underwood saw the change in Jess's eyes but it was too late now. Jess fired both barrels of the scattergun at the same time and Underwood's head disappeared. The headless corpse fell to the right side of his horse but Underwood's right boot got caught in the stirrup. Underwood's horse began walking down the trail and Jess moved to let the horse pass. He watched as Underwood's body dragged on the ground, leaving a streak of blood in the dirt. Jess watched as the horse rounded a bend in the trail and was out of sight. One more down, Jess thought to himself.

Jess rode back to the spot where he had shot Galt Dixon and the other four men. He tied Gray up about two hundred feet into the woods, took his Sharps and his Winchester, and walked to the covered hole. He lifted the thatched cover that he had made, removed his hat, and dropped down into the hole. He didn't have to wait very long. Only about two hours had passed when Jess spotted two men coming from the direction of town. They were quite a ways off, probably about a thousand yards. Jess lifted the cover of his hole just enough to peek out with his telescope. He could see their faces enough to know that they were Madden's men. He remembered seeing these two in the group standing around the body of the man Jess had shot with the Sharps from his hiding spot in the cave.

Jess put the telescope away, brought the Sharps up, and laid it on the ground, still keeping the thatched cover resting on his head. He waited until the two men were about one hundred yards off. Jess fired the Sharps and the man on the left flew back off his saddle. The other man, surprised at the loud boom of the Sharps and remembering the ambush that had taken place here the other day, turned his horse back toward town at a full gallop. Jess quickly put another round in and took careful aim at the man. The man was about two hundred yards off now and Jess knew that he would probably have only one good shot. He gently squeezed the trigger until the Sharps boomed again. The man flew forward toward the horse's neck. Then he fell off his horse and rolled a few times before he finally came to a halt. Jess retrieved Gray and rode over to the first man. He was dead. Then, he rode to the second man who was lying face down but still breathing. Jess's shot had hit him in the right side of his back. Jess rolled him over but not before making sure that the man's pistol was still in its holster.

The man tried to speak but couldn't. His eyes rolled back and forth and his mouth was moving but no sound was coming out. It was as though the man was having a conversation with someone who wasn't there. Then, his breathing stopped and so did the movement of his eyes. Jess closed the dead man's eyes, swung himself back up on Gray, and rode off in the direction of town. He figured that this ambush spot was no longer a good one so he abandoned it. He headed back to where he had stashed Sharps and then he rode up the slope and back into the cave. He figured the cave was good for only one more ambush before Madden's men figured it out. For now, he used it to check out the town some more.

He watched the town for the remainder of the day. He observed the movements of the men watching the jail. He studied the movement of Madden's men coming and going from Jed's Saloon and coming and going in and out of town. Jess noticed that all of Madden's men came and went from the east. Thornton's ranch was to the west and none of Madden's men went that way. He tried to pick out Madden, but he couldn't figure it out yet. Several times a man who seemed to be in charge came out and gave orders to the other men, but Jess didn't know if it was Rance Madden or not.

Then he spotted Pattie just before it was almost too dark to see. She came out from the doctor's office, walked back to Jed's Saloon, and climbed up the stairs to her little room. He knew what he had to do. He went back down the hill, rode back to the spot where he had tied up Sharps, and moved down along the little stream. That would give the horses some more fresh grass to eat. Jess figured he would go out to Thornton's in the morning, give his horses a break, and get them some good feed. He ate some cold beans and stale biscuits. He longed for a hot meal, but he couldn't afford to shoot any meat or cook anything for fear that he might be spotted.

He waited until about two o'clock in the morning and rode Gray to within one hundred yards of the edge of the woods. He tied off Gray and walked to the edge of the woods. He propped his Winchester against a tree and pulled out his telescope. He watched for about fifteen minutes but he didn't see much movement. There was a guard posted outside each end of town and one on top of a building. Once in a while a man would come out of Jed's Saloon, walk around town, and then return to the saloon. Jess waited until the man repeated his walk, and as soon as the man went back into the saloon, Jess slowly and carefully made his way behind the saloon. He worked his way to the stairs, quickly climbed up them, stooped down below the window of Pattie Nate's room, and tapped gently on the window. He heard footsteps coming toward the door. When he heard the footsteps stop, he slowly stood up, his pistol in his hand.

Pattie almost screamed but she put her hands over her mouth before anything could come out. She quickly opened the door to let Jess in, and Jess quietly closed and locked the door and peeked out for a moment to see if anyone had seen or heard anything. Once he was satisfied that no one had seen him, he turned to Pattie, who rushed forward and hugged him as if she would never let him go. He held her and she was shivering badly, but not from being cold. She was shivering with absolute fear.

Jess finally got her to let go and set her down on the bed. He pulled the chair over and sat in front of her. She lifted both of her hands and gently placed one on each side of Jess's face. "Jess, I prayed that it was you killing Madden's men. I can't tell you how good it is to know that you're here. For a while, I thought all hope was lost and that we would all be murdered by Madden," she sobbed quietly.

"I headed here as soon as I got your message. Things are really bad, the way I see it."

"It's worse than bad. Mark hasn't come out of a coma yet and Doc doesn't think he ever will. He's so weak and his breathing is sometimes erratic. Marshal Reedy and his men, along with Mark's deputies, are still locked up over at the jail. They won't let me feed them anything but bread and water. Tex is still pretty bad, even though Madden has let me feed him some soup. I heard Madden say that when this is all over he's going to murder them all and bury them way out of town. What are we going to do?" she asked, as she put her hands in her lap, clenching and wringing them nervously.

"Well, I've been knocking off Madden's men at a pretty good pace. I've lost count but I think I took out a dozen men so far."

"Are you the one who shot one of Madden's men the other day, out in the street? Was that you?"

"Yes, and I'm glad to hear it was one of Madden's men. I couldn't be certain when I took the shot. I was hoping I didn't take down one of the townsfolk by mistake."

"No, it was one of his men. None of the townsfolk stay in the street. They run from one place to the other and only when absolutely necessary. If you see any armed men in the street, you can be sure it's one of Madden's men. He won't let any of the men in town who aren't working for him wear or carry guns."

"That's good information that I can use. I need some more information. How many men does Madden have in town right now?"

"I'm not sure. I think about ten. He always has at least two men at the jail and three or four posted around town. He usually keeps four or five men downstairs in the saloon. They're all armed and most of them are seasoned gunmen."

"Can you tell me how to pick out Rance Madden?"

"He's a large man with a scar over his right eye. He wears the nicest pair of boots I've ever seen and a dark brown hat and a black leather necktie."

"Who is the man who slapped you on the side of your face the other day on the boardwalk?"

"You saw that?"

Jess put his head down as if in shame. "Yes, but I couldn't do anything about it at the time, Pattie. I'm sorry, but I didn't want to give away my hiding spot."

Pattie took her right hand and lifted Jess's face up. "Don't you ever feel ashamed of that. At least you're still alive to help. I can take a little roughing up if that means protecting you and saving Mark."

"Thanks, Pattie, but I still want to know who did it."

"That was that bastard Vernon Foster. He's a real piece of work. He beats on women because he's a coward. Madden keeps him around because he'll do whatever Madden asks him to do. He'd shoot a man in the back but I don't think he would face one down fair."

"Well, you have my guarantee that he will pay for what he did to you."

"Jess, are you going to try to get Reedy out of jail?"

"I'm not sure that's a good idea."

"Why?"

"Because he would probably arrest me for what I've been doing and prevent me from what I plan to do. He's a U.S. marshal and he's taken an oath to uphold the law. What I've done so far isn't what you would call following the law."

"Yes, but these are desperate circumstances that require desperate measures. Don't you think he would understand that?"

"He might, and maybe he would let me walk away for what I've done so far, but the minute he's out of jail with a gun in his hand, he'll want to handle the situation his way and if I don't listen to him, he'll have me arrested for sure."

"You're going to need help soon. Madden has a dozen more men coming to town to work for him as hired guns. You can't kill them all. Eventually, they will find you and kill you."

Jess thought about it for a minute. "Maybe you're right. Listen, why don't you get dressed and come with me. I don't think you're safe here in town. I can take you out to Thornton's ranch. I think I can get a few of Thornton's men to help me break Reedy out of jail. At least that way, the town will have a chance."

"I hate to leave Mark here with that madman, Madden."

"Pattie, what do you think you can do anyway? Whatever Madden decides to do about Sheriff Steele can't be changed by you staying here. The sheriff would tell you to leave if you had the chance, and you know it."

She thought about it for a moment. "You're right. You turn around and I'll get dressed."

CHAPTER EIGHTEEN

"Two riders coming in," hollered Dana Stevens, "and one of 'em is a woman."

"Let them come on in," yelled out Henry Thornton from the window on the second floor of his ranch house. "I think it's that young fellow that was here the other day."

Jess and Pattie walked their horses up to Dana Stevens. He was carrying a scattergun across his lap, but when he saw it was Jess, he relaxed. "Welcome back, Mr. Williams. Pattie, I'm surprised to see you here. What's the news on the sheriff and the marshal?"

"Let's talk about that in the house with Mr. Thornton," replied Pattie. "No sense in telling the tale twice."

"I suppose not. Come on, I'm sure the boss is itching to find out what's happening."

Jess and Pattie followed Stevens up to the house. Stumpy Watson grabbed the reins of Jess's two horses and started walking them to the barn when Jess spoke.

"Stumpy, will you do me a favor?"

"Anything for you, Mr. Williams. You just ask."

"Those horses have had saddles on them since I last saw you and they haven't had a good bucket of grain, either. Could you give them some good feed and brush them down for me?"

"I'll dig into the best feed we got and I'll brush them down like they was my own."

"I sure appreciate it and so will they," Jess replied as he headed into the house.

Thornton stood up when they walked into the kitchen. "It's nice to see you again, Mr. Williams. Pattie, this is a most pleasant surprise, indeed. I didn't expect to see you visit my humble abode, but it's nice to have a woman around for a change."

"I'd like to say it's a pleasure to visit, but under the circumstances, I can't. For all we know, Rance Madden is right behind us with a dozen hired killers ready to shoot every one of us."

"I can't argue with you on that. He attacked again the other night and tried to burn us out, but we were ready for him that time. We got four of his men and he got two of ours."

"I heard the shooting that night. I got three more of Madden's men as they rode back to town," said Jess.

"Really? Does that mean that you've decided to take sides, Mr. Williams?"

"No, I just don't like people like Madden who think they own the world, and please, call me Jess."

"All right, but thanks for your help anyway. We sure need it."

"You'll be happy to know that I took out a dozen of Madden's men so far since I saw you last, Mr. Thornton."

Henry Thornton looked at Dana Stevens and Lemore Taft, who walked into the kitchen and sat down. "That might explain why Madden hasn't attacked again. He's waiting for reinforcements for the men you killed. You say you killed a dozen of his men?"

"Yes, sir."

"And you're still alive to talk about it?"

"I'm here, drinking your coffee and it doesn't seem to be draining out anywhere."

"I guess you are as good as they say."

"One of the men I killed the day I left here was Galt Dixon."

"Jesus Christ," said Lemore Taft. "If Madden's hiring the likes of Galt Dixon, we have a bigger problem than we thought. Dixon was one of the best. Did you face him down fair?"

"Nope, I just shot him along with four of Madden's men who were riding with him," replied Jess, as though it was nothing, which it was as far as Jess was concerned.

Lemore Taft was going to say something, but a feeling inside him stopped him from saying it. He just stared at Jess with a puzzled look. Dana Stevens said nothing, but the look on his face was one of agreement in what Jess had done.

Thornton looked at Pattie Nate with a look of compassion. "Pattie, I never wanted any of this to happen. I did what the sheriff asked me to. I stayed on my land and let him handle it. I'm sorry that the sheriff was shot. How is he, by the way?"

Pattie hung her head. "For all I know, he might be dead. He hasn't come out of the coma he's been in for several days now and he's getting weaker. Madden might have killed him by now because I left town. I don't know but I'm scared."

"How about the marshal and his deputies? What happened to them?"

"That's why I came out here, Mr. Thornton," interjected Jess. "Madden has them locked up in the jail. I'd like to borrow a few of your men and sneak into town and break them out."

"How in the hell do you plan on doing that with Madden and his men being in town? You'll just get yourself killed along with my men. I finally have a few more men to protect my property and I can't afford to lose any of them."

"Mr. Thornton, you can't afford not to use them. If we don't get the marshal and his deputies out, Madden will hire enough guns to finish you and everyone who stands in his way, and that will be the end of it. You can't hire enough men to stop him, but with Marshal Reedy and his deputies, along with me and your men, maybe we'll have a fighting chance if we act now. We can't let Madden strengthen his forces and that is exactly what he's doing. I found one of his hired guns heading for his ranch yesterday, so I know he's got more men heading his way as we speak."

"Are you talking about Galt Dixon?"

"No, it was another man who was riding alone."

"Who was it?"

"He said his name was Clint Underwood."

"So, where is he now?"

"I don't know for sure. The last time I saw him, he was headless and being dragged by his horse."

"How the hell did that happen?" asked Dana Stevens.

"It seems his face ran into a hail of buckshot from my scattergun."

"I like your style, Mr. Williams," replied Stevens.

"Well, you're in the minority," Jess replied. "Marshal Reedy would have probably arrested me by now."

"Boss," Stevens said, "I think we should help Jess here and go break the marshal out. I volunteer and I'm sure you'll get a few more who will volunteer."

"I'm in, too," said Lemore Taft, "but on one condition."

"What's that?" asked Jess.

"That you don't just plug me if you get pissed off."

"Don't worry about that. I won't plug you unless you give me a reason to."

"Well, that won't happen. I can promise you that."

"All right, let's hear your plan," said Thornton.

Jess and four of Thornton's men headed out toward Timber at about midnight. They arrived at the wooded edge south of town in about two hours. The four men with Jess were Stumpy Watson, Lemore Taft, Dana Stevens and Lawrence Fields. Stumpy and Lemore circled around town to the east. Their job was to create a disturbance. Jess, Dana and Lawrence stayed close to the jail waiting for the disturbance. They had four extra horses and four extra Winchesters with them.

Jess had explained the plan to the men before they left the Thornton ranch. First, Stumpy and Lemore were to fire off a few rounds in the air. When they were done, they were to make their way back to the jail as quickly as they could. As soon as the shooting started, Jess figured that the men inside the jail would come out and Jess and Dana Stevens would be there waiting. Dana was to cover the saloon and Jess would deal with the two men who would come out of the jail. If they didn't come out, Jess would blow the door with his scattergun and go in. At the same instant as the shooting started, Lawrence Fields would hand the four Winchesters into the jail cell from the small barred window for Reedy and his men to use.

Stumpy Watson and Lemore Taft got to their position and began firing off a few rounds. A second later, Jess ran toward the front of the jail and Dana Stevens propped himself against the side of the jail wall, his Winchester aimed at the front door of Jed's Saloon. Dana picked off one of Madden's men as he ran up the street toward the saloon. The door of the jail flew open and Jess plugged the first man as he ran out to the porch. The man fell forward off the porch. That's when Jess saw another man going for the door to slam it shut. Jess heard a rifle shot ring out from inside the jail and the man fell forward, hitting his head on the door.

Jess hollered to the inside of the jail as Dana Stevens and Lawrence Fields started firing off rounds in the direction of Jed's Saloon. "Marshal Reedy, it's Jess Williams! I'm coming in to unlock the cell. Don't fire!"

"Come on in. We won't shoot," a voice bellowed back.

Jess ran inside the door and found the keys to the cell hanging up behind the small desk. He threw the keys to Marshal Reedy, who quickly unlocked the cell he and the three deputies were in. Buck unlocked the cell that Tex was in. As they were doing that, Jess fired off his Winchester through one of the windows at the men in Jed's Saloon. Within seconds, Frank Reedy and his three deputies were firing from the windows and the door of the jail. Dana Stevens had hit the guard on the top of the saloon and Jess had killed the man on top of the building to his left.

"Marshal, we have horses for your men out back. As soon as our other two men get back, we plan to open up with scatterguns while they lay down rifle fire. That should hold them back until you get a start out of town. Me and Stevens here will leave last and that will give you at least a two-minute head start. Just make sure you don't take the two horses that are tied to the small tree. Those are long horses and they will outrun any of the horses Madden's men have."

"Sounds like you planned this right down to every little detail," replied Reedy, as he stopped to reload the Winchester.

"I'm kind of like that."

"So I've learned."

Reedy finished reloading and started firing again. Stumpy Watson and Lemore Taft returned from the other end of town, came from the back of the jail, and started firing as fast as they could. They had Madden and his men pinned down pretty good in the saloon. At the peak of the firing, Jess told them to get on their horses and ride out to the Thornton ranch. They did and that left Jess and Dana Stevens alone. They emptied their Winchesters and grabbed their scatterguns. They fired off one barrel at a time three times, taking turns, one shooting while the other man reloaded. Then they ran behind the jail. Jess mounted Gray and Stevens jumped on Sharps and they spurred the horses into a dead run. It was silent for the first five minutes or so. Madden and his men were waiting to see if the shooting was over yet. They had taken over a hundred rounds in less than five minutes and lost two men in the saloon to the gunfire.

"Vernon, take a look outside," hollered Madden.

Vernon Foster carefully worked his way toward the door of the saloon and peeked out. He saw the jail door wide open and a dead man on the porch of the jail. "They broke the marshal out of jail, boss. One of our men is lying dead on the boardwalk."

"Jesus Christ! How in the hell could that happen? Get some men and go after them."

"Boss, we already lost two men in here and probably three out there. We ain't got enough men to go chasing after them in the night. Besides, they might have an ambush planned for us along the trail. I think we should wait until morning to decide what to do. Maybe some more men will show up tomorrow. We're getting a little short on men."

Madden was so riled up he threw his rifle clear across the room. "When I find out who the hell did this, I'll have him skinned in the middle of town and let him bake in the sun for all to see!"

Madden was mad as hell but he knew that Vernon Foster was right. He grabbed a bottle from behind the bar, sat down at his table, and poured himself a drink. After he had had several shots, he finally cooled down a little. "Vernon, get these bodies out of here and go assess the rest of the damage. Gilroy, ride out to the ranch and bring every available man back here. Just leave two men there to feed the stock." Foster went out to check the dead and Gilroy ran to the livery and saddled up and rode out of town.

Jess and Stevens rode like the wind. Gray had to jump over the dead body of the guard that Madden had posted at the west end of town. Jess had snuck up and slit his throat with his bowie knife earlier.

"Damn, I don't think I've ever ridden a horse that could run so damn fast," exclaimed Stevens.

"Hang on to your hat because they don't slow down none for a long time," replied Jess.

It didn't take them long to catch up with the other six men. They rode fast all the way to the Thornton ranch where Thornton's other men were waiting for them. They rode their horses straight into the barn and ran into the ranch house and took up positions at the windows, waiting for any attack which might or might not happen. By now, it was past three o'clock and they waited until four in the morning before coming to the conclusion that Madden would not attack, at least, not tonight. They posted guards around the ranch property and finally relaxed...a little.

CHAPTER NINETEEN

The sky had a beautiful orange and reddish glow to it as the sun finally started to rise high enough above the horizon to see it. Pattie Nate had been busy in the kitchen whipping up some tempting food. She had cooked biscuits, flapjacks, eggs, bacon, ham and fresh bread along with four large apple pies. The men were all drooling like a bunch of starving animals. They weren't used to getting this kind of food here. Stumpy was an okay cook, but he was an amateur compared to Pattie. She allowed him to make the coffee and help serve, but that was about it.

The table would only accommodate eight people so the other men would be eating later. For now it was Henry Thornton, Frank Reedy and his two deputies, Buck Hern, Tex, Dana Stevens and Jess. Stumpy always ate standing up, picking up pieces of food from the plates as he put them down and eating it while he was pouring coffee or replenishing the food on the table.

Thornton looked over at Marshal Reedy who was carefully putting some fresh butter on a biscuit and trying not to break it apart. "Marshal, a few days ago you were here warning me about my little war with Rance Madden and now, here you are, a guest at my table. Isn't it funny how things work out sometimes?"

Reedy broke the biscuit and it fell on the plate in a few pieces. "Yeah, who would have thought that would happen. Of course, I might not have had another meal if it weren't for Jess here. Thanks for breaking me out of that hole."

"You're welcome, Marshal, and you can show me just how thankful you are by not arresting me for some of the things I had to do concerning Rance Madden and his hired guns."

Reedy finally got another biscuit and successfully buttered it. "Yeah, I heard about most of it from the two men who were guarding us in the jail. Some of the things you did are actions that I normally would have arrested you for, but I suppose this ain't exactly a normal situation. I couldn't have done what you did, that's for sure. If I did, they'd yank this badge off me in a second and I've kind of gotten used to wearing it."

"Is it true that you just plugged Galt Dixon without even giving him so much as a warning?" asked Tex.

"Yes, that's true. He had four other men with him so I couldn't take the chance. Besides, they ain't been exactly playing fair, so why should we?" replied Jess.

"Well, just so you know, I would've done the same damn thing, knowing what I know now," said Tex.

"Maybe," added Buck, "but we wear badges and we can't do things like that. We're supposed to follow the law and all."

Pattie Nate brought another platter of flapjacks over to the table. "You lawmen are something else. If it weren't for Jess and his way of doing things, you men would all be under the ground and never heard from again, Sheriff Steele would be dead, if he ain't already, and I would have been raped and buried in a deep grave, too. Rance Madden would own this whole town along with Mr. Thornton's ranch. Is that what you lawmen want? Do you want the bad guys to win all the time because you're too damn proud of those shiny tin badges you wear and all the rules that go along with them? Those badges only mean something to law-abiding people, not murderers the likes of Madden. When are you men going to finally get it? When you are all dead? And what about all the innocent people who get killed in the process? Don't their lives count? According to the law you men are so concerned about following, you can't do anything until a crime has been committed, even when you know for sure that Madden is going to commit a crime. The only reason that Mark Steele is lying in Doctor Hammond's office, in a coma and near death, is because of his belief in following the law. All of this could have been prevented if you all did things the way Jess here does. Hell, he's been here just a few days and he's done more to stop Madden than all the rest of you combined. I think you all need to do some serious thinking about what you're going to do next, because I can guarantee that Rance Madden is going to commit another crime and it won't be long before he does it either."

Pattie turned around, almost in tears, and went back to cooking. Everyone in the room was speechless. No one knew what to say because they all knew that she was right. The only one who was still eating was Jess; the other seven men were watching him eat. He finally noticed it.

"Why are you all looking at me like that?" asked Jess.

"Because we all just got an ass-chewing, except you," answered Reedy.

"Well, that's because you all deserved it."

"Yeah, maybe," said Reedy, "but we're sworn to uphold the law and that means following it, too."

"Tell that to Sheriff Steele. Tell that to all the other men who have died at the hands of Madden's hired killers. Hell, I would have shot Rance Madden right from the start. You knew what he was when you let him out of jail, and you knew exactly what he was going to do."

"Well, what would you have done?"

"I would have gone over to the jail and plugged his sorry ass, strapped him on his horse, and sent him back to his ranch. Hired killers don't work for free; when there isn't someone to pay them, they leave."

Frank Reedy wanted to argue the point further but he knew that he couldn't win the argument. Hell, he couldn't even win the argument within his own head. The truth was, that was exactly what Frank Reedy wanted to do about Madden but Marshal Reedy couldn't allow himself to just shoot Madden in the jail cell. They all ate in silence for about five minutes, every one of them letting what Pattie Nate and Jess had said sink into their brains.

Henry Thornton finally finished his meal. "Pattie, that was the best food I've had in a long time. If you don't want to go back to work at the saloon, you have a job right here as my full-time cook."

"Why, thank you, Mr. Thornton, but I like working over at Jed's place. Of course, by the time you men do something to stop Madden, Jed might be dead and the place burned to the ground," she replied, with a sarcastic tone in her voice.

"I heard you the first time, Pattie," said Frank Reedy.

"Good, I'm glad you were paying attention."

"How could we not? Well, Jess," said Reedy, "what do you think we ought to do about Madden and his men?"

Jess stopped eating and Pattie turned around to hear what Jess would say. "Hey, I'm not the leader of this group and I don't wear a badge. You and your men have to decide for yourselves what you want to do. I do things my way and I usually work alone."

Reedy folded his arms, which is what he usually did when he was getting frustrated. "Okay, let me put it to you this way. What are you planning on doing about Madden and his men?"

Jess placed his hands on the table and let out a sigh. "Well, Marshal, unless you plan on arresting me, I plan on going back to town and killing every one of Madden's men, and then I'm going to put a bullet in Madden's head and I ain't going to do it nicely either. Rance Madden made up his own set of rules and I'm simply going to use his rules against him and his men. And, I'm planning on leaving in about ten minutes to get started, so if you're going to arrest me, you had better do it before I leave because once I do, you'll never catch me."

"Well, don't you just get to the point," said Reedy.

"No sense putting off the inevitable or waiting around for something to happen. Pattie is right; Madden is plotting as we speak. It's either him or me, and I'd rather it be him. He started this war and I plan to finish it, even if I have to do it alone. "

Reedy unfolded his arms. "Well, I don't want to arrest you and I'm not sure that I want to stop you from what you want to do."

"I'll tell you what, Marshal. I'm going over to the barn and spending about a half hour cleaning and getting my weapons ready. You try to make up your mind about things. I'm going to assume that if you let me ride out, you won't arrest me for anything I've done or anything I'm going to do."

"I guess that's fair enough," said Reedy.

Jess pushed the chair back and kissed Pattie on her still bruised cheek. Then he gently brushed his right index finger over the bruise. "I'm not forgetting who did this either, Pattie."

Jess went out to the barn, sat at a small table, and went through his ritual of cleaning and checking all his weapons. He had plenty of ammunition for his Winchesters as well as the Sharps Big Fifty. Frank Reedy and the rest were still sitting at the table.

"Mr. Thornton, how many men do you have left now?" Reedy asked.

"Stumpy here got me five new men. Add that to the five I have left and that gives me ten men who can shoot a gun. None of them are gunslingers but every one of them will fight."

"Well, when you add me and my two deputies along with Buck, it gives us fourteen men."

Torrey Abel looked at his boss. "What are you planning, Frank?"

"I'm not exactly sure yet but I'm thinking about it. Mr. Thornton, would you excuse me and my two deputies? We need to have a private meeting."

"You can use my study if you wish."

"Thanks, but I think we'll just go out back and have a smoke."

Frank Reedy, Torrey Abel, Hal Banks and Buck went out back behind the Thornton Ranch. Buck and Abel took out the makings and rolled themselves smokes.

Torrey took a long drag from his cigarette and slowly let it out. "What do you think we ought to do, Boss?"

"Well, we have fourteen men. I figure that Madden has at least that many men and more on the way. Madden has us outnumbered and his men are hardened killers. That puts us at a disadvantage."

"Maybe not," said Buck.

"What do you mean?"

"We got Jess Williams. Hell, from what I've seen so far, he counts as ten men."

"Yeah, that's true, but I can't let him loose while I wear this badge."

"Well, you'd better make a decision pretty soon 'cause our friend is saddling up to ride out right now and once he does, we'll have no control over what he might do unless we arrest him. Somehow I don't think he would allow that to happen."

Reedy folded his arms again. "I don't think we have much control over what he does anyway, but I do think that he will work along with us if we ask him."

Torrey Abel and Hal Banks looked back and forth at one another and then Banks looked at Reedy. "You mean if *you* ask him."

Reedy looked at his two deputies who had been working under him for a while now. They were both as tough as they come and seasoned gunmen. "You don't mean to imply that the two of you are afraid of him, are you?"

"No," answered Banks quickly. "We just have a lot of respect for that right hand of his."

"Yeah," added Abel.

"Well, so do I, but I know him better than you two. He wouldn't take on either one of you unless you gave him no choice. He's not like that. As a matter of fact, as much as I don't always agree with how he does things, he ain't never killed a man who didn't need killing. Anyway, enough of that. I've made a decision. Torrey, Hal, you're both fired. Take those badges off."

Both Abel and Banks looked at their boss as if he had gone loco. "What the hell you say?" asked Banks.

"You heard me right. Take them off," replied Reedy who also removed his U.S. marshal's badge from his shirt and placed it in his back pocket.

"Why are we being fired?" Abel asked, taking his badge off and handing it to Reedy. Banks followed suit but said nothing.

"Because what we are about to do might tarnish these badges and I won't allow that to happen. Maybe we can put them back on later but for now, until we get this problem with Rance Madden settled, we don't represent the U.S. marshal's office. We are officially off the payroll."

"Damn it," said Banks, kicking a small rock about ten feet. "I need this job."

"Well, I know someone who is hiring and paying a whole lot more money than a deputy U.S. marshal gets paid," said Buck, who had been silent during the entire conversation until now.

Banks and Abel looked at one another with that unspoken language and then they looked over at their boss. "Frank, you got a problem with us working for Thornton since we've been fired?" asked Banks.

"The way I see it, you two are free to pursue any line of work you wish to. I have officially relieved you of your duties as of this moment."

"Frank, what are you going to do?" asked Buck.

Frank Reedy looked down at the ground for a moment. "Well, I just quit so I am relieved of my duties as a U.S. marshal as of now, so I guess I'm looking for a new job and Thornton is paying pretty well."

Buck looked at Reedy, Abel and Banks. He smiled as he took off his deputy sheriff's badge and stuck it in his back pocket. "I guess I'm in too."

"What about Tex?"

"I don't think he should ride yet. He's still bleeding from his wounds. I think it's best if he stays here and helps guard the ranch. It will be up to him to decide whether or not he wants to take his badge off."

Jess was coming out of the barn with both of his horses saddled up and ready to ride. "Marshal Reedy, I sure enjoyed seeing you again but I have to ride out. I hope you won't try to stop me."

"I have no intention of stopping you. I intend to join you."

Jess noticed that Reedy's badge was missing. He looked at the other three and noticed that all three had removed their badges. Jess smiled. "Just what do you have in mind, Marshal?"

Reedy smiled back. "Just call me Frank from now on."

CHAPTER TWENTY

Rance Madden hadn't slept all night. He was still livid over losing his prisoners, and even more livid over losing three more of his men. He had sent Vernon Foster out to his ranch to wait for the new arrival of hired guns that he hoped would show up soon. He had Jed working the bar and the kitchen both and Jed was getting worn out trying to keep Madden's men fed and full of whiskey. The only good thing is that there were less of Madden's men right now.

Madden had posted two men on the top of the two last buildings going out of town to the east and two more on the top of the two last buildings going out of town to the west. He kept three men with him in the saloon and two more walking along each side of the main street of Timber. He would know instantly of another ambush attack like last night at the jail cell. He waited all day but nothing happened.

It was just about dusk when Gus Gilroy rode up to Jed's Saloon followed by ten of the meanest-looking men you could lay eyes on. Each man was a seasoned gunman and itching to make some good money by plying his skills. Gilroy strutted into the saloon and motioned to the ten men to join him. They all walked in and stood in a semi-circle around the large table where Rance Madden was seated with one of his other men, Vernon Foster.

"Boss," said Gilroy, "these are the men I was telling you about the other day. Each and every one of these men is as tough as they come and they are looking to make some money. I've already explained the situation to them and they ain't got any problems with shooting whoever you want shot, as long as they get paid well for it."

Madden stood up and looked the ten men over. They did, indeed, look like hardened men. All of them had six guns worn low and strapped down tight. "If there is any man here who hasn't killed at least one man in his life, I don't want to hire you, so speak up now."

The ten men looked at one another and no one spoke up. The truth was, each of them had killed more than their share of men and a few of them had killed and raped their share of women. These were hard cases for sure. Madden motioned for them to put some tables together and sit down. The ten men introduced themselves to Madden. The men were Lane Myers, Jon Stidham, Smitty Morrison, Vreeland Summers, Ernest Winslow, Gorden Barry, Lyle Bitters, Reginald Sharky, Hatch Simpson and Griff Clark. Vreeland Summers, who was probably the worst of the lot and probably the deadliest of them with a pistol, was the first to speak up.

"Mr. Madden, we've all been told that you're paying well for hired guns. I've talked with all the other men and they agreed to let me speak for them. We all had jobs we were being hired for and we canceled them because we heard you would pay more. The question is, how much are you paying?"

Madden poured himself a drink. "I don't like to admit this, but I'm desperate for men so I will pay more than you would make hiring your gun out to anyone else. I guarantee it. I have the sheriff of this town lying over at the doctor's office, and Thornton's men broke Marshal Frank Reedy and three deputies out of the jail last night. I've lost a lot of men over the last several days."

Vreeland Summers stiffened at the mention of Frank Reedy. "Did I hear you right? Did you say Marshal Frank Reedy?"

"Yes."

"U.S. Marshal Frank Reedy?"

"Yes, do you know him?"

"I ought to. He put a bullet in me and locked me up for six months just because I killed a man over in Leavenworth. Man attacked me with a knife so I had to shoot him. Reedy wouldn't listen to my side of the story and when I wouldn't go willingly, he put a bullet in my right side. I owe him one, but if you want us to take on a U.S. marshal and two of his deputies, you'd better be willing to pay real good. A man kills a U.S. marshal and the rest of them damn marshals take it real personal. They will keep coming for you until they get you, no matter how long it takes them."

"Not if we can ambush them first and kill them. Then we go out and bury them deep out in the forest where no one will ever find their bodies."

"We would have to kill all the witnesses because if one person knows, he'll tell someone eventually. You're going to have to pay us enough to hide out for quite a while."

"I will pay each of you five hundred dollars now and another five hundred when your work is finished. On top of that, I will pay one hundred per day for each man and I will cover all your expenses along with that. You men can go to the mercantile store and take whatever you need and charge it to my account. The same goes for the saloon here as well as the hotel. How does that sound?"

Vreeland looked around at the other nine men and they all looked satisfied with the offer. He turned back to Rance Madden. "How long do you think this job will take?"

"I figure that Marshal Reedy will ride straight into town tomorrow with some of Thornton's men and try to arrest me and my men. He figures I'm low on hired guns and he has no idea that you men showed up so fast, so I figure he won't waste any time."

"Well, how do you want us to go about it?"

"We've got about twenty men now with your ten in the fold. My man Vernon here will show you around town. I'd like you to keep at least two of your men on the rooftops at all times, day and night. They can take turns. I figure that Reedy will come in at the west end of town since that's the way to the Thornton ranch. I want you to use the rest of your men to wait outside of town to ambush Reedy and his men when they come to town. Take three or four of my other men with you."

"Do you want us to warn them before we start shooting?"

"Hell no. I want you and your men to open fire on them and hopefully, you'll get four or five of them before they know what hit them. Then, finish them off, drag their sorry asses out in the woods, and bury them deep so the coyotes won't dig them up. We don't want any evidence."

"What if they come in the other way?"

"Then we'll just have to deal with it. My men can hold out until your men can get here. That's why I need two of your men up on the rooftops and I need them to be your best shooters."

"Hell, just pick any of them; they're all expert shooters with a rifle or pistol. I'll leave you four men for the rooftops. They can rotate every six hours."

"It sounds like we have a deal and a plan."

"Yeah, but I ain't seen any money yet." Vreeland said, holding his hand out.

Madden smiled. "Vernon, go over to the bank and bring me back six thousand dollars. That should cover your pay, including today's wages. You and your men get something to eat and you'll all have your money in your pockets before you finish your meals."

Vernon Foster had already headed for the bank and Madden motioned for Jed to take care of his newly acquired hired guns. Madden looked them over and smiled. He felt good that he had the upper hand again. It wouldn't be long before he would be rid of Thornton, Reedy, Steele and everyone else who was getting in his way. He sat back and poured himself another drink.

"So what is the plan, Frank?" Jess asked.

"Jess, the way I see it, Madden figures that I'm going to waltz right in there and arrest him and his men. Well, we ain't going to dance to that tune this time. I think we're going to play it your way."

"It's about time you came to your senses, Frank. You can't deal with a man like Madden and follow the law. Don't you remember

Dick Carter or Paul Mason? They were cut out of the same bolt of cloth that Madden was, although I actually think that Madden isn't playing with a full deck."

"I'm beginning to see it that way too. I know one thing for sure. He intends on killing me and my men here no matter what. I figure it's either me or him and it ain't going to be me."

Jess looked at the other three men. "Are the rest of you men in on this? I don't see any badges on any of your shirts."

Torrey Abel, Hal Banks and Buck Hern all shook their heads in agreement.

"All right, I'll go along with it, but I still need to work alone most of the time."

"Jess, where were you when you shot that man down in the street back in town? Everyone was looking around to see where the shot came from, but no one figured it out."

"You're still not going to figure it out because I'm not telling anyone, and that includes you. What I will tell you is that I do plan on doing some shooting with my Sharps today. I figure I can pick off a few of Madden's men before they can figure it out."

"Jess, go ahead and get into your position and do whatever you think you need to do. Here is what I plan on doing. I'm going to take these three men and four of Thornton's men and attack Madden tonight just after dark. Banks and I will sneak into town from the north. We'll take out two or three easy targets and then run like hell for the woods. I figure that Madden's men will follow and my other men will be positioned at the edge of the woods where they can open fire with their Winchesters at Madden's men. We'll get as many of them as we can and then we'll all split up and head through the woods. They might find one or two of us, but they won't get all of us. I don't think they will follow us into the woods anyway. They'll probably figure we have another ambush set up for them."

Jess thought about it for a moment. "I wouldn't have planned it any other way myself, Frank. I'll be able to give you and your men some cover from my position. It will be dark so they might see the muzzle flash and give my position away, but if that happens, I'll be able to get away and meet you back at the Thornton ranch."

"Good luck to you, Jess," Reedy said as he shook Jess's hand.

"Luck doesn't have much to do with it, Frank," Jess replied as he swung up in the saddle. "I hope to see you tomorrow for breakfast."

"You will. I don't want to miss out on those fresh flapjacks Pattie makes."

Jess headed out and Reedy and the other three men went back into Thornton's ranch to explain what they were planning to do. The rest of Thornton's men were done eating and already out at their designated spots. Henry Thornton was sitting at the table with Stumpy Watson, Tex and Pattie Nate, drinking coffee. Thornton noticed that none of the four men was wearing a badge.

"Marshal, what happened to your badge?"

"I took it off," Reedy said as he reached into his back pocket and pulled out his marshal's badge and placed it in the middle of the table. Abel, Banks and Buck all followed suit. "I think it's best if we leave those badges here until this matter is finished for good."

"Well, I'm glad you men finally came to your senses," exclaimed Pattie.

Tex took off his badge and threw it onto the pile. "I'm in for whatever you decide, Marshal."

"Tex, I need you to keep wearing that badge and I want you to stay here and help protect the ranch. Any hard riding will surely open up those wounds and you'd bleed to death. Besides, if things go okay, we'll need a lawman to make legal arrests and lock up prisoners."

Tex thought about it for a moment. Then he picked his badge up and pinned it back on. "I suppose you're right, Marshal. I can do more good here than out there. I would probably slow you down."

"I'm glad you agree. Don't call me marshal anymore; just call me Frank. Mr. Thornton, I need your best four men. I plan on attacking Madden in town tonight."

Henry Thornton smiled at the thought. "You can take Stevens, Fields, Taft and one of the new men, Cotton. That only leaves me with six men and Tex here to guard the ranch. We won't be able to fight off a large attack from Madden and his men."

"Hopefully, you won't have to. We should have Madden and his men too busy to attack you tonight. Pattie, I expect a big breakfast tomorrow morning, including some of those flapjacks."

"Frank, if you come back tomorrow, I'll cook up anything you want. Is Jess going with you?"

"No, he decided to go ahead and work alone for now. I think he's planning on giving Madden a little grief before we get there tonight."

"Good, that bastard deserves all the grief he gets."

"Okay men, let's go get the other four and all get some rest. We'll ride out right after dark," said Reedy.

CHAPTER TWENTY-ONE

Jess took the long way toward Timber, following along the edge of the woods. That way, he could duck into cover if he saw anyone coming along the trail. He saw no one. He thought of Eddie Sloan and how he had missed him again back in Abilene, Kansas. Jess had been so distracted by the current turn of events that he had almost forgotten about his hunt for Eddie Sloan, almost. Jess figured that Sloan was finished with his high-stakes poker game in St. Louis and off to somewhere else. It didn't matter to Jess. He would pick up Sloan's trail again and it didn't matter how long it took.

He worked himself behind the high ridge on the north side of Timber. He tied Sharps up about two hundred feet into the woods by the same little stream and rode Gray up the gentle slope until he reached the hole going into the cave. He walked through the cave to the other side and leaned his Sharps Big Fifty against the wall. He put the leather bag down, opened the large flap, and placed several cartridges on the flap, all pointing in the same direction. He took his telescope and looked down at the town.

Timber was a small town with only one main street and about a dozen buildings along each side. There were a few scattered houses around the town in no particular order. Most of them were mere one-room shacks and just had a bed, a stove or a fireplace for heat and cooking and not much more than that. A few were larger and looked fairly nice, with porches and flowers planted around the houses. Jess had noticed that hardly any of the townsfolk came out of their homes or businesses. They were afraid to walk the streets with Madden's men all around. Jess noticed that there were more

men than before. It was obvious that Madden had hired more gunmen and by the looks of it, quite a few.

Jess could also see that Madden had a large group of men at the
west end of town and a small group at the east end. Jess knew why
Madden had placed the larger group at the west end of town. It was
because he figured that any attack from Thornton or Reedy would
most likely come from that direction and that would give Madden
the perfect ambush. They were far enough out of town that Jess
could hardly see them through the telescope, but he could see that
they were hiding behind trees and large boulders. They were out of
range for the Sharps.

The two men he had spotted on the rooftops, however, were not
out of his range. Jess looked them over very carefully. He had not
seen either of them before and they looked like seasoned gunmen.
Probably new, Jess thought to himself. Well, time to get things moving, Jess decided.

He chambered the first round into the Sharps and lifted the
front sight up. He checked the wind; it was blowing gently to the
east. He sighted in on the first target. He was smoking a cigarette
and sitting on a ledge that was about two feet high and went around
three sides on top of the mercantile store. The man's Winchester
was leaning against the ledge within easy reach.

Jess propped the Sharps in the fork of the large branch he had
cut and left there before. It held the Sharps nice and steady and
allowed Jess to fire about five feet back from the opening of the
cave. That way, the muzzle flash and smoke would not be seen in
the daylight. He took careful aim above and to the right a little to
make up for the wind and the drop of the round on its way to its
target. He was firing downward at about a forty-five degree angle.
He slowly put pressure on the trigger of the Sharps until it barked.
Jess looked up and the man flew off the building and fell between
the mercantile store and the building next to it.

Jess put the Sharps against the cave wall and took the telescope
and watched the flurry of activity that took place next. The other
man who was on the rooftop of the livery ducked down for cover.

Two men came running out of Jed's Saloon trying to find out who had been hit. The man Jess had killed was Lane Myers, one of the new men. Vernon Foster went to check on Myers who lay dead in the three-foot gap between the two buildings. Myers had fallen backward with a full turn before hitting the ground, so his back was propped up against one building and his feet were propped up against the mercantile store. There was a very large hole in his chest. Vernon ran back over to the saloon where Rance Madden was standing on the porch, a rifle in his hands.

"Who the hell got hit?" asked Madden.

"One of the new men, Lane Myers. Shot right in the middle of his chest, Boss."

"Where the hell did the shot come from?"

"That's what we're trying to figure out right now. It's just like the last time; no one has seen a thing. I got a few men looking around town now but so far, I haven't a clue."

"Well find one, damn it! I can't start losing men again."

Jess watched a man walk over to Jed's Saloon and talk to a tall man who was wearing a brown hat. Jess looked down at the man's boots and they were, indeed, a fine-looking pair. Then Jess looked at the man's face, but from this distance he couldn't see if he had a scar over his right eye. Jess figured that this might be Rance Madden and even though he couldn't be sure, it didn't matter. If it wasn't Madden, it surely was one of his men and that made him a good target. Jess grabbed the Sharps again and propped it up in the fork of the large branch. He sighted the man in but just as he was beginning to put pressure on the trigger, the man walked back inside the saloon. "Well, Mr. Madden, if that was you, that was your one break," Jess said to no one but himself.

Jess figured he would wait and watch. A man from each end of the town rode in to find out what had happened, and then rode out again. The other man on the rooftop of the livery had been staying down, but he was slowly getting more comfortable now that the shooting was over. Jess watched the rotation take place with the guards on the rooftops. The one who was left on the rooftop of the livery came down and two new guards took over. One man replaced the man on the livery and the other man went up to the rooftop of the mercantile store. Jess also watched as some of the men from each end of town rode in. For each one that rode in, one rode out to take the other man's place. "Well, Mr. Madden, you seem to have set up quite an elaborate plan for your men," he said, again, to no one but himself.

It had been four hours since Jess had shot the first man. He figured that Reedy and his men would come into town a few hours after dark. Jess couldn't do anything to help from his position in the cave. All he could do was to keep any other men from riding out of town. He figured it was time to take another man away from Madden. He propped the Sharps up in the fork of the branch and sighted in his target. He picked out the meanest-looking of the two who were on the rooftops. The man was Smitty Morrison, and he was on top of Jed's Saloon. Jess took careful aim and pulled the trigger back slowly until the Sharps barked. He hit the man in the middle of his back since he was turned away from Jess. Morrison fell forward and fell flat onto the rooftop.

Vernon Foster and Gus Gilroy came running out of the saloon again, trying to see where the shot had come from. They had heard the loud thump of Morrison's body hitting the rooftop. Foster ran up the side steps and onto the rooftop to find Smitty Morrison in a puddle of blood with a large hole in the middle of his back. Jess watched as the man he thought to be Rance Madden climbed the steps to see about Morrison. Jess put the sights of the Sharps on the man all the way up the steps. When he stopped to look at the body of Smitty Morrison, Jess pulled the trigger back and the Sharps exploded. But a split second before it did, a small rock under the branch moved and threw the shot off ever so slightly. The round hit Madden in his left arm, spinning him around and down on the roof.

Vernon Foster turned in the direction of where the shot had come from but he still didn't think to look up to the top of the rock cliff. Jess focused the telescope on the man and that's when

Jess recognized him as the one who had slapped Pattie so hard that she fell. I owe you one, Mister, Jess thought to himself as he chambered another round into the Sharps. Foster helped Madden up and was taking him down the steps when the Sharps barked loudly again, the round hitting Vernon Foster in his right side just below his elbow. Foster and Madden tumbled down the steps like two rag dolls, Madden cussing all the way. Gus Gilroy and Denny Shank ran over to Madden and got him into the saloon as quickly as they could. One look at Vernon Foster told them he was dead. They sat Madden down in a chair and sent for Doctor Hammond.

"I want you men to find out who in the hell has been doing the shooting!" hollered Madden.

"Boss, we've been trying," Gilroy replied, "but whoever it is, he must have one heck of a hiding spot."

Doctor Hammond came in and checked out Madden's wound. "You'll live; it's just a flesh wound. It didn't even hit the bone. The bullet went clean through the muscle." Hammond began cleaning the wound when he noticed something funny. "That's a little strange," Hammond said.

"What's so strange about a flesh wound, Doc?" Madden asked.

"It's the angle of the bullet. It looks like it hit your arm at a forty-five degree angle. See here at the entry point and then look at the exit point."

Madden looked at the wound and it was obvious. He thought about it for a moment and then he remembered that the shot seemed to have come from above. "That son of a bitch is on that rock cliff to the north side of town."

Gilroy looked at Denny Shank and then back to Madden. "Boss, that cliff has to be about six or seven hundred yards out. Even a Winchester in an expert's hand couldn't reach that far and kill anyone. The shots couldn't have come from up there."

"Yeah, but a buffalo rifle could make a shot like that, especially if the right man is doing the shooting. I used to hunt with a buffalo hunter for a few months, and you wouldn't believe how far those damn things shoot," said Denny Shank.

"Gilroy, take Shank and two more men and go around the other side of that cliff. The slope is easy enough to climb with a horse. If you find someone up there, bring him to me. I want to cut his gonads off and make him eat them right here while we watch."

"You got it, Boss," said Gilroy as he and Denny Shank headed out. They took Richard Braun and Grant Hull with them, rode out the west end of town, and headed for the backside of the rock cliff where Jess was hiding. It didn't take long for Jess to realize what was happening. They had figured it out. He had just enough time to get out of the cave, back down to the bottom, and into the cover of the woods. When he got there, he tied Gray up to a tree about fifty feet inside the woods and then he grabbed his Sharps and both of his Winchesters and ran back out to the edge and waited.

He didn't have to wait long. The four men were riding fast and coming around the bottom of the rock cliff. They were about two hundred fifty yards out. He raised the sights and his first target was Gus Gilroy. The Sharps barked and knocked Gilroy backward out of the saddle. The other three men stopped momentarily to see where the shot had come from. Jess knew that he didn't have much time, so he chambered another round into the Sharps. He fired again and Denny Shank hit the ground, his horse running off back toward town. The other two men started running their horses at a full gallop. Richard Braun was firing his Winchester and Hull was firing his pistol. They were about one hundred fifty yards out when Jess's third shot took out Braun and silenced the Winchester, which had been slamming rounds into the tree Jess was standing behind. That left only one man, Grant Hull, who had emptied his pistol and pulled his Winchester out of its scabbard. Hull was levering a round into the chamber when Jess's fourth shot slammed into his chest, knocking him off the saddle. His body hit the ground not more than fifty yards from Jess. Jess knew that the men at the west end of town would be coming so he grabbed his weapons, jumped on Gray, retrieved his other horse, and headed through the thick woods as fast as he could.

He could hear the hollering and the beating of hoofs heading in the direction of where he had been. Jess made it to a clearing. He spurred Gray and made it across the clearing in two minutes. He reached the heavily wooded area on the other side of the clearing and still rode as fast as he could through the trees. He wanted to put as much distance from the men as he could. He knew that they would not follow him too far because they would have to go back to their ambush location. He took a turn to the right and rode about five more miles before he found a creek and made camp. He kept both of his horses saddled and ready to ride at a moment's notice. He opened up a cold can of beans and ate them.

CHAPTER TWENTY-TWO

Vreeland Summers had taken his men to the site of the shooting. He found the dead bodies of Hull, Shank, Gilroy and Braun scattered on the ground. He sent a few men into the woods to look for the shooter, but he didn't want to keep them there long. He had left only two men back at their ambush spot and he wanted the rest of his men to get back to it as soon as possible. He sent his men back to the ambush point and he rode back to Jed's Saloon to inform Madden of what had happened. When he walked into the saloon, Madden had a bandage covering his left arm. He was in a foul mood, which was evident from the nasty scowl he had on his face.

"Mr. Madden, I have some bad news for you."

"That's a surprise; it seems like that's all I'm getting today, including getting shot myself! I just sent four men up to the top of that rock cliff to find the son of a bitch who has been doing all the shooting."

"I heard a few gunshots but I figured you and the other men had it covered. As for the four men you sent to find out about the shooting, well, they didn't make it."

"What do you mean?"

"I found all four of them at the base of that hill, dead."

"All four of them?"

"Yes, sir, all four."

"Who the hell could pick off four men by himself? It has to be more than one shooter. All I know is I've lost seven more men today and got myself shot too. That damn Thornton must've hired some damn good men."

"Mr. Madden, I don't mean to tell you your business, but I would suggest that you keep the men in town hidden and off them rooftops until this is over. Let's hope that Thornton or the marshal come to town soon. We're getting a little light on men."

Madden looked down at his drink on the table, "I think that's good advice, Vreeland. I know I ain't going outside unless I have to. Why don't you take the men from the east end of town with your other men at the west end? If they come in from the east, you and your men can make it here in a few minutes anyway."

"I agree. I'll go and get them and head back out to the ambush point. That will give me a dozen men including myself. My guess is that if Reedy comes in, he will have fewer men than that. If you hear gunshots, send the rest of your men out to join us." Madden nodded in agreement. Vreeland Summers headed out and Madden went back to drinking his whiskey.

⚑ ⚐

It was dark now and Reedy and his men were saddling up to ride into Timber. He had no idea that Jess had already taken out seven of Madden's men and wounded Madden himself. They rode along the trees and entered the woods about a mile out from where Vreeland Summers and his men were waiting to ambush them. Reedy and his men worked their way slowly and quietly until they reached the edge of the woods to the north of the town right about in the middle. They could see the back of Jed's Saloon. They tied their horses up about a hundred yards inside the dense woods and made their way to the edge.

"Torrey, you're the best man with a Winchester I know, so go and position yourself about fifty feet off to our right. That will give you a few shots before they spot you. The rest of you men go about a hundred feet in the other direction. I'm going to take Buck and Hal with me to the back of the saloon and check things out. Then, we'll work ourselves across the street and open fire on the front of the saloon. When the shooting starts, the rest of the men here will start firing, but all of you wait until you see a target before you fire. We'll be straight across the street from the saloon. That way, both you and the other men will be shooting from different angles and with a little luck, you won't hit us."

"That's a good plan, as long as the three of you stay across the street from the saloon," replied Torrey.

"We'll do the best we can. My guess is that some of them will sneak out the back door of the saloon when we start firing at the front and that will be your chance to pick off a few."

"All right, but be careful. You don't know how many men he has in town. You might just be running into an ambush."

"We'll just have to take that chance."

Reedy, Buck and Banks started crawling on their bellies toward the back of Jed's Saloon. When they finally reached it, Banks peeked through the back door. He could see Madden and two other men sitting at a large table. He couldn't tell if there were any more men inside from his vantage point, so he worked his way around the side of the saloon and peeked in. He saw two more men at the bar and Jed behind the bar. He worked his way back to Reedy and Buck, who had ducked behind and below the little room that Pattie usually stayed in.

"I count five men inside along with the bartender. Madden is sitting at a table with two men and there are two more at the bar. Madden is wearing a bloody bandage on his left arm, though."

"That's interesting, but you didn't see any more men?" asked Reedy.

"Nope, just those five. Maybe he has more men hiding in the other buildings."

Reedy took a moment to think about it. "Well, let's see if we can get across the street. Let's go down several buildings and cross toward the end of town."

They slowly worked their way to the east end of town. They took turns running across the street, one at a time. Reedy went first, Buck second and Banks last. They ducked behind the mercantile store, which was directly across from Jed's Saloon.

"I don't see any other men," said Buck. "Where the hell do you think they all are?"

"I'm betting that Madden's men are waiting out at the west end of town for us to ride straight into an ambush," replied Reedy.

"You just might be right," said Banks.

"Well, this certainly changes things a little," said Reedy. "Buck, I hate to ask you to do this, but I need you to make it back to the other men. Tell them to leave Abel there to pick off the men I'm certain will come out the back door of that saloon. Then, tell the rest of them to get themselves over to the west end of town as quickly as they can and position themselves on both sides of the street and wait for Madden's men to come riding in when they hear all the shooting. When they do, our men will have them in a cross fire."

"I'm on my way. It's going to take a while, so don't start the fireworks without me."

Buck worked his way along the backs of the buildings. He looked both ways and ran across the street. As far as he knew, no one had spotted him. He was looking back and forth at the backs of the buildings on the north side of town before doing another belly crawl through the grass. Just as he was about to get down he felt a gun barrel in his back and the cocking of the hammer at the same instant. Before he realized it, a large bowie knife was at his throat; the pressure of the blade just slight enough to push the skin in, but not enough to cut it.

"Make one sound and I promise it will be your last," the unknown figure said, in a very low whisper. "I want to know where Rance Madden is. You've got five seconds to tell me before I slit your throat."

"Take it easy, Mister. Rance Madden is in the saloon with four more men. If you're asking about Madden, then maybe we're on the same side."

"Who are you?" the man behind Buck asked.

"I'm Buck Hern, one of Sheriff Steele's deputies. I'm here with Frank Reedy and we're getting ready to go after Madden."

The bowie knife disappeared as fast as it had appeared at Buck's throat. Buck slowly turned around when he didn't feel the barrel in his back and when he did, he was looking at Jess Williams. Buck let out a sigh. "Well, ain't you a sight for sorry eyes. Where the hell you been all day?"

"Up on the rock cliff, killing more of Madden's men."

"How many did you get?"

"Seven. Plus, I had the pleasure of putting a slug in Madden in the process."

"Seven? You killed seven of Madden's men all by yourself and you're still walking upright?"

"Yep."

"Damn, you don't mess around none, do you?"

"Nope."

"So, why were you here in town?"

"I was working my way toward the saloon to kill Madden and finish this. That's when I spotted you running across the street."

"Well, you'll have help, but I need to fill you in on what's going to happen." Buck told Jess the entire plan, including the fact about Madden having most of his men at the west end of town.

"Tell Frank Reedy that I'm going to put myself up on top of the mercantile store with my Sharps. It's only a half moon so it's not very light out, but I might be able to pick off a few of them as they come into town."

"He'll be happy to hear it, but you can tell him yourself. He's back behind the mercantile store with Banks waiting for me to return."

Buck got down on his belly and started to crawl through the grass, but before he got two feet, he stopped and turned his head around. "You really were going to slit my throat, weren't you?"

"Well...you did have one second left," replied Jess, with a smirk.

"A damn good thing I don't stutter," said Buck, as he started crawling.

Jess worked his way across the street and to the back of the mercantile store where he spotted two men sitting on the ground with their backs against the back of the building. As soon as he got close enough, the two men began to point their Winchesters in his direction. "Easy, Frank, don't open up with those rifles. It's Jess Williams."

Reedy was not one to take chances. He continued to keep his Winchester pointed at Jess until he could actually see his face. "Well, I'm glad you decided to join the party."

"Hell, I've been here all day. You're the one who's late. I already took down seven of Madden's men."

"I guess you've been a little busy then."

"Yeah, I would still be up in my little hiding spot, but when I saw Madden, I just had to take the shot and it gave my position away."

"Well, you didn't get him because he's still over there at the saloon, but he is sporting a nice bandage on his left arm."

"Yeah, I gave him that. The only reason he isn't dead is that a rock moved under the forked branch I was using to support the Sharps and it threw the shot off. I won't miss the next time."

"Buck should be back soon and when he arrives, we plan to open up on the front of the saloon. I have Torrey Abel back behind the saloon at the edge of the woods ready to open up when any of them go out the back. Madden has only four men with him in the saloon. I have a hunch he has the rest of his men out at the west end of town to ambush us if we rode in. I sent the rest of my men to the buildings at the end of the street and they'll turn the tables by ambushing Madden's men as they ride in."

"I can tell you for sure that's where they are. I spotted them from the cliff at the north of town. They were out of range of the Sharps so I couldn't take any of them out. I was hoping you were smart enough not to ride in on the main trail."

"I let them ambush me once. If I had prevented that, this whole thing would have never gotten this far. I'm not going to let that happen again. We came in along the woods to the north."

"I see you still haven't pinned that badge back on yet."

"No, and I don't plan to until this is over. I'm done playing fair with that madman."

"I'm glad to hear it. Frank, I'm going up top with my Sharps. I met Buck on his way to your other men and he told me about you sending your people to the west end to wait for Madden's men to come riding in. I figure that I might be able to pick off one or two before they get into range of your men."

"Okay, but wait until the shooting starts. I figure it won't take but a few minutes before Madden's men come riding straight in at a full gallop."

"I'll use my Winchester and help you pick off the men in the saloon, but I want to ask you a favor."

"Anything you want. What is it?"

"If it's possible, I'd like you to leave Madden alive for me."

"I'll try, but once the shooting starts, he'll probably be hit before it's over with."

"I know, but if he makes it, leave him to me."

"Why?"

"I like to finish what I start."

CHAPTER TWENTY-THREE

Rance Madden was just lifting his shot glass to down his whiskey when bullets started hitting the front of the saloon. The first bullet whizzed right by his right ear, missing him by mere inches. Treat Knudsen and Denzel Matheny flipped the large table they were sitting at on its side and pushed it up to the window using the thick tabletop for extra cover. Madden ran behind the bar and grabbed the scattergun that Jed kept there. Jed was crouching down behind the bar, shivering like a scared cat.

"Rory and Clevis, you two run out the back and work your way around the front of the next building and fire from there," shouted Madden.

Treat Knudsen and Denzel Matheny fired off shots at the two openings of the mercantile store where the incoming shots were coming from. Jess took aim at one of the men behind the table, but he was having trouble keeping him in his sights because both men were ducking down and coming up to fire a few quick rounds. He fired off a few rounds with the Winchester, but the rounds wouldn't go through the thick tabletop after going through the wall. He grabbed the Sharps and chambered a round. It barked and Treat Knudsen fell back from behind the table, dead.

"Jesus Christ, I think someone is on top of that building with a cannon or something," exclaimed Matheny as he ran behind the bar where Madden was still crouching. Bullets were flying everywhere, hitting behind the bar, breaking glasses and bottles of whiskey, the glass falling on Madden and Matheny who were ducking from the shots and the glass both.

Rory Clement and Clevis Danville ran out the back door of the saloon but they had not made it very far. Torry Abel hit Clement first. When Danville tried to go back inside, Abel hit him with a second round from the Winchester, throwing Danville into the screen door hard enough that he pushed the screen out and his body was lying halfway inside the doorway. Abel fired a few more rounds into the back of the saloon. Then he headed out at a dead run for the other men who were positioned at the last buildings at the west end of town.

Jess turned his attention to the sound of running horses. He crouched down and propped the Sharps on top of the side of the building. When he could finally see the shadowy figures atop the running horses, he took aim and fired. He couldn't tell if he had delivered a fatal shot, but the rider did fall off his horse. He took aim at another figure and fired, this time missing the man. Then, he heard gunfire erupting from the end of the street.

Frank Reedy had sent Buck Hern and Hal Banks to the end of town to help his other men. He stayed on the side of the mercantile store to keep Madden, and whoever he had left in the saloon, pinned down. He could see through the front saloon door all the way to the back door. If anyone tried to go out the back, he would know it. Besides, anyone who tried would have to move Danville's body out of the way or try to jump over his body.

Vreeland Summers was leading the pack into town. He was riding next to Jeramiah Paxton when he saw Paxton get hit and go down. They rode straight through the gunfire and Reedy's men took out four more of Madden's men. Murphy Monroe, Taylor Stowe, Ernest Winslow and Gorden Berry all went down. Vreeland and his men rode past Jess who was still on top of the mercantile store. Jess aimed his Winchester at a man and the bullet slammed into his back. He fell forward, bounced off the neck of his horse, and hit the ground. Lyle Bitters was dead two seconds after he had been hit. Jess fired another round and Mike Winters flew off his horse, the slug entering the back of his head and exiting out his left eye. That left Vreeland Summers and four other men. They all jumped off their horses and scattered between buildings, firing back at Jess and the other men, who were now making their way up the street, ducking between buildings one at a time and laying down cover fire for the other men to advance up the street.

Buck Hern and Hal Banks made it back to Reedy's position. Frank was reloading his Winchester and his pistol. "Glad to see you boys are still breathing."

"Yeah, but we lost two men. Dana Stevens took one in the chest and Lawrence Fields took one in the gut. He ain't dead yet, but he will be soon," said Buck.

"The good news though," added Banks, "is that we got six of Madden's men, so we're raising our odds of surviving this thing. Your boy upstairs took out three of them himself."

"Actually he got four. He took out one in the bar with that Sharps rifle of his. That round went right through the wall of the saloon and through a thick wooden table and still knocked the man backward."

"Who's left in the bar?"

"As far as I can tell, Madden is still in there with at least one other man. One man is lying halfway inside the back door, dead."

"That was Abel's work. He told me he got two men who came out of the back door of the saloon."

"Well," Banks said, "let's not get too awfully excited about this. We still have five of Madden's men to deal with and they're hiding in town right now taking pot shots at us. We have five men left, unless you want to count Jess and that makes it six."

"It seems like we have more work to do," said Reedy as he started to work his way behind the mercantile store. Hern and Banks separated and went looking for Madden's men. Reedy slowly worked himself forward staying as low as possible, until he got past three more buildings. He heard the sound of gunfire from all around town as Madden's and Reedy's men fought it out. He peeked around the building he was behind and found one of Madden's men aiming a rifle down toward the mercantile store where he had just come from. Reedy put the sights of his Winchester on the man.

"Hey, who you shooting at?" Reedy asked, nonchalantly.

The man, Jon Stidham, was so startled by the voice he turned to his left to see who it was. When he did, the rifle barrel hit the side of the building, knocking his rifle out of his hands and it fell to the ground. Stidham's right hand went for the butt of his pistol, but he knew he didn't have a chance so he stopped and raised both his hands.

"You got me, Marshal. I give up."

Frank Reedy smiled at Stidham. "Do you see a badge on this shirt?"

Stidham understood what that meant and he went for his pistol, but Reedy pulled the trigger on the Winchester, putting a hole in Stidham's chest and knocking him backward. He fell to the ground on his back. Dan Cotton, one of Thornton's men, took a shot at Reginald Sharky, who was leaning on the side of the jail and firing off rounds from a rifle, but his shot was high and Sharkey ran back behind the jail where he found Hatch Simpson.

"Hatch, let's me and you go up on the top of the jail."

"I'm right behind you," said Hatch.

Sharky and Hatch Simpson took the stairs up to the roof of the jail. Jess had watched them run across the roof and take up positions at each end of the front wooden wall that protruded up about five feet above the roof. Sharky and Simpson were firing their rifles as fast as they could, and Simpson hit Dan Cotton in the right shoulder. Cotton ran back behind the building. Sharky was firing at Lemore Taft, keeping him pinned down behind a wagon that was in front of the livery.

Jess took careful aim and the slug from his Winchester hit Simpson, who fell backward onto the roof. Jess couldn't see Reginald Sharky from his angle. Sharky was behind the far end of the roof of the jail, but Jess knew he was there because he could see the muzzle flash as Sharky kept firing at Lemore Taft. Jess put the Winchester down and grabbed the Sharps. He took aim at the wooden wall right about where he figured the man would be standing and the Sharps exploded with a loud boom. Jess saw a rifle fall off the roof and land on the cover of the porch of the jail. He heard a thump when the body hit the ground.

Lyle Bitters and Griff Clark made their way back to Jed's Saloon. They had to move the body of Clevis Danville before they could get in the back door. They took up positions behind the bar with their boss and Denzel Matheny.

"How many men do we have left?" Madden asked.

Bitters shook his head. "We got slaughtered, Boss. I don't think we have but one or two men left out there besides us."

"God damn it!" hollered Madden. "Where the hell is Vreeland?"

"I haven't seen him since we ran into town. Everyone just scattered."

"How many men does Thornton have?"

"Thornton? Hell, he didn't even come in. Frank Reedy brought a bunch into town and ambushed our ambush. I don't know how many men he has, but I'm guessing about six or seven. I'm thinking we should surrender right about now and beg for mercy."

"They can kiss my ass! I ain't going to surrender and let Thornton win. I'd rather take a bullet first."

Just as Madden said that, a few rounds hit the shelves behind the bar and one of the rounds busted one of the few bottles of whiskey left.

"I'm afraid it just might come to that in the very near future, Boss," replied Bitters.

Vreeland Summers was just taking aim at Lemore Taft's back with his Winchester when he felt the end of a gun in his back. He had spotted Taft behind the wagon and made his way around to the back of the livery to get a clean shot at him.

"I wouldn't pull that trigger if I were you," said Frank Reedy.

Summers dropped his rifle to the ground and as he did, he turned, spinning to his right knocking the rifle out of Reedy's hands with his right hand and grabbing Reedy's throat with his left hand. Summers pushed him back against the back wall of the livery. He grabbed Reedy's pistol out of its holster but Reedy knocked it out of Summers' hand. Summers landed a right fist to Reedy's jaw and it stunned him. Summers went for his own pistol. Reedy grabbed his hand and pulled it up, but Summers was strong and he was slowly pulling it down to level it with Reedy's face. Then all Frank Reedy saw was a flash of light from something that looked like silver. Jess's bowie knife cut through the left carotid artery of Summers' neck and the blood pumped out with each beat of his heart. Summers was trying to hold his hand on it to stop the flow of blood, but it was hopeless. He staggered a little as he turned around to look at who had cut him and he saw Jess Williams, as cool as could be. Jess was waving his hand to the right.

Summers looked back to Reedy now who had understood what Jess was trying to tell him. Reedy moved out of the line of fire and Summers also understood. When he turned his head back, Jess had pulled his scattergun out of its back sling. He fired both barrels, hitting Summers in the gut, nearly cutting his body in half. Jess reloaded his scattergun and put it back in the sling. He picked up his bowie knife and wiped the blood off the blade on Summers' pants and placed it back in its sheath.

"That's the second time you pulled my ass out of the fire, Jess."

"Yeah, but who's counting?"

"I sure am. I owe you a couple of favors already and I don't like owing favors all that much."

"Don't worry, Frank. You'll get a chance to use them all up pretty soon."

"I don't like the sound of that."

"You're going to like it even less when I call those favors in."

"Now you're really scaring me."

"Rance Madden's the one who needs to be afraid."

"I sure wouldn't want to be him today."

Reedy and Jess made their way back to the mercantile store where Buck Hern and Hal Banks were. Banks had sent Torry Abel out behind Jed's Saloon to pick off anyone who tried to escape. Lemore Taft and Dan Cotton showed up about the same time. Cotton had a handkerchief stuck inside his shirt, which was bloody from his gunshot wound.

"How bad are you hit, Cotton?" Reedy asked.

"It hurts like hell, but I'm all right."

"Well, Buck, who do you think is left in the saloon?" asked Reedy.

"As far as I can tell, Madden and maybe two or three of his men along with Jed are still inside."

"Well, let's see if we can get them to give it up."

They all walked between the buildings. Buck, Hal and Lemore went to the right of the mercantile store while Reedy, Cotton and Jess walked to the left side of the store. There was no shooting going on and it was eerily quiet compared to the last five or ten minutes when gunfire had been erupting and bullets flying through the air in all directions, most of them missing their intended targets.

Reedy cupped his hands around his mouth and talked as loud as he could. "Madden, this is Frank Reedy. You and your men are surrounded from all sides. I have six men behind you with rifles and ten more out here. You haven't got a chance. Come on out with your hands up and we'll spare your lives."

Buck looked at Hal. "We ain't got sixteen men."

"He's just trying to scare Madden. Frank always says that he don't often tell the truth, but he never lies."

Madden hollered out back at Reedy. "Kiss my ass, Marshal. You ain't locking me up in that jail cell again!"

Reedy looked at Jess for a moment. "Madden, that jail cell might be the only place you'll be safe right about now."

A few minutes of silence passed as if Madden was thinking it over. Madden wasn't really thinking anything over in his mind, he was simply stalling to see if any of his men were still out there. If they were, they would start shooting anytime soon. No shots came, only Frank Reedy's voice again.

"I'm still waiting for an answer, Madden!"

"You want an answer? Well here it is." Madden let both barrels of the scattergun go off, blowing off what was left of the swinging saloon batwings, with lead pellets flying all over the place. Reedy and his men ducked back farther between the two buildings.

Jess looked at Frank Reedy. "I think it's my turn now, don't you agree?"

Frank Reedy didn't even have to respond. He just put his head down. He knew exactly what Jess meant. He looked back up to Jess but still said nothing. He didn't have to; his eyes said all Jess needed to hear.

CHAPTER TWENTY-FOUR

"Rance Madden, this is Jess Williams. I'm only going to give you one minute to come out of there. If you don't, I will surely come in there and kill you."

"Who the hell is Jess Williams?" Madden asked Lyle Bitters.

"Shit, I bet he's the one who's been killing our men all along. He's a bounty hunter and they say he's faster than lightning and one tough hombre to deal with. Boss, I think you might want to give it up."

"He can kiss my ass too, right along with Frank Reedy. As a matter of fact, I got two cheeks, and they can each pick one out and pucker on up."

"Boss, your ass ain't the only one in here, you know."

Madden raised his head slightly above the bar. "Listen, Mr. Williams, I don't care who you are, I ain't coming out. We've got good cover in here and I know you won't burn us out 'cause poor Jed is still in here with us."

"You're right, Mr. Madden, we won't burn you out. But you're dead wrong about that thing you said about having good cover."

"Hell, this bar is made of thick wood and there are three walls behind us. You can shoot all day but you won't hit any of us."

"Mister Madden, you obviously don't know much about me, but do you know anything about buffalo rifles?"

"I know some things about 'em. Why?"

"Well, I have a really nice one here. They call it a Sharps Big Fifty. That's because it shoots a fifty caliber round. I've killed men at some pretty long distances with it and more than once. As a matter of fact, I shot you in the left arm all the way from the top of the north cliff behind you."

Jess chambered a round in the Sharps and nonchalantly walked out in the street right in front of the window of the saloon. He knew that he was putting himself in harm's way, but he just didn't care anymore. He was going to end this matter once and for all, and right now. "I have some bad news for you, Mister Madden."

"Yeah, and just what is that?"

"It seems that you just ran out of time."

Jess aimed at the front of the bar and the Sharps exploded. Madden ducked back down. The round went through the solid wood front of the bar and the slug still had enough force to hit Denzel Matheny in his side. The shot didn't kill him, but he was bleeding badly. Denzel ran out the back door holding his side and Torrey Abel took him down with one shot to the chest. Jess didn't know that Denzel had run out and he didn't care. He was in forward motion, and when he got like that, a steam locomotive couldn't hold him back.

He knew that the shot through the bar would let them know that they were no longer safe. He dropped the Sharps on the ground in the street and walked quickly toward the saloon. He pulled his scattergun out of its sling and as he continued walking, he fired off one round through the window and then the second one through the door of the saloon. He grabbed two shells from the front of his shirt, after pulling the spent ones out, and reloaded the scattergun. Jess had long ago learned to be able to grab two shotgun shells from the special pockets he had sewn on the front of his shirt, and load them both with his left hand simultaneously. He didn't have to look at the shells or the scattergun to do it; he could do it with his eyes closed, which is exactly how he practiced doing it so that he could keep his eyes on his target.

Buck Hern and Hal Banks were now trying to cover Jess, throwing lead with their rifles through the window. Jess knew what they were doing but he didn't let it distract him in the least. As soon as he reloaded the scattergun, he walked up to the door and let one barrel go, lead buckshot peppering all around the bar. He walked into the saloon and he let the other barrel go. As soon as he did, he dropped the scattergun on the floor and slicked his pistol out just as Griff Clark tried to peek above the bar to see if he could take a shot. Jess fired his first round and hit Clark in the top of his head, scattering some of his brains behind the bar. Lyle Bitters threw his rifle and pistol out from behind the bar.

"I give up. Don't shoot. I'm coming out." As soon as he stood up, Jess plugged him square in his chest and Bitters' dead body fell against Rance Madden who was still crouched behind the bar. It knocked Madden over and he dropped his scattergun just as Jess came around the corner of the bar. He saw Madden reaching for the scattergun and Jess shot Madden in his left hand.

"You crazy son of a bitch! All right. I give up, damn it!" Madden slowly rose up and turned around. He was looking at a young man who looked as though he could scarcely be twenty years old, but the look in the young man's eyes was that of a much older man, a look that actually scared Madden for the very first time in his life.

Frank Reedy and his men walked into the bar. Reedy looked at Jess with a pleading look. "Jess, it's over. We can lock Madden up and take him to a judge. I'm sure we can get him hanged."

Jess never took his eyes off Madden. "Frank, you know those favors we spoke about?"

"Yeah?"

"Well, consider them paid in full."

Madden was now visibly shaking with fear. "Marshal, he's loco. He shot an unarmed man. It's him you should be arresting."

"In case you haven't noticed, I ain't wearing any badge and neither is anyone else in here. The only men who still have a badge pinned on are the sheriff lying in a coma in Doctor Hammond's office, thanks to you, and Tex who is still recuperating from two gunshot wounds that he got from...now, who was that...oh, I remember now...you. If you're looking for justice, you're looking at him now right in front of you. It just so happens that it ain't the kind of justice you figured on."

Jess looked at Jed, still crouched on the floor. "Jed, come on out of there."

Jed slowly got up and walked around Madden. Rance Madden was terrified now. He had never felt helpless before and he didn't like it. He had always been able to buy anything with his money but now, all the money in the world wouldn't help him.

Jess fired a round into Madden's right arm. "That one is for Sheriff Steele."

Madden spun around and his back hit the wall. "God damn it Reedy, do something! You can't just let him kill me like this!"

Jess fired another round into Madden left thigh, missing the bone but going through the muscle. "That one is for Pattie Nate."

Madden went down on his right knee. "You rotten bastard! You don't even have the courage to face me fair. Give me a gun and I swear I'll kill you!"

"Fair ain't here right now, but I am. Mr. Madden, your killing days are over for good. Someone should have done this a long time ago. This last one—is just for me."

Jess fired a round that hit Madden in the middle of his forehead. Madden fell backward onto his back and his right leg flipped out from under him as he went down. Jess reloaded and put his pistol back in its holster and placed the hammer strap on, all the while looking at Madden's boots. "Those are some pretty nice boots he has there. Someone should claim them."

Jess looked at Reedy and the other men who were looking at him with a stunned silence. "What?"

Frank Reedy shook his head. "Madden might have been right about that loco thing. What the hell were you thinking, walking right in here blasting away? You're not invincible, you know. Didn't you ever consider the fact that you might have gotten yourself killed?"

"I wasn't really thinking about it all that much. I just figured that I was coming in here and killing Rance Madden and anyone who got in my way and that was that."

"You sure live dangerously, I'll tell you that."

"Maybe."

"So, are we even now?"

"Yeah, until you get your ass in a sling again and I have to come and pull it out."

"That's not going to happen again. Jed, you got any good whiskey left in here?"

Jed, who was still quite shaken by what had just happened, finally responded. "Oh…yeah, I keep some in the back. I'll go and get some."

"Jess, let's sit for a spell and have a drink. Gunfightin' is damn hard work and a man has to rest up a bit after it's over."

"That sounds like a good idea, Frank." They all sat at a table and Jed brought out the last few bottles, which hadn't been broken by gunfire, along with the last shot glasses he had in the place. They sat around for hours and talked about all that had happened. Even some of the townsmen who had been afraid to come out of their homes or shops came in for a drink to celebrate the fact that the town had finally been released from Madden's grip. Everyone turned in early for a well-deserved good night's rest. Thornton's men went back to the ranch to tell Henry Thornton the good news. The war was over and Madden was dead.

The light was just peeking through the curtains in the hotel room and that was all that was needed to wake Jess. He had taken a long hot bath last night before turning in and it had felt so good. He got up, splashed some cold water on his face, and wiped off with a small towel. He looked at his youthful stubble and decided that he would get a shave and a haircut today before leaving town. He had to get back to looking for Eddie Sloan. He moved the chair that he had placed in front of the door and walked downstairs and out of the only hotel in Timber. He saw Frank Reedy and Tex walking out of the jail. Tex still looked a little pale but at least he was walking on his own, even though he was still limping on his right leg a little.

"Good morning, men. Tex, I didn't expect to see you in town yet. When did you get in?"

"Pattie wouldn't wait until morning. As soon as Thornton's men came back to the ranch last night, she asked Thornton for a wagon and made me bring her into town so that she could see the sheriff."

"That doesn't surprise me at all. I'm still pissed off at Madden for what he did to the sheriff. As a matter of fact, I wish that I could bring him back from the dead just so I could have the pleasure of shooting him again."

"The good news is," interjected Reedy, "the sheriff finally woke up last night. Doctor Hammond was sleeping in the back of his office when the shooting started and he came out to peek out the window. He said when you fired the Sharps rifle at the bar, Steele started moaning. He's been drinking water and eating some soup that Pattie made for him last night. He's real weak and can hardly talk, but the doctor thinks that he might just pull through."

Jess put his arm around Frank Reedy and smiled. "That's the best news I've heard in a long time. Let's go and see him right now."

Tex, Reedy and Jess walked into Doctor Hammond's office and Mark Steele was still lying down but his head was propped up with some pillows. Jess walked up to him, grabbed his right hand, and squeezed it very gently. "Damn good to see your eyes open, my friend."

Sheriff Steele squeezed Jess's hand a little. Then he looked at Jess with a serious look as he gathered up enough strength to speak. "I hear you've been up to your normal tactics. Most lawmen would arrest you for some of what you did."

"Well, the marshal here took off his badge and so did Buck, and Tex wasn't there last night so I guess I'm still a free man, unless you intend to arrest me."

Frank Reedy shook his head as he laughed. "Yeah, like you'd let that happen. Sheriff, he did what needed to be done and if it weren't for him, a lot of us would be eatin' dirt about now, including Pattie Nate, and I know you wouldn't want that." Sheriff Steele shook his head as if to say no.

"Well, Sheriff, we'll let you get some rest. I'm planning on leaving town in a little bit so this is goodbye, my good friend. If you ever need help again, you know you can count on me."

Sheriff Steele nodded his head affirmatively. Reedy and Jess had almost gotten to the door when the sheriff got up enough strength to speak again.

"Jess, thanks, especially for saving Pattie."

"No thanks necessary, Sheriff. When a friend calls for help, I consider it an obligation to respond."

Jess and Frank Reedy walked over to Jed's Saloon. Tex stayed behind to keep the sheriff company. Jed had restocked the bar with what little whiskey he had left. Reedy and Jess sat at a little table by the window, which was still broken out. Jed brought over a coffee pot and two cups and filled them. "I've got some men coming over today to replace the windows and fix the place up a little. You boys sure shot it up pretty good."

"Sorry about that, Jed. I'm willing to pay for all the damages," replied Jess.

"You don't have to apologize. I'm glad you did what you did. I have a dozen horses and a lot of guns and rifles from Madden's men that I'm going to sell or trade for the work needed to fix this place up. Plus, Madden had five hundred dollars in cash on him as well as a few of his other men, and I figure he owed it to me. I'll be all right. Hell, I'll be able to fix this place up right nice, and I plan to order a brand new mirror for the bar, too."

Jess looked at Jed as he walked away. "Mighty fine boots you have there, Jed."

Jed turned around and smiled as he looked down at his new boots. "Yeah, and I have a pretty nice hat to go with 'em, too. Figured they might as well not go to waste and that's what they were doing on Madden's feet."

Just then, Pattie Nate came out from the kitchen. She walked right over to the table. "Jess Williams, stand up right this minute." Jess did as he was told and Pattie grabbed his face with both hands, kissed him right on the lips, and then hugged him for a long time. "I owe you my life, young Mr. Williams. I will never forget what you did for me and everyone else and especially for saving my man. If you hadn't showed up, Madden would have killed him for sure." She finally let go of him and she had tears in her eyes.

Jess was still stunned by the kiss. It was the first time that he could remember being kissed by any other woman except for his ma, and it was a very new and strange feeling for him. "Uh...well, you're certainly welcome, Pattie."

"Well, I suppose you two are hungry. Would you like me to fix you some breakfast?"

"I don't know about Frank here, but I'm starving."

"He's speaking for the both of us, Pattie," Frank added.

Pattie headed back into the kitchen to fix them some food. She would make them a breakfast that would feed ten men. She was deliriously happy now with Sheriff Steele out of his coma and Madden dead. Things were beginning to feel a little normal at last.

Jake Morgan had been on the trail for several days now. He was on his way to meet with a man by the name of Rance Madden who was going to pay Jake his customary one thousand dollar fee per man. Jake had long ago stopped caring who it was he killed, as long as he got paid well for it. When he was fired from the gun company he worked at, he got so angry that it changed his way of thinking and looking at things, but not in a good way. He knew that his design of the pistol he now wore would have been revolutionary and way ahead of its time, but the owner wouldn't take a chance on putting it into production.

He bought the pistol from the owner and then went and had a special holster designed for it as a gun-tipping holster. The holster swiveled on a round piece of metal so that he did not have to remove the pistol from the holster to shoot it; he only needed to cock the hammer back as he swiveled the holster up ninety degrees and pull the trigger. The holster was cut short at the top and the bottom and it was cut out so that he could easily reach the trigger. It was also designed to allow the cylinder to revolve. It was quite difficult to learn how to use it at first, but he practiced with it for almost two years and became very fast with it before he began to hire out his gun for money.

He sold off all his other belongings and made his way out West. He took a train to Missouri, bought himself a horse and headed farther west. Since then, he had killed over a dozen men in gunfights. His first gunfight was in Wichita, Kansas, and he wasn't being paid for it. A man had challenged him because the man wanted to buy Jake's gun and holster and of course, Jake wouldn't sell it. Then, the man challenged Jake to a gunfight, leaving the gun and holster to the man left standing. Jake was still wearing it when he left Wichita, killing the man by putting a bullet in his chest before the other man even got his own gun out of his holster.

He had already been to the Madden ranch and found out all about what had happened. There were only a few ranch hands there and they couldn't pay Jake Morgan his fee. Once he learned that Jess Williams was responsible for the demise of Madden and most of his hired guns, his interest piqued. He knew of Jess Williams and had heard stories about a very unique pistol and holster that he wore. Jake Morgan just had to see it so he headed into Timber to check it out for himself.

Jess and Frank were holding their stomachs as if they were trying to keep them from bursting. They had consumed two plates of flapjacks, one plate of biscuits, eight eggs and over a pound of salt pork between the two of them.

"You were right about that gun fighting thing last night, Frank."

"Huh, what do you mean?"

"You know, that thing you said about gun fighting being hard work. Well, we've rested and we've eaten more than our share of good food, so I guess we have fully recuperated."

Frank had been listening to part of what Jess was saying but in the middle of Jess saying it, he was distracted by the man he saw through the broken window of the saloon over at the livery. He knew the man very well and he knew that it spelled trouble. "Jess, the gun fighting might not be over just yet."

"What do you mean? Do you know something that I don't?"

"It's more like I know someone you don't."

"Who?"

Reedy pointed to the livery. "The man over at the livery is Jake Morgan and if I haven't lost my touch, I would say that he's not here by accident. I would wager that Madden hired him and that he got here a little too late."

Jess looked the man over and he could see the same thing in the man that Reedy saw. He was wearing a very strange holster, one that Jess had not seen before. "Well, Madden is dead so he can't get paid. Maybe he's just stopping by to supply up and get a hot meal before moving on."

"Unlikely, especially if he knows you're here. Some men call him the Reaper. At last count, he's killed at least a dozen men. He's what they call a gun-tipper. That's why his holster looks so strange. He doesn't have to draw his pistol from the holster; he just swivels it up and fires. He's pretty damn fast with it, too."

"So, how come you or some other lawman hasn't arrested him yet?"

"Because every gunfight he's been in has been a fair showdown."

Jess shook his head. "You lawmen with all your rules you have to follow sometimes just don't make much sense to me. You'll hang a starving man for stealing a cow, but you have to let men like that go around killing other men as long as he can goad them into the street for a showdown."

"Hey, I don't make the laws. I just enforce them."

"By the way, when are you going to pin that marshal's badge back on?"

"Obviously not today by the looks of things."

Jake Morgan was asking the livery man something and the livery man pointed over at Jed's Saloon. Morgan slowly walked toward the saloon.

"I shouldn't have eaten that last stack of flapjacks," said Jess.

"Why not?"

"I hate gun fighting on a full stomach."

CHAPTER TWENTY-FIVE

Jake Morgan stepped onto the porch and examined all the damage from the bullet holes. The batwing doors were almost completely gone from the pounding of bullets and buckshot. He walked inside and looked at Jess and Frank, taking his time looking over both of them methodically. Jess did the same, looking Morgan over at the same time. Morgan was very neatly dressed and wore fine clothing. He had a slim build and wore what looked to be a new hat. Jess noticed that his hands were not rough like most men, but very clean. The gun and holster were, indeed, different from what he had ever seen before with the exception of his own. The holster was not tied to the thigh. When Morgan finished looking the two over, he walked up to the bar and ordered a whiskey. As he walked, the pistol swiveled a little back and forth.

Morgan finished his whiskey and ordered one more. He turned to face Jess and Frank Reedy. "My name is Jake Morgan. I'm looking for a young man by the name of Jess Williams, and I would assume by looking at that pistol and holster that I've found him," Morgan said, his eyes fixed on Jess.

Jess turned to face Morgan but did not get out of his chair. "Mr. Morgan, you have found me. The smartest thing that you could do right now is to finish up your drink and leave town before something bad happens."

Jake Morgan downed his shot of whiskey and placed the shot glass on the counter. "I'll leave when I'm good and ready."

"Have it your way."

"I usually do."

Frank Reedy, who had been silent up to now, turned to face Morgan directly. "Morgan, I'm a U.S. marshal and I know all about you. I would suggest that you leave town like my friend here has asked."

"I don't see any badge pinned on your shirt."

"I'm officially off the job, so to speak, but I could pin it back on anytime I want."

"What difference would that make? If I decide to call him out in the street fair, what the hell you going to do about it?"

"Yeah," added Jess, with a slight hint of friendly sarcasm, "what the hell could you do about it anyway if you did pin that badge on?"

"All right, I admit it, not a damn thing as long as it's a fair fight, but there's been enough gunplay in this town already. Besides, Rance Madden is dead so he won't be paying you any money anyway. You working for free these days, Morgan?"

Morgan grinned as he looked at Jess's pistol and holster. "I have plenty of money in the bank, but what I don't have is that thing right there," he said, as he pointed at Jess's pistol.

"And that's one thing you'll never have, Morgan," said Jess.

"We'll see about that now, won't we?"

"Only if you force it, Morgan, because I'm not looking for any fight with you."

"Are you gonna run from it?"

"You already know the answer to that question, but do you know the answer to this one? Are you prepared to die over this thing here?" Jess said, as he tapped his pistol with his right hand.

"Who say's I'm going to be the one to die?"

"That would be me, Mr. Morgan. You can't beat me even with that fancy tipping holster you got there."

"Well, I think I can. I've gotten pretty fast with it and I'm thinkin' I can beat you fair and square on the draw."

"You sure I can't talk you out of this?"

"I don't believe so."

"Then let's quit wasting time on it."

Jess stood up and so did Reedy. Jess walked out into the street and Reedy followed and stood on the wooden walkway. It didn't take long for Morgan to follow. He stopped on the walkway and glanced over at Reedy. "You plan on involving yourself in this, Mr. Reedy?"

"No, I'm just here to make sure things are fair." This was another example of Frank Reedy's phrase—I don't often tell the truth, but I never lie. Reedy had every intention of plugging Morgan if something went wrong and Jess was gunned down.

"I'm always fair when it comes to gun fighting. I do have rules that I play by."

"Yeah, so do I and I'm getting a little tired about it, too," replied Reedy, a hint of frustration in his voice.

Pattie Nate came out and stood next to Frank Reedy. "Why does this always keep happening? Jess didn't start anything with that man. Why doesn't he just leave?"

Tex came hobbling up the street with a scattergun. "Hold on there, men. What the hell is going on?"

Jess removed his hammer strap. "Tex, it's okay. This is Jake Morgan and he's decided today that he is going to challenge me to a gunfight. Why don't you get on the porch with Frank and Pattie and let it go?"

"To hell with that. I'm still wearing a badge and I don't give two shits about the law right about now. I would've been dead if it weren't for you. I swear, I'll blow him in half with both barrels if you just give me the word. We can bury his ass out back with the rest of those assholes and Madden."

"No, that won't be necessary, Tex. I'll give him what he wants. He might not like it when he gets it, but it is his choice."

"You sound awfully sure of yourself for such a young man."

"You're about to find out, once you go for that pistol. Hey, Tex, how would you like a nice gun-tipping holster?"

"Hell, I wouldn't say no to that," Tex replied, as he joined Reedy, Pattie and Jed who had since come out from behind the bar. They were watching Jess and Morgan who were now about thirty feet apart and just staring at one another. Pattie could not believe what was happening. A moment ago, Jess was finishing up a nice breakfast and now, here he was again, facing down yet another gunslinger.

"It's your move, Morgan."

"No, why don't you go first?"

"Not a chance. This is your play. I won't walk away, but I won't draw first, either. Your life is in your hands right now. Once you touch the butt of your pistol, it will be in mine."

Morgan waited a few more moments. Jess didn't know exactly why; maybe he was thinking about leaving town and giving it up or maybe he just needed to wait until he felt he was ready. It mattered little to Jess, however; he had been at this very moment so many times before that it almost felt natural, as if killing another man should ever feel natural. Then, Jess saw the look that came over Morgan's eyes. Morgan went for his gun, cocked the hammer back and had the holster at a forty-five degree angle when the bullet from Jess's gun slammed into Morgan's chest, knocking him off balance. Morgan actually got to pull the trigger but his slug hit the ground about twenty feet from Jess. Morgan got his balance back but he was still wobbling a little.

"Damn, that sure was fast," Morgan said. Morgan looked over at Tex. "You make sure you take real good care of my pistol and holster, you hear?"

"I'll do just that," responded Tex, as Morgan slowly dropped to his knees and fell forward into the dirt.

Jess reloaded the spent cartridge, put his pistol back in the holster, and put the hammer strap in place. He walked over to Morgan, turned him over and removed the pistol and holster from Morgan's dead body. "Here you go, Tex, it's all yours. Just don't shoot your foot off when you try it out."

"I'll be real careful, Jess, and thank you."

Tex hollered to a few of the local men to remove Jake Morgan's body from the middle of the street. One of them used his boots to kick some dry soil over the blood now seeping into the dirt. Tex had a big smile on his face like a kid standing at a counter full of penny candy.

"Pattie, do you have some more hot coffee brewing?" asked Jess.

Pattie, who had been mesmerized by the whole event, was a little befuddled. "Coffee? Oh...sure, I got coffee, Jess."

"Maybe you could throw in a biscuit or two?" asked Jess.

"For Christ's sake, Jess, you just shot a man dead and now you're hungry again? You two just finished up enough food to feed four men," said Pattie.

"Well, like Frank here says, gun fighting is hard work."

"Come on, I'll make you another biscuit," said Pattie, as she headed back into the saloon.

"Hey, maybe you could make a few more while you're at it?" asked Reedy.

"Oh hell, I'll just make a dozen. Will that make you happy?"

Frank Reedy and Jess had made it up the two steps to the porch of the saloon when they spotted a lone rider coming into town. Reedy recognized him right off. It was U.S. Deputy Marshal Cray Pittman. He rode up to where Reedy was standing with Jess.

"Well, it's about damn time someone came to check on us," said Reedy.

Cray Pittman got off his horse, walked up the two steps, and shook hands with Reedy. "Where is your badge, Marshal?"

"Come on inside and join us and I'll explain everything. By the way, this is a good friend of mine, Jess Williams."

Pittman shook Jess's hand. "I've heard a lot about you, Mr. Williams. Not all of it good."

"It depends on how you look at it, I guess."

The three of them walked into Jed's Saloon and Pattie brought out a platter of biscuits and a slab of butter. "I see you have more company."

"This is U.S. Deputy Marshal Cray Pittman. Cray, this is Pattie Nate."

Pittman stood up and took off his hat. "Pleasure to meet you, ma'am."

"Would you like some eggs and flapjacks to go with those biscuits, Mr. Pittman?"

"Ma'am, that's sounds wonderful. I would be most appreciative." Pittman turned to Reedy as Pattie went back to the kitchen. "Now, Frank, you want to tell me what the hell happened here. We've been sending messages here and getting messages back from you telling us everything was fine. After a while, we got suspicious and the marshal's office decided to send me down to check on you."

Frank Reedy explained the entire chain of events to Pittman as he gulped his food. Pittman washed his breakfast down with several cups of strong hot coffee. "Sounds like this Madden fellow was quite a piece of work, but you still haven't explained where your badge is."

Reedy took it out of his back pocket and shined it up a little and set it down on the table. "Well, I took myself off the clock for a while and I fired my two deputies."

"What the hell did you go and do that for?"

Reedy looked at Jess, then back to Pittman. "Because desperate times call for desperate measures, and we had to do some things that I just couldn't do while having a U.S. marshal's badge pinned on my shirt."

Pittman looked at Reedy as if he understood. "Whatever it was, I don't want to know about it. You can put whatever you want in your report. Are you going to pin that badge back on?"

"I don't know just yet. Jess, are we done here?"

"I sure hope so. I don't know if Madden has any more hired guns coming to town or not, but I can't wait around to find out. I have to get back on Eddie Sloan's trail."

Cray Pittman put his coffee cup down. "Did you say you were looking for Eddie Sloan, the gambler?"

"Yes I did, why? Do you know him?"

"Yeah, and I know where he is right now. He's over in Largo trying to get a poker game going. I stopped in to see Sheriff A.J. Rubel on my way here and Rubel was grumbling about Sloan being there.

I went to the saloon with the sheriff and we both warned Sloan that if he caused any trouble he would be locked up. You know Sheriff Rubel, he don't cotton to troublemakers."

"What are the chances that he still might be there?" Jess asked.

"I'd say the chances are pretty good. He was waiting on a few players who were riding into town a day or so after I spoke with him, and it's only a day and a half's ride there from here. The game was supposed to last two days so if you headed out now, I think you'd have a good chance of finding him, not that you'd want to. He ain't the friendliest guy you've ever met and he still has a fast right hand, even though he is getting up there in years. What business do you have with him anyway?"

"Let's just say it's personal."

"I know what that usually means. If you go to Largo and cause any ruckus with Sloan, you'll either get shot by Sloan or arrested or even shot by Sheriff Rubel. He don't take no shit."

"I've met Sheriff Rubel before and I don't think I'll have any problem with him. As for Eddie Sloan, he's the one who'll have a problem. Well, Frank, I guess I'd better start riding. I'd like to get there before Sloan leaves Largo."

Reedy picked up his badge and put it back in his back pocket. "Wait up. I'm going with you to Largo."

"I don't need any help, Frank. Go ahead and pin that badge back on and get back to being a lawman."

"I will, as soon as you finish your business in Largo."

"I told you I don't need any help."

"I know that, but you were here for me and you saved my life, twice. I think I owe it to you to make sure you get a fair shake when you get there. That means I might have to do something that might go against being a lawman with a badge on his shirt."

"All right, I guess I can't stop you from coming along. What about your two deputies?"

Frank looked over at Pittman. "Cray, why don't you go back and inform the marshal's office that I'll be back there to make out my report. I'm going to leave Abel and Banks here with Sheriff Steele's two deputies just in case any more of Rance Madden's hired guns come into town. When I'm finished up with Jess in Largo, I'll come back and get them."

"All right, I guess I'll head back and tell them that you're okay."

Cray Pittman got up, walked out, and got on his horse. Frank Reedy walked over to talk to Abel and Banks and asked them to stay in town with Buck and Tex. They had to volunteer to do it since they officially weren't on the payroll. They agreed to stay because they were loyal to Frank Reedy. Jess said goodbye to Pattie Nate and then walked over to see Sheriff Steele once more. He walked into Doctor Hammond's office and Steele was sitting a little more upright now.

"Well, Sheriff, you still look like shit, but you do look a little better."

"I still feel like shit. At least I got an appetite and can keep down some food now. Pattie is making me some more homemade soup for lunch. She sure is taking good care of me."

"Well, you best get out of that bed soon or you just might lose her to old River Bend Bill."

The name of River Bend Bill always got under Sheriff Steele's skin and Jess knew that, which is exactly why he did it. "Damn it, Jess. If I could get out of this bed I'd whip your ass a good one."

Jess laughed. "Yeah, but you can't, so you won't. I have to leave, Sheriff. Frank Reedy's going to leave his two men here with your deputies just in case there's any more trouble. I'm going over to Largo to find Eddie Sloan so if you need me again for anything else, send a message to Largo and I'll be back here as fast as I can."

"Thanks Jess. I don't think anything else will happen. This town owes you a debt of gratitude, as well as me. We won't forget what you did for us."

"That's what friends are for, Sheriff. You take care now, you hear?"

"Between the doc and Pattie, I'll be up and running around in no time."

Jess walked out and met Reedy at the livery. They mounted up and headed for Largo. Reedy could see anxiousness in Jess as they rode. Reedy had gained a lot of respect for this young man he was riding next to and he hoped that Jess would find what he was looking for in Largo.

CHAPTER TWENTY-SIX

The ride to Largo was a quiet and uneventful one. Reedy and Jess covered as much distance as they could the first day. Reedy's horse was having a hard time keeping up with Jess's horses. Jess had to slow the pace once in a while to give Reedy's horse a break. They even rode a few hours after the sun went down. They finally made camp at a small clearing in a wooded area where a small stream ran out of the woods and into a large meadow. They had cover from three sides, which always made Jess more comfortable. Reedy gathered some wood and made a small fire to boil some coffee and warm up some beans while Jess went about checking the perimeter and placing a few of his cans on strings around the area. After the coffee was done and the beans were warm enough, they both sat down to eat.

"You're mighty darn careful about your surroundings, Jess. I never seen anyone put up cans and string around a camp before. Where did you get that idea from?"

"It just came to me one day. I figure if someone is going to sneak up on me, he'll never suspect the cans and it might just give me enough warning to stay alive."

Reedy thought about it for a moment. "Well, I can't say it's not a good idea; I just never thought about it before."

"Well, maybe you should start thinking a little more about such things. I would've never gotten ambushed back in Timber like you did, that's for sure."

"Yeah, I sure let my guard down that time. I won't let that happen again. You can be sure of that."

Reedy finished his beans and filled his coffee cup again. "Jess, can I talk with you about something?"

"Sure, Frank, what's on your mind?"

"Well, you've killed quite a lot of men already and you ain't even hit twenty years yet. How long are you going to keep on this trail of vengeance? You already killed the three men who murdered your family, and you've killed your brother that you didn't know you had, and tomorrow you plan on riding into Largo and my guess is that you will brace your father. Your reputation is growing with every kill and there'll be more men gunning for you than ever. Have you ever thought about just quitting and going back home and starting up the old homestead and farming some fields and raising some cattle?"

Jess had been finishing his beans while Reedy was talking. He put his tin plate down and filled his cup with more hot coffee. "Frank, you're a lawman so you'll understand it more than most. I didn't ask for this life; fate just threw it at me. Maybe there is some reason for it. I'm not sure, but I do think about it all the time. I mean, the way I got this gun and holster is something that can't be explained, but here it is and it came to me after my family was murdered. It was like as though it was supposed to find me when I needed it the most. I can't explain it, and probably never will understand it, but that don't matter.

There are plenty of farmers and cattle ranchers. There are plenty of sheepherders and other people in all walks of life. There are lawmen like you, although not enough to enforce the law out here, and there are plenty of bad men who deserve to die for the awful things that they do. That's where I fit in and I'm comfortable with it. Frank, everyone has his place in life and I believe I've found mine. There are men who need to be brought to justice and too many of them never get caught. They continue to kill innocent men and rape innocent women, and the law can't catch them all. I can't go back to farming now. I have a different sort of talent and it just happens to be killing bad men who deserve to die. I will not waste that talent on farming. I suppose some people might consider me as evil, but I guess I'm what some people would call a necessary evil. I get the job done that you and other lawmen can't or won't. I believe in what I'm doing and I don't intend to stop until either I die or I kill the last man that needs killing."

Reedy leaned back against his saddle and thought about what Jess had said for a few minutes. "Well, it's damn hard to argue with your view about such things and I have to agree that you are damn good at what you do. You have an unnatural ability to kill men and it doesn't seem to bother you. I also can't argue that the men you've killed didn't deserve to die because each one of them surely did. I guess until you start killing men who don't deserve to die, I will consider you a good man and a good friend."

"I'm glad you feel that way, Frank. I'd always like to consider you a friend, too. I don't have very many, so I need every one I can get."

"I have a hunch you have more friends than you think. You may have killed a lot of men but you have helped a whole lot of people in the process. Well, I'm ready to turn in. Tomorrow will be an interesting day, I believe."

"Frank, you're right about that. I can't wait to have my little chat with Eddie Sloan."

They put out the fire and both pulled blankets up to keep warm from the cool night air. They both went off to sleep, Frank wondering how things were in Timber and Jess wondering about what he would say to Eddie Sloan tomorrow. They awoke at sunrise and made coffee but no breakfast. They saddled up and headed straight for Largo.

The saloon was no different than any other saloon that one would find in many of the small towns scattered throughout the West. It reeked of cheap whiskey, and cigar smoke lingered heavily in the air. There was one bartender behind the bar and a few women sitting around waiting for one of the men to take them upstairs for a little attention. One of the women was sitting next to a man who was playing poker at a table with three other men. They had been playing for several hours now, and it was obvious to everyone in the game who was in control.

Eddie Sloan always liked to have a whore sitting next to him when he was playing cards and he always liked to control the game. Most of the time he could control it simply through his well-honed skill at the game. When that didn't work, he could always fall back on his cheating skills. Sloan had honed his cheating skills over the years to a level of perfection that most men would never acquire. He could palm cards, hide them and make them disappear without anyone else noticing. He would practice those skills in his hotel room every day so that he could always keep sharp and way ahead of the best of players.

He would often ride out of whatever town he was staying in and practice his pistol skills for hours. It was another skill that went along with his profession as an expert poker player, especially when someone at the table would finally get fed up with losing every hand and make the mistake of calling Eddie Sloan a cheat or a liar. That was exactly the mistake Brad Tillman was making at this very moment.

"Jesus Christ!" exclaimed Tillman. "How in the hell did you get another two pair? Hell, I've never had that many good hands in a row in any game and I've played a lot of poker. You just can't be that lucky. It ain't natural."

Sloan leaned back in his chair, picked up his cigar, took a long pull on it, and let it out slowly, savoring the flavor. He enjoyed a good cigar much like he enjoyed a good whore once in a while. He looked completely relaxed and completely within his environment. He looked at the other two men to see if they were going to start complaining. Sloan could tell from their faces that they wanted to say something, but they would not. They knew all too well that Eddie Sloan was not a man to cross or especially to call a cheat. They would be no problem for Sloan. They would simply lose all their money to Sloan and walk away, which is exactly what most of the men who played poker against Sloan did.

Poker was a little like being a gunslinger. Even though you knew the man you were up against was a better player, you just had to try your luck to see if you could be the one who could brag that you beat the best poker player in the West—Eddie Sloan. To this day, no one had ever beaten Sloan at poker and this day would be no different. The pot on the table had grown to almost two hundred dollars before Tillman called Sloan's hand. Tillman thought he finally had a winning hand with a pair of kings and a pair of fours. His smile had quickly faded when Sloan laid his pair of aces and pair of eights on the table. It was the very same hand that Wild Bill Hickok was holding when Jack McCall shot Hickok in the back while Hickok was playing in a poker game in Deadwood, South Dakota on August 2, 1876.

Sloan looked squarely into Brad Tillman's eyes and found what he was looking for. "So, what are you saying, Tillman? Are you saying that I'm unnaturally lucky?"

Tillman leaned forward in his chair. "I'm saying anyone who can win that many hands and have that many good hands in that short of a time has got to be cheating."

It was the one thing that Brad Tillman shouldn't have said, but he had said it now and there was no taking the words back. Sloan motioned for his whore to go to the bar. She knew what that meant and she did not linger. She had seen this before and knew that it would not be long before lead flew and someone died. She walked up to the bar next to a tall man who had a full head of golden hair along with a beard and a mustache. He was sipping whiskey and watching the event unfold as if he had bought a ticket for it. When she placed herself to the left of the man, she partially blocked his view of the poker table and the man politely asked her if she could move to his right.

She looked up at him curiously. "You've never seen a gunfight before?" she asked, somewhat nonchalantly.

Frank Reedy looked her over. She was prettier than most of the women who worked in her profession. "Normally, I don't much care to watch one man shoot it out with another for no good reason, but I have a vested interest in this one."

Her curiosity grew a little more. "What do you mean? Do you know those men?"

"I know one of them. Eddie Sloan, the man you were sitting with. You know, the one who keeps winning hand after hand."

She laughed. "I don't know what you'd call it. He is either the luckiest man I've ever met or the best poker player anywhere in the West, but he never loses a game. What is your interest in him? If you're looking to get into the game, I believe there'll be an empty seat real soon," she said, looking past Reedy's shoulder at the unfolding argument.

Eddie Sloan had put down his cigar. He was now glaring at Brad Tillman. "Mister, did I hear you correctly. Did you just call me a cheat?"

Tillman pushed back his chair and slowly stood up. "I do believe that's what I called you—a cheat. I heard about you before and that's why I got into this game. I wanted to know if the great Eddie Sloan was really the best poker player in the West or if he was a cheat. Now I know the answer. I've played a lot of poker and no one is that lucky for that long of a time."

Frank Reedy watched intently as Eddie Sloan slowly stood up to face Brad Tillman. "I'm going to do you a favor," said Sloan. "I'm going to give you a chance to apologize for your remarks and then ask you to leave the game and the saloon. Also, don't ever sit at a game that I'm playing in, ever. If you do, I will plug you before your ass hits the chair."

"And what if I don't?" replied Tillman, a growing defiance in his voice.

Sloan sneered at Tillman. "Then we will have to see if you can handle that side iron better than a deck of cards."

"I can play just fine, when everyone at the table is playing fair and with the same deck of cards."

Sloan lowered his head a little. "Now, there you go again, saying something that you ought not to. I warned you once; I'm not going to warn you again."

"You can kiss my ass, Sloan. I can beat you in a fair card game and I think I can beat you on the draw, too."

"You might be making a big mistake thinking that, Tillman. You ain't got a chance in hell of beating me. I'm telling you, if you snake that thing out, I'll plug you before you clear leather."

"Yeah…let's just see about that."

Brad Tillman went for his Colt .45. His hand reached the butt of his pistol and he had barely started to get it out of the holster when Sloan's Colt .45 barked loudly, punching a hole right through the middle of Tillman's chest. Tillman stumbled backward and Sloan put another slug into his chest as he was falling over, making sure he would not get back up from the floor. Sloan looked around the room to see if anyone else was going to challenge him and when he saw none, he simply whirled his Colt .45 back into his holster and began to sit back down and collect his pot of money. That was when Frank Reedy spoke.

"Mr. Sloan, that was mighty impressive. I've seen some fast guns and you are one of the fastest men on the draw I've seen in a long time," said Reedy, keeping both hands on the bar so as not to give Sloan the wrong idea.

Sloan had stopped his movement toward his seat and stood back up and looked Frank Reedy over for a moment. "You look like you might be one of them bounty hunters. Are you planning on trying my hand, too?"

Reedy shook his head. "No, sir, not me. I know my limitations and I know I can't beat you on the draw. That's for sure."

"Well, good. You're a smart man to admit it. It's too bad Tillman there wasn't as smart," remarked Sloan, glancing over at the now dead body of Brad Tillman. Sloan again started the movement of sitting back down in his chair and was stopped by Frank Reedy's next statement.

"I do, however, know someone who is faster than you."

That got Sloan's attention right away and he stood straight back up. Then he smiled. "You must be talking about my boy, Tim. He's about the only one I know that might have a chance against me and that's because I taught him everything I know about drawing and shooting a pistol."

"Evidently, you didn't teach him enough."

Sloan's demeanor turned somewhat darker. "What the hell does that mean?"

"Tim Sloan seems to have managed to get himself killed." replied Reedy, still keeping his hands on the bar so as not to give Eddie Sloan any reason to think that Reedy was going to challenge him.

Sloan looked down at the table, talking to himself. "I wondered why I hadn't seen him. Hell, I thought he went out East to play poker and was having too much fun and hadn't made it back yet..." Then Sloan looked up at Reedy with a glare. "Are you the one who killed my boy?"

Reedy shook his head no as he answered. "No, I didn't kill your boy, but I know who did."

"Who?" demanded Sloan.

"Your only living son," answered Reedy, with a mischievous grin.

Sloan was thoroughly confused, which wasn't something he was used to. "What the hell are you talking about? I only had one son, and now you're telling me he was killed by my only living son? That doesn't make any sense to me." Sloan thought again for a minute and then it finally came to him. He remembered about leaving Tim's brother back with the woman who had given him his two sons. He had taken the one son who looked to be the stronger of the two. "I'll be damned. I haven't seen or heard from my other boy since he was a baby. And now you tell me that he's gone and killed his own brother, Tim?"

Reedy looked at Sloan with that same strange grin. "I know it sounds kind of crazy, but yes, that's what I'm telling you."

"Well, why the hell do you suppose he went and did that?"

"You'll be able to ask him that yourself in a moment or so. He's probably walking up the street as we speak."

"What the hell is he doing here?"

"He's looking for you."

CHAPTER TWENTY-SEVEN

When Frank and Jess had arrived in Largo, Jess sent Frank to the only saloon in town to find out if Eddie Sloan was still there. While Frank was doing that, Jess visited Sheriff A.J. Rubel's office. The deputy, who recognized Jess right off, waved him in and Jess walked up to Sheriff Rubel's desk.

"Why, I'll be damned. If it ain't Jess Williams himself come back to visit," said Sheriff Rubel, as he stood up and stuck his hand out to shake hands with Jess.

"It's nice to see you again, Sheriff, but I'm not here on a visit, I'm here on business."

"Is that right? Who might you be looking for here?"

"I'm looking for a man by the name of Eddie Sloan. I heard he was in a poker game here in town. Is he here?"

Just then a gunshot boomed, followed by a second one. The sound was coming from the saloon. "Eddie Sloan is here in town and over at the saloon in a poker game. I'll bet my month's pay that he's got something to do with the gunshots we just heard. Elias," Rubel hollered out to the deputy on the front porch, "get your ass over to the Mustang Bar and see what's going on. I'll be right behind you."

Sheriff Rubel grabbed a scattergun from behind his desk and loaded both barrels. "Nothing like a scattergun to quiet things down. I see you've cut the stock down on yours."

"Yeah, I like it that way. It seems less cumbersome and easier to handle. Sheriff, can I ask you a favor?"

"Sure, Jess, what do you need?"

"If that is Eddie Sloan involved in a gunfight over there, will you not arrest him but instead, tell him to meet me out in the street?"

"What business do you have with Eddie Sloan, anyway?"

"I don't like to admit it, but he is actually my father, although I have a hard time bringing myself to saying it."

"Eddie Sloan is your father? I thought the last time I saw you, you said your entire family was murdered."

"It's kind of a long and complicated story, Sheriff. I never knew about Eddie Sloan or my brother Tim Sloan until a few years back. I found my brother and now I have finally caught up with my so-called father who abandoned me when I was just an infant."

"I bet you were happy to finally find you still had some family left. How did you and your brother get along after you met?"

"Actually, not too well, Sheriff."

"Why not? What happened?"

"I killed him."

"You killed your brother? Did he deserve killing?"

"Yes, he did. I can assure you of that."

"You plan on killing Eddie Sloan, too?"

"I can't say for sure until I get to talk to him, but I wouldn't be surprised if that's the way it goes down."

"Well, I'll give him your message and as long as it's a fair fight, I got no problem with it. I doubt there will be any people crying at his funeral."

Sheriff Rubel walked out and headed for the Mustang Bar. Jess checked his pistol, walked out, and waited outside the Mustang Bar. When Sheriff Rubel walked into the Mustang holding the scatter-gun, everyone went silent. Everyone in town knew about his short fuse and they weren't taking any chances, not even Eddie Sloan, who had been engaged in a conversation with a man at the bar. Rubel recognized him right away.

"When did you get into town, Frank, and where is that U.S. marshal's badge?"

"It's in my back pocket taking a little siesta," said Reedy, with a look that Rubel understood.

Sheriff Rubel turned his attention to Eddie Sloan. "Sloan, what did I tell you about keeping this game clean and no gunplay?"

"Sheriff, I had no choice. Tillman drew on me."

"Frank, did you witness it? Is that the way it went down?"

"He's telling the truth, Sheriff. That Tillman fellow forced the fight." Rubel's deputy, who was standing next to Reedy, nodded in agreement.

Rubel had a smile on his face, which was not a very common sight to see. "Well, then, I guess I'm just going to have to let you go."

Eddie Sloan was somewhat confused by the sheriff's attitude and comment. Usually the sheriff would have locked him up for a night, even if it was a fair fight. "Well, thank you, Sheriff. I appreciate the fact that you agree with me." Sloan started to sit back down again and join the poker game.

"I didn't mean that I was letting you go back to your game, Sloan. I meant that I was letting you go outside."

"Why do you want me to go outside?"

"Because there is someone out there who wants to meet you. I believe he said he was your son and his name is Jess Williams."

Sloan looked over to Frank Reedy who just nodded his head as if to confirm it. Eddie Sloan looked back over at Sheriff Rubel who was pointing the scattergun toward the door of the bar going outside. Sloan, knowing that there was no point in delaying this thing, whatever it was, put his hat on and slowly walked outside the batwing doors of the Mustang Bar, with Reedy following close behind. Sheriff Rubel decided to sit and watch from a window while sipping on some whiskey. Frank Reedy walked out of the bar behind Sloan and leaned against one of the posts on the edge of the boardwalk just outside the saloon's batwing doors. Sloan stood on the other side of the other post, one hand below his pistol and the other hand holding the buckle of his gun belt.

Sloan watched Reedy out of the corner of his eyes. "Are you getting involved in whatever this is, Frank?"

"I'm just here to watch and make sure everything goes fair," Reedy replied, leaning his left shoulder lightly on the post and placing his other hand on the butt of his pistol, his thumb on the hammer. Reedy had already made up his mind that he would kill Sloan if anything went wrong. He figured he owed it to Jess, even though he had not discussed it with him.

Eddie Sloan simply stared at Jess who was standing in the street, only a few feet from Sloan. Sloan looked Jess over and saw a remarkable resemblance to his other son, Tim. Sloan noticed the unusual pistol and holster that Jess was wearing. Sloan slightly leaned up against the post and said nothing; he just kept glaring at Jess and neither of them spoke for a minute or so.

Sloan looked up at Jess. "Frank Reedy here said you killed my boy, Tim? Is that true?"

"He told you straight. I killed him."

Sloan moved away from the post. "Now, why in the hell would you go and do something like that? Family don't kill family; he was your brother."

"Maybe by blood but that doesn't matter much to me. He was still a bad man and he was involved with one of the men who killed my ma, pa and little sister Samantha."

Sloan looked surprised. "You mean Becky is dead? Last I heard she got married to an old law dog and was living with him outside of Black Creek. What happened?"

"Why do you care? You never came back or helped her in any way. You abandoned me when I was an infant and you took one of her two sons away from her and raised him to be a bad one."

"I take what's mine, boy, and I don't answer to anyone for it."

"That's going to change today."

Sloan's demeanor turned somewhat darker now. "What the hell did you come here for, boy?"

"I came to find out if you were just like my brother."

"Well, I'm not. I'm worse than he ever was."

"I'll bet that's one of the first times you've ever told the truth. A man who abandons his family and lives a life of gambling, cheating, lying and killing other men over a card game isn't really a man in my book."

"You kiss my ass, boy. You ain't got any right talking to me like that."

"I have all the right I need right here," Jess said, tapping his right index finger on his pistol.

"Do you really think so? Do you think that fancy pistol is going to do you any good against me?"

"Why don't you come on down off that boardwalk and find out?"

Sloan slowly stepped off the boardwalk and walked out into the street about thirty feet from where Jess stood, waiting patiently.

"Boy, you done killed your brother and now you want to brace me in a gunfight? That makes you just as bad as me or your brother."

"Don't even try to compare me to you or Tim Sloan. I don't go around killing people without a good reason. Tim Sloan deserved to die and so do you."

"I've got some bad news for you, boy. I don't plan on dying today."

"Actually, the bad news is that there is a slight change in plans and I don't think you're going to like it."

"You've got salt, I'll give you that. Well, if that's what you really want, go ahead and slick that pistol of yours out and let's see who is left standing when the smoke clears."

"I'm the one making the challenge, so I think it's only fair to give you the first move."

Sloan had an evil smile on his lips. "Awe, is that out of respect for your father?" he said, sarcastically.

"No, it's because you're going to need that extra split second."

Sloan glared at Jess, who was glaring straight back at Sloan. Jess had a look of stone on his face but it didn't bother Sloan. He slowly lowered his right hand until it was in position to draw. Jess's right hand had been at the ready all along.

679

"Last chance to back out of this, boy."

"That's not going to happen, so you might as well stop talking and start shooting."

Eddie Sloan went for his gun just as Jess finished talking. He was using that as an advantage to beat Jess on the draw. It didn't work, as Jess's first shot hit Eddie Sloan in the right side of his chest before Sloan had gotten his pistol completely out of the holster, collapsing his right lung. Sloan staggered back and his pistol slipped from his right hand. Jess had not missed his target; he had intended to wound Sloan with his first shot.

"Well," said Sloan, his voice weak, "you are damn fast with that pistol, but your aim is a little off."

"I hit exactly what I was aiming at."

"I don't understand."

"You don't have to. I just want to ask you a question."

"What?"

"Do you remember my ma?"

"Yeah."

"Can you picture her in your head right now?"

Sloan searched his head for a moment. "Yeah, I can picture her."

"Good, because that's the last thing I want you to remember."

Jess fanned two shots at Sloan, the first one hitting him in the forehead and the second one in the neck. Sloan fell back and hit the dirt. Jess walked over to him as he replaced the spent cartridges from his pistol. He holstered his pistol and removed Sloan's gun belt. Jess looked up at Frank Reedy who said nothing. Jess stepped up onto the boardwalk and into the bar, ordered a beer, and slung Sloan's holster on the bar. Reedy walked up next to him.

"Well, do you feel any better now?" asked Reedy.

Jess thought about it for a moment. "No, not really, but it does feel as though things are finally right somehow."

"So, what are you going to do now?" asked Reedy, as he ordered a whiskey.

"Well, I'm still a bounty hunter so I guess I'll keep on doing that. I do think, though, that I will take a little time to go and visit a real nice family I met out on the trail recently. They were going to build a cabin outside of Abilene, Kansas. I don't figure they're done with it yet, so I think I'll go and help them finish building it."

"I think that's a wonderful idea. You need to find out that there are other things that you can do with those hands besides killing."

"What about you, Frank? Are you going to pin that marshal's badge back on now?"

"I think I might just do that," said Frank, as he took out his badge and pinned it back on his shirt.

Jess smiled at Frank. "It looks right nice on you, Marshal."

"It feels right nice, too."

Jess and Reedy finished their drinks and turned to face Sheriff Rubel and his deputy, who were sitting at a table by the window of the bar. "Sheriff," said Jess, "thanks for not interfering."

"Hell, it was my pleasure, Jess. Watching you slick that pistol out was worth it alone and besides, Sloan needed killing anyway. If it hadn't been you, someone would have killed him sooner or later."

Jess and Frank walked back to the livery and mounted their horses. They slowly walked them to the end of the main street. "Marshal Reedy, it was a pleasure to work with you," said Jess, as he stuck his hand out and shook Reedy's hand. "Don't hesitate to call on me if you ever need to."

"The same goes for me, Jess. You take care of yourself, you hear?"

Jess tipped his hat and turned his horse to the north. Reedy watched him until he was out of sight. He tried to imagine what Jess felt like inside after killing his brother and his father but he couldn't get his head around it. Once Jess was out of sight, he headed back toward Timber to retrieve his two deputies and give them the good news that they were officially back on the payroll.

Jess made his way slowly, not being in any hurry. He made camp the first day early, next to a quiet river and he caught a few fish on a string and a hook, using a few kernels of corn that he always kept on hand for fishing. He had a tasty meal of pan-fried trout and pan bread along with a helping of beans. As he lay back on his saddle sipping coffee and looking at the dancing flames of the fire, he finally felt as though he was at peace with himself. Sure, he had killed his brother and his father but they were just two more bad men and nothing else to him. Then he thought about the nice family he had rescued recently. He was looking forward to visiting Hadley, Jane, Harold and little Jessica Brown and helping them work on their new house.

CHAPTER TWENTY-EIGHT

Jess had taken his time getting to Abilene. He was in no real hurry; he was no longer on the trail hunting down a killer for bounty. He had stopped early each day so that he could practice with his pistol, as well as with the Sharps. He spent some time practicing throwing his bowie knife and he had gotten pretty accurate with it, too. He was constantly honing his skills with his weapons.

He rode into Abilene in the late afternoon and found Sheriff Bad Axe McCoy sitting on a rocking chair outside his office. He reined Gray up, tied Gray and Sharps to the post, walked up, and shook hands with the sheriff.

"Nice to see you again, young Mister Williams. Did you finally catch up with your father?"

"I'm afraid so, Sheriff."

"Well, that doesn't sound good."

"It wasn't, especially for my father...I mean Eddie Sloan."

"Are you just stopping by or are you looking for someone who has a bounty on his head, 'cause if you are, I have some bounties on some real bad ones."

"No, Sheriff. I'm actually here to visit with that nice family, the Browns who are building a home just outside of town."

Sheriff McCoy hung his head and frowned. "Oh, yeah, the Browns, Hadley and Jane and their two children. You haven't heard?"

"Heard what, Sheriff?"

"It was an awful thing, what happened to that poor family. Hadley Brown had come into town to get some more lumber and when he did, he got into an argument with three cowboys in the saloon. Hadley didn't even wear a gun and those three cowboys were hell-bent for starting trouble. Hadley told them to kiss his ass and Hadley threw his whiskey in one of their faces. Well, the three of them went to giving him the beating of his life. I wasn't here at the time and by the time my deputies heard about it, those three cowboys rode out of town. I got back here the next day and decided to ride out and check on him and when I got there, the only thing standing was the stone fireplace. I found the four bodies all stacked together so I figure they must have been shot and then the cabin set on fire. They were burned beyond recognition but we did bury them separately, although it was a real mess getting the four bodies apart. We buried them in the local cemetery here in town."

Jess felt sick to his stomach. He let out a long sigh and sat down on the chair next to the sheriff. Sheriff McCoy didn't say anything; he knew that Jess needed a moment to let it all sink in. Jess took off his hat and fidgeted with it. Jess's thoughts turned back to his family and then to the Browns. There were so many similarities that he wondered if fate was again playing a role in his life. He thought about little Harold Brown and compared Harold to himself. Jess had been away and came back to find his family murdered, but Harold had been at home and suffered the same fate as his family. Jess wondered which way was better, to die together as a family or to be the only one left to face the loneliness and the hatred and the rage. Then he thought of little Jessica and compared her to his little sister, Samantha.

He wondered if the men who were responsible for the death of the Browns had raped the little girl or the mother, Jane, or just killed the family and robbed them. He would find out, no matter how much pain he would cause the cold-blooded murderers, before he killed each one of them. He put his hat back on, leaned back in the rocker, closed his eyes, and sat silent for almost ten minutes. Sheriff McCoy said nothing.

Jess finally opened his eyes, leaned forward in the rocker, placed his elbows on his knees, and closed his hands tightly. "Sheriff, do you know who did this?"

"We're pretty sure it was the three cowboys who gave Hadley the beating. After it was all over, someone said they spotted the three of them heading toward the Browns' homestead and they recognized them as the Bolin boys. Their names are Felix, Lance, and Burt Bolin, to be exact. All bad ones, if you know what I mean. We formed a posse and chased them for days but we couldn't catch up with them. They split up and went in three different directions to throw us off, but it was the rain that finally washed away all the tracks. I've had my ear to the ground but haven't heard any news about them since it happened. They're probably holed up somewhere waiting for things to blow over."

Jess looked over at Sheriff McCoy and McCoy saw a look in Jess's eyes that unnerved even him. "Sheriff, there isn't any hole deep enough for those boys to hole up in. Do you have any description of them that I can get?"

"The man who saw them heading for the Browns' place runs the local newspaper here in town and he is sort of an artist. He drew us some pictures for wanted posters. I have copies in my office if you would like them. Those were the bounties I mentioned to you before."

"Yes, I would like a copy of each one of them. I don't much care about the bounty on their heads. This is personal."

The sheriff walked inside his office, came back out, and handed Jess three pencil sketches of the Bolin brothers. Jess looked at each one of them, folded them and put them in his back pocket. "Sheriff, it was nice seeing you again, but I have to go."

"Won't you stay the night and leave in the morning? I'd like to buy you some lunch over at the café."

"I don't think I would be very good company right now, Sheriff. I have to go and pay my respects to the Browns and then I'm going to go look for the Bolin brothers. When I find them, I'll give them one chance to convince me they aren't the ones who did the killing and the burning of the Brown family. If they don't, they will pay dearly for what they did."

"I hope you catch up with them. I hear they like to hang around Dodge City a lot. Last I heard the law there hadn't seen them lately."

"I'll find them, one way or another. It doesn't matter how long it takes me."

"Good hunting, Jess. You keep in touch with me back here and I'll let you know if I find out any news about them."

Jess untied both horses and swung up onto Gray. "I will, Sheriff. And maybe next time I see you, we can have that lunch. I'd like that."

Sheriff McCoy nodded at Jess. Jess walked Gray slowly toward the east end of town and stopped at the little local cemetery. He got off his horse and walked around until he found the gravesites of Hadley, Jane, Harold and Jessica Brown. He knelt down at Jessica's headstone and placed his right hand on the dirt over her grave. "I swear to you on my life that I will bring justice to the men responsible for you and your family's deaths. You have my word on it. He stood back up and began to walk back to Gray when he saw one of McCoy's deputies, Elias, walking toward him.

"Damn shame about that poor family, Jess," said Elias as he reached Jess and shook his hand.

"Yeah, they didn't deserve that. They were just trying to live their lives and build a new homestead."

"I hear that you're going after the men who did it?"

"Yes, and I don't plan on wasting one more minute."

"I hope you find them."

Jess climbed up in the saddle and headed Gray in the direction of Dodge City. Elias watched until Jess was out of sight. Then he looked over at the gravesites of the Browns. When he looked back up in the direction that Jess had went, he said in a low voice that no one could heard, "I surely wouldn't want to be one of them Bolin brothers."

EPILOGUE

It had been four years now since Dave Walters had lost his custom pistol and holster from his gun locker. The gun disappeared in 2002 from the gun locker that he was now staring at, which is something he did quite often, still wondering if some unknown spirit or entity would somehow come out from it, grab him and take him to some unknown time or place. His hands literally shook every time he opened the gun locker. He finished his beer and headed for the fridge for another one. His wife, Jean, had been working on the computer all day trying to finish a project that she had started a few months ago. She finally turned off the computer, grabbed several sheets of paper from the printer, and walked into the kitchen just as Dave was popping the top off another cold beer.

"Why thank you, dear," she said playfully, as she grabbed the beer from his hand.

"Well, I guess you're welcome, sweetie," said Dave, as he went back to the fridge again and grabbed another beer. "How's the family tree going?"

Jean made some unrecognizable grunting sound as she plopped down in one of the chairs at the kitchen table. "If I had known how much work this was going to be, I wouldn't have started it in the first place."

"So what did you find? Are we related to some famous rich people or royalty somewhere?"

"No, I didn't find anything really unusual, no kings, no queens and no royalty."

"Damn, I guess I'll have to keep buying my lottery tickets," said Dave as he sat down at the table with Jean.

"I did find out something interesting, though."

"What?"

"Well, on my side of the family, I was able to go all the way back to the early 1700s. All of the relatives I could find were from a common background and all were fairly poor people. A few of the men in my family tree were in the military but no high-ranking positions. I had a distant cousin who was killed in the Civil War but for the most part, nothing worth talking about. I did find something interesting in your family tree, though."

"Really, what did you find?" Dave asked, his interest piquing a little.

"Well, you have this avid interest in Western history and the gunfighters from back then, and you compete in fast draw and cowboy action shooting, and I found out something that might be interesting to you."

Dave's interest piqued a little more. "Go on, what did you find out?"

Jean shuffled some papers until she found the one she wanted. "Here it is. It seems that you are related somehow to a gunfighter in the late 1800s. He was born around 1860, as far as I can tell from the records, and he died in 1921. He married a woman by the name of Martha Heller…"

Dave cut her off in mid-sentence. "Heller is my mother's maiden name."

"Well, if you'll let me finish, I'll make the connection."

Dave shut up but his interest now turned to excitement. Jean continued her explanation. "As I said, he married a Martha Heller and they had one son who passed away in 1959. Martha Heller is related to your mother and that means that you are related in some way to this gunfighter Jess Williams."

Some of the beer squirted out of Dave's mouth at the mention of Jess Williams' name.

"What the hell—are you okay, dear?" Jean asked.

"Did you say his name was Jess Williams?"

"Yes, do you know of him? You've never mentioned that you had a real Old West gunfighter in your family."

Dave didn't answer. He couldn't answer. His head was reeling with thoughts darting around and around. He was trying to get his brain wrapped around what Jean had just told him. He remembered back a few months earlier when he and Jean had taken a trip through Yellowstone National Park. He remembered how after going through Yellowstone they had stayed overnight in Cody, Wyoming. The day they left, they had stopped at the old man's big white house in Wapiti, just outside of Cody. He remembered paying the five dollars to see the old man's gun collection in the man's basement and he remembered seeing his gun and holster, his gun that had disappeared four years earlier, in the case in the basement. He remembered how the old man, Steve, had told him how his Uncle Henry had gotten the gun from a Jess Williams Jr., and that Steve's uncle had given Steve the gun in 1969. Steve told Dave the whole story, which had been told to him by his Uncle Henry about Jess Williams and how he had found the pistol and holster right after his family was brutally murdered. Dave, who had been facing his wife all this time, but really looking into some far beyond that Jean could not see, finally spoke.

"You said he had a son. What was his name? Wait, don't tell me; let me guess. His son's name was Jess Williams Jr., wasn't it?"

Jean looked back down at the papers. "Why yes, that was his name but how did you know that? Dave, are you okay? You have that same look on your face that you had that day you walked out of that man's house after looking at his old gun collection when we were out in Wyoming. I always wondered about that."

Dave looked at her but he didn't respond. His mind was reeling now. So, this was the connection, Dave thought to himself. He had purchased the custom gun and holster and somehow, it went back in time to Jess Williams. And now, he had discovered that he was related to Jess Williams through his mother's side. His mother was related to Jess Williams and somehow, for some unknown reason, fate had taken the gun from Dave and delivered it to Jess Williams when he had needed it the most. Dave almost ran to the gun locker in the bedroom and started twisting the dial on the locker. Jean followed him, a worried look on her face now. Dave had never told her about finding his gun and holster in the man's basement in Wapiti, Wyoming.

"What are you doing?" asked Jean.

"Just wait a minute. I need to find out."

"Find out what for God's sake!"

"Just give me a minute," he said, as he finally finished up the combination and put his hand on the handle, with little beads of nervous sweat now beginning to form on his forehead. He slowly opened it up. When he did, he gasped, stumbled backward from the gun locker, and sat down on the bed, a contorted look on his face. There, in all its glory, were the custom gun and holster he had purchased four years ago. The same custom gun and holster that he had seen in the old man's house in Wapiti, Wyoming a few months back. They were worn quite a bit but that was understandable knowing what he knew now.

Jean walked up to the cabinet. "Oh my God, whose gun is that? I've never seen it before. And how did it get in there? Did you buy another gun after losing that last one and you've been hiding it from me all this time?" Dave couldn't speak yet but shook his head as if to say no.

Jean looked the gun and holster over carefully. "Well, this one has sure been used a lot. It looks pretty worn out but it looks just like most of the guns you guys shoot with at all the fast draw competitions."

Dave finally regained enough composure to speak. "You know me well enough to know that it wouldn't look like that if I had been using it the last four years. You know how meticulous I am about taking care of my guns and holsters."

Jean looked at the other gun and holster that were hanging in the locker that Dave had continued to use after losing the new one he had gotten from Bob Graham and Bob Mernickle. They were in better condition than the now older and worn-out gun and holster that had appeared, seemingly out of nowhere. "Well, I have to agree with you on that. You do take care of your guns and holsters. So what is the explanation for this?" she said, pointing to the gun that Dave had lost four years ago.

Dave thought about telling her the whole story but he couldn't bring himself to do it. Hell, he couldn't believe it himself. At least he finally understood the connection and why the gun had disappeared and found its way back to Jess Williams, and now back to him. He stood up, walked over to the gun locker, and closed it.

"You're not going to look at it?" asked Jean.

"Not right now," said Dave as he headed back to the kitchen and grabbed his cold beer. He took a sip and just stood there in front of the fridge and stared at the ceiling.

Jean sat back down at the kitchen table and kept staring at her husband, still worried about him. She decided to try to lighten up the conversation. "Well, you've had an interesting moment. Maybe one day you'll tell me the rest of what you know, but I'll leave it up to you. I did find one interesting tidbit on my family tree, or maybe you would call it more of a coincidence."

"What did you find?"

"Remember when we took that vacation and went to Yellowstone and all through Wyoming?"

"Yeah?" replied Dave, looking more nervous, if that was at all possible.

"Well, when we left Cody, Wyoming, you stopped in a little town call Wapiti. I only remember it because you stopped at some old guy's house to see some old guns and stuff and when you came back out to the car, you looked as white as a ghost, kind of like you do right now."

"Yeah, but what about it?"

"When I was doing my family tree, I found out I'm related to someone who lived in Wapiti, Wyoming. What are the odds of that?"

Dave, who had been taking a swallow of beer almost chocked on it. He coughed several times, trying to clear his throat. "Who the hell are you related to in Wapiti, Wyoming?"

"His name is Henry Meyers and I remember it because when I looked at his death certificate it said he died in 1969 but they listed his name on the death certificate as "Uncle" Henry Meyers. I thought that kind of odd but maybe that's what everybody called him or something."

When the beer can hit the floor the beer splashed all the way to the ceiling.

⚐⚐

The day before in Wapiti, Wyoming...

A red car pulled up in the driveway and Steve heard it. He had been watching television but he clicked it off and slowly walked to the door and opened it. An old man stood at the door and was just about to knock when Steve opened it.

"I'm here to see your gun collection, Mister."

"That's fine. It's in the basement, but it'll cost you five bucks."

The man pulled out a five-dollar bill from his wallet and Steve motioned for him to come in and follow him. The man did and Steve led him down the stairs to the basement.

"Look around all you want. I have some pretty nice stuff."

"Yeah, you do, I love all this stuff. I used to compete in fast draw competition but I'm getting a little older and slower now, so I mostly do Cowboy Action Shooting. Hey, what do you have in the display case over there?" the man asked, as he walked over to the display case.

"Oh, that's my best piece. Everyone who sees it says the same thing. I had a guy stop here a couple of months ago and claimed it was his and that he bought it four years ago and..."

The other man cut him off in mid-sentence. "Mister, there's nothing in this case."

Steve almost tripped over his own feet as he rushed over to the man's side. He gasped at the sight of the empty display case. "I don't understand. It was there last night when I was cleaning down here. I have the only key and the display case is still locked."

"Maybe you moved it and don't remember."

"No, I always leave it in the display case. I never take it out. I just don't understand."

"Maybe you should call the police and report it as stolen. You have insurance, don't you?"

"Yeah, but they couldn't replace it, no matter how much money they paid."

Steve thought about the history of the gun and the man who had shown up before claiming it was his gun and holster. He remembered that the man knew the serial number on the gun and the holster and how strange the whole story was. Steve looked at the man in his basement. "Mister, do you believe in destiny and fate and that sometimes things happen for a reason, even though we may never understand why?"

"Yeah, I think everything happens for a reason. Sometimes we don't know why but that's just the way it is."

"So do I."

"So, what are you going to do about your missing gun and holster?"

Steve looked down at the case, thought about it for a moment, and then looked back up at the man in his basement. "Not a damned thing," said Steve, finality in his voice.

The End

READ THE ENTIRE SERIES OF JESS WILLIAMS WESTERNS (LISTED IN ORDER)...